Marie-Henri Beyle, known as STENDHAL (1783-1842), French novelist, essayist, and pamphleteer, has earned his place among the great for writings that are informed by superior intelligence and on his intimate understanding of human behavior. He was a brilliant conversationalist, but he never rose above the post of a minor government official. In the service of Napoleon, he saw much of Europe and was present at the burning of Moscow. He had a passion for Italy and it was there he settled after the Restoration. Stendhal's work is a curious combination. It looks back to the philosophy and ideology of the eighteenth century; yet in its psychological analysis it foreshadows the orientation of our own century—a century in which the author rightly predicted would come the true estimation and appreciation of his work. Stendhal died in Paris in 1842.

Marie-Henri Beyle,
known as STENDHAL
(1783-1842), French

novelist, essayist, and biographer, has earned his
place among the great for writings that are informed by superior intelligence and on his intimate
understanding of human behavior. He was a brilliant conversationalist, but he never rose above the
post of a minor government official. In the service
of Napoleon, he saw much of Europe, and was
present at the burning of Moscow. He had a passion for Italy, and it was there he settled after the
Restoration. Stendhal's work is a curious combination. It looks back to the philosophy and ideology
of the eighteenth century, yet in its psychological
analysis it foreshadows the orientation of our own
century—a century in which the author highly
predicted would sense the true estimation and appreciation of his works. Stendhal died in Paris in
1842.

STENDHAL
(Marie-Henri Beyle)

THE
CHARTERHOUSE
OF
PARMA

TRANSLATED FROM THE FRENCH BY
C. K. SCOTT-MONCRIEFF

WITH AN AFTERWORD BY
JACQUES BARZUN

A SIGNET CLASSIC
Published by The New American Library

TO THE READER

IT WAS IN THE winter of 1830 and three hundred leagues from Paris that this tale was written; thus it contains no allusion to the events of 1839.

Many years before 1830, at the time when our Armies were overrunning Europe, chance put me in possession of a billeting order on the house of a Canon: this was at Padua, a charming town in Italy; my stay being prolonged, we became friends.

Passing through Padua again towards the end of 1830, I hastened to the house of the good Canon: he himself was dead, that I knew, but I wished to see once again the room in which we had passed so many pleasant evenings, evenings on which I had often looked back since. I found there the Canon's nephew and his wife who welcomed me like an old friend. Several people came in, and we did not break up until a very late hour; the nephew sent out to the Caffè Pedrocchi for an excellent *zabaione*. What more than anything kept us up was the story of the Duchessa Sanseverina, to which someone made an allusion, and which the nephew was good enough to relate from beginning to end, in my honour.

"In the place to which I am going," I told my friends, "I am not likely to find evenings like this, and, to while away the long hours of darkness, I shall make a novel out of your story."

"In that case," said the nephew, "let me give you my uncle's journal, which, under the heading *Parma*, mentions several of the intrigues of that court, in the days when the Duchessa's word was law there; but, have a care! this story is anything but moral, and now that you pride yourselves in France on your gospel purity, it may win you the reputation of an *assassin*."

I publish this tale without any alteration from the manuscript of 1830, a course which may have two drawbacks:

The first for the reader: the characters being Italians will perhaps interest him less, hearts in that country differing con-

vii

siderably from hearts in France: the Italians are sincere, honest folk and, not taking offence, say what is in their minds; it is only when the mood seizes them that they shew any vanity; which then becomes passion, and goes by the name of *puntiglio*. Lastly, poverty is not, with them, a subject for ridicule.

The second drawback concerns the author.

I confess that I have been so bold as to leave my characters with their natural asperities; but, on the other hand—this I proclaim aloud—I heap the most moral censure upon many of their actions. To what purpose should I give them the exalted morality and other graces of French characters, who love money above all things, and sin scarcely ever from motives of hatred or love? The Italians in this tale are almost the opposite. Besides, it seems to me that, whenever one takes a stride of two hundred leagues from South to North, the change of scene that occurs is tantamount to a fresh tale. The Canon's charming niece had known and indeed had been greatly devoted to the Duchessa Sanseverina, and begs me to alter nothing in her adventures, which are reprehensible.

23rd January, 1839.

THE
CHARTERHOUSE
OF
PARMA

VOLUME ONE

CHAPTER ONE

O<small>N THE</small> 15<small>TH</small> of May, 1796, General Bonaparte made his entry into Milan at the head of that young army which had shortly before crossed the Bridge of Lodi and taught the world that after all these centuries Cæsar and Alexander had a successor. The miracles of gallantry and genius of which Italy was a witness in the space of a few months aroused a slumbering people; only a week before the arrival of the French, the Milanese still regarded them as a mere rabble of brigands, accustomed invariably to flee before the troops of His Imperial and Royal Majesty; so much at least was reported to them three times weekly by a little news-sheet no bigger than one's hand, and printed on soiled paper.

In the Middle Ages the Republicans of Lombardy had given proof of a valour equal to that of the French, and deserved to see their city rased to the ground by the German Emperors. Since they had become *loyal subjects,* their great occupation was the printing of sonnets upon handkerchiefs of rose-coloured taffeta whenever the marriage occurred of a young lady belonging to some rich or noble family. Two or three years after that great event in her life, the young lady in question used to engage a devoted admirer: sometimes the

name of the *cicisbeo* chosen by the husband's family occupied an honourable place in the marriage contract. It was a
far cry from these effeminate ways to the profound emotions
aroused by the unexpected arrival of the French army. Presently there sprang up a new and passionate way of life. A
whole people discovered, on the 15th of May, 1796, that
everything which until then it had respected was supremely
ridiculous, if not actually hateful. The departure of the last
Austrian regiment marked the collapse of the old ideas: to
risk one's life became the fashion. People saw that in order to
be really happy after centuries of cloying sensations, it was
necessary to love one's country with a real love and to seek
out heroic actions. They had been plunged in the darkest
night by the continuation of the jealous despotism of Charles
V and Philip II; they overturned these monarchs' statues
and immediately found themselves flooded with daylight.
For the last half-century, as the *Encyclopædia* and Voltaire
gained ground in France, the monks had been dinning into
the ears of the good people of Milan that to learn to read, or
for that matter to learn anything at all was a great waste of
labour, and that by paying one's exact tithe to one's parish
priest and faithfully reporting to him all one's little misdeeds, one was practically certain of having a good place
in Paradise. To complete the debilitation of this people
once so formidable and so rational, Austria had sold them,
on easy terms, the privilege of not having to furnish any re-
cruits to her army.

In 1796, the Milanese army was composed of four and
twenty rapscallions dressed in scarlet, who guarded the town
with the assistance of four magnificent regiments of Hun-
garian Grenadiers. Freedom of morals was extreme, but
passion very rare; otherwise, apart from the inconvenience of
having to repeat everything to one's parish priest, on pain of
ruin even in this world, the good people of Milan were still
subjected to certain little monarchical interferences which
could not fail to be vexatious. For instance, the Archduke,
who resided at Milan and governed in the name of the Emper-
or, his cousin, had had the lucrative idea of trading in corn.
In consequence, an order prohibiting the peasants from selling their grain until His Highness had filled his granaries.

In May, 1796, three days after the entry of the French,
a young painter in miniature, slightly mad, named Gros,
afterwards famous, who had come with the army, overhear-
ing in the great Caffè dei Servi (which was then in fashion)

an account of the exploits of the Archduke, who moreover
was extremely stout, picked up the list of ices which was
printed on a sheet of coarse yellow paper. On the back of this
he drew the fat Archduke; a French soldier was stabbing
him with his bayonet in the stomach, and instead of blood
there gushed out an incredible quantity of corn. What we call
a lampoon or caricature was unknown in this land of crafty
despotism. The drawing, left by Gros on the table of the
Caffè dei Servi, seemed a miracle fallen from heaven; it was
engraved and printed during the night, and next day twenty
thousand copies of it were sold.

The same day, there were posted up notices of a forced
loan of six millions, levied to supply the needs of the French
army which, having just won six battles and conquered a
score of provinces, wanted nothing now but shoes, breeches,
jackets and caps.

The mass of prosperity and pleasure which burst into
Lombardy in the wake of these French ragamuffins was so
great that only the priests and a few nobles were conscious
of the burden of this levy of six millions, shortly to be followed by a number of others. These French soldiers
laughed and sang all day long; they were all under twenty-
five years of age, and their Commander in Chief, who had
reached twenty-seven, was reckoned the oldest man in his
army. This gaiety, this youthfulness, this irresponsibility furnished a jocular reply to the furious preachings of the monks,
who, for six months, had been announcing from the pulpit
that the French were monsters, obliged, upon pain of death,
to burn down everything and to cut off everyone's head.
With this object, each of their regiments marched with a
guillotine at its head.

In the country districts one saw at the cottage doors the
French soldier engaged in dandling the housewife's baby in
his arms, and almost every evening some drummer, scraping
a fiddle, would improvise a ball. Our country dances proving
a great deal too skilful and complicated for the soldiers, who
for that matter barely knew them themselves, to be able to
teach them to the women of the country, it was the latter
who shewed the young Frenchmen the *Monferrina*, *Salterello*
and other Italian dances.

The officers had been lodged, as far as possible, with the
wealthy inhabitants; they had every need of comfort. A certain lieutenant, for instance, named Robert, received a billeting order on the *palazzo* of the Marchesa del Dongo. This

officer, a young conscript not over-burdened with scruples, possessed as his whole worldly wealth, when he entered this *palazzo,* a scudo of six francs which he had received at Piacenza. After the crossing of the Bridge of Lodi he had taken from a fine Austrian officer, killed by a ball, a magnificent pair of nankeen pantaloons, quite new, and never did any garment come more opportunely. His officer's epaulettes were of wool, and the cloth of his tunic was stitched to the lining of the sleeves so that its scraps might hold together; but there was something even more distressing; the soles of his shoes were made out of pieces of soldiers' caps, likewise picked up on the field of battle, somewhere beyond the Bridge of Lodi. These makeshift soles were tied on over his shoes with pieces of string which were plainly visible, so that when the major-domo appeared at the door of Lieutenant Robert's room bringing him an invitation to dine with the Signora Marchesa, the officer was thrown into the utmost confusion. He and his orderly spent the two hours that divided him from this fatal dinner in trying to patch up the tunic a little and in dyeing black, with ink, those wretched strings round his shoes. At last the dread moment arrived. "Never in my life did I feel more ill at ease," Lieutenant Robert told me; "the ladies expected that I would terrify them, and I was trembling far more than they were. I looked down at my shoes and did not know how to walk gracefully. The Marchesa del Dongo," he went on, "was then in the full bloom of her beauty: you have seen her for yourself, with those lovely eyes of an angelic sweetness, and the dusky gold of her hair which made such a perfect frame for the oval of that charming face. I had in my room a *Herodias* by Leonardo da Vinci, which might have been her portrait. Mercifully, I was so overcome by her supernatural beauty that I forgot all about my clothes. For the last two years I had been seeing nothing that was not ugly and wretched, in the mountains behind Genoa: I ventured to say a few words to her to express my delight.

"But I had too much sense to waste any time upon compliments. As I was turning my phrases I saw, in a dining-room built entirely of marble, a dozen flunkeys and footmen dressed in what seemed to me then the height of magnificence. Just imagine, the rascals had not only good shoes on their feet, but silver buckles as well. I could see them all, out of the corner of my eye, staring stupidly at my coat and perhaps at my shoes also, which cut me to the heart. I could

have frightened all these fellows with a word; but how was I
to put them in their place without running the risk of offending the ladies? For the Marchesa, to fortify her own courage
a little, as she has told me a hundred times since, had sent
to fetch from the convent where she was still at school Gina
del Dongo, her husband's sister, who was afterwards that
charming Contessa Pietranera: no one, in prosperity, surpassed her in gaiety and sweetness of temper, just as no one
surpassed her in courage and serenity of soul when fortune
turned against her.

"Gina, who at that time might have been thirteen but
looked more like eighteen, a lively, downright girl, as you
know, was in such fear of bursting out laughing at the sight
of my costume that she dared not eat; the Marchesa, on the
other hand, loaded me with constrained civilities; she could
see quite well the movements of impatience in my eyes. In a
word, I cut a sorry figure, I chewed the bread of scorn, a
thing which is said to be impossible for a Frenchman. At
length, a heaven-sent idea shone in my mind: I set to work
to tell the ladies of my poverty and of what we had suffered
for the last two years in the mountains behind Genoa where
we were kept by idiotic old Generals. There, I told them, we
were paid in *assignats* which were not legal tender in the
country, and given three ounces of bread daily. I had not
been speaking for two minutes before there were tears in the
good Marchesa's eyes, and Gina had grown serious.

" 'What, Lieutenant,' she broke in, 'three ounces of bread!'

" 'Yes, Signorina; but to make up for that the issue ran
short three days in the week, and as the peasants on whom
we were billeted were even worse off than ourselves, we used
to hand on some of our bread to them.'

"On leaving the table, I offered the Marchesa my arm as far
as the door of the drawing-room, then hurried back and gave
the servant who had waited upon me at dinner that solitary
scudo of six francs upon the spending of which I had built so
many castles in the air.

"A week later," Robert went on, "when it was satisfactorily established that the French were not guillotining anyone, the Marchese del Dongo returned from his castle of
Grianta on the Lake of Como, to which he had gallantly
retired on the approach of the army, abandoning to the fortunes of war his young and beautiful wife and his sister. The
hatred that this Marchese felt for us was equal to his fear, that
is to say immeasurable: his fat face, pale and pious, was an

amusing spectacle when he was being polite to me. On the day after his return to Milan, I received three ells of cloth and two hundred francs out of the levy of six millions; I renewed my wardrobe, and became cavalier to the ladies, for the season of balls was beginning."

Lieutenant Robert's story was more or less that of all the French troops; instead of laughing at the wretched plight of these poor soldiers, people were sorry for them and came to love them.

This period of unlooked-for happiness and wild excitement lasted but two short years; the frenzy had been so excessive and so general that it would be impossible for me to give any idea of it, were it not for this historical and profound reflexion: these people had been living in a state of boredom for the last hundred years.

The thirst for pleasure natural in southern countries had prevailed in former times at the court of the Visconti and Sforza, those famous Dukes of Milan. But from the year 1524, when the Spaniards conquered the Milanese, and conquered them as taciturn, suspicious, arrogant masters, always in dread of revolt, gaiety had fled. The subject race, adopting the manners of their masters, thought more of avenging the least insult by a dagger-blow than of enjoying the fleeting hour.

This frenzied joy, this gaiety, this thirst for pleasure, this tendency to forget every sad or even reasonable feeling, were carried to such a pitch, between the 15th of May, 1796, when the French entered Milan, and April, 1799, when they were driven out again after the battle of Cassano, that instances have been cited of old millionaire merchants, old moneylenders, old scriveners who, during this interval, quite forgot to pull long faces and to amass money.

At the most it would have been possible to point to a few families belonging to the higher ranks of the nobility, who had retired to their palaces in the country, as though in a sullen revolt against the prevailing high spirits and the expansion of every heart. It is true that these noble and wealthy families had been given a distressing prominence in the allocation of the forced loans exacted for the French army.

The Marchese del Dongo, irritated by the spectacle of so much gaiety, had been one of the first to return to his magnificent castle of Grianta, on the farther side of Como, whither his ladies took with them Lieutenant Robert. This castle, standing in a position which is perhaps unique in the world, on a plateau one hundred and fifty feet above that sublime lake, a great part of which it commands, had been originally a fortress. The del Dongo family had constructed it in the fifteenth century, as was everywhere attested by marble tablets charged with their arms; one could still see the drawbridges and deep moats, though the latter, it must be admitted, had been drained of their water; but with its walls eighty feet in height and six in thickness, this castle was safe from assault, and it was for this reason that it was dear to the timorous Marchese. Surrounded by some twenty-five or thirty retainers whom he supposed to be devoted to his person, presumably because he never opened his mouth except to curse them, he was less tormented by fear than at Milan.

This fear was not altogether groundless: he was in most active correspondence with a spy posted by Austria on the Swiss frontier three leagues from Grianta, to contrive the escape of the prisoners taken on the field of battle; conduct which might have been viewed in a serious light by the French Generals.

The Marchese had left his young wife at Milan; she looked after the affairs of the family there, and was responsible for providing the sums levied on the *casa del Dongo* (as they say in Italy); she sought to have these reduced, which obliged her to visit those of the nobility who had accepted public office, and even some highly influential persons who were not of noble birth. A great event now occurred in this family. The Marchese had arranged the marriage of his young sister Gina with a personage of great wealth and the very highest birth; but he powdered his hair; in virtue of which, Gina received him with shouts of laughter, and presently took the rash step of marrying the Conte Pietranera. He was, it is true, a very fine gentleman, of the most personable appearance, but ruined for generations past in estate, and to complete the disgrace of the match, a fervent supporter of the new ideas. Pietranera was a sub-lieutenant in the Italian Legion; this was the last straw for the Marchese.

After these two years of folly and happiness, the Directory in Paris, giving itself the airs of a sovereign firmly enthroned, began to shew a mortal hatred of everything that was not commonplace. The incompetent Generals whom it imposed on the Army of Italy lost a succession of battles on those same plains of Verona, which had witnessed two years before the prodigies of Arcole and Lonato. The Austrians again drew near to Milan; Lieutenant Robert, who had been promoted to the command of a battalion and had been wounded at the battle of Cassano, came to lodge for the last time in the house of his friend the Marchesa del Dongo. Their parting was a sad one; Robert set forth with Conte Pietranera, who followed the French in their retirement on Novi. The young Contessa, to whom her brother refused to pay her marriage portion, followed the army, riding in a cart.

Then began that period of reaction and a return to the old ideas, which the Milanese call *i tredici mesi* (the thirteen months), because as it turned out their destiny willed that this return to stupidity should endure for thirteen months only, until Marengo. Everyone who was old, bigoted, morose, reappeared at the head of affairs, and resumed the leadership of society; presently the people who had remained faithful to the sound doctrines published a report in the villages that Napoleon had been hanged by the Mamelukes in Egypt, as he so richly deserved.

Among these men who had retired to sulk on their estates and came back now athirst for vengeance, the Marchese del Dongo distinguished himself by his rabidity; the extravagance of his sentiments carried him naturally to the head of his party. These gentlemen, quite worthy people when they were not in a state of panic, but who were always trembling, succeeded in getting round the Austrian General: a good enough man at heart, he let himself be persuaded that severity was the best policy, and ordered the arrest of one hundred and fifty patriots: quite the best man to be found in Italy at the time.

They were speedily deported to the Bocche di Cattaro, and, flung into subterranean caves, the moisture and above all the want of bread did prompt justice to each and all of these rascals.

The Marchese del Dongo had an exalted position, and, as he combined with a host of other fine qualities a sordid avarice, he would boast publicly that he never sent a scudo to his sister, the Contessa Pietranera: still madly in love, she refused to leave her husband, and was starving by his side in France. The good Marchesa was in despair; finally she managed to abstract a few small diamonds from her jewel case, which her husband took from her every evening to stow away under his bed, in an iron coffer: the Marchesa had brought him a dowry of 800,000 francs, and received 80 francs monthly for her personal expenses. During the thirteen months in which the French were absent from Milan, this most timid of women found various pretexts and never went out of mourning.

We must confess that, following the example of many grave authors, we have begun the history of our hero a year before his birth. This essential personage is none other than Fabrizio Valserra, Marchesino del Dongo, as the style is at Milan.[1] He had taken the trouble to be born just when the French were driven out, and found himself, by the accident of birth, the second son of that Marchese del Dongo who was so great a gentleman, and with whose fat, pasty face, false smile and unbounded hatred for the new ideas the reader is already acquainted. The whole of the family fortune was already settled upon the elder son, Ascanio del Dongo, the worthy image of his father. He was eight years old and Fabrizio two when all of a sudden that General Bonaparte, whom everyone of good family understood to have been hanged long ago, came down from the Mont Saint-Bernard. He entered Milan: that moment is still unique in history; imagine a whole populace madly in love. A few days later, Napoleon won the battle of Marengo. The rest needs no telling. The frenzy of the Milanese reached its climax; but this time it was mingled with ideas of vengeance: these good people had been taught to hate. Presently they saw arrive in their midst all that remained of the patriots deported to the Bocche di Cattaro; their return was celebrated with a national *festa*. Their pale faces, their great startled eyes, their shrunken limbs were in strange contrast to the joy that broke out on every side. Their arrival was the signal for departure for the families most deeply compromised. The Marchese del Dongo was one of the first to flee to his castle of Grianta. The heads of the great families were filled with hatred and fear; but their wives, their daughters, remembered the joys of the former French occupation, and thought with regret of Milan and those gay balls, which, immediately after Marengo, were organised afresh at the *casa Tanzi*. A few days after the victory, the French General responsible for maintaining order in Lombardy discovered that all the farmers on the noblemen's estates, all the old wives in the villages, so far from still thinking of this astonishing victory at

[1] By the local custom, borrowed from Germany, this title is given to every son of a Marchese; *Contino* to the son of a Conte, *Contessina* to the daughter of a Conte, etc.

Marengo, which had altered the destinies of Italy and recaptured thirteen fortified positions in a single day, had their minds occupied only by a prophecy of San Giovita, the principal Patron Saint of Brescia. According to this inspired utterance, the prosperity of France and of Napoleon was to cease just thirteen weeks after Marengo. What does to some extent excuse the Marchese del Dongo and all the nobles sulking on their estates is that literally and without any affectation they believed in the prophecy. Not one of these gentlemen had read as many as four volumes in his life; quite openly they were making their preparations to return to Milan at the end of the thirteen weeks; but time, as it went on, recorded fresh successes for the cause of France. Returning to Paris, Napoleon, by wise decrees, saved the country from revolution at home as he had saved it from its foreign enemies at Marengo. Then the Lombard nobles, in the safe shelter of their castles, discovered that at first they had misinterpreted the prophecy of the holy patron of Brescia; it was a question not of thirteen weeks, but of thirteen months. The thirteen months went by, and the prosperity of France seemed to increase daily.

We pass lightly over ten years of progress and happiness, from 1800 to 1810. Fabrizio spent the first part of this decade at the castle of Grianta, giving and receiving an abundance of fisticuffs among the little *contadini* of the village, and learning nothing, not even how to read. Later on, he was sent to the Jesuit College at Milan. The Marchese, his father, insisted on his being shewn the Latin tongue, not on any account in the works of those ancient writers who are always talking about Republics, but in a magnificent volume adorned with more than a hundred engravings, a masterpiece of seventeenth-century art; this was the Latin genealogy of the Valserra, Marchesi del Dongo, published in 1650 by Fabrizio del Dongo, Archbishop of Parma. The fortunes of the Valserra being pre-eminently military, the engravings represented any number of battles, and everywhere one saw some hero of the name dealing mighty blows with his sword. This book greatly delighted the young Fabrizio. His mother, who adored him, obtained permission, from time to time, to pay him a visit at Milan; but as her husband never offered her any money for these journeys, it was her sister-in-law, the charming Contessa Pietranera, who lent her what she required. After the return of the French, the Contessa had

become one of the most brilliant ladies at the court of Prince
Eugène, the Viceroy of Italy.

When Fabrizio had made his First Communion, she obtained leave from the Marchese, still in voluntary exile, to
invite him out, now and again, from his college. She found
him unusual, thoughtful, very serious, but a nice-looking
boy and not at all out of place in the drawing-room of a
lady of fashion; otherwise, as ignorant as one could wish,
and barely able to write. The Contessa, who carried her impulsive character into everything, promised her protection to
the head of the establishment provided that her nephew
Fabrizio made astounding progress and carried off a number
of prizes at the end of the year. So that he should be in a
position to deserve them, she used to send for him every
Saturday evening, and often did not restore him to his masters
until the following Wednesday or Thursday. The Jesuits, although tenderly cherished by the Prince Viceroy, were ex-
pelled from Italy by the laws of the Kingdom, and the Superior of the College, an able man, was conscious of all that
might be made out of his relations with a woman all-
powerful at court. He never thought of complaining of the
absences of Fabrizio, who, more ignorant than ever, at the
end of the year was awarded five first prizes. This being so,
the Contessa, escorted by her husband, now the General
commanding one of the Divisions of the Guard, and by five or
six of the most important personages at the viceregal court,
came to attend the prize-giving at the Jesuit College. The
Superior was complimented by his chiefs.

The Contessa took her nephew with her to all those brilliant festivities which marked the too brief reign of the sociable Prince Eugène. She had on her own authority created
him an officer of hussars, and Fabrizio, now twelve years
old, wore that uniform. One day the Contessa, enchanted by
his handsome figure, besought the Prince to give him a post
as page, a request which implied that the del Dongo family
was coming round. Next day she had need of all her credit
to secure the Viceroy's kind consent not to remember this
request, which lacked only the consent of the prospective
page's father, and this consent would have been emphatically
refused. After this act of folly, which made the sullen Marchese shudder, he found an excuse to recall young Fabrizio
to Grianta. The Contessa had a supreme contempt for her
brother, she regarded him as a melancholy fool, and one
who would be troublesome if ever it lay in his power. But

she was madly fond of Fabrizio, and, after ten years of silence, wrote to the Marchese reclaiming her nephew; her letter was left unanswered.

On his return to this formidable palace, built by the most bellicose of his ancestors, Fabrizio knew nothing in the world except how to drill and how to sit on a horse. Conte Pietranera, as fond of the boy as was his wife, used often to put him on a horse and take him with him on parade.

On reaching the castle of Grianta, Fabrizio, his eyes still red with the tears that he had shed on leaving his aunt's fine rooms, found only the passionate caresses of his mother and sisters. The Marchese was closeted in his study with his elder son, the Marchesino Ascanio; there they composed letters in cipher which had the honour to be forwarded to Vienna; father and son appeared in public only at meal-times. The Marchese used ostentatiously to repeat that he was teaching his natural successor to keep, by double entry, the accounts of the produce of each of his estates. As a matter of fact, the Marchese was too jealous of his own power ever to speak of these matters to a son, the necessary inheritor of all these entailed properties. He employed him to cipher despatches of fifteen or twenty pages which two or three times weekly he had conveyed into Switzerland, where they were put on the road for Vienna. The Marchese claimed to inform his rightful Sovereign of the internal condition of the Kingdom of Italy, of which he himself knew nothing, and his letters were invariably most successful, for the following reason: the Marchese would have a count taken on the high road, by some trusted agent, of the number of men in a certain French or Italian regiment that was changing its station, and in reporting the fact to the court of Vienna would take care to reduce by at least a quarter the number of the troops on the march. These letters, in other respects absurd, had the merit of contradicting others of greater accuracy, and gave pleasure. And so, a short time before Fabrizio's arrival at the castle, the Marchese had received the star of a famous order: it was the fifth to adorn his Chamberlain's coat. As a matter of fact, he suffered from the chagrin of not daring to sport this garment outside his study; but he never allowed himself to dictate a despatch without first putting on the gold-laced coat, studded with all his orders. He would have felt himself to be wanting in respect had he acted otherwise.

The Marchesa was amazed by her son's graces. But she had kept up the habit of writing two or three times every year to General Comte d'A——, which was the title now borne by Lieutenant Robert. The Marchesa had a horror of lying to the people to whom she was attached; she examined her son and was appalled by his ignorance.

"If he appears to me to have learned little," she said to herself, "to me who know nothing, Robert, who is so clever, would find that his education had been entirely neglected; and in these days one must have merit." Another peculiarity, which astonished her almost as much, was that Fabrizio had taken seriously all the religious teaching that had been instilled into him by the Jesuits. Although very pious herself, the fanaticism of this child made her shudder; "If the Marchese has the sense to discover this way of influencing him, he will take my son's affection from me." She wept copiously, and her passion for Fabrizio was thereby increased.

Life in this castle, peopled by thirty or forty servants, was extremely dull; accordingly Fabrizio spent all his days in pursuit of game or exploring the lake in a boat. Soon he was on intimate terms with the coachmen and grooms; these were all hot supporters of the French, and laughed openly at the pious valets, attached to the person of the Marchese or to that of his elder son. The great theme for wit at the expense of these solemn personages was that, in imitation of their masters, they powdered their heads.

CHAPTER TWO

. . . Alors que Vesper vient embrunir nos yeux,
Tout épris d'avenir, je contemple les cieux,
En qui Dieu nous escrit, par notes non obscures,
Les sorts et les destins de toutes créatures.
Car lui, du fond des cieux regardant un humain,
Parfois mû de pitié, lui montre le chemin;
Par les astres du ciel qui sont ses caractères,
Les choses nous prédit et bonnes et contraires;
Mais les hommes chargés de terre et de trépas,
Méprisent tel écrit, et ne le lisent pas.

RONSARD.

THE MARCHESE professed a vigorous hatred of enlightenment: "It is ideas," he used to say, "that have ruined Italy"; he did not know quite how to reconcile this holy horror of instruction with his desire to see his son Fabrizio perfect the education so brilliantly begun with the Jesuits. In order to incur the least possible risk, he charged the good Priore Blanès, parish priest of Grianta, with the task of continuing Fabrizio's Latin studies. For this it was necessary that the priest should himself know that language; whereas it was to him an object of scorn; his knowledge in the matter being confined to the recitation, by heart, of the prayers in his missal, the meaning of which he could interpret more or less to his flock. But this priest was nevertheless highly respected and indeed feared throughout the district; he had always said that it was by no means in thirteen weeks, nor even in thirteen months that they would see the fulfilment of the famous prophecy of San Giovita, the Patron Saint of Brescia. He added, when he was speaking to friends whom he could trust, that this number *thirteen* was to be interpreted in a fashion which would astonish many people, if it were permitted to say all that one knew (1813).

The fact was that the Priore Blanès, a man whose honesty and virtue were primitive, and a man of parts as well, spent all his nights up in his belfry; he was mad on astrology. After using up all his days in calculating the conjunctions and positions of the stars, he would devote the greater part of his nights to following their course in the sky. Such was his poverty, he had no other instrument than a long telescope with pasteboard tubes. One may imagine the contempt that was felt for the study of languages by a man who spent his time discovering the precise dates of the fall of empires and the revolutions that change the face of the world. "What more do I know about a horse," he asked Fabrizio, "when I am told that in Latin it is called *equus?*"

The *contadini* looked upon Priore Blanès with awe as a great magician: for his part, by dint of the fear that his nightly stations in the belfry inspired, he restrained them from stealing. His clerical brethren in the surrounding parishes, intensely jealous of his influence, detested him; the Marchese del Dongo merely despised him, because he reasoned too much for a man of such humble station. Fabrizio adored him: to gratify him he sometimes spent whole evenings in doing enormous sums of addition or multiplication. Then he would go up to the belfry: this was a great favour and one that Priore Blanès had never granted to anyone; but he liked the boy for his simplicity. "If you do not turn out a hypocrite," he would say to him, "you will perhaps be a man."

Two or three times in a year, Fabrizio, intrepid and passionate in his pleasures, came within an inch of drowning himself in the lake. He was the leader of all the great expeditions made by the young *contadini* of Grianta and Cadenabbia. These boys had procured a number of little keys, and on very dark nights would try to open the padlocks of the chains that fastened the boats to some big stone or to a tree growing by the water's edge. It should be explained that on the Lake of Como the fishermen in the pursuit of their calling put out night-lines at a great distance from the shore. The upper end of the line is attached to a plank kept afloat by a cork keel, and a supple hazel twig, fastened to this plank, supports a little bell which rings whenever a fish, caught on the line, gives a tug to the float.

The great object of these nocturnal expeditions, of which

Fabrizio was commander in chief, was to go out and visit the night-lines before the fishermen had heard the warning note of the little bells. They used to choose stormy weather, and for these hazardous exploits would embark in the early morning, an hour before dawn. As they climbed into the boat, these boys imagined themselves to be plunging into the greatest dangers; this was the finer aspect of their behaviour; and, following the example of their fathers, would devoutly repeat a *Hail, Mary*. Now it frequently happened that at the moment of starting, and immediately after the *Hail, Mary*, Fabrizio was struck by a foreboding. This was the fruit which he had gathered from the astronomical studies of his friend Priore Blanès, in whose predictions he had no faith whatsoever. According to his youthful imagination, this foreboding announced to him infallibly the success or failure of the expedition; and, as he had a stronger will than any of his companions, in course of time the whole band had so formed the habit of having forebodings that if, at the moment of embarking, one of them caught sight of a priest on the shore, or if someone saw a crow fly past on his left, they would hasten to replace the padlock on the chain of the boat, and each would go off to his bed. Thus Priore Blanès had not imparted his somewhat difficult science to Fabrizio; but, unconsciously, had infected him with an unbounded confidence in the signs by which the future can be foretold.

The Marchese felt that any accident to his ciphered correspondence might put him at the mercy of his sister; and so every year, at the feast of Sant'Angela, which was Contessa Pietranera's name-day, Fabrizio was given leave to go and spend a week at Milan. He lived through the year looking hopefully forward or sadly back to this week. On this great occasion, to carry out this politic mission, the Marchese handed over to his son four scudi, and, in accordance with his custom, gave nothing to his wife, who took the boy. But one of the cooks, six lackeys and a coachman with a pair of horses started for Como the day before, and every day at Milan the Marchesa found a carriage at her disposal and a dinner of twelve covers.

The sullen sort of life that was led by the Marchese del Dongo was certainly by no means entertaining, but it had this advantage that it permanently enriched the families who were kind enough to sacrifice themselves to it. The Marchese, who had an income of more than two hundred thousand lire,

did not spend a quarter of that sum; he was living on hope.
Throughout the thirteen years from 1800 to 1813, he
constantly and firmly believed that Napoleon would be over-
thrown within six months. One may judge of his rapture
when, at the beginning of 1813, he learned of the disasters
of the Beresima! The taking of Paris and the fall of Napoleon almost made him lose his head; he then allowed himself to make the most outrageous remarks to his wife and
sister. Finally, after fourteen years of waiting, he had that
unspeakable joy of seeing the Austrain troops re-enter Milan.
In obedience to orders issued from Vienna, the Austrian
General received the Marchese del Dongo with a consideration
akin to respect; they hastened to offer him one of the
highest posts in the government; and he accepted it as the
payment of a debt. His elder son obtained a lieutenancy in
one of the smartest regiments of the Monarchy, but the
younger repeatedly declined to accept a cadetship which
was offered him. This triumph, in which the Marchese exulted
with a rare insolence, lasted but a few months, and was
followed by a humiliating reverse. Never had he had any
talent for business, and fourteen years spent in the country
among his footmen, his lawyer and his doctor, added to the
crustiness of old age which had overtaken him, had left
him totally incapable of conducting business in any form.
Now it is not possible, in an Austrian country, to keep
an important place without having the kind of talent that is
required by the slow and complicated, but highly reasonable
administration of that venerable Monarchy. The blunders
made by the Marchese del Dongo scandalised the staff of his
office, and even obstructed the course of public business. His
ultra-monarchist utterances irritated the populace which the
authorities sought to lull into a heedless slumber. One fine
day he learned that His Majesty had been graciously pleased
to accept the resignation which he had submitted of his post
in the administration, and at the same time conferred on
him the place of *Second Grand Major-domo Major* of the
Lombardo-Venetian Kingdom. The Marchese was furious at
the atrocious injustice of which he had been made a victim;
he printed an open letter to a friend, he who so inveighed
against the liberty of the press. Finally, he wrote to the
Emperor that his Ministers were playing him false, and were
no better than Jacobins. These things accomplished, he went
sadly back to his castle of Grianta. He had one consolation.
After the fall of Napoleon, certain powerful personages at

Milan planned an assault in the streets on Conte Prina, a former Minister of the King of Italy, and a man of the highest merit. Conte Pietranera risked his own life to save that of the Minister, who was killed by blows from umbrellas after five hours of agony. A priest, the Marchese del Dongo's confessor, could have saved Prina by opening the wicket of the church of San Giovanni, in front of which the unfortunate Minister was dragged, and indeed left for a moment in the gutter, in the middle of the street; but he refused with derision to open his wicket, and, six months afterwards, the Marchese was happily able to secure for him a fine advancement.

He execrated Conte Pietranera, his brother-in-law, who, not having an income of 50 louis, had the audacity to be quite content, made a point of showing himself loyal to what he had loved all his life, and had the insolence to preach that spirit of justice without regard for persons, which the Marchese called an infamous piece of Jacobinism. The Conte had refused to take service in Austria; this refusal was remembered against him, and, a few months after the death of Prina, the same persons who had hired the assassins contrived that General Pietranera should be flung into prison. Whereupon the Contessa, his wife, procured a passport and sent for posthorses to go to Vienna to tell the Emperor the truth. Prina's assassins took fright, and one of them, a cousin of Signora Pietranera, came to her at midnight, an hour before she was to start for Vienna, with the order for her husband's release. Next day, the Austrian General sent for Conte Pietranera, received him with every possible mark of distinction, and assured him that his pension as a retired officer would be issued to him without delay and on the most liberal scale. The gallant General Bubna, a man of sound judgement and warm heart, seemed quite ashamed of the assassination of Prina and the Conte's imprisonment.

After this brief storm, allayed by the Contessa's firmness of character, the couple lived, for better or worse, on the retired pay for which, thanks to General Bubna's recommendation, they were not long kept waiting.

Fortunately, it so happened that, for the last five or six years, the Contessa had been on the most friendly terms with a very rich young man, who was also an intimate friend of the Conte, and never failed to place at their disposal the finest team of English horses to be seen in Milan at the time, his box in the theatre *alla Scala* and his villa in the country. But the Conte had a sense of his own valour, he was full of generous impulses, he was easily carried away, and at such times allowed himself to make imprudent speeches. One day when he was out shooting with some young men, one of them, who had served under other flags than his, began to belittle the courage of the soldiers of the Cisalpine Republic. The Conte struck him, a fight at once followed, and the Conte, who was without support among all these young men, was killed. This species of duel gave rise to a great deal of talk, and the persons who had been engaged in it took the precaution of going for a tour in Switzerland.

That absurd form of courage which is called resignation, the courage of a fool who allows himself to be hanged without a word of protest, was not at all in keeping with the Contessa's character. Furious at the death of her husband, she would have liked Limercati, the rich young man, her intimate friend, to be seized also by the desire to travel in Switzerland, and there to shoot or otherwise assault the murderer of Conte Pietranera.

Limercati thought this plan the last word in absurdity, and the Contessa discovered that in herself contempt for him had killed her affection. She multiplied her attentions to Limercati; she sought to rekindle his love, and then to leave him stranded and so make him desperate. To render this plan of vengeance intelligible to French readers, I should explain that at Milan, in a land widely remote from our own, people are still made desperate by love. The Contessa, who, in her widow's weeds, easily eclipsed any of her rivals, flirted with all the young men of rank and fashion, and one of these, Conte N——, who, from the first, had said that he felt Limercati's good qualities to be rather heavy, rather starched for so spirited a woman, fell madly in love with her. She wrote to Limercati:

"Will you for once act like a man of spirit? Please to consider that you have never known me.

"I am, with a trace of contempt perhaps, your most humble servant,

"GINA PIETRANERA."

After reading this missive, Limercati set off for one of his country seats, his love rose to a climax, he became quite mad and spoke of blowing out his brains, an unheard-of thing in

countries where hell is believed in. Within twenty-four hours
of his arrival in the country, he had written to the Contessa
offering her his hand and his rent-roll of 200,000 francs. She
sent him back his letter, with its seal unbroken, by Conte
N——'s groom. Whereupon Limercati spent three years on
his estates, returning every other month to Milan, but without
ever having the courage to remain there, and boring all his
friends with his passionate love for the Contessa and his detailed accounts of the favours she had formerly bestowed on
him. At first, he used to add that with Conte N—— she was
ruining herself, and that such a connexion was degrading to
her.

The fact of the matter was that the Contessa had no sort
of love for Conte N——, and she told him as much when
she had made quite sure of Limercati's despair. The Conte,
who was no novice, besought her upon no account to
divulge the sad truth which she had confided to him. "If you
will be so extremely indulgent," he added, "as to continue to
receive me with all the outward distinctions accorded to a
reigning lover, I may perhaps be able to find a suitable
position."

After this heroic declaration the Contessa declined to avail
herself any longer either of Conte N——'s horses or of his
box. But for the last fifteen years she had been accustomed to
the most fashionable style of living; she had now to solve
that difficult, or rather impossible, problem: how to live in
Milan on a pension of 1,500 francs. She left her *palazzo,*
took a pair of rooms on a fifth floor, dismissed all her servants, including even her own maid whose place she filled
with a poor old woman to do the housework. This sacrifice
was as a matter of fact less heroic and less painful than it appears to us; at Milan poverty is not a thing to laugh at, and
therefore does not present itself to trembling souls as the
worst of evils. After some months of this noble poverty, besieged by incessant letters from Limercati, and indeed from
Conte N——, who also wished to marry her, it came to pass
that the Marchese del Dongo, miserly as a rule to the last
degree, bethought himself that his enemies might find a
cause for triumph in his sister's plight. What! A del Dongo
reduced to living upon the pension which the court of Vienna,
of which he had so many grounds for complaint, grants to the
widows of its Generals!

He wrote to inform her that an apartment and an allowance worthy of his sister awaited her at the castle of Grianta.

The Contessa's volatile mind embraced with enthusiasm the idea of this new mode of life; it was twenty years since she had lived in that venerable castle that rose majestically from among its old chestnuts planted in the days of the Sforza. "There," she told herself, "I shall find repose, and, at my age, is not that in itself happiness?" (Having reached one-and-thirty, she imagined that the time had come for her to retire.) "On that sublime lake by which I was born, there awaits me at last a happy and peaceful existence."

I cannot say whether she was mistaken, but one thing certain is that this passionate soul, which had just refused so lightly the offer of two vast fortunes, brought happiness to the castle of Grianta. Her two nieces were wild with joy. "You have renewed the dear days of my youth," the Marchesa told her, as she took her in her arms; "before you came, I was a hundred." The Contessa set out to revisit, with Fabrizio, all those enchanting spots in the neighbourhood of Grianta, which travellers have made so famous: the Villa Melzi on the other shore of the lake, opposite the castle, and commanding a fine view of it; higher up, the sacred wood of the Sfrondata, and the bold promontory which divides the two arms of the lake, that of Como, so voluptuous, and the other, which runs towards Lecco, grimly severe: sublime and charming views which the most famous site in the world, the Bay of Naples, may equal, but does not surpass. It was with ecstasy that the Contessa recaptured the memories of her earliest childhood and compared them with her present sensations. "The Lake of Como," she said to herself, "is not surrounded, like the Lake of Geneva, by wide tracts of land enclosed and cultivated according to the most approved methods, which suggest money and speculation. Here, on every side, I see hills of irregular height covered with clumps of trees that have grown there at random, which the hand of man has never yet spoiled and forced to *yield a return*. Standing among these admirably shaped hills which run down to the lake at such curious angles, I can preserve all the illusions of Tasso's and Ariosto's descriptions. All is noble and tender, everything speaks of love, nothing recalls the ugliness of civilisation. The villages halfway up their sides are hidden in tall trees, and above the tree-tops rises the charming architecture of their picturesque belfries. If some little field fifty yards across comes here and there to interrupt the clumps of chestnuts and wild cherries, the satisfied eye sees growing on it plants more vigorous and happier than else-

where. Beyond these hills, the crests of which offer one her-
mitages in all of which one would like to dwell, the astonished
eye perceives the peaks of the Alps, always covered in snow,
and their stern austerity recalls to one so much of the sorrows of life as is necessary to enhance one's immediate
pleasure. The imagination is touched by the distant sound
of the bell of some little village hidden among the trees:
these sounds, borne across the waters which soften their tone,
assume a tinge of gentle melancholy and resignation, and
seem to be saying to man: 'Life is fleeting: do not therefore
show yourself so obdurate towards the happiness that is offered you, make haste to enjoy it.'" The language of these
enchanting spots, which have not their like in the world, restored to the Contessa the heart of a girl of sixteen. She
could not conceive how she could have spent all these years
without revisiting the lake. "Is it then to the threshold of
old age," she asked herself, "that our happiness takes flight?"
She bought a boat which Fabrizio, the Marchesa and she
decorated with their own hands, having no money to spend
on anything, in the midst of this most luxurious establishment; since his disgrace the Marchese del Dongo had doubled
his aristocratic state. For example, in order to reclaim ten
yards of land from the lake, near the famous plane avenue, in
the direction of Cadenabbia, he had an embankment built
the estimate for which ran to 80,000 francs. At the end of
this embankment there rose, from the plans of the famous
Marchese Cagnola, a chapel built entirely of huge blocks of
granite, and in this chapel Marchesi, the sculptor then in
fashion at Milan, built him a tomb on which a number of
bas-reliefs were intended to represent the gallant deeds of his
ancestors.

Fabrizio's elder brother, the Marchesino Ascanio, sought
to join the ladies in their excursions; but his aunt flung
water over his powdered hair, and found some fresh dart
every day with which to puncture his solemnity. At length
he delivered from the sight of his fat, pasty face the merry
troop who did not venture to laugh in his presence. They
supposed him to be the spy of the Marchese, his father, and
care had to be taken in handling that stern despot, always in a
furious temper since his enforced retirement.

Ascanio swore to be avenged on Fabrizio.

There was a storm in which they were all in danger; although they were infinitely short of money, they paid the
two boatmen generously not to say anything to the Marchese,

who already was showing great ill humour at their taking
his two daughters with them. They encountered a second
storm; the storms on this lake are terrible and unexpected:
gusts of wind sweep out suddenly from the two mountain
gorges which run down into it on opposite sides and join
battle on the water. The Contessa wished to land in the midst
of the hurricane and pealing thunder; she insisted that, if
she were to climb to a rock that stood up by itself in the
middle of the lake and was the size of a small room, she
would enjoy a curious spectacle; she would see herself as-
sailed on all sides by raging waves; but in jumping out of the
boat she fell into the water. Fabrizio dived in after her to
save her, and both were carried away for some distance. No
doubt it is not a pleasant thing to feel oneself drowning;
but the spirit of boredom, taken by surprise, was banished
from the feudal castle. The Contessa conceived a passionate
enthusiasm for the primitive nature of the Priore Blanès and
for his astrology. The little money that remained to her after
the purchase of the boat had been spent on buying a spy-
glass, and almost every evening, with her nieces and
Fabrizio, she would take her stand on the platform of one
of the Gothic towers of the castle. Fabrizio was the learned
one of the party, and they spent many hours there very pleas-
antly, out of reach of the spies.

It must be admitted that there were days on which the
Contessa did not utter a word to anyone; she would be seen
strolling under the tall chestnuts lost in sombre meditations;
she was too clever a woman not to feel at times the tedium
of having no one with whom to exchange ideas. But next
day she would be laughing as before: it was the lamentations
of her sister-in-law, the Marchesa, that produced these
sombre impressions on a mind naturally so active.

"Are we to spend all the youth that is left to us in this
gloomy castle?" the Marchesa used to exclaim.

Before the Contessa came, she had not had the courage
even to feel these regrets.

Such was their life during the winter of 1814 and 1815. On
two occasions, in spite of her poverty, the Contessa went to
spend a few days at Milan; she was anxious to see a sublime
ballet by Vigano, given at the Scala, and the Marchese raised
no objections to his wife's accompanying her sister-in-law.
They went to draw the arrears of the little pension, and it
was the penniless widow of the Cisalpine General who lent
a few sequins to the millionaire Marchesa del Dongo. These

parties were delightful; they invited old friends to dinner, and consoled themselves by laughing at everything, just like children. This Italian gaiety, full of surprise and *brio,* made them forget the atmosphere of sombre gloom which the stern faces of the Marchese and his elder son spread around them at Grianta. Fabrizio, though barely sixteen, represented the head of the house admirably.

On the 7th of March, 1815, the ladies had been back for two days after a charming little excursion to Milan; they were strolling under the fine avenue of plane trees, then recently extended to the very edge of the lake. A boat appeared, coming from the direction of Como, and made strange signals. One of the Marchese's agents leaped out upon the bank: Napoleon had just landed from the Gulf of Juan. Europe was kind enough to be surprised at this event, which did not at all surprise the Marchese del Dongo; he wrote his Sovereign a letter full of the most cordial effusion; he offered him his talents and several millions of money, and informed him once again that his Ministers were Jacobins and in league with the ringleaders in Paris.

On the 8th of March, at six o'clock in the morning, the Marchese, wearing all his orders, was making his elder son dictate to him the draft of a third political despatch; he was solemnly occupied in transcribing this in his fine and careful hand, upon paper that bore the Sovereign's effigy as a watermark. At the same moment, Fabrizio was knocking at Contessa Pietranera's door.

"I am off," he informed her, "I am going to join the Emperor who is also King of Italy; he was such a good friend to your husband! I shall travel through Switzerland. Last night, at Menaggio, my friend Vasi, the dealer in barometers, gave me his passport; now you must give me a few napoleons, for I have only a couple on me; but if necessary I shall go on foot."

The Contessa wept with joy and grief. "Great Heavens! What can have put that idea into your head?" she cried, seizing Fabrizio's hands in her own.

She rose and went to fetch from the linen-cupboard, where it was carefully hidden, a little purse embroidered with pearls; it was all that she possessed in the world.

"Take it," she said to Fabrizio; "but, in heaven's name, do not let yourself be killed. What will your poor mother and I have left, if you are taken from us? As for Napoleon's succeeding, that, my poor boy, is impossible; our gentlemen will certainly manage to destroy him. Did you not hear, a week ago, at Milan the story of the twenty-three plots to assassinate him, all so carefully planned, from which it was only by a miracle that he escaped? And at that time he was all-powerful. And you have seen that it is not the will to destroy him that is lacking in our enemies; France ceased to count after he left it."

It was in a tone of the keenest emotion that the Contessa spoke to Fabrizio of the fate in store for Napoleon. "In allowing you to go to join him, I am sacrificing to him the dearest thing I have in the world," she said. Fabrizio's eyes grew moist, he shed tears as he embraced the Contessa, but his determination to be off was never for a moment shaken. He explained with effusion to this beloved friend all the reasons that had led to his decision, reasons which we take the liberty of finding highly attractive.

"Yesterday evening, it wanted seven minutes to six, we were strolling, you remember, by the shore of the lake along the plane avenue, below the *casa Sommariva,* and we were facing the south. It was there that I first noticed, in the distance, the boat that was coming from Como, bearing such great tidings. As I looked at this boat without thinking of the Emperor, and only envying the lot of those who are free to travel, suddenly I felt myself seized by a profound emotion. The boat touched ground, the agent said something in a low tone to my father, who changed colour, and took us aside to announce the *terrible news.* I turned towards the lake with no other object but to hide the tears of joy that were flooding my eyes. Suddenly, at an immense height in the sky and on my right-hand side, I saw an eagle, the bird of Napoleon; he flew majestically past making for Switzerland, and consequently for Paris. 'And I too,' I said to myself at that moment, 'will fly across Switzerland with the speed of an eagle, and will go to offer that great man a very little thing, but the only thing, after all, that I have to offer him, the support of my feeble arm. He wished to give us a country, and he loved my uncle.' At that instant, while I was gazing at the eagle, in some strange way my tears ceased to flow; and the proof that this idea came from above is that at the same moment, without any discussion, I made up my mind to go, and saw how the journey might be made. In the twinkling of an eye all the sorrows that, as you know, are poisoning my life, especially on Sundays, seemed to be swept away by a breath from heaven. I saw that mighty figure of Italy raise herself from the mire in which the Germans keep her plunged; [1] she stretched out her mangled arms still half loaded with chains towards her King and Liberator. 'And I,' I said to myself, 'a son as yet unknown to fame of that unhappy Mother, I shall go forth to die or to conquer with that man marked out by destiny, who sought to cleanse us from the scorn that is heaped upon us by even the most enslaved and the vilest among the inhabitants of Europe.'

"You know," he added in a low tone drawing nearer to the Contessa, and fastening upon her a pair of eyes from which fire darted, "you know that young chestnut which my mother, in the winter in which I was born, planted with her own hands beside the big spring in our forest, two leagues from here; before doing anything else I wanted to visit it. 'The spring is not far advanced,' I said to myself, 'very well, if my tree is in leaf, that shall be a sign for me. I also must emerge from the state of torpor in which I am languishing in this cold and dreary castle.' Do you not feel that these old blackened walls, the symbols now as they were once the instruments of despotism, are a perfect image of the dreariness of winter? They are to me what winter is to my tree.

"Would you believe it, Gina? Yesterday evening at half past seven I came to my chestnut; it had leaves, pretty little leaves that were quite big already! I kissed them, carefully so as not to hurt them. I turned the soil reverently round the dear tree. At once filled with a fresh enthusiasm, I crossed the mountain; I came to Menaggio: I needed a passport to enter Switzerland. The time had flown, it was already one o'clock in the morning when I found myself at Vasi's door. I thought that I should have to knock for a long time to arouse him, but he was sitting up with three of his friends. At the first word I uttered: 'You are going to join Napoleon,' he cried; and he fell on my neck. The others too embraced me with rapture. 'Why am I married?' I heard one of them say."

Signora Pietranera had grown pensive. She felt that she must offer a few objections. If Fabrizio had had the slightest experience of life, he would have seen quite well that the Contessa herself did not believe in the sound reasons which she hastened to urge on him. But, failing experience, he had resolution; he did not condescend even to hear what those

[1] The speaker is carried away by passion; he is rendering in prose some lines of the famous Monti.

reasons were. The Contessa presently came down to making
him promise that at least he would inform his mother of his
intention.

"She will tell my sisters, and those women will betray me
without knowing it!" cried Fabrizio with a sort of heroic
grandeur.

"You should speak more respectfully," said the Contessa,
smiling through her tears, "of the sex that will make your
fortune; for you will never appeal to men, you have too much
fire for prosaic souls."

The Marchesa dissolved in tears on learning her son's
strange plan; she could not feel its heroism, and did everything in her power to keep him at home. When she was
convinced that nothing in the world, except the walls of a
prison, could prevent him from starting, she handed over to
him the little money that she possessed; then she remembered that she had also, the day before, received nine or ten
small diamonds, worth perhaps ten thousand francs, which
the Marchese had entrusted to her to take to Milan to be set.
Fabrizio's sisters came into their mother's room while the
Contessa was sewing these diamonds into our hero's travelling coat; he handed the poor women back their humble napoleons. His sisters were so enthusiastic over his plan, they
kissed him with so clamorous a joy that he took in his hand
the diamonds that had still to be concealed and was for
starting off there and then.

"You will betray me without knowing it," he said to his
sisters. "Since I have all this money, there is no need to take
clothes; one can get them anywhere." He embraced these
dear ones and set off at once without even going back to his
own room. He walked so fast, afraid of being followed by
men on horseback, that before night he had entered Lugano.
He was now, thank heaven, in a Swiss town, and had no longer any fear of being waylaid on the lonely road by constables in his father's pay. From this haven, he wrote him a
fine letter, a boyish weakness which gave strength and substance to the Marchese's anger. Fabrizio took the post,
crossed the Saint-Gothard; his progress was rapid, and he entered France by Pontarlier. The Emperor was in Paris. There
Fabrizio's troubles began; he had started out with the firm intention of speaking to the Emperor: it had never occurred to
him that this might be a difficult matter. At Milan, ten times
daily he used to see Prince Eugène, and could have
spoken to him had he wished. In Paris, every morning he

went to the courtyard of the Tuileries to watch the reviews held by Napoleon; but never was he able to come near the Emperor. Our hero imagined all the French to be profoundly disturbed, as he himself was, by the extreme peril in which their country lay. At table in the hotel in which he was staying, he made no mystery about his plans; he found several young men with charming manners, even more enthusiastic than himself, who, in a very few days, did not fail to rob him of all the money that he possessed. Fortunately, out of pure modesty, he had said nothing of the diamonds given him by his mother. On the morning when, after an orgy overnight, he found that he had been decidedly robbed, he bought a fine pair of horses, engaged as servant an old soldier, one of the dealer's grooms, and, filled with contempt for the young men of Paris with their fine speeches, set out to join the army. He knew nothing except that it was concentrated near Maubeuge. No sooner had he reached the frontier than he felt that it would be absurd for him to stay in a house, toasting himself before a good fire, when there were soldiers in bivouac outside. In spite of the remonstrances of his servant, who was not lacking in common sense, he rashly made his way to the bivouacs on the extreme frontier, on the road into Belgium. No sooner had he reached the first battalion that was resting by the side of the road than the soldiers began to stare at the sight of this young civilian in whose appearance there was nothing that suggested uniform. Night was falling, a cold wind blew. Fabrizio went up to a fire and offered to pay for hospitality. The soldiers looked at one another amazed more than anything at the idea of payment, and willingly made room for him by the fire. His servant constructed a shelter for him. But, an hour later, the *adjudant* of the regiment happening to pass near the bivouac, the soldiers went to report to him the arrival of this stranger speaking bad French. The *adjudant* questioned Fabrizio, who spoke to him of his enthusiasm for the Emperor in an accent which aroused grave suspicion; whereupon this under-officer requested our hero to go with him to the Colonel, whose headquarters were in a neighbouring farm. Fabrizio's servant came up with the two horses. The sight of them seemed to make so forcible an impression upon the *adjudant* that immediately he changed his mind and began to interrogate the servant also. The latter, an old soldier, guessing his questioner's plan of campaign from the first, spoke of the powerful protection which his master enjoyed, adding that certainly they would not *bone* his fine horses. At once a soldier called by the *adjutant* put his hand on the servant's collar; another soldier took charge of the horses, and, with an air of severity, the *adjutant* ordered Fabrizio to follow him and not to answer back.

After making him cover a good league on foot, in the darkness rendered apparently more intense by the fires of the bivouacs which lighted the horizon on every side, the adjutant handed Fabrizio over to an officer of *gendarmerie* who, with a grave air, asked for his papers. Fabrizio showed his passport, which described him as a dealer in barometers travelling with his wares.

"What fools they are!" cried the officer; "this really is too much."

He put a number of questions to our hero, who spoke of the Emperor and of Liberty in terms of the keenest enthusiasm; whereupon the officer of *gendarmerie* went off in peals of laughter.

"Gad! You're no good at telling a tale!" he cried. "It is a bit too much of a good thing their daring to send us young mugs like you!" And despite all the protestations of Fabrizio, who was dying to explain that he was not really a dealer in barometers, the officer sent him to the prison of B——, a small town in the neighbourhood, where our hero arrived at about three o'clock in the morning, beside himself with rage and half dead with exhaustion.

Fabrizio, astonished at first, then furious, understanding absolutely nothing of what was happening to him, spent thirty-three long days in this wretched prison; he wrote letter after letter to the town commandant, and it was the gaoler's wife, a handsome Fleming of six-and-thirty, who undertook to deliver them. But as she had no wish to see so nice-looking a boy shot, and as moreover he paid well, she put all these letters without fail in the fire. Late in the evening, she would deign to come in and listen to the prisoner's complaints; she had told her husband that the young greenhorn had money, after which the prudent gaoler allowed her a free hand. She availed herself of this licence and received several gold napoleons in return, for the *adjutant* had taken only the horses, and the officer of *gendarmerie* had confiscated nothing at all. One afternoon in the month of June, Fabrizio heard a violent cannonade at some distance. So they were fighting at last! His heart leaped with impatience. He heard also a great deal of noise in the town; as a matter of fact a big movement of troops was being effected; three divisions were passing through B——. When, about eleven o'clock, the gaoler's wife came in to share his griefs, Fabrizio was even more friendly than usual; then, seizing hold of her hands:

"Get me out of here; I swear on my honour to return to prison as soon as they have stopped fighting."

"Stuff and nonsense! Have you the *quibus?*" He seemed worried; he did not understand the word *quibus*. The gaoler's wife, noticing his dismay, decided that he must be in low water, and instead of talking in gold napoleons as she had intended talked now only in francs.

"Listen," she said to him, "if you can put down a hundred francs, I will place a double napoleon on each eye of the corporal who comes to change the guard during the night. He won't be able to see you breaking out of prison, and if his regiment is to march to-morrow he will accept."

The bargain was soon struck. The gaoler's wife even consented to hide Fabrizio in her own room, from which he could more easily make his escape in the morning.

Next day, before dawn, the woman, who was quite moved, said to Fabrizio:

"My dear boy, you are still far too young for that dirty trade; take my advice, don't go back to it."

"What!" stammered Fabrizio, "is it a crime then to wish to defend one's country?"

"Enough said. Always remember that I saved your life; your case was clear, you would have been shot. But don't say a word to anyone, or you will lose my husband and me our job; and whatever you do, don't go about repeating that silly tale about being a gentleman from Milan disguised as a dealer in barometers, it's too stupid. Listen to me now, I'm going to give you the uniform of a hussar who died the other day in the prison; open your mouth as little as you possibly can; but if a serjeant or an officer asks you questions so that you have to answer, say that you've been lying ill in the house of a peasant who took you in out of charity when you were shivering with fever in a ditch by the roadside. If that does not satisfy them, you can add that you are going back to your regiment. They may perhaps arrest you because of your accent; then say that you were born in Piedmont, that you're a conscript who was left in France last year, and all that sort of thing."

For the first time, after thirty-three days of blind fury, Fabrizio grasped the clue to all that had happened. They took

him for a spy. He argued with the gaoler's wife, who, that
morning, was most affectionate; and finally, while armed with
a needle she was taking in the hussar's uniform to fit him,
he told his whole story in so many words to the astonished
woman. For an instant she believed him; he had so innocent an air, and looked so nice dressed as a hussar.

"Since you have such a desire to fight," she said to him
at length half convinced, "what you ought to have done as
soon as you reached Paris was to enlist in a regiment. If
you had paid for a serjeant's drink, the whole thing would
have been settled." The gaoler's wife added much good advice for the future, and finally, at the first streak of dawn,
let Fabrizio out of the house, after making him swear
a hundred times over that he would never mention her
name, whatever happened. As soon as Fabrizio had left the
little town, marching boldly with the hussar's sabre under his
arm, he was seized by a scruple. "Here I am," he said to
himself, "with the clothes and the marching orders of a
hussar who died in prison, where he was sent, they say,
for stealing a cow and some silver plate! I have, so to speak,
inherited his identity . . . and without wishing it or expecting
it in any way! Beware of prison! The omen is clear, I shall
have much to suffer from prisons!"

Not an hour had passed since Fabrizio's parting from his
benefactress when the rain began to fall with such violence
that the new hussar was barely able to get along, hampered
by a pair of heavy boots which had not been made for him.
Meeting a peasant mounted upon a sorry horse, he bought
the animal, explaining by signs what he wanted; the gaoler's
wife had recommended him to speak as little as possible,
in view of his accent.

That day the army, which had just won the battle of
Ligny, was marching straight on Brussels. It was the eve
of the battle of Waterloo. Towards midday, the rain still continuing to fall in torrents, Fabrizio heard the sound of the
guns; this joy made him completely oblivious of the fearful
moments of despair in which so unjust an imprisonment had
plunged him. He rode on until late at night, and, as he
was beginning to have a little common sense, went to seek
shelter in a peasant's house a long way from the road. This
peasant wept and pretended that everything had been taken
from him; Fabrizio gave him a crown, and he found some
barley. "My horse is no beauty," Fabrizio said to himself,
"but that makes no difference, he may easily take the fancy

of some *adjutant*," and he went to lie down in the stable by its side. An hour before dawn Fabrizio was on the road, and, by copious endearments, succeeded in making his horse trot. About five o'clock, he heard the cannonade: it was the preliminaries of Waterloo.

CHAPTER THREE

FABRIZIO SOON came upon some *vivandières*, and the extreme gratitude that he felt for the gaoler's wife of B—— impelled him to address them; he asked one of them where he would find the 4th Hussar Regiment, to which he belonged.

"You would do just as well not to be in such a hurry, young soldier," said the *cantinière*, touched by Fabrizio's pallor and glowing eyes. "Your wrist is not strong enough yet for the sabre-thrusts they'll be giving to-day. If you had a musket, I don't say, maybe you could let off your round as well as any of them."

This advice displeased Fabrizio; but however much he urged on his horse, he could go no faster than the *cantinière* in her cart. Every now and then the sound of the guns seemed to come nearer and prevented them from hearing each other speak, for Fabrizio was so beside himself with enthusiasm and delight that he had renewed the conversation. Every word uttered by the *cantinière* intensified his happiness by making him understand it. With the exception of his real name and his escape from prison, he ended by confiding everything to this woman who seemed such a good soul. She was greatly surprised and understood nothing at all of what this handsome young soldier was telling her.

"I see what it is," she exclaimed at length with an air of triumph. "You're a young gentleman who has fallen in love with the wife of some captain in the 4th Hussars. Your mistress will have made you a present of the uniform you're wearing, and you're going after her. As sure as God's in heaven, you've never been a soldier; but, like the brave boy you are, seeing your regiment's under fire, you want to be there too, and not let them think you a chicken."

Fabrizio agreed with everything; it was his only way of procuring good advice. "I know nothing of the ways of these French people," he said to himself, "and if I am not guided by someone I shall find myself being put in prison again, and they'll steal my horse."

"First of all, my boy," said the *cantinière*, who was becoming more and more of a friend to him, "confess that you're not one-and-twenty: at the very most you might be seventeen."

This was the truth, and Fabrizio admitted as much with good grace.

"Then, you aren't even a conscript; it's simply because of Madame's pretty face that you're going to get your bones broken. Plague it, she can't be particular. If you've still got some of the *yellow-boys* she sent you, you must first of all buy yourself another horse; look how your screw pricks up his ears when the guns sound at all near; that's a peasant's horse, and will be the death of you as soon as you reach the line. That white smoke you see over there above the hedge, that's the infantry firing, my boy. So prepare for a fine fright when you hear the bullets whistling over you. You'll do as well to eat a bit while there's still time."

Fabrizio followed this advice and, presenting a napoleon to the *vivandière,* asked her to accept payment.

"It makes one weep to see him!" cried the woman; "the poor child doesn't even know how to spend his money! It would be no more than you deserve if I pocketed your napoleon and put Cocotte into a trot; damned if your screw could catch me up. What would you do, stupid, if you saw me go off? Bear in mind, when the *brute* growls, never to show your gold. Here," she went on, "here's 18 francs, 50 centimes, and your breakfast costs you 30 sous. Now, we shall soon have some horses for sale. If the beast is a small one, you'll give ten francs, and, in any case, never more than twenty, not if it was the horse of the Four Sons of Aymon."

The meal finished, the *vivandière,* who was still haranguing, was interrupted by a woman who had come across the fields and passed them on the road.

"Hallo there, hi!" this woman shouted. "Hallo, Margot! Your 6th Light are over there on the right."

"I must leave you, my boy," said the *vivandière* to our

hero; "but really and truly I pity you; I've taken quite a fancy to you, upon my word I have. You don't know a thing about anything, you're going to get a wipe in the eye, as sure as God's in heaven! Come along to the 6th Light with me."

"I quite understand that I know nothing," Fabrizio told her, "but I want to fight, and I'm determined to go over there towards that white smoke."

"Look how your horse is twitching his ears! As soon as he gets over there, even if he's no strength left, he'll take the bit in his teeth and start galloping, and heaven only knows where he'll land you. Will you listen to me now? As soon as you get to the troops, pick up a musket and a cartridge pouch, get down among the men and copy what you see them do, exactly the same: But, good heavens, I'll bet you don't even know how to open a cartridge."

Fabrizio, stung to the quick, admitted nevertheless to his new friend that she had guessed aright.

"Poor boy! He'll be killed straight away; sure as God! It won't take long. You've got to come with me, absolutely," went on the *cantinière* in a tone of authority.

"But I want to fight."

"You shall fight too; why, the 6th Light are famous fighters, and there's fighting enough to-day for everyone."

"But shall we come soon to the regiment?"

"In a quarter of an hour at the most."

"With this honest woman's recommendation," Fabrizio told himself, "my ignorance of everything won't make them take me for a spy, and I shall have a chance of fighting." At this moment the noise of the guns redoubled, each explosion coming straight on top of the last. "It's like a Rosary," said Fabrizio.

"We're beginning to hear the infantry fire now," said the *vivandière,* whipping up her little horse, which seemed quite excited by the firing.

The *cantinière* turned to the right and took a side road that ran through the fields; there was a foot of mud in it; the little cart seemed about to be stuck fast: Fabrizio pushed the wheel. His horse fell twice; presently the road, though with less water on it, was nothing more than a bridle path through the grass. Fabrizio had not gone five hundred yards when his nag stopped short: it was a corpse, lying across the path, which terrified horse and rider alike.

Fabrizio's face, pale enough by nature, assumed a markedly green tinge; the *cantinière*, after looking at the dead man, said, as though speaking to herself: "That's not one of our Division." Then, raising her eyes to our hero, she burst out laughing.

"Aha, my boy! There's a titbit for you!" Fabrizio sat frozen. What struck him most of all was the dirtiness of the feet of this corpse which had already been stripped of its shoes and left with nothing but an old pair of trousers all clotted with blood.

"Come nearer," the *cantinière* ordered him, "get off your horse, you'll have to get accustomed to them; look," she cried, "he's stopped one in the head."

A bullet, entering on one side of the nose, had gone out at the opposite temple, and disfigured the corpse in a hideous fashion. It lay with one eye still open.

"Get off your horse then, lad," said the *cantinière*, "and give him a shake of the hand to see if he'll return it."

Without hesitation, although ready to yield up his soul with disgust, Fabrizio flung himself from his horse and took the hand of the corpse which he shook vigorously; then he stood still as though paralysed. He felt that he had not the strength to mount again. What horrified him more than anything was that open eye.

"The *vivandière* will think me a coward," he said to himself bitterly. But he felt the impossibility of making any movement; he would have fallen. It was a frightful moment; Fabrizio was on the point of being physically sick. The *vivandière* noticed this, jumped lightly down from her little carriage, and held out to him, without saying a word, a glass of brandy which he swallowed at a gulp; he was able to mount his screw, and continued on his way without speaking. The *vivandière* looked at him now and again from the corner of her eye.

"You shall fight to-morrow, my boy," she said at length; "to-day you're going to stop with me. You can see now that you've got to learn the business before you can become a soldier."

"On the contrary, I want to start fighting at once," exclaimed our hero with a sombre air which seemed to the *vivandière* to augur well. The noise of the guns grew twice as loud and seemed to be coming nearer. The explosions began to form a continuous bass; there was no interval between one and the next, and above this running bass, which suggested the roar of a torrent in the distance, they could make out quite plainly the rattle of musketry.

At this point the road dived down into a clump of trees. The *vivandière* saw three or four soldiers of our army who were coming towards her as fast as their legs would carry them; she jumped nimbly down from her cart and ran into cover fifteen or twenty paces from the road. She hid herself in a hole which had been left where a big tree had recently been uprooted. "Now," thought Fabrizio, "we shall see whether I am a coward!" He stopped by the side of the little cart which the woman had abandoned, and drew his sabre. The soldiers paid no attention to him and passed at a run along the wood, to the left of the road.

"They're ours," said the *vivandière* calmly, as she came back, quite breathless, to her little cart. . . . "If your horse was capable of galloping, I should say: push ahead as far as the end of the wood, and see if there's anyone on the plain." Fabrizio did not wait to be told twice, he tore off a branch from a poplar, stripped it and started to lash his horse with all his might; the animal broke into a gallop for a moment, then fell back into its regular slow trot. The *vivandière* had put her horse into a gallop. "Stop, will you, stop!" she called after Fabrizio. Presently both were clear of the wood. Coming to the edge of the plain, they heard a terrifying din, guns and muskets thundered on every side, right, left, behind them. And as the clump of trees from which they emerged grew on a mound rising nine or ten feet above the plain, they could see fairly well a corner of the battle; but still there was no one to be seen in the meadow beyond the wood. This meadow was bordered, half a mile away, by a long row of willows, very bushy; above the willows appeared a white smoke which now and again rose eddying into the sky.

"If I only knew where the regiment was," said the *cantinière,* in some embarrassment. "It won't do to go straight ahead over this big field. By the way," she said to Fabrizio, "if you see one of the enemy, stick him with the point of your sabre, don't play about with the blade."

At this moment, the *cantinière* caught sight of the four soldiers whom we mentioned a little way back; they were coming out of the wood on to the plain to the left of the road. One of them was on horseback.

"There you are," she said to Fabrizio. "Hallo there!" she

called to the mounted man, "come over here and have a glass of brandy." The soldiers approached.

"Where are the 6th Light?" she shouted.

"Over there, five minutes away, across that canal that runs along by the willows; why, Colonel Macon has just been killed."

"Will you take five francs for your horse, you?"

"Five francs! That's not a bad one, *ma!* An officer's horse I can sell in ten minutes for five napoleons."

"Give me one of your napoleons," said the *vivandière* to Fabrizio. Then going up to the mounted soldier: "Get off, quickly," she said to him, "here's your napoleon."

The soldier dismounted, Fabrizio sprang gaily on to the saddle, the *vivandière* unstrapped the little portmanteau which was on his old horse.

"Come and help me, all of you!" she said to the soldiers, "is that the way you leave a lady to do the work?"

But no sooner had the captured horse felt the weight of the portmanteau than he began to rear, and Fabrizio, who was an excellent horseman, had to use all his strength to hold him.

"A good sign!" said the *vivandière*, "the gentleman is not accustomed to being tickled by portmanteaus."

"A general's horse," cried the man who had sold it, "a horse that's worth ten napoleons if it's worth a liard."

"Here are twenty francs," said Fabrizio, who could not contain himself for joy at feeling between his legs a horse that could really move.

At that moment a shot struck the line of willows, through which it passed obliquely, and Fabrizio had the curious spectacle of all those little branches flying this way and that as though mown down by a stroke of the scythe.

"Look, there's the *brute* advancing," the soldier said to him as he took the twenty francs. It was now about two o'clock.

Fabrizio was still under the spell of this strange spectacle when a party of generals, followed by a score of hussars, passed at a gallop across one corner of the huge field on the edge of which he had halted: his horse neighed, reared several times in succession, then began violently tugging the bridle that was holding him. "All right, then," Fabrizio said to himself.

The horse, left to his own devices, dashed off hell for leather to join the escort that was following the generals.

Fabrizio counted four gold-laced hats. A quarter of an hour later, from a few words said by one hussar to the next, Fabrizio gathered that one of these generals was the famous Marshal Ney. His happiness knew no bounds; only he had no way of telling which of the four generals was Marshal Ney; he would have given everything in the world to know, but he remembered that he had been told not to speak. The escort halted, having to cross a wide ditch left full of water by the rain overnight; it was fringed with tall trees and formed the left-hand boundary of the field at the entrance to which Fabrizio had bought the horse. Almost all the hussars had dismounted; the bank of the ditch was steep and very slippery and the water lay quite three or four feet below the level of the field. Fabrizio, distracted with joy, was thinking more of Marshal Ney and of glory than of his horse, which, being highly excited, jumped into the canal, thus splashing the water up to a considerable height. One of the generals was soaked to the skin by the sheet of water, and cried with an oath: "Damn the f—— brute!" Fabrizio felt deeply hurt by this insult. "Can I ask him to apologise?" he wondered. Meanwhile, to prove that he was not so clumsy after all, he set his horse to climb the opposite bank of the ditch; but it rose straight up and was five or six feet high. He had to abandon the attempt; then he rode up stream, his horse being up to its head in water, and at last found a sort of drinking-place. By this gentle slope he was easily able to reach the field on the other side of the canal. He was the first man of the escort to appear there; he started to trot proudly down the bank; below him, in the canal, the hussars were splashing about, somewhat embarrassed by their position, for in many places the water was five feet deep. Two or three horses took fright and began to swim, making an appalling mess. A serjeant noticed the manœuvre that this youngster, who looked so very unlike a soldier, had just carried out.

"Up here! There is a watering-place on the left!" he shouted, and in time they all crossed.

On reaching the farther bank, Fabrizio had found the generals there by themselves; the noise of the guns seemed to him to have doubled; and it was all he could do to hear the general whom he had given such a good soaking and who now shouted in his ear:

"Where did you get that horse?"

Fabrizio was so much upset that he answered in Italian:

"L'ho comprato poco fa." (I bought it just now.)

"What's that you say?" cried the general.

But the din at that moment became so terrific that Fabrizio could not answer him. We must admit that our hero was very little of a hero at that moment. However, fear came to him only as a secondary consideration; he was principally shocked by the noise, which hurt his ears. The escort broke into a gallop; they crossed a large batch of tilled land which lay beyond the canal. And this field was strewn with dead.

"Red-coats! red-coats!" the hussars of the escort exclaimed joyfully, and at first Fabrizio did not understand; then he noticed that as a matter of fact almost all these bodies wore red uniforms. One detail made him shudder with horror; he observed that many of these unfortunate red-coats were still alive; they were calling out, evidently asking for help, and no one stopped to give it them. Our hero, being most humane, took every possible care that his horse should not tread upon any of the red-coats. The escort halted; Fabrizio, who was not paying sufficient attention to his military duty, galloped on, his eyes fixed on a wounded wretch in front of him.

"Will you halt, you young fool!" the serjeant shouted after him. Fabrizio discovered that he was twenty paces on the generals' right front, and precisely in the direction in which they were gazing through their glasses. As he came back to take his place behind the other hussars, who had halted a few paces in rear of them, he noticed the biggest of these generals, who was speaking to his neighbour, a general also, in a tone of authority and almost of reprimand; he was swearing. Fabrizio could not contain his curiosity; and, in spite of the warning not to speak, given him by his friend the gaoler's wife, he composed a short sentence in good French, quite correct, and said to his neighbour:

"Who is that general who is *chewing up* the one next to him?"

"Gad, it's the Marshal!"

"What Marshal?"

"Marshal Ney, you fool! I say, where have you been serving?"

Fabrizio, although highly susceptible, had no thought of resenting this insult; he was studying, lost in childish admiration, the famous Prince de la Moskowa, the "Bravest of the Brave."

Suddenly they all moved off at full gallop. A few minutes later Fabrizio saw, twenty paces ahead of him, a ploughed field the surface of which was moving in a singular fashion. The furrows were full of water and the soil, very damp, which formed the ridges between these furrows kept flying off in little black lumps three or four feet into the air. Fabrizio noticed as he passed this curious effect; then his thoughts turned to dreaming of the Marshal and his glory. He heard a sharp cry close to him; two hussars fell struck by shot; and, when he looked back at them, they were already twenty paces behind the escort. What seemed to him horrible was a horse streaming with blood that was struggling on the ploughed land, its hooves caught in its own entrails; it was trying to follow the others: its blood ran down into the mire.

"Ah! So I am under fire at last!" he said to himself. "I have seen shots fired!" he repeated with a sense of satisfaction. "Now I am a real soldier." At that moment, the escort began to go hell for leather, and our hero realised that it was shot from the guns that was making the earth fly up all round him. He looked vainly in the direction from which the balls were coming, he saw the white smoke of the battery at an enormous distance, and, in the thick of the steady and continuous rumble produced by the artillery fire, he seemed to hear shots discharged much closer at hand: he could not understand in the least what was happening.

At that moment, the generals and their escort dropped into a little road filled with water which ran five feet below the level of the fields.

The Marshal halted and looked again through his glasses. Fabrizio, this time, could examine him at his leisure. He found him to be very fair, with a big red face. "We don't have any faces like that in Italy," he said to himself. "With my pale cheeks and chestnut hair, I shall never look like that," he added despondently. To him these words implied: "I shall never be a hero." He looked at the hussars; with a solitary exception, all of them had yellow moustaches. If Fabrizio was studying the hussars of the escort, they were all studying him as well. Their stare made him blush, and, to get rid of his embarrassment, he turned his head towards the enemy. They consisted of widely extended lines of men in red, but, what greatly surprised him, these men seemed to be quite minute. Their long files, which were regiments or divisions, appeared no taller than hedges. A line of red cavalry were trotting in the direction of the sunken road along which the Marshal and his escort had begun to move at a walk, splashing through the mud. The smoke made it impossible to distinguish anything in the direction in which they were advancing; now and then one saw men moving at a gallop against this background of white smoke.

Suddenly, from the direction of the enemy, Fabrizio saw four men approaching hell for leather. "Ah! We are attacked," he said to himself; then he saw two of these men speak to the Marshal. One of the generals on the latter's staff set off at a gallop towards the enemy, followed by two hussars of the escort and by the four men who had just come up. After a little canal which they all crossed, Fabrizio found himself riding beside a serjeant who seemed a good-natured fellow. "I must speak to this one," he said to himself, "then perhaps they'll stop staring at me." He thought for a long time.

"Sir, this is the first time that I have been present at a battle," he said at length to the serjeant. "But is this a real battle?"

"Something like. But who are you?"

"I am the brother of a captain's wife."

"And what is he called, your captain?"

Our hero was terribly embarrassed; he had never anticipated this question. Fortunately, the Marshal and his escort broke into a gallop. "What French name shall I say?" he wondered. At last he remembered the name of the innkeeper with whom he had lodged in Paris; he brought his horse up to the serjeant's, and shouted to him at the top of his voice:

"Captain Meunier!" The other, not hearing properly in the roar of the guns, replied: "Oh, Captain Teulier? Well, he's been killed." "Splendid," thought Fabrizio. "Captain Teulier; I must look sad."

"Good God!" he cried; and assumed a piteous mien. They had left the sunken road and were crossing a small meadow, they were going hell for leather, shots were coming over again, the Marshal headed for a division of cavalry. The escort found themselves surrounded by dead and wounded men; but this sight had already ceased to make any impression on our hero; he had other things to think of.

While the escort was halted, he caught sight of the little cart of a *cantinière*, and his affection for this honourable corps sweeping aside every other consideration, set off at a gallop to join her.

"Stay where you are, curse you," the serjeant shouted after him.

"What can he do to me here?" thought Fabrizio, and he continued to gallop towards the *cantinière*. When he put spurs to his horse, he had had some hope that it might be his good *cantinière* of the morning; the horse and the little cart bore a strong resemblance, but their owner was quite different, and our hero thought her appearance most forbidding. As he came up to her, Fabrizio heard her say: "And he was such a fine-looking man, too!" A very ugly sight awaited the new recruit; they were sawing off a cuirassier's leg at the thigh, a handsome young fellow of five feet ten. Fabrizio shut his eyes and drank four glasses of brandy straight off.

"How you do go for it, you boozer!" cried the *cantinière*. The brandy gave him an idea: "I must buy the goodwill of my comrades, the hussars of the escort."

"Give me the rest of the bottle," he said to the *vivandière*.

"What do you mean," was her answer, "what's left there costs ten francs, on a day like this."

As he rejoined the escort at a gallop:

"Ah! You're bringing us a drop of drink," cried the serjeant. "That was why you deserted, was it? Hand it over."

The bottle went round, the last man to take it flung it in the air after drinking. "Thank you, chum!" he cried to Fabrizio. All eyes were fastened on him kindly. This friendly gaze lifted a hundredweight from Fabrizio's heart; it was one of those hearts of too delicate tissue which require the friendship of those around it. So at last he had ceased to be looked at askance by his comrades; there was a bond between them! Fabrizio breathed a deep sigh of relief, then in a bold voice said to the serjeant:

"And if Captain Teulier has been killed, where shall I find my sister?" He fancied himself a little Machiavelli to be saying Teulier so naturally instead of Meunier.

"That's what you'll find out to-night," was the serjeant's reply.

The escort moved on again and made for some divisions of infantry. Fabrizio felt quite drunk; he had taken too much brandy, he was rolling slightly in his saddle: he remembered most opportunely a favourite saying of his mother's coachman: "When you've been lifting your elbow, look straight between your horse's ears, and do what the man next you does." The Marshal stopped for some time beside a number of cavalry units which he ordered to charge; but for an hour or two our hero was barely conscious of what was going on round about him. He was feeling extremely tired, and when his horse galloped he fell back on the saddle like a lump of lead.

Suddenly the serjeant called out to his men: "Don't you see the Emperor, curse you!" Whereupon the escort shouted: *"Vive l'Empereur!"* at the top of their voices. It may be imagined that our hero stared till his eyes started out of his head, but all he saw was some generals galloping, also followed by an escort. The long floating plumes of horsehair which the dragoons of the bodyguard wore on their helmets prevented him from distinguishing their faces. "So I have missed seeing the Emperor on a field of battle, all because of those cursed glasses of brandy!" This reflexion brought him back to his senses.

They went down into a road filled with water, the horses wished to drink.

"So that was the Emperor who went past then?" he asked the man next to him.

"Why, surely, the one with no braid on his coat. How is it you didn't see him?" his comrade answered kindly. Fabrizio felt a strong desire to gallop after the Emperor's escort and embody himself in it. What a joy to go really to war in the train of that hero! It was for that that he had come to France. "I am quite at liberty to do it," he said to himself, "for after all I have no other reason for being where I am but the will of my horse, which started galloping after these generals."

What made Fabrizio decide to stay where he was was that the hussars, his new comrades, seemed so friendly towards him; he began to imagine himself the intimate friend of all the troopers with whom he had been galloping for the last few hours. He saw arise between them and himself that noble friendship of the heroes of Tasso and Ariosto. If he were to attach himself to the Emperor's escort, there would be fresh acquaintances to be made, perhaps they would look at him askance, for these other horsemen were dragoons, and he was wearing the hussar uniform like all the rest that were following the Marshal. The way in which they now looked at him set our hero on a pinnacle of happiness; he would have done anything in the world for his comrades; his mind and soul were in the clouds. Everything seemed to have assumed a new aspect now that he was among friends; he was dying to ask them various questions. "But I am still a little drunk," he said to himself, "I must bear in mind what the gaoler's wife told me." He noticed on leaving the sunken road that the escort was no longer with Marshal Ney; the general whom they were following was tall and thin, with a dry face and an awe-inspiring eye.

This general was none other than Comte d'A——, the Lieutenant Robert of the 15th of May, 1796. How delighted he would have been to meet Fabrizio del Dongo!

It was already some time since Fabrizio had noticed the earth flying off in black crumbs on being struck by shot; they came in rear of a regiment of cuirassiers, he could hear distinctly the rattle of the grapeshot against their breastplates, and saw several men fall.

The sun was now very low and had begun to set when the escort, emerging from a sunken road, mounted a little bank three or four feet high to enter a ploughed field. Fabrizio heard an odd little sound quite close to him: he turned his head, four men had fallen with their horses; the general himself had been unseated, but picked himself up, covered in blood. Fabrizio looked at the hussars who were lying on the ground: three of them were still making convulsive movements, the fourth cried: "Pull me out!" The serjeant and two or three men had dismounted to assist the general, who, leaning upon his aide-de-camp, was attempting to walk a few steps; he was trying to get away from his horse, which lay on the ground struggling and kicking out madly.

The serjeant came up to Fabrizio. At that moment our hero heard a voice say behind him and quite close to his ear: "This is the only one that can still gallop." He felt himself seized by the feet; they were taken out of the stirrups at the same time as someone caught him underneath the arms; he was lifted over his horse's tail and then allowed to slip to the ground, where he landed sitting.

The aide-de-camp took Fabrizio's horse by the bridle; the general, with the help of the serjeant, mounted and rode off at a gallop; he was quickly followed by the six men who were left of the escort. Fabrizio rose up in a fury, and began to run after them shouting: *"Ladri! Ladri!"* (Thieves! Thieves!) It was an amusing experience to run after horse-stealers across a battlefield.

The escort and the general, Comte d'A——, disappeared presently behind a row of willows. Fabrizio, blind with rage, also arrived at this line of willows; he found himself brought to a halt by a canal of considerable depth which he crossed. Then, on reaching the other side, he began swearing again as he saw once more, but far away in the distance, the general and his escort vanishing among the trees. "Thieves! Thieves!" he cried, in French this time. In desperation, not so much at the loss of his horse as at the treachery to himself, he let himself sink down on the side of the ditch, tired out and dying of hunger. If his fine horse had been taken from him by the enemy, he would have thought no more about it; but to see himself betrayed and robbed by that serjeant whom he liked so much and by those hussars whom he regarded as brothers! That was what broke his heart. He could find no consolation for so great an infamy, and, leaning his back against a willow, began to shed hot tears. He abandoned one by one all those beautiful dreams of a chivalrous and sublime friendship, like that of the heroes of the *Gerusalemme Liberata*. To see death come to one was nothing, surrounded by heroic and tender hearts, by noble friends who clasp one by the hand as one yields one's dying breath! But to retain one's enthusiasm surrounded by a pack of vile scoundrels! Like all angry men Fabrizio exaggerated. After a quarter of an hour of this melting mood, he noticed that the guns were beginning to range on the row of trees in the shade of which he sat meditating. He rose and tried to find his bearings. He scanned those fields bounded by a wide canal and the row of pollard willows: he thought he knew where he was. He saw a body of infantry crossing the ditch and marching over the fields, a quarter of a league in front of him. "I was just falling asleep," he said to himself; "I must see that I'm not taken prisoner." And he put his best foot foremost. As he advanced, his mind was set at rest; he recognized the uniforms, the regiments by which he had been afraid of being cut off were French. He made a right incline so as to join them.

After the moral anguish of having been so shamefully betrayed and robbed, there came another which, at every moment, made itself felt more keenly; he was dying of hunger. It was therefore with infinite joy that after having walked, or rather run, for ten minutes, he saw that the column of infantry, which also had been moving very rapidly, was halting to take up a position. A few minutes later, he was among the nearest of the soldiers.

"Friends, could you sell me a mouthful of bread?"

"I say, here's a fellow who thinks we're bakers!"

This harsh utterance and the general guffaw that followed it had a crushing effect on Fabrizio. So war was no longer that noble and universal uplifting of souls athirst for glory which he had imagined it to be from Napoleon's proclamations! He sat down, or rather let himself fall on the grass; he turned very pale. The soldier who had spoken to him, and who had stopped ten paces off to clean the lock of his musket with his handkerchief, came nearer and flung him a lump of bread; then, seeing that he did not pick it up, broke off a piece which he put in our hero's mouth. Fabrizio opened his eyes, and ate the bread without having the strength to speak. When at length he looked round for the soldier to pay him, he found himself alone; the men nearest to him were a hundred yards off and were marching. Mechanically he rose and followed them. He entered a wood; he was dropping with exhaustion, and already had begun to look round for a comfortable resting-place; but what was his delight on recognising first of all the horse, then the cart, and finally the *cantinière* of that morning! She ran to him and was frightened by his appearance.

"Still going, my boy," she said to him; "you're wounded then? And where's your fine horse?" So saying she led him towards the cart, upon which she made him climb, supporting him under the arms. No sooner was he in the cart than our hero, utterly worn out, fell fast asleep.

CHAPTER FOUR

NOTHING COULD awaken him, neither the muskets fired close to the cart nor the trot of the horse which the *cantinière* was flogging with all her might. The regiment, attacked unexpectedly by swarms of Prussisn cavalry, after imagining all day that they were winning the battle, was beating a retreat or rather fleeing in the direction of France.

The colonel, a handsome young man, well turned out, who had succeeded Macon, was sabred; the battalion commander who took his place, an old man with white hair, ordered the regiment to halt. "Damn you," he cried to his men, "in the days of the Republic we waited till we were forced by the enemy before running away. Defend every inch of ground, and get yourselves killed!" he shouted, and swore at them. "It is the soil of the Fatherland that these Prussians want to invade now!"

The little cart halted; Fabrizio awoke with a start. The sun had set some time back; he was quite astonished to see that it was almost night. The troops were running in all directions in a confusion which greatly surprised our hero; they looked shame-faced, he thought.

"What is happening?" he asked the *cantinière*.

"Nothing at all. Only that we're in the soup, my boy; it's the Prussian cavalry mowing us down, that's all. The idiot of a general thought at first they were our men. Come, quick, help me to mend Cocotte's trace; it's broken."

Several shots were fired ten yards off. Our hero, cool and composed, said to himself: "But really, I haven't fought at all, the whole day; I have only escorted a general.—I must go and fight," he said to the *cantinière*.

"Keep calm, you shall fight, and more than you want! We're done for."

"Aubry, my lad," she called out to a passing corporal, "keep an eye on the little cart now and then."

"Are you going to fight?" Fabrizio asked Aubry.

"Oh, no, I'm putting my pumps on to go to a dance!"

"I shall follow you."

"I tell you, he's all right, the little hussar," cried the *cantinière*. "The young gentleman has a stout heart." Corporal Aubry marched on without saying a word. Eight or nine soldiers ran up and joined him; he led them behind a big oak surrounded by brambles. On reaching it he posted them along the edge of the wood, still without uttering a word, on a widely extended front, each man being at least ten paces from the next.

"Now then, you men," said the corporal, opening his mouth for the first time, "don't fire till I give the order: remember you've only got three rounds each."

"Why, what is happening?" Fabrizio wondered. At length, when he found himself alone with the corporal, he said to him: "I have no musket."

"Will you hold your tongue? Go forward there: fifty paces in front of the wood you'll find one of the poor fellows of the Regiment who've been sabred; you will take his cartridge-pouch and his musket. Don't strip a wounded man, though; take the pouch and musket from one who's properly dead, and hurry up or you'll be shot in the back by our fellows." Fabrizio set off at a run and returned the next minute with a musket and a pouch.

"Load your musket and stick yourself behind this tree, and whatever you do don't fire till you get the order from me. . . . Great God in heaven!" the corporal broke off, "he doesn't even know how to load!" He helped Fabrizio to do this while going on with his instructions. "If one of the enemy's cavalry gallops at you to cut you down, dodge round your tree and don't fire till he's within three paces: wait till your bayonet's practically touching his uniform.

"Throw that great sabre away," cried the corporal. "Good God, do you want it to trip you up? Fine sort of soldiers they're sending us these days!" As he spoke he himself took hold of the sabre which he flung angrily away.

"You there, wipe the flint of your musket with your handkerchief. Have you never fired a musket?"

"I am a hunter."

"Thank God for that!" went on the corporal with a loud

sigh. "Whatever you do, don't fire till I give the order." And he moved away.

Fabrizio was supremely happy. "Now I'm going to do some real fighting," he said to himself, "and kill one of the enemy. This morning they were sending cannonballs over, and I did nothing but expose myself and risk getting killed; that's a fool's game." He gazed all round him with extreme curiosity. Presently he heard seven or eight shots fired quite close at hand. But receiving no order to fire he stood quietly behind his tree. It was almost night; he felt he was in a *look-out,* bear-shooting, on the mountain of Tramezzina, above Grianta. A hunter's idea came to him: he took a cartridge from his pouch and removed the ball. "If I see him," he said, "it won't do to miss him," and he slipped this second ball into the barrel of his musket. He heard shots fired close to his tree; at the same moment he saw a horseman in blue pass in front of him at a gallop, going from right to left. "It is more than three paces," he said to himself, "but at that range I am certain of my mark." He kept the trooper carefully sighted with his musket and finally pressed the trigger: the trooper fell with his horse. Our hero imagined he was stalking game: he ran joyfully out to collect his bag. He was actually touching the man, who appeared to him to be dying, when, with incredible speed, two Prussian troopers charged down on him to sabre him. Fabrizio dashed back as fast as he could go to the wood; to gain speed he flung his musket away. The Prussian troopers were not more than three paces from him when he reached another plantation of young oaks, as thick as his arm and quite upright, which fringed the wood. These little oaks delayed the horsemen for a moment, but they passed them and continued their pursuit of Fabrizio along a clearing. Once again they were just overtaking him when he slipped in among seven or eight big trees. At that moment his face was almost scorched by the flame of five or six musket shots fired from in front of him. He ducked his head; when he raised it again he found himself face to face with the corporal.

"Did you kill your man?" Corporal Aubry asked him.

"Yes; but I've lost my musket."

"It's not muskets we're short of. You're not a bad b——; though you do look as green as a cabbage you've won the day all right, and these men here have just missed the two who were chasing you and coming straight at them. I didn't see them myself. What we've got to do now is to get away

at the double; the Regiment must be half a mile off, and
there's a bit of a field to cross, too, where we may find ourselves surrounded."

As he spoke, the corporal marched off at a brisk pace at
the head of his ten men. Two hundred yards farther on, as
they entered the little field he had mentioned, they came upon
a wounded general who was being carried by his aide-de-
camp and an orderly.

"Give me four of your men," he said to the corporal in a
faint voice, "I've got to be carried to the ambulance; my leg
is shattered."

"Go and f—— yourself!" replied the corporal, "you and
all your generals. You've all of you betrayed the Emperor to-
day."

"What," said the general, furious, "you dispute my orders.
Do you know that I am General Comte B——, commanding
your Division," and so on. He waxed rhetorical. The aide-de-
camp flung himself on the men. The corporal gave him a
thrust in the arm with his bayonet, then made off with his
party at the double. "I wish they were all in your boat," he
repeated with an oath; "I'd shatter their arms and legs for
them. A pack of puppies! All of them bought by the Bourbons,
to betray the Emperor!" Fabrizio listened with a thrill of
horror to this frightful accusation.

About ten o'clock that night the little party overtook their
regiment on the outskirts of a large village which divided
the road into several very narrow streets; but Fabrizio noticed that Corporal Aubry avoided speaking to any of the
officers. "We can't get on," he called to his men. All these
streets were blocked with infantry, cavalry, and, worst of all,
by the limbers and wagons of the artillery. The corporal tried
three of these streets in turn; after advancing twenty yards
he was obliged to halt. Everyone was swearing and losing
his temper.

"Some traitor in command here, too!" cried the corporal:
"if the enemy has the sense to surround the village, we shall
all be caught like rats in a trap. Follow me, you." Fabrizio
looked round; there were only six men left with the corporal.
Through a big gate which stood open they came into a huge
courtyard; from this courtyard they passed into a stable, the
back door of which let them into a garden. They lost their way
for a moment and wandered blindly about. But finally, going
through a hedge, they found themselves in a huge field of
buckwheat. In less than half an hour, guided by the shouts

and confused noises, they had regained the high road on the other side of the village. The ditches on either side of this road were filled with muskets that had been thrown away; Fabrizio selected one: but the road, although very broad, was so blocked with stragglers and transport that in the next half-hour the corporal and Fabrizio had not advanced more than five hundred yards at the most; they were told that this road led to Charleroi. As the village clock struck eleven:

"Let us cut across the fields again," said the corporal. The little party was reduced now to three men, the corporal and Fabrizio. When they had gone a quarter of a league from the high road: "I'm done," said one of the soldiers.

"Me, too!" said another.

"That's good news! We're all in the same boat," said the corporal; "but do what I tell you and you'll get through all right." His eye fell on five or six trees marking the line of a little ditch in the middle of an immense cornfield. "Make for the trees!" he told his men; "lie down," he added when they had reached the trees, "and not a sound, remember. But before you go to sleep, who's got any bread?"

"I have," said one of the men.

"Give it here," said the corporal in a tone of authority. He divided the bread into five pieces and took the smallest himself.

"A quarter of an hour before dawn," he said as he ate it, "you'll have the enemy's cavalry on your backs. You've got to see you're not sabred. A man by himself is done for with cavalry after him on these big plains, but five can get away; keep in close touch with me, don't fire till they're at close range, and to-morrow evening I'll undertake to get you to Charleroi." The corporal roused his men an hour before daybreak and made them recharge their muskets. The noise on the high road still continued; it had gone on all night: it was like the sound of a torrent heard from a long way off.

"They're like a flock of sheep running away," said Fabrizio with a guileless air to the corporal.

"Will you shut your mouth, you young fool!" said the corporal, greatly indignant. And the three soldiers who with Fabrizio composed his whole force scowled angrily at our hero as though he had uttered blasphemy. He had insulted the nation.

"That is where their strength lies!" thought our hero. "I noticed it before with the Viceroy at Milan; they are not running away, oh, no! With these Frenchmen you must never speak the truth if it shocks their vanity. But as for their savage scowls, they don't trouble me, and I must let them understand as much." They kept on their way, always at an interval of five hundred yards from the torrent of fugitives that covered the high road. A league farther on, the corporal and his party crossed a road running into the high road in which a number of soldiers were lying. Fabrizio purchased a fairly good horse which cost him forty francs, and among all the sabres that had been thrown down everywhere made a careful choice of one that was long and straight. "Since I'm told I've got to stick them," he thought, "this is the best." Thus equipped, he put his horse into a gallop and soon overtook the corporal who had gone on ahead. He sat up in his stirrups, took hold with his left hand of the scabbard of his straight sabre, and said to the four Frenchmen:

"Those people going along the high road look like a flock of sheep . . . they are running like frightened sheep. . . ."

In spite of his dwelling upon the word *sheep*, his companions had completely forgotten that it had annoyed them an hour earlier. Here we see one of the contrasts between the Italian character and the French; the Frenchman is no doubt the happier of the two; he glides lightly over the events of life and bears no malice afterwards.

We shall not attempt to conceal the fact that Fabrizio was highly pleased with himself after using the word *sheep*. They marched on, talking about nothing in particular. After covering two leagues more, the corporal, still greatly astonished to see no sign of the enemy's cavalry, said to Fabrizio:

"You are our cavalry; gallop over to that farm on the little hill; ask the farmer if he will *sell* us breakfast: mind you tell him there are only five of us. If he hesitates, put down five francs of your money in advance; but don't be frightened, we'll take the dollar back from him after we've eaten."

Fabrizio looked at the corporal; he saw in his face an imperturbable gravity and really an air of moral superiority; he obeyed. Everything fell out as the commander in chief had anticipated; only, Fabrizio insisted on their not taking back by force the five francs he had given to the farmer.

"The money is mine," he said to his friends; "I'm not paying for you, I'm paying for the oats he's given my horse."

Fabrizio's French accent was so bad that his companions thought they detected in his words a note of superiority; they were keenly annoyed, and from that moment a duel began to take shape in their minds for the end of the day. They found

him very different from themselves, which shocked them;
Fabrizio, on the contrary, was beginning to feel a warm
friendship towards them.

They had marched without saying a word for a couple of
hours when the corporal, looking across at the high road,
exclaimed in a transport of joy: "There's the Regiment!"
They were soon on the road; but, alas, round the eagle were
mustered not more than two hundred men. Fabrizio's eye
soon caught sight of the *vivandière:* she was going on foot,
her eyes were red and every now and again she burst into
tears. Fabrizio looked in vain for the little cart and Cocotte.

"Stripped, ruined, robbed!" cried the *vivandière,* in answer
to our hero's inquiring glance. He, without a word, got down
from his horse, took hold of the bridle and said to the
vivandière: "Mount!" She did not have to be told twice.

"Shorten the stirrups for me," was her only remark.

As soon as she was comfortably in the saddle she began
to tell Fabrizio all the disasters of the night. After a narrative
of endless length but eagerly drunk in by our hero who, to tell
the truth, understood nothing at all of what she said but had
a tender feeling for the *vivandière,* she went on:

"And to think that they were Frenchmen who robbed me,
beat me, destroyed me. . . ."

"What! It wasn't the enemy?" said Fabrizio with an air of
innocence which made his grave, pale face look charming.

"What a fool you are, you poor boy!" said the *vivandière,*
smiling through her tears; "but you're very nice, for all that."

"And such as he is, he brought down his Prussian properly,"
said Corporal Aubry, who, in the general confusion round
them, happened to be on the other side of the horse on which
the *cantinière* was sitting. "But he's proud," the corporal
went on. . . . Fabrizio made an impulsive movement. "And
what's your name?" asked the corporal; "for if there's a report going in I should like to mention you."

"I'm called Vasi," replied Fabrizio, with a curious expression on his face. "Boulot, I mean," he added, quickly correcting himself.

Boulot was the name of the late possessor of the marching
orders which the gaoler's wife at B—— had given him; on
his way from B—— he had studied them carefully, for he
was beginning to think a little and was no longer so easily
surprised. In addition to the marching orders of Trooper
Boulot, he had stowed away in a safe place the precious
Italian passport according to which he was entitled to the

noble appellation of Vasi, dealer in barometers. When the corporal had charged him with being proud, it had been on the tip of his tongue to retort: "I proud! I, Fabrizio Volterra, Marchesino del Dongo, who consent to go by the name of a Vasi, dealer in barometers!"

While he was making these reflexions and saying to himself: "I must not forget that I am called Boulot, or look out for the prison fate threatens me with," the corporal and the *cantinière* had been exchanging a few words with regard to him.

"Don't say I'm inquisitive," said the *cantinière*, ceasing to address him in the second person singular, "it's for your good I ask you these questions. Who are you, now, really?"

Fabrizio did not reply at first. He was considering that never again would he find more devoted friends to ask for advice, and he was in urgent need of advice from someone. "We are coming into a fortified place, the governor will want to know who I am, and ware prison if I let him see by my answers that I know nobody in the 4th Hussar Regiment, whose uniform I am wearing!" In his capacity as an Austrian subject, Fabrizio knew all about the importance to be attached to a passport. Various members of his family, although noble and devout, although supporters of the winning side, had been in trouble a score of times over their passports; he was therefore not in the least put out by the question which the *cantinière* had addressed to him. But as, before answering, he had to think of the French words which would express his meaning most clearly, the *cantinière*, pricked by a keen curiosity, added, to induce him to speak: "Corporal Aubry and I are going to give you some good advice."

"I have no doubt you are," replied Fabrizio. "My name is Vasi and I come from Genoa; my sister, who is famous for her beauty, is married to a captain. As I am only seventeen, she made me come to her to let me see something of France, and form my character a little; not finding her in Paris, and knowing that she was with this army, I came on here. I've searched for her everywhere and haven't found her. The soldiers, who were puzzled by my accent, had me arrested. I had money then, I gave some to the *gendarme*, who let me have some marching orders and a uniform, and said to me: 'Get away with you, and swear you'll never mention my name.'"

"What was he called?" asked the *cantinière*.

"I've given my word," said Fabrizio.

"He's right," put in the corporal, "the *gendarme* is a sweep, but our friend ought not to give his name. And what is the other one called, this captain, your sister's husband? If we knew his name, we could try to find him."

"Teulier, Captain in the 4th Hussars," replied our hero.

"And so," said the corporal, with a certain subtlety, "from your foreign accent the soldiers took you for a spy?"

"That's the abominable word!" cried Fabrizio, his eyes blazing. "I who love the Emperor so and the French people! And it was that insult that annoyed me more than anything."

"There's no insult about it; that's where you're wrong; the soldiers' mistake was quite natural," replied Corporal Aubry gravely.

And he went on to explain in the most pedantic manner that in the army one must belong to some corps and wear a uniform, failing which it was quite simple that people should take one for a spy. "The enemy sends us any number of them; everybody's a traitor in this war." The scales fell from Fabrizio's eyes; he realised for the first time that he had been in the wrong in everything that had happened to him during the last two months.

"But make the boy tell us the whole story," said the *cantinière,* her curiosity more and more excited. Fabrizio obeyed. When he had finished:

"It comes to this," said the *cantinière,* speaking in a serious tone to the corporal, "this child is not a soldier at all; we're going to have a bloody war now that we've been beaten and betrayed. Why should he go and get his bones broken free, gratis and for nothing?"

"Especially," put in the corporal, "as he doesn't even know how to load his musket, neither by numbers, nor in his own time. It was I put in the shot that brought down the Prussian."

"Besides, he lets everyone see the colour of his money," added the *cantinière;* "he will be robbed of all he has as soon as he hasn't got us to look after him."

"The first cavalry non-com he comes across," said the corporal, "will take it from him to pay for his drink, and perhaps they'll enlist him for the enemy; they're all traitors. The first man he meets will order him to follow, and he'll follow him; he would do better to join our Regiment."

"No, please, if you don't mind, Corporal!" Fabrizio exclaimed with animation; "I am more comfortable on a horse.

And, besides, I don't know how to load a musket, and you have seen that I can manage a horse."

Fabrizio was extremely proud of this little speech. We need not report the long discussion that followed between the corporal and the *cantinière* as to his future destiny. Fabrizio noticed that in discussing him these people repeated three or four times all the circumstances of his story: the soldiers' suspicions, the *gendarme* selling him marching orders and a uniform, the accident by which, the day before, he had found himself forming part of the Marshal's escort, the glimpse of the Emperor as he galloped past, the horse that had been *scoffed* from him, and so on indefinitely.

With feminine curiosity the *cantinière* kept harking back incessantly to the way in which he had been dispossessed of the good horse which she had made him buy.

"You felt yourself seized by the feet, they lifted you gently over your horse's tail, and sat you down on the ground!" "Why repeat so often," Fabrizio said to himself, "what all three of us know perfectly well?" He had not yet discovered that this is how, in France, the lower orders proceed in quest of ideas.

"How much money have you?" the *cantinière* asked him suddenly. Fabrizio had no hesitation in answering. He was sure of the nobility of the woman's nature; that is the fine side of France.

"Altogether, I may have got left thirty napoleons in gold, and eight or nine five-franc pieces."

"In that case, you have a clear field!" exclaimed the *cantinière*. "Get right away from this rout of an army; clear out, take the first road with ruts on it that you come to on the right; keep your horse moving and your back to the army. At the first opportunity, buy some civilian clothes. When you've gone nine or ten leagues and there are no more soldiers in sight, take the mail-coach, and go and rest for a week and eat beefsteaks in some nice town. Never let anyone know that you've been in the army, or the police will take you up as a deserter; and, nice as you are, my boy, you're not quite clever enough yet to stand up to the police. As soon as you've got civilian clothes on your back, tear up your marching orders into a thousand pieces and go back to your real name: say that you're Vasi. And where ought he to say he comes from?" she asked the corporal.

"From Cambrai on the Scheldt: it's a good town and quite

small, if you know what I mean. There's a cathedral there, and Fénelon."

"That's right," said the *cantinière*. "Never let on to anyone that you've been in battle, don't breathe a word about B——, or the *gendarme* who sold you the marching orders. When you're ready to go back to Paris, make first for Versailles, and pass the Paris barrier from that side in a leisurely way, on foot, as if you were taking a stroll. Sew up your napoleons inside your breeches, and remember, when you have to pay for anything, shew only the exact sum that you want to spend. What makes me sad is that they'll take you and rob you and strip you of everything you have. And whatever will you do without money, you that don't know how to look after yourself . . ." and so on.

The good woman went on talking for some time still; the corporal indicated his support by nodding his head, not being able to get a word in himself. Suddenly the crowd that was packing the road first of all doubled its pace, then, in the twinkling of an eye, crossed the little ditch that bounded the road on the left and fled helter-skelter across country. Cries of "The Cossacks! The Cossacks!" rose from every side.

"Take back your horse!" the *cantinière* shouted.

"God forbid!" said Fabrizio. "Gallop! Away with you! I give him to you. Do you want someting to buy another cart with? Half of what I have is yours."

"Take back your horse, I tell you!" cried the *cantinière* angrily; and she prepared to dismount. Fabrizio drew his sabre. "Hold on tight!" she shouted to him, and gave two or three strokes with the flat of his sabre to the horse, which broke into a gallop and followed the fugitives.

Our hero stood looking at the road; a moment ago, two or three thousand people had been jostling along it, packed together like peasants at the tail of a procession. After the shout of: "Cossacks!" he saw not a soul on it; the fugitives had cast away shakoes, muskets, sabres, everything. Fabrizio, quite bewildered, climbed up into a field on the right of the road and twenty or thirty feet above it; he scanned the line of the road in both directions, and the plain, but saw no trace of the Cossacks. "Funny people, these French!" he said to himself. "Since I have got to go to the right," he thought, "I may as well start off at once; it is possible that these people have a reason for running away that I don't know." He picked up a musket, saw that it was charged, shook up the powder in the priming, cleaned the flint, then

chose a cartridge-pouch that was well filled and looked round
him again in all directions; he was absolutely alone in the
middle of this plain which just now had been so crowded
with people. In the far distance he could see the fugitives,
who were beginning to disappear behind the trees, and were
still running. "That's a very odd thing," he said to himself,
and remembering the tactics employed by the corporal the
night before, he went and sat down in the middle of a field
of corn. He did not go farther because he was anxious to see
again his good friends the *cantinière* and Corporal Aubry.

In this cornfield, he made the discovery that he had no
more than eighteen napoleons, instead of thirty as he had
supposed; but he still had some small diamonds which he had
stowed away in the lining of the hussar's boots, before dawn,
in the gaoler's wife's room at B——. He concealed his
napoleons as best he could, pondering deeply the while on the
sudden disappearance of the others. "Is that a bad omen for
me?" he asked himself. What distressed him most was that
he had not asked Corporal Aubry the question: "Have I
really taken part in a battle?" It seemed to him that he had,
and his happiness would have known no bounds could he
have been certain of this.

"But even if I have," he said to himself, "I took part in
it bearing the name of a prisoner, I had a prisoner's marching
orders in my pocket, and, worse still, his coat on my back!
That is the fatal threat to my future: what would the Priore
Blanès say to it? And that wretched Boulot died in prison.
It is all of the most sinister augury; fate will lead me to
prison." Fabrizio would have given anything in the world to
know whether Trooper Boulot had really been guilty; when he
searched his memory, he seemed to recollect that the gaoler's
wife had told him that the hussar had been taken up not only
for the theft of silver plate but also for stealing a cow from
a peasant and nearly beating the peasant to death: Fabrizio
had no doubt that he himself would be sent to prison some
day for a crime which would bear some relation to that of
Trooper Boulot. He thought of his friend the *parroco* Blanès:
what would he not have given for an opportunity of consulting him! Then he remembered that he had not written
to his aunt since leaving Paris. "Poor Gina!" he said to himself. And tears stood in his eyes, when suddenly he heard a
slight sound quite close to him: a soldier was feeding three
horses on the standing corn; he had taken the bits out of
their mouths and they seemed half dead with hunger; he was

holding them by the snaffle. Fabrizio got up like a partridge; the soldier seemed frightened. Our hero noticed this, and yielded to the pleasure of playing the hussar for a moment.

"One of those horses belongs to me, f—— you, but I don't mind giving you five francs for the trouble you've taken in bringing it here."

"What are you playing at?" said the soldier. Fabrizio took aim at him from a distance of six paces.

"Let go the horse, or I'll blow your head off."

The soldier had his musket slung on his back; he reached over his shoulder to seize it.

"If you move an inch, you're a dead man!" cried Fabrizio, rushing upon him.

"All right, give me the five francs and take one of the horses," said the embarrassed soldier, after casting a rueful glance at the high road, on which there was absolutely no one to be seen. Fabrizio, keeping his musket raised in his left hand, with the right flung him three five-franc pieces.

"Dismount, or you're a dead man. Bridle the black, and go farther off with the other two. . . . If you move, I fire."

The soldier looked savage but obeyed. Fabrizio went up to the horse and passed the rein over his left arm, without losing sight of the soldier, who was moving slowly away; when our hero saw that he had gone fifty paces, he jumped nimbly on to the horse. He had barely mounted and was feeling with his foot for the off stirrup when he heard a bullet whistle past close to his head: it was the soldier who had fired at him. Fabrizio, beside himself with rage, started galloping after the soldier who ran off as fast as his legs could carry him, and presently Fabrizio saw him mount one of his two horses and gallop away. "Good, he's out of range now," he said to himself. The horse he had just bought was a magnificent animal, but seemed half starved. Fabrizio returned to the high road, where there was still not a living soul; he crossed it and put his horse into a trot to reach a little fold in the ground on the left, where he hoped to find the *cantinière;* but when he was at the top of the little rise he could see nothing save, more than a league away, a few scattered troops. "It is written that I shall not see her again," he said to himself with a sigh, "the good, brave woman!" He came to a farm which he had seen in the distance on the right of the road. Without dismounting, and after paying for it in advance, he made the farmer produce some oats for his poor horse, which was so famished that it began to gnaw the manger. An hour later, Fabrizio was trotting along the high road, still in the hope of meeting the *cantinière,* or at any rate Corporal Aubry. Moving all the time and keeping a look-out all round him, he came to a marshy river crossed by a fairly narrow wooden bridge. Between him and the bridge, on the right of the road, was a solitary house bearing the sign of the White Horse. "There I shall get some dinner," thought Fabrizio. A cavalry officer with his arm in a sling was guarding the approach to the bridge; he was on horseback and looked very melancholy; ten paces away from him, three dismounted troopers were filling their pipes.

"There are some people," Fabrizio said to himself, "who look to me very much as though they would like to buy my horse for even less than he cost me." The wounded officer and the three men on foot watched him approach and seemed to be waiting for him. "It would be better not to cross by this bridge, but to follow the river bank to the right; that was the way the *cantinière* advised me to take to get clear of difficulties. . . . Yes," thought our hero, "but if I take to my heels now, to-morrow I shall be thoroughly ashamed of myself; besides, my horse has good legs, the officer's is probably tired; if he tries to make me dismount I shall gallop." Reasoning thus with himself, Fabrizio pulled up his horse and moved forward at the slowest possible pace.

"Advance, you, hussar!" the officer called to him with an air of authority.

Fabrizio went on a few paces and then halted.

"Do you want to take my horse?" he shouted.

"Not in the least; advance."

Fabrizio examined the officer; he had a white moustache, and looked the best fellow in the world; the handkerchief that held up his left arm was drenched with blood, and his right hand also was bound up in a piece of bloodstained linen. "It is the men on foot who are going to snatch my bridle," thought Fabrizio; but, on looking at them from nearer, he saw that they too were wounded.

"On your honour as a soldier," said the officer, who wore the epaulettes of a colonel, "stay here on picket, and tell all the dragoons, chasseurs and hussars that you see that Colonel Le Baron is in the inn over there, and that I order them to come and report to me." The old colonel had the air of a man broken by suffering; with his first words he had made a conquest of our hero, who replied with great good sense:

"I am very young, sir, to make them listen to me; I ought to have a written order from you."

"He is right," said the colonel, studying him closely; "make out the order, La Rose, you've got the use of your right hand."

Without saying a word, La Rose took from his pocket a little parchment book, wrote a few lines, and, tearing out a leaf, handed it to Fabrizio; the colonel repeated the order to him, adding that after two hours on duty he would be relieved, as was right and proper, by one of the three wounded troopers he had with him. So saying he went into the inn with his men. Fabrizio watched them go and sat without moving at the end of his wooden bridge, so deeply impressed had he been by the sombre, silent grief of these three persons. "One would think they were under a spell," he said to himself. At length he unfolded the paper and read the order, which ran as follows:

"Colonel Le Baron, 6th Dragoons, Commanding the 2nd Brigade of the 1st Cavalry Division of the XIV Corps, orders all cavalrymen, dragoons, chasseurs and hussars, on no account to cross the bridge, and to report to him at the White Horse Inn, by the bridge, which is his headquarters.

"Headquarters, by the bridge of La Sainte, June 19, 1815.
     "For Colonel Le Baron, wounded in the right arm,
          and by his orders,
                              "LA ROSE, Serjeant."

Fabrizio had been on guard at the bridge for barely half an hour when he saw six chasseurs approaching him mounted, and three on foot; he communicated the colonel's order to them. "We're coming back," said four of the mounted men, and crossed the bridge at a fast trot. Fabrizio then spoke to the other two. During the discussion, which grew heated, the three men on foot crossed the bridge. Finally, one of the two mounted troopers who had stayed behind asked to see the order again, and carried it off, with:

"I am taking it to the others, who will come back without fail; wait for them here." And off he went at a gallop; his companion followed him. All this had happened in the twinkling of an eye.

Fabrizio was furious, and called to one of the wounded soldiers, who appeared at a window of the White Horse.

This soldier, on whose arm Fabrizio saw the stripes of a cavalry serjeant, came down and shouted to him: "Draw your sabre, man, you're on picket." Fabrizio obeyed, then said: "They've carried off the order."

"They're out of hand after yesterday's affair," replied the other in a melancholy tone. "I'll let you have one of my pistols; if they force past you again, fire it in the air; I shall come, or the colonel himself will appear."

Fabrizio had not failed to observe the serjeant's start of surprise on hearing of the theft of the order. He realised that it was a personal insult to himself, and promised himself that he would not allow such a trick to be played on him again.

Armed with the serjeant's horse-pistol, Fabrizio had proudly resumed his guard when he saw coming towards him seven hussars, mounted. He had taken up a position that barred the bridge; he read them the colonel's order, which seemed greatly to annoy them; the most venturesome of them tried to pass. Fabrizio, following the wise counsel of his friend the *vivandière*, who, the morning before, had told him that he must thrust and not slash, lowered the point of his long, straight sabre and made as though to stab with it the man who was trying to pass him.

"Oh, so he wants to kill us, the baby!" cried the hussars, "as if we hadn't been killed quite enough yesterday!" They all drew their sabres at once and fell on Fabrizio: he gave himself up for dead; but he thought of the serjeant's surprise, and was not anxious to earn his contempt again. Drawing back on to his bridge, he tried to reach them with his sabre-point. He looked so absurd when he tried to wield this huge, straight heavy-dragoon sabre, a great deal too heavy for him, that the hussars soon saw with what sort of soldier they had to deal; they then endeavoured not to wound him but to slash his clothing. In this way Fabrizio received three or four slight sabre-cuts on his arms. For his own part, still faithful to the *cantinière's* precept, he kept thrusting the point of his sabre at them with all his might. As ill luck would have it, one of these thrusts wounded a hussar in the hand: highly indignant at being touched by so raw a recruit, he replied with a downward thrust which caught Fabrizio in the upper part of the thigh. What made this blow effective was that our hero's horse, so far from avoiding the fray, seemed to take pleasure in it and to be flinging himself on the assailants. These, seeing Fabrizio's blood streaming along his right arm, were afraid that they might have carried the game too far, and, pushing him against the left-hand parapet of the bridge, crossed at a gallop. As soon as Fabrizio had a moment to himself he fired his pistol in the air to warn the colonel.

Four mounted hussars and two on foot, of the same regiment as the others, were coming towards the bridge and were still two hundred yards away from it when the pistol went off. They had been paying close attention to what was happening on the bridge, and, imagining that Fabrizio had fired at their comrades, the four mounted men galloped upon him with raised sabres: it was a regular cavalry charge. Colonel Le Baron, summoned by the pistol-shot, opened the door of the inn and rushed on to the bridge just as the galloping hussars reached it, and himself gave them the order to halt.

"There's no colonel here now!" cried one of them, and pressed on his horse. The colonel in exasperation broke off the reprimand he was giving them, and with his wounded right hand seized the rein of this horse on the off side.

"Halt! You bad soldier," he said to the hussar; "I know you, you're in Captain Henriot's squadron."

"Very well, then! The captain can give me the order himself! Captain Henriot was killed yesterday," he added with a snigger, "and you can go and f—— yourself!"

So saying, he tried to force a passage, and pushed the old colonel, who fell in a sitting position on the roadway of the bridge. Fabrizio, who was a couple of yards farther along upon the bridge, but facing the inn, pressed his horse, and, while the breast-piece of the assailant's harness threw down the old colonel, who never let go the off rein, Fabrizio, indignant, bore down upon the hussar with a driving thrust. Fortunately the hussar's horse, feeling itself pulled towards the ground by the rein which the colonel still held, made a movement sideways, with the result that the long blade of Fabrizio's heavy-cavalry sabre slid along the hussar's jacket, and the whole length of it passed beneath his eyes. Furious, the hussar turned round and, using all his strength, dealt Fabrizio a blow which cut his sleeve and went deep into his arm: our hero fell.

One of the dismounted hussars, seeing the two defenders of the bridge on the ground, seized the opportunity, jumped on to Fabrizio's horse and tried to make off with it by starting at a gallop across the bridge.

The serjeant, as he hurried from the inn, had seen his colonel fall, and supposed him to be seriously wounded. He ran after Fabrizio's horse and plunged the point of his sabre into the thief's entrails; he fell. The hussars, seeing no one now on the bridge but the serjeant, who was on foot, crossed at a gallop and rapidly disappeared. The one on foot bolted into the fields.

The serjeant came up to the wounded men. Fabrizio was already on his feet; he was not in great pain, but was bleeding profusely. The colonel got up more slowy; he was quite stunned by his fall, but had received no injury. "I feel nothing," he said to the serjeant, "except the old wound in my hand."

The hussar whom the serjeant had wounded was dying.

"The devil take him!" exclaimed the colonel. "But," he said to the serjeant and the two troopers who came running out, "look after this young man whose life I have risked, most improperly. I shall stay on the bridge myself and try to stop these madmen. Take the young man to the inn and tie up his arm. Use one of my shirts."

CHAPTER FIVE

THE WHOLE OF this adventure had not lasted a minute. Fabrizio's wounds were nothing; they tied up his arm with bandages torn from the colonel's shirt. They wanted to make up a bed for him upstairs in the inn.

"But while I am tucked up here on the first floor," said Fabrizio to the serjeant, "my horse, who is down in the stable, will get bored with being left alone and will go off with another master."

"Not bad for a conscript!" said the serjeant. And they deposited Fabrizio on a litter of clean straw in the same stall as his horse.

Then, as he was feeling very weak, the serjeant brought him a bowl of mulled wine and talked to him for a little. Several compliments included in this conversation carried our hero to the seventh heaven.

Fabrizio did not wake until dawn on the following day; the horses were neighing continuously and making a frightful din; the stable was filled with smoke. At first Fabrizio could make nothing of all this noise, and did not even know where he was: finally, half stifled by the smoke, it occurred to him that the house was on fire; in the twinkling of an eye he was out of the stable and in the saddle. He raised his head; smoke was belching violently from the two windows over the stable; and the roof was covered by a black smoke which rose curling into the air. A hundred fugitives had arrived during the night at the White Horse; they were all shouting and swearing. The five or six whom Fabrizio could see close at hand seemed to him to be completely drunk; one of them tried to stop him and called out to him: "Where are you taking my horse?"

When Fabrizio had gone a quarter of a league, he turned

his head. There was no one following him; the building was in flames. Fabrizio caught sight of the bridge; he remembered his wound, and felt his arm compressed by bandages and very hot. "And the old colonel, what has become of him? He gave his shirt to tie up my arm." Our hero was this morning the coolest man in the world; the amount of blood he had shed had liberated him from all the romantic element in his character.

"To the right!" he said to himself, "and no time to lose." He began quietly following the course of the river which, after passing under the bridge, ran to the right of the road. He remembered the good *cantinière's* advice. "What friendship!" he said to himself, "what an open nature!"

After riding for an hour he felt very weak. "Oho! Am I going to faint?" he wondered. "If I faint, someone will steal my horse, and my clothes, perhaps, and my money and jewels with them." He had no longer the strength to hold the reins, and was trying to keep his balance in the saddle when a peasant who was digging in a field by the side of the high road noticed his pallor and came up to offer him a glass of beer and some bread.

"When I saw you look so pale, I thought you must be one of the wounded from the great battle," the peasant told him. Never did help come more opportunely. As Fabrizio was munching the piece of bread his eyes began to hurt him when he looked straight ahead. When he felt a little better he thanked the man. "And where am I?" he asked. The peasant told him that three quarters of a league farther on he would come to the township of Zonders, where he would be very well looked after. Fabrizio reached the town, not knowing quite what he was doing and thinking only at every step of not falling off his horse. He saw a big door standing open; he entered. It was the Woolcomb Inn. At once there ran out to him the good lady of the house, an enormous woman; she called for help in a voice that throbbed with pity. Two girls came and helped Fabrizio to dismount; no sooner had his feet touched the ground than he fainted completely. A surgeon was fetched, who bled him. For the rest of that day and the days that followed Fabrizio scarcely knew what was being done to him; he slept almost without interruption.

The sabre wound in his thigh threatened to form a serious abscess. When his mind was clear again, he asked them to look after his horse, and kept on repeating that he would pay them well, which shocked the good hostess and her daughters. For a fortnight he was admirably looked after and he was beginning to be himself again when he noticed one evening that his hostesses seemed greatly upset. Presently a German officer came into his room: in answering his questions they used a language which Fabrizio did not understand, but he could see that they were speaking about him; he pretended to be asleep. A little later, when he thought that the officer must have gone, he called his hostesses.

"That officer came to put my name on a list, and make me a prisoner, didn't he?" The landlady assented with tears in her eyes.

"Very well, there is money in my dolman!" he cried, sitting up in bed; "buy me some civilian clothes and tonight I shall go away on my horse. You have already saved my life once by taking me in just as I was going to drop down dead in the street; save it again by giving me the means of going back to my mother."

At this point the landlady's daughters began to dissolve in tears; they trembled for Fabrizio; and, as they barely understood French, they came to his bedside to question him. They talked with their mother in Flemish; but at every moment pitying eyes were turned on our hero; he thought he could make out that his escape might compromise them seriously, but that they would gladly incur the risk. A Jew in the town supplied a complete outfit, but when he brought it to the inn about ten o'clock that night, the girls saw, on comparing it with Fabrizio's dolman, that it would require an endless amount of alteration. At once they set to work; there was no time to lose. Fabrizio showed them where several napoleons were hidden in his uniform, and begged his hostesses to stitch them into the new garments. With these had come a fine pair of new boots. Fabrizio had no hesitation in asking these kind girls to slit open the hussar's boots at the place which he shewed them, and they hid the little diamonds in the lining of the new pair.

One curious result of his loss of blood and the weakness that followed from it was that Fabrizio had almost completely forgotten his French; he used Italian to address his hostesses, who themselves spoke a Flemish dialect, so that their conversation had to be conducted almost entirely in signs. When the girls, who for that matter were entirely disinterested, saw the diamonds, their enthusiasm for Fabrizio knew no bounds; they imagined him to be a prince in disguise. Aniken, the younger and less sophisticated, kissed him

without ceremony. Fabrizio, for his part, found them charming, and towards midnight, when the surgeon had allowed
him a little wine in view of the journey he had to take, he
felt almost inclined not to go. "Where could I be better off
than here?" he asked himself. However, about two o'clock in
the morning, he rose and dressed. As he was leaving the
room, his good hostess informed him that his horse had been
taken by the officer who had come to search the house that
afternoon.

"Ah! The swine!" cried Fabrizio with an oath, "robbing
a wounded man!" He was not enough of a philosopher, this
young Italian, to bear in mind the price at which he himself
had acquired the horse.

Aniken told him with tears that they had hired a horse
for him. She would have liked him not to go. Their farewells
were tender. Two big lads, cousins of the good landlady,
helped Fabrizio into the saddle: during the journey they
supported him on his horse, while a third, who walked a
few hundred yards in advance of the little convoy, searched
the roads for any suspicious patrol. After going for a couple
of hours, they stopped at the house of a cousin of the landlady of the Woolcomb. In spite of anything that Fabrizio
might say, the young men who accompanied him refused
absolutely to leave him; they claimed that they knew better
than anyone the hidden paths through the woods.

"But to-morrow morning, when my flight becomes known,
and they don't see you anywhere in the town, your absence
will make things awkward for you," said Fabrizio.

They proceeded on their way. Fortunately, when day broke
at last, the plain was covered by a thick fog. About eight
o'clock in the morning they came in sight of a little town.
One of the young men went on ahead to see if the post-horses
there had been stolen. The postmaster had had time to make
them vanish and to raise a team of wretched screws with
which he had filled his stables. Grooms were sent to find a
pair of horses in the marshes where they were hidden, and
three hours later Fabrizio climbed into a little cabriolet which
was quite dilapidated but had harnessed to it a pair of good
post-horses. He had regained his strength. The moment of
parting with the young men, his hostess's cousins, was
pathetic in the extreme; on no account, whatever friendly
pretext Fabrizio might find, would they consent to take any
money.

"In your condition, sir, you need it more than we do,"

was the invariable reply of these worthy young fellows. Finally they set off with letters in which Fabrizio, somewhat emboldened by the agitation of the journey, had tried to convey to his hostesses all that he felt for them. Fabrizio wrote with tears in his eyes, and there was certainly love in the letter addressed to little Aniken.

In the rest of the journey there was nothing out of the common. He reached Amiens in great pain from the cut he had received in his thigh; it had not occurred to the country doctor to lance the wound, and in spite of the bleedings an abscess had formed. During the fortnight that Fabrizio spent in the inn at Amiens, kept by an obsequious and avaricious family, the Allies were invading France, and Fabrizio became another man, so many and profound were his reflexions on the things that had happened to him. He had remained a child upon one point only: what he had seen, was it a battle; and, if so, was that battle Waterloo? For the first time in his life he found pleasure in reading; he was always hoping to find in the newspapers, or in the published accounts of the battle, some description which would enable him to identify the ground he had covered with Marshal Ney's escort, and afterwards with the other general. During his stay at Amiens he wrote almost every day to his good friends at the Woolcomb. As soon as his wound was healed, he came to Paris. He found at his former hotel a score of letters from his mother and aunt, who implored him to return home as soon as possible. The last letter from Contessa Pietranera had a certain enigmatic tone which made him extremely uneasy; this letter destroyed all his tender fancies. His was a character to which a single word was enough to make him readily anticipate the greatest misfortunes; his imagination then stepped in and depicted these misfortunes to him with the most horrible details.

"Take care never to sign the letters you write to tell us what you are doing," the Contessa warned him. "On your return you must on no account come straight to the Lake of Como. Stop at Lugano, on Swiss soil." He was to arrive in this little town under the name of Cavi; he would find at the principal inn the Contessa's footman, who would tell him what to do. His aunt ended her letter as follows: "Take every possible precaution to keep your mad escapade secret, and above all do not carry on you any printed or written document; in Switzerland you will be surrounded by the

friends of Santa Margherita.[1] If I have enough money," the
Contessa told him, "I shall send someone to Geneva, to the
Hôtel des Balances, and you shall have particulars which I
cannot put in writing but which you ought to know before
coming here. But, in heaven's name, not a day longer in
Paris; you will be recognised there by our spies." Fabrizio's
imagination set to work to construct the wildest hypotheses,
and he was incapable of any other pleasure save that of trying to guess what the strange information could be that his
aunt had to give him. Twice on his passage through France
he was arrested, but managed to get away; he was indebted,
for these unpleasantnesses, to his Italian passport and to
that strange description of him as a dealer in barometers,
which hardly seemed to tally with his youthful face and the
arm which he carried in a sling.

Finally, at Geneva, he found a man in the Contessa's service, who gave him a message from her to the effect that he,
Fabrizio, had been reported to the police at Milan as having
gone abroad to convey to Napoleon certain proposals drafted
by a vast conspiracy organised in the former Kingdom of
Italy. If this had not been the object of his journey, the report went on, why should he have gone under an assumed
name? His mother was endeavouring to establish the truth,
as follows:

1st, that he had never gone beyond Switzerland.

2ndly, that he had left the castle suddenly after a quarrel
with his elder brother.

On hearing this story Fabrizio felt a thrill of pride. "I
am supposed to have been a sort of ambassador to Napoleon,"
he said to himself; "I should have had the honour of speaking to that great man: would to God I had!" He recalled
that his ancestor seven generations back, a grandson of him
who came to Milan in the train of the Sforza, had had the
honour of having his head cut off by the Duke's enemies,
who surprised him as he was on his way to Switzerland to
convey certain proposals to the Free Cantons and to raise
troops there. He saw in his mind's eye the print that illus-
trated this exploit in the genealogy of the family. Fabrizio,
questioning the servant, found him shocked by a detail which
finally he allowed to escape him, despite the express order,
several times repeated to him by the Contessa, not to reveal

---

[1] Silvio Pellico has given this name a European notoriety: it
is that of the street in Milan in which the police headquarters and
prisons are situated.

it. It was Ascanio, his elder brother, who had reported him to the Milan police. This cruel news almost drove our hero out of his mind. From Geneva, in order to go to Italy, one must pass through Lausanne; he insisted on setting off at once on foot, and thus covering ten to twelve leagues, although the mail from Geneva to Lausanne was starting in two hours' time. Before leaving Geneva he picked a quarrel in one of the melancholy cafés of the place with a young man who, he said, stared at him in a singular fashion. Which was perfectly true: the young Genevan, phlegmatic, rational and interested only in money, thought him mad; Fabrizio on coming in had glared furiously in all directions, then had upset the cup of coffee that was brought to him over his breeches. In this quarrel Fabrizio's first movement was quite of the sixteenth century: instead of proposing a duel to the young Genevan, he drew his dagger and rushed upon him to stab him with it. In this moment of passion, Fabrizio forgot everything he had ever learned of the laws of honour and reverted to instinct, or, more properly speaking, to the memories of his earliest childhood.

The confidential agent whom he found at Lugano increased his fury by furnishing him with fresh details. As Fabrizio was beloved at Grianta, no one there had mentioned his name, and, but for his brother's kind intervention, everyone would have pretended to believe that he was at Milan, and the attention of the police in that city would not have been drawn to his absence.

"I expect the *doganieri* have a description of you," his aunt's envoy hinted, "and if we keep to the main road, when you come to the frontier of the Lombardo-Venetian Kingdom, you will be arrested."

Fabrizio and his party were familiar with every footpath over the mountain that divides Lugano from the Lake of Como; they disguised themselves as hunters, that is to say as poachers, and as they were three in number and had a fairly resolute bearing, the *doganieri* whom they passed gave them a greeting and nothing more. Fabrizio arranged things so as not to arrive at the castle until nearly midnight; at that hour his father and all the powdered footmen had long been in bed. He climbed down without difficulty into the deep moat and entered the castle by the window of a cellar: it was there that his mother and aunt were waiting for him; presently his sisters came running in. Transports of affection alternated with tears for some time, and they had scarcely begun to talk reasonably when the first light of dawn came to warn these people who thought themselves so unfortunate that time was flying.

"I hope your brother won't have any suspicion of your being here," Signora Pietranera said to him; "I have scarcely spoken to him since that fine escapade of his, and his vanity has done me the honour of taking offence. This evening, at supper, I condescended to say a few words to him; I had to find some excuse to hide my frantic joy, which might have made him suspicious. Then, when I noticed that he was quite proud of this sham reconciliation, I took advantage of his happiness to make him drink a great deal too much, and I am certain he will never have thought of taking any steps to carry on his profession of spying."

"We shall have to hide our hussar in your room," said the Marchesa; "he can't leave at once; we haven't sufficient command of ourselves at present to make plans, and we shall have to think out the best way of putting those terrible Milan police off the track."

This plan was adopted; but the Marchese and his elder son noticed, next day, that the Marchesa was constantly in her sister-in-law's room. We shall not stop to depict the transports of affection and joy which continued, all that day, to convulse these happy creatures. Italian hearts are, far more than ours in France, tormented by the suspicions and wild ideas which a burning imagination presents to them, but on the other hand their joys are far more intense and more lasting. On the day in question the Contessa and Marchesa were literally out of their minds; Fabrizio was obliged to begin all his stories over again; finally they decided to go away and conceal their general joy at Milan, so difficult did it appear to be to keep it hidden any longer from the scrutiny of the Marchese and his son Ascanio.

They took the ordinary boat of the household to go to Como; to have acted otherwise would have aroused endless suspicions. But on arriving at the harbour of Como the Marchesa remembered that she had left behind at Grianta papers of the greatest importance: she hastened to send the boatmen back for them, and so these men could give no account of how the two ladies were spending their time at Como. No sooner had they arrived in the town than they selected haphazard one of the carriages that ply for hire near that tall mediæval tower which rises above the Milan gate. They started off at once, without giving the coachman time to speak to anyone. A quarter of a league from the town they found a young sportsman of their acquaintance who, out of courtesy to them as they had no man with them, kindly consented to act as their escort as far as the gates of Milan, whither he was bound for the shooting. All went well, and the ladies were conversing in the most joyous way with the young traveller when, at a bend which the road makes to pass the charming hill and wood of San Giovanni, three constables in plain clothes sprang at the horses' heads. "Ah! My husband has betrayed us," cried the Marchesa, and fainted away. A serjeant who had remained a little way behind came staggering up to the carriage and said, in a voice that reeked of the *trattoria*:

"I am sorry, sir, but I must do my duty and arrest you, General Fabio Conti."

Fabrizio thought that the serjeant was making a joke at his expense when he addressed him as "General." "You shall pay for this!" he said to himself. He examined the men in plain clothes and watched for a favourable moment to jump down from the carriage and dash across the fields.

The Contessa smiled—a smile of despair, I fancy—then said to the serjeant:

"But, my dear serjeant, is it this boy of sixteen that you take for General Conti?"

"Aren't you the General's daughter?" asked the serjeant.

"Look at my father," said the Contessa, pointing to Fabrizio. The constables went into fits of laughter.

"Show me your passports and don't argue the point," said the serjeant, stung by the general mirth.

"These ladies never take passports to go to Milan," said the coachman with a calm and philosophical air: "they are coming from their castle of Grianta. This lady is the Signora Contessa Pietranera; the other is the Signora Marchesa del Dongo."

The serjeant, completely disconcerted, went forward to the horses' heads and there took counsel with his men. The conference had lasted for fully five minutes when the Contessa asked if the gentlemen would kindly allow the carriage to be moved forward a few yards and stopped in the shade; the heat was overpowering, though it was only eleven o'clock in the morning. Fabrizio, who was looking out most attentively in all directions, seeking a way of escape, saw coming out of a little path through the fields and on to the high road a girl of fourteen or fifteen, who was crying timidly into her handkerchief. She came forward walking between two constables in uniform, and, three paces behind her, also between constables, stalked a tall, lean man who assumed an air of dignity, like a Prefect following a procession.

"Where did you find them?" asked the serjeant, for the moment completely drunk.

"Running away across the fields, with not a sign of a passport about them."

The serjeant appeared to lose his head altogether; he had before him five prisoners, instead of the two that he was expected to have. He went a little way off, leaving only one man to guard the male prisoner who put on the air of majesty, and another to keep the horses from moving.

"Wait," said the Contessa to Fabrizio, who had already jumped out of the carriage. "Everything will be settled in a minute."

They heard a constable exclaim: "What does it matter! If they have no passports, they're fair game whoever they are." The serjeant seemed not quite so certain; the name of Contessa Pietranera made him a little uneasy: he had known the General, and had not heard of his death. "The General is not the man to let it pass, if I arrest his wife without good reason," he said to himself.

During this deliberation, which was prolonged, the Contessa had entered into conversation with the girl, who was standing on the road, and in the dust by the side of the carriage; she had been struck by her beauty.

"The sun will be bad for you, Signorina. This gallant soldier," she went on, addressing the constable who was posted at the horses' heads, "will surely allow you to get into the carriage."

Fabrizio, who was wandering round the vehicle, came up to help the girl to get in. Her foot was already on the step, her arm supported by Fabrizio, when the imposing man, who was six yards behind the carriage, called out in a voice magnified by the desire to preserve his dignity:

"Stay in the road; don't get into a carriage that does not belong to you!"

Fabrizio had not heard this order; the girl, instead of climbing into the carriage, tried to get down again, and, as Fabrizio continued to hold her up, fell into his arms. He smiled; she blushed a deep crimson; they stood for a moment looking at one another after the girl had disengaged herself from his arms.

"She would be a charming prison companion," Fabrizio said to himself. "What profound thought lies behind that brow! She would know how to love."

The serjeant came up to them with an air of authority: "Which of these ladies is named Clelia Conti?"

"I am," said the girl.

"And I," cried the elderly man, "am General Fabio Conti, Chamberlain to H.S.H. the Prince of Parma; I consider it most irregular that a man in my position should be hunted down like a thief."

"The day before yesterday, when you embarked at the harbour of Como, did you not tell the police inspector who asked for your passport to go away? Very well, his orders to-day are that you are not to go away."

"I had already pushed off my boat, I was in a hurry, there was a storm threatening, a man not in uniform shouted to me from the quay to put back into harbour, I told him my name and went on."

"And this morning you escaped from Como."

"A man like myself does not take a passport when he goes from Milan to visit the lake. This morning, at Como, I was told that I should be arrested at the gate. I left the town on foot with my daughter; I hoped to find on the road some carriage that would take me to Milan, where the first thing I shall do will certainly be to call on the General commanding the Province and lodge a complaint."

A heavy weight seemed to have been lifted from the serjeant's mind.

"Very well, General, you are under arrest and I shall take you to Milan. And you, who are you?" he said to Fabrizio.

"My son," replied the Contessa; "Ascanio, son of the Divisional General Pietranera."

"Without a passport, Signora Contessa?" said the serjeant, in a much gentler tone.

"At his age, he has never had one; he never travels alone, he is always with me."

During this colloquy General Conti was standing more and more on his dignity with the constables.

"Not so much talk," said one of them; "you are under arrest, that's enough!"

"You will be glad to hear," said the serjeant, "that we allow you to hire a horse from some *contadino*; otherwise, never mind all the dust and the heat and the Chamberlain of

Parma, you would have to put your best foot foremost to keep pace with our horses."

The General began to swear.

"Will you kindly be quiet!" the constable repeated. "Where is your general's uniform? Anybody can come along and say he's a general."

The General grew more and more angry. Meanwhile things were looking much brighter in the carriage.

The Contessa kept the constables running about as if they had been her servants. She had given a scudo to one of them to go and fetch wine, and, what was better still, cold water from a cottage that was visible two hundred yards away. She had found time to calm Fabrizio, who was determined, at all costs, to make a dash for the wood that covered the hill. "I have a good brace of pistols," he said. She obtained the infuriated General's permission for his daughter to get into the carriage. On this occasion the General, who loved to talk about himself and his family, told the ladies that his daughter was only twelve years old, having been born in 1803, on the 27th of October, but that, such was her intelligence, everyone took her to be fourteen or fifteen.

"A thoroughly common man," the Contessa's eyes signalled to the Marchesa. Thanks to the Contessa, everything was settled, after a colloquy that lasted an hour. A constable, who discovered that he had some business to do in the neighbouring village, lent his horse to General Conti, after the Contessa had said to him: "You shall have ten francs." The serjeant went off by himself with the General; the other constables stayed behind under a tree, accompanied by four huge bottles of wine, almost small demi-johns, which the one who had been sent to the cottage had brought back, with the help of a *contadino*. Clelia Conti was authorised by the proud Chamberlain to accept, for the return journey to Milan, a seat in the ladies' carriage, and no one dreamed of arresting the son of the gallant General Pietranera. After the first few minutes had been devoted to an exchange of courtesies and to remarks on the little incident that had just occurred, Clelia Conti observed the note of enthusiasm with which so beautiful a lady as the Contessa spoke to Fabrizio; certainly, she was not his mother. The girl's attention was caught most of all by repeated allusions to something heroic, bold, dangerous to the last degree, which he had recently done; but for all her cleverness little Clelia could not discover what this was.

She gazed with astonishment at this young hero, whose eyes seemed to be blazing still with all the fire of action. For his part, he was somewhat embarrassed by the remarkable beauty of this girl of twelve, and her steady gaze made him blush.

A league outside Milan Fabrizio announced that he was going to see his uncle, and took leave of the ladies.

"If I ever get out of my difficulties," he said to Clelia, "I shall pay a visit to the beautiful pictures at Parma, and then will you deign to remember the name: Fabrizio del Dongo?"

"Good!" said the Contessa, "that is how you keep your identity secret. Signorina, deign to remember that this scapegrace is my son, and is called Pietranera, and not del Dongo."

That evening, at a late hour, Fabrizio entered Milan by the Porta Renza, which leads to a fashionable gathering-place. The despatch of their two servants to Switzerland had exhausted the very modest savings of the Marchesa and her sister-in-law; fortunately, Fabrizio had still some napoleons left, and one of the diamonds, which they decided to sell.

The ladies were highly popular, and knew everyone in the town. The most important personages in the Austrian and religious party went to speak on behalf of Fabrizio to Barone Binder, the Chief of Police. These gentlemen could not conceive, they said, how anyone could take seriously the escapade of a boy of sixteen who left the paternal roof after a dispute with an elder brother.

"My business is to take everything seriously," replied Barone Binder gently; a wise and solemn man, he was then engaged in forming the Milan police, and had undertaken to prevent a revolution like that of 1746, which drove the Austrians from Genoa. This Milan police, since rendered so famous by the adventures of Silvio Pellico and M. Andryane, was not exactly cruel; it carried out, reasonably and without pity, harsh laws. The Emperor Francis II wished these over-bold Italian imaginations to be struck by terror.

"Give me, day by day," repeated Barone Binder to Fabrizio's protectors, "a *certified* account of what the young Marchesino del Dongo has been doing; let us follow him from the moment of his departure on the 8th of March to his arrival last night in this city, where he is hidden in one of the rooms of his mother's apartment, and I am prepared to treat him as the most well-disposed and most frolicsome young man in town. If you cannot furnish me with the young man's itinerary during all the days following his departure from Grianta, however exalted his birth may be, however great the respect I owe to the friends of his family, obviously it is my duty to order his arrest. Am I not bound to keep him in prison until he has furnished me with proofs that he did not go to convey a message to Napoleon from such disaffected persons as may exist in Lombardy among the subjects of His Imperial and Royal Majesty? Note farther, gentlemen, that if young del Dongo succeeds in justifying himself on this point, he will still be liable to be charged with having gone abroad without a passport properly issued to himself, and also with assuming a false name and deliberately making use of a passport issued to a common workman, that is to say to a person of a class greatly inferior to that to which he himself belongs."

This declaration, cruelly reasonable, was accompanied by all the marks of deference and respect which the Chief of Police owed to the high position of the Marchesa del Dongo and of the important personages who were intervening on her behalf.

The Marchesa was in despair when Barone Binder's reply was communicated to her.

"Fabrizio will be arrested," she sobbed, "and once he is in prison, God knows when he will get out! His father will disown him!"

Signora Pietranera and her sister-in-law took counsel with two or three intimate friends, and, in spite of anything these might say, the Marchesa was absolutely determined to send her son away that very night.

"But you can see quite well," the Contessa pointed out to her, "that Barone Binder knows that your son is here; he is not a bad man."

"No; but he is anxious to please the Emperor Francis."

"But, if he thought it would lead to his promotion to put Fabrizio in prison, the boy would be there now; it is showing an insulting defiance of the Barone to send him away."

"But his admission to us that he knows where Fabrizio is, is as much as to say: 'Send him away!' No, I shan't feel alive until I can no longer say to myself: 'In a quarter of an hour my son may be within prison walls.' Whatever Barone Binder's ambition may be," the Marchesa went on, "he thinks it useful to his personal standing in this country to make certain concessions to oblige a man of my husband's rank, and I see a proof of this in the singular frankness with which he admits that he knows where to lay hands on my son. Besides, the Barone has been so kind as to let us know the two offences with which Fabrizio is charged, at the instigation of his unworthy brother; he explains that each of these offences means prison: is not that as much as to say that if we prefer exile it is for us to choose?"

"If you choose exile," the Contessa kept on repeating, "we shall never set eyes on him again as long as we live." Fabrizio, who was present at the whole conversation, with an old friend of the Marchesa, now a counsellor on the tribunal set up by Austria, was strongly inclined to take the key of the street and go; and, as a matter of fact, that same evening he left the *palazzo,* hidden in the carriage that was taking his mother and aunt to the Scala theatre. The coachman, whom they distrusted, went as usual to wait in an *osteria,* and while the footmen, on whom they could rely, were looking after the horses, Fabrizio, disguised as a *contadino,* slipped out of the carriage and escaped from the town. Next morning he crossed the frontier with equal ease, and a few hours later had established himself on a property which his mother owned in Piedmont, near Novara, to be precise, at Romagnano, where Bayard was killed.

It may be imagined how much attention the ladies, on reaching their box in the Scala, paid to the performance. They had gone there solely to be able to consult certain of their friends who belonged to the Liberal party and whose appearance at the *palazzo* del Dongo might have been misconstrued by the police. In the box it was decided to make a fresh appeal to Barone Binder. There was no question of offering a sum of money to this magistrate who was a perfectly honest man; moreover, the ladies were extremely poor; they had forced Fabrizio to take with him all the money that remained from the sale of the diamond.

It was of the utmost importance that they should be kept constantly informed of the Barone's latest decisions. The Contessa's friends reminded her of a certain Canon Borda, a most charming young man who at one time had tried to make advances to her, in a somewhat violent manner; finding himself unsuccessful he had reported her friendship for Limercati to General Pietranera, whereupon he had been dismissed from the house as a rascal. Now, at present this Canon was in the habit of going every evening to play *tarocchi* with Baronessa Binder, and was naturally the intimate friend of her husband. The Contessa made up her mind to take the horribly unpleasant step of going to see this Canon; and the following morning, at an early hour, before he had left the house, she sent in her name.

When the Canon's one and only servant announced: "Contessa Pietranera," his master was so overcome as to be incapable of speech; he made no attempt to repair the disorder of a very scanty attire.

"Shew her in, and leave us," he said in faint accents. The Contessa entered the room; Borda fell on his knees.

"It is in this position that an unhappy madman ought to receive your orders," he said to the Contessa, who, that morning, in a plain costume that was almost a disguise, was irresistibly attractive. Her intense grief at Fabrizio's exile, the violence that she was doing to her own feelings in coming to the house of a man who had behaved treacherously towards her, all combined to give an incredible brilliance to her eyes.

"It is in this position that I wish to recieve your orders," cried the Canon, "for it is obvious that you have some service to ask of me, otherwise you would not have honoured with your presence the poor dwelling of an unhappy madman; once before, carried away by love and jealousy, he behaved towards you like a scoundrel, as soon as he saw that he could not win your favour."

The words were sincere, and all the more handsome in that the Canon now enjoyed a position of great power; the Contessa was moved to tears by them; humiliation and fear had frozen her spirit; now in a moment affection and a gleam of hope took their place. From a most unhappy state she passed in a flash almost to happiness.

"Kiss my hand," she said, as she held it out to the Canon, "and rise." (She used the second person singular, which in Italy, it must be remembered, indicates a sincere and open friendship just as much as a more tender sentiment.) "I have come to ask your favour for my nephew Fabrizio. This is the whole truth of the story without the slightest concealment, as one tells it to an old friend. At the age of sixteen and a half he has done an intensely stupid thing. We were at the castle of Grianta on the Lake of Como. One evening at seven o'clock we learned by a boat from Como of the Emperor's landing on the shore of the Gulf of Juan. Next morning Fabrizio went off to France, after borrowing the passport of one of his plebeian friends, a dealer in barometers, named Vasi. As he does not exactly resemble a dealer in barometers, he had hardly gone ten leagues into France when he was arrested on sight; his outbursts of enthusiasm in bad French seemed suspicious. After a time he escaped and managed to reach Geneva; we sent to meet him at Lugano. . . ."

"That is to say, Geneva," put in the Canon with a smile. The Contessa finished her story.

"I will do everything for you that is humanly possible," replied the Canon effusively; "I place myself entirely at your disposal. I will even do imprudent things," he added. "Tell me, what am I to do as soon as this poor parlour is deprived of this heavenly apparition which marks an epoch in the history of my life?"

"You must go to Barone Binder and tell him that you have loved Fabrizio ever since he was born, that you saw him in his cradle when you used to come to our house, and that accordingly, in the name of the friendship he has shown for you, you beg him to employ all his spies to discover whether, before his departure for Switzerland, Fabrizio was in any sort of communication whatsoever with any of the Liberals whom he has under supervision. If the Barone's information is of any value, he is bound to see that there is nothing more in this than a piece of boyish folly. You know that I used to have, in my beautiful apartment in the *palazzo* Dugnani, prints of the battles won by Napoleon: it was by spelling out the legends engraved beneath them that my nephew learned to read. When he was five years old, my poor husband used to explain these battles to him; we put my husband's helmet on his head, the boy strutted about trailing his big sabre. Very well, one fine day he learns that my husband's god, the Emperor, has returned to France, he starts out to join him, like a fool, but does not succeed in reaching him. Ask your Barone with what penalty he proposes to punish this moment of folly?"

"I was forgetting one thing," said the Canon, "you shall see that I am not altogether unworthy of the pardon that you grant me. Here," he said, looking on the table among his papers, "here is the accusation by that infamous *collo-torto*" (that is, hypocrite), "see, signed *Ascanio Valserra del* DONGO, which gave rise to the whole trouble; I found it yesterday at the police headquarters, and went to the Scala in the hope of finding someone who was in the habit of going to your box, through whom I might be able to communicate it to you. A copy of this document reached Vienna long ago.

There is the enemy that we have to fight." The Canon read the accusation through with the Contessa, and it was agreed that in the course of the day he would let her have a copy by the hand of some trustworthy person. It was with joy in her heart that the Contessa returned to the *palazzo* del Dongo.

"No one could possibly be more of a gentleman than that reformed rake," she told the Marchesa. "This evening at the Scala, at a quarter to eleven by the theatre clock, we are to send everyone away from our box, put out the candles, and shut our door, and at eleven the Canon himself will come and tell us what he has managed to do. We decided that this would be the least compromising course for him."

This Canon was a man of spirit; he was careful to keep the appointment; he shewed when he came a complete good nature and an unreserved openness of heart such as are scarcely to be found except in countries where vanity does not predominate over every other sentiment. His denunciation of the Contessa to her husband, General Pietranera, was one of the great sorrows of his life, and he had now found a means of getting rid of that remorse.

That morning, when the Contessa had left his room, "So she's in love with her nephew, is she," he had said to himself bitterly, for he was by no means cured. "With her pride, to have come to me! . . . After that poor Pietranera died, she repulsed with horror my offers of service, though they were most polite and admirably presented by Colonel Scotti, her old lover. The beautiful Pietranera reduced to living on fifteen hundred francs!" the Canon went on, striding vigorously up and down the room. "And then to go and live in the castle of Grianta, with an abominable *seccatore* like that Marchese del Dongo! . . . I can see it all now! After all, that young Fabrizio is full of charm, tall, well built, always with a smile on his face . . . and, better still, a deliciously voluptuous expression in his eye . . . a Correggio face," the Canon added bitterly.

"The difference in age . . . not too great . . . Fabrizio born after the French came, about '98, I fancy; the Contessa might be twenty-seven or twenty-eight: no one could be better looking, more adorable. In this country rich in beauties, she defeats them all, the Marini, the Gherardi, the Ruga, the Aresi, the Pietragrua, she is far and away above any of them. They were living happily together, hidden away by that beautiful Lake of Como, when the young man took it into his

head to join Napoleon. . . . There are still souls in Italy!
In spite of everything! Dear country! No," went on this heart
inflamed by jealousy, "impossible to explain in any other way
her resigning herself to vegetating in the country, with the
disgusting spectacle, day after day, at every meal, of that
horrible face of the Marchese del Dongo, as well as that
unspeakable pasty physiognomy of the Marchesino Ascanio,
who is going to be worse than his father! Well, I shall serve
her faithfully. At least I shall have the pleasure of seeing
her otherwise than through an opera-glass."

Canon Borda explained the whole case very clearly to the
ladies. At heart, Binder was as well disposed as they could
wish; he was delighted that Fabrizio should have taken the
key of the street before any orders could arrive from Vienna;
for Barone Binder had no power to make any decision, he
awaited orders in this case as in every other. He sent every
day to Vienna an exact copy of all the information that
reached him; then he waited.

It was necessary that, in his exile at Romagnano, Fabrizio

(1) Should hear mass daily without fail, take as his confessor a man of spirit, devoted to the cause of the Monarchy,
and should confess to him, at the tribunal of penitence, only
the most irreproachable sentiments.

(2) Should consort with no one who bore any reputation
for intelligence, and, were the need to arise, must speak of
rebellion with horror as a thing that no circumstances could
justify.

(3) Must never let himself be seen in the *caffè*, must
never read any newspaper other than the official *Gazette* of
Turin and Milan; in general he should shew a distaste for
reading, and never open any book printed later than 1720,
with the possible exception of the novels of Walter Scott.

(4) "Finally" (the Canon added with a touch of malice),
"it is most important that he should pay court openly to one
of the pretty women of the district, of the noble class, of
course; this will shew that he has not the dark and dissatisfied mind of an embryo conspirator."

Before going to bed, the Contessa and the Marchesa each
wrote Fabrizio an endless letter, in which they explained to
him with a charming anxiety all the advice that had been
given them by Borda.

Fabrizio had no wish to be a conspirator: he loved Napoleon, and, in his capacity as a young noble, believed that he
had been created to be happier than his neighbour, and

thought the middle classes absurd. Never had he opened a book since leaving school, where he had read only texts arranged by the Jesuits. He established himself at some distance from Romagnano, in a magnificent *palazzo*, one of the masterpieces of the famous architect Sanmicheli; but for thirty years it had been uninhabited, so that the rain came into every room and not one of the windows would shut. He took possession of the agent's horses, which he rode without ceremony at all hours of the day; he never spoke, and he thought about things. The recommendation to take a mistress from an *ultra* family appealed to him, and he obeyed it to the letter. He chose as his confessor a young priest given to intrigue who wished to become a bishop (like the confessor of the Spielberg[1]); but he went three leagues on foot and wrapped himself in a mystery which he imagined to be impenetrable, in order to read the *Constitutionnel,* which he thought sublime. "It is as fine as Alfieri and Dante!" he used often to exclaim. Fabrizio had this in common with the young men of France, that he was far more seriously taken up with his horse and his newspaper than with his politically *sound* mistress. But there was no room as yet for *imitation of others* in this simple and sturdy nature, and he made no friends in the society of the large country town of Romagnano; his simplicity passed as arrogance: no one knew what to make of his character. *"He is a younger son who feels himself wronged because he is not the eldest,"* was the *parroco's* comment.

[1] See the curious Memoirs of M. Andryane, as entertaining as a novel, and as lasting as Tacitus.

CHAPTER SIX

LET US ADMIT frankly that Canon Borda's jealousy was not altogether unfounded: on his return from France, Fabrizio appeared to the eyes of Contessa Pietranera like a handsome stranger whom she had known well in days gone by. If he had spoken to her of love she would have loved him; had she not already conceived, for his conduct and his person, a passionate and, one might say, unbounded admiration? But Fabrizio embraced her with such an effusion of innocent gratitude and good-fellowship that she would have been horrified with herself had she sought for any other sentiment in this almost filial friendship. "After all," she said to herself, "some of my friends who knew me six years ago, at Prince Eugène's court, may still find me good-looking and even young, but for him I am a respectable woman—and, if the truth must be told without any regard for my vanity, a woman of a certain age." The Contessa was under an illusion as to the period of life at which she had arrived, but it was not the illusion of common women. "Besides, at his age," she went on, "boys are apt to exaggerate the ravages of time. A man with more experience of life . . ."

The Contessa, who was pacing the floor of her drawing-room, stopped before a mirror, then smiled. It must be explained that, some months since, the heart of Signora Pietranera had been attacked in a serious fashion, and by a singular personage. Shortly after Fabrizio's departure for France, the Contessa who, without altogether admitting it to herself, was already beginning to take a great interest in him, had fallen into a profound melancholy. All her occupations seemed to her to lack pleasure, and, if one may use the word, savour; she told herself that Napoleon, wishing to secure the attachment of his Italian peoples, would take

Fabrizio as his aide-de-camp. "He is lost to me!" she exclaimed, weeping, "I shall never see him again; he will write to me, but what shall I be to him in ten years' time?"

It was in this frame of mind that she made an expedition to Milan; she hoped to find there some more immediate news of Napoleon, and, for all she knew, incidentally news of Fabrizio. Without admitting it to herself, this active soul was beginning to be very weary of the monotonous life she was leading in the country. "It is a postponement of death," she said to herself, "it is not life." Every day to see those powdered heads, her brother, her nephew Ascanio, their footmen! What would her excursions on the lake be without Fabrizio? Her sole consolation was based on the ties of friendship that bound her to the Marchesa. But for some time now this intimacy with Fabrizio's mother, a woman older than herself and with no hope left in life, had begun to be less attractive to her.

Such was the singular position in which Signora Pietranera was placed: with Fabrizio away, she had little hope for the future. Her heart was in need of consolation and novelty. On arriving in Milan she conceived a passion for the fashionable opera; she would go and shut herself up alone for hours on end, at the Scala, in the box of her old friend General Scotti. The men whom she tried to meet in order to obtain news of Napoleon and his army seemed to her vulgar and coarse. Going home, she would improvise on her piano until three o'clock in the morning. One evening, at the Scala, in the box of one of her friends to which she had gone in search of news from France, she made the acquaintance of Conte Mosca, a Minister from Parma; he was an agreeable man who spoke of France and Napoleon in a way that gave her fresh reasons for hope or fear. She returned to the same box the following evening; this intelligent man reappeared and throughout the whole performance she talked to him with enjoyment. Since Fabrizio's departure she had not found any evening so lively. This man who amused her, Conte Mosca della Rovere Sorezana, was at that time Minister of Police and Finance to that famous Prince of Parma, Ernesto IV, so notorious for his severities, which the Liberals of Milan called cruelties. Mosca might have been forty or forty-five; he had strongly marked features, with no trace of self-importance, and a simple and light-hearted manner which was greatly in his favour; he would have looked very well indeed, if a whim on the part of his Prince had not obliged him to wear powder on his hair as a proof of his soundness in politics. As people have little fear of wounding one another's vanity, they quickly arrive in Italy at a tone of intimacy, and make personal observations. The antidote to this practice is not to see the other person again if one's feelings have been hurt.

"Tell me, Conte, why do you powder your hair?" Signora Pietranera asked him at their third meeting. "Powder! A man like you, attractive, still young, who fought on our side in Spain!"

"Because, in the said Spain, I stole nothing, and one must live. I was athirst for glory; a flattering word from the French General, Gouvion Saint-Cyr, who commanded us, was everything to me then. When Napoleon fell, it so happened that while I was eating up my patrimony in his service, my father, a man of imagination, who pictured me as a general already, had been building me a *palazzo* at Parma. In 1813 I found that my whole worldly wealth consisted of a huge *palazzo*, half finished, and a pension."

"A pension: 3,500 francs, like my husband's?"

"Conte Pietranera commanded a Division. My pension, as a humble squadron commander, has never been more than 800 francs, and even that has been paid to me only since I became Minister of Finance."

As there was nobody else in the box but the lady of extremely liberal views to whom it belonged, the conversation continued with the same frankness. Conte Mosca, when questioned, spoke of his life at Parma. "In Spain, under General Saint-Cyr, I faced the enemy's fire to win a cross and a little glory besides, now I dress myself up like an actor in a farce to win a great social position and a few thousand francs a year. Once I had started on this sort of political chessboard, stung by the insolence of my superiors, I determined to occupy one of the foremost posts; I have reached it. But the happiest days of my life will always be those which, now and again, I manage to spend at Milan; here, it seems to me, there still survives the spirit of your Army of Italy."

The frankness, the *disinvoltura* with which this Minister of so dreaded a Prince spoke pricked the Contessa's curiosity; from his title she had expected to find a pedant filled with self-importance; what she saw was a man who was ashamed of the gravity of his position. Mosca had promised to let her have all the news from France that he could collect; this was a grave indiscretion at Milan, during the month that preceded Waterloo; the question for Italy at that time was to be or not to be; everyone at Milan was in a fever, a fever of hope or fear. Amid this universal disturbance, the Contessa started to make inquiries about a man who spoke thus lightly of so coveted a position, and one which, moreover, was his sole means of livelihood.

Certain curious information of an interesting oddity was reported to Signora Pietranera. "Conte Mosca della Rovere Sorezana," she was told, "is on the point of becoming Prime Minister and declared favourite of Ranuccio-Ernesto IV, the absolute sovereign of Parma and one of the wealthiest Princes in Europe to boot. The Conte would already have attained to this exalted position if he had cared to shew a more solemn face: they say that the Prince often lectures him on this failing.

"'What do my manners matter to Your Highness,' he answers boldly, 'so long as I conduct his affairs?'

"This favourite's bed of roses," her informant went on, "is not without its thorns. He has to please a Sovereign, a man of sense and intelligence, no doubt, but a man who, since his accession to an absolute throne, seems to have lost his head altogether and shews, for instance, suspicions worthy of an old woman.

"Ernesto IV is courageous only in war. On the field of battle he has been seen a score of times leading a column to the attack like a gallant general; but after the death of his father, Ernesto III, on his return to his States, where, unfortunately for him, he possesses unlimited power, he set to work to inveigh in the most senseless fashion against Liberals and liberty. Presently he began to imagine that he was hated; finally, in a moment of ill temper, he had two Liberals hanged, who may or may not have been guilty, acting on the advice of a wretch called Rassi, a sort of Minister of Justice.

"From that fatal moment the Prince's life changed; we find him tormented by the strangest suspicions. He is not fifty, and fear has so reduced him, if one may use the expression, that whenever he speaks of Jacobins, and the plans of the Central Committee in Paris, his face becomes like that of an old man of eighty; he relapses into the fantastic fears of childhood. His favourite, Rassi, the Fiscal General (or Chief Justice), has no influence except through his master's fear; and whenever he is alarmed for his own position, he makes haste to discover some fresh conspiracy of the blackest and most fantastic order. Thirty rash fellows have banded themselves together to read a number of the *Constitutionnel,* Rassi declares them to be conspirators, and sends them off to prison in that famous citadel of Parma, the terror of the whole of Lombardy. As it rises to a great height, a hundred and eighty feet, people say, it is visible from a long way off in the middle of that immense plain; and the physical outlines of the prison, of which horrible things are reported, makes it the queen, governing by fear, of the whole of that plain, which extends from Milan to Bologna."

"Would you believe," said another traveller to the Contessa, "that at night, on the third floor of his palace, guarded by eighty sentinels who every quarter of an hour cry aloud a whole sentence, Ernesto IV trembles in his room. All the doors fastened with ten bolts, and the adjoining rooms, above as well as below him, packed with soldiers, he is afraid of the Jacobins. If a plank creaks in the floor, he snatches up his pistols and imagines there is a Liberal hiding under his bed. At once all the bells in the castle are set ringing, and an aide-de-camp goes to awaken Conte Mosca. On reaching the castle, the Minister of Police takes good care not to deny the existence of any conspiracy; on the contrary, alone with the Prince, and armed to the teeth, he inspects every corner of the rooms, looks under the beds, and, in a word, gives himself up to a whole heap of ridiculous actions worthy of an old woman. All these precautions would have seemed highly degrading to the Prince himself in the happy days when he used to go to war and had never killed anyone except in open combat. As he is a man of infinite spirit, he is ashamed of these precautions; they seem to him ridiculous, even at the moment when he is giving way to them, and the source of Conte Mosca's enormous reputation is that he devotes all his skill to arranging that the Prince shall never have occasion to blush in his presence. It is he, Mosca, who, in his capacity as Minister of Police, insists upon looking under the furniture, and, so people say in Parma, even in the cases in which the musicians keep their double-basses. It is the Prince who objects to this and teases his Minister over his excessive punctiliousness. 'It is a challenge,' Conte Mosca replies; 'think of the satirical sonnets the Jacobins would shower on us if we allowed you to be killed. It is not only your life that we are defending, it is our honour.'

But it appears that the Prince is only half taken in by this, for if anyone in the town should take it into his head to remark that they have passed a sleepless night at the castle, the Grand Fiscal Rassi sends the impertinent fellow to the citadel, and once in that lofty abode, and *in the fresh air*, as they say at Parma, it is a miracle if anyone remembers the prisoner's existence. It is because he is a soldier, and in Spain got away a score of times, pistol in hand, from a tight corner, that the Prince prefers Conte Mosca to Rassi, who is a great deal more flexible and baser. Those unfortunate prisoners in the citadel are kept in the most rigorously secret confinement, and all sort of stories are told about them. The Liberals assert that (and this, they say, is one of Rassi's ideas) the gaolers and confessors are under orders to assure them, about once a month, that one of them is being led out to die. That day the prisoners have permission to climb to the platform of the huge tower, one hundred and eighty feet high, and from there they see a procession file along the plain with some spy who plays the part of a poor devil going to his death."

These stories and a score of others of the same nature and of no less authenticity keenly interested Signora Pietranera: on the following day she asked Conte Mosca, whom she rallied briskly, for details. She found him amusing, and maintained to him that at heart he was a monster without knowing it. One day as he went back to his inn the Conte said to himself: "Not only is this Contessa Pietranera a charming woman; but when I spend the evening in her box I manage to forget certain things at Parma the memory of which cuts me to the heart."—This Minister, in spite of his frivolous air and his polished manners, was not blessed with a soul of the French type; he could not *forget* the things that annoyed him. When there was a thorn in his pillow, he was obliged to break it off and to blunt its point by repeated stabbings of his throbbing limbs. (I must apologise for the last two sentences, which are translated from the Italian.) On the morrow of this discovery, the Conte found that, notwithstanding the business that had summoned him to Milan, the day spun itself out to an enormous length; he could not stay in one place, he wore out his carriage-horses. About six o'clock he mounted his saddle-horse to ride to the *Corso;* he had some hope of meeting Signora Pietranera there; seeing no sign of her, he remembered that at eight o'clock the Scala Theatre opened; he entered it, and did not see ten persons in that immense auditorium. He felt somewhat ashamed of himself for being there. "Is it possible," he asked himself, "that at forty-five and past I am committing follies at which a sub-lieutenant would blush? Fortunately nobody suspects them." He fled, and tried to pass the time by strolling up and down the attractive streets that surround the Scala. They are lined with *caffè* which at that hour are filled to overflowing with people. Outside each of these *caffè* crowds of curious idlers perched on chairs in the middle of the street sip ices and criticise the passers-by. The Conte was a passer-by of importance; at once he had the pleasure of being recognised and addressed. Three or four importunate persons of the kind that one cannot easily shake off seized this opportunity to obtain an audience of so powerful a Minister. Two of them handed him petitions; the third was content with pouring out a stream of long-winded advice as to his political conduct.

"One does not sleep," he said to himself, "when one has such a brain; one ought not to walk about when one is so powerful." He returned to the theatre, where it occurred to him that he might take a box in the third tier; from there his gaze could plunge, unnoticed by anyone, into the box in the second tier in which he hoped to see the Contessa arrive. Two full hours of waiting did not seem any too long to this lover; certain of not being seen he abandoned himself joyfully to the full extent of his folly. "Old age," he said to himself, "is not that, more than anything else, the time when one is no longer capable of these delicious puerilities?"

Finally the Contessa appeared. Armed with his glasses, he studied her with rapture: "Young, brilliant, light as a bird," he said to himself, "she is not twenty-five. Her beauty is the least of her charms: where else could one find that soul, always sincere, which never acts *with prudence,* which abandons itself entirely to the impression of the moment, which asks only to be carried away towards some new goal? I can understand Conte Nani's foolish behaviour."

The Conte supplied himself with excellent reasons for behaving foolishly, so long as he was thinking only of capturing the happiness which he saw before his eyes. He did not find any quite so satisfactory when he came to consider his age and the anxieties, sometimes of the saddest nature, that burdened his life. "A man of ability, whose spirit has been destroyed by fear, gives me a sumptuous life and plenty of money to be his Minister; but were he to dismiss me to-

morrow, I should be left old and poor, that is to say everything that the world despises most; there's a fine partner to
offer the Contessa!" These thoughts were too dark, he came
back to Signora Pietranera; he could not tire of gazing at
her, and, to be able to think of her better, did not go down
to her box. "Her only reason for taking Nani, they tell me,
was to put that imbecile Limercati in his place when he could
not be prevailed upon to run a sword, or to hire someone
else to stick a dagger into her husband's murderer. I would
fight for her twenty times over!" cried the Conte in a transport of enthusiasm. Every moment he consulted the theatre
clock which, with illuminated figures upon a black background, warned the audience every five minutes of the approach of the hour at which it was permissible for them to
visit a friend's box. The Conte said to himself: "I cannot
spend more than half an hour at the most in the box, seeing
that I have known her so short a time; if I stay longer, I
shall attract attention, and, thanks to my age and even more
to this accursed powder on my hair, I shall have all the be-
witching allurements of a Cassandra." But a sudden thought
made up his mind once and for all. "If she were to leave
that box to pay someone else a visit, I should be well rewarded for the avarice with which I am hoarding up this
pleasure." He rose to go down to the box in which he could
see the Contessa; all at once he found that he had lost almost all his desire to present himself to her.

"Ah! this is really charming," he exclaimed with a smile
at his own expense, and coming to a halt on the staircase;
"an impulse of genuine shyness! It must be at least five and
twenty years since an adventure of this sort last came my
way."

He entered the box, almost with an effort to control himself; and, making the most, like a man of spirit, of the condition in which he found himself, made no attempt to appear
at ease, or to display his wit by plunging into some entertaining story; he had the courage to be shy, he employed
his wits in letting his disturbance be apparent without making himself ridiculous. "If she should take it amiss," he said
to himself, "I am lost for ever. What! Shy, with my hair
covered with powder, hair which, without the disguise of the
powder, would be visibly grey! But, after all, it is a fact; it
cannot therefore be absurd unless I exaggerate it or make a
boast of it." The Contessa had spent so many weary hours at
the castle of Grianta, facing the powdered heads of her

brother and nephew, and of various politically *sound* bores of the neighbourhood, that it never occurred to her to give a thought to her new adorer's style in hairdressing.

The Contessa's mind having this protection against the impulse to laugh on his entry, she paid attention only to the news from France which Mosca always had for her in detail, on coming to her box; no doubt he used to invent it. As she discussed this news with him, she noticed this evening the expression in his eyes, which was good and kindly.

"I can imagine," she said to him, "that at Parma, among your slaves, you will not wear that friendly expression; it would ruin everything and give them some hope of not being hanged!"

The entire absence of any sense of self-importance in a man who passed as the first diplomat in Italy seemed strange to the Contessa; she even found a certain charm in it. Moreover, as he talked well and with warmth, she was not at all displeased that he should have thought fit to take upon himself for one evening, without ulterior consequences, the part of squire of dames.

It was a great step forward, and highly dangerous; fortunately for the Minister, who, at Parma, never met a cruel fair, the Contessa had arrived from Grianta only a few days before: her mind was still stiff with the boredom of a country life. She had almost forgotten how to make fun; and all those things that appertain to a light and elegant way of living had assumed in her eyes as it were a tint of novelty which made them sacred; she was in no mood to laugh at anyone, even a lover of forty-five, and shy. A week later, the Conte's temerity might have met with a very different sort of welcome.

At the Scala, it is not usual to prolong for more than twenty minutes or so these little visits to one's friends' boxes; the Conte spent the whole evening in the box in which he had been so fortunate as to meet Signora Pietranera. "She is a woman," he said to himself, "who revives in me all the follies of my youth!" But he was well aware of the danger. "Will my position as an all-powerful Bashaw in a place forty leagues away induce her to pardon me this stupid behaviour? I get so bored at Parma!" Meanwhile, every quarter of an hour, he registered a mental vow to get up and go.

"I must explain to you, Signora," he said to the Contessa with a laugh, "that at Parma I am bored to death, and I ought to be allowed to drink my fill of pleasure when the cup comes my way. So, without involving you in anything and simply for this evening, permit me to play the part of lover in your company. Alas, in a few days I shall be far away from this box which makes me forget every care and indeed, you will say, every convention."

A week after this monstrous visit to the Contessa's box, and after a series of minor incidents the narration of which here would perhaps seem tedious, Conte Mosca was absolutely mad with love, and the Contessa had already begun to think that his age need offer no objection if the suitor proved attractive in other ways. They had reached this stage when Mosca was recalled by a courier from Parma. One would have said that his Prince was afraid to be left alone. The Contessa returned to Grianta; her imagination no longer serving to adorn that lovely spot, it appeared to her a desert. "Should I be attached to this man?" she asked herself. Mosca wrote to her, and had not to play a part; absence had relieved him of the source of all his anxious thoughts; his letters were amusing, and, by a little piece of eccentricity which was not taken amiss, to escape the comments of the Marchese del Dongo, who did not like having to pay for the carriage of letters, he used to send couriers who would post his at Como or Lecco or Varese or some other of those charming little places on the shores of the lake. This was done with the idea that the courier might be employed to take back her replies. The move was successful.

Soon the days when the couriers came were events in the Contessa's life; these couriers brought her flowers, fruit, little presents of no value, which amused her, however, and her sister-in-law as well. Her memory of the Conte was blended with her idea of his great power; the Contessa had become curious to know everything that people said of him; the Liberals themselves paid a tribute to his talents.

The principal source of the Conte's reputation for evil was that he passed as the head of the *Ultra* Party at the Court of Parma, while the Liberal Party had at its head an intriguing woman capable of anything, even of succeeding, the Marchesa Raversi, who was immensely rich. The Prince made a great point of not discouraging that one of the two parties which happened not to be in power; he knew quite well that he himself would always be the master, even with a Ministry formed in Signora Raversi's drawing-room. Endless details of these intrigues were reported at Grianta. The bodily absence of Mosca, whom everyone described as a

Minister of supreme talent and a man of action, made it possible not to think any more of his powdered head, a symbol of everything that is dull and sad; it was a detail of no consequence, one of the obligations of the court at which, moreover, he was playing so distinguished a part. "It is a ridiculous thing, a court," said the Contessa to the Marchesa, "but it is amusing; it is a game that it is interesting to play, but one must agree to the rules. Who ever thought of protesting against the absurdity of the rules of piquet? And yet, once you are accustomed to the rules, it is delightful to beat your adversary with *repique* and *capot*."

The Contessa often thought about the writer of these entertaining letters; the days on which she received them were delightful to her; she would take her boat and go to read them in one of the charming spots by the lake, the Pliniana, Belan, the wood of the Sfrondata. These letters seemed to console her to some extent for Fabrizio's absence. She could not, at all events, refuse to allow the Conte to be deeply in love; a month had not passed before she was thinking of him with tender affection. For his part, Conte Mosca was almost sincere when he offered to hand in his resignation, to leave the Ministry and to come and spend the rest of his life with her at Milan or elsewhere. "I have 400,000 francs," he added, "which will always bring us in an income of 15,000." —"A box at the play again, horses, everything," thought the Contessa; they were pleasant dreams. The sublime beauty of the different views of the Lake of Como began to charm her once more. She went down to dream by its shores of this return to a brilliant and distinctive life, which, most unexpectedly, seemed to be coming within the bounds of possibility. She saw herself on the Corso, at Milan, happy and gay as in the days of the Viceroy: "Youth, or at any rate a life of action, would begin again for me."

Sometimes her ardent imagination concealed things from her, but never did she have those deliberate illusions which cowardice induces. She was above all things a woman who was honest with herself. "If I am a little too old to be doing foolish things," she said to herself, "envy, which creates illusions as love does, may poison my stay in Milan for me. After my husband's death, my noble poverty was a success, as was my refusal of two vast fortunes. My poor little Conte Mosca had not a twentieth part of the opulence that was cast at my feet by those two worms, Limercati and Nani. The meagre widow's pension which I had to struggle to obtain, the dismissal of my servants, which made some sensation, the little fifth-floor room, which brought a score of carriages to the door, all went to form at the time a striking spectacle. But I shall have unpleasant moments, however skilfully I may handle things, if, never possessing any fortune beyond my widow's pension, I go back to live at Milan on the snug little middle-class comfort which we can secure with the 15,000 lire that Mosca will have left after he retires. One strong objection, out of which envy will forge a terrible weapon, is that the Conte, although separated long ago from his wife, is still a married man. This separation is known at Parma, but at Milan it will come as news, and they will put it down to me. So, my dear Scala, my divine Lake of Como, adieu! adieu!"

In spite of all these forebodings, if the Contessa had had the smallest income of her own she would have accepted Mosca's offer to resign his office. She regarded herself as a middle-aged woman, and the idea of the court alarmed her; but what will appear in the highest degree improbable on this side of the Alps is that the Conte would have handed in that resignation gladly. So, at least, he managed to make his friend believe. In all his letters he implored, with an ever increasing frenzy, a second interview at Milan; it was granted him. "To swear that I feel an insane passion for you," the Contessa said to him one day at Milan, "would be a lie; I should be only too glad to love to-day at thirty odd as I used to love at two and twenty! But I have seen so many things decay that I had imagined to be eternal! I have the most tender regard for you, I place an unbounded confidence in you, and of all the men I know, you are the one I like best." The Contessa believed herself to be perfectly sincere; and yet, in the final clause, this declaration embodied a tiny falsehood. Fabrizio, perhaps, had he chosen, might have triumphed over every rival in her heart. But Fabrizio was nothing more than a boy in Conte Mosca's eyes: he himself reached Milan three days after the young hothead's departure for Novara, and he hastened to intercede on his behalf with Barone Binder. The Conte considered that his exile was now irrevocable.

He had not come to Milan alone; he had in his carriage the Duca Sanseverina-Taxis, a handsome little old man of sixty eight, dapple-grey, very polished, very neat, immensely rich but not quite as noble as he ought to have been. It was his grandfather, only, who had amassed millions from the office of Farmer General of the Revenues of the State of Parma. His father had had himself made Ambassador of the Prince of Parma to the Court of ——, by advancing the following argument: "Your Highness allots 30,000 francs to his Representative at the Court of ——, where he cuts an extremely modest figure. Should Your Highness deign to appoint me to the post, I will accept 6,000 francs as salary. My expenditure at the Court of —— will never fall below 100,000 francs a year, and my agent will pay over 20,000 francs every year to the Treasurer for Foreign Affairs at Parma. With that sum they can attach to me whatever Secretary of Embassy they choose, and I shall shew no curiosity to inquire into diplomatic secrets, if there are any. My object is to shed lustre on my house, which is still a new one, and to give it the distinction of having filled one of the great public offices."

The present Duca, this Ambassador's son and heir, had made the stupid mistake of coming out as a semi-Liberal, and for the last two years had been in despair. In Napoleon's time, he had lost two or three millions owing to his obstinacy in remaining abroad, and even now, after the re-establishment of order in Europe, he had not managed to secure a certain Grand Cordon which adorned the portrait of his father. The want of this Cordon was killing him by inches.

At the degree of intimacy which in Italy follows love, there was no longer any obstacle in the nature of vanity between the lovers. It was therefore with the most perfect simplicity that Mosca said to the woman he adored:

"I have two or three plans of conduct to offer you, all pretty well thought out; I have been thinking of nothing else for the last three months.

"First: I hand in my resignation, and we retire to a quiet life at Milan or Florence or Naples or wherever you please. We have an income of 15,000 francs, apart from the Prince's generosity, which will continue for some time, more or less.

"Secondly: You condescend to come to the place in which I have some authority; you buy a property, Sacca, for example, a charming house in the middle of a forest, commanding the valley of the Po; you can have the contract signed within a week from now. The Prince then attaches you to his court. But here I can see an immense objection. You will be well received at court; no one would think of refusing, with me there; besides, the Princess imagines she is unhappy, and I have recently rendered her certain services with an eye to your future. But I must remind you of one paramount objection: the Prince is a bigoted churchman, and, as you already know, ill luck will have it that I am a married man. From which will arise a million minor unpleasantnesses. You are a widow; it is a fine title which would have to be exchanged for another, and this brings me to my third proposal.

"One might find a new husband who would not be a nuisance. But first of all he would have to be considerably advanced in years, for why should you deny me the hope of some day succeeding him? Very well, I have made this curious arrangement with the Duca Sanseverina-Taxis, who, of course, does not know the name of his future Duchessa. He knows only that she will make him an Ambassador and will procure him the Grand Cordon which his father had and the lack of which makes him the most unhappy of mortals. Apart from this, the Duca is by no means an absolute idiot; he gets his clothes and wigs from Paris. He is not in the least the sort of man who would do anything *deliberately* mean, he seriously believes that honour consists in his having a Cordon, and he is ashamed of his riches. He came to me a year ago proposing to found a hospital, in order to get this Cordon; I laughed at him then, but he did not by any means laugh at me when I made him a proposal of marriage; my first condition was, you can understand, that he must never set foot again in Parma."

"But do you know that what you are proposing is highly immoral?" said the Contessa.

"No more immoral than everything else that is done at our court and a score of others. Absolute Power has this advantage, that it sanctifies everything in the eyes of the public: what harm can there be in a thing that nobody notices? Our policy for the next twenty years is going to consist in fear of the Jacobins—and such fear, too! Every year, we shall fancy ourselves on the eve of '93. You will hear, I hope, the fine speeches I make on the subject at my receptions! They are beautiful! Everything that can in any way reduce this fear will be *supremely moral* in the eyes of the nobles and the bigots. And you see, at Parma, everyone who is not either a noble or a bigot is in prison, or is packing up to go there; you may be quite sure that this marriage will not be thought odd among us until the day on which I am disgraced. This arrangement involves no dishonesty towards anyone; that is the essential thing, it seems to me. The Prince, on whose favour we are trading, has placed only one condition on his consent, which is that the future Duchessa shall be of noble birth. Last year my office, all told, brought me in 107,000 francs; my total income would therefore be 122,000; I invested 20,000 at Lyons. Very well, chose for yourself; either a life of luxury based on our having 122,000 francs to spend, which, at Parma, go as far as at least 400,000 at Milan, but with this marriage which will give you the name of a passable man on whom you will never set eyes after you leave the altar; or else the simple middle-class existence on 15,000 francs at Florence or Naples, for I am of your opinion, you have been too much admired at Milan; we should be persecuted here by envy, which might perhaps succeed in souring our tempers. Our grand life at Parma will, I hope, have some touches of novelty, even in your eyes, which have seen the court of Prince Eugène; you would be wise to try it before shutting the door on it for ever. Do not think that I am seeking to influence your opinion. As for me, my mind is quite made up: I would rather live on a fourth floor with you than continue that grand life by myself."

The possibility of this strange marriage was debated by the loving couple every day. The Contessa saw the Duca Sanseverina-Taxis at the Scala Ball, and thought him highly presentable. In one of their final conversations, Mosca summed up his proposals in the following words: "We must take some decisive action if we wish to spend the rest of our lives in an enjoyable fashion and not grow old before our time. The Prince has given his approval; Sanseverina is a person who might easily be worse; he possesses the finest *palazzo* in Parma, and a boundless fortune; he is sixty-eight, and has an insane passion for the Grand Cordon; but there is one great stain on his character: he once paid 10,000 francs for a bust of Napoleon by Canova. His second sin, which will be the death of him if you do not come to his rescue, is that he lent 25 napoleons to Ferrante Palla, a lunatic of our country but also something of a genius, whom we have since sentenced to death, fortunately in his absence. This Ferrante has written a couple of hundred lines in his time which are like nothing in the world; I will repeat them to you, they are as fine as Dante. The Prince then sends Sanseverina to the Court of ——, he marries you on the day of his departure, and in the second year of his stay

abroad, which he calls an Embassy, he receives the Grand
Cordon of the ——, without which he cannot live. You will
have in him a brother who will give you no trouble at all;
he signs all the papers I require in advance, and besides
you will see nothing of him, or as little as you choose. He
asks for nothing better than never to shew his face at Parma,
where his grandfather the tax-gatherer and his own profession of Liberalism stand in his way. Rassi, our hangman,
makes out that the Duca was a secret subscriber to the
Constitutionnel through Ferrante Palla the poet, and this
slander was for a long time a serious obstacle in the way of
the Prince's consent."

Why should the historian who follows faithfully all the
most trivial details of the story that has been told him be
held responsible? Is it his fault if his characters, led astray
by passions which he, unfortunately for himself, in no way
shares, descend to conduct that is profoundly immoral? It
is true that things of this sort are no longer done in a
country where the sole passion that has outlived all the rest
is that for money, as an excuse for vanity.

Three months after the events we have just related, the
Duchessa Sanseverina-Taxis astonished the court of Parma
by her easy affability and the noble serenity of her mind;
her house was beyond comparison the most attractive in the
town. This was what Conte Mosca had promised his master.
Ranuccio-Ernesto IV, the Reigning Prince, and the Princess
his Consort, to whom she was presented by two of the
greatest ladies in the land, gave her a most marked welcome.
The Duchessa was curious to see this Prince, master of the
destiny of the man she loved, she was anxious to please
him, and in this was more than successful. She found a man
of tall stature but inclined to stoutness; his hair, his moustache, his enormous whiskers were of a fine gold, according
to his courtiers; elsewhere they had provoked, by their faded
tint, the ignoble word *flaxen*. From the middle of a plump
face there projected to no distance at all a tiny nose that
was almost feminine. But the Duchessa observed that, in
order to notice all these points of ugliness, one had first to
attempt to catalogue the Prince's features separately. Taken
as a whole, he had the air of a man of sense and of firm
character. His carriage, his way of holding himself were by
no means devoid of majesty, but often he sought to impress
the person he was addressing; at such times he grew embarrassed himself, and fell into an almost continuous sway-

ing motion from one leg to the other. For the rest, Ernesto IV had a piercing and commanding gaze; his gestures with his arms had nobility, and his speech was at once measured and concise.

Mosca had warned the Duchessa that the Prince had, in the large cabinet in which he gave audiences, a full-length portrait of Louis XIV, and a very fine table by Scagliola of Florence. She found the imitation striking; evidently he sought to copy the gaze and the noble utterance of Louis XIV, and he leaned upon the Scagliola table so as to give himself the pose of Joseph II. He sat down as soon as he had uttered his greeting to the Duchessa, to give her an opportunity to make use of the *tabouret* befitting her rank. At this court, duchesses, princesses, and the wives of Grandees of Spain alone have the right to sit; other women wait until the Prince or Princess invites them; and, to mark the difference in rank, these August Personages always take care to allow a short interval to elapse before inviting the ladies who are not duchesses to be seated. The Duchessa found that at certain moments the imitation of Louis XIV was a little too strongly marked in the Prince; for instance, in his way of smiling good-naturedly and throwing back his head.

Ernesto IV wore an evening coat in the latest fashion, that had come from Paris; every month he had sent to him from that city, which he abhorred, an evening coat, a frock coat, and a hat. But by an odd blend of costume, on the day on which the Duchessa was received he had put on red breeches, silk stockings and very close-fitting shoes, models for which might be found in the portraits of Joseph II.

He received Signora Sanseverina graciously; the things he said to her were shrewd and witty; but she saw quite plainly that there was no superfluity of warmth in his reception of her.—"Do you know why?" said Conte Mosca on her return from the audience, "it is because Milan is a larger and finer city than Parma. He was afraid, had he given you the welcome that I expected and he himself had led me to hope, of seeming like a provincial in ecstasies before the charms of a beautiful lady who has come down from the capital. No doubt, too, he is still upset by a detail which I hardly dare mention to you; the Prince sees at his court no woman who can vie with you in *beauty*. Yesterday evening, when he retired to bed, that was his sole topic of conversation with Pernice, his principal valet, who is good enough to confide in me. I foresee a little revolution in etiquette; my chief enemy at this court is a fool who goes by the name of General Fabio Conti. Just imagine a creature who has been on active service for perhaps one day in his life, and sets out from that day to copy the bearing of Frederick the Great. In addition to which, he aims also at copying the noble affability of General La Fayette, and that because he is the leader, here, of the Liberal Party (God knows what sort of Liberals!)."

"I know your Fabio Conti," said the Duchessa; "I had a good view of him once near Como; he was quarrelling with the police." She related the little adventure which the reader may perhaps remember.

"You will learn one day, Signora, if your mind ever succeeds in penetrating the intricacies of our etiquette, that young ladies do not appear at court here until after their marriage. At the same time, the Prince has, for the superiority of his city of Parma over all others, a patriotism so ardent that I would wager that he will find some way of having little Clelia Conti, our La Fayette's daughter, presented to him. She is charming, upon my soul she is; and was still reckoned, a week ago, the best-looking person in the States of the Prince.

"I do not know," the Conte went on, "whether the horrors that the enemies of our Sovereign have disseminated against him have reached the castle of Grianta; they make him out a monster, an ogre. The truth is that Ernesto IV was full of dear little virtues, and one may add that, had he been invulnerable like Achilles, he would have continued to be the model of a potentate. But in a moment of boredom and anger, and also a little in imitation of Louis XIV cutting off the head of some hero or other of the Fronde, who was discovered living in peaceful solitude on a plot of land near Versailles, fifty years after the Fronde, one fine day Ernesto IV had two Liberals hanged. It seems that these rash fellows used to meet on fixed days to speak evil of the Prince and address ardent prayers to heaven that the plague might visit Parma and deliver them from the tyrant. The word *tyrant* was proved. Rassi called this conspiracy; he had them sentenced to death, and the execution of one of them, Conte L——, was atrocious. All this happened before my time. Since that fatal hour," the Conte went on, lowering his voice, "the Prince has been subject to fits of panic *unworthy of a man*, but these are the sole source of the favour that I enjoy. But for this royal fear, mine would be a kind of merit too abrupt, too harsh for this court, where idiocy runs rampant. Would you believe that the Prince looks under the beds in his room before going to sleep, and spends a million, which at Parma is the equivalent of four millions at Milan, to have a good police force; and you see before you, Signora Duchessa, the Chief of that terrible Police. By the police, that is to say by fear, I have become Minister of War and Finance; and as the Minister of the Interior is my nominal chief, in so far as he has the police under his jurisdiction, I have had that portfolio given to Conte Zurla-Contarini, an imbecile who is a glutton for work and gives himself the pleasure of writing eighty letters a day. I received one only this morning on which Conte Zurla-Contarini has had the satisfaction of writing with his own hand the number 20,715."

The Duchessa Sanseverina was presented to the melancholy Princess of Parma, Clara-Paolina, who, because her husband had a mistress (quite an attractive woman, the Marchesa Balbi), imagined herself to be the most unhappy person in the universe, a belief which had made her perhaps the most trying. The Duchessa found a very tall and very thin woman, who was not thirty-six and appeared fifty. A symmetrical and noble face might have passed as beautiful, though somewhat spoiled by the large round eyes which could barely see, if the Princess had not herself abandoned every attempt at beauty. She received the Duchessa with a shyness so marked that certain courtiers, enemies of Conte Mosca, ventured to say that the Princess looked like the woman who was being presented and the Duchessa like the sovereign. The Duchessa, surprised and almost disconcerted, could find no language that would put her in a place inferior to that which the Princess assumed for herself. To restore some self-possession to this poor Princess, who at heart was not wanting in intelligence, the Duchessa could think of nothing better than to begin, and keep going, a long dissertation on botany. The Princess was really learned in this science; she had some very fine hothouses with quantities of tropical plants. The Duchessa, while seeking simply for a way out of a difficult position, made a lifelong conquest of Princess Clara-Paolina, who, from the shy and speechless creature that she had been at the beginning of the audience, found herself towards the end so much at her ease that, in defiance of all the rules of etiquette, this first audience lasted for no less than an hour and a quarter. Next day, the Duchessa sent out to purchase some exotic plants, and posed as a great lover of botany.

The Princess spent all her time with the venerable Father Landriani, Archbishop of Parma, a man of learning, a man of intelligence even, and a perfectly honest man, but one who presented a singular spectacle when he was seated in his chair of crimson velvet (it was the privilege of his office) opposite the armchair of the Princess, surrounded by her maids of honour and her two ladies *of company*. The old prelate, with his flowing white locks, was even more timid, were such a thing possible, than the Princess; they saw one another every day, and every audience began with a silence that lasted fully a quarter of an hour. To such a state had they come that the Contessa Alvizi, one of the ladies of company, had become a sort of favourite, because she possessed the art of encouraging them to talk and so breaking the silence.

To end the series of presentations, the Duchessa was admitted to the presence of H.S.H. the Crown Prince, a personage of taller stature than his father and more timid than his mother. He was learned in mineralogy, and was sixteen years old. He blushed excessively on seeing the Duchessa come in, and was so put off his balance that he could not think of a word to say to that beautiful lady. He was a fine-looking young man, and spent his life in the woods, hammer in hand. At the moment when the Duchessa rose to bring this silent audience to an end:

"My God! Signora, how pretty you are!" exclaimed the Crown Prince; a remark which was not considered to be in too bad taste by the lady presented.

The Marchesa Balbi, a young woman of five-and-twenty, might still have passed for the most perfect type of *leggiadria italiana*, two or three years before the arrival of the Duchessa Sanseverina at Parma. As it was, she had still the finest eyes in the world and the most charming airs, but, viewed close at hand, her skin was netted with countless fine little wrinkles which made the Marchesa look like a young grandmother. Seen from a certain distance, in the theatre for instance, in her box, she was still a beauty, and the people in the pit thought that the Prince shewed excellent taste. He spent every evening with the Marchesa Balbi, but often without opening his lips, and the boredom she saw on the Prince's face had made this poor woman decline into an extraordinary thinness. She laid claim to an unlimited subtlety, and was always smiling a bitter smile; she had the prettiest teeth in the world, and in season and out, having little or no sense, would attempt by an ironical smile to give some hidden meaning to her words. Conte Mosca said that it was these continual smiles, while inwardly she was yawning, that gave her all her wrinkles. The Balbi had a finger in every pie, and the State never made a contract for 1,000 francs without there being some little *ricordo* (this was the polite expression at Parma) for the Marchesa. Common report would have it that she had invested six millions in England, but her fortune, which indeed was of recent origin, did not in reality amount to 1,500,000 francs. It was to be out of reach of her stratagems, and to have her dependent upon himself, that Conte Mosca had made himself Minister of Finance. The Marchesa's sole passion was fear disguised in sordid avarice: *"I shall die on straw!"* she used occasionally to say to the Prince, who was shocked by such a remark. The Duchessa noticed that the ante-room, resplendent with gilding, of the Balbi's *palazzo*, was lighted by a single candle which guttered on a priceless marble table, and that the doors of her drawing-room were blackened by the footmen's fingers.

"She received me," the Duchessa told her lover, "as though she expected me to offer her a gratuity of 50 francs."

The course of the Duchessa's successes was slightly interrupted by the reception given her by the shrewdest woman of the court, the celebrated Marchesa Raversi, a consummate intriguer who had established herself at the head of the party opposed to that of Conte Mosca. She was anxious to overthrow him, all the more so in the last few months, since she was the niece of the Duca Sanseverina, and was afraid of seeing her prospects impaired by the charms of his new Duchessa. "The Raversi is by no means a woman to be ignored," the Conte told his mistress; "I regard her as so far capable of sticking at nothing that I separated from my wife solely because she insisted on taking as her lover Cavaliere Bentivoglio, a friend of the Raversi." This lady, a tall virago with very dark hair, remarkable for the diamonds which she wore all day, and the rouge with which she covered her cheeks, had declared herself in advance the Duchessa's enemy, and when she received her in her own house made it her business to open hostilities. The Duca Sanseverina, in the letters he wrote from ——, appeared so delighted with his Embassy and, above all, with the prospect of the Grand Cordon, that his family were afraid of his leaving part of his fortune to his wife, whom he loaded with little presents. The Raversi, although definitely ugly, had for a lover Conte Baldi, the handsomest man at court; generally speaking, she was successful in all her undertakings.

The Duchessa lived in the greatest style imaginable. The *palazzo* Sanseverina had always been one of the most magnificent in the city of Parma, and the Duca, to celebrate the occasion of his Embassy and his future Grand Cordon, was spending enormous sums upon its decoration; the Duchessa directed the work in person.

The Conte had guessed aright; a few days after the presentation of the Duchessa, young Clelia Conti came to court; she had been made a Canoness. In order to parry the blow which this favour might be thought to have struck at the Conte's influence, the Duchessa gave a party, on the pretext of throwing open the new garden of her *palazzo*, and by the exercise of her most charming manners made Clelia, whom she called her young friend of the Lake of Como, the queen of the evening. Her monogram was displayed, as though by accident, upon the principal transparencies. The young Clelia, although slightly pensive, was pleasant in the way in which she spoke of the little adventure by the Lake, and of her warm gratitude. She was said to be deeply religious and very fond of solitude. "I would wager," said the Conte, "that she has enough sense to be ashamed of her father." The Duchessa made a friend of this girl; she felt attracted towards her, she did not wish to appear jealous, and included her in all her pleasure parties; after all, her plan was to seek to diminish all the enmities of which the Conte was the object.

Everything smiled on the Duchessa; she was amused by this court existence where a sudden storm is always to be feared; she felt as though she were beginning life over again. She was tenderly attached to the Conte, who was literally mad with happiness. The pleasing situation had bred in him an absolute impassivity towards everything in which only his professional interests were concerned. And so, barely two months after the Duchessa's arrival, he obtained the patent and honours of Prime Minister, honours which come very near to those paid to the Sovereign himself. The Conte had complete control of his master's will; they had a proof of this at Parma by which everyone was impressed.

To the southeast, and within ten minutes of the town

rises that famous citadel so renowned throughout Italy, the main tower of which stands one hundred and eighty feet high and is visible from so far. This tower, constructed on the model of Hadrian's Tomb, at Rome, by the Farnese, grandsons of Paul III, in the first half of the sixteenth century, is so large in diameter that on the platform in which it ends it has been possible to build a *palazzo* for the governor of the citadel and a new prison called the Farnese tower. This prison, erected in honour of the eldest son of Ranuccio-Ernesto II, who had become the accepted lover of his stepmother, is regarded as a fine and singular monument throughout the country. The Duchessa was curious to see it; on the day of her visit the heat was overpowering in Parma, and up there, in that lofty position, she found fresh air, which so delighted her that she stayed for several hours. The officials made a point of throwing open to her the rooms of the Farnese tower.

The Duchessa met on the platform of the great tower a poor Liberal prisoner who had come to enjoy the half-hour's outing that was allowed him every third day. On her return to Parma, not having yet acquired the discretion necessary in an absolute court, she spoke of this man, who had told her the whole history of his life. The Marchesa Raversi's party seized hold of these utterances of the Duchessa and repeated them broadcast, greatly hoping that they would shock the Prince. Indeed, Ernesto IV was in the habit of repeating that the essential thing was to impress the imagination. "*Perpetual* is a big word," he used to say, "and more terrible in Italy than elsewhere": accordingly, never in his life had he granted a pardon. A week after her visit to the fortress the Duchessa received a letter commuting a sentence, signed by the Prince and by his Minister, with a blank left for the name. The prisoner whose name she chose to write in this space would obtain the restoration of his property, with permission to spend the rest of his days in America. The Duchessa wrote the name of the man who had talked to her. Unfortunately this man turned out to be half a rogue, a weak-kneed creature; it was on the strength of his confession that the famous Ferrante Palla had been sentenced to death.

The unprecedented nature of this pardon set the seal upon Signora Sanseverina's position. Conte Mosca was wild with delight; it was a great day in his life and one that had a decisive influence on Fabrizio's destiny. He, meanwhile, was still at Romagnano, near Novara, going to confession, hunting, reading nothing, and paying court to a lady of noble birth, as was laid down in his instructions. The Duchessa was still a trifle shocked by this last essential. Another sign which boded no good to the Conte was that, while she would speak to him with the utmost frankness about everyone else, and would think aloud in his presence, she never mentioned Fabrizio to him without first carefully choosing her words.

"If you like," the Conte said to her one day, "I will write to that charming brother you have on the Lake of Como, and I will soon force that Marchese del Dongo, if I and my friends in a certain quarter apply a little pressure, to ask for the pardon of your dear Fabrizio. If it be true, as I have not the least doubt that it is, that Fabrizio is somewhat superior to the young fellows who ride their English thoroughbreds about the streets of Milan, what a life, at eighteen, to be doing nothing with no prospect of ever having anything to do! If heaven had endowed him with a real passion for anything in the world, were it only for angling, I should respect it; but what is he to do at Milan, even after he has obtained his pardon? He will get on a horse, which he will have had sent to him from England, at a certain hour of the day; at another, idleness will take him to his mistress, for whom he will care less than he will for his horse. . . . But, if you say the word, I will try to procure this sort of life for your nephew."

"I should like him to be an officer," said the Duchessa.

"Would you recommend a Sovereign to entrust a post which, at a given date, may be of some importance to a young man who, in the first place, is liable to enthusiasm, and, secondly, has shewn enthusiasm for Napoleon to the extent of going to join him at Waterloo? Just think where we should all be if Napoleon had won at Waterloo! We should have no Liberals to be afraid of, it is true, but the Sovereigns of ancient Houses would be able to keep their thrones only by marrying the daughters of his Marshals. And so military life for Fabrizio would be the life of a squirrel in a revolving cage: plenty of movement with no progress. He would have the annoyance of seeing himself cut out by all sorts of plebeian devotion. The essential quality in a young man of the present day, that is to say for the next fifty years perhaps, so long as we remain in a state of fear and religion has not been re-established, is not to be liable to enthusiasm and not to shew any spirit.

"I have thought of one thing, but one that will begin by

making you cry out in protest, and will give me infinite trouble for many a day to come: it is an act of folly which I am ready to commit for you. But tell me, if you can, what folly would I not commit to win a smile?"

"Well?" said the Duchessa.

"Well, we have had as Archbishops of Parma three members of your family: Ascanio del Dongo who wrote a book in sixteen-something, Fabrizio in 1699, and another Ascanio in 1740. If Fabrizio cares to enter the prelacy, and to make himself conspicuous for virtues of the highest order, I can make him a Bishop somewhere, and then Archbishop here, provided that my influence lasts. The real objection is this: shall I remain Minister for long enough to carry out this fine plan, which will require several years? The Prince may die, he may have the bad taste to dismiss me. But, after all, it is the only way open to me of securing for Fabrizio something that is worthy of you."

They discussed the matter at length: the idea was highly repugnant to the Duchessa.

"Prove to me again," she said to the Conte, "that every other career is impossible for Fabrizio." The Conte proved it.

"You regret," he added, "the brilliant uniform; but as to that, I do not know what to do."

After a month in which the Duchessa had asked to be allowed to think things over, she yielded with a sigh to the sage views of the Minister. "Either ride stiffly upon an English horse through the streets of some big town," repeated the Conte, "or adopt a calling that is not unbefitting his birth; I can see no middle course. Unfortunately, a gentleman cannot become either a doctor or a barrister, and this age is made for barristers.

"Always bear in mind, Signora," the Conte went on, "that you are giving your nephew, on the streets of Milan, the lot enjoyed by the young men of his age who pass for the most fortunate. His pardon once procured, you will give him fifteen, twenty, thirty thousand francs; the amount does not matter; neither you nor I make any pretence of saving money."

The Duchessa was susceptible to the idea of fame; she did not wish Fabrizio to be simply a young man living on an allowance; she reverted to her lover's plan.

"Observe," the Conte said to her, "that I do not pretend to turn Fabrizio into an exemplary priest, like so many that you see. No, he is a great gentleman, first and foremost; he can remain perfectly ignorant if it seems good to him, and will none the less become Bishop and Archbishop, if the Prince continues to regard me as a useful person.

"If your orders deign to transform my proposal into an immutable decree," the Conte went on, "our *protégé* must on no account be seen in Parma living with modest means. His subsequent promotion will cause a scandal if people have seen him here as an ordinary priest; he ought not to appear in Parma until he has his *violet stockings* [1] and a suitable establishment. Then everyone will assume that your nephew is destined to be a Bishop, and nobody will be shocked.

"If you will take my advice, you will send Fabrizio to take his theology and spend three years at Naples. During the vacations of the Ecclesiastical Academy he can go if he likes to visit Paris and London, but he must never shew his face in Parma." This sentence made the Duchessa shudder.

She sent a courier to her nephew, asking him to meet her at Piacenza. Need it be said that this courier was the bearer of all the means of obtaining money and all the necessary passports?

Arriving first at Piacenza, Fabrizio hastened to meet the Duchessa, and embraced her with transports of joy which made her dissolve in tears. She was glad that the Conte was not present; since they had fallen in love, it was the first time that she had experienced this sensation.

Fabrizio was profoundly touched, and then distressed by the plans which the Duchessa had made for him; his hope had always been that, his affair at Waterloo settled, he might end by becoming a soldier. One thing struck the Duchessa, and still further increased the romantic opinion that she had formed of her nephew; he refused absolutely to lead a *caffè*-haunting existence in one of the big towns of Italy.

"Can't you see yourself on the *Corso* of Florence or Naples," said the Duchessa, "with thoroughbred English horses? For the evenings a carriage, a charming apartment," and so forth. She dwelt with exquisite relish on the details of this vulgar happiness, which she saw Fabrizio thrust from him with disdain. "He is a hero," she thought.

[1] In Italy, young men with influence or brains become *Monsignori* and *prelati*, which does not mean bishop; they then wear violet stockings. A man need not take any vows to become *Monsignore;* he can discard his violet stockings and marry.

"And after ten years of this agreeable life, what shall I have done?" said Fabrizio; "what shall I be? A young man *of a certain age,* who will have to move out of the way of the first good-looking boy who makes his appearance in society, also mounted upon an English horse."

Fabrizio at first utterly rejected the idea of the Church. He spoke of going to New York, of becoming an American citizen and a soldier of the Republic.

"What a mistake you are making! You won't have any war, and you'll fall back into the *caffè* life, only without smartness, without music, without love affairs," replied the Duchessa. "Believe me, for you just as much as for myself, it would be a wretched existence there in America." She explained to him the cult of the god *Dollar,* and the respect that had to be shewn to the artisans in the street who by their votes decided everything. They came back to the idea of the Church.

"Before you fly into a passion," the Duchessa said to him, "just try to understand what the Conte is asking you to do; there is no question whatever of your being a poor priest of more or less exemplary and virtuous life, like Priore Blanès. Remember the example of your uncles, the Archbishops of Parma; read over again the accounts of their lives in the supplement to the Genealogy. First and foremost, a man with a name like yours has to be a great gentleman, noble, generous, an upholder of justice, destined from the first to find himself at the head of his order . . . and in the whole of his life doing only one dishonourable thing, and that a very useful one."

"So all my illusions are shattered," said Fabrizio, heaving a deep sigh; "it is a cruel sacrifice! I admit, I had not taken into account this horror of enthusiasm and spirit, even when wielded to their advantage, which from now onwards is going to prevail amongst absolute monarchs."

"Remember that a proclamation, a caprice of the heart flings the enthusiast into the bosom of the opposite party to the one he has served all his life!"

"I an enthusiast!" repeated Fabrizio; "a strange accusation! I cannot manage even to be in love!"

"What!" exclaimed the Duchessa.

"When I have the honour to pay my court to a beauty, even if she is of good birth and sound religious principles, I cannot think about her except when I see her."

This avowal made a strange impression upon the Duchessa.

"I ask for a month," Fabrizio went on, "in which to take leave of Signora C——, of Novara, and, what will be more difficult still, of all the castles I have been building in the air all my life. I shall write to my mother, who will be so good as to come and see me at Belgirate, on the Piedmontese shore of Lake Maggiore, and, in thirty-one days from now, I shall be in Parma incognito."

"No, whatever you do!" cried the Duchessa. She did not wish Conte Mosca to see her talking to Fabrizio.

The same pair met again at Piacenza. The Duchessa this time was highly agitated: a storm had broken at court; the Marchesa Raversi's party was on the eve of a triumph; it was on the cards that Conte Mosca might be replaced by General Fabio Conti, the leader of what was called at Parma the *Liberal Party*. Omitting only the name of the rival who was growing in the Prince's favour, the Duchessa told Fabrizio everything. She discussed afresh the chances of his future career, even with the prospect of his losing the all-powerful influence of the Conte.

"I am going to spend three years in the Ecclesiastical Academy at Naples," exclaimed Fabrizio; "but since I must be before all things a young gentleman, and you do not oblige me to lead the life of a virtuous seminarist, the prospect of this stay at Naples does not frighten me in the least; the life there will be in every way as pleasant as life at Romagnano; the best society of the neighbourhood was beginning to class me as a Jacobin. In my exile I have discovered that I know nothing, not even Latin, not even how to spell. I had planned to begin my education over again at Novara; I shall willingly study theology at Naples; it is a complicated science." The Duchessa was overjoyed. "If we are driven out of Parma," she told him, "we shall come and visit you at Naples. But since you agree, until further orders, to try for the violet stockings, the Conte, who knows the Italy of to-day through and through, has given me an idea to suggest to you. Believe or not, as you choose, what they teach you, *but never raise any objection*. Imagine that they are teaching you the rules of the game of whist; would you raise any objection to the rules of whist? I have told the Conte that you do believe, and he is delighted to hear it; it is useful in this world and in the next. But, if you believe, do not fall into the vulgar habit of speaking with horror of Voltaire, Diderot, Raynal and all those harebrained Frenchmen who paved the way to the Dual Chamber. Their names should not be allowed to pass your lips, but if you must mention them, speak of these gentlemen with a calm irony: they are people who have long since been refuted and whose attacks are no longer of any consequence. Believe blindly everything that they tell you at the Academy. Bear in mind that there are people who will make a careful note of your slightest objections; they will forgive you a little amorous intrigue if it is done in the proper way, but not a doubt: age stifles intrigue but encourages doubt. Act on this principle at the tribunal of penitence. You shall have a letter of recommendation to a Bishop who is factotum to the Cardinal Archbishop of Naples: to him alone you should admit your escapade in France and your presence on the 18th of June in the neighbourhood of Waterloo. Even then, cut it as short as possible, confess it only so that they cannot reproach you with having kept it secret. You were so young at the time!

"The second idea which the Conte sends you is this: if there should occur to you a brilliant argument, a triumphant retort that will change the course of the conversation, do not give in to the temptation to shine; remain silent: people of any discernment will see your cleverness in your eyes. It will be time enough to be witty when you are a Bishop."

Fabrizio began his life at Naples with an unpretentious carriage and four servants, good Milanese, whom his aunt had sent him. After a year of study, no one said of him that he was a man of parts: people looked upon him as a great nobleman, of a studious bent, extremely generous, but something of a libertine.

That year, amusing enough for Fabrizio, was terrible for the Duchessa. The Conte was three or four times within an inch of ruin; the Prince, more timorous than ever, because he was ill that year, believed that by dismissing him he could free himself from the odium of the executions carried out before the Conte had entered his service. Rassi was the cherished favourite who must at all costs be retained. The Conte's perils won him the passionate attachment of the Duchessa; she gave no more thought to Fabrizio. To lend colour to their possible retirement, it appeared that the air of Parma, which was indeed a trifle damp as it is everywhere in Lombardy, did not at all agree with her. Finally, after intervals of disgrace which went so far as to make the Conte, though Prime Minister, spend sometimes twenty whole days without seeing his master privately, Mosca

won; he secured the appointment of General Fabio Conti,
the so-called Liberal, as governor of the citadel in which
were imprisoned the Liberals condemned by Rassi. "If Conti
shows any leniency towards his prisoners," Mosca observed
to his lady, "he will be disgraced as a Jacobin whose political
theories have made him forget his duty as a general; if he
shows himself stern and pitiless, and that, to my mind, is the
direction in which he will tend, he ceases to be the leader of
his own party and alienates all the families that have a
relative in the citadel. This poor man has learned how to
assume an air of awed respect on the approach of the
Prince; if necessary, he changes his clothes four times a
day; he can discuss a question of etiquette, but his is not
a head capable of following the difficult path by which alone
he can save himself from destruction; and in any case, I
am there."

The day after the appointment of General Fabio Conti,
which brought the ministerial crisis to an end, it was announced that Parma was to have an ultra-monarchist newspaper.

"What feuds the paper will create!" said the Duchessa.

"This paper, the idea of which is perhaps my masterpiece," replied the Conte with a smile, "I shall gradually and
quite against my will allow to pass into the hands of the
ultra-rabid section. I have attached some good salaries to
the editorial posts. People are coming from all quarters to
beg for employment on it; the excitement will help us
through the next month or two, and people will forget the
danger I have been in. Those seriously minded gentlemen
P—— and D—— are already on the list."

"But this paper will be quite revoltingly absurd."

"I am reckoning on that," replied the Conte. "The Prince
will read it every morning and admire the doctrines taught
by myself as its founder. As to the details, he will approve
or be shocked; of the hours which he devotes every day to
work, two will be taken up in this way. The paper will get
itself into trouble, but when the serious complaints begin to
come in, in eight or ten months' time, it will be entirely in
the hands of the ultra-rabids. It will be this party, which is
annoying me, that will have to answer; as for me, I shall
raise objections to the paper; but after all I greatly prefer a
hundred absurdities to one hanging. Who remembers an
absurdity two years after the publication of the official
gazette! It is better than having the sons and family of the

hanged men vowing a hatred which will last as long as I shall and may perhaps shorten my life."

The Duchessa, always passionately interested in something, always active, never idle, had more spirit than the whole court of Parma put together; but she lacked the patience and impassivity necessary for success in intrigue. However, she had managed to follow with passionate excitement the interests of the various groups, she was beginning even to establish a certain personal reputation with the Prince. Clara-Paolina, the Princess Consort, surrounded with honours but a prisoner to the most antiquated etiquette, looked upon herself as the unhappiest of women. The Duchessa Sanseverina paid her various attentions and tried to prove to her that she was by no means so unhappy as she supposed. It should be explained that the Prince saw his wife only at dinner: this meal lasted for thirty minutes, and the Prince would spend whole weeks without saying a word to Clara-Paolina. Signora Sanseverina attempted to change all this; she amused the Prince, all the more as she had managed to retain her independence intact. Had she wished to do so, she could not have succeeded in never hurting any of the fools who swarmed about this court. It was this utter inadaptability on her part that led to her being execrated by the common run of courtiers, all Conti or Marchesi, with an average income of 5,000 lire. She realised this disadvantage after the first few days, and devoted herself exclusively to pleasing the Sovereign and his Consort, the latter of whom was in absolute control of the Crown Prince. The Duchessa knew how to amuse the Sovereign, and profited by the extreme attention he paid to her lightest word to put in some shrewd thrusts at the courtiers who hated her. After the foolish actions that Rassi had made him commit, and for foolishness that sheds blood there is no reparation, the Prince was sometimes afraid and was often bored, which had brought him to a state of morbid envy; he felt that he was deriving little amusement from life, and grew sombre when he saw other people amused; the sight of happiness made him furious. "We must keep our love secret," she told her admirer, and gave the Prince to understand that she was only very moderately attached to the Conte, who for that matter was so thoroughly deserving of esteem.

This discovery had given His Highness a happy day. From time to time, the Duchessa let fall a few words about the plan she had in her mind of taking a few months' holiday

every year, to be spent in seeing Italy, which she did not
know at all; she would visit Naples, Florence, Rome. Now
nothing in the world was more capable of distressing the
Prince than an apparent desertion of this sort: it was
one of his most pronounced weaknesses; any action that
might be interpreted as showing contempt for his capital
city pierced him to the heart. He felt that he had no way of
holding Signora Sanseverina, and Signora Sanseverina was by
far the most brilliant woman in Parma. A thing without
parallel in the lazy Italian character, people used to drive
in from the surrounding country to attend her *Thursdays;*
they were regular festivals; almost every week the Duchessa had something new and sensational to present. The
Prince was dying to see one of these *Thursdays* for himself;
but how was it to be managed? Go to the house of a
private citizen! That was a thing that neither his father nor
he had ever done in their lives!

There came a certain Thursday of cold wind and rain;
all through the evening the Prince heard carriages rattling
over the pavement of the *piazza* outside the Palace, on their
way to Signora Sanseverina's. He moved petulantly in his
chair: other people were amusing themselves, and he, their
sovereign Prince, their absolute master, who ought to find
more amusement than anyone in the world, he was tasting
the fruit of boredom! He rang for his aide-de-camp: he was
obliged to wait until a dozen trustworthy men had been
posted in the street that led from the Royal Palace to the *palazzo* Sanseverina. Finally, after an hour that seemed to the
Prince an age, during which he had been minded a score of
times to brave the assassins' daggers and to go boldly out without any precaution, he appeared in the first of Signora Sanseverina's drawing-rooms. A thunderbolt might have fallen upon
the carpet and not produced so much surprise. In the twinkling of an eye, and as the Prince advanced through them,
these gay and noisy rooms were hushed to a stupefied silence; every eye, fixed on the Prince, was strained with attention. The courtiers appeared disconcerted; the Duchessa
alone shewed no sign of surprise. When finally her guests
had recovered sufficient strength to speak, the great preoccupation of all present was to decide the important question:
had the Duchessa been warned of this visit, or had she like
everyone else been taken by surprise?

The Prince was amused, and the reader may now judge
of the utterly impulsive character of the Duchessa, and of

the boundless power which vague ideas of departure, adroitly disseminated, had enabled her to assume.

As she went to the door with the Prince, who was making her the prettiest speeches, an odd idea came to her which she ventured to put into words quite simply, and as though it were the most natural thing in the world.

"If Your Serene Highness would address to the Princess three or four of these charming utterances which he lavishes on me, he could be far more certain of giving me pleasure than by telling me that I am pretty. I mean that I would not for anything in the world have the Princess look with an unfriendly eye on the signal mark of his favour with which His Highness has honoured me this evening."

The Prince looked fixedly at her and replied in a dry tone:

"I was under the impression that I was my own master and could go where I pleased."

The Duchessa blushed.

"I wished only," she explained, instantly recovering herself, "not to expose His Highness to the risk of a bootless errand, for this Thursday will be the last; I am going for a few days to Bologna or Florence."

When she reappeared in the rooms, everyone imagined her to be at the height of favour, whereas she had just taken a risk upon which, in the memory of man, no one had ever ventured. She made a sign to the Conte, who rose from the whist-table and followed her into a little room that was lighted but empty.

"You have done a very bold thing," he informed her; "I should not have advised it myself, but when hearts are really inflamed," he added with a smile, "happiness enhances love, and if you leave to-morrow morning, I shall follow you to-morrow night. I shall be detained here only by that burden of a Ministry of Finance which I was stupid enough to take on my shoulders; but in four hours of hard work, one can hand over a good many accounts. Let us go back, dear friend, and play at ministerial fatuity with all freedom and without reserve; it may be the last performance that we shall give in this town. If he thinks he is being defied, the man is capable of anything; he will call it *making an example*. When these people have gone, we can decide on a way of barricading you for to-night; the best plan perhaps would be to set off without delay for your house at Sacca, by the Po, which has the advantage of being within half an hour of Austrian territory."

For the Duchessa's love and self-esteem this was an exquisite moment; she looked at the Conte, and her eyes brimmed with tears. So powerful a Minister, surrounded by this swarm of courtiers who loaded him with homage equal to that which they paid to the Prince himself, to leave everything for her sake, and with such unconcern!

When she returned to the drawing-room she was beside herself with joy. Everyone bowed down before her.

"How prosperity has changed the Duchessa!" was murmured everywhere by the courtiers, "one would hardly recognise her. So that Roman spirit, so superior to everything in the world, does, after all, deign to appreciate the extraordinary favour that has just been conferred upon her by the Sovereign!"

Towards the end of the evening the Conte came to her: "I must tell you the latest news." Immediately the people who happened to be standing near the Duchessa withdrew.

"The Prince, on his return to the Palace," the Conte went on, "had himself announced at the door of his wife's room. Imagine the surprise! 'I have come to tell you,' he said to her, 'about a really most delightful evening I have spent at the Sanseverina's. It was she who asked me to give you a full description of the way in which she has decorated that grimy old *palazzo*.' Then the Prince took a seat and went into a description of each of your rooms in turn.

"He spent more than twenty-five minutes with his wife, who was in tears of joy; for all her intelligence, she could not think of anything to keep the conversation going in the light tone which His Highness was pleased to impart to it."

This Prince was by no means a wicked man, whatever the Liberals of Italy might say of him. As a matter of fact, he had cast a good number of them into prison, but that was from fear, and he used to repeat now and then, as though to console himself for certain unpleasant memories: "It is better to kill the devil than to let the devil kill you." The day after the party we have been describing, he was supremely happy; he had done two good actions: he had gone to the *Thursday*, and he had talked to his wife. At dinner, he addressed her again; in a word, this *Thursday* at Signora Sanseverina's brought about a domestic revolution with which the whole of Parma rang; the Raversi was in consternation, and the Duchessa doubly delighted: she had contrived to be of use to her lover, and had found him more in love with her than ever.

"All this owing to a thoroughly rash idea which came into my mind!" she said to the Conte. "I should be more free, no doubt, in Rome or Naples, but should I find so fascinating a game to play there? No, indeed, my dear Conte, and you provide me with all my joy in life."

CHAPTER SEVEN

I T IS WITH trifling details of court life as insignificant as
those related in the last chapter that we should have to
fill up the history of the next four years. Every spring the
Marchesa came with her daughters to spend a couple of
months at the *palazzo* Sanseverina or on the property of
Sacca, by the bank of the Po; there they spent some very
pleasant hours and used to talk of Fabrizio, but the Conte
would never allow him to pay a single visit to Parma. The
Duchessa and the Minister had indeed to make amends for
certain acts of folly, but on the whole Fabrizio followed
soberly enough the line of conduct that had been laid down
for him: that of a great nobleman who is studying theology
and does not rely entirely on his virtues to bring him advancement. At Naples, he had acquired a keen interest in the
study of antiquity, he made excavations; this new passion
had almost taken the place of his passion for horses. He
had sold his English thoroughbreds in order to continue his
excavations at Miseno, where he had turned up a bust of
Tiberius as a young man which had been classed among the
finest relics of antiquity. The discovery of this bust was almost the keenest pleasure that had come to him at Naples.
He had too lofty a nature to seek to copy the other young
men he saw, to wish for example to play with any degree
of seriousness the part of lover. Of course he never lacked
mistresses, but these were of no consequence to him, and, in
spite of his years, one might say of him that he still knew
nothing of love: he was all the more loved on that account.
Nothing prevented him from behaving with the most perfect
coolness, for to him a young and pretty woman was always
equivalent to any other young and pretty woman; only the
latest comer seemed to him the most exciting. One of the

most generally admired ladies in Naples had done all sorts of foolish things in his honour during the last year of his stay there, which at first had amused him, and had ended by boring him to tears, so much so that one of the joys of his departure was the prospect of being delivered from the attentions of the charming Duchessa d'A——. It was in 1821 that, having satisfactorily passed all his examinations, his director of studies, or governor, received a Cross and a gratuity, and he himself started out to see at length that city of Parma of which he had often dreamed. He was *Monsignore*, and he had four horses drawing his carriage; at the stage before Parma he took only two, and on entering the town made them stop outside the church of San Giovanni. There was to be found the costly tomb of Archbishop Ascanio del Dongo, his great-granduncle, the author of the Latin genealogy. He prayed beside the tomb, then went on foot to the *palazzo* of the Duchessa, who did not expect him until several days later. There was a large crowd in her drawing-room; presently they were left alone.

"Well, are you satisfied with me?" he asked her as he flung himself into her arms; "thanks to you, I have spent four quite happy years at Naples, instead of eating my head off at Novara with my mistress authorised by the police."

The Duchessa could not get over her astonishment; she would not have known him had she seen him go by in the street; she discovered him to be, what as a matter of fact he was, one of the best-looking men in Italy; his physiognomy in particular was charming. She had sent him to Naples a devil-may-care young rough-rider; the horsewhip he invariably carried at that time had seemed an inherent part of his person: now he had the noblest and most measured bearing before strangers, while in private conversation she found that he had retained all the ardour of his boyhood. This was a diamond that had lost nothing by being polished. Fabrizio had not been in the room an hour when Conte Mosca appeared; he arrived a little too soon. The young man spoke to him with so apt a choice of terms of the Cross of Parma that had been conferred on his governor, and expressed his lively gratitude for certain other benefits of which he did not venture to speak in so open a fashion, with so perfect a restraint, that at the first glance the Minister formed an excellent impression of him. "This nephew," he murmured to the Duchessa, "is made to adorn all the exalted posts to which you will raise him in due course." So far, all had gone wonderfully well, but when the Minister, thoroughly satisfied with Fabrizio, and paying attention so far only to his actions and gestures, turned to the Duchessa, he noticed a curious look in her eyes. "This young man is making a strange impression here," he said to himself. This reflexion was bitter; the Conte had reached the *fifties,* a cruel word of which perhaps only a man desperately in love can feel the full force. He was a thoroughly good man, thoroughly deserving to be loved, apart from his severities as a Minister. But in his eyes that cruel word *fifties* threw a dark cloud over his whole life and might well have made him cruel on his own account. In the five years since he had persuaded the Duchessa to settle at Parma, she had often aroused his jealousy, especially at first, but never had she given him any real grounds for complaint. He believed indeed, and rightly, that it was with the object of making herself more certain of his heart that the Duchessa had had recourse to those apparent bestowals of her favour upon various young *beaux* of the court. He was sure, for instance, that she had rejected the offers of the Prince, who, indeed, on that occasion, had made a significant utterance.

"But if I were to accept Your Highness's offer," the Duchessa had said to him with a smile, "how should I ever dare to look the Conte in the face afterwards?"

"I should be almost as much out of countenance as you. The dear Conte! My friend! But there is a very easy way out of that difficulty, and I have thought of it: the Conte would be put in the citadel for the rest of his days."

At the moment of Fabrizio's arrival, the Duchessa was so beside herself with joy that she never even thought of the ideas which the look in her eyes might put into the Conte's head. The effect was profound and the suspicions it aroused irremediable.

Fabrizio was received by the Prince two hours after his arrival; the Duchessa, foreseeing the good effect which this impromptu audience would have on the public, had been begging for it for the last two months; this favour put Fabrizio beyond all rivalry from the first; the pretext for it had been that he would only be passing through Parma on his way to visit his mother in Piedmont. At the moment when a charming little note from the Duchessa arrived to inform the Prince that Fabrizio awaited his orders, the Prince was feeling bored. "I shall see," he said to himself, "a saintly little simpleton, a mean or a sly face." The Town Commandant had already reported the newcomer's first visit to the tomb of his archiepiscopal uncle. The Prince saw enter the room a tall young man whom, but for his violet stockings, he would have taken for some young officer.

This little surprise dispelled his boredom: "Here is a fellow," he said to himself, "for whom they will be asking me heaven knows what favours, everything that I have to bestow. He is just come, he probably feels nervous: I shall give him a little dose of Jacobin politics; we shall see how he replies."

After the first gracious words on the Prince's part:

"Well, *Monsignore*," he said to Fabrizio, "and the people of Naples, are they happy? Is the King loved?"

"Serene Highness," Fabrizio replied without a moment's hesitation, "I used to admire, when they passed me in the street, the excellent bearing of the troops of the various regiments of His Majesty the King; the better classes are respectful towards their masters, as they ought to be; but I must confess that, all my life, I have never allowed the lower orders to speak to me about anything but the work for which I am paying them."

"Plague!" said the Prince, "what a *slyboots!* This is a well-trained bird, I recognise the Sanseverina touch." Becoming interested, the Prince employed great skill in leading Fabrizio on to discuss this scabrous topic. The young man, animated by the danger he was in, was so fortunate as to hit upon some admirable rejoinders: "It is almost insolence to boast of one's love for one's King," he said; "it is blind obedience that one owes to him." At the sight of so much prudence the Prince almost lost his temper: "Here, it seems, is a man of parts come among us from Naples, and I don't like *that breed;* a man of parts may follow the highest principles and even be quite sincere; all the same on one side or the other he is always first cousin to Voltaire and Rousseau."

This Prince felt himself almost defied by such correctness of manner and such unassailable rejoinders coming from a youth fresh from college; what he had expected never occurred; in an instant he assumed a tone of good-fellowship and, reverting in a few words to the basic principles of society and government, repeated, adapting them to the matter in hand, certain phrases of Fénelon which he had been made to learn by heart in his boyhood for use in public audiences.

"These principles surprise you, young man," he said to Fabrizio (he had called him *Monsignore* at the beginning of

the audience, and intended to give him his *Monsignore* again
in dismissing him, but in the course of the conversation he
felt it to be more adroit, better suited to moving turns of
speech, to address him in an informal and friendly style).
"These principles surprise you, young man. I admit that
they bear little resemblance to the *bread and butter absolut-
ism*" (this was the expression in use) "which you can read
every day in my official newspaper. . . . But, great heavens,
what is the good of my quoting that to you? Those writers
in my newspaper must be quite unknown to you."

"I beg Your Serene Highness's pardon; not only do I read
the Parma newspaper, which seems to me to be very well
written, but I hold, moreover, with it, that everything that
has been done since the death of Louis XIV, in 1715, has
been at once criminal and foolish. Man's chief interest in
life is his own salvation, there can be no two ways of looking
at it, and that is a happiness that lasts for eternity. The
words *Liberty, Justice,* the *Good of the Greatest Number,*
are infamous and criminal: they form in people's minds the
habits of discussion and want of confidence. A Chamber of
Deputies votes *no confidence* in what these people call *the
Ministry*. This fatal habit of *want of confidence* once con-
tracted, human weakness applies it to everything, man loses
confidence in the Bible, the Orders of the Church, Tradition
and everything else; from that moment he is lost. Even upon
the assumption—which is abominably false, and criminal
even to suggest—that this want of confidence in the authority of the Princes *by God established* were to secure one's
happiness during the twenty or thirty years of life which any
of us may expect to enjoy, what is half a century, or a
whole century even, compared with an eternity of torment?"
And so on.

One could see, from the way in which Fabrizio spoke,
that he was seeking to arrange his ideas so that they should
be grasped as quickly as possible by his listener; it was clear
that he was not simply repeating a lesson.

Presently the Prince lost interest in his contest with this
young man whose simple and serious manner had begun to
irritate him.

"Good-bye, *Monsignore,*" he said to him abruptly, "I can
see that they provide an excellent education at the Ecclesiastical Academy of Naples, and it is quite simple when these
good precepts fall upon so distinguished a mind, one secures
brilliant results. Good-bye." And he turned his back on him.

"I have quite failed to please this animal," thought Fabrizio.

"And now, it remains to be seen," said the Prince as soon as he was once more alone, "whether this fine young man is capable of passion for anything; in that case, he would be complete. . . . Could anyone repeat with more spirit the lessons he has learned from his aunt? I felt I could hear her speaking; should we have a revolution here, it would be she that would edit the *Monitore*, as the Sanfelice did at Naples! But the Sanfelice, in spite of her twenty-five summers and her beauty, got a bit of a hanging all the same! A warning to women with brains." In supposing Fabrizio to be his aunt's pupil, the Prince was mistaken: people with brains who are born on the throne or at the foot of it soon lose all fineness of touch; they proscribe, in their immediate circle, freedom of conversation which seems to them coarseness; they refuse to look at anything but masks and pretend to judge the beauty of complexions; the amusing part of it is that they imagine their touch to be of the finest. In this case, for instance, Fabrizio believed practically everything that we have heard him say; it is true that he did not think twice in a month of these great principles. He had keen appetites, he had brains, but he had faith.

The desire for liberty, the fashion and cult of the *greatest good of the greatest number,* after which the nineteenth century has run mad, were nothing in his eyes but a heresy which, like other heresies, would pass away, though not until it had destroyed many souls, as the plague while it reigns unchecked in a country destroys many bodies. And in spite of all this Fabrizio read the French newspapers with keen enjoyment, even taking rash steps to procure them.

Fabrizio having returned quite flustered from his audience at the Palace, and having told his aunt of the various attacks launched on him by the Prince:

"You ought," she told him, "to go at once to see Father Landriani, our excellent Archbishop; go there on foot; climb the staircase quietly, make as little noise as possible in the ante-rooms; if you are kept waiting, so much the better, a thousand times better! In a word, be *apostolic!*"

"I understand," said Fabrizio, "our man is a Tartuffe."

"Not the least bit in the world, he is virtue incarnate."

"Even after the way he behaved," said Fabrizio in some bewilderment, "when Conte Palanza was executed?"

"Yes, my friend, after the way he behaved: the father of

our Archbishop was a clerk in the Ministry of Finance, a man of humble position, and that explains everything. Monsignor Landriani is a man of keen, extensive and deep intelligence; he is sincere, he loves virtue; I am convinced that if an Emperor Decius were to reappear in the world he would undergo martyrdom like Polyeuctes in the opera they played last week. So much for the good side of the medal, now for the reverse: as soon as he enters the Sovereign's, or even the Prime Minister's presence, he is dazzled by the sight of such greatness, he becomes confused, he begins to blush; it is physically impossible for him to say no. This accounts for the things he has done, things which have won him that cruel reputation throughout Italy; but what is not generally known is that, when public opinion had succeeded in enlightening him as to the trial of Conte Palanza, he set himself the penance of living upon bread and water for thirteen weeks, the same number of weeks as there are letters in the name *Davide Palanza*. We have at this court a rascal of infinite cleverness named *Rassi*, a Chief Justice or Fiscal General, who at the time of Conte Palanza's death cast a spell over Father Landriani. During his thirteen weeks' penance, Conte Mosca, from pity and also a little out of malice, used to ask him to dinner once and even twice a week: the good Archbishop, in deference to his host, ate like everyone else; he would have thought it rebellious and Jacobinical to make a public display of his penance for an action that had the Sovereign's approval. But we knew that, for each dinner at which his duty as a loyal subject had obliged him to eat like everyone else, he set himself a penance of two days more of bread and water.

"Monsignor Landriani, a man of superior intellect, a scholar of the first order, has only one weakness: *he likes to be loved:* therefore, grow affectionate as you look at him, and, on your third visit, shew your love for him outright. That, added to your birth, will make him adore you at once. Shew no sign of surprise if he accompanies you to the head of the staircase, assume an air of being accustomed to such manners: he is a man who was born on his knees before the nobility. For the rest, be simple, apostolic, no cleverness, no brilliance, no prompt repartee; if you do not startle him at all, he will be delighted with you; do not forget that it must be on his own initiative that he makes you his Grand Vicar. The Conte and I will be surprised and even annoyed at so rapid an advancement; that is essential in dealing with the Sovereign."

Fabrizio hastened to the Archbishop's Palace: by a singular piece of good fortune, the worthy prelate's footman, who was slightly deaf, did not catch the name *del Dongo;* he announced a young priest named Fabrizio; the Archbishop happened to be closeted with a parish priest of by no means exemplary morals, for whom he had sent in order to scold him. He was in the act of delivering a reprimand, a most painful thing for him, and did not wish to be distressed by it longer than was necessary; accordingly he kept waiting for three quarters of an hour the great-nephew of the Archbishop Ascanio del Dongo.

How are we to depict his apologies and despair when, after having conducted the priest to the farthest ante-room, and on asking, as he returned, the man who was waiting *what he could do to serve him,* he caught sight of the violet stockings and heard the name Fabrizio del Dongo? This accident seemed to our hero so fortunate that on this first visit he ventured to kiss the saintly prelate's hand, in a transport of affection. He was obliged to hear the Archbishop repeat in a tone of despair: "A del Dongo kept waiting in my anteroom!" The old man felt obliged, by way of apology, to relate to him the whole story of the parish priest, his misdeeds, his replies to the charges, and so forth.

"Is it really possible," Fabrizio asked himself as he made his way back to the *palazzo* Sanseverina, "that this is the man who hurried on the execution of that poor Conte Palanza?"

"What is Your Excellency's impression?" Conte Mosca inquired with a smile, as he saw him enter the Duchessa's drawing-room. (The Conte would not allow Fabrizio to address him as Excellency.)

"I have fallen from the clouds; I know nothing at all about human nature: I would have wagered, had I not known his name, that that man could not bear to see a chicken bleed."

"And you would have won your wager," replied the Conte; "but when he is with the Prince, or merely with myself, he cannot say no. To be quite honest, in order for me to create my full effect, I have to slip the yellow riband of my Grand Cordon over my coat; in plain evening dress he would contradict me, and so I always put on a uniform to receive him. It is not for us to destroy the prestige of power, the French newspapers are demolishing it quite fast enough; it is doubtful whether the *mania of respect* will last out our time, and you, my dear nephew, will outlive respect altogether. You will be simply a fellow-man!"

Fabrizio delighted greatly in the Conte's society; he was the first superior person who had condescended to talk to him frankly, without make-believe; moreover they had a taste in common, that for antiquities and excavations. The Conte, for his part, was flattered by the extreme attention with which the young man listened to him; but there was one paramount objection: Fabrizio occupied a set of rooms in the *palazzo* Sanseverina, spent his whole time with the Duchessa, let it be seen in all innocence that this intimacy constituted his happiness in life, and Fabrizio had eyes and a complexion of a freshness that drove the older man to despair.

For a long time past Ranuccio-Ernesto IV, who rarely encountered a cruel fair, had felt it to be an affront that the Duchessa's virtue, which was well known at court, had not made an exception in his favour. As we have seen, the mind and the presence of mind of Fabrizio had shocked him at their first encounter. He took amiss the extreme friendship which Fabrizio and his aunt heedlessly displayed in public; he gave ear with the closest attention to the remarks of his courtiers, which were endless. The arrival of this young man and the unprecedented audience which he had obtained provided the court with news and a sensation for the next month; which gave the Prince an idea.

He had in his guard a private soldier who carried his wine in the most admirable way; this man spent his time in the *trattorie*, and reported the spirit of the troops directly to his Sovereign. Carlone lacked education, otherwise he would long since have obtained promotion. Well, his duty was to be in the Palace every day when the strokes of twelve sounded on the great clock. The Prince went in person a little before noon to arrange in a certain way the shutters of a *mezzanino* communicating with the room in which His Highness dressed. He returned to this *mezzanino* shortly after twelve had struck, and there found the soldier; the Prince had in his pocket writing materials and a sheet of paper; he dictated to the soldier the following letter:

"Your Excellency has great intelligence, doubtless, and it is thanks to his profound sagacity that we see this State so well governed. But, my dear Conte, such great success never comes unaccompanied by a little envy, and I am seriously afraid that people will be laughing a little at your expense if your sagacity does not discern that a certain handsome young man has had the good fortune to inspire, unintentionally it may be, a passion of the most singular order. This happy mortal is, they say, only twenty-three years old, and, dear Conte, what complicates the question is that you and I are considerably more than twice that age. In the evening, at a certain distance, the Conte is charming, scintillating, a wit, as attractive as possible; but in the morning, in an intimate scene, all things considered, the newcomer has perhaps greater attractions. Well, we poor women, we make a great point of this youthful freshness, especially when we have ourselves passed thirty. Is there not some talk already of settling this charming youth at our court, in some fine post? And if so, who is the person who speaks of it most frequently to Your Excellency?"

The Prince took the letter and gave the soldier two scudi. "This is in addition to your pay," he said in a grim tone. "Not a single word of this to anyone, or you will find yourself in the dampest dungeon in the citadel." The Prince had in his desk a collection of envelopes bearing the addresses of most of the persons at his court, in the handwriting of this same soldier who was understood to be illiterate, and never even wrote out his own police reports: the Prince picked out the one he required.

A few hours later, Conte Mosca received a letter by post; the hour of its delivery had been calculated, and just as the postman, who had been seen going in with a small envelope in his hand, came out of the ministerial palace, Mosca was summoned to His Highness. Never had the favourite appeared to be in the grip of a blacker melancholy: to enjoy this at his leisure, the Prince called out to him, as he saw him come in:

"I want to amuse myself by talking casually to my friend and not working with my Minister. I have a maddening headache this evening, and all sorts of gloomy thoughts keep coming into my mind."

I need hardly mention the abominable ill-humour which agitated the Prime Minister, Conte Mosca della Rovere, when at length he was permitted to take leave of his august master. Ranuccio-Ernesto IV was a past-master in the art of torturing a heart, and it would not be unfair at this point to make the comparison of the tiger which loves to play with its victim.

The Conte made his coachman drive him home at a gallop; he called out as he crossed the threshold that not a living soul was to be allowed upstairs, sent word to the *auditor* on duty that he might take himself off (the knowledge that there was a human being within earshot was hateful to him), and hastened to shut himself up in the great picture gallery. There at length he could give full vent to his fury; there he spent an hour without lights, wandering about the room like a man out of his mind. He sought to impose silence on his heart, to concentrate all the force of his attention upon deliberating what action he ought to take. Plunged in an anguish that would have moved to pity his most implacable enemy, he said to himself: "The man I abhor is living in the Duchessa's house; he spends every hour of the day with her. Ought I to try to make one of her women speak? Nothing could be more dangerous; she is so good to them; she pays them well; she is adored by them (and by whom, great God, is she not adored?)! The question is," he continued, raging: "Ought I to let her detect the jealousy that is devouring me, or not to speak of it?

"If I remain silent, she will make no attempt to keep anything from me. I know Gina, she is a woman who acts always on the first impulse; her conduct is incalculable, even by herself; if she tries to plan out a course in advance, she goes all wrong; invariably, when it is time for action, a new idea comes into her head which she follows rapturously as though it were the most wonderful thing in the world, and upsets everything.

"If I make no mention of my suffering, nothing will be kept back from me, and I shall see all that goes on. . . .

"Yes, but by speaking I bring about a change of circumstances: I make her reflect; I give her fair warning of all the horrible things that may happen. . . . Perhaps she will send him away" (the Conte breathed a sigh of relief), "then I shall practically have won; even allowing her to be a little out of temper for the moment, I shall soothe her . . . and a little ill-temper, what could be more natural? . . . she has loved him like a son for fifteen years. There lies all my hope: *like a son* . . . but she had ceased to see him after his dash to Waterloo; now, on his return from Naples, especially for her, he is a different man. *A different man!*" he repeated with fury, "and that man is charming; he has, apart from everything else, that simple and tender air and that smiling eye which hold out such a promise of happiness! And those eyes—the Duchessa cannot be accustomed to see eyes like those at this court! . . . Our substitute for them is a gloomy or sardonic stare. I myself, pursued everywhere by official business, governing only by my influence over a man who would like to turn me to ridicule, what a look there must often be in mine! Ah! whatever pains I may take to conceal it, it is in my eyes that age will always shew. My gaiety, does it not always border upon irony? . . . I will go farther, I must be sincere with myself; does not my gaiety allow a glimpse to be caught, as of something quite close to it, of absolute power . . . and irresponsibility? Do I not sometimes say to myself, especially when people irritate me: 'I can do what I like!' and indeed go on to say what is foolish: 'I ought to be happier than other men, since I possess what others have not, sovereign power in three things out of four . . . ?' Very well, let us be just! The habit of thinking thus must affect my smile, must give me a selfish, satisfied air. And, how charming his smile is! It breathes the easy happiness of extreme youth, and engenders it."

Unfortunately for the Conte, the weather that evening was hot, stifling, with the threat of a storm in the air; the sort of weather, in short, that in those parts carries people to extremes. How am I to find space for all the arguments, all the ways of looking at what was happening to him, which, for three mortal hours on end, kept this impassioned man in torment? At length the side of prudence prevailed, solely as a result of this reflexion: "I am in all probability mad; when I think I am reasoning, I am not, I am simply turning about in search of a less painful position, I pass by without seeing it some decisive argument. Since I am blinded by excessive grief, let us obey the rule, approved by every sensible man, which is called *Prudence*.

"Besides, once I have uttered the fatal word *jealousy,* my course is traced for me for ever. If on the contrary I say nothing to-day, I can speak to-morrow, I remain master of the situation." The crisis was too acute; the Conte would have gone mad had it continued. He was comforted for a few moments, his attention came to rest on the anonymous letter. From whose hand could it have come? There followed then a search for possible names, and a personal judgement of each, which created a diversion. In the end, the Conte remembered a gleam of malice that had darted from the eyes of the Sovereign, when it had occurred to him to say, towards the end of the audience: "Yes, dear friend, let us be agreed on this point: the pleasures and cares of the most amply rewarded ambition, even of unbounded power, are as nothing compared with the intimate happiness that is afforded by relations of affection and love. I am a man first, and a Prince afterwards, and, when I have the good fortune to be in love, my mistress speaks to the man and not to the Prince." The Conte compared that moment of malicious joy with the phrase in the letter: "It is thanks to your profound sagacity that we see this State so well governed." "Those are the Prince's words!" he exclaimed; "in a courtier they would be a gratuitous piece of imprudence; the letter comes from His Highness."

This problem solved, the faint joy caused by the pleasure of guessing the solution was soon effaced by the cruel spectre of the charming graces of Fabrizio, which returned afresh. It was like an enormous weight that fell back on the heart of the unhappy man. "What does it matter from whom the anonymous letter comes?" he cried with fury; "does the fact that it discloses to me exist any the less? This caprice may alter my whole life," he said, as though to excuse himself for being so mad. "At the first moment, if she cares for him in a certain way, she will set off with him for Belgirate, for Switzerland, for the ends of the earth. She is rich, and besides, even if she had to live on a few louis a year, what would that matter to her? Did she not admit to me, not a week ago, that her *palazzo*, so well arranged, so magnificent, bored her? Novelty is essential to so youthful a spirit! And with what simplicity does this new form of happiness offer itself! She will be carried away before she has begun to think of the danger, before she has begun to think of being sorry for me! And yet I am so wretched!" cried the Conte, bursting into tears.

He had sworn to himself that he would not go to the Duchessa's that evening; never had his eyes thirsted so to gaze on her. At midnight he presented himself at her door; he found her alone with her nephew; at ten o'clock she had sent all her guests away and had closed her door.

At the sight of the tender intimacy that prevailed between these two creatures, and of the Duchessa's artless joy, a frightful difficulty arose before the eyes of the Conte, and one that was quite unforeseen. He had never thought of it

during his long deliberation in the picture gallery: how was he
to conceal his jealousy?

Not knowing what pretext to adopt, he pretended that he
had found the Prince that evening excessively ill-disposed towards him, contradicting all his assertions, and so forth. He
had the distress of seeing the Duchessa barely listen to him,
and pay no attention to these details which, forty-eight hours
earlier, would have plunged her in an endless stream of discussion. The Conte looked at Fabrizio: never had that handsome Lombard face appeared to him so simple and so noble!
Fabrizio paid more attention than the Duchessa to the
difficulties which he was relating.

"Really," he said to himself, "that head combines extreme
good-nature with the expression of a certain artless and
tender joy which is irresistible. It seems to be saying: 'Love
and the happiness it brings are the only serious things in
this world.' And yet, when one comes to some detail which
requires thought, the light wakes in his eyes and surprises
one, and one is left dumbfounded.

"Everything is simple in his eyes, because everything is
seen from above. Great God! how is one to fight against
an enemy like this? And after all, what is life without Gina's
love? With what rapture she seems to be listening to the
charming sallies of that mind, which is so boyish and must,
to a woman, seem without a counterpart in the world!"

An atrocious thought gripped the Conte like a sudden
cramp. "Shall I stab him here, before her face, and then kill
myself?"

He took a turn through the room, his legs barely supporting him, but his hand convulsively gripping the hilt of
his dagger. Neither of the others paid any attention to what
he might be doing. He announced that he was going to
give an order to his servant; they did not even hear him;
the Duchessa was laughing tenderly at something Fabrizio
had just said to her. The Conte went up to a lamp in the
outer room, and looked to see whether the point of his
dagger was well sharpened. "One must behave graciously,
and with perfect manners to this young man," he said to
himself as he returned to the other room and went up to
them.

He became quite mad; it seemed to him that, as they
leaned their heads together, they were kissing each other,
there, before his eyes. "That is impossible in my presence,"
he told himself; "my wits have gone astray. I must calm

myself; if I behave rudely, the Duchessa is quite capable, simply out of injured vanity, of following him to Belgirate; and there, or on the way there, a chance word may be spoken which will give a name to what they now feel for one another; and after that, in a moment, all the consequences.

"Solitude will render that word decisive, and besides, once the Duchessa has left my side, what is to become of me? And if, after overcoming endless difficulties on the Prince's part, I go and shew my old and anxious face at Belgirate, what part shall I play before these people both mad with happiness?

"Here even, what else am I than the *terzo incomodo?*" (That beautiful Italian language is simply made for love: *terzo incomodo,* a third person when two are company.) What misery for a man of spirit to feel that he is playing that execrable part, and not to be able to muster the strength to get up and leave the room!

The Conte was on the point of breaking out, or at least of betraying his anguish by the discomposure of his features. When in one of his circuits of the room he found himself near the door, he took his flight, calling out, in a genial, intimate tone: "Good-bye, you two!— Once must avoid bloodshed," he said to himself.

The day following this horrible evening, after a night spent half in compiling a detailed sum of Fabrizio's advantages, half in the frightful transports of the most cruel jealousy, it occurred to the Conte that he might send for a young servant of his own; this man was keeping company with a girl named Cecchina, one of the Duchessa's personal maids, and her favourite. As good luck would have it, this young man was very sober in his habits, indeed miserly, and was anxious to find a place as porter in one of the public institutions of Parma. The Conte ordered the man to fetch Cecchina, his mistress, instantly. The man obeyed, and an hour later the Conte appeared suddenly in the room where the girl was waiting with her lover. The Conte frightened them both by the amount of gold that he gave them, then he addressed these few words to the trembling Cecchina, looking her straight in the face:

"Is the Duchessa in love with Monsignore?"

"No," said the girl, gaining courage to speak after a moment's silence. . . . "No, *not yet,* but he often kisses the Signora's hands, laughing, it is true, but with real feeling."

This evidence was completed by a hundred answers to as many furious questions from the Conte; his uneasy passion made the poor couple earn in full measure the money that he had flung them: he ended by believing what they told him, and was less unhappy. "If the Duchessa ever has the slightest suspicion of what we have been saying," he told Cecchina, "I shall send your lover to spend twenty years in the fortress, and when you see him again his hair will be quite white."

Some days elapsed, during which Fabrizio in turn lost all his gaiety.

"I assure you," he said to the Duchessa, "that Conte Mosca feels an antipathy for me."

"So much the worse for His Excellency," she replied with a trace of temper.

This was by no means the true cause of the uneasiness which had made Fabrizio's gaiety vanish. "The position in which chance has placed me is not tenable," he told himself. "I am quite sure that she will never say anything, she would be as much horrified by a too significant word as by an incestuous act. But if, one evening, after a rash and foolish day, she should come to examine her conscience, if she believes that I may have guessed the feeling that she seems to have formed for me, what part should I then play in her eyes? Nothing more nor less than the *casto Giuseppe!*" (An Italian expression alluding to the ridiculous part played by Joseph with the wife of the eunuch Potiphar.)

"Should I give her to understand by a fine burst of confidence that I am not capable of serious affection? I have not the necessary strength of mind to announce such a fact so that it shall not be as like as two peas to a gross impertinence. The sole resource left to me is a great passion left behind at Naples; in that case, I should return there for twenty-four hours: such a course is wise, but is it really worth the trouble? There remains a minor affair with some one of humble rank at Parma, which might annoy her; but anything is preferable to the appalling position of a man who will not see the truth. This course may, it is true, prejudice my future; I should have, by the exercise of prudence and the purchase of discretion, to minimise the danger." What was so cruel an element among all these thoughts was that really Fabrizio loved the Duchessa far above anyone else in the world. "I must be very clumsy," he told himself angrily, "to have such misgivings as to my ability to persuade her of what is so glaringly true!" Lacking the skill to extricate himself from this position, he grew sombre and sad. "What would become of me, Great God, if I quarrelled with the one person in the world for whom I feel a passionate attachment?" From another point of view, Fabrizio could not bring himself to spoil so delicious a happiness by an indiscreet word. His position abounded so in charm! The intimate friendship of so beautiful and attractive a woman was so pleasant! Under the most commonplace relations of life, her protection gave him so agreeable a position at this court, the great intrigues of which, thanks to her who explained them to him, were as amusing as a play! "But at any moment I may be awakened by a thunderbolt," he said to himself. "These gay, these tender evenings, passed almost in privacy with so thrilling a woman, if they lead to something better, she will expect to find in me a lover; she will call on me for frenzied raptures, for acts of folly, and I shall never have anything more to offer her than friendship, of the warmest kind, but without love; nature has not endowed me with that sort of sublime folly. What reproaches have I not had to bear on that account! I can still hear the Duchessa d'A—— speaking, and I used to laugh at the Duchessa! She will think that I am wanting in love for her, whereas it is love that is wanting in me; never will she make herself understand me. Often after some story about the court, told by her with that grace, that abandonment which she alone in the world possesses, and which is a necessary part of my education besides, I kiss her hand and sometimes her cheek. What is to happen if that hand presses mine in a certain fashion?"

Fabrizio put in an appearance every day in the most respectable and least amusing drawing-rooms in Parma. Guided by the able advice of the Duchessa, he paid a sagacious court to the two Princes, father and son, to the Princess Clara-Paolina and Monsignore the Archbishop. He met with successes, but these did not in the least console him for his mortal fear of falling out with the Duchessa.

CHAPTER EIGHT

So, LESS THAN a month after his arrival at court, Fabrizio had tasted all the sorrows of a courtier, and the intimate friendship which constituted the happiness of his life was poisoned. One evening, tormented by these thoughts, he left that drawing-room of the Duchessa in which he had too much of the air of a reigning lover; wandering at random through the town, he came opposite the theatre, in which he saw lights; he went in. It was a gratuitous imprudence in a man of his cloth and one that he had indeed vowed that he would avoid in Parma, which, after all, is only a small town of forty thousand inhabitants. It is true that after the first few days he had got rid of his official costume; in the evenings, when he was not going into the very highest society, he used simply to dress in black like a layman in mourning.

At the theatre he took a box on the third tier, so as not to be noticed; the play was Goldoni's *La Locanderia*. He examined the architecture of the building, scarcely did he turn his eyes to the stage. But the crowded audience kept bursting into laughter at every moment; Fabrizio gave a glance at the young actress who was playing the part of the landlady, and found her amusing. He looked at her more closely; she seemed to him quite attractive, and, above all, perfectly natural; she was a simple-minded young girl who was the first to laugh at the witty lines Goldoni had put into her mouth, lines which she appeared to be quite surprised to be uttering. He asked what her name was, and was told: "Marietta Valserra."

"Ah!" he thought; "she has taken my name; that is odd." In spite of his intentions he did not leave the theatre until the end of the piece. The following evening he returned; three days later he knew Marietta Valserra's address.

On the evening of the day on which, with a certain amount of trouble, he had procured this address, he noticed that the Conte was looking at him in the most friendly way. The poor jealous lover, who had all the trouble in the world in keeping within the bounds of prudence, had set spies on the young man's track, and this theatrical escapade pleased him. How are we to depict the Conte's joy when, on the day following that on which he had managed to bring himself to look amicably at Fabrizio, he learned that the latter, in the partial disguise, it must be admitted, of a long blue frock-coat, had climbed to the wretched apartment which Marietta Valserra occupied on the fourth floor of an old house behind the theatre? His joy was doubled when he heard that Fabrizio had presented himself under a false name, and had had the honour to arouse the jealousy of a scapegrace named Giletti, who in town played Third Servant, and in the villages danced on the tight rope. This noble lover of Marietta cursed Fabrizio most volubly and expressed a desire to kill him.

Opera companies are formed by an *impresario* who engages in different places the artists whom he can afford to pay or has found unemployed, and the company collected at random remains together for one season or two at most. It is not so with *comedy companies;* while passing from town to town and changing their address every two or three months, they nevertheless form a family of which all the members love or loathe one another. There are in these companies united couples whom the *beaux* of the towns in which the actors appear find it sometimes exceedingly difficult to sunder. This is precisely what happened to our hero. Little Marietta liked him well enough, but was horribly afraid of Giletti, who claimed to be her sole lord and master and kept a close watch over her. He protested everywhere that he would kill the *Monsignore*, for he had followed Fabrizio, and had succeeded in discovering his name. This Giletti was quite the ugliest creature imaginable and the least fitted to be a lover: tall out of all proportion, he was horribly thin, strongly pitted by smallpox, and inclined to squint. In addition, being endowed with all the graces of his profession, he was continually coming into the wings where his fellow-actors were assembled, turning cartwheels on his feet and hands or practising some other pretty trick. He triumphed in those parts in which the actor has to appear with his face whitened with flour and to give or receive a countless number of blows with a cudgel. This worthy rival of Fabrizio drew a monthly salary of 32 francs, and thought himself extremely well off.

Conte Mosca felt himself drawn up from the gate of the tomb when his watchers gave him the full authority for all these details. His kindly nature reappeared; he seemed more gay and better company than ever in the Duchessa's drawing-room, and took good care to say nothing to her of the little adventure which had restored him to life. He even took steps to ensure that she should be informed of everything that occurred with the greatest possibly delay. Finally he had the courage to listen to the voice of reason, which had been crying to him in vain for the last month that, whenever a lover's lustre begins to fade, it is time for that lover to travel.

Urgent business summoned him to Bologna, and twice a day cabinet messengers brought him not so much the official papers of his departments as the latest news of the love affairs of little Marietta, the rage of the terrible Giletti and the enterprises of Fabrizio.

One of the Conte's agents asked several times for *Arlecchino fantasma e pasticcio,* one of Giletti's triumphs (he emerges from the pie at the moment when his rival Brighella is sticking the knife into it, and gives him a drubbing); this was an excuse for making him earn 100 francs. Giletti, who was riddled with debts, took care not to speak of this windfall, but became astonishing in his arrogance.

Fabrizio's whim changed to a wounded pride (at his age, his anxieties had already reduced him to the state of having whims!). Vanity led him to the theatre; the little girl acted in the most sprightly fashion and amused him; on leaving the theatre, he was in love for an hour. The Conte returned to Parma on receiving the news that Fabrizio was in real danger; Giletti, who had served as a trooper in that fine regiment the Dragoni Napoleone, spoke seriously of killing him, and was making arrangements for a subsequent flight to Romagna. If the reader is very young, he will be scandalised by our admiration for this fine mark of virtue. It was, however, no slight act of heroism on the part of Conte Mosca, his return from Bologna; for, after all, frequently in the morning he presented a worn appearance, and Fabrizio was always so fresh, so serene! Who would ever have dreamed of reproaching him with the death of Fabrizio, occurring in his absence and from so stupid a cause? But his was one of those rare spirits which make an everlasting remorse out of a generous action which they might have done and did not do; besides, he could not bear the thought of seeing the Duchessa look sad, and by any fault of his.

He found her, on his arrival, taciturn and gloomy. This is what had occurred: the little lady's maid, Cecchina, tormented by remorse and estimating the importance of her crime by the immensity of the sum that she had received for committing it, had fallen ill. One evening the Duchessa, who was devoted to her, went up to her room. The girl could not hold out against this mark of kindness; she dissolved in tears, was for handing over to her mistress all that she still possessed of the money she had received, and finally had the courage to confess to her the questions asked by the Conte and her own replies to them. The Duchessa ran to the lamp, which she blew out, then said to little Cecchina that she forgave her, but on condition that she never uttered a word about this strange episode to anyone in the world. "The poor Conte," she added in a careless tone, "is afraid of being laughed at; all men are like that."

The Duchessa hastened downstairs to her own apartments. No sooner had she shut the door of her bedroom than she burst into tears; there seemed to her something horrible in the idea of her making love to Fabrizio, whom she had seen brought into the world; and yet what else could her behaviour imply?

This had been the primary cause of the black melancholy in which the Conte found her plunged; on his arrival she suffered fits of impatience with him, and almost with Fabrizio; she would have liked never to set eyes on either of them again; she was contemptuous of the part, ridiculous in her eyes, which Fabrizio was playing with the little Marietta; for the Conte had told her everything, like a true lover, incapable of keeping a secret. She could not grow used to this disaster; her idol had a fault; finally, in a moment of frank friendship, she asked the Conte's advice; this was for him a delicious instant, and a fine reward for the honourable impulse which had made him return to Parma.

"What could be more simple?" said the Conte, smiling. "Young men want to have every woman they see, and next day they do not give her a thought. Ought he not to be going to Belgirate, to see the Marchesa del Dongo? Very well, let him go. During his absence, I shall request the company of comedians to take their talents elsewhere, I shall pay their travelling expenses; but presently we shall see him in love with the first pretty woman that may happen to come his way: it is in the nature of things, and I should not care to see him act otherwise. . . . If necessary, get the Marchesa to write to him."

This suggestion, offered with the air of a complete indifference, came as a ray of light to the Duchessa; she was frightened of Giletti. That evening, the Conte announced, as though by chance, that one of his couriers, on his way to Vienna, would be passing through Milan; three days later Fabrizio received a letter from his mother. He seemed greatly annoyed at not having yet been able, thanks to Giletti's jealousy, to profit by the excellent intentions, assurance of which little Marietta had conveyed to him through a *mammaccia,* an old woman who acted as her mother.

Fabrizio found his mother and one of his sisters at Belgirate, a large village in Piedmont, on the right shore of Lake Maggiore; the left shore belongs to the Milanese, and consequently to Austria. This lake, parallel to the Lake of Como, and also running from north to south, is situated some ten leagues farther to the west. The mountain air, the majestic and tranquil aspect of this superb lake which recalled to him that other on the shores of which he had spent his childhood, all helped to transform into a tender melancholy Fabrizio's grief, which was akin to anger. It was with an infinite tenderness that the memory of the Duchessa now presented itself to him; he felt that in separation he was acquiring for her that love which he had never felt for any woman; nothing would have been more painful to him than to be separated from her for ever, and, he being in this frame of mind, if the Duchessa had deigned to have recourse to the slightest coquetry, she could have conquered this heart by—for instance—presenting it with a rival. But, far from taking any so decisive a step, it was not without the keenest self-reproach that she found her thoughts constantly following in the young traveller's footsteps. She reproached herself for what she still called a fancy, as though it had been something horrible; she redoubled her forethought for and attention to the Conte, who, captivated by such a display of charm, paid no heed to the sane voice of reason which was prescribing a second visit to Bologna.

The Marchesa del Dongo, busy with preparations for the

wedding of her elder daughter, whom she was marrying to a Milanese Duca, could give only three days to her beloved son; never had she found in him so tender an affection. Through the cloud of melancholy that was more and more closely enwrapping Fabrizio's heart, an odd and indeed ridiculous idea had presented itself, and he had suddenly decided to adopt it. Dare we say that he wished to consult Priore Blanès? That excellent old man was totally incapable of understanding the sorrows of a heart torn asunder by boyish passions more or less equal in strength; besides, it would have taken a week to make him gather even a faint impression of all the conflicting interests that Fabrizio had to consider at Parma; but in the thought of consulting him Fabrizio recaptured the freshness of his sensations at the age of sixteen. Will it be believed? It was not simply as to a man full of wisdom, to an old and devoted friend, that Fabrizio wished to speak to him; the object of this expedition, and the feelings that agitated our hero during the fifty hours that it lasted are so absurd that, doubtless, in the interests of our narrative, it would have been better to suppress them. I am afraid that Fabrizio's credulity may make him forfeit the sympathy of the reader; but after all thus it was; why flatter him more than another? I have not flattered Conte Mosca, nor the Prince.

Fabrizio, then, since the whole truth must be told, Fabrizio escorted his mother as far as the port of Laveno, on the left shore of Lake Maggiore, the Austrian shore, where she landed about eight o'clock in the evening. (The lake is regarded as neutral territory, and no passport is required of those who do not set foot on shore.) But scarcely had night fallen when he had himself ferried to this same Austrian shore, and landed in a little wood which juts out into the water. He had hired a *sediola,* a sort of rustic and fast-moving tilbury, by means of which he was able, at a distance of five hundred yards, to keep up with his mother's carriage; he was disguised as a servant of the *casa* del Dongo, and none of the many police or customs officials ever thought of asking him for his passport. A quarter of a league before Como, where the Marchesa and her daughter were to stop for the night, he took a path to the left which, making a circuit of the village of Vico, afterwards joined a little road recently made along the extreme edge of the lake. It was midnight, and Fabrizio could count upon not meeting any of the police. The trees of the various thickets into which

the little road kept continually diving traced the black outline of their foliage against a sky bright with stars but
veiled by a slight mist. Water and sky were of a profound
tranquillity. Fabrizio's soul could not resist this sublime
beauty; he stopped, then sat down on a rock which ran out
into the lake, forming almost a little promontory. The universal silence was disturbed only, at regular intervals, by the
faint ripple of the lake as it lapped on the shore. Fabrizio
had an Italian heart; I crave the reader's pardon for him:
this defect, which will render him less attractive, consisted mainly in this: he had no vanity, save by fits
and starts, and the mere sight of sublime beauty melted him
to a tender mood and took from his sorrows their hard and
bitter edge. Seated on his isolated rock, having no longer
any need to be on his guard against the police, protected by
the profound night and the vast silence, gentle tears
moistened his eyes, and he found there, with little or no
effort, the happiest moments that he had tasted for many a
day.

He resolved never to tell the Duchessa any falsehood, and
it was because he loved her to adoration at that moment that
he vowed to himself never to say to her *that he loved her;*
never would he utter in her hearing the word love, since the
passion which bears that name was a stranger to his heart.
In the enthusiasm of generosity and virtue which formed
his happiness at that moment, he made the resolution to tell
her, at the first opportunity, everything: his heart had never
known love. Once this courageous plan had been definitely
adopted, he felt himself delivered of an enormous burden.
"She will perhaps have something to say to me about
Marietta; very well, I shall never see my little Marietta
again," he assured himself blithely.

The overpowering heat which had prevailed throughout
the day was beginning to be tempered by the morning
breeze. Already dawn was outlining in a faint white glimmer the Alpine peaks that rise to the north and east of Lake
Como. Their massive shapes, bleached by their covering
of snow, even in the month of June, stand out against
the pellucid azure of a sky which at those immense altitudes
is always pure. A spur of the Alps stretching southwards into
smiling Italy separates the sloping shores of Lake Como from
those of the Lake of Garda. Fabrizio followed with his eye all
the branches of these sublime mountains, the dawn as it
grew brighter came to mark the valleys that divide them,

gilding the faint mist which rose from the gorges beneath.

Some minutes since, Fabrizio had taken the road again; he passed the hill that forms the peninsula of Durini, and at length there met his gaze that *campanile* of the village of Grianta in which he had so often made observations of the stars with Priore Blanès. "What bounds were there to my ignorance in those days? I could not understand," he reminded himself, "even the ridiculous Latin of those treatises on astrology which my master used to pore over, and I think I respected them chiefly because, understanding only a few words here and there, my imagination stepped in to give them a meaning, and the most romantic sense imaginable."

Gradually his thoughts entered another channel. "May not there be something genuine in this science? Why should it be different from the rest? A certain number of imbeciles and quick-witted persons agree among themselves that they know (shall we say) *Mexican;* they impose themselves with this qualification upon society which respects them and governments which pay them. Favours are showered upon them precisely because they have no real intelligence, and authority need not fear their raising the populace and creating an atmosphere of rant by the aid of generous sentiments! For instance, Father Bari, to whom Ernesto IV has just awarded a pension of 4,000 francs and the Cross of his Order for having restored nineteen lines of a Greek dithyramb!

"But, Great God, have I indeed the right to find such things ridiculous? Is it for me to complain?" he asked himself, suddenly, stopping short in the road, "has not that same Cross just been given to my governor at Naples?" Fabrizio was conscious of a feeling of intense disgust; the fine enthusiasm for virtue which had just been making his heart beat high changed into the vile pleasure of having a good share in the spoils of a robbery. "After all," he said to himself at length, with the lustreless eyes of a man who is dissatisfied with himself, "since my birth gives me the right to profit by these abuses, it would be a signal piece of folly on my part not to take my share, but I must never let myself denounce them in public." This reasoning was by no means unsound; but Fabrizio had fallen a long way from that elevation of sublime happiness to which he had found himself transported an hour earlier. The thought of privilege had withered that plant, always so delicate, which we name happiness.

"If we are not to believe in astrology," he went on, seeking to calm himself; "if this science is, like three quarters of the sciences that are not mathematical, a collection of enthusiastic simpletons and adroit hypocrites paid by the masters they serve, how does it come about that I think so often and with emotion of this fatal circumstance: I did make my escape from the prison at B——, but in the uniform and with the marching orders of a soldier who had been flung into prison with good cause?"

Fabrizio's reasoning could never succeed in penetrating farther; he went a hundred ways round the difficulty without managing to surmount it. He was too young still; in his moments of leisure, his mind devoted itself with rapture to enjoying the sensations produced by the romantic circumstances with which his imagination was always ready to supply him. He was far from employing his time in studying with patience the actual details of things in order to discover their causes. Reality still seemed to him flat and muddy; I can understand a person's not caring to look at it, but then he ought not to argue about it. Above all, he ought not to fashion objections out of the scattered fragments of his ignorance.

Thus it was that, though not lacking in brains, Fabrizio could not manage to see that his half-belief in omens was for him a religion, a profound impression received at his entering upon life. To think of this belief was to feel, it was a happiness. And he set himself resolutely to discover how this could be a *proved*, a real science, in the same category as geometry, for example. He searched his memory strenuously for all the instances in which omens observed by him had not been followed by the auspicious or inauspicious events which they seemed to herald. But all this time, while he believed himself to be following a line of reasoning and marching towards the truth, his attention kept coming joyfully to rest on the memory of the occasions on which the foreboding had been amply followed by the happy or unhappy accident which it had seemed to him to predict, and his heart was filled with respect and melted; and he would have felt an invincible repugnance for the person who denied the value of omens, especially if in doing so he had had recourse to irony.

Fabrizio walked on without noticing the distance he was

covering, and had reached this point in his vain reasonings when, raising his head, he saw the wall of his father's garden. This wall, which supported a fine terrace, rose to a height of more than forty feet above the road, on its right. A cornice of wrought stone along the highest part, next to the balustrade, gave it a monumental air. "It is not bad," Fabrizio said to himself dispassionately, "it is good architecture, a little in the Roman style"; he applied to it his recently acquired knowledge of antiquities. Then he turned his head away in disgust; his father's severities, and especially the denunciation of himself by his brother Ascanio on his return from his wanderings in France, came back to his mind.

"That unnatural denunciation was the origin of my present existence; I may detest, I may despise it; when all is said and done, it has altered my destiny. What would have become of me once I had been packed off to Novara, and my presence barely tolerated in the house of my father's agent, if my aunt had not made love to a powerful Minister? If the said aunt had happened to possess merely a dry, conventional heart instead of that tender and passionate heart which loves me with a sort of enthusiasm that astonishes me? Where should I be now if the Duchessa had had the heart of her brother the Marchese del Dongo?"

Oppressed by these cruel memories, Fabrizio began now to walk with an uncertain step; he came to the edge of the moat immediately opposite the magnificent façade of the castle. Scarcely did he cast a glance at that great building, blackened by time. The noble language of architecture left him unmoved, the memory of his brother and father stopped his heart to every sensation of beauty, he was attentive only to the necessity of keeping on his guard in the presence of hypocritical and dangerous enemies. He looked for an instant, but with a marked disgust, at the little window of the bedroom which he had occupied until 1815 on the third storey. His father's character had robbed of all charm the memory of his early childhood. "I have not set foot in it," he thought, "since the 7th of March, at eight o'clock in the evening. I left it to go and get the passport from Vasi, and next morning my fear of spies made me hasten my departure. When I passed through again after my visit to France, I had not time to go upstairs, even to look at my prints again, and that thanks to my brother's denouncing me."

Fabrizio turned away his head in horror. "Priore Blanès is eighty-three at the very least," he said sorrowfully to himself; "he hardly ever comes to the castle now, from what my sister tells me; the infirmities of old age have had their effect on him. That heart, once so strong and noble, is frozen by age. Heaven knows how long it is since he last went up to his *campanile!* I shall hide myself in the cellar, under the vats or under the wine-press, until he is awake; I shall not go in and disturb the good old man in his sleep; probably he will have forgotten my face, even; six years mean a great deal at his age! I shall find only the tomb of a friend! And it is really childish of me," he added, "to have come here to provoke the disgust that the sight of my father's castle gives me."

Fabrizio now came to the little *piazza* in front of the church; it was with an astonishment bordering on delirium that he saw, on the second stage of the ancient *campanile,* the long and narrow window lighted by the little lantern of Priore Blanès. The Priore was in the habit of leaving it there when he climbed to the cage of planks which formed his observatory, so that the light should not prevent him from reading the face of his plain sphere. This chart of the heavens was stretched over a great jar of terracotta which had originally belonged to one of the orange-trees at the castle. In the opening, at the bottom of the jar, burned the tiniest of lamps, the smoke of which was carried away from the jar through a little tin pipe, and the shadow of the pipe indicated the north on the chart. All these memories of things so simple in themselves deluged Fabrizio's heart with emotions and filled him with happiness.

Almost without thinking, he put his hands to his lips and gave the little, short, low whistle which had formerly been the signal for his admission. At once he heard several tugs given to the cord which, from the observatory above, opened the latch of the *campanile* door. He dashed headlong up the staircase, moved to a transport of excitement; he found the Priore in his wooden armchair in his accustomed place; his eye was fixed on the little glass of a mural quadrant. With his left hand the Priore made a sign to Fabrizio not to interrupt him in his observation; a moment later, he wrote down a figure upon a playing card, then, turning round in his chair, opened his arms to our hero, who flung himself into them, dissolved in tears. Priore Blanès was his true father.

"I expected you," said Blanès, after the first warm words of affection. Was the Priore speaking in his character as a diviner, or, indeed, as he often thought of Fabrizio, had some astrological sign, by pure chance, announced to him the young man's return?

"This means that my death is at hand," said Priore Blanès.

"What!" cried Fabrizio, quite overcome.

"Yes," the Priore went on in a serious but by no means sad tone: "five months and a half, or six months and a half after I have seen you again, my life having found its full complement of happiness will be extinguished

Come face al mancar dell'alimento"

(as the little lamp is when its oil runs dry). "Before the supreme moment, I shall probably pass a month or two without speaking, after which I shall be received into Our Father's Bosom; provided always that He finds that I have performed my duty in the post in which He has placed me as a sentinel.

"But you, you are worn out with exhaustion, your emotion makes you ready for sleep. Since I began to expect you, I have hidden a loaf of bread and a bottle of brandy for you in the great chest which holds my instruments. Give yourself that sustenance, and try to collect enough strength to listen to me for a few moments longer. It lies in my power to tell you a number of things before night shall have given place altogether to days; at present I see them a great deal more distinctly than perhaps I shall see them to-morrow. For, my child, we are at all times frail vessels, and we must always take that frailty into account. To-morrow, it may be, the old man, the earthly man in me will be occupied with preparations for my death, and to-morrow evening at nine o'clock, you will have to leave me."

Fabrizio having obeyed him in silence, as was his custom:

"Then, it is true," the old man went on, "that when you tried to see Waterloo you found nothing at first but a prison?"

"Yes, Father," replied Fabrizio in amazement.

"Well, that was a rare piece of good fortune, for, warned by my voice, your soul can prepare itself for another prison, far different in its austerity, far more terrible! Probably you will escape from it only by a crime; but, thanks be to heaven, that crime will not have been committed by you. Never fall into crime, however violently you may be tempted; I seem to see that it will be a question of killing an innocent man, who, without knowing it, usurps your rights; if you resist the violent temptation which will seem to be justified by the laws of honour, your life will be most happy in the eyes of men . . . and reasonably happy in the eyes of the sage," he added after a moment's reflexion; "you will die like me, my son, sitting upon a wooden seat, far from all luxury and having seen the hollowness of luxury, and like me not having to reproach yourself with any grave sin.

"And now, the discussion of your future state is at an end between us, I could add nothing of any importance. It is in vain that I have tried to see how long this imprisonment is to last; is it to be for six months, a year, ten years? I have been able to discover nothing; apparently I have made some error, and heaven has wished to punish me by the distress of this uncertainty. I have seen only that after your prison, but I do not know whether it is to be at the actual moment of your leaving it, there will be what I call a crime; but, fortunately, I believe I can be sure that it will not be committed by you. If you are weak enough to involve yourself in this crime, all the rest of my calculations becomes simply one long error. Then you will not die with peace in your soul, on a wooden seat and clad in white." As he said these words, Priore Blanès attempted to rise; it was then that Fabrizio noticed the ravages of time; it took him nearly a minute to get upon his feet and to turn towards Fabrizio. Our hero allowed him to do this, standing motionless and silent. The Priore flung himself into his arms again and again; he embraced him with extreme affection. After which he went on, with all the gaiety of the old days: "Try to make a place for yourself among all my instruments where you can sleep with some comfort; take my furs; you will find several of great value which the Duchessa Sanseverina sent me four years ago. She asked me for a forecast of your fate, which I took care not to give her, while keeping her furs and her fine quadrant. Every announcement of the future is a breach of the rule, and contains this danger, that it may alter the event, in which case the whole science falls to the ground, like a child's card-castle; and besides, there were things that it was hard to say to that Duchessa who is always so charming. But let me warn you, do not be startled in your sleep by the bells, which will make a terrible din in your ear when the men come to ring for the seven o'clock mass; later on, in the stage below, they will set the big *campanone* going, which shakes all my instruments. To-day is the feast of San Giovita, Martyr and Soldier. As you know, the little village of Grianta has the same patron as the great city of Brescia, which, by the way, led to a most amusing mistake on the part of my illustrious master, Giacomo Marini of Ravenna. More than once he announced to me that I should have quite a fine career in the church; he believed that I was to be the curate of the magnificent church of San Giovita, at Brescia; I have been the curate of a little village of seven hundred and fifty chimneys! But all has been for the best. I have seen, and not ten years ago, that if I had been curate at Brescia, my destiny would have been to be cast into prison on a hill in Moravia, the Spielberg. To-morrow I shall bring you all manner of delicacies pilfered from the great dinner which I am giving to all the clergy of the district who are coming to sing at my high mass. I shall leave them down below, but do not make any attempt to see me, do not come down to take possession of the good things until you have heard me go out again. You must not see me again *by daylight,* and as the sun sets to-morrow at twenty-seven minutes past seven, I shall not come up to embrace you until about eight, and it is necessary that you depart while the hours are still numbered by nine, that is to say before the clock has struck ten. Take care that you are not seen in the windows of the *campanile*: the police have your description, and they are to some extent under the orders of your brother, who is a famous tyrant. The Marchese del Dongo is growing feeble," added Blanès with a sorrowful air, "and if he were to see you again, perhaps he would let something pass to you, from hand to hand. But such benefits, tainted with deceit, do not become a man like yourself, whose strength will lie one day in his conscience. The Marchese abhors his son Ascanio, and it is on that son that the five or six millions that he possesses will devolve. That is justice. You, at his death, will have a pension of 4,000 francs, and fifty ells of black cloth for your servants' mourning."

CHAPTER NINE

FABRIZIO'S SOUL was exalted by the old man's speech, by his own keen attention to it, and by his extreme exhaustion. He had great difficulty in getting to sleep, and his slumber was disturbed by dreams, presages perhaps of the future; in the morning, at ten o'clock, he was awakened by the whole belfry's beginning to shake; an alarming noise seemed to come from outside. He rose in bewilderment and at first imagined that the end of the world had come; then he thought that he was in prison; it took him some time to recognise the sound of the big bell, which forty peasants were setting in motion in honour of the great San Giovita; ten would have been enough.

Fabrizio looked for a convenient place from which to see without being seen; he discovered that from this great height his gaze swept the gardens, and even the inner courtyard of his father's castle. He had forgotten this. The idea of that father arriving at the ultimate bourne of life altered all his feelings. He could even make out the sparrows that were hopping in search of crumbs upon the wide balcony of the dining-room. "They are the descendants of the ones I used to tame long ago," he said to himself. This balcony, like every balcony in the mansion, was decorated with a large number of orange-trees in earthenware tubs, of different sizes: this sight melted his heart; the view of that inner courtyard thus decorated, with its sharply defined shadows outlined by a radiant sun, was truly majestic.

The thought of his father's failing health came back to his mind. "But it is really singular," he said to himself, "my father is only thirty-five years older than I am; thirty-five and twenty-three make only fifty-eight!" His eyes, fixed on the windows of the bedroom of that stern man who had never loved him, filled with tears. He shivered, and a sudden chill ran through his veins when he thought he saw his father crossing a terrace planted with orange-trees which was on a level with his room; but it was only one of the servants. Close underneath the *campanile* a number of girls dressed in white and split up into different bands were occupied in tracing patterns with red, blue and yellow flowers on the pavement of the streets through which the procession was to pass. But there was a spectacle which spoke with a more living voice to Fabrizio's soul: from the *campanile* his gaze shot down to the two branches of the lake, at a distance of several leagues, and this sublime view soon made him forget all the others; it awakened in him the most lofty sentiments. All the memories of his childhood came crowding to besiege his mind; and this day which he spent imprisoned in a belfry was perhaps one of the happiest days of his life.

Happiness carried him to an exaltation of mind quite foreign to his nature; he considered the incidents of life, he, still so young, as if already he had arrived at its farthest goal. "I must admit that, since I came to Parma," he said to himself at length after several hours of delicious musings, "I have known no tranquil and perfect joy such as I used to find at Naples in galloping over the roads of Vomero or pacing the shores of Miseno. All the complicated interests of that nasty little court have made me nasty also. . . . I even believe that it would be a sorry happiness for me to humiliate my enemies if I had any; but I have no enemy. . . . Stop a moment!" he suddenly interjected, "I have got an enemy, Giletti. . . . And here is a curious thing," he said to himself, "the pleasure that I should feel in seeing such an ugly fellow go to all the devils in hell has survived the very slight fancy that I had for little Marietta. . . . She does not come within a mile of the Duchessa d'A——, to whom I was obliged to make love at Naples, after I had told her that I was in love with her. Good God, how bored I have been during the long assignations which that fair Duchessa used to accord me; never anything like that in the tumbledown bedroom, serving as a kitchen as well, in which little Marietta received me twice, and for two minutes on each occasion.

"Oh, good God, what on earth can those people have to eat? They make one pity them! . . . I ought to have settled on her and the *mammaccia* a pension of three beefsteaks, payable daily. . . . Little Marietta," he went on, "used to distract me from the evil thoughts which the proximity of that court put in my mind.

"I should perhaps have done well to adopt the *caffè* life, as the Duchessa said; she seemed to incline in that direction, and she has far more intelligence than I. Thanks to her generosity, or indeed merely with that pension of 4,000 francs and that fund of 40,000 invested at Lyons, which my mother intends for me, I should always have a horse and a few scudi to spend on digging and collecting a cabinet. Since it appears that I am not to know the taste of love, there will always be those other interests to be my great sources of happiness; I should like, before I die, to go back to visit the battlefield of Waterloo and try to identify the meadow where I was so neatly lifted from my horse and left sitting on the ground. That pilgrimage accomplished, I should return constantly to this sublime lake; nothing else as beautiful is to be seen in the world, for my heart at least. Why go so far afield in search of happiness? It is there, beneath my eyes!

"Ah," said Fabrizio to himself, "there is this objection: the police drive me away from the Lake of Como, but I am younger than the people who are setting those police on my track. Here," he added with a smile, "I should certainly not find a Duchessa d'A——, but I should find one of those little girls down there who are strewing flowers on the pavement, and, to tell the truth, I should care for her just as much. Hypocrisy freezes me, even in love, and our great ladies aim at effects that are too sublime. Napoleon has given them new ideas as to conduct and constancy.

"The devil!" he suddenly exclaimed, drawing back his head from the window, as though he had been afraid of being recognised despite the screen of the enormous wooden shutter which protected the bells from rain, "here comes a troop of police in full dress." And indeed, ten policemen, of whom four were non-commissioned officers, had come into sight at the top of the village street. The serjeant distributed them at intervals of a hundred yards along the course which the procession was to take. "Everyone knows me here; if they see me, I shall make but one bound from the shores of the Lake of Como to the Spielberg, where they will fasten to each of my legs a chain weighing a hundred and ten pounds: and what a grief for the Duchessa!"

It took Fabrizio two or three minutes to realise that, for one thing, he was stationed at a height of more than eighty feet, that the place in which he stood was comparatively dark, that the eyes of the people who might be looking up at him were blinded by a dazzling sun, in addition to which they were walking about, their eyes wide open, in streets all the houses of which had just been whitewashed with lime, in honour of the *festa* of San Giovita. Despite all these clear and obvious reasons, Fabrizio's Italian nature would not have been in a state, from that moment, to enjoy any pleasure in the spectacle, had he not interposed between himself and the policemen a strip of old cloth which he nailed to the frame of the window, piercing a couple of holes in it for his eyes.

The bells had been making the air throb for ten minutes, the procession was coming out of the church, the *mortaretti* started to bang. Fabrizio turned his head and recognised that little terrace, adorned with a parapet and overlooking the lake, where so often, when he was a boy, he had risked his life to watch the *mortaretti* go off between his legs, with the result that on the mornings of public holidays his mother liked to see him by her side.

It should be explained that the *mortaretti* (or little mortars) are nothing else than gun-barrels which are sawn through so as to leave them only four inches long; that is why the peasants greedily collect all the gun-barrels which, since 1796, European policy has been sowing broadcast over the plains of Lombardy. Once they have been reduced to a length of four inches, these little guns are loaded to the muzzle, they are planted in the ground in a vertical position, and a train of powder is laid from one to the next; they are drawn up in three lines like a battalion, and to the number of two or three hundred, in some suitable emplacement near the route along which the procession is to pass. When the Blessed Sacrament approaches, a match is put to the train of powder, and then begins a running fire of sharp explosions, utterly irregular and quite ridiculous; the women are wild with joy. Nothing is so gay as the sound of these *mortaretti*, heard at a distance on the lake and softened by the rocking of the water; this curious sound, which had so often been the delight of his boyhood, banished the somewhat too solemn thoughts by which our hero was being besieged; he went to find the Priore's big astronomical telescope, and recognised the majority of the men and women who were following the procession. A number of charming little girls, whom Fabrizio had last seen at the age of eleven or twelve, were now superb women in the full flower of the most vigorous youth; they made our hero's courage revive, and to speak to them he would readily have braved the police.

After the procession had passed and had re-entered the church by a side door which was out of Fabrizio's sight, the heat soon became intense even up in the belfry; the inhabitants returned to their homes, and a great silence fell upon the village. Several boats took on board loads of *contadini* returning to Bellagio, Menaggio and other villages situated on the lake; Fabrizio could distinguish the sound of each stroke of the oars: so simple a detail as this sent him into an ecstasy; his present joy was composed of all the unhappiness, all the irritation that he found in the complicated life of a court. How happy he would have been at this moment to be sailing for a league over that beautiful lake which looked so calm and reflected so clearly the depth of the sky above! He heard the door at the foot of the *campanile* opened: it was the Priore's old servant who brought in a great hamper, and he had all the difficulty in the world in restraining himself from speaking to her. "She is almost as fond of me as of her master," he said to himself, "and besides, I am leaving to-night at nine o'clock; would she not keep the oath of secrecy I should make her swear, if only for a few hours? But," Fabrizio reminded himself, "I should be vexing my friend! I might get him into trouble with the police!" and he let Ghita go without speaking to her. He made an excellent dinner, then settled himself down to sleep for a few minutes: he did not awake until half-past eight in the evening; the Priore Blanès was shaking him by the arm; it was dark.

Blanès was extremely tired, and looked fifty years older than the night before. He said nothing more about serious matters, sitting in his wooden armchair. "Embrace me," he said to Fabrizio. He clasped him again and again in his arms. "Death," he said at last, "which is coming to put an end to this long life, will have nothing about it so painful as this separation. I have a purse which I shall leave in Ghita's custody, with orders to draw on it for her own needs, but to hand over to you what is left, should you ever come to ask for it. I know her; after those instructions, she is capable, from economy on your behalf, of not buying meat four times in the year, if you do not give her quite definite orders. You may yourself be reduced to penury, and the obol of your aged friend will be of service to you. Expect nothing from your brother but atrocious behaviour, and try to earn money by some work which will make you useful to society. I foresee strange storms; perhaps, in fifty years' time, the world will have no more room for idlers! Your mother and aunt may fail you, your sisters will have to obey their husbands. . . . Away with you, away with you, fly!" exclaimed Blanès urgently; he had just heard a little sound in the clock which warned him that ten was about to strike, and he would not even allow Fabrizio to give him a farewell embrace.

"Hurry, hurry!" he cried to him; "it will take you at least a minute to get down the stair; take care not to fall, that would be a terrible omen." Fabrizio dashed down the staircase and emerging on to the *piazza* began to run. He had scarcely arrived opposite his father's castle when the bell sounded ten times; each stroke reverberated in his bosom, where it left a singular sense of disturbance. He stopped to think, or rather to give himself up to the passionate feelings inspired in him by the contemplation of that majestic edifice which he had judged so coldly the night before. He was recalled from his musings by the sound of footsteps; he looked up and found himself surrounded by four constables. He had a brace of excellent pistols, the priming of which he had renewed while he dined; the slight sound that he made in cocking them attracted the attention of one of the constables, and he was within an inch of being arrested. He saw the danger he ran, and decided to fire the first shot; he would be justified in doing so, for this was the sole method open to him of resisting four well-armed men. Fortunately, the constables, who were going round to clear the *osteria*, had not shown themselves altogether irresponsive to the hospitality that they had received in several of those sociable resorts; they did not make up their minds quickly enough to do their duty. Fabrizio took to his heels and ran. The constables went a few yards, running also, and shouting "Stop! Stop!" then everything relapsed into silence. After every three hundred yards Fabrizio halted to recover his breath. "The sound of my pistols nearly made me get caught; this is just the sort of thing that would make the Duchessa tell me, should it ever be granted me to see her lovely eyes again, that my mind finds pleasure in contemplating what is going to happen in ten years' time, and forgets to look out for what is actually happening beneath my nose."

Fabrizio shuddered at the thought of the danger he had

just escaped; he increased his pace, and presently found himself impelled to run, which was not over-prudent, as it attracted the attention of several *contadini* who were going back to their homes. He could not bring himself to stop until he had reached the mountain, more than a league from Grianta, and even when he had stopped, he broke into a cold sweat at the thought of the Spielberg.

"There's a fine fright!" he said aloud: on hearing the sound of this word, he was almost tempted to feel ashamed. "But does not my aunt tell me that the thing I most need is to learn to make allowances for myself? I am always comparing myself with a model of perfection, which cannot exist. Very well, I forgive myself my fright, for, from another point of view, I was quite prepared to defend my liberty, and certainly all four of them would not have remained on their feet to carry me off to prison. What I am doing at this moment," he went on, "is not military; instead of retiring rapidly, after having attained my object, and perhaps given the alarm to my enemies, I am amusing myself with a fancy more ridiculous perhaps than all the good Priore's predictions."

For indeed, instead of retiring along the shortest line, and gaining the shore of Lake Maggiore, where his boat was awaiting him, he made an enormous circuit to go and visit *his tree*. The reader may perhaps remember the love that Fabrizio bore for a chestnut tree planted by his mother twenty-three years earlier. "It would be quite worthy of my brother," he said to himself, "to have had the tree cut down; but those creatures are incapable of delicate shades of feeling; he will never have thought of it. And besides, that would not be a bad augury," he added with firmness. Two hours later he was shocked by what he saw; mischief-makers or a storm had broken one of the main branches of the young tree, which hung down withered; Fabrizio cut it off reverently, using his dagger, and smoothed the cut carefully, so that the rain should not get inside the trunk. Then, although time was highly precious to him, for day was about to break, he spent a good hour in turning the soil round his dear tree. All these acts of folly accomplished, he went rapidly on his way towards Lake Maggiore. All things considered, he was not at all sad; the tree was coming on well, was more vigorous than ever, and in five years had almost doubled in height. The branch was only an accident of no consequence; once it had been cut off, it did no more harm to the tree, which indeed would grow all the better if its spread began higher from the ground.

Fabrizio had not gone a league when a dazzling band of white indicated to the east the peaks of the Resegon di Lec, a mountain famous throughout the district. The road which he was following became thronged with *contadini;* but, instead of adopting military tactics, Fabrizio let himself be melted by the sublime or touching aspect of these forests in the neighbourhood of Lake Como. They are perhaps the finest in the world; I do not mean to say those that bring in most *new mon*ey, as the Swiss would say, but those that speak most eloquently to the soul. To listen to this language in the position in which Fabrizio found himself, an object for the attentions of the gentlemen of the Lombardo-Venetian police, was really childish. "I am half a league from the frontier," he reminded himself at length, "I am going to meet *doganieri* and constables making their morning rounds: this coat of fine cloth will look suspicious, they will ask me for my passport; now that passport is inscribed at full length with my name, which is marked down for prison; so here I am under the regrettable necessity of committing a murder. If, as is usual, the police are going about in pairs, I cannot wait quietly to fire until one of them tries to take me by the collar; he has only to clutch me for a moment while he falls, and off I go to the Spielberg." Fabrizio, horrified most of all by the necessity of firing first, possibly on an old soldier who had served under his uncle, Conte Pietranera, ran to hide himself in the hollow trunk of an enormous chestnut; he was renewing the priming of his pistols, when he heard a man coming towards him through the wood, singing very well a delicious air from *Mercadante,* which was popular at that time in Lombardy.

"There is a good omen for me," he said to himself. This air, to which he listened religiously, took from him the little spark of anger which was finding its way into his reasonings. He scrutinised the high road carefully, in both directions, and saw no one: "The singer must be coming along some side road," he said to himself. Almost at that moment, he saw a footman, very neatly dressed in the English style and mounted on a hack, who was coming towards him at a walk, leading a fine thoroughbred, which however was perhaps a little too thin.

"Ah! If I reasoned like Conte Mosca," thought Fabrizio, "when he assures me that the risks a man runs are always

the measure of his rights over his neighbours, I should blow
out this servant's brains with a pistol-shot, and, once I was
mounted on the thin horse, I should laugh aloud at all the
police in the world. As soon as I was safely in Parma, I
should send money to the man, or to his widow . . . but it
would be a horrible thing to do!"

CHAPTER TEN

MORALISING THUS, Fabrizio sprang down on to the high road which runs from Lombardy into Switzerland: at this point, it is fully four or five feet below the level of the forest. "If my man takes fright," he said to himself, "he will go off at a gallop, and I shall be stranded here looking the picture of a fool." At this moment he found himself only ten yards from the footman, who had stopped singing: Fabrizio could see in his eyes that he was frightened, he was perhaps going to turn his horses. Still without having come to any decision, Fabrizio made a bound, and seized the thin horse by the bridle.

"My friend," he said to the footman, "I am not an ordinary thief, for I am going to begin by giving you twenty francs, but I am obliged to borrow your horse; I shall be killed if I don't get away pretty quickly. I have the four Riva brothers on my heels, those great hunters whom you probably know; they caught me just now in their sister's bedroom, I jumped out of the window, and here I am. They dashed out into the forest with their dogs and guns. I hid myself in that big hollow chestnut because I saw one of them cross the road; their dogs will track me down. I am going to mount your horse and gallop a league beyond Como; I am going to Milan to throw myself at the Viceroy's feet. I shall leave your horse at the post-house with two napoleons for yourself, if you consent with good grace. If you offer the slightest resistance, I shall kill you with these pistols you see here. If, after I have gone, you set the police on my track, my cousin, the gallant Conte Alari, Equerry to the Emperor, will take good care to break your bones for you."

Fabrizio invented the substance of this speech as he went on, uttering it in a wholly pacific tone.

"As far as that goes," he went on with a laugh, "my name is no secret; I am the Marchesino Ascanio del Dongo, my castle is quite close to here, at Grianta. Damn you!" he cried, raising his voice, "will you let go the horse!" The servant, stupefied, never breathed a word. Fabrizio transferred the pistol to his left hand, seized the bridle which the other dropped, sprang into the saddle, and made off at a canter. When he had gone three hundred yards, it occurred to him that he had forgotten to give the man the twenty francs he had promised him; he stopped; there was still no one upon the road but the footman, who was following him at a gallop; he signalled to him with his handkerchief to come on, and when he judged him to be fifty yards off, flung a handful of small change on to the road and went on again. From a distance he looked and saw the footman gathering up the money. "There is a truly reasonable man," Fabrizio said to himself with a laugh, "not an unnecessary word." He proceeded rapidly southwards, halted, towards midday, at a lonely house, and took the road again a few hours later. At two o'clock in the morning he was on the shore of Lake Maggiore; he soon caught sight of his boat, which was tacking to and fro; at the agreed signal, it made for the shore. He could see no *contadino* to whom to hand over the horse, so he gave the noble animal its liberty, and three hours later was at Belgirate. There, finding himself on friendly soil, he took a little rest; he was exceedingly joyful, everything had proved a complete success. Dare we indicate the true causes of his joy? His tree showed a superb growth, and his soul had been refreshed by the deep affection which he had found in the arms of Priore Blanès. "Does he really believe," he asked himself, "in all the predictions he has made me? Or was he, since my brother has given me the reputation of a Jacobin, a man without law or honour, sticking at nothing, was he seeking simply to bind me not to yield to the temptation to break the head of some animal who may have done me a bad turn?" Two days later, Fabrizio was at Parma, where he greatly amused the Duchessa and the Conte, when he related to them, with the utmost exactitude, which he always observed, the whole story of his travels.

On his arrival, Fabrizio found the porter and all the servants of the *palazzo* Sanseverina wearing the tokens of the deepest mourning.

"Whom have we lost?" he inquired of the Duchessa.

"That excellent man whom people called my husband has just died at Baden. He has left me this *palazzo*, that had been arranged beforehand, but as a sign of good fellowship he has added a legacy of 300,000 francs, which embarrasses me greatly; I have no desire to surrender it to his niece, the Marchesa Raversi, who plays the most damnable tricks on me every day. You are interested in art, you must find me some good sculptor; I shall erect a tomb to the Duca which will cost 300,000 francs." The Conte began telling ancedotes about the Raversi.

"I have tried to win her by kindness, but all in vain," said the Duchessa. "As for the Duca's nephews, I have made them all colonels or generals. In return for which, not a month passes without their sending me some abominable anonymous letter; I have been obliged to engage a secretary simply to read letters of that sort."

"And these anonymous letters are their mildest offence," the Conte joined in; "they make a regular business of inventing infamous accusations. A score of times I could have brought the whole gang before the courts, and Your Excellency may imagine," he went on, addressing Fabrizio, "whether my good judges would have convicted them."

"Ah, well, that is what spoils it all for me," replied Fabrizio with a simplicity which was quite refreshing at court; "I should prefer to see them sentenced by magistrates judging according to their conscience."

"You would oblige me greatly, since you are travelling with a view to gaining instruction, if you would give me the addresses of such magistrates; I shall write to them before I go to bed."

"If I were Minister, this absence of judges who were honest men would wound my self-respect."

"But it seems to me," said the Conte, "that Your Excellency, who is so fond of the French, and did indeed once lend them the aid of his invincible arm, is forgetting for the moment one of their great maxims: 'It is better to kill the devil than to let the devil kill you.' I should like to see how you would govern these burning souls, who read every day the *History of the Revolution in France,* with judges who would acquit the people whom I accuse. They would reach the point of not convicting the most obviously guilty scoundrels, and would fancy themselves Brutuses. But I should like to pick a crow with you; does not your delicate soul feel a touch of remorse at the thought of that fine (though perhaps a little too thin) horse which you have just abandoned on the shore of Lake Maggiore?"

"I fully intend," said Fabrizio, with the utmost seriousness, "to send whatever is necessary to the owner of the horse to recompense him for the cost of advertising and any other expenses which he may be made to incur by the *contadini* who may have found it; I shall study the Milan newspaper most carefully to find the announcement of a missing horse; I know the description of that one very well."

"He is truly *primitive*," said the Conte to the Duchessa. "And where would Your Excellency be now," he went on with a smile, "if, while he was galloping away hell for leather on this borrowed horse, it had taken it into its head to make a false step? You would be in the Spielberg, my dear young nephew, and all my authority would barely have managed to secure the reduction by thirty pounds of the weight of the chain attached to each of your legs. You would have had some ten years to spend in that pleasure-resort; perhaps your legs would have become swollen and gangrened, then they would have cut them clean off."

"Oh, for pity's sake, don't go any farther with so sad a romance!" cried the Duchessa, with tears in her eyes. "Here he is back again. . . ."

"And I am more delighted than you, you may well believe," replied the Minister with great seriousness, "but after all why did not this cruel boy come to me for a passport in a suitable name, since he was anxious to penetrate into Lombardy? On the first news of his arrest, I should have set off for Milan, and the friends I have in those parts would have obligingly shut their eyes and pretended to believe that their police had arrested a subject of the Prince of Parma. The story of your adventures is charming, amusing, I readily agree," the Conte went on, adopting a less sinister tone; "your rush from the wood on to the high road quite thrills me; but, between ourselves, since this servant held your life in his hands, you had the right to take his. We are about to arrange a brilliant future for Your Excellency; at least, the Signora here orders me to do so, and I do not believe that my greatest enemies can accuse me of having ever disobeyed her commands. What a bitter grief for her and for myself if, in this sort of steeplechase which you appear to have been riding on this thin horse, he had made a false step! It would almost have been better," the Conte added, "if the horse had broken your neck for you."

"You are very tragic this evening, my friend," said the Duchessa, quite overcome.

"That is because we are surrounded by tragic events," replied the Conte, also with emotion; "we are not in France, where everything ends in song, or in imprisonment for a year or two, and really it is wrong of me to speak of all this to you in a jocular tone. Well, now, my young nephew, just suppose that I find a chance to make you a Bishop, for really I cannot begin with the Archbishopric of Parma, as is desired, most reasonably, by the Signora Duchessa here present; in that Bishopric, where you will be far removed from our sage counsels, just tell us roughly what your policy will be?"

"To kill the devil rather than let him kill me, in the admirable words of my friends the French," replied Fabrizio with blazing eyes; "to keep, by every means in my power, including pistols, the position you will have secured for me. I have read in the del Dongo genealogy the story of that ancestor of ours who built the castle of Grianta. Towards the end of his life, his good friend Galeazzo, Duke of Milan, sent him to visit a fortress on our lake; they were afraid of another invasion by the Swiss. 'I must just write a few civil words to the governor,' the Duke of Milan said to him as he was sending him off. He wrote and handed our ancestor a note of a couple of lines; then he asked for it back to seal it. 'It will be more polite,' the Prince explained. Vespasiano del Dongo started off, but, as he was sailing over the lake, an old Greek tale came into his mind, for he was a man of learning; he opened his liege lord's letter and found inside an order addressed to the governor of the castle to put him to death as soon as he should arrive. The Sforza, too much intent on the trick he was playing our ancestor, had left a space between the end of the letter and his signature; Vespasiano del Dongo wrote in this space an order proclaiming himself Governor General of all the castles on the lake, and tore off the original letter. Arriving at the fort, where his authority was duly acknowledged, he flung the commandant down a well, declared war on the Sforza, and after a few years exchanged his fortress for those vast estates which have made the fortune of every branch of our family, and one day will bring in to me, personally, an income of four thousand lire."

"You talk like an academician," exclaimed the Conte, laughing; "that was a bold stroke with a vengeance; but it is only once in ten years that one has a chance to do anything so sensational. A creature who is half an idiot, but who keeps a sharp look-out, and acts prudently all his life, often enjoys the pleasure of triumphing over men of imagination. It was by a foolish error of imagination that Napoleon was led to surrender to the prudent *John Bull,* instead of seeking to conquer America. John Bull, in his counting-house, had a hearty laugh at his letter in which he quotes Themistocles. In all ages, the base Sancho Panza triumphs, you will find, in the long run, over the sublime Don Quixote. If you are willing to agree to do nothing extraordinary, I have no doubt that you will be a highly respected, if not a highly respectable Bishop. In any case, what I said just now holds good: Your Excellency acted with great levity in the affair of the horse; he was within a finger's breadth of perpetual imprisonment."

This statement made Fabrizio shudder. He remained plunged in a profound astonishment. "Was that," he wondered, "the prison with which I am threatened? Is that the crime which I was not to commit?" The predictions of Blanès, which as prophecies he utterly derided, assumed in his eyes all the importance of authentic forecasts.

"Why, what is the matter with you?" the Duchessa asked him, in surprise; "the Conte has plunged you in a sea of dark thoughts."

"I am illuminated by a new truth, and, instead of revolting against it, my mind adopts it. It is true, I passed very near to an endless imprisonment! But that footman looked so nice in his English jacket! It would have been such a pity to kill him!"

The Minister was enchanted with his little air of wisdom.

"He is excellent in every respect," he said, with his eyes on the Duchessa. "I may tell you, my friend, that you have made a conquest, and one that is perhaps the most desirable of all."

"Ah!" thought Fabrizio, "now for some joke about little Marietta." He was mistaken; the Conte went on to say:

"Your *Gospel* simplicity has won the heart of our venerable Archbishop, Father Landriani. One of these days we are going to make a Grand Vicar of you, and the charming part of the whole joke is that the three existing Grand Vicars, all most deserving men, workers, two of whom, I fancy, were Grand Vicars before you were born, will demand, in a finely worded letter addressed to their Archbishop, that you shall rank first among them. These gentlemen base their plea in the first place upon your virtues, and also upon the fact that you are the great-nephew of the famous Archbishop Ascanio del Dongo. When I learned the respect that they felt for your virtues, I immediately made the senior Vicar General's nephew a captain; he had been a lieutenant ever since the siege of Tarragona by Marshal Suchet."

"Go right away now, dressed as you are, and pay a friendly visit to your Archbishop!" exclaimed the Duchessa. "Tell him about your sister's wedding; when he hears that she is to be a Duchessa, he will think you more apostolic than ever. But, remember, you know nothing of what the Conte has just told you about your future promotion."

Fabrizio hastened to the archiepiscopal palace; there he shewed himself simple and modest, a tone which he assumed only too easily; whereas it required an effort for him to play the great gentleman. As he listened to the somewhat prolix stories of Monsignor Landriani, he was saying to himself: "Ought I to have fired my pistol at the footman who was leading the thin horse?" His reason said to him: "Yes," but his heart could not accustom itself to the bleeding image of the handsome young man, falling from his horse, all disfigured.

"That prison in which I should have been swallowed up, if the horse had stumbled, was that the prison with which I was threatened by all those forecasts?"

This question was of the utmost importance to him, and the Archbishop was gratified by his air of profound attention.

CHAPTER ELEVEN

O N LEAVING the Archbishop's Palace, Fabrizio hastened to see little Marietta; he could hear from the street the loud voice of Giletti, who had sent out for wine and was regaling himself with his friends the prompter and the candle-snuffers. The *mammaccia,* who played the part of mother, came alone in answer to his signal.

"A lot has happened since you were here," she cried; "two or three of our actors are accused of having celebrated the great Napoleon's *festa* with an orgy, and our poor company, which they say is Jacobin, has been ordered to leave the States of Parma, and *evviva Napoleone!* But the Minister has had a finger in that pie, they say. One thing certain is that Giletti has got money, I don't know how much, but I've seen him with a fistful of scudi. Marietta has had five scudi from our manager to pay for the journey to Mantua and Venice, and I have had one. She is still in love with you, but Giletti frightens her; three days ago, at the last performance we gave, he absolutely wanted to kill her; he dealt her two proper blows, and, what was abominable of him, tore her blue shawl. If you would care to give her a blue shawl, you would be a very good boy, and we can say that we won it in a lottery. The drum-major of the *carabinieri* is giving an assault-at-arms to-morrow, you will find the hour posted up at all the street corners. Come and see us; if he has gone to the assault, and we have any reason to hope that he will stay away for some time, I shall be at the window, and I shall give you a signal to come up. Try to bring us something really nice, and Marietta will be madly in love with you."

As he made his way down the winding staircase of this foul rookery, Fabrizio was filled with compunction. "I have not altered in the least," he said to himself; "all the fine resolutions I made on the shore of our lake, when I looked at life with so philosophic an eye, have gone to the winds. My mind has lost its normal balance; the whole thing was a dream, and vanishes before the stern reality. Now would be the time for action," he told himself as he entered the *palazzo* Sanseverina about eleven o'clock that evening. But it was in vain that he sought in his heart for the courage to speak with that sublime sincerity which had seemed to him so easy, the night he spent by the shore of the Lake of Como. "I am going to vex the person whom I love best in the world; if I speak, I shall simply seem to be jesting in the worst of taste; I am not worth anything, really, except in certain moments of exaltation."

"The Conte has behaved admirably towards me," he said to the Duchessa, after he had given her an account of his visit to the Archbishop's Palace; "I appreciate his conduct all the more, in that I think I am right in saying that personally I have made only a very moderate impression on him: my behaviour towards him ought therefore to be strictly correct. He has his excavations at Sanguigna, about which he is still madly keen, if one is to judge, that is, by his expedition the day before yesterday: he went twelve leagues at a gallop in order to spend a couple of hours with his workmen. If they find fragments of statues in the ancient temple, the foundations of which he has just laid bare, he is afraid of their being stolen; I should like to propose to him that I should go and spend a night or two at Sanguigna. To-morrow, about five, I have to see the Archbishop again; I can start in the evening and take advantage of the cool night air for the journey."

The Duchessa did not at first reply.

"One would think you were seeking excuses for staying away from me," she said to him at length with extreme affection: "No sooner do you come back from Belgirate than you find a reason for going off again."

"Here is a fine opportunity for speaking," thought Fabrizio. "But by the lake I was a trifle mad; I did not realise, in my enthusiasm for sincerity, that my compliment ended in an impertinence. It was a question of saying: 'I love you with the most devoted friendship, etc., etc., but my heart is not susceptible to love.' Is not that as much as to say: 'I see that you are in love with me: but take care, I cannot pay you back in the same coin.' If it is love that she feels, the Duchessa may be annoyed at its being guessed, and she will be revolted by my impudence if all that she feels for me is friendship pure and simple . . . and that is one of the offences people never forgive."

While he weighed these important thoughts in his mind, Fabrizio, quite unconsciously, was pacing up and down the drawing-room with the grave air, full of dignity, of a man who sees disaster staring him in the face.

The Duchessa gazed at him with admiration; this was no longer the child she had seen come into the world, this was no longer the nephew always ready to obey her; this was a serious man, a man whom it would be delicious to make fall in love with her. She rose from the ottoman on which she was sitting, and, flinging herself into his arms in a transport of emotion:

"So you want to run away from me?" she asked him.

"No," he replied with the air of a Roman Emperor, "but I want to act wisely."

This speech was capable of several interpretations; Fabrizio did not feel that he had the courage to go any farther and to run the risk of wounding this adorable woman. He was too young, too susceptible to sudden emotion; his brain could not supply him with any elegant turn of speech to give expression to what he wished to say. By a natural transport, and in defiance of all reason, he took this charming woman in his arms and smothered her in kisses. At that moment the Conte's carriage could be heard coming into the courtyard, and almost immediately the Conte himself entered the room; he seemed greatly moved.

"You inspire very singular passions," he said to Fabrizio, who stood still, almost dumbfounded by this remark.

"The Archbishop had this evening the audience which His Serene Highness grants him every Thursday; the Prince has just been telling me that the Archbishop, who seemed greatly troubled, began with a set speech, learned by heart, and extremely clever, of which at first the Prince could understand nothing at all. Landriani ended by declaring that it was important for the Church in Parma that *Monsignor* Fabrizio del Dongo should be appointed his First Vicar General, and, in addition, as soon as he should have completed his twenty-fourth year, his Coadjutor *with eventual succession*.

"The last clause alarmed me, I must admit," said the Conte: "it is going a little too fast, and I was afraid of an outburst from the Prince; but he looked at me with a smile, and said to me in French: *'Ce sont là de vos coups, monsieur!'*

" 'I can take my oath, before God and before Your Highness,' I exclaimed with all the unction possible, 'that I knew absolutely nothing about the words *eventual succession.*' Then I told him the truth, what in fact we were discussing together here a few hours ago; I added, impulsively, that, so far as the future was concerned, I should regard myself as most bounteously rewarded with His Highness's favour if he would deign to allow me a minor Bishopric to begin with. The Prince must have believed me, for he thought fit to be gracious; he said to me with the greatest possible simplicity: 'This is an official matter between the Archbishop and myself; you do not come into it at all; the worthy man delivered me a kind of report, of great length and tedious to a degree, at the end of which he came to an official proposal; I answered him very coldly that the person in question was extremely young, and, moreover, a very recent arrival at my court, that I should almost be giving the impression that I was honouring a bill of exchange drawn upon me by the Emperor, in giving the prospect of so high a dignity to the son of one of the principal officers of his Lombardo-Venetian Kingdom. The Archbishop protested that no recommendation of that sort had been made. That was a pretty stupid thing to say to *me.* I was surprised to hear it come from a man of his experience; but he always loses his head when he speaks to me, and this evening he was more troubled than ever, which gave me the idea that he was passionately anxious to secure the appointment. I told him that I knew better than he that there had been no recommendation from any high quarter in favour of this del Dongo, that nobody at my court denied his capacity, that they did not speak at all too badly of his morals, but that I was afraid of his being liable to *enthusiasm,* and that I had made it a rule never to promote to considerable positions fools of that sort, with whom a Prince can never be sure of anything. Then,' His Highness went on, 'I had to submit to a fresh tirade almost as long as the first; the Archbishop sang me the praises of the enthusiasm of the *Casa di Dio.* Clumsy fellow, I said to myself, you are going astray, you are endangering an appointment which was almost confirmed; you ought to have cut your speech short and thanked me effusively. Not a bit of it; he continued his homily with a ridiculous intrepidity; I had to think of a reply which would not be too unfavourable to young del Dongo; I found one, and by no means a bad one, as you shall judge for yourself. Monsignore, I said to him, Pius VII was a great Pope and a great saint: among all the Sovereigns, he alone dared to say *No* to the tyrant who saw Europe at his feet: very well, he was liable to enthusiasm, which led him, when he was Bishop of Imola, to write that famous Pastoral of the *Citizen-Cardinal* Chiaramonti, in support of the Cisalpine Republic.

" 'My poor Archbishop was left stupefied, and, to complete his stupefaction, I said to him with a very serious air: Good-bye, Monsignore, I shall take twenty-four hours to consider your proposal. The poor man added various supplications, by no means well expressed and distinctly inopportune after the word *Good-bye* had been uttered by me. Now, Conte Mosca della Rovere, I charge you to inform the Duchessa that I have no wish to delay for twenty-four hours a decision which may be agreeable to her; sit down there and write the Archbishop the letter of approval which will bring the whole matter to an end.' I wrote the letter, he signed it, and said to me: 'Take it, immediately, to the Duchessa.' Here, Signora, is the letter, and it is this that has given me an excuse for taking the pleasure of seeing you again this evening."

The Duchessa read the letter with rapture. While the Conte was telling his long story, Fabrizio had had time to collect himself: he shewed no sign of astonishment at the incident, he took the whole thing like a true nobleman who naturally has always supposed himself entitled to these extraordinary advancements, these strokes of fortune which would unhinge a plebeian mind; he spoke of his gratitude, but in polished terms, and ended by saying to the Conte:

"A good courtier ought to flatter the ruling passion; yesterday you expressed the fear that your workmen at Sanguigna might steal any fragments of ancient sculpture they brought to light; I am extremely fond of excavation, myself; with your kind permission, I will go to superintend the workmen. To-morrow evening, after suitably expressing my thanks at the Palace and to the Archbishop, I shall start for Sanguigna."

"But can you guess," the Duchessa asked the Conte, "what can have given rise to this sudden passion on our good Archbishop's part for Fabrizio?"

"I have no need to guess; the Grand Vicar whose nephew I made a captain said to me yesterday: 'Father Landriani

starts from this absolute principle, that the titular is superior
to the coadjutor, and is beside himself with joy at the
prospect of having a del Dongo under his orders, and of
having done him a service.' Everything that can draw attention to Fabrizio's noble birth adds to his secret happiness:
that he should have a man like that as his aide-de-camp! In
the second place, Monsignor Fabrizio has taken his fancy,
he does not feel in the least shy before him; finally, he has
been nourishing for the last ten years a very vigorous hatred
of the Bishop of Piacenza, who openly boasts of his claim
to succeed him in the see of Parma, and is moreover the
son of a miller. It is with a view to this eventual succession
that the Bishop of Piacenza has formed very close relations
with the Marchesa Raversi, and now their intimacy is making
the Archbishop tremble for the success of his favourite
scheme, to have a del Dongo on his staff and to give him
orders."

Two days after this, at an early hour in the morning,
Fabrizio was directing the work of excavation at Sanguigna,
opposite Colorno (which is the Versailles of the Princes of
Parma); these excavations extended over the plain close to
the high road which runs from Parma to the bridge of
Casalmaggiore, the first town on Austrian territory. The workmen were intersecting the plain with a long trench, eight
feet deep and as narrow as possible: they were engaged in
seeking, along the old Roman Way, for the ruins of a second
temple which, according to local reports, had still been in
existence in the Middle Ages. Despite the Prince's orders,
many of the *contadini* looked with misgivings on these long
ditches running across their property. Whatever one might
say to them, they imagined that a search was being made
for treasure, and Fabrizio's presence was especially desirable
with a view to preventing any little unrest. He was by no
means bored, he followed the work with keen interest; from
time to time they turned up some medal, and he saw to it
that the workmen did not have time to arrange among themselves to make off with it.

The day was fine, the time about six o'clock in the morning: he had borrowed an old gun, single-barrelled; he shot
several larks; one of them, wounded, was falling upon the
high road. Fabrizio, as he went after it, caught sight, in the
distance, of a carriage that was coming from Parma and
making for the frontier at Casalmaggiore. He had just re-
loaded his gun when, the carriage which was extremely di-

lapidated coming towards him at a snail's pace, he recognised little Marietta; she had, on either side of her, the big bully Giletti and the old woman whom she passed off as her mother.

Giletti imagined that Fabrizio had posted himself there in the middle of the road, and with a gun in his hand, to insult him, and perhaps even to carry off his little Marietta. Like a man of valour, he jumped down from the carriage; he had in his left hand a large and very rusty pistol, and held in his right a sheathed sword, which he used when the limitations of the company obliged them to cast him for the part of some Marchese.

"Ha! Brigand!" he shouted, "I am very glad to find you here, a league from the frontier; I'll settle your account for you, right away; you're not protected here by your violet stockings."

Fabrizio was engaged in smiling at little Marietta, and barely heeding the jealous shouts of Giletti, when suddenly he saw within three feet of his chest the muzzle of the rusty pistol; he was just in time to aim a blow at it, using his gun as a club: the pistol went off, but did not hit anyone.

"Stop, will you, you ——," cried Giletti to the *vetturino;* at the same time he was quick enough to spring to the muzzle of his adversary's gun and to hold it so that it pointed away from his body; Fabrizio and he pulled at the gun, each with his whole strength. Giletti, who was a great deal the more vigorous of the two, placing one hand in front of the other, kept creeping forward towards the lock, and was on the point of snatching away the gun when Fabrizio, to prevent him from making use of it, fired. He had indeed seen, first, that the muzzle of the gun was more than three inches above Giletti's shoulder: still, the detonation occurred close to the man's ear. He was somewhat startled at first, but at once recovered himself:

"Oh, so you want to blow my head off, you scum! Just let me settle your reckoning." Giletti flung away the scabbard of his Marchese's sword, and fell upon Fabrizio with admirable swiftness. Our hero had no weapon, and gave himself up for lost.

He made for the carriage, which had stopped some ten yards beyond Giletti; he passed to the left of it, and, grasping the spring of the carriage in his hand, made a quick turn which brought him level with the door on the right-hand side, which stood open. Giletti, who had started off on his long legs and had not thought of checking himself by catching hold of the spring, went on for several paces in the same direction before he could stop. As Fabrizio passed by the open door, he heard Marietta whisper to him:

"Take care of yourself; he will kill you. Here!"

As he spoke, Fabrizio saw fall from the door a sort of big hunting knife, he stooped to pick it up, but as he did so was wounded in the shoulder by a blow from Giletti's sword. Fabrizio, on rising to his feet, found himself within six inches of Giletti, who struck him a furious blow in the face with the hilt of his sword; this blow was delivered with so much force that it completely took away Fabrizio's senses. At that moment, he was on the point of being killed. Fortunately for him, Giletti was still too near to be able to give him a thrust with the point. Fabrizio, when he came to himself, took to flight, and ran as fast as his legs would carry him; as he ran, he flung away the sheath of the hunting knife, and then, turning smartly round, found himself three paces ahead of Giletti, who was in pursuit. Giletti rushed on, Fabrizio struck at him with the point of his knife; Giletti was in time to beat up the knife a little with his sword, but he received the point of the blade full in the left cheek. He passed close by Fabrizio, who felt his thigh pierced: it was Giletti's knife, which he had found time to open. Fabrizio sprang to the right; he turned round, and at last the two adversaries found themselves at a proper fighting distance.

Giletti swore like a lost soul: "Ah! I shall slit your throat for you, you rascally priest," he kept on repeating every moment. Fabrizio was quite out of breath and could not speak: the blow on his face from the sword-hilt was causing him a great deal of pain, and his nose was bleeding abundantly. He parried a number of strokes with his hunting knife, and made a number of passes without knowing quite what he was doing. He had a vague feeling that he was at a public display. This idea had been suggested to him by the presence of the workmen, who, to the number of twenty-five or thirty, formed a circle round the combatants, but at a most respectful distance; for at every moment they saw them start to run, and spring upon one another.

The fight seemed to be slackening a little; the strokes no longer followed one another with the same rapidity, when Fabrizio said to himself: "To judge by the pain which I feel in my face, he must have disfigured me." In a spasm of rage at this idea, he leaped upon his enemy with the poi' of his hunting knife forwards. This point entered Giletti's chest on the right side and passed out near his left shoulder; at the same moment Giletti's sword passed right to the hilt through the upper part of Fabrizio's arm, but the blade glided under the skin and the wound was not serious.

Giletti had fallen; as Fabrizio advanced towards him, looking down at his left hand which was clasping a knife, that hand opened mechanically and let the weapon slip to the ground.

"The rascal is dead," said Fabrizio to himself. He looked at Giletti's face: blood was pouring from his mouth. Fabrizio ran to the carriage.

"Have you a mirror?" he cried to Marietta. Marietta stared at him, deadly pale, and made no answer. The old woman with great coolness opened a green workbag and handed Fabrizio a little mirror with a handle, no bigger than his hand. Fabrizio as he looked at himself felt his face carefully: "My eyes are all right," he said to himself, "that is something, at any rate." He examined his teeth; they were not broken at all. "Then how is it that I am in such pain?" he asked himself, half aloud.

The old woman answered him:

"It is because the top of your cheek has been crushed between the hilt of Giletti's sword and the bone we keep there. Your cheek is horribly swollen and blue: put leeches on it instantly, and it will be all right."

"Ah! Leeches, instantly!" said Fabrizio with a laugh, and recovered all his coolness. He saw that the workmen had gathered round Giletti, and were gazing at him, without venturing to touch him.

"Look after that man there!" he called to them; "take his coat off." He was going to say more, but, on raising his eyes, saw five or six men at a distance of three hundred yards on the high road, who were advancing on foot and at a measured pace towards the scene of action.

"They are police," he thought, "and, as there has been a man killed, they will arrest me, and I shall have the honour of making a solemn entry into the city of Parma. What a story for the Raversi's friends at court who detest my aunt!"

Immediately, with the rapidity of a flash of lightning, he flung to the open-mouthed workmen all the money that he had in his pockets and leaped into the carriage.

"Stop the police from pursuing me!" he cried to his men,

"and your fortunes are all made; tell them that I am innocent, that this man *attacked me and wanted to kill me*.

"And you," he said to the *vetturino*, "make your horses gallop; you shall have four golden napoleons if you cross the Po before these people behind can overtake me."

"Right you are," said the man; "but there's nothing to be afraid of: those men back there are on foot, and my little horses have only to trot to leave them properly in the lurch." So saying, he put the animals into a gallop.

Our hero was shocked to hear the word "afraid" used by the driver: the fact being that really he had been extremely afraid after the blow from the sword-hilt which had struck him in the face.

"We may run into people on horseback coming towards us," said the prudent *vetturino*, thinking of the four napoleons, "and the men who are following us may call out to them to stop us. . . ." Which meant, in other words: "Reload your weapons."

"Oh, how brave you are, my little Abate!" cried Marietta as she embraced Fabrizio. The old woman was looking out through the window of the carriage; presently she drew in her head.

"No one is following you, sir," she said to Fabrizio with great coolness; "and there is no one on the road in front of you. You know how particular the officials of the Austrian police are: if they see you arrive like this at a gallop, along the embankment by the Po, they will arrest you, no doubt about it."

Fabrizio looked out of the window.

"Trot," he said to the driver. "What passport have you?" he asked the old woman.

"Three, instead of one," she replied, "and they cost us four francs apiece; a dreadful thing, isn't it, for poor dramatic artists who are kept travelling all the year round! Here is the passport of Signor Giletti, dramatic artist: that will be you; here are our two passports, Marietta's and mine. But Giletti had all our money in his pocket; what is to become of us?"

"What had he?" Fabrizio asked.

"Forty good scudi of five francs," said the old woman.

"You mean six, and some small change," said Marietta with a smile: "I won't have my little Abate cheated."

"Isn't it only natural, sir," replied the old woman with great coolness, "that I should try to tap you for thirty-four

scudi? What are thirty-four scudi to you, and we—we have
lost our protector. Who is there now to find us lodgings, to
beat down prices with the *vetturini* when we are on the road,
and to put the fear of God into everyone? Giletti was not
beautiful, but he was most useful; and if the little girl there
hadn't been a fool, and fallen in love with you from the first,
Giletti would never have noticed anything, and you would
have given us good money. I can assure you that we are very
poor."

Fabrizio was touched; he took out his purse and gave
several napoleons to the old woman.

"You see," he said to her, "I have only fifteen left, so it is
no use your trying to pull my leg any more."

Little Marietta flung her arms round his neck, and the
old woman kissed his hands. The carriage was moving all this
time at a slow trot. When they saw in the distance the yellow
barriers striped with black which indicated the beginning of
Austrian territory, the old woman said to Fabrizio:

"You would do best to cross the frontier on foot with
Giletti's passport in your pocket; as for us, we shall stop for
a minute, on the excuse of making ourselves tidy. And besides, the *dogana* will want to look at our things. If you will
take my advice, you will go through Casalmaggiore at a careless stroll; even go into the *caffè* and drink a glass of
brandy; once you are past the village, put your best foot
foremost. The police are as sharp as the devil in an Austrian
country; they will pretty soon know there has been a man
killed; you are travelling with a passport which is not yours,
that is more than enough to get you two years in prison.
Make for the Po on your right after you leave the town, hire
a boat and get away to Ravenna or Ferrara; get clear of the
Austrian States as quickly as ever you can. With a couple of
louis you should be able to buy another passport from some
doganiere; it would be fatal to use this one; don't forget that
you have killed the man."

As he approached, on foot, the bridge of boats at Casalmaggiore, Fabrizio carefully reread Giletti's passport. Our
hero was in great fear, he recalled vividly all that Conte
Mosca had said to him about the danger involved in his
entering Austrian territory; well, two hundred yards ahead of
him he saw the terrible bridge which was about to give him
access to that country, the capital of which, in his eyes, was
the Spielberg. But what else was he to do? The Duchy of
Modena, which marches with the State of Parma on the

South, returned its fugitives in compliance with a special convention; the frontier of the State which extends over the mountains in the direction of Genoa was too far off; his misadventure would be known at Parma long before he could reach those mountains; there remained therefore nothing but the Austrian States on the left bank of the Po. Before there was time to write to the Austrian authorities asking them to arrest him, thirty-six hours, or even two days must elapse. All these considerations duly weighed, Fabrizio set a light with his cigar to his own passport; it was better for him, on Austrian soil, to be a vagabond than to be Fabrizio del Dongo, and it was possible that they might search him.

Quite apart from the very natural repugnance which he felt towards entrusting his life to the passport of the unfortunate Giletti, this document presented material difficulties. Fabrizio's height was, at the most, five feet five inches, and not five feet ten inches as was stated on the passport. He was not quite twenty-four, and looked younger. Giletti had been thirty-nine. We must confess that our hero paced for a good half-hour along a flood-barrier of the Po near the bridge of boats before making up his mind to go down on to it. "What should I advise anyone else to do in my place?" he asked himself finally. "Obviously, to cross: there is danger in remaining in the State of Parma; a constable may be sent in pursuit of the man who has killed another man, even in self-defence." Fabrizio went through his pocket, tore up all his papers, and kept literally nothing but his handkerchief and his cigar-case; it was important for him to curtail the examination which he would have to undergo. He thought of a terrible objection which might be raised, and to which he could find no satisfactory answer: he was going to say that his name was Giletti, and all his linen was marked F. D.

As we have seen, Fabrizio was one of those unfortunates who are tormented by their imagination; it is a characteristic fault of men of intelligence in Italy. A French soldier of equal or even inferior courage would have gone straight to the bridge and have crossed it without more ado, without thinking beforehand of any possible difficulties; but also he would have carried with him all his coolness, and Fabrizio was far from feeling cool when, at the end of the bridge, a little man, dressed in grey, said to him: "Go into the police office and shew your passport."

This office had dirty walls studded with nails from which hung the pipes and the soiled hats of the officials. The big

deal table behind which they were installed was spotted all
over with stains of ink and wine; two or three fat registers
bound in raw hide bore stains of all colours, and the margins
of the pages were black with finger-marks. On top of the
registers which were piled one on another lay three magnificent wreaths of laurel which had done duty a couple of
days before for one of the Emperor's festivals.

Fabrizio was impressed by all these details; they gave him
a tightening of the heart; this was the price he must pay for
the magnificent luxury, so cool and clean, that caught the
eye in his charming rooms in the *palazzo* Sanseverina. He
was obliged to enter this dirty office and to appear there as
an inferior; he was about to undergo an examination.

The official who stretched out a yellow hand to take his
passport was small and dark. He wore a brass pin in his
necktie. "This is an ill-tempered fellow," thought Fabrizio.
The gentleman seemed excessively surprised as he read the
passport, and his perusal of it lasted fully five minutes.

"You have met with an accident," he said to the stranger,
looking at his cheek.

"The *vetturino* flung us out over the embankment."

Then the silence was resumed, and the official cast sour
glances at the traveller.

"I see it now," Fabrizio said to himself, "he is going to inform me that he is sorry to have bad news to give me, and
that I am under arrest." All sorts of wild ideas surged
simultaneously into our hero's brain, which at this moment
was not very logical. For instance, he thought of escaping by
a door in the office which stood open. "I get rid of my coat, I
jump into the Po, and no doubt I shall be able to swim
across it. Anything is better than the Spielberg." The police
official was staring fixedly at him, while he calculated the
chances of success of this dash for safety; they furnished
two interesting types of the human countenance. The presence
of danger gives a touch of genius to the reasoning man,
places him, so to speak, above his own level: in the imagina-
tive man it inspires romances, bold, it is true, but frequently
absurd.

You ought to have seen the indignant air of our hero under
the searching eye of this police official, adorned with his
brass jewelry. "If I were to kill him," thought Fabrizio, "I
should be convicted of murder and sentenced to twenty
years in the galleys, or to death, which is a great deal less
terrible than the Spielberg with a chain weighing a hundred

and twenty pounds on each foot and nothing but eight ounces of bread to live on; and that lasts for twenty years; so that I should not get out until I was forty-four." Fabrizio's logic overlooked the fact that, as he had burned his own passport, there was nothing to indicate to the police official that he was the rebel, Fabrizio del Dongo.

Our hero was sufficiently alarmed, as we have seen; he would have been a great deal more so could he have read the thoughts that were disturbing the official's mind. This man was a friend of Giletti; one may judge of his surprise when he saw his friend's passport in the hands of a stranger; his first impulse was to have that stranger arrested, then he reflected that Giletti might easily have sold his passport to this fine young man who apparently had just been doing something disgraceful at Parma. "If I arrest him," he said to himself, "Giletti will get into trouble; they will at once discover that he has sold his passport; on the other hand, what will my chiefs say if it is proved that I, a friend of Giletti, put a *visa* on his passport when it was carried by someone else." The official got up with a yawn and said to Fabrizio: "Wait a minute, sir"; then, adopting a professional formula, added: "A difficulty has arisen." On which Fabrizio murmured: "What is going to arise is my escape."

As a matter of fact, the official went out of the office, leaving the door open; and the passport was left lying on the deal table. "The danger is obvious," thought Fabrizio; "I shall take my passport and walk slowly back across the bridge; I shall tell the constable, if he questions me, that I forgot to have my passport examined by the commissary of police in the last village in the State of Parma." Fabrizio had already taken the passport in his hand when, to his unspeakable astonishment, he heard the clerk with the brass jewelry say:

"Upon my soul, I can't do any more work; the heat is stifling; I am going to the *caffè* to have half a glass. Go into the office when you have finished your pipe, there's a passport to be stamped; the party is in there."

Fabrizio, who was stealing out on tiptoe, found himself face to face with a handsome young man who was saying to himself, or rather humming: "Well, let us see this passport; I'll put my scrawl on it.

"Where does the gentleman wish to go?"

"To Mantua, Venice and Ferrara."

"Ferrara it is," said the official, whistling; he took up a die,

stamped the *visa* in blue ink on the passport, rapidly wrote
in the words: "Mantua, Venice and Ferrara," in the space
left blank by the stamp, then waved his hand several times
in the air, signed, and dipped his pen in the ink to make his
flourish, which he executed slowly and with infinite pains.
Fabrizio followed every movement of his pen; the clerk
studied his flourish with satisfaction, adding five or six finishing touches, then handed the passport back to Fabrizio, saying
in a careless tone: "A good journey, sir!"

Fabrizio made off at a pace the alacrity of which he was
endeavouring to conceal, when he felt himself caught by the
left arm: instinctively his hand went to the hilt of his dagger,
and if he had not observed that he was surrounded by
houses he might perhaps have done something rash. The
man who was touching his left arm, seeing that he appeared
quite startled, said by way of apology:

"But I called the gentleman three times, and got no
answer; has the gentleman anything to declare before the
customs?"

"I have nothing on me but my handkerchief; I am going to
a place quite near here, to shoot with one of my family."

He would have been greatly embarrassed had he been
asked to name this relative. What with the great heat and his
various emotions, Fabrizio was as wet as if he had fallen
into the Po. "I am not lacking in courage to face actors, but
clerks with brass jewelry send me out of my mind; I shall
make a humorous sonnet out of that to amuse the Duchessa."

Entering Casalmaggiore, Fabrizio at once turned to the
right along a mean street which leads down to the Po. "I am
in great need," he said to himself, "of the succour of Bacchus
and Ceres," and he entered a shop outside which there hung
a grey clout fastened to a stick; on the clout was inscribed
the word *Trattoria*. A meagre piece of bed-linen supported
on two slender wooden hoops and hanging down to within
three feet of the ground sheltered the doorway of the *Trattoria* from the vertical rays of the sun. There, a half-un-
dressed and extremely pretty woman received our hero with
respect, which gave him the keenest pleasure; he hastened to
inform her that he was dying of hunger. While the woman
was preparing his breakfast, there entered a man of about
thirty; he had given no greeting on coming in; suddenly he
rose from the bench on which he had flung himself down
with a familiar air, and said to Fabrizio: *"Eccellenza, la ri-
verisco!"* (Excellency, your servant!) Fabrizio was in the

highest spirits at the moment, and, instead of forming sinister plans, replied with a laugh: "And how the devil do you know my Excellency?"

"What! Doesn't Your Excellency remember Lodovico, one of the Signora Duchessa Sanseverina's coachmen? At Sacca, the place in the country where we used to go every year, I always took fever; I asked the Signora for a pension, and retired from service. Now I am rich; instead of the pension of twelve scudi a year, which was the most I was entitled to expect, the Signora told me that, to give me the leisure to compose sonnets, for I am a poet in the *lingua volgare,* she would allow me twenty-four scudi and the Signor Conte told me that if ever I was in difficulties I had only to come and tell him. I have had the honour to drive Monsignore for a stage, when he went to make his retreat, like a good Christian, in the Certosa of Velleja."

Fabrizio studied the man's face and began to recognise him. He had been one of the smartest coachmen in the Sanseverina establishment; now that he was what he called rich his entire clothing consisted of a coarse shirt, in holes, and a pair of cloth breeches, dyed black at some time in the past, which barely came down to his knees; a pair of shoes and a villainous hat completed his equipment. In addition to this, he had not shaved for a fortnight. As he ate his omelette Fabrizio engaged in conversation with him, absolutely as between equals; he thought he detected that Lodovico was in love with their hostess. He finished his meal rapidly, then said in a low voice to Lodovico: "I want a word with you."

"Your Excellency can speak openly before her, she is a really good woman," said Lodovico with a tender air.

"Very well, my friends," said Fabrizio without hesitation, "I am in trouble, and have need of your help. First of all, there is nothing political about my case; I have simply and solely killed a man who wanted to murder me because I spoke to his mistress."

"Poor young man!" said the landlady.

"Your Excellency can count on me!" cried the coachman, his eyes ablaze with the most passionate devotion; "where does His Excellency wish to go?"

"To Ferrara. I have a passport, but I should prefer not to speak to the police, who may have received information of what has happened."

"When did you despatch this fellow?"

"This morning, at six o'clock."

"Your Excellency has no blood on his clothes, has he," asked the landlady.

"I was thinking of that," put in the coachman, "and besides, the cloth of that coat is too fine; you don't see many like that in the country round here, it would make people stare at us; I shall go and buy some clothes from the Jew. Your Excellency is about my figure, only thinner."

"For pity's sake, don't go on calling me Excellency, it may attract attention."

"Very good, Excellency," replied the coachman, as he left the tavern.

"Here, here," Fabrizio called after him, "and what about the money! Come back!"

"What do you mean—money!" said the landlady; "he has sixty-seven scudi which are entirely at your service. I myself," she went on, lowering her voice, "have forty scudi which I offer you with the best will in the world; one doesn't always have money on one when these accidents happen."

On account of the heat, Fabrizio had taken off his coat on entering the *Trattoria*.

"You have a waistcoat on you which might land us in trouble if anyone came in: that fine *English cloth* would attract attention." She gave our fugitive a stuff waistcoat, dyed black, which belonged to her husband. A tall young man came into the tavern by an inner door; he was dressed with a certain style.

"This is my husband," said the landlady. "Pietro-Antonio," she said to her husband, "this gentleman is a friend of Lodovico; he met with an accident this morning, across the river, and he wants to get away to Ferrara."

"Oh, we'll get him there," said the husband with an air of great gentility; "we have Carlo-Giuseppe's boat."

Owing to another weakness in our hero which we shall confess as naturally as we have related his fear in the police office at the end of the bridge, there were tears in his eyes; he was profoundly moved by the perfect devotion which he found among these *contadini;* he thought also of this characteristic generosity of his aunt; he would have liked to be able to make these people's fortune. Lodovico returned, carrying a packet.

"So that's finished," the husband said to him in a friendly tone.

"It's not that," replied Lodovico in evident alarm, "people

are beginning to talk about you, they noticed that you hesitated before turning down our *vicolo* and leaving the big street, like a man who was trying to hide."

"Go up quick to the bedroom," said the husband.

This room, which was very large and fine, had grey cloth instead of glass in its two windows; it contained four beds, each six feet wide and five feet high.

"Be quick! Be quick!" said Lodovico, "there is a swaggering fool of a constable who has just been posted here and began trying to make love to the pretty lady downstairs; and I've told him that when he goes travelling about the country he may find himself stopping a bullet. If the dog hears any mention of Your Excellency, he'll want to do us a bad turn, he will try to arrest you here, so as to get Teodolinda's *Trattoria* a bad name.

"What's this?" Lodovico went on, seeing Fabrizio's shirt all stained with blood and his wounds bandaged with handkerchiefs, "so the *porco* shewed fight, did he? That's a hundred times more that you need to get yourself arrested, and I haven't bought you any shirt." Without ceremony he opened the husband's wardrobe and gave one of his shirts to Fabrizio, who was soon attired like a prosperous countryman. Lodovico took down a net that was hanging on the wall, placed Fabrizio's clothes in the basket in which the fish are put, went downstairs at a run and hastened out of the house by a back door; Fabrizio followed him.

"Teodolinda," he called out as he passed by the bar, "hide what I've left upstairs, we are going to wait among the willows, and you, Pietro-Antonio, send us a boat quickly, we'll pay well for it."

Lodovico led Fabrizio across more than a score of ditches. There were planks, very long and very elastic, which served as bridges across the wider of these ditches; Lodovico took up these planks after crossing by them. On coming to the last canal he took up the plank with haste. "Now we can stop and breathe," he said; "that dog of a constable will have to go two leagues and more to reach Your Excellency. Why, you're quite pale," he said to Fabrizio; "I haven't forgotten the little bottle of brandy."

"It comes in most useful; the wound in my thigh is beginning to hurt me; and besides, I was in a fine fright in the police office by the bridge."

"I can well believe it," said Lodovico; "with a shirt covered in blood, as yours was, I can't conceive how you ever even dared to set foot in such a place. As for your wounds, I know what to do; I am going to put you in a cool place where you can sleep for an hour; the boat will come for us there, if there is any way of getting a boat; if not, when you have rested a little, we shall go on two short leagues, and I shall take you to a mill where I shall take a boat myself. Your Excellency knows far more than I do: the Signora will be in despair when she hears of the accident; they will tell her that you are mortally wounded, perhaps even that you killed the other man by foul play. The Marchesa Raversi will not fail to circulate all the evil reports that can hurt the Signora. Your Excellency might write."

"And how should I get the letter delivered?"

"The boys at the mill where we are going earn twelve soldi a day; in a day and a half they can be at Parma; say four francs for the journey; two francs for the wear and tear of their shoe-leather: if the errand was being done for a poor man like me, that would be six francs; as it is in the service of a Signore, I shall give them twelve."

When they had reached the resting-place in a clump of alders and willows, very leafy and very cool, Lodovico went to a house more than an hour's journey away in search of ink and paper. "Great heavens, how comfortable I am here," cried Fabrizio. "Fortune, farewell! I shall never be an Archbishop!"

On his return, Lodovico found him fast asleep and did not like to arouse him. The boat did not arrive until the sun had almost set; as soon as Lodovico saw it appear in the distance he called Fabrizio, who wrote a couple of letters.

"Your Excellency knows far more than I do," said Lodovico with a troubled air, "and I am very much afraid of displeasing him seriously, whatever he may say, if I add a certain remark."

"I am not such a fool as you think me," replied Fabrizio, "and, whatever you may say, you will always be in my eyes a faithful servant of my aunt, and a man who has done everything in the world to get me out of a very awkward scrape."

Many more protestations still were required before Lodovico could be prevailed upon to speak, and when at last he had made up his mind, he began with a preamble which lasted for quite five minutes. Fabrizio grew impatient, then said to himself: "After all, whose fault is it? It is due to our vanity, which this man has very well observed from his seat on the box." Lodovico's devotion at last impelled him to run the risk of speaking plainly.

"What would not the Marchesa Raversi give to the messenger you are going to send to Parma to have these two letters? They are in your handwriting, and consequently furnish legal evidence against you. Your Excellency will take me for an inquisitive and indiscreet fellow; in the second place, he will perhaps feel ashamed of setting before the eyes of the Signora Duchessa the wretched handwriting of a coachman like myself; but after all, the thought of your safety opens my mouth, although you may think me impertinent. Could not Your Excellency dictate those two letters to me? Then I am the only person compromised, and that very little; I can say, at a pinch, that you appeared to me in the middle of a field with an inkhorn in one hand and a pistol in the other, and that you ordered me to write."

"Give me your hand, my dear Lodovico," cried Fabrizio, "and to prove to you that I wish to have no secret from a friend like yourself, copy these two letters just as they are." Lodovico fully appreciated this mark of confidence, and was extremely grateful for it, but after writing a few lines, as he saw the boat coming rapidly downstream:

"The letters will be finished sooner," he said to Fabrizio, "if Your Excellency will take the trouble to dictate them to me." The letters written, Fabrizio wrote an A and a B on the closing lines, and on a little scrap of paper which he afterwards crumpled up, put in French: *"Croyez A et B."* The messenger would be told to hide this scrap of paper in his clothing.

The boat having come within hailing distance, Lodovico called to the boatmen by names which were not theirs; they made no reply, and put into the bank a thousand yards lower down, looking all round them to make sure that they had not been seen by some *doganiere*.

"I am at your orders," said Lodovico to Fabrizio; "would you like me to take these letters myself to Parma? Or would you prefer me to accompany you to Ferrara?"

"To accompany me to Ferrara is a service which I was hardly daring to ask of you. I shall have to land, and try to enter the town without shewing my passport. I may tell you that I feel the greatest repugnance towards travelling under the name of Giletti, and I can think of no one but yourself who would be able to buy me another passport."

"Why didn't you speak at Casalmaggiore? I know a spy there who would have sold me an excellent passport, and not dear, for forty or fifty francs."

One of the two boatmen, whose home was on the right bank of the Po, and who consequently had no need of a foreign passport to go to Parma, undertook to deliver the letters. Lodovico, who knew how to handle the oars, set to work to propel the boat with the other man.

"We shall find on the lower reaches of the Po," he said, "several armed vessels belonging to the police, and I shall manage to avoid them." Ten times at least they were obliged to hide among little islets flush with the water, covered with willows. Three times they set foot on shore in order to let the boat drift past the police vessels empty. Lodovico took advantage of these long intervals of leisure to recite to Fabrizio several of his sonnets. The sentiments were true enough, but were so to speak blunted by his expression of them, and were not worth the trouble of putting them on paper; the curious thing was that this ex-coachman had passions and points of view that were vivid and picturesque; he became cold and commonplace as soon as he began to write. "It is the opposite of what we see in society," thought Fabrizio; "people know nowadays how to express everything gracefully, but their hearts have nothing to say." He realised that the greatest pleasure he could give to this faithful servant would be to correct the mistakes in spelling in his sonnets.

"They laugh at me when I lend them my copy-book," said Lodovico; "but if Your Excellency would deign to dictate to me the spelling of the words letter by letter, the envious fellows wouldn't have anything left to say: spelling doesn't make genius." It was not until the third night of his journey that Fabrizio was able to land in complete safety in a thicket of alders, a league above Pontelagoscuro. All the next day he remained hidden in a hempfield, while Lodovico went ahead to Ferrara; he there took some humble lodgings in the house of a poor Jew, who at once realised that there was money to be earned if one knew how to keep one's mouth shut. That evening, as the light began to fail, Fabrizio entered Ferrara riding upon a pony; he had every need of this support, for he had been touched by the sun on the

river; the knife-wound that he had in his thigh, and the
sword-thrust that Giletti had given him in the shoulder, at
the beginning of their duel, were inflamed and had brought
on a fever.

CHAPTER TWELVE

THE JEW, the owner of the house, had procured a discreet surgeon, who, realising in his turn that there was money in the case, informed Lodovico that his *conscience* obliged him to make his report to the police on the injuries of the young man whom he, Lodovico, called his brother.

"The law is clear on the subject," he added; "it is evident that your brother cannot possibly have injured himself, as he says, by falling from a ladder while he was holding an open knife in his hand."

Lodovico replied coldly to this honest surgeon that, if he should decide to yield to the inspirations of his conscience, he, Lodovico, would have the honour, before leaving Ferrara, of falling upon him in precisely the same way, with an open knife in his hand. When he reported this incident to Fabrizio, the latter blamed him strongly, but there was not a moment to be lost; they must fly. Lodovico told the Jew that he wished to try the effect of a little fresh air on his brother; he went to fetch a carriage, and our friends left the house never to return. The reader is no doubt finding these accounts of all the manœuvres that the absence of a passport renders necessary extremely wearisome; this sort of anxiety does not exist in France; but in Italy, and especially in the neighbourhood of the Po, people talk about passports all day long. Once they had left Ferrara without hindrance, as though they were taking a drive, Lodovico sent the carriage back, then re-entered the town by another gate and returned to pick up Fabrizio with a *sediola* which he had hired to take them a dozen leagues. Coming near Bologna, our friends had themselves taken through the fields to the road which leads from Florence to Bologna; they spent the night in the most wretched inn they could find, and on the following day, Fabrizio feeling strong enough to walk a little, they entered Bologna like ordinary pedestrians. They had burned Giletti's passport; the comedian's death must by now be common knowledge, and there was less danger in being arrested as people without passports than as bearing the passport of a man who had been killed.

Lodovico knew at Bologna two or three servants in great houses; it was decided that he should go to the them and find out how the land lay. He explained to them that, while he was on his way from Florence, travelling with his younger brother, the latter, wanting to sleep, had let him come on by himself an hour before sunrise. He was to have joined him in the village where he, Lodovico, would stop to escape the midday heat. But Lodovico, seeing no sign of his brother, had decided to retrace his steps; he had found his brother injured by a blow from a stone and with several knife-wounds, and, in addition, robbed by some men who had picked a quarrel with him. This brother was a good-looking boy, knew how to groom and drive horses, read and write, and was anxious to find a place with some good family. Lodovico reserved for use on a future occasion the detail that, when Fabrizio was on the ground, the robbers had fled, taking with them the little bag in which the brothers had put their linen and their passports.

On arriving in Bologna, Fabrizio, feeling extremely tired and not venturing, without a passport, to shew his face at an inn, had gone into the huge church of San Petronio. He found there a delicious coolness; presently he felt quite revived. "Ungrateful wretch that I am," he said to himself suddenly, "I go into a church, simply to sit down, as it might be in a *caffè*!" He threw himself on his knees and thanked God effusively for the evident protection with which he had been surrounded ever since he had had the misfortune to kill Giletti. The danger which still made him shudder had been that of his being recognised in the police office at Casalmaggiore. "How," he asked himself, "did that clerk, whose eyes were so full of suspicion, who read my passport through at least three times, fail to notice that I am not five feet ten inches tall, that I am not thirty-nine years old, and that I am not strongly pitted by small-pox? What thanks I owe to Thee, O my God! And I have actually refrained until this moment from casting the nonentity that I am at Thy feet. My pride has chosen to believe that it was to a vain human prudence that I owed the good fortune of escaping the Spielberg, which was already opening to engulf me."

Fabrizio spent more than an hour in this state of extreme emotion, in the presence of the immense bounty of God. Lodovico approached, without his hearing him, and took his stand opposite him. Fabrizio, who had buried his face in his hands, raised his head, and his faithful servant could see the tears streaming down his cheeks.

"Come back in an hour," Fabrizio ordered him, somewhat harshly.

Lodovico forgave this tone in view of the speaker's piety. Fabrizio repeated several times the Seven Penitential Psalms, which he knew by heart; he stopped for a long time at the verses which had a bearing on his situation at the moment.

Fabrizio asked pardon of God for many things, but what is really remarkable is that it never entered his head to number among his faults the plan of becoming Archbishop simply because Conte Mosca was Prime Minister and felt that office and all the importance it implied to be suitable for the Duchessa's nephew. He had desired it without passion, it is true, but still he had thought of it, exactly as one might think of being made a Minister or a General. It had never entered his thoughts that his conscience might be concerned in this project of the Duchessa. This is a remarkable characteristic of the religion which he owed to the instruction given him by the Jesuits of Milan. That religion *deprives one of the courage to think of unfamiliar things,* and especially forbids *personal examination,* as the most enormous of sins; it is a step towards Protestantism. To find out of what sins one is guilty, one must question one's priest, or read the list of sins, as it is to be found printed in the books entitled, *Preparation for the Sacrament of Penance.* Fabrizio knew by heart the list of sins, rendered into the Latin tongue, which he had learned at the Ecclesiastical Academy of Naples. So, when going through that list, on coming to the article, *Murder,* he had most forcibly accused himself before God of having killed a man, but in defence of his own life. He had passed rapidly, and without paying them the slightest attention, over the various articles relating to the sin of *Simony* (the procuring of ecclesiastical dignities with money). If anyone had suggested to him that he should pay a hundred louis to become First Grand Vicar of the Archbishop of Parma, he would have rejected such an idea with horror; but, albeit he was not wanting in intelligence, nor above all in logic, it never once occurred to his mind that the employment on his behalf of Conte Mosca's influence was a form of Simony. This is where the Jesuitical education triumphs: it forms the habit of not paying attention to things that are clearer than daylight. A Frenchman, brought up among conflicting personal interests and in the prevailing irony of Paris, might, without being deliberately unfair, have accused Fabrizio of hypocrisy at the very moment when our hero was opening his soul to God with the utmost sincerity and the most profound emotion.

Fabrizio did not leave the church until he had prepared the confession which he proposed to make the next day. He found Lodovico sitting on the steps of the vast stone peristyle which rises above the great *piazza* opposite the front of San Petronio. As after a storm the air becomes more pure, so now Fabrizio's soul was tranquil and happy and so to speak refreshed.

"I feel quite well now, I hardly notice my wounds," he said to Lodovico as he approached him; "but first of all I have to apologise to you; I answered you crossly when you came and spoke to me in the church; I was examining my conscience. Well, how are things going?"

"Excellently: I have taken lodgings, to tell the truth not at all worthy of Your Excellency, with the wife of one of my friends, who is a very pretty woman and, better still, on the best of terms with one of the heads of the police. Tomorrow I shall go to declare how our passports came to be stolen; my declaration will be taken in good part; but I shall pay the carriage of the letter which the police will write to Casalmaggiore, to find out whether there exists in that *comune* a certain San Micheli, Lodovico, who has a brother, named Fabrizio, in service with the Signora Duchessa Sanseverina at Parma. All is settled, *siamo a cavallo.*" (An Italian proverb meaning: "We are saved.")

Fabrizio had suddenly assumed a most serious air: he begged Lodovico to wait a moment, almost ran back into the church, and when barely past the door flung himself down on his knees; he humbly kissed the stone slabs of the floor. "It is a miracle, Lord," he cried with tears in his eyes: "when Thou sawest my soul disposed to return to the path of duty, Thou hast saved me. Great God! It is possible that one day I may be killed in some quarrel; in the hour of my death remember the state in which my soul is now." It was with transports of the keenest joy that Fabrizio recited afresh the Seven Penitential Psalms. Before leaving the building he went up to an old woman who was seated before a great Madonna and by the side of an iron triangle rising vertically from a stand on the same metal. The sides of this triangle bristled with a large number of spikes intended to support the little candles which the piety of the faithful keeps burning before the famous Madonna of Cimabue. Seven candles only were lighted when Fabrizio approached the stand; he registered this fact in his memory, with the intention of meditating upon it later on when he had more leisure.

"What do the candles cost?" he asked the woman.

"Two bajocchi each."

As a matter of fact they were scarcely thicker than quills and were not a foot in length.

"How many candles can still go on your triangle?"

"Sixty-three, since there are seven alight."

"Ah!" thought Fabrizio, "sixty-three and seven make seventy; that also is to be borne in mind." He paid for the candles, placed the first seven in position himself, and lighted them, then fell on his knees to make his oblation, and said to the old woman as he rose:

"It is *for grace received*."

"I am dying of hunger," he said to Lodovico as he joined him outside.

"Don't let us go to an *osteria*, let us go to our lodgings; the woman of the house will go out and buy you everything you want for your meal; she will rob you of a score of soldi, and will be all the more attached to the newcomer in consequence."

"All this means simply that I shall have to go on dying of hunger for a good hour longer," said Fabrizio, laughing with the serenity of a child; and he entered an *osteria* close to San Petronio. To his extreme suprise, he saw at a table near the one at which he had taken his seat, Peppe, his aunt's first footman, the same who on a former occasion had come to meet him at Geneva. Fabrizio made a sign to him to say nothing; then, having made a hasty meal, a smile of happiness hovering over his lips, he rose; Peppe followed him, and, for the third time, our hero entered the church of San Petronio. Out of discretion, Lodovico remained outside, strolling in the *piazza*.

"Oh, Lord, Monsignore! How are your wounds? The Signora Duchessa is terribly upset: for a whole day she thought you were dead, and had been left lying on some island in the Po; I must go and send off a messenger to her this very instant. I have been looking for you for the last six days; I spent three at Ferrara, searching all the inns."

"Have you a passport for me?"

"I have three different ones: one with Your Excellency's names and titles, a second with your name only, and the other in a false name, Giuseppe Bossi; each passport is made out in duplicate, according to whether Your Excellency prefers to have come from Florence or from Modena. You have only to go for a turn outside the town. The Signor Conte would be glad if you would lodge at the Albergo del Pellegrino; the landlord is a friend of his."

Fabrizio, with the air of a casual visitor, advanced along the right aisle of the church to the place where his candles were burning; he fastened his eyes on Cimabue's Madonna, then said to Peppe as he fell on his knees: "I must just give thanks for a moment." Peppe followed his example. When they left the church, Peppe noticed that Fabrizio gave a twenty-franc piece to the first pauper who asked him for alms: this mendicant uttered cries of gratitude which drew into the wake of the charitable stranger the swarms of paupers of every kind who generally adorn the Piazza San Petronio. All of them were anxious to have a share in the napoleon. The women, despairing of making their way through the crowd that surrounded him, flung themselves on Fabrizio, shouting to him to know whether it was not the fact that he had intended to give his napoleon to be divided among all the *poveri del buon Dio*. Peppe, brandishing his gold-headed cane, ordered them to leave His Excellency alone.

"Oh! Excellency!" all the women proceeded to cry in still more piercing accents, "give another gold napoleon for the poor women!" Fabrizio increased his pace, the women followed him, screaming, and a number of male paupers, running in from every street, created a sort of tumult. All this crowd, horribly dirty and energetic, cried out: *"Eccellenza!"* Fabrizio had great difficulty in escaping from the rabble; the scene brought his imagination back to earth. "I have got only what I deserve," he said to himself; "I have rubbed shoulders with the mob."

Two women followed him as far as the Porta Saragozza, by which he left the town: Peppe stopped them by threatening them seriously with his cane and flinging them some small

change; Fabrizio climbed the charming hill of San Michele in
Bosco, made a partial circuit of the town outside the walls,
took a path which brought him in five hundred yards to the
Florence road, then re-entered Bologna and gravely handed
to the police official a passport in which his description was
given in the fullest detail. This passport gave him the name
of Giuseppe Bossi, student of theology. Fabrizio noticed a
little spot of red ink dropped, as though by accident, at the
foot of the sheet, near the right-hand corner. A couple of
hours later he had a spy on his heels, on account of the
title of *Eccellenza* which his companion had given him in
front of the beggars of San Petronio, although his passport
bore none of the titles which give a man the right to make
his servants address him as Excellency.

Fabrizio saw the spy and made light of him; he gave no
more thought either to passports or to police, and amused
himself with everything, like a boy. Peppe, who had orders
to stay beside him, seeing that he was more than satisfied
with Lodovico, preferred to go back in person to convey
these good tidings to the Duchessa. Fabrizio wrote two very
long letters to his dear friends; then it occurred to him to
write a third to the venerable Archbishop Landriani. This
letter produced a marvellous effect; it contained a very
exact account of the affair with Giletti. The good Archbishop, deeply moved, did not fail to go and read this
letter to the Prince, who was quite ready to listen to it, being
somewhat curious to know what line this young Monsignore
took to excuse so shocking a murder. Thanks to the many
friends of the Marchesa Raversi, the Prince, as well as the
whole city of Parma, believed that Fabrizio had procured the
assistance of twenty or thirty peasants to overpower a bad
actor who had had the insolence to challenge him for the
favours of little Marietta. In despotic courts, the first skilful
intriguer controls the *Truth,* as the fashion controls it in
Paris.

"But, what in the devil's name!" exclaimed the Prince to
the Archbishop; "one gets things of that sort done for one
by somebody else; but to do them oneself is not the custom;
besides, one doesn't kill a comedian like Giletti, one buys
him."

Fabrizio had not the slightest suspicion of what was going
on at Parma. As a matter of fact, the question there was
whether the death of this comedian, who in his lifetime
had earned a monthly salary of thirty-two francs, was not

going to bring about the fall of the Ultra Ministry, and of
its leader, Conte Mosca.

On learning of the death of Giletti, the Prince, stung
by the independent airs which the Duchessa was giving herself, had ordered the Fiscal General Rassi to treat the whole
case as though the person charged were a Liberal. Fabrizio,
for his part, thought that a man of his rank was
superior to the laws; he did not take into account that in
countries where bearers of great names are never punished,
intrigue can do anything, even against them. He often spoke
to Lodovico of his perfect innocence, which would very
soon be proclaimed; his great argument being that he was
not guilty. Whereupon Lodovico said to him: "I cannot conceive how Your Excellency, who has so much intelligence and
education, can take the trouble to say all that before me
who am his devoted servant; Your Excellency adopts too
many precautions; that sort of thing is all right to say in
public, or before a court." "This man believes me to be
a murderer, and loves me none the less for it," thought
Fabrizio, falling from the clouds.

Three days after Peppe's departure, he was greatly
astonished to receive an enormous letter, sealed with a plait
of silk, as in the days of Louis XIV, and addressed *a Sua
Eccellenza reverendissima monsignor Fabrizio del Dongo,
primo gran vicario della diocesi di Parma, canonico,* etc.

"Why, am I still all that?" he asked himself with a laugh.
Archbishop Landriani's letter was a masterpiece of logic
and lucidity; it filled nevertheless nineteen large pages, and
gave an extremely good account of all that had occurred
in Parma on the occasion of the death of Giletti.

"A French army commanded by Marshal Ney, and marching upon the town, would not have had a greater effect,"
the good Archbishop informed him; "with the exception of
the Duchessa and myself, my dearly beloved son, everyone
believes that you gave yourself the pleasure of killing the
histrion Giletti. Had this misfortune befallen you, it is one
of those things which one hushes up with two hundred louis
and six months' absence abroad; but the Marchesa Raversi
is seeking to overthrow Conte Mosca with the help of this
incident. It is not at all with the dreadful sin of murder that
the public blames you, it is solely with the *clumsiness,* or
rather the insolence of not having condescended to have
recourse to a *bulo*" (a sort of hired assassin). "I give you a
summary here in clear terms of the things that I hear said

all around me, for since this ever deplorable misfortune, I go every day to three of the principal houses in the town to have an opportunity of justifying you. And never have I felt that I was making a more blessed use of the scanty eloquence with which heaven has deigned to endow me."

The scales fell from Fabrizio's eyes; the Duchessa's many letters, filled with transports of affection, never condescended to tell him anything. The Duchessa swore to him that she would leave Parma for ever, unless presently he returned there in triumph. "The Conte will do for you," she wrote to him in the letter that accompanied the Archbishop's, "everything that is humanly possible. As for myself, you have changed my character with this fine escapade of yours; I am now as great a miser as the banker Tombone; I have dismissed all my workmen, I have done more, I have dictated to the Conte the inventory of my fortune, which turns out to be far less considerable than I supposed. After the death of the excellent Conte Pietranera, whom, by the way, you would have done far better to avenge, instead of exposing your life to a creature of Giletti's sort, I was left with an income of twelve hundred francs and five thousand francs of debts; I remember, among other things, that I had two and a half dozen white satin slippers coming from Paris and not a single pair of shoes to wear in the street. I have almost made up my mind to take the three hundred thousand francs which the Duca has left me, the whole of which I intended to use in erecting a magnificent tomb to him. Besides, it is the Marchesa Raversi who is your principal enemy, that is to say mine; if you find life dull by yourself at Bologna, you have only to say the word, I shall come and join you. Here are four more bills of exchange," and so on.

The Duchessa said not a word to Fabrizio of the opinion that was held in Parma of his affair, she wished above all things to comfort him, and in any event the death of a ridiculous creature like Giletti did not seem to her the sort of thing that could be seriously charged against a del Dongo. "How many Gilettis have not our ancestors sent into the other world," she said to the Conte, "without anyone's ever taking it into his head to reproach them with it?"

Fabrizio, taken completely by surprise, and getting for the first time a glimpse of the true state of things, set himself down to study the Archbishop's letter. Unfortunately the Archbishop himself believed him to be better informed than he actually was. Fabrizio gathered that the principal cause of the Marchesa Raversi's triumph lay in the fact that it was impossible to find any eye-witnesses of the fatal combat. The footman who had been the first to bring the news to Parma had been at the village inn at Sanguigna when the fight occurred; little Marietta and the old woman who acted as her mother had vanished, and the Marchesa had bought the *vetturino* who drove the carriage, and who had now made an abominable deposition. "Although the proceedings are enveloped in the most profound mystery," wrote the Archbishop in his Ciceronian style, "and directed by the Fiscal General, Rassi, of whom Christian charity alone can restrain me from speaking evil, but who has made his fortune by harrying his wretched prisoners as the greyhound harries the hare; although this Rassi, I say, whose turpitude and venality your imagination would be powerless to exaggerate, has been appointed to take charge of the case by an angry Prince, I have been able to read the three depositions of the *vetturino*. By a signal piece of good fortune, the wretch contradicts himself. And I shall add, since I am addressing my Grand Vicar, him who, after myself, is to have the charge of this Diocese, that I have sent for the curate of the parish in which this straying sinner resides. I shall tell you, my dearly beloved son, but under the seal of the confessional, that this curate already knows, through the wife of the *vetturino*, the number of scudi that he has received from the Marchesa Raversi; I shall not venture to say that the Marchesa insisted upon his slandering you, but that is probable. The scudi were transmitted to him through a wretched priest who performs functions of a base order in the Marchesa's household, and whom I have been obliged to banish from the altar for the second time. I shall not weary you with an account of various other actions which you might expect from me, and which, moreover, enter into my duty. A Canon, your colleague at the Cathedral, who is a little too prone at times to remember the influence conferred upon him by the wealth of his family, to which, by divine permission, he is now the sole heir, having allowed himself to say in the house of Conte Zurla, the Minister of the Interior, that he regarded this *bagattella* (he referred to the killing of the unfortunate Giletti) as proved against you, I summoned him to appear before me, and there, in the presence of my three other Vicars General, of my Chaplain and of two curates who happened to be in the waiting-room, I requested him to communicate to us his brethren the elements of the complete

conviction which he professed to have acquired against one
of his colleagues at the Cathedral; the unhappy man was
able to articulate only the most inconclusive arguments;
every voice was raised against him, and, although I did not
think it my duty to add more than a very few words, he
burst into tears and made us the witnesses of his full confession of his complete error, upon which I promised him
secrecy in my name and in the names of the persons who
had been present at the discussion, always on the condition
that he would devote all his zeal to correcting the false impressions that might have been created by the language employed by him during the previous fortnight.

"I shall not repeat to you, my dear son, what you must
long have known, namely that of the thirty-four *contadini*
employed on the excavations undertaken by Conte Mosca,
whom the Raversi pretends to have been paid by you to assist you in a crime, thirty-two were at the bottom of their
trench, wholly taken up with their work, when you armed
yourself with the hunting knife and employed it to defend
your life against the man who had attacked you thus unawares. Two of their number, who were outside the trench,
shouted to the others: 'They are murdering Monsignore!'
This cry alone reveals your innocence in all its whiteness.
Very well, the Fiscal General Rassi maintains that these two
men have disappeared; furthermore, they have found eight of
the men who were at the bottom of the trench; at their first
examination, six declared that they had heard the cry: 'They
are murdering Monsignore!' I know, through indirect chan-
nels, that at their fifth examination, which was held yesterday evening, five declared that they could not remember
distinctly whether they had heard the cry themselves or
whether it had been reported to them by their comrades.
Orders have been given that I am to be informed of the
place of residence of these excavators, and their parish
priests will make them understand that they are damning
themselves if, in order to gain a few soldi, they allow themselves to alter the truth."

The good Archbishop went into endless details, as may be
judged by those we have extracted from his letter. Then he
added, using the Latin tongue:

"This affair is nothing less than an attempt to bring about
a change of government. If you are sentenced, it can be
only to the galleys or to death, in which case I should inter-
vene by declaring from my Archepiscopal Throne that I

know you to be innocent, that you simply and solely defended your life against a brigand, and that finally I have forbidden you to return to Parma for so long as your enemies shall be triumphant there; I propose even to stigmatise, as he deserves, the Fiscal General; the hatred felt for that man is as common as esteem for his character is rare. But finally, on the eve of the day on which this Fiscal is to pronounce so unjust a sentence, the Duchessa Sanseverina will leave the town, and perhaps even the States of Parma: in that event, no doubt is felt that the Conte will hand in his resignation. Then, very probably, General Fabio Conti will come into office and the Marchesa Raversi will be triumphant. The great mistake in your case is that no skilled person has been appointed to take charge of the procedure necessary to bring your innocence into the light of day, and to foil the attempts that have been made to suborn witnesses. The Conte believes that he is playing this part; but he is too great a gentleman to stoop to certain details; besides, in his capacity as Minister of Police, he was obliged to issue, at the first moment, the most severe orders against you. Lastly, dare I say it, our Sovereign Lord believes you to be guilty, or at least feigns that belief, and has introduced a certain bitterness into the affair." (The words corresponding to "our Sovereign Lord" and "feigns that belief" were in Greek, and Fabrizio felt infinitely obliged to the Archbishop for having had the courage to write them. With a pen-knife he cut this line out of the letter, and destroyed it on the spot.)

Fabrizio broke off a score of times while reading this letter; he was carried away by transports of the liveliest gratitude: he replied at once in a letter of eight pages. Often he was obliged to raise his head so that his tears should not fall on the paper. Next day, as he was sealing this letter, he felt that it was too worldly in tone. "I shall write it in Latin," he said to himself, "that will make it appear more seemly to the worthy Archbishop." But, while he was seeking to construct fine Latin phrases of great length, in the true Ciceronian style, he remembered that one day the Archbishop, in speaking to him of Napoleon, had made a point of calling him Buonaparte; at that instant there vanished all the emotion that, on the previous day, had moved him to tears. "O King of Italy!" he exclaimed, "that loyalty which so many others swore to thee in thy lifetime, I shall preserve for thee after thy death. He is fond of me, no doubt, but because I am a del Dongo and he a son of the people." So that his fine letter in Italian might not be wasted, Fabrizio made a few necessary alterations in it, and addressed it to Conte Mosca.

That same day, Fabrizio met in the street little Marietta; she flushed with joy and made a sign to him to follow her without speaking. She made swiftly for a deserted archway; there, she pulled forward the black lace shawl which, following the local custom, covered her head, so that she could not be recognised; then turning round quickly:

"How is it," she said to Fabrizio, "that you are walking freely in the street like this?" Fabrizio told her his story.

"Good God! You were at Ferrara! And there was I looking for you everywhere in the place! You must know that I quarrelled with the old woman, because she wanted to take me to Venice, where I knew quite well that you would never go, because you are on the Austrian black list. I sold my gold necklace to come to Bologna, I had a presentiment that I should have the happiness of meeting you here; the old woman arrived two days after me. And so I shan't ask you to come and see us, she would go on making those dreadful demands for money which make me so ashamed. We have lived very comfortably since the fatal day you remember, and haven't spent a quarter of what you gave us. I would rather not come and see you at the Albergo del Pellegrino, it would be a *pubblicità*. Try to find a little room in a quiet street, and at the Ave Maria" (nightfall) "I shall be here, under this same archway." So saying, she took to her heels.

CHAPTER THIRTEEN

ALL SERIOUS thoughts were forgotten on the unexpected appearance of this charming person. Fabrizio settled himself to live at Bologna in a joy and security that were profound. This artless tendency to take delight in everything that entered into his life shewed through in the letters which he wrote to the Duchessa; to such an extent that she began to take offence. Fabrizio paid little attention; he wrote, however, in abridged symbols on the face of his watch: "When I write to the D., must never say *When I was prelate, when I was in the Church:* that annoys her." He had bought a pair of ponies with which he was greatly pleased: he used to harness them to a hired carriage whenever little Marietta wished to pay a visit to any of the enchanting spots in the neighbourhood of Bologna; almost every evening he drove her to the *Cascata del Reno.* On their way back, he would call on the friendly Crescentini, who regarded himself as to some extent Marietta's father.

"Upon my soul, if this is the *caffè* life which seemed to me so ridiculous for a man of any worth, I did wrong to reject it," Fabrizio said to himself. He forgot that he never went near a *caffè* except to read the *Constitutionnel,* and that, since he was a complete stranger to everyone in Bologna, the gratification of vanity did not enter at all into his present happiness. When he was not with little Marietta, he was to be seen at the Observatory, where he was taking a course in astronomy; the Professor had formed a great affection for him, and Fabrizio used to lend him his ponies on Sundays, to cut a figure with his wife on the *Corso della Montagnola.*

He loathed the idea of harming any living creature, however undeserving that creature might be. Marietta was resolutely opposed to his seeing the old woman, but one day, when she was at church, he went up to visit the *Mammaccia,* who flushed with anger when she saw him enter the room. "This is a case where one plays the del Dongo," he said to himself.

"How much does Marietta earn in a month when she is working?" he cried, with the air with which a self-respecting young man, in Paris, enters the balcony at the Bouffes.

"Fifty scudi."

"You are lying, as usual; tell the truth, or, by God, you shall not have a centesimo!"

"Very well, she was getting twenty-two scudi in our company at Parma, when we had the bad luck to meet you; I was getting twelve scudi, and we used to give Giletti, our protector, a third of what each of us earned. Out of which, every month almost, Giletti would make Marietta a present; the present might be worth a couple of scudi."

"You're lying still; you never had more than four scudi. But if you are good to Marietta, I will engage you as though I were an *impresario;* every month you shall have twelve scudi for yourself and twenty-two for her; but if I see her with red eyes, I make you bankrupt."

"You're very stiff and proud; very well, your fine generosity will be the ruin of us," replied the old woman in a furious tone; "we lose our *avviamento"* (our connexion). "When we have the enormous misfortune to be deprived of Your Excellency's protection, we shall no longer be known in any of the companies, they will all be filled up; we shall not find any engagement, and, all through you, we shall starve to death."

"Go to the devil," said Fabrizio as he left the room.

"I shall not go to the devil, you impious wretch! But I will go straight away to the police office, where they shall learn from me that you are a Monsignore who has flung his cassock to the winds, and that you are no more Giuseppe Bossi than I am." Fabrizio had already gone some way down the stairs. He returned.

"In the first place, the police know better than you what my real name may be; but if you take it into your head to denounce me, if you do anything so infamous," he said to her with great seriousness, "Lodovico shall talk to you, and it is not six slashes with the knife that your old carcass shall get, but two dozen, and you will be six months in hospital, and no tobacco."

The old woman turned pale, and dashed at Fabrizio's hand, which she tried to kiss.

"I accept with gratitude the provision that you are making for Marietta and me. You look so good that I took you for a fool; and, you bear in mind, others besides myself may make the same error; I advise you always to adopt a more noblemanly air." Then she added with an admirable impudence: "You will reflect upon this good advice, and, as the winter is not far off, you will make Marietta and me a present of two good jackets of that fine English stuff which they sell at the big shop in the Piazza San Petronio."

The love of the pretty Marietta offered Fabrizio all the charms of the most delightful friendship, which set him dreaming of the happiness of the same order which he might have been finding in the Duchessa's company.

"But is it not a very pleasant thing," he asked himself at times, "that I am not susceptible to that exclusive and passionate preoccupation which they call love? Among the intimacies into which chance has brought me at Novara or at Naples, have I ever met a woman whose company, even in the first few days, was to my mind preferable to riding a good horse that I did not know? What they call love," he went on, "can that be just another lie? I feel myself in love, no doubt, as I feel a good appetite at six o'clock! Can it be out of this slightly vulgar propensity that those liars have fashioned the love of Othello, the love of Tancred? Or am I indeed to suppose that I am constructed differently from other men? That my soul should be lacking in one passion, why should that be? It would be a singular destiny!"

At Naples, especially in the latter part of his time there, Fabrizio had met women who, proud of their rank, their beauty and the position held in society by the adorers whom they had sacrificed to him, had attempted to lead him. On discovering their intention, Fabrizio had broken with them in the most summary and open fashion. "Well," he said to himself, "if I ever allow myself to be carried away by the pleasure, which no doubt is extremely keen, of being on friendly terms with that charming woman who is known as the Duchessa Sanseverina, I shall be exactly like that stupid Frenchman who killed the goose that was laying the golden eggs. It is to the Duchessa that I owe the sole happiness which has ever come to me from sentiments of affection: my friendship for her is my life, and besides, without her, what am I? A poor exile reduced to living from hand to mouth in a tumble-down country house outside Novara. I remember how, during the heavy autumn rains, I used to be obliged, at night, for fear of accidents, to fix up an umbrella over the tester of my bed. I rode the agent's horses, which he was good enough to allow out of respect for my blue blood (for my influence, that is), but he was beginning to find my stay there a trifle long; my father had made me an allowance of twelve hundred francs, and thought himself damned for having given bread to a Jacobin. My poor mother and sisters let themselves go without new clothes to keep me in a position to make a few little presents to my mistresses. This way of being generous pierced me to the heart. And besides, people were beginning to suspect my poverty, and the young noblemen of the district would have been feeling sorry for me next. Sooner or later some prig would have let me see his contempt for a poor Jacobin whose plans had come to grief, for in those people's eyes I was nothing more than that. I should have given or received some doughty thrust with a sword which would have carried me off to the fortress of Fenestrelle, or else I should have been obliged to take refuge again in Switzerland, still on my allowance of twelve hundred francs. I have the good fortune to be indebted to the Duchessa for the absence of all these evils; besides, it is she who feels for me the transports of affection which I ought to be feeling for her.

"Instead of that ridiculous, pettifogging existence which would have made me a sad dog, a fool, for the last four years I have been living in a big town, and have an excellent carriage, which things have preserved me from feelings of envy and all the base sentiments of a provincial life. This too indulgent aunt is always scolding me because I do not draw enough money from the banker. Do I wish to ruin for all time so admirable a position? Do I wish to lose the one friend that I have in the world? All I need do is to utter a *falsehood;* all I need do is to say to a charming woman, a woman who is perhaps without a counterpart in the world, and for whom I feel the most passionate friendship: '*I love you,*' I who do not know what it is to love amorously. She would spend the day finding fault with me for the absence of these transports which are unknown to me. Marietta, on the other hand, who does not see into my heart, and takes a caress for a transport of the soul, thinks me madly in love and looks upon herself as the most fortunate of women.

"As a matter of fact, the only slight acquaintance I have

ever had with that tender obsession which is called, I believe, *love*, was with the young Aniken in the inn at Zonders, near the Belgian frontier."

It is with regret that we have to record here one of Fabrizio's worst actions; in the midst of this tranquil life, a wretched *pique* of vanity took possession of this heart rebellious to love and led it far astray. Simultaneously with himself there happened to be at Bologna the famous Fausta F——, unquestionably one of the finest singers of the day and perhaps the most capricious woman that was ever seen. The excellent poet Burati, of Venice, had composed the famous satirical sonnet about her, which at that time was to be heard on the lips alike of princes and of the meanest street Arabs:

"To wish and not to wish, to adore and on the same day to detest, to find contentment only in inconstancy, to scorn what the world worships, while the world worships it: Fausta has these defects and many more. Look not therefore upon that serpent. If thou seest her, imprudent man, thou forgettest her caprices. Hast thou the happiness to hear her voice, thou dost forget thyself, and love makes of thee, in a moment, what Circe in days of yore made of the companions of Ulysses."

For the moment, this miracle of beauty had come under the spell of the enormous whiskers and haughty insolence of the young Conte M——, to such an extent as not to be revolted by his abominable jealousy. Fabrizio saw this Conte in the streets of Bologna and was shocked by the air of superiority with which he took up the pavement and deigned to display his graces to the public. This young man was extremely rich, imagined that everything was permitted him, and, as his *prepotenze* had brought him threats of punishment, never appeared in public save with the escort of nine or ten *buli* (a sort of cut-throat) clad in his livery, whom he had brought from his estates in the environs of Brescia. Fabrizio's eye had met once or twice that of this terrible Conte, whence chance led him to hear Fausta sing. He was astonished by the angelic sweetness of her voice: he had never imagined anything like it; he was indebted to it for sensations of supreme happiness, which made a pleasing contrast to the *placidity* of his life at the time. Could this at last be love? he asked himself. Thoroughly curious to taste that sentiment, and amused moreover by the thought of braving Conte M——, whose expression was more terrifying than that of any drum-major, our hero let himself fall into the childish habit of passing a great deal too often in front of the *palazzo* Tanari, which Conte M—— had taken for Fausta.

One day, as night was beginning to fall, Fabrizio, seeking to catch Fausta's eye, was greeted by peals of laughter of the most pointed kind proceeding from the Conte's *buli*, who were assembled by the door of the *palazzo* Tanari. He hastened home, armed himself well, and again passed before the *palazzo*. Fausta, concealed behind her shutters, was awaiting his return, and gave him due credit for it. M——, jealous of the whole world, became specially jealous of Signor Giuseppe Bossi, and indulged in ridiculous utterances; whereupon every morning our hero had delivered at his door a letter which contained only these words:

"Signor Giuseppe Bossi destroys troublesome insects and is staying at the Pellegrino, Via Larga, No. 79."

Conte M——, accustomed to the respect which was everywhere assured him by his enormous fortune, his blue blood and the physical courage of his thirty servants, declined altogether to understand the language of this little missive.

Fabrizio wrote others of the sort to Fausta; M—— posted spies round this rival, who perhaps was not unattractive; first of all, he learned his true name, and later that, for the present, he could not shew his face at Parma. A few days after this, Conte M——, his *buli*, his magnificent horses and Fausta set off together for Parma.

Fabrizio, becoming excited, followed them next day. In vain did the good Lodovico utter pathetic remonstrances: Fabrizio turned a deaf ear, and Lodovico, who was himself extremely brave, admired him for it; besides, this removal brought him nearer to the pretty mistress he had left at Casalmaggiore. Through Lodovico's efforts, nine or ten old soldiers of Napoleon's regiments re-enlisted under Signor Giuseppe Bossi, in the capacity of servants. "Provided," Fabrizio told himself, when committing the folly of going after Fausta, "that I have no communication either with the Minister of Police, Conte Mosca, or with the Duchessa, I expose only myself to risk. I shall explain later on to my aunt that I was going in search of love, that beautiful thing which I have never encountered. The fact is that I think of Fausta even when I am not looking at her. But is it the memory of her voice that I love, or her person?" Having ceased to think of an ecclesiastical career, Fabrizio had grown a pair of moustaches and whiskers almost as terrible as those of Conte M——, and these disguised him to some extent. He set up his headquarters not at Parma—that would have been too imprudent—but in a neighbouring village, in the woods, on the road to Sacca, where his aunt had her country house. Following Lodovico's advice, he gave himself out in this village as the valet of a great English nobleman of original tastes, who spent a hundred thousand francs a year on providing himself with the pleasures of the chase, and would arrive shortly from the Lake of Como, where he was detained by the trout-fishing. Fortunately for him, the charming little *palazzo* which Conte M—— had taken for the fair Fausta was situated at the southern extremity of the city of Parma, precisely on the road to Sacca, and Fausta's windows looked out over the fine avenues of tall trees which extend beneath the high tower of the citadel. Fabrizio was completely unknown in this little frequented quarter; he did not fail to have Conte M—— followed, and one day when that gentleman had just emerged from the admirable singer's door, he had the audacity to appear in the street in broad daylight; it must be admitted that he was mounted upon an excellent horse, and well armed. A party of musicians, of the sort that frequent the streets in Italy and are sometimes excellent, came and planted their viols under Fausta's window; after playing a prelude they sang, and quite well too, a cantata composed in her honour. Fausta came to the window and had no difficulty in distinguishing a young man of extremely polite manners, who, stopping his horse in the middle of the street, bowed to her first of all, then began to direct at her a gaze that could have but one meaning. In spite of the exaggeratedly English costume adopted by Fabrizio, she soon recognised the author of the passionate letters that had brought about her departure from Bologna. "That is a curious creature," she said to herself; "it seems to me that I am going to fall in love with him. I have a hundred louis in hand, I can quite well give that terrible Conte M—— the slip; if it comes to that, he has no spirit, he never does anything unexpected, and is only slightly amusing because of the bloodthirsty appearance of his escort."

On the following day Fabrizio, having learned that every morning at eleven o'clock Fausta went to hear mass in the centre of the town, in that same church of San Giovanni which contained the tomb of his great-uncle, Archbishop Ascanio del Dongo, made bold to follow her there. To tell the truth, Lodovico had procured him a fine English wig with hair of the most becoming red. Inspired by the colour of his wig, which was that of the flames that were devouring his heart, he composed a sonnet which Fausta thought charming; an unseen hand had taken care to place it upon her piano. This little war lasted for quite a week; but Fabrizio found that, in spite of the steps he was taking in every direction, he was making no real progress; Fausta refused to see him. He strained the effect of singularity; she admitted afterwards that she was afraid of him. Fabrizio was kept going now only by a faint hope of coming to feel what is known as *love*, but frequently he felt bored.

"Let us leave this place, Signore," Lodovico used to urge him; "you are not in the least in love: I can see that you have the most desperate coolness and common sense. Besides, you are making no headway; if only for shame, let us clear out." Fabrizio was ready to go at the first moment of ill-humour, when he heard that Fausta was to sing at the Duchessa Sanseverina's. "Perhaps that sublime voice will succeed in softening my heart," he said to himself; and he actually ventured to penetrate in disguise into the *palazzo* where he was known to every eye. We may imagine the Duchessa's emotion when, right at the end of the concert, she noticed a man in the full livery of a *chasseur*, standing by the door of the big drawing-room: that pose reminded her of someone. She went to look for Conte Mosca, who only then informed her of the signal and truly incredible folly of Fabrizio. He took it extremely well. This love for another than the Duchessa pleased him greatly; the Conte, a perfect *galantuomo*, apart from politics, acted upon the maxim that he could himself find happiness only so long as the Duchessa was happy. "I shall save him from himself," he said to his mistress; "judge of our enemies' joy if he were arrested in this *palazzo!* Also I have more than a hundred men with me here, and that is why I made them ask you for the keys of the great reservoir. He gives out that he is madly in love with Fausta, and up to the present has failed to get her away from Conte M——, who lets the foolish woman live the life of a queen." The Duchessa's features betrayed the keenest grief; so Fabrizio was nothing more than a libertine, utterly incapable of any tender and serious feeling. "And not to come and see us! That is what I shall never be able to

forgive him!" she said at length; "and I writing to him every
day to Bologna!"

"I greatly admire his restraint," replied the Conte; "he
does not wish to compromise us by his escapade, and it will
be amusing to hear him tell us about it."

Fausta was too great a fool to be able to keep quiet
about what was on her mind; the day after the concert,
every melody in which her eyes had addressed to that tall
young man dressed as a *chasseur*, she spoke to Conte
M—— of an unknown admirer. "Where do you see him?"
asked the Conte in a fury. "In the streets, in church," replied
Fausta, at a loss for words. At once she sought to atone
for her imprudence, or at least to eliminate from it anything that could suggest Fabrizio: she dashed into an endless description of a tall young man with red hair; he had
blue eyes; no doubt he was some Englishman, very rich
and very awkward, or some prince. At this word Conte
M——, who did not shine in the accuracy of his percep-
tions, conceived the idea, deliciously flattering to his vanity,
that this rival was none other than the Crown Prince of
Parma. This poor melancholy young man, guarded by five
or six governors, under-governors, preceptors, etc., etc., who
never allowed him out of doors until they had first held
council together, used to cast strange glances at all the passable women whom he was permitted to approach. At the
Duchessa's concert, his rank had placed him in front of all
the rest of the audience in an isolated armchair within three
yards of the fair Fausta, and his stare had been supremely
shocking to Conte M——. This hallucination of an exquisite
vanity, that he had a Prince for a rival, greatly amused
Fausta, who took delight in confirming it with a hundred
details artlessly supplied.

"Your race," she asked the Conte, "is surely as old as
that of the Farnese, to which this young man belongs?"

"What do you mean? As old? I have no bastardy in my
family, thank you." [1]

As luck would have it, Conte M—— never had an opportunity of studying this pretended rival at his leisure, which
confirmed him in the flattering idea of his having a Prince
for antagonist. The fact was that whenever the interests of
his enterprise did not summon Fabrizio to Parma, he re-

[1] Pier-Luigi, the first sovereign of the Farnese family, so renowned for his virtues, was, as is generally known, a natural son
of His Holiness Pope Paul III.

mained in the woods round Sacca and on the bank of the
Po. Conte M—— was indeed more proud, but was also more
prudent since he had imagined himself to be on the way to
disputing the heart of Fausta with a Prince; he begged her
very seriously to observe the greatest restraint in all her
doings. After flinging himself on his knees like a jealous
and impassioned lover, he declared to her in so many words
that his honour was involved in her not being made the
dupe of the young Prince.

"Excuse me, I should not be his dupe if I cared for him;
I must say, I have never yet seen a Prince at my feet."

"If you yield," he went on with a haughty stare, "I may
not perhaps be able to avenge myself on the Prince but I
will, most assuredly, be avenged"; and he went out, slam-
ming the doors behind him. Had Fabrizio presented himself at that moment, he would have won his cause.

"If you value your life," her lover said to her that evening as he bade her good night after the performance, "see
that it never comes to my ears that the young Prince has
been inside your house. I can do nothing to him, curse
him, but do not make me remember that I can do everything to you!"

"Ah, my little Fabrizio," cried Fausta, "if I only knew
where to find you!"

Wounded vanity may carry a young man far who is rich
and from his cradle has always been surrounded by flat-
terers. The very genuine passion that Conte M—— felt for
Fausta revived with furious intensity; it was in no way
checked by the dangerous prospect of his coming into conflict with the only son of the Sovereign in whose dominions
he happened to be staying; at the same time he had not the
courage to try to see this Prince, or at least to have him
followed. Not being able to attack him in any other way,
M—— dared to consider making him ridiculous. "I shall be
banished for ever from the States of Parma," he said to
himself; "Pshaw! What does that matter?" Had he sought
to reconnoitre the enemy's position, he would have learned
that the poor young Prince never went out of doors without
being followed by three or four old men, tiresome guardians
of etiquette, and that the one pleasure of his choice that
was permitted him in the world was mineralogy. By day,
as by night, the little *palazzo* occupied by Fausta, to which
the best society of Parma went in crowds, was surrounded
by watchers; M—— knew, hour by hour, what she was

doing, and, more important still, what others were doing round about her. There is this to be said in praise of the precautions taken by her jealous lover: this eminently capricious woman had at first no idea of the multiplication of his vigilance. The reports of all his agents informed Conte M—— that a very young man, wearing a wig of red hair, appeared very often beneath Fausta's windows, but always in a different disguise. "Evidently, it is the young Prince," thought M——, "otherwise, why the disguise? And, by gad, a man like me is not made to give way to him. But for the usurpations of the Venetian Republic, I should be a Sovereign Prince myself."

On the feast of Santo Stefano, the reports of the spies took on a more sombre hue; they seemed to indicate that Fausta was beginning to respond to the stranger's advances. "I can go away this instant, and take the woman with me!" M—— said to himself; "but no! At Bologna I fled from del Dongo; here I should be fleeing before a Prince. But what could the young man say? He might think that he had succeeded in making me afraid. And, by God, I come of as good a family as he." M—— was furious, but, to crown his misery, he made a particular point of not letting himself appear in the eyes of Fausta, whom he knew to be of a mocking spirit, in the ridiculous character of a jealous lover. On Santo Stefano's day, then, after having spent an hour with her and been welcomed by her with an ardour which seemed to him the height of insincerity, he left her, shortly before eleven o'clock, getting ready to go and hear mass in the church of San Giovanni. Conte M—— returned home, put on the shabby black coat of a young student of theology, and hastened to San Giovanni; he chose a place behind one of the tombs that adorn the third chapel on the right; he could see everything that went on in the church beneath the arm of a cardinal who is represented as kneeling upon his tomb; this statue kept the light from the back of the chapel and gave him sufficient concealment. Presently he saw Fausta arrive, more beautiful than ever. She was in full array, and a score of admirers, drawn from the highest ranks of society, furnished her with an escort. Joyous smiles broke from her eyes and lips. "It is evident," thought the jealous wretch, "that she counts upon meeting here the man she loves, whom for a long time, perhaps, thanks to me, she has been prevented from seeing." Suddenly, the keen look of happiness in her eyes seemed to double

in intensity; "My rival is here," muttered M——, and the
fury of his outraged vanity knew no bounds. "What sort of
figure do I cut here, serving as pendant to a young Prince
in disguise?" But despite every effort on his part, he could
never succeed in identifying this rival, for whom his famished gaze kept seeking in every direction.

All through the service Fausta, after letting her eyes wander over the whole church, would end by bringing her gaze
to rest, charged with love and happiness, on the dim corner
in which M—— was concealed. In an impassioned heart,
love is liable to exaggerate the slightest shades of meaning;
it draws from them the most ridiculous conclusions; did not
poor M—— end by persuading himself that Fausta had seen
him, that, having in spite of his efforts perceived his deadly
jealousy, she wished to reproach him with it and at the
same time to console him for it with these tender glances?

The tomb of the cardinal, behind which M—— had taken
his post of observation, was raised four or five feet above
the marble floor of San Giovanni. The fashionable mass ending about one o'clock, the majority of the faithful left the
church, and Fausta dismissed the *beaux* of the town, on a
pretext of devotion; as she remained kneeling on her chair,
her eyes, which had grown more tender and more brilliant,
were fixed on M——; since there were now only a few people left in the building, she no longer put her eyes to the
trouble of ranging over the whole of it before coming joyfully to rest on the cardinal's statue. "What delicacy!"
thought Conte M——, imagining that he was the object
of her gaze. At length Fausta rose and quickly left the
church after first making some odd movements with her
hands.

M——, blind with love and almost entirely relieved of his
mad jealousy, had left his post to fly to his mistress's
palazzo and thank her a thousand, thousand times, when,
as he passed in front of the cardinal's tomb, he noticed a
young man all in black: this funereal being had remained
until then on his knees, close against the epitaph on the
tomb, in such a position that the eyes of the jealous lover,
in their search for him, must pass over his head and miss
him altogether.

This young man rose, moved briskly away, and was immediately surrounded by seven or eight persons, somewhat
clumsy in their gait, of a singular appearance, who seemed
to belong to him. M—— hurried after him, but, without

any marked sign of obstruction, was stopped in the narrow passage formed by the wooden drum of the door by these clumsy men who were protecting his rival; and when finally, at the tail of their procession, he reached the street, he was in time only to see someone shut the door of a carriage of humble aspect, which, by an odd contrast, was drawn by a pair of excellent horses, and in a moment had passed out of sight.

He returned home panting with fury; presently there arrived his watchers, who reported impassively that that morning the mysterious lover, disguised as a priest, had been kneeling in an attitude of great devotion against a tomb which stood in the entrance of a dark chapel in the church of San Giovanni. Fausta had remained in the church until it was almost empty, and had then rapidly exchanged certain signs with the stranger; with her hands she had seemed to be making a series of crosses. M—— hastened to the faithless one's house; for the first time she could not conceal her uneasiness; she told him, with the artless mendacity of a passionate woman, that, as usual, she had gone to San Giovanni, but that she had seen no sign there of that man who was persecuting her. On hearing these words, M——, beside himself with rage, railed at her as at the vilest of creatures, told her everything that he had seen himself, and, the boldness of her lies increasing with the force of his accusations, took his dagger and flung himself upon her. With great coolness Fausta said to him:

"Very well, everything you complain of is the absolute truth, but I have tried to keep it from you so that you should not go rushing desperately into mad plans of vengeance which may ruin us both; for, let me tell you once for all, as far as I can make out, the man who is persecuting me with his attentions is one who is accustomed not to meet with any opposition to his wishes, in this country at any rate." Having very skilfully reminded M—— that, after all, he had no legal authority over her, Fausta ended by saying that probably she would not go again to the church of San Giovanni. M—— was desperately in love; a trace of coquetry had perhaps combined itself with prudence in the young woman's heart; he felt himself disarmed. He thought of leaving Parma; the young Prince, however powerful he might be, could not follow him, or if he did follow him would cease to be anything more than his equal. But pride represented to him afresh that this departure must inevitably have the appearance of a flight, and Conte M—— forbade himself to think of it.

"He has no suspicion that my little Fabrizio is here," the singer said to herself, delighted, "and now we can make a fool of him in the most priceless fashion!"

Fabrizio had no inkling of his good fortune; finding next day that the singer's windows were carefully shuttered, and not seeing her anywhere, he began to feel that the joke was lasting rather too long. He felt some remorse. "In what sort of position am I putting that poor Conte Mosca, and he the Minister of Police! They will think he is my accomplice, I shall have come to this place to ruin his career! But if I abandon a project I have been following for so long, what will the Duchessa say when I tell her of my essays in love?"

One evening when, on the point of giving up everything, he was moralising thus to himself, as he strolled under the tall trees which divided Fausta's *palazzo* from the citadel, he observed that he was being followed by a spy of diminutive stature; in vain did he attempt to shake him off by turning down various streets, this microscopic being seemed always to cling to his heels. Growing impatient, he dashed into a lonely street running along the bank of the Parma, where his men were ambushed; on a signal from him they leaped out upon the poor little spy, who flung himself at their feet; it was Bettina, Fausta's maid; after three days of boredom and seclusion, disguised as a man to escape the dagger of Conte M——, of whom her mistress and she were in great dread, she had undertaken to come out and tell Fabrizio to see someone who loved him passionately and was burning to see him, but that the said person could not appear any more in the church of San Giovanni. "The time has come," Fabrizio said to himself, "hurrah for persistence!"

The little maid was exceedingly pretty, a fact which took Fabrizio's mind from his moralisings. She told him that the avenue and all the streets through which he had passed that evening were being jealously watched, though quite unobtrusively, by M——'s spies. They had taken rooms on the ground floors or on the first storeys of the houses; hidden behind the shutters and keeping absolutely silent, they observed everything that went on in the apparently quite deserted street, and heard all that was said.

"If those spies had recognised my voice," said little Bettina, "I should have been stabbed without mercy as soon as I got back to the house, and my poor mistress with me, perhaps."

This terror rendered her charming in Fabrizio's eyes.

"Conte M——," she went on, "is furious, and the Signora knows that he will stick at nothing. . . . She told me to say to you that she would like to be a hundred leagues away from here with you."

Then she gave an account of the scene on St. Stephen's day, and of the fury of M——, who had missed none of the glances and signs of affection which Fausta, madly in love that day with Fabrizio, had directed towards him. The Conte had drawn his dagger, had seized Fausta by the hair, and, but for her presence of mind, she must have perished.

Fabrizio made the pretty Bettina come up to a little apartment which he had near there. He told her that he came from Turin, and was the son of an important personage who happened at that moment to be in Parma, which meant that he had to be most careful in his movements. Bettina replied with a smile that he was a far grander gentleman than he chose to appear. It took our hero some little time to realise that the charming girl took him for no less a personage than the Crown Prince himself. Fausta was beginning to be frightened, and to love Fabrizio; she had taken the precaution of not mentioning his name to her maid, but of speaking to her always of the Prince. Finally Fabrizio admitted to the pretty girl that she had guessed aright: "But if my name gets out," he added, "in spite of the great passion of which I have furnished your mistress with so many proofs, I shall be obliged to cease to see her, and at once my father's Ministers, those rascally jokers whom I shall bring down from their high places some day, will not fail to send her an order to quit the country which up to now she has been adorning with her presence."

Towards morning, Fabrizio arranged with the little lady's maid a number of plans by which he might gain admission to Fausta's house. He summoned Lodovico and another of his retainers, a man of great cunning, who came to an understanding with Bettina while he himself wrote the most extravagant letter to Fausta; the situation allowed all the exaggerations of tragedy, and Fabrizio did not miss the opportunity. It was not until day was breaking that he parted from the little lady's maid, whom he left highly satisfied with the ways of the young Prince.

It had been repeated a hundred times over that, Fausta

having now come to an understanding with her lover, the latter was no longer to pass to and fro beneath the windows of the little *palazzo* except when he could be admitted there, and that then a signal would be given. But Fabrizio, in love with Bettina, and believing himself to have come almost to the point with Fausta, could not confine himself to his village two leagues outside Parma. The following evening, about midnight, he came on horseback and with a good escort to sing under Fausta's windows an air then in fashion, the words of which he altered. "Is not this the way in which our friends the lovers behave?" he asked himself.

Now that Fausta had shewn a desire to meet him, all this pursuit seemed to Fabrizio very tedious. "No, I am not really in love in the least," he assured himself as he sang (none too well) beneath the windows of the little *palazzo;* "Bettina seems to me a hundred times preferable to Fausta, and it is by her that I should like to be received at this moment." Fabrizio, distinctly bored, was returning to his village when, five hundred yards from Fausta's *palazzo,* fifteen or twenty men flung themselves upon him; four of them seized his horse by the bridle, two others took hold of his arms. Lodovico and Fabrizio's *bravi* were attacked, but managed to escape; they fired several shots with their pistols. All this was the affair of an instant: fifty lighted torches appeared in the street in the twinkling of an eye, as though by magic. All these men were well armed. Fabrizio had jumped down from his horse in spite of the men who were holding him; he tried to clear a space round him; he even wounded one of the men who was gripping his arms in hands like a pair of vices; but he was greatly surprised to hear this man say to him, in the most respectful tone:

"Your Highness will give me a good pension for this wound, which will be better for me than falling into the crime of high treason by drawing my sword against my Prince."

"So this is the punishment I get for my folly," thought Fabrizio; "I shall have damned myself for a sin which did not seem to me in the least attractive."

Scarcely had this little attempt at a battle finished, when a number of lackeys in full livery appeared with a sedan-chair gilded and painted in an odd fashion. It was one of those grotesque chairs used by masked revellers at carnival time. Six men, with daggers in their hands, requested His Highness to get into it, telling him that the cold night air might be injurious to his voice: they affected the most reverential forms, the title "Prince" being every moment repeated and almost shouted. The procession began to move on. Fabrizio counted in the street more than fifty men carrying lighted torches. It might be about one o'clock in the morning; all the populace was gazing out of the windows, the whole thing went off with a certain gravity. "I was afraid of dagger-thrusts on Conte M——'s part," Fabrizio said to himself; "he contents himself with making a fool of me; I had not suspected him of such good taste. But does he really think that he has the Prince to deal with? If he knows that I am only Fabrizio, ware the dirk!"

These fifty men carrying torches and the twenty armed men, after stopping for a long interval under Fausta's windows, proceeded to parade before the finest *palazzi* in the town. A pair of *maggiordomi,* posted one on either side of the sedan-chair, asked His Highness from time to time whether he had any order to give them. Fabrizio took care not to lose his head; by the light which the torches cast he saw that Lodovico and his men were following the procession as closely as possible. Fabrizio said to himself: "Lodovico has only nine or ten men, and dares not attack." From the interior of his sedan-chair he could see quite plainly that the men responsible for carrying out this practical joke were armed to the teeth. He made a show of talking and laughing with the *maggiordomi* who were looking after him. After more than two hours of this triumphal march, he saw that they were about to pass the end of the street in which the *palazzo* Sanseverina stood.

As they turned the corner, he quickly opened the door in the front of the chair, jumped out over one of the carrying poles, felled with a blow from his dagger one of the flunkeys who thrust a torch into his face; he received a stab in the shoulder from a dirk; a second flunkey singed his beard with his lighted torch, and finally Fabrizio reached Lodovico, to whom he shouted: "Kill! Kill everyone carrying a torch!" Lodovico used his sword, and delivered Fabrizio from two men who had started in pursuit of him. He arrived, running, at the door of the *palazzo* Sanseverina; out of curiosity the porter had opened the little door, three feet high, that was cut in the big door, and was gazing in bewilderment at this great mass of torches. Fabrizio sprang inside and shut this miniature door behind him; he ran to the garden and escaped by a gate which opened on to an unfrequented street. An hour later, he was out of the town; at daybreak he crossed the frontier of the States of Modena, and was safe. That evening he entered Bologna. "Here is a fine expedition," he said to himself; "I never even managed to speak to my charmer." He made haste to write letters of apology to the Conte and the Duchessa, prudent letters which, while describing all that was going on in his heart, could not give away any information to an enemy. "I was in love with love," he said to the Duchessa, "I have done everything in the world to acquire knowledge of it; but it appears that nature has refused me a heart to love, and to be melancholy; I cannot raise myself above the level of vulgar pleasure," and so forth.

It would be impossible to give any idea of the stir that this escapade caused in Parma. The mystery of it excited curiosity: innumerable people had seen the torches and the sedan-chair. But who was the man they were carrying away, to whom every mark of respect was paid? No one of note was missing from the town next day.

The humble folk who lived in the street from which the prisoner had made his escape did indeed say that they had seen a corpse; but in daylight, when they ventured out of their houses, they found no other traces of the fray than quantities of blood spilled on the pavement. More than twenty thousand sight-seers came to visit the street that day. Italian towns are accustomed to singular spectacles, but the *why* and the *wherefore* of these are always known. What shocked Parma about this occurrence was that even a month afterwards, when people had ceased to speak of nothing but the torchlight procession, nobody, thanks to the prudence of Conte Mosca, had been able to guess the name of the rival who had sought to carry off Fausta from Conte M——. This jealous and vindictive lover had taken flight at the beginning of the parade. By the Conte's order, Fausta was sent to the citadel. The Duchessa laughed heartily over a little act of injustice which the Conte was obliged to commit to put a stop to the curiosity of the Prince, who otherwise might have succeeded in hitting upon the name of Fabrizio.

There was to be seen at Parma a scholar, arrived there from the North to write a History of the Middle Ages; he was in search of manuscripts in the libraries, and the Conte had given him every possible facility. But this scholar, who was still quite young, shewed a violent temper; he believed, for one thing, that everybody in Parma was trying to make a fool of him. It was true that the boys in the streets sometimes followed him on account of an immense shock of bright red hair which he displayed with pride. This scholar imagined that at his inn they were asking exaggerated prices for everything, and he never paid for the smallest trifle without first looking up its price in the *Travels* of a certain Mrs. Starke, a book which has gone into its twentieth edition because it indicates to the prudent Englishman the price of a turkey, an apple, a glass of milk, and so forth.

The scholar with the fiery crest, on the evening of the very day on which Fabrizio made this forced excursion, flew into a rage at his inn, and drew from his pocket a brace of small pistols to avenge himself on the *cameriere* who demanded two soldi for an indifferent peach. He was arrested, for to carry pocket pistols is a serious crime!

As this irascible scholar was long and lean, the Conte conceived the idea, next morning, of making him pass in the Prince's eyes as the rash fellow who, having tried to steal away Fausta from Conte M——, had afterwards been hoaxed. The carrying of pocket pistols is punishable at Parma with three years in the galleys; but this punishment is never enforced. After a fortnight in prison, during which time the scholar had seen no one but a lawyer who had put in him a terrible fright by his account of the atrocious laws aimed by the pusillanimity of those in power against the bearers of hidden arms, another lawyer visited the prison and told him of the expedition inflicted by Conte M—— on a rival who had not yet been identified. "The police do not wish to admit to the Prince that they have not been able to find out who this rival is. Confess that you were seeking to find favour with Fausta; that fifty brigands carried you off while you were singing beneath her window; that for an hour they took you about the town in a sedan-chair without saying anything to you that was not perfectly proper. There is nothing humiliating about this confession, you are asked to say only one word. As soon as, by saying it, you have relieved the police from their difficulty, you will be put into a post-chaise and driven to the frontier, where they will bid you good-bye."

The scholar held out for a month; two or three times the Prince was on the point of having him brought to the Ministry of the Interior, and of being present in person at his examination. But at last he gave no more thought to the matter when the scholar, losing patience, decided to confess everything, and was conveyed to the frontier. The Prince remained convinced that Conte M——'s rival had a forest of red hair.

Three days after the escapade, while Fabrizio, who was in hiding at Bologna, was planning with the faithful Lodovico the best way to catch Conte M——, he learned that he too was hiding in a village in the mountains on the road to Florence. The Conte had only two or three of his *buli* with him; next day, just as he was coming home from his ride, he was seized by eight men in masks who gave him to understand that they were *sbirri* from Parma. They conducted him, after bandaging his eyes, to an inn two leagues farther up the mountains, where he found himself treated with the utmost possible respect, and an abundant supper awaiting him. He was served with the best wines of Italy and Spain.

"Am I a State prisoner then?" asked the Conte.

"Nothing of the sort," the masked Lodovico answered him, most politely. "You have given offence to a private citizen by taking upon yourself to have him carried about in a sedan-chair; to-morrow morning he wishes to fight a duel with you. If you kill him, you will find a pair of good horses, money, and relays prepared for you along the road to Genoa."

"What is the name of this fire-eater?" asked the Conte with irritation.

"He is called *Bombace*. You will have the choice of weapons and good seconds, thoroughly loyal, but it is essential that one of you die!"

"Why, it is murder, then!" said the Conte; growing frightened.

"Please God, no! It is simply a duel to the death with the young man whom you have had carried about the streets of Parma in the middle of the night, and whose honour would be tarnished if you remained alive. One or other of you is superfluous on this earth, therefore try to kill him; you shall have swords, pistols, sabres, all the weapons that can be procured at a few hours' notice, for we have to make haste; the police at Bologna are most diligent, as you perhaps know, and they must on no account interfere with this duel which is necessary to the honour of the young man whom you have made to look foolish."

"But if this young man is a Prince. . . ."

"He is a private citizen like yourself, and indeed a great

deal less wealthy than you, but he wishes to fight to the
death, and he will force you to fight, I warn you."

"Nothing in the world frightens me!" cried M——.

"That is just what your adversary most passionately desires," replied Lodovico. "To-morrow, at dawn, prepare to
defend your life; it will be attacked by a man who has good
reason to be extremely angry, and will not let you off lightly;
I repeat that you will have the choice of weapons; and remember to make your will."

Next morning, about six o'clock, breakfast was brought to
Conte M——, a door was then opened in the room in which
he was confined, and he was made to step into the courtyard of a country inn; this courtyard was surrounded by
hedges and walls of a certain height, and its doors had been
carefully closed.

In a corner, upon a table which the Conte was requested
to approach, he found several bottles of wine and brandy,
two pistols, two swords, two sabres, paper and ink; a score
of *contadini* stood in the windows of the inn which overlooked the courtyard. The Conte implored their pity. "They
want to murder me," he cried, "save my life!"

"You deceive yourself, or you wish to deceive others,"
called out Fabrizio, who was at the opposite corner of the
courtyard, beside a table strewn with weapons. He was in
his shirtsleeves, and his face was concealed by one of those
wire masks which one finds in fencing-rooms.

"I require you," Fabrizio went on, "to put on the wire
mask which is lying beside you, then to advance towards
me with a sword or with pistols; as you were told yesterday
evening, you have the choice of weapons."

Conte M—— raised endless difficulties, and seemed most
reluctant to fight; Fabrizio, for his part, was afraid of the
arrival of the police, although they were in the mountains
quite five leagues from Bologna. He ended by hurling at his
rival the most atrocious insults; at last he had the good
fortune to enrage Conte M——, who seized a sword and advanced upon him. The fight began quietly enough.

After a few minutes, it was interrupted by a great tumult.
Our hero had been quite aware that he was involving himself in an action which, for the rest of his life, might be
a subject of reproach or at least of slanderous imputations.
He had sent Lodovico into the country to procure witnesses.
Lodovico gave money to some strangers who were working
in a neighbouring wood; they ran to the inn shouting, think-

ing that the game was to kill an enemy of the man who had paid them. When they reached the inn, Lodovico asked them to keep their eyes open and to notice whether either of the two young men who were fighting acted treacherously and took an unfair advantage over the other.

The fight, which had been interrupted for the time being by the cries of murder uttered by the *contadini*, was slow in beginning again. Fabrizio offered fresh insults to the fatuity of the Conte. "Signor Conte," he shouted to him, "when one is insolent, one ought to be brave also. I feel that the conditions are hard on you; you prefer to pay people who are brave." The Conte, once more stung to action, began to shout to him that he had for years frequented the fencing-school of the famous Battistini at Naples, and that he was going to punish his insolence. Conte M——'s anger having at length reappeared, he fought with a certain determination, which did not however prevent Fabrizio from giving him a very pretty thrust in the chest with his sword, which kept him in bed for several months. Lodovico, while giving first aid to the wounded man, whispered in his ear: "If you report this duel to the police, I will have you stabbed in your bed."

Fabrizio withdrew to Florence; as he had remained in hiding at Bologna, it was only at Florence that he received all the Duchessa's letters of reproach; she could not forgive his having come to her concert and made no attempt to speak to her. Fabrizio was delighted by Conte Mosca's letters; they breathed a sincere friendship and the most noble sentiments. He gathered that the Conte had written to Bologna, in such a way as to clear him of any suspicion which might attach to him as a result of the duel. The police behaved with perfect justice: they reported that two strangers, of whom one only, the wounded man, was known to them (namely Conte M——), had fought with swords, in front of more than thirty *contadini*, among whom there had arrived towards the end of the fight the curate of the village, who had made vain efforts to separate the combatants. As the name of Giuseppe Bossi had never been mentioned, less than two months afterwards Fabrizio returned to Bologna, more convinced than ever that his destiny condemned him never to know the noble and intellectual side of love. So much he gave himself the pleasure of explaining at greath length to the Duchessa; he was thoroughly tired of his solitary life and now felt a passionate desire to return to those charming evenings which he used to pass with the Conte and his aunt. Since then he had never tasted the delights of good society.

"I am so bored with the thought of the love which I sought to give myself, and of Fausta," he wrote to the Duchessa, "that now, even if her fancy were still to favour me, I would not go twenty leagues to hold her to her promise; so have no fear, as you tell me you have, of my going to Paris, where I see that she has now made her appearance and has created a *furore*. I would travel all the leagues in the world to spend an evening with you and with that Conte who is so good to his friends."

END OF VOLUME I

THE
CHARTERHOUSE
OF
PARMA

VOLUME TWO

CHAPTER FOURTEEN

WHILE FABRIZIO was in pursuit of love, in a village near Parma, the Fiscal General Rassi, who did not know that he was so near, continued to treat his case as though he had been a Liberal: he pretended to be unable to find—or, rather, he intimidated—the witnesses for the defence; and finally, after the most ingenious operations, carried on for nearly a year, and about two months after Fabrizio's final return to Bologna, on a certain Friday, the Marchesa Raversi, mad with joy, announced publicly in her drawing-room that next day the sentence which had just been pronounced, in the last hour, on young del Dongo would be presented to the Prince for his signature and approved by him. A few minutes later the Duchessa was informed of this utterance by her enemy.

"The Conte must be extremely ill served by his agents!" she said to herself; "only this morning he thought that the sentence could not be passed for another week. Perhaps he would not be sorry to see my young Grand Vicar kept out of Parma; but," she added, breaking into song, "we shall see him come again; and one day he will be our Archbishop." The Duchessa rang:

"Collect all the servants in the waiting-room," she told her footman, "including the kitchen staff; go to the town commandant and get the necessary permit to procure four post-horses, and have those horses harnessed to my landau within half an hour." All the women of the household were set to work packing trunks: the Duchessa hastily chose a travelling dress, all without sending any word to the Conte; the idea of playing a little joke on him sent her into a transport of joy.

"My friends," she said to the assembled servants, "I learn that my poor nephew is to be condemned in his absence for having had the audacity to defend his life against a raging madman; I mean Giletti, who was trying to kill him. You have all of you had opportunities of seeing how mild and inoffensive Fabrizio's nature is. Rightly indignant at this atrocious outrage, I am going to Florence; I leave for each of you ten years' wages; if you are in distress, write to me, and, so long as I have a sequin, there will be something for you."

The Duchessa meant exactly what she said, and, at her closing words, the servants dissolved in tears; her eyes too were moist: she added in a voice faint with emotion: "Pray to God for me and for Monsignor Fabrizio del Dongo, First Grand Vicar of the Diocese, who to-morrow morning is going to be condemned to the galleys, or, which would be less stupid, to the penalty of death."

The tears of the servants flowed in double volume, and gradually changed into cries that were almost seditious; the Duchessa stepped into her carriage and drove to the Prince's Palace. Despite the unusual hour, she sent in a request for an audience by General Fontana, the Aide-de-Camp in waiting; she was by no means in court dress, a fact which threw this Aide-de-Camp into a profound stupor. As for the Prince, he was not at all surprised, still less annoyed by this request for an audience. "We shall see tears flowing from fine eyes," he said to himself, rubbing his hands. "She comes to sue for pardon; at last that proud beauty is going to humble herself! She was, really, too insupportable with her little airs of independence! Those speaking eyes seemed always to be saying to me, when the slightest thing offended her: 'Naples or Milan would have very different attractions as a residence from your little town of Parma.' In truth, I do not reign over Naples, nor over Milan; but now at last this great lady is coming to ask me for something which depends upon me alone, and which she is burning to obtain;

I always thought that nephew's coming here would bring me some advantage."

While the Prince was smiling at these thoughts, and giving himself up to all these agreeable anticipations, he walked up and down his cabinet, at the door of which General Fontana remained standing stiff and erect like a soldier presenting arms. Seeing the sparkling eyes of the Prince, and remembering the Duchessa's travelling dress, he imagined a dissolution of the Monarchy. His bewilderment knew no bounds when he heard the Prince say: "Ask the Signora Duchessa to wait for a quarter of an hour." The General Aide-de-Camp made his half-turn, like a soldier on parade; the Prince was still smiling: "Fontana is not accustomed," he said to himself, "to see that proud Duchessa kept waiting. The face of astonishment with which he is going to tell her about the *quarter of an hour to wait* will pave the way for the touching tears which this cabinet is going to see her shed." This quarter of an hour was exquisite for the Prince; he walked up and down with a firm and steady pace; he *reigned.* "It will not do at this point to say anything that is not perfectly correct; whatever my feelings for the Duchessa may be, I must never forget that she is one of the greatest ladies of my court. How used Louis XIV to speak to the Princesses, his daughters, when he had occasion to be displeased with them?" And his eyes came to rest on the portrait of the Great King.

The amusing thing was that the Prince never thought of asking himself whether he should shew clemency to Fabrizio, or what form that clemency should take. Finally, at the end of twenty minutes, the faithful Fontana presented himself again at the door, but without saying a word. "The Duchessa Sanseverina may enter," cried the Prince, with a theatrical air. "Now for the tears," he added inwardly, and, as though to prepare himself for such a spectacle, took out his handkerchief.

Never had the Duchessa been so gay or so pretty; she did not seem five and twenty. Seeing her light and rapid little step scarcely brush the carpet, the poor Aide-de-Camp was on the point of losing his reason altogether.

"I have a thousand pardons to ask of Your Serene Highness," said the Duchessa in her light and gay little voice; "I have taken the liberty of presenting myself before him in a costume which is not exactly conventional, but Your Highness has so accustomed me to his kindnesses that I have ventured to hope that he will be pleased to accord me this pardon also."

The Duchessa spoke quite slowly so as to give herself time to enjoy the spectacle of the Prince's face; it was delicious, by reason of the profound astonishment and of the traces of the grand manner which the position of his head and arms still betrayed. The Prince sat as though struck by a thunderbolt; in a shrill and troubled little voice he exclaimed from time to time, barely articulating the words: *"What's that! What's that!"* The Duchessa, as though out of respect, having ended her compliment, left him ample time to reply; then went on:

"I venture to hope that Your Serene Highness deigns to pardon me the incongruity of my costume"; but, as she said the words, her mocking eyes shone with so bright a sparkle that the Prince could not endure it; he studied the ceiling, an act which with him was the final sign of the most extreme embarrassment.

"What's that! What's that!" he said again; then he had the good fortune to hit upon a phrase:—"Signora Duchessa, pray be seated"; he himself drew forward a chair for her, not ungraciously. The Duchess was by no means insensible to this courtesy; she moderated the petulance of her gaze.

"What's that! What's that!" the Prince once more repeated, moving uneasily in his chair, in which one would have said that he could find no solid support.

"I am going to take advantage of the cool night air to travel by post," went on the Duchessa, "and as my absence may be of some duration, I have not wished to leave the States of His Serene Highness without thanking him for all the kindnesses which, in the last five years, he has deigned to shew me." At these words the Prince at last understood; he grew pale; he was the one man in the world who really suffered when he saw himself proved wrong in his calculations. Then he assumed an air of grandeur quite worthy of the portrait of Louis XIV which hung before his eyes. "Very good," thought the Duchessa, "there is a man."

"And what is the reason for this sudden departure?" said the Prince in a fairly firm tone.

"I have long had the plan in my mind," replied the Duchessa, "and a little insult which has been offered to *Monsignor* del Dongo, whom to-morrow they are going to sentence to death or to the galleys, makes me hasten my departure."

"And to what town are you going?"

"To Naples, I think." She added as she rose to her feet: "It only remains for me to take leave of Your Serene Highness and to thank him most humbly for his *former* kindnesses." She, in turn, spoke with so firm an air that the Prince saw that in two minutes all would be over; once the sensation of her departure had occurred, he knew that no further arrangement was possible; she was not a woman to retrace her steps. He ran after her.

"But you know well, Signora Duchessa," he said, taking her hand, "that I have always felt a regard for you, a regard to which it rested only with you to give another name. A murder has been committed; that is a fact which no one can deny; I have entrusted the sifting of the evidence to my best judges. . . ."

At these words the Duchessa rose to her full height; every sign of respect and even of urbanity disappeared in the twinkling of an eye; the outraged woman became clearly apparent, and the outraged woman addressing a creature whom she knew to have broken faith with her. It was with an expression of the most violent anger, and indeed of contempt that she said to the Prince, dwelling on every word:

"I am leaving the States of Your Serene Highness for ever, so as never to hear the names of the Fiscal Rassi and of the other infamous assassins who have condemned my nephew and so many others to death; if Your Serene Highness does not wish to introduce a feeling of bitterness into the last moments that I shall pass in the presence of a Prince who is courteous and intelligent when he is not led astray, I beg him most humbly not to recall to me the thought of those infamous judges who sell themselves for a thousand scudi or a Cross."

The admirable—and, above all, genuine—accent in which these words were uttered made the Prince shudder; he feared for a moment to see his dignity compromised by an accusation even more direct, but on the whole his sensation soon became one of pleasure; he admired the Duchessa; her face and figure attained at that moment to a sublime beauty. "Great God! How beautiful she is!" the Prince said to himself; "one ought to make some concessions to a woman who is so unique, when there probably is not another like her in the whole of Italy. Oh well, with a little policy it might not be impossible one day to make her my mistress: there is a wide gulf between a creature like this and that doll of a

Marchesa Balbi, who moreover robs my poor subjects of at least three hundred thousand francs every year. . . . but did I hear aright?" he thought suddenly; "she said: 'condemned my nephew and so many others.' " Then his anger boiled over, and it was with a stiffness worthy of his supreme rank that the Prince said, after an interval of silence: "And what would one have to do to make the Signora not leave us?"

"Something of which you are not capable," replied the Duchessa in an accent of the most bitter irony and the most unconcealed contempt.

The Prince was beside himself, but his professional training as an Absolute Sovereign gave him the strength to overcome his first impulse. "I must have this woman," he said to himself; "so much I owe to myself, then she must be made to die of shame. . . . If she leaves this cabinet, I shall never see her again." But, mad with rage and hatred as he was at this moment, where was he to find an answer that would at once satisfy the requirements of what he owed to himself and induce the Duchessa not to abandon his court immediately? "She cannot," he said to himself, "repeat or turn to ridicule a gesture," and he placed himself between the Duchessa and the door of his cabinet. Presently he heard a tap at this door.

"Who is the creature," he cried, shouting with the full force of his lungs, "who is the creature who comes here to thrust his fatuous presence upon me?" Poor General Fontana shewed a pallid face of complete discomfiture, and it was with the air of a man in his last agony that he stammered these inarticulate words: "His Excellency the Conte Mosca solicits the honour of being introduced."

"Let him come in," said, or rather shouted, the Prince, and, as Mosca bowed:

"Well," he said to him, "here is the Signora Duchessa Sanseverina, who informs me that she is leaving Parma immediately to go and settle at Naples, and who, incidentally, is being most impertinent to me."

"What!' said Mosca turning pale.

"Oh! So you did not know of this plan of departure?"

"Not a word; I left the Signora at six o'clock, happy and content."

This statement had an incredible effect on the Prince. First of all he looked at Mosca; his increasing pallor shewed the Prince that he was telling the truth and was in no way an accomplice of the Duchessa's desperate action. "In that case," he said to himself, "I lose her for ever; pleasure and

vengeance, all goes in a flash. At Naples she will make
epigrams with her nephew Fabrizio about the great fury of
the little Prince of Parma." He looked at the Duchessa: the
most violent scorn and anger were disputing the possession
of her heart; her eyes were fixed at that moment on Conte
Mosca, and the exquisite curves of that lovely mouth expressed the bitterest disdain. The whole face seemed to be
saying: "Vile courtier!" "So," thought the Prince after he had
examined her, "I lose this means of bringing her back to my
country. At this moment again, if she leaves this cabinet, she
is lost to me; God knows the things she will say about my
judges at Naples. . . . And with that spirit, and that divine
power of persuasion which heaven has bestowed on her, she
will make everyone believe her. I shall be obliged to her for
the reputation of a ridiculous tyrant, who gets up in the
middle of the night to look under his bed. . . ." Then, by
an adroit move and as though he were intending to walk
up and down the room to reduce his agitation, the Prince
took his stand once again in front of the door of the
cabinet; the Conte was on his right, at a distance of three
paces, pale, shattered, and trembling so that he was obliged
to seek support from the back of the armchair in which the
Duchessa had been sitting during the earlier part of the
audience, and which the Prince in a moment of anger had
pushed across the floor. The Conte was in love. "If the
Duchessa goes, I follow her," he said to himself; "but will
she want me in her train? That is the question."

On the Prince's left, the Duchessa, erect, her arms folded
and pressed to her bosom, was looking at him with an
admirable impatience: a complete and intense pallor
had taken the place of the vivid colours which a moment
earlier animated that sublime face.

The Prince, in contrast to the other two occupants of the
room, had a red face and a troubled air; his left hand played
convulsively with the Cross attached to the Grand Cordon of
his Order which he wore under his coat: with his right hand
he caressed his chin.

"What is to be done?" he asked the Conte, without knowing quite what he himself was doing, and carried away by
the habit of consulting this other in everything.

"I can think of nothing, truly, Serene Highness," replied
the Conte with the air of a man yielding up his last breath.
It was all he could do to pronounce the words of his
answer. The tone of his voice gave the Prince the first

consolation that his wounded pride had received during this audience, and this grain of happiness furnished him with a speech that gratified his vanity.

"Very well," he said, "I am the most reasonable of the three; I choose to make a complete elimination of my position in the world. I am going to speak *as a friend"*; and he added, with a fine smile of condescension, beautifully copied from the brave days of Louis XIV, *"like a friend speaking to friends.* Signora Duchessa," he went on, "what is to be done to make you forget an untimely resolution?"

"Truly, I can think of nothing," replied the Duchessa with a deep sigh, "truly, I can think of nothing, I have such a horror of Parma." There was no epigrammatic intention in this speech; one could see that sincerity itself spoke through her lips.

The Conte turned sharply towards her; his courtier's soul was scandalised; then he addressed a suppliant gaze to the Prince. With great dignity and coolness the Prince allowed a moment to pass; then, addressing the Conte:

"I see," he said, "that your charming friend is altogether beside herself; it is quite simple, she *adores* her nephew." And, turning towards the Duchessa, he went on with a glance of the utmost gallantry and at the same time with the air which one adopts when quoting a line from a play: *"What must one do to please those lovely eyes?"*

The Duchessa had had time for reflexion; in a firm and measured tone, and as though she were dictating her *ultimatum*, she replied:

"His Highness might write me a gracious letter, as he knows so well how to do; he might say to me that, not being at all convinced of the guilt of Fabrizio del Dongo, First Grand Vicar of the Archbishop, he will not sign the sentence when it is laid before him, and that these unjust proceedings shall have no consequences in the future."

"What, *unjust!*" cried the Prince, colouring to the whites of his eyes, and recovering his anger.

"That is not all," replied the Duchessa, with a Roman pride, *"this very evening,* and," she added, looking at the clock, "it is already a quarter past eleven, this very evening His Serene Highness will send word to the Marchesa Raversi that he advises her to retire to the country to recover from the fatigue which must have been caused her by a certain prosecution of which she was speaking in her drawing-room in the early hours of the evening." The Prince was pacing the floor of his cabinet like a madman.

"Did anyone ever see such a woman?" he cried. "She is wanting in respect for me!"

The Duchessa replied with inimitable grace:

"Never in my life have I had a thought of shewing want of respect for His Serene Highness; His Highness has had the extreme condescension to say that he was speaking *as a friend to friends*. I have, moreover, no desire to remain at Parma," she added, looking at the Conte with the utmost contempt. This look decided the Prince, hitherto highly uncertain, though his words had seemed to promise a pledge; he paid little attention to words.

There was still some further discussion; but at length Conte Mosca received the order to write the gracious note solicited by the Duchessa. He omitted the phrase: *these unjust proceedings shall have no consequences in the future.* "It is enough," the Conte said to himself, "that the Prince shall promise not to sign the sentence which will be laid before him." The Prince thanked him with a quick glance as he signed.

The Conte was greatly mistaken; the Prince was tired and would have signed anything. He thought that he was getting well out of the difficulty, and the whole affair was coloured in his eyes by the thought: "If the Duchessa goes, I shall find my court become boring within a week." The Conte noticed that his master altered the date to that of the following day. He looked at the clock: it pointed almost to midnight. The Minister saw nothing more in this correction of the date than a pedantic desire to show a proof of exactitude and good government. As for the banishment of the Marchesa Raversi, he made no objection; the Prince took a particular delight in banishing people.

"General Fontana!" he cried, opening the door a little way.

The General appeared with a face shewing so much astonishment and curiosity, that a merry glance was exchanged by the Duchessa and Conte, and this glance made peace between them.

"General Fontana," said the Prince, "you will get into my carriage, which is waiting under the colonnade; you will go to the Marchesa Raversi's, you will send in your name; if she is in bed, you will add that you come from me, and, on entering her room, you will say these precise words and no others: 'Signora Marchesa Raversi, His Serene Highness requests you to leave to-morrow morning, before eight o'clock, for your *castello* at Velleja; His Highness will let you know when you may return to Parma.' "

The Prince's eyes sought those of the Duchessa, who, without giving him the thanks he expected, made him an extremely respectful curtsey, and swiftly left the room.

"What a woman!" said the Prince, turning to Conte Mosca.

The latter, delighted at the banishment of the Marchesa Raversi, which simplified all his ministerial activities, talked for a full half-hour like a consummate courtier; he sought to console his Sovereign's injured vanity, and did not take his leave until he saw him fully convinced that the historical anecdotes of Louis XIV included no fairer page than that with which he had just provided his own future historians.

On reaching home the Duchessa shut her doors, and gave orders that no one was to be admitted, not even the Conte. She wished to be left alone with herself, and to consider for a little what idea she ought to form of the scene that had just occurred. She had acted at random and for her own immediate pleasure; but to whatever course she might have let herself be induced to take she would have clung with tenacity. She had not blamed herself in the least on recovering her coolness, still less had she repented; such was the character to which she owed the position of being still, in her thirty-seventh year, the best-looking woman at court.

She was thinking at this moment of what Parma might have to offer in the way of attractions, as she might have done on returning after a long journey, so fully, between nine o'clock and eleven, had she believed that she was leaving the place for ever.

"That poor Conte did cut a ludicrous figure when he learned of my departure in the Prince's presence. . . . After all, he is a pleasant man, and has a very rare warmth of heart. He would have given up his Ministries to follow me. . . . But on the other hand, during five whole years, he has not had to find fault with me for a single aberration. How many women married before the altar could say as much to their lords and masters? It must be admitted that he is not self-important, he is no pedant; he gives one no desire to be unfaithful to him; when he is with me, he seems always to be ashamed of his power. . . . He cut a funny figure in the presence of his lord and master; if he was in the room now, I should kiss him. . . . But not for anything in the world would I undertake to amuse a Minister who had lost his portfolio; that is a malady which only death can cure, and . . . one which kills. What a misfortune it would be to become Minister when one was young! I must write to him; it is one of the things that he ought to know officially before he quarrels with his Prince. . . . But I am forgetting my good servants."

The Duchessa rang. Her women were still at work packing trunks; the carriage had drawn up under the portico, and was being loaded; all the servants who had nothing else to do were gathered round this carriage, with tears in their eyes. Cecchina, who on great occasions had the sole right to enter the Duchessa's room, told her all these details.

"Call them upstairs," said the Duchessa.

A moment later she passed into the waiting-room.

"I have been promised," she told them, "that the sentence passed on my nephew will not be signed by the Sovereign" (such is the term used in Italy), "and I am postponing my departure. We shall see whether my enemies have enough influence to alter this decision."

After a brief silence, the servants began to shout: *"Evviva la Signora Duchessa!"* and to applaud furiously. The Duchessa, who had gone into the next room, reappeared like an actress taking a *call,* made a little curtsey, full of grace, to her people, and said to them: *"My friends, I thank you."* Had she said the word, all of them at that moment would have marched on the Palace to attack it. She beckoned to a postilion, an old smuggler and a devoted servant, who followed her.

"You will disguise yourself as a *contadino* in easy circumstances, you will get out of Parma as best you can, hire a *sediola* and proceed as quickly as possible to Bologna. You will enter Bologna as a casual visitor and by the Florence gate, and you will deliver to Fabrizio, who is at the Pellegrino, a packet which Cecchina will give you. Fabrizio is in hiding, and is known there as Signor Giuseppe Bossi; do not give him away by any stupid action, do not appear to know him; my enemies will perhaps set spies on your track. Fabrizio will send you back here after a few hours or a few days: and it is on your return journey especially that you must use every precaution not to give him away."

"Ah! Marchesa Raversi's people!" cried the postilion. "We

are on the look-out for them, and if the Signora wished, they would soon be exterminated."

"Some other day, perhaps; but don't, as you value your life, do anything without orders from me."

It was a copy of the Prince's note which the Duchessa wished to send to Fabrizio; she could not resist the pleasure of making him amused, and added a word about the scene which had led up to the note; this word became a letter of ten pages. She had the postilion called back.

"You cannot start," she told him, "before four o'clock, when the gates are opened."

"I was thinking of going out by the big conduit; I should be up to my neck in water, but I should get through. . . ."

"No," said the Duchessa, "I do not wish to expose one of my most faithful servants to the risk of fever. Do you know anyone in the Archbishop's household?"

"The second coachman is a friend of mine."

"Here is a letter for that saintly prelate; make your way quietly into his Palace, get them to take you to his valet; I do not wish Monsignore to be awakened. If he has retired to his room, spend the night in the Palace, and, as he is in the habit of rising at dawn, to-morrow morning, at four o'clock, have yourself announced as coming from me, ask the holy Archbishop for his blessing, hand him the packet you see here, and take the letters that he will perhaps give you for Bologna."

The Duchessa addressed to the Archbishop the actual original of the Prince's note; as this note concerned his First Grand Vicar, she begged him to deposit it among the archives of the Palace, where she hoped that their Reverences the Grand Vicars and Canons, her nephew's colleagues, would be so good as to acquaint themselves with its contents; the whole transaction to be kept in the most profound secrecy.

The Duchessa wrote to Monsignor Landriani with a familiarity which could not fail to charm that honest plebeian; the signature alone filled three lines; the letter, couched in the most friendly tone, was followed by the words: *Angelina-Cornelia-Isotta Valserra del Dongo, Duchessa Sanseverina.*

"I don't believe I have signed all that," the Duchessa said to herself, "since my marriage contract with the poor Duca; but one only gets hold of those people with that sort of thing, and in the eyes of the middle classes the caricature looks like beauty." She could not bring the evening to an end without yielding to the temptation to write to the poor Conte; she announced to him officially, for his *guidance*, she said, *in his relations with crowned heads*, that she did not feel herself to be capable of amusing a Minister in disgrace. "The Prince frightens you; when you are no longer in a position to see him, will it be my business to frighten you?" She had this letter taken to him at once.

For his part, that morning at seven o'clock, the Prince sent for Conte Zurla, the Minister of the Interior.

"Repeat," he told him, "the strictest orders to every *podestà* to have Signor Fabrizio del Dongo arrested. We are informed that possibly he may dare to reappear in our States. This fugitive being now at Bologna, where he seems to defy the judgement of our tribunals, post the *sbirri* who know him by sight: (1) in the villages on the road from Bologna to Parma; (2) in the neighbourhood of Duchessa Sanseverina's *castello* at Sacca, and of her house at Castelnuovo; (3) round Conte Mosca's *castello*. I venture to hope from your great sagacity, Signor Conte, that you will manage to keep all knowledge of these, your Sovereign's orders, from the curiosity of Conte Mosca. Understand that I wish Signor Fabrizio del Dongo to be arrested."

As soon as the Minister had left him, a secret door introduced into the Prince's presence the Fiscal General, Rassi, who came towards him bent double, and bowing at every step. The face of this rascal was a picture; it did full justice to the infamy of the part he had to play, and, while the rapid and extravagant movements of his eyes betrayed his consciousness of his own merits, the arrogant and grimacing assurance of his mouth showed that he knew how to fight against contempt.

As this personage is going to acquire a considerable influence over Fabrizio's destiny, we may say a word here about him. He was tall, he had fine eyes that shewed great intelligence, but a face ruined by smallpox; as for brains, he had them in plenty, and of the finest quality; it was admitted that he had an exhaustive knowledge of the law, but it was in the quality of resource that he specially shone. Whatever the aspect in which a case might be laid before him, he easily and in a few moments discovered the way, thoroughly well founded in law, to arrive at a conviction or an acquittal; he was above all a past-master of the hair-splittings of a prosecutor.

In this man, whom great Monarchs might have envied the

Prince of Parma, one passion only was known to exist: he loved to converse with eminent personages and to please them by buffooneries. It mattered little to him whether the powerful personage laughed at what he said or at his person, or uttered revolting pleasantries at the expense of Signora Rassi; provided that he saw the great man laugh and was himself treated as a familiar, he was content. Sometimes the Prince, at a loss how further to insult the dignity of this Chief Justice, would actually kick him; if the kicks hurt him, he would begin to cry. But the instinct of buffoonery was so strong in him that he might be seen every day frequenting the drawing-room of a Minister who scoffed at him, in preference to his own drawing-room where he exercised a despotic rule over all the stuff gowns of the place. This Rassi had above all created for himself a place apart, in that it was impossible for the most insolent noble to humiliate him; his method of avenging himself for the insults which he had to endure all day long was to relate them to the Prince, in whose presence he had acquired the privilege of saying anything; it is true that the reply often took the form of a well-directed cuff, which hurt him, but he stood on no ceremony about that. The presence of this Chief Justice used to distract the Prince in his moments of ill-humour; then he amused himself by outraging him. It can be seen that Rassi was almost the perfect courtier: a man without honour and without humour.

"Secrecy is essential above all things," the Prince shouted to him without greeting him, treating him, in fact, exactly as he would have treated a scullion, he who was so polite to everybody. "From when is your sentence dated?"

"Serene Highness, from yesterday morning."

"By how many judges is it signed?"

"By all five."

"And the penalty?"

"Twenty years in a fortress, as Your Serene Highness told me."

"The death penalty would have given offence," said the Prince, as though speaking to himself; "it is a pity! What an effect on that woman! But he is a del Dongo, and that name is revered in Parma, on account of the three Archbishops, almost in direct sequence. . . . You say twenty years in a fortress?"

"Yes, Serene Highness," replied the Fiscal, still on his feet and bent double; "with, as a preliminary, a public apology before His Serene Highness's portrait; and, in addition, a diet of bread and water every Friday and on the Vigils of the principal Feasts, *the accused being notorious for his impiety.* This is with an eye to the future and to put a stop to his career."

"Write," said the Prince: " 'His Serene Highness having deigned to turn a considerate ear to the most humble supplications of the Marchesa del Dongo, the culprit's mother, and of the Duchessa Sanseverina, his aunt, which ladies have represented to him that at the date of the crime their son and nephew was extremely young, and in addition led astray by an insensate passion conceived for the wife of the unfortunate Giletti, has been graciously pleased, notwithstanding the horror inspired by such a murder, to commute the penalty to which Fabrizio del Dongo has been sentenced to that of twelve years in a fortress.' "

"Give it to me to sign."

The Prince signed and dated the sentence from the previous day; then, handing it back to Rassi, said to him: "Write immediately beneath my signature: 'The Duchessa Sanseverina having once again thrown herself before the knees of His Highness, the Prince has given permission that every Thursday the prisoner may take exercise for one hour on the platform of the square tower, commonly called Torre Farnese.'

"Sign that," said the Prince, "and, don't forget, keep your mouth shut, whatever you may hear said in the town. You will tell Councillor De' Capitani, who voted for two years in a fortress, and even made a speech upholding so ridiculous a sentence, that I expect him to refresh his memory of the laws and regulations. Once again silence, and good night." Fiscal Rassi performed with great deliberation three profound reverences to which the Prince paid no attention.

This happened at seven o'clock in the morning. A few hours later, the news of the Marchesa Raversi's banishment spread through the town and among the *caffè*: everyone was talking at once of this great event. The Marchesa's banishment drove away for some time from Parma that implacable enemy of small towns and small courts, boredom. General Fabio Conti, who had regarded himself as a Minister already, feigned an attack of gout, and for several days did not emerge from his fortress. The middle classes, and consequently the populace, concluded from what was happening that it was clear that the Prince had decided to confer the

Archbishopric of Parma on Monsignor del Dongo. The shrewd politicians of the *caffè* went so far as to assert that Father Landriani, the reigning Archbishop, had been ordered to plead ill health and to send in his resignation; he was to be awarded a fat pension from the tobacco duty, they were positive about it; this report reached the Archbishop himself, who was greatly alarmed, and for several days his zeal for our hero was considerably paralysed. Two months later, this fine piece of news found its way into the Paris newspapers, with the slight alteration that it was Conte Mosca, nephew of the Duchessa Sanseverina, who was to be made Archbishop.

The Marchesa Raversi meanwhile was raging in her Castello di Velleja; she was by no means one of those little feather-pated women who think that they are avenging themselves when they say damaging things about their enemies. On the day following her disgrace, Cavaliere Riscara and three more of her friends presented themselves before the Prince by her order, and asked him for permission to go to visit her at her *castello*. His Highness received these gentlemen with perfect grace, and their arrival at Velleja was a great consolation to the Marchesa. Before the end of the second week, she had thirty people in her *castello,* all those whom the Liberal Ministry was going to bring into power. Every evening, the Marchesa held a regular council with the better informed of her friends. One day, on which she had received a number of letters from Parma and Bologna, she retired to bed early: her maid let into the room, first of all the reigning lover, Conte Baldi, a young man of admirable appearance and complete insignificance, and, later on, Cavaliere Riscara, his predecessor: this was a small man dark in complexion and in character, who, having begun by being instructor in geometry at the College of Nobles at Parma, now found himself a Councillor of State and a Knight of several Orders.

"I have the good habit," the Marchesa said to these two men, "of never destroying any paper; and well it has served me; here are nine letters which the Sanseverina has written me on different occasions. You will both of you proceed to Genoa, you will look among the gaol-birds there for an ex-lawyer named Burati, like the great Venetian poet, or else Durati. You, Conte Baldi, sit down at my desk and write what I am going to dictate to you.

" 'An idea has occurred to me, and I write you a line. I am going to my cottage, by Castelnuovo; if you care to come over and spend a day with me, I shall be most delighted; there is, it seems to me, no great danger after what has just happened; the clouds are lifting. However, stop before you come to Castelnuovo; you will find one of my people on the road; they are all madly devoted to you. You will, of course, keep the name Bossi for this little expedition. They tell me that you have grown a beard like the most perfect Capuchin, and nobody has seen you at Parma except with the decent countenance of a Grand Vicar.'

"Do you follow me, Riscara?"

"Perfectly; but the journey to Genoa is an unnecessary extravagance; I know a man in Parma who, to be accurate, is not yet in the galleys, but cannot fail to get there in the end. He will counterfeit the Sanseverina's hand to perfection."

At these words, Conte Baldi opened those fine eyes of his to their full extent; he had only just understood.

"If you know this worthy personage of Parma, who, you hope, will obtain advancement," said the Marchesa to Riscara, "presumably he knows you also: his mistress, his confessor, his bosom friend may have been bought by the Sanseverina: I should prefer to postpone this little joke for a few days and not to expose myself to any risk. Start in a couple of hours like good little lambs, don't see a living soul at Genoa, and return quickly." Cavaliere Riscara fled from the room laughing, and squeaking through his nose like Punchinello. *"We must pack up our traps!"* he said as he ran in a burlesque fashion. He wished to leave Baldi alone with the lady. Five days later, Riscara brought the Marchesa back her Conte Baldi, flayed alive; to cut off six leagues, they had made him cross a mountain on mule-back; he vowed that nothing would ever induce him again to take *long journeys*. Baldi handed the Marchesa three copies of the letter which she had dictated to him, and five or six other letters in the same hand, composed by Riscara, which might perhaps be put to some use later on. One of these letters contained some very pretty witticisms with regard to the fears from which the Prince suffered at night, and to the deplorable thinness of the Marchesa Balbi, his mistress, who left a dint in the sofa-cushions, it was said, like the mark made by a pair of tongs, after she had sat on them for a moment. Anyone would have sworn that all these letters came from the hand of Signora Sanseverina.

"Now I know, beyond any doubt," said the Marchesa, "that the favoured lover, Fabrizio, is at Bologna or in the immediate neighbourhood. . . ."

"I am too unwell," cried Conte Baldi, interrupting her; "I ask as a favour to be excused this second journey, or at least I should like to have a few days' rest to recover my health."

"I shall go and plead your cause," said Riscara.

He rose and spoke in an undertone to the Marchesa.

"Oh, very well, then, I consent," she replied with a smile. "Reassure yourself, you shall not go at all," she told Baldi, with a certain air of contempt.

"Thank you," he cried in heart-felt accents. In the end, Riscara got into a post-chaise by himself. He had scarcely been a couple of days in Bologna when he saw, in an open carriage, Fabrizio and little Marietta. "The devil!" he said to himself, "it seems our future Archbishop doesn't let the time hang on his hands; we must let the Duchessa know about this, she will be charmed." Riscara had only to follow Fabrizio to discover his address; next morning our hero received from a courier the letter forged at Genoa; he thought it a trifle short, but apart from that suspected nothing. The thought of seeing the Duchessa and Conte again made him wild with joy, and in spite of anything Lodovico might say he took a post-horse and went off at a gallop. Without knowing it, he was followed at a short distance by Cavaliere Riscara, who on coming to a point six leagues from Parma, at the stage before Castelnuovo, had the satisfaction of seeing a crowd on the *piazza* outside the local prison; they had just led in our hero, recognised at the post-house, as he was changing horses, by two *sbirri* who had been selected and sent there by Conte Zurla.

Cavaliere Riscara's little eyes sparkled with joy; he informed himself, with exemplary patience, of everything that had occurred in the little village, then sent a courier to the Marchesa Raversi. After which, roaming the streets as though to visit the church, which was of great interest, and then to look for a picture by the Parmigianino which, he had been told, was to be found in the place, he finally ran into the *podestà*, who was obsequious in paying his respects to a Councillor of State. Riscara appeared surprised that he had not immediately despatched to the citadel of Parma the conspirator whose arrest he had had the good fortune to secure.

"There is reason to fear," Riscara added in an indifferent tone, "that his many friends, who were endeavouring, the day before yesterday, to facilitate his passage through the States of His Highness, may come into conflict with the police; there were at least twelve or fifteen of these rebels, mounted."

"*Intelligenti pauca!*" cried the *podestà* with a cunning air.

CHAPTER FIFTEEN

A COUPLE OF HOURS later, the unfortunate Fabrizio, fitted with handcuffs and actually attached by a long chain to the *sediola* into which he had been made to climb, started for the citadel of Parma, escorted by eight constables. These had orders to take with them all the constables stationed in the villages through which the procession had to pass; the *podestà* in person followed this important prisoner. About seven o'clock in the evening the *sediola*, escorted by all the little boys in Parma and by thirty constables, came down the fine avenue of trees, passed in front of the little *palazzo* in which Fausta had been living a few months earlier, and finally presented itself at the outer gate of the citadel just as General Fabio Conti and his daughter were coming out. The governor's carriage stopped before reaching the drawbridge to make way for the *sediola* to which Fabrizio was attached; the General instantly shouted for the gates to be shut, and hastened down to the turnkey's office to see what was the matter; he was not a little surprised when he recognised the prisoner, who had grown quite stiff after being fastened to his *sediola* throughout such a long journey; four constables had lifted him down and were carrying him into the turnkey's office. "So I have in my power," thought the feather-pated governor, "that famous Fabrizio del Dongo, with whom anyone would say that for the last year the high society of Parma had taken a vow to occupy themselves exclusively!"

The General had met him a score of times at court, at the Duchessa's and elsewhere; but he took good care not to shew any sign that he knew him; he was afraid of compromising himself.

"Have a report made out," he called to the prison clerk,

"in full detail of the surrender made to me of the prisoner by his worship the *podestà* of Castelnuovo."

Barbone, the clerk, a terrifying personage owing to the volume of his beard and his martial bearing, assumed an air of even greater importance than usual; one would have called him a German gaoler. Thinking he knew that it was chiefly the Duchessa Sanseverina who had prevented his master from becoming Minister of War, he was behaving with more than his ordinary insolence towards the prisoner; in speaking to him he used the pronoun *voi,* which in Italy is the formula used in addressing servants.

"I am a prelate of the Holy Roman Church," Fabrizio said to him firmly, "and Grand Vicar of this Diocese; my birth alone entitles me to respect."

"I know nothing about that!" replied the clerk pertly; "prove your assertions by shewing the brevets which give you a right to those highly respectable titles."

Fabrizio had no such documents and did not answer. General Fabio Conti, standing by the side of his clerk, watched him write without raising his eyes to the prisoner, so as not to be obliged to admit that he was really Fabrizio del Dongo.

Suddenly Clelia Conti, who was waiting in the carriage, heard a tremendous racket in the guard-room. The clerk, Barbone, in making an insolent and extremely long description of the prisoner's person, ordered him to undo his clothing in order to verify and put on record the number and condition of scars received by him in his fight with Giletti.

"I cannot," said Fabrizio, smiling bitterly; "I am not in a position to obey the gentleman's orders, these handcuffs make it impossible."

"What!" cried the General with an innocent air, "the prisoner is handcuffed! Inside the fortress! That is against the rules, it requires an order *ad hoc;* take the handcuffs off him."

Fabrizio looked at him: "There's a nice Jesuit," he thought; "for the last hour he has seen me with these handcuffs, which have been hurting me horribly, and he pretends to be surprised!"

The handcuffs were taken off by the constables; they had just learned that Fabrizio was the nephew of the Duchessa Sanseverina, and made haste to shew him a honeyed politeness which formed a sharp contrast to the rudeness

of the clerk; the latter seemed annoyed by this and said to
Fabrizio, who stood there without moving:

"Come along, there! Hurry up, shew us those scratches
you got from poor Giletti, the time he was murdered." With
a bound, Fabrizio sprang upon the clerk, and dealt him such
a blow that Barbone fell from his chair against the General's
legs. The constables seized hold of the arms of Fabrizio, who
made no attempt to resist them; the General himself and
two constables who were standing by him hastened to pick
up the clerk, whose face was bleeding copiously. Two subordinates who stood farther off ran to shut the door of the
office, in the idea that the prisoner was trying to escape.
The *brigadiere* who was in command of them thought that
young del Dongo could not make a serious attempt at flight,
since after all he was in the interior of the citadel; at the
same time, he went to the window to put a stop to any
disorder, and by a professional instinct. Opposite this open
window and within a few feet of it the General's carriage
was drawn up: Clelia had shrunk back inside it, so as not to
be a witness of the painful scene that was being enacted in
the office; when she heard all this noise, she looked out.

"What is happening?" she asked the *brigadiere*.

"Signorina, it is young Fabrizio del Dongo who has just
given that insolent Barbone a proper smack!"

"What! It is Signor del Dongo that they are taking to
prison?"

"Eh! No doubt about that," said the *brigadiere;* "it is because of the poor young man's high birth that they are
making all this fuss; I thought the Signorina knew all about
it." Clelia remained at the window: when the constables
who were standing round the table moved away a little
she caught a glimpse of the prisoner. "Who would ever have
said," she thought, "that I should see him again for the
first time in this sad plight, when I met him on the road from
the Lake of Como? . . . He gave me his hand to help me into
his mother's carriage. . . . He had the Duchessa with him
even then! Had they begun to love each other as long ago as
that?"

It should be explained to the reader that the members of
the Liberal Party swayed by the Marchesa Raversi and General Conti affected to entertain no doubt as to the tender
intimacy that must exist between Fabrizio and the Duchessa.
Conte Mosca, whom they abhorred, was the object of endless pleasantries for the way in which he was being deceived.

"So," thought Clelia, "there he is a prisoner, and a prisoner in the hands of his enemies. For after all, Conte Mosca, angel as one would like to think him, will be delighted when he hears of this capture."

A loud burst of laughter sounded from the guard-room.

"Jacopo," she said to the *brigadiere* in a voice that quivered with emotion, "what in the world is happening?"

"The General asked the prisoner sharply why he had struck Barbone: Monsignor Fabrizio answered calmly: 'He called me *assassino;* let him produce the titles and brevets which authorise him to give me that title'; and they all laughed."

A gaoler who could write took Barbone's place; Clelia saw the latter emerge mopping with his handkerchief the blood that streamed in abundance from his hideous face; he was swearing like a heathen: "That f— Fabrizio," he shouted at the top of his voice, "I'll have his life, I will, if I have to steal the hangman's rope." He had stopped between the office window and the General's carriage, and his oaths redoubled.

"Move along there," the *brigadiere* told him; "you mustn't swear in front of the Signorina."

Barbone raised his head to look at the carriage, his eyes met those of Clelia who could not repress a cry of horror; never had she seen at such close range so atrocious an expression upon any human face. "He will kill Fabrizio!" she said to herself, "I shall have to warn Don Cesare." This was her uncle, one of the most respected priests in the town; General Conti, his brother, had procured for him the post of *economo* and principal chaplain in the prison.

The General got into the carriage.

"Would you rather stay at home," he said to his daughter, "or wait for me, perhaps for some time, in the courtyard of the Palace? I must go and report all this to the Sovereign."

Fabrizio came out of the office escorted by three constables; they were taking him to the room which had been allotted to him. Clelia looked out of the window, the prisoner was quite close to her. At that moment she answered her father's question in the words: "*I will go with you.*" Fabrizio, hearing these words uttered close to his ear, raised his eyes and met the girl's gaze. He was struck, especially, by the expression of melancholy on her face. "How she has improved," he thought, "since our meeting near

Como! What an air of profound thought! . . . They are
quite right to compare her with the Duchessa; what angelic
features!" Barbone, the bloodstained clerk, who had not
taken his stand beside the carriage without a purpose, held up
his hand to stop the three constables who were leading Fabrizio away, and, moving round behind the carriage until
he reached the window next which the General was sitting:

"As the prisoner has committed an act of violence in the
interior of the citadel," he said to him, "in consideration of
Article 157 of the regulations, would it not be as well to put
the handcuffs on him for three days?"

"Go to the devil!" cried the General, still considerably
embarrassed by this arrest. It was important for him that
he should not drive either the Duchessa or Conte Mosca to
extremes; and besides, what attitude was the Conte going to
adopt towards this affair? After all, the murder of a
Giletti was a mere trifle, and only intrigue had succeeded in
magnifying it into anything of importance.

During this brief dialogue, Fabrizio stood superb among
the group of constables, his expression was certainly the
proudest and most noble that one could imagine; his fine and
delicate features and the contemptuous smile that strayed
over his lips made a charming contrast with the coarse appearance of the constables who stood round him. But all
this formed, so to speak, only the external part of his
physiognomy; he was enraptured by the heavenly beauty
of Clelia, and his eyes betrayed his surprise to the full.
She, profoundly pensive, had never thought of drawing
back her head from the window; he bowed to her with a
half-smile of the utmost respect; then, after a moment's
silence:

"It seems to me, Signorina," he said to her, "that, once
before, near a lake, I had the honour of meeting you, in the
company of the police."

Clelia blushed, and was so taken aback that she could
find no words in which to reply. "What a noble air among
all those coarse creatures," she had been saying to herself
at the moment when Fabrizio spoke to her. The profound
pity, we might almost say the tender emotion in which she
was plunged deprived her of the presence of mind necessary
to find words, no matter what; she became conscious of her
silence and blushed all the deeper. At this moment the
bolts of the great gate of the citadel were drawn back
with a clang; had not His Excellency's carriage been wait-

ing for at least a minute? The echo was so loud in this vaulted passage that even if Clelia had found something to say in reply Fabrizio could not have caught her words.

Borne away by the horses which had broken into a gallop immediately after crossing the drawbridge, Clelia said to herself: "He must have thought me very silly!" Then suddenly she added: "Not only silly; he must have felt that I had a base nature, he must have thought that I did not respond to his greeting because he is a prisoner and I am the governor's daughter."

The thought of such a thing was terrible to this girl of naturally lofty soul. "What makes my behaviour absolutely degrading," she went on, "is that before, when we met for the first time, also *in the company of the police*, as he said just now, it was I who was the prisoner, and he did me a service, and helped me out of a very awkward position. . . . Yes, I am bound to admit, my behaviour was quite complete, it combined rudeness and ingratitude. Alas, poor young man! Now that he is in trouble, everybody is going to behave disgracefully to him. Even if he did say to me then: 'You will remember my name, I hope, at Parma?' how he must be despising me at this moment! It would have been so easy to say a civil word! Yes, I must admit, my conduct towards him has been atrocious. The other time, but for the generous offer of his mother's carriage, I should have had to follow the constables on foot through the dust, or, what would have been far worse, ride pillion behind one of them; it was my father then who was under arrest, and I defenceless! Yes, my behaviour is complete. And how keenly a nature like his must have felt it! What a contrast between his noble features and my behaviour! What nobility! What serenity! How like a hero he looked, surrounded by his vile enemies! Now I understand the Duchessa's passion: if he looks like that in distressing circumstances which may end in frightful disaster, what must he be like when his heart is happy!"

The governor's carriage waited for more than an hour and a half in the courtyard of the Palace, and yet, when the General returned from his interview with the Prince, Clelia by no means felt that he had stayed there too long.

"What is His Highness's will?" asked Clelia.

"His tongue said: Prison! His eyes: Death!"

"Death! Great God!" exclaimed Clelia.

"There now, be quiet!" said the General crossly; "what a fool I am to answer a child's questions."

Meanwhile Fabrizio was climbing the three hundred and eighty steps which led to the Torre Farnese, a new prison built on the platform of the great tower, at a prodigious height from the ground. He never once thought, distinctly that is to say, of the great change that had just occurred in his fortunes. "What eyes!" he said to himself: "What a wealth of expression in them! What profound pity! She looked as though she were saying: 'Life is such a tangled skein of misfortunes! Do not distress yourself too much about what is happening to you! Are we not sent here below to be unhappy?' How those fine eyes of hers remained fastened on me, even when the horses were moving forward with such a clatter under the arch!"

Fabrizio completely forgot to feel wretched.

Clelia accompanied her father to various houses; in the early part of the evening no one had yet heard the news of the arrest of the *great culprit,* for such was the name which the courtiers bestowed a couple of hours later on this poor, rash young man.

It was noticed that evening that there was more animation than usual in Clelia's face; whereas animation, the air of taking part in what was going on round her, was just what was chiefly lacking in that charming young person. When you compared her beauty with that of the Duchessa, it was precisely that air of not being moved by anything, that manner as though of a person superior to everything, which weighed down the balance in her rival's favour. In England, in France, lands of vanity, the general opinion would probably have been just the opposite. Clelia Conti was a young girl still a trifle too slim, who might be compared to the beautiful models of Guido Reni. We make no attempt to conceal the fact that, according to Greek ideas of beauty, the objection might have been made that her head had certain features a trifle too strongly marked; the lips, for instance, though full of the most touching charm, were a little too substantial.

The admirable peculiarity of this face in which shone the artless graces and the heavenly imprint of the most noble soul was that, albeit of the rarest and most singular beauty, it did not in any way resemble the heads of Greek sculpture. The Duchessa had, on the other hand, a little too much of the *recognised* beauty of the ideal type, and her truly Lombard head recalled the voluptuous smile and tender melancholy of Leonardo's lovely paintings of Herodias. Just as the Duchessa shone, sparkled with wit and irony, attaching herself passionately, if one may use the expression, to all the subjects which the course of the conversation brought before her mind's eye, so Clelia showed herself calm and slow to move, whether from contempt for her natural surroundings or from regret for some unfulfilled dream. It had long been thought that she would end by embracing the religious life. At twenty she was observed to show a repugnance towards going to balls, and if she accompanied her father to these entertainments it was only out of obedience to him and in order not to jeopardise the interests of his career.

"It is apparently going to be impossible for me," the General in his vulgarity of spirit was too prone to repeat, "heaven having given me as a daughter the most beautiful person in the States of our Sovereign, and the most virtuous, to derive any benefit from her for the advancement of my fortune! I live in too great isolation, I have only her in the world, and what I must absolutely have is a family that will support me socially, and will procure for me a certain number of houses where my merit, and especially my aptitude for ministerial office shall be laid down as unchallengeable postulates in any political discussion. And there is my daughter, so beautiful, so sensible, so religious, taking offence whenever a young man well established at court attempts to find favour in her sight. If the suitor is dismissed, her character becomes less sombre, and I see her appear almost gay, until another champion enters the lists. The handsomest man at court, Conte Baldi, presented himself and failed to please; the richest man in His Highness's States, the Marchese Crescenzi, has now followed him; she insists that he would make her miserable.

"Decidedly," the General would say at other times, "my daughter's eyes are finer than the Duchessa's, particularly as, on rare occasions, they are capable of assuming a more profound expression; but that magnificent expression, when does anyone ever see it? Never in a drawing-room where she might do justice to it; but simply out driving alone with me, when she lets herself be moved, for instance, by the miserable state of some hideous rustic. 'Keep some reflexion of that sublime gaze,' I tell her at times, 'for the drawing-rooms in which we shall be appearing this evening.' Not a bit of it: should she condescend to accompany me into society, her pure and noble features present the somewhat haughty and scarcely encouraging expression of passive obedience." The General spared himself no trouble, as we can see, in his search for a suitable son-in-law, but what he said was true.

Courtiers, who have nothing to contemplate in their own hearts, notice every little thing that goes on round about them; they had observed that it was particularly on those days when Clelia could not succeed in making herself emerge from her precious musings and feign an interest in anything that the Duchessa chose to stop beside her and tried to make her talk. Clelia had hair of an ashen fairness, which stood out with a charming effect against cheeks that were delicately tinted but, as a rule, rather too pale. The mere shape of her brow might have told an attentive observer that that air, so instinct with nobility, that manner, so far superior to vulgar charms, sprang from a profound indifference to everything that was vulgar. It was the absence and not the impossibility of interest in anything. Since her father had become governor of the citadel, Clelia had found happiness, or at least freedom from vexations in her lofty abode. The appalling number of steps that had to be climbed in order to reach this official residence of the governor, situated on the platform of the main tower, kept away tedious visitors, and Clelia, for this material reason, enjoyed the liberty of the convent; she found there almost all the ideal of happiness which at one time she had thought of seeking from the religious life. She was seized by a sort of horror at the mere thought of putting her beloved solitude and her secret thoughts at the disposal of a young man whom the title of husband would authorise to disturb all this inner life. If, by her solitude, she did not attain to happiness, at least she had succeeded in avoiding sensations that were too painful.

On the evening after Fabrizio had been taken to the fortress, the Duchessa met Clelia at the party given by the Minister of the Interior, Conte Zurla; everyone gathered round them; that evening, Clelia's beauty outshone the Duchessa's. The beautiful eyes of the girl wore an expression so singular and so profound as to be almost indiscreet; there was pity, there were indignation also and anger in her gaze. The gaiety and brilliant ideas of the Duchessa seemed to plunge Clelia into spells of grief that bordered on horror. "What will be the cries and groans of this poor woman," she said to herself, "when she learns that her lover, that young man with so great a heart and so noble a countenance, has just been flung into prison? And that look in the Sovereign's eyes which condemns him to death! O Absolute Power, when wilt thou cease to crush down Italy! O base and venal souls! And I am the daughter of a gaoler! And I have done nothing to deny that noble station, for I did not deign to answer Fabrizio! And once before he was my benefactor! What can he be thinking of me at this moment, alone in his room with his little lamp for sole companion?" Revolted by this idea, Clelia cast a look of horror at the magnificent illumination of the drawing-rooms of the Minister of the Interior.

"Never," the word went round the circle of courtiers who had gathered round the two reigning beauties, and were seeking to join in their conversation, "never have they talked to one another with so animated and at the same time so intimate an air. Can the Duchessa, who is always so careful to smooth away the animosities aroused by the Prime Minister, can she have thought of some great marriage for Clelia?" This conjecture was founded upon a circumstance which until then had never presented itself to the observation of the court: the girl's eyes shewed more fire, and indeed, if one may use the term, more passion than those of the beautiful Duchessa. The latter, for her part, was astonished, and, one may say it to her credit, delighted by the discovery of charms so novel in the young recluse; for an hour she had been gazing at her with a pleasure by no means commonly felt in the sight of a rival. "Why, what can have happened?" the Duchessa asked herself; "never has Clelia looked so beautiful, or, one might say, so touching: can her heart have spoken? . . . But in that case, certainly, it is an unhappy love, there is a dark grief at the root of this strange animation. . . . But unhappy love keeps silent. Can it be a question of recalling a faithless lover by shining in society?" And the Duchessa gazed with attention at all the young men who stood round them. Nowhere could she see any unusual expression, every face shone with a more or less pleased fatuity. "But a miracle must have happened," the Duchessa told herself, vexed by her inability to solve the mystery. "Where is Conte Mosca, that man of discernment? No, I am not mistaken, Clelia is looking at me attentively, and as if I was for her the object of a quite novel interest. Is it the effect of some order received from her father, that vile courtier? I supposed that young and noble mind to be incapable of lowering itself to any pecuniary consideration. Can General Fabio Conti have some decisive request to make of the Conte?"

About ten o'clock, a friend of the Duchessa came up to her and murmured a few words; she turned extremely pale: Clelia took her hand and ventured to press it.

"I thank you, and I understand you now . . . you have a noble heart," said the Duchessa, making an effort to control herself; she had barely the strength to utter these few words. She smiled profusely at the lady of the house, who rose to escort her to the door of the outermost drawing-room: such honours were due only to Princesses of the Blood, and were for the Duchessa an ironical comment on her position at the moment. And so she continued to smile at Contessa Zurla, but in spite of untold efforts did not succeed in uttering a single word.

Clelia's eyes filled with tears as she watched the Duchessa pass through these rooms, thronged at the moment with all the most brilliant figures in society. "What is going to happen to that poor woman," she wondered, "when she finds herself alone in her carriage? It would be an indiscretion on my part to offer to accompany her, I dare not. . . . And yet, what a consolation it would be to the poor prisoner, sitting in some wretched cell, if he knew that he was loved to such a point! What a frightful solitude that must be in which they have plunged him! And we, we are here in these brilliant rooms, how horrible! Can there be any way of conveying a message to him? Great God! That would be treachery to my father; his position is so delicate between the two parties! What will become of him if he exposes himself to the passionate hatred of the Duchessa, who controls the will of the Prime Minister, who in three out of every four things here is the master? On the other hand, the Prince takes an unceasing interest in everything that goes on at the fortress, and will not listen to any jest on that subject; fear makes him cruel. . . . In any case, Fabrizio" (Clelia no longer thought of him as Signor del Dongo) "is greatly to be pitied. . . . It is a very different thing for him from the risk of losing a lucrative post! . . . And the Duchessa! . . . What a terrible passion love is! . . . And yet all those liars in society speak of it as a source of happiness! One is sorry for elderly women because they can no longer feel or inspire love. . . . Never shall I forget what I have just seen; what a sudden change! How those beautiful, radiant eyes of the Duchessa turned dull and dead after the fatal word which

Marchese N—— came up and said to her! . . . Fabrizio
must indeed be worthy of love!"

Breaking in upon these highly serious reflexions, which
were absorbing the whole of Clelia's mind, the complimen-
tary speeches which always surrounded her seemed to her
even more distasteful than usual. To escape from them she
went across to an open window, half screened by a taffeta
curtain; she hoped that no one would be so bold as to
follow her into this sort of sanctuary. This window opened
upon a little grove of orange-trees planted in the ground:
as a matter of fact, every winter they had to be protected
by a covering. Clelia inhaled with rapture the scent of their
blossom, and this pleasure seemed to restore a little calm
to her spirit. "I felt that he had a very noble air," she
thought, "but to inspire such passion in so distinguished a
woman! She has had the glory of refusing the Prince's
homage, and if she had deigned to consent, she would have
reigned as queen over his States. . . . My father says that
the Sovereign's passion went so far as to promise to marry
her if ever he became free to do so. . . . And this love for
Fabrizio has lasted so long! For it is quite five years since
we met them by the Lake of Como. . . . Yes, it is quite five
years," she said to herself after a moment's reflexion. "I was
struck by it even then, when so many things passed unnoticed before my childish eyes. How those two ladies seemed
to admire Fabrizio! . . ."

Clelia remarked with joy that none of the young men
who had been speaking to her with such earnestness had
ventured to approach her balcony. One of them, the Marchese Crescenzi, had taken a few steps in that direction, but
had then stopped by a card-table. "If only," she said to
herself, "under my window in our *palazzo* in the fortress,
the only one that has any shade, I had some pretty orange-
trees like these to look at, my thoughts would be less sad:
but to have as one's sole outlook the huge blocks of stone
of the Torre Farnese. . . . Ah!" she cried with a convulsive
movement, "perhaps that is where they have put him. I must
speak about it at once to Don Cesare! He will be less severe
than the General. My father is certain to tell me nothing
on our way back to the fortress, but I shall find out everything from Don Cesare. . . . I have money, I could buy a
few orange-trees, which, placed under the window of my
aviary, would prevent me from seeing that great wall of
the Torre Farnese. How infinitely more hateful still it will

be to me now that I know one of the people whom it hides
from the light of day! . . . Yes, it is just the third time I
have seen him. Once at court, at the ball on the Princess's
birthday; to-day, hemmed in by three constables, while that
horrible Barbone was begging for handcuffs to be put on
him, and the other time by the Lake of Como. That is quite
five years ago. What a hang-dog air he had then! How
he stared at the constables, and what curious looks his mother
and his aunt kept giving him. Certainly there must have
been some secret that day, some special knowledge which
they were keeping to themselves; at the time, I had an idea
that he too was afraid of the police. . . ." Clelia shuddered;
"But how ignorant I was! No doubt at that time the Duchessa had already begun to take an interest in him. How he
made us laugh after the first few minutes, when the ladies,
in spite of their obvious anxiety, had begun to grow more
accustomed to the presence of a stranger! . . . And this
evening I had not a word to say in reply when he spoke to
me. . . . O ignorance and timidity! How often you have
the appearance of the blackest cowardice! And I am like
this at twenty, yes and past twenty! . . . I was well-advised
to think of the cloister; really I am good for nothing but
retirement. 'Worthy daughter of a gaoler!' he will have
been saying to himself. He despises me, and, as soon as he
is able to write to the Duchessa, he will tell her of my want
of consideration, and the Duchessa will think me a very de-
ceitful little girl; for, after all, this evening she must have
thought me full of sympathy with her in her trouble."

Clelia noticed that someone was approaching, apparently
with the intention of taking his place by her side on the
iron balcony of this window; she could not help feeling
annoyed, although she blamed herself for being so; the meditations in which she was disturbed were by no means without
their pleasant side. "Here comes some troublesome fellow
to whom I shall give a warm welcome!" she thought. She
was turning her head with a haughty stare, when she caught
sight of the timid face of the Archbishop, who was approaching the balcony by a series of almost imperceptible little
movements. "This saintly man has no manners," thought
Clelia. "Why come and disturb a poor girl like me? My
tranquillity is the only thing I possess." She was greeting
him with respect, but at the same time with a haughty air,
when the prelate said to her:

"Signorina, have you heard the terrible news?"

The girl's eyes had at once assumed a totally different expression; but, following the instructions repeated to her a hundred times over by her father, she replied with an air of ignorance which the language of her eyes loudly contradicted:

"I have heard nothing, Monsignore."

"My First Grand Vicar, poor Fabrizio del Dongo, who is no more guilty than I am of the death of that brigand Giletti, has been arrested at Bologna where he was living under the assumed name of Giuseppe Bossi; they have shut him up in your citadel; he arrived there actually *chained* to the carriage that brought him. A sort of gaoler, named Barbone, who was pardoned some time ago after murdering one of his own brothers, chose to attempt an act of personal violence against Fabrizio, but my young friend is not the man to take an insult quietly. He flung his infamous adversary to the ground, whereupon they cast him into a dungeon, twenty feet underground, after first putting handcuffs on his wrists."

"Not handcuffs, no!"

"Ah! Then you do know something," cried the Archbishop. And the old man's features lost their intense expression of discouragement. "But, before we go any farther, someone may come out on to this balcony and interrupt us: would you be so charitable as to convey personally to Don Cesare my pastoral ring here?"

The girl took the ring, but did not know where to put it for fear of losing it.

"Put it on your thumb," said the Archbishop; and he himself slipped the ring into position. "Can I count upon you to deliver this ring?"

"Yes, Monsignore."

"Will you promise me to keep secret what I am going to say, even if circumstances should arise in which you may find it inconvenient to agree to my request?"

"Why, yes, Monsignore," replied the girl, trembling all over as she observed the sombre and serious air which the old man had suddenly assumed. . . .

"Our estimable Archbishop," she went on, "can give me no orders that are not worthy of himself and me."

"Say to Don Cesare that I commend to him my adopted son; I know that the *sbirri* who carried him off did not give him time to take his breviary with him, I therefore request Don Cesare to let him have his own, and if your uncle will send to-morrow to my Palace, I promise to replace the book given by him to Fabrizio. I request Don Cesare also to convey the ring which this pretty hand is now wearing to Signor del Dongo." The Archibishop was interrupted by General Fabio Conti, who came in search of his daughter to take her to the carriage; there was a brief interval of conversation in which the prelate shewed a certain adroitness. Without making any reference to the latest prisoner, he so arranged matters that the course of the conversation led naturally to the utterance of certain moral and political maxims by himself; for instance: "There are moments of crisis in the life of a court which decide for long periods the existence of the most exalted personages; it would be distinctly imprudent to change into *personal hatred* the state of political aloofness which is often the quite simple result of diametrically opposite positions." The Archbishop, letting himself be carried away to some extent by the profound grief which he felt at so unexpected an arrest, went so far as to say that one must undoubtedly strive to retain the position one holds, but that it would be a quite gratuitous imprudence to attract to oneself furious hatreds in consequence of lending oneself to certain actions which are never forgotten.

When the General was in the carriage with his daughter: "Those might be described as threats," he said to her. . . . "Threats, to a man of my sort!"

No other words passed between father and daughter for the next twenty minutes.

On receiving the Archbishop's pastoral ring, Clelia had indeed promised herself that she would inform her father, as soon as she was in the carriage, of the little service which the prelate had asked of her; but after the word *threats,* uttered with anger, she took it for granted that her father would intercept the token; she covered the ring with her left hand and pressed it passionately. During the whole of the time that it took them to drive from the Ministry of the Interior to the citadel, she was asking herself whether it would be criminal on her part not to speak of the matter to her father. She was extremely pious, extremely timorous, and her heart, usually so tranquil, beat with an unaccustomed violence; but in the end the *chi va là* of the sentry posted on the rampart above the gate rang out on the approach of the carriage before Clelia had found a form of words calculated to incline her father not to refuse, so much afraid was she of his refusing. As they climbed the three hundred and sixty steps which led to the governor's residence, Clelia could think of nothing.

She hastened to speak to her uncle, who rebuked her and refused to lend himself to anything.

CHAPTER SIXTEEN

"WELL," CRIED the General, when he caught sight of his brother Don Cesare, "here is the Duchessa going to spend a hundred thousand scudi to make a fool of me and help the prisoner to escape!"

But, for the moment, we are obliged to leave Fabrizio in his prison, at the very summit of the citadel of Parma; he is well guarded and we shall perhaps find him a little altered when we return to him. We must now concern ourselves first of all with the court, where certain highly complicated intrigues, and in particular the passions of an unhappy woman are going to decide his fate. As he climbed the three hundred and ninety steps to his prison in the Torre Farnese, beneath the eyes of the governor, Fabrizio, who had so greatly dreaded this moment, found that he had no time to think of his misfortunes.

On returning home after the party at Conte Zurla's, the Duchessa dismissed her women with a wave of the hand; then, letting herself fall, fully dressed, on to her bed, "Fabrizio," she cried aloud, *"is in the power of his enemies, and perhaps to spite me they will give him poison!"* How is one to depict the moment of despair that followed this statement of the situation in a woman so far from reasonable, so much the slave of every passing sensation, and, without admitting it to herself, desperately in love with the young prisoner? There were inarticulate cries, paroxysms of rage, convulsive movements, but never a tear. She had sent her women away to conceal her tears; she thought that she was going to break into sobs as soon as she found herself alone; but tears, those first comforters in hours of great sorrow, completely failed her. Anger, indignation, the sense of her

269

own inferiority when matched with the Prince, had too firm a mastery of this proud soul.

"Am I not humiliated enough?" she kept on exclaiming; "I am outraged, and, worse still, Fabrizio's life is in danger; and I have no means of vengeance! Wait a moment, my Prince; you kill me, well and good, you have the power to do so; but afterwards I shall have your life. Alas! Poor Fabrizio, how will that help you? What a difference from the day when I was proposing to leave Parma, and yet even then I thought I was unhappy . . . what blindness! I was going to break with all the habits and customs of a pleasant life; alas! without knowing it, I was on the edge of an event which was to decide my fate for ever. Had not the Conte, with the miserable fawning instinct of a courtier, omitted the words *unjust proceedings* from that fatal note which the Prince's vanity allowed me to secure, we should have been saved. I had had the good fortune (rather than the skill, I must admit) to bring into play his personal vanity on the subject of his beloved town of Parma. Then I threatened to leave, then I was free. . . . Great God! What sort of slave am I now? Here I am now nailed down in this foul sewer, and Fabrizio in chains in the citadel, in that citadel which for so many eminent men has been the ante-room of death; and I can no longer keep that tiger cowed by the fear of seeing me leave his den.

"He has too much sense not to realise that I will never move from the infamous tower in which my heart is enchained. Now, the injured vanity of the man may put the oddest ideas into his head; their fantastic cruelty would but whet the appetite of his astounding vanity. If he returns to his former programme of insipid love-making, if he says to me: 'Accept the devotion of your slave or Fabrizio dies,'— well, there is the old story of Judith. . . . Yes, but if it is only suicide for me, it will be murder for Fabrizio; his fool of a successor, our Crown Prince, and the infamous headsman Rassi will have Fabrizio hanged as my accomplice."

The Duchessa wailed aloud: this dilemma, from which she could see no way of escape, was torturing her unhappy heart. Her distracted head could see no other probability in the future. For ten minutes she writhed like a madwoman; then a sleep of utter exhaustion took the place for a few moments of this horrible state, life was crushed out. A few minutes later she awoke with a start and found herself sitting on her bed; she had dreamed that, in her presence, the Prince was going to cut off Fabrizio's head. With what haggard eyes the

Duchessa stared round her! When at length she was convinced that neither Fabrizio nor the Prince was in the room with her, she fell back on her bed and was on the point of fainting. Her physical exhaustion was such, that she could not summon up enough strength to change her position. "Great God! If I could die!" she said to herself. . . . "But what cowardice, for me to abandon Fabrizio in his trouble! My wits are straying. . . . Come, let us get back to the facts; let us consider calmly the execrable position in which I have plunged myself, as though of my own free will. What a lamentable piece of stupidity to come and live at the court of an Absolute Prince! A tyrant who knows all his victims; every look they give him he interprets as a defiance of his power. Alas, that is what neither the Conte nor I took into account when we left Milan: I thought of the attractions of an amusing court; something inferior, it is true, but something in the same style as the happy days of Prince Eugène.

"Looking from without, we can form no idea of what is meant by the authority of a despot who knows all his subjects by sight. The outward form of despotism is the same as that of the other kinds of government: there are judges, for instance, but they are Rassis: the monster! He would see nothing extraordinary in hanging his own father if the Prince ordered him to do so. . . . He would call it his duty. . . . Seduce Rassi! Unhappy wretch that I am! I possess no means of doing so. What can I offer him? A hundred thousand francs, possibly: and they say that, after the last dagger-blow which the wrath of heaven against this unhappy country allowed him to escape, the Prince sent him ten thousand golden sequins in a casket. Besides, what sum of money would seduce him? That soul of mud, which has never read anything but contempt in the eyes of men, enjoys here the pleasure of seeing now fear, and even respect there; he may become Minister of Police, and why not? Then three-fourths of the inhabitants of the place will be his base courtiers, and will tremble before him in as servile a fashion as he himself trembles before his Sovereign.

"Since I cannot fly this detested spot, I must be of use here to Fabrizio: live alone, in solitude, in despair!—what can I do then for Fabrizio? Come; *forward, unhappy woman!* Do your duty; go into society, pretend to think no more of Fabrizio. . . . Pretend to forget him, the dear angel!"

So speaking, the Duchessa burst into tears; at last she

could weep. After an hour set apart for human frailty, she saw with some slight consolation that her mind was beginning to grow clearer. "To have the magic carpet," she said to herself, "to snatch Fabrizio from the citadel and fly with him to some happy place where we could not be pursued, Paris for instance. We should live there, at first, on the twelve hundred francs which his father's agent transmits to me with so pleasing a regularity. I could easily gather together a hundred thousand francs from the remains of my fortune!" The Duchessa's imagination passed in review, with moments of unspeakable delight, all the details of the life which she would lead three hundred leagues from Parma. "There," she said to herself, "he could enter the service under an assumed name. . . . Placed in a regiment of those gallant Frenchmen, the young Valserra would speedily win a reputation; at last he would be happy."

These blissful pictures brought on a second flood of tears, but they were tears of joy. So happiness did exist then somewhere in the world! This state lasted for a long time; the poor woman had a horror of coming back to the contemplation of the grim reality. At length, as the light of dawn began to mark with a white line the tops of the trees in her garden, she forced herself into a state of composure. "In a few hours from now," she told herself, "I shall be on the field of battle; it will be a case for action, and if anything should occur to irritate me, if the Prince should take it into his head to say anything to me about Fabrizio, I am by no means certain that I can keep myself properly in control. I must therefore, here and now, *make plans*.

"If I am declared a State criminal, Rassi will seize everything there is in this *palazzo;* on the first of this month the Conte and I burned, as usual, all papers of which the police might make any improper use; and he is Minister of Police! That is the amusing part of it. I have three diamonds of some value; to-morrow, Fulgenzio, my old boatman from Grianta, will set off for Geneva, where he will deposit them in a safe place. Should Fabrizio ever escape (Great God, be Thou propitious to me!" She crossed herself), "the unutterable meanness of the Marchese del Dongo will decide that it is a sin to supply food to a man pursued by a lawful Sovereign: then he will at least find my diamonds, he will have bread.

"Dismiss the Conte . . . being left alone with him, after what has happened, is the one thing I cannot face. The

poor man! He is not bad really, far from it; he is only
weak. That commonplace soul does not rise to the level of
ours. Poor Fabrizio! Why cannot you be here for a moment
with me to discuss our perils?

"The Conte's meticulous prudence would spoil all my
plans, and besides, I must on no account involve him in my
downfall. . . . For why should not the vanity of that tyrant
cast me into prison? I shall have conspired . . . what could
be easier to prove? If it should be to his citadel that he sent
me, and I could manage, by bribery, to speak to Fabrizio,
were it only for an instant, with what courage would we step
out together to death! But enough of such follies: his Rassi
would advise him to make an end of me with poison; my
appearance in the streets, riding upon a cart, might touch
the hearts of his dear Parmesans. . . . But what is this? Still
romancing? Alas! These follies must be forgiven a poor
woman whose actual lot is so piteous! The truth of all this is
that the Prince will not send me to my death; but nothing
could be more easy than to cast me into prison and keep me
there; he will make his people hide all sorts of suspicious
papers in some corner of my *palazzo,* as they did with that
poor L——. Then three judges—not too big rascals, for they
will have what is called *documentary evidence*—and a dozen
false witnesses will be all he needs. So I may be sentenced to
death as having conspired, and the Prince, in his boundless
clemency, taking into consideration the fact that I have had
the honour of being admitted to his court, will commute my
punishment to ten years in a fortress. But I, so as not to fall
short in any way of that violent character which has led the
Marchesa Raversi and my other enemies to say so many stupid
things about me, will poison myself bravely. So, at least, the
public will be kind enough to believe; but I wager that Rassi
will appear in my cell to bring me gallantly, in the Prince's
name, a little bottle of strychnine, or Perugia opium.

"Yes, I must quarrel in the most open manner with the
Conte, for I do not wish to involve him in my downfall—that
would be a scandalous thing; the poor man has loved me
with such candour! My mistake lay in thinking that a true
courtier would have sufficient heart left to be capable of love.
Very probably the Prince will find some excuse for casting
me into prison; he will be afraid of my perverting public
opinion with regard to Fabrizio. The Conte is a man of perfect
honour; at once he will do what the sycophants of this court,
in their profound astonishment, will call madness, he will

leave the court. I braved the Prince's authority on the evening of the note; I may expect anything from his wounded vanity: does a man who is born a Prince ever forget the sensation I gave him that evening? Besides, the Conte, once he has quarrelled with me, is in a stronger position for being of use to Fabrizio. But if the Conte, whom this decision of mine must plunge in despair, should avenge himself? . . . There, now, is an idea that would never occur to him; his is not a fundamentally base nature like the Prince's; the Conte may, with a sigh of protest, countersign a wicked decree, but he is a man of honour. And besides, avenge himself for what? Simply because, after loving him for five years without giving the slightest offence to his love, I say to him: 'Dear Conte, I had the good fortune to be in love with you: very well, that flame is burning low; I no longer love you, but I know your heart through and through; I retain a profound regard for you and you will always be my best friend."

"What answer can a *galantuomo* make to so sincere a declaration?

"I shall take a new lover, or so at least people will suppose; I shall say to this lover: 'After all, the Prince does right to punish Fabrizio's folly; but on the day of his *festa*, no doubt our gracious Sovereign will set him at liberty.' Thus I gain six months. The new lover whom prudence suggests to me would be that venal judge, that foul hangman of a Rassi. . . . He would find himself ennobled and, as far as that goes, I shall give him the right of entry into good society. Forgive me, dear Fabrizio; such an effort, for me, is beyond the bounds of possibility. What! That monster, still all bespattered with the blood of Conte P—— and of D——! I should faint with horror whenever he came near me, or rather I should seize a knife and plunge it into his vile heart. Do not ask of me things that are impossible!

"Yes, that is the first thing to do: forget Fabrizio! And not the least trace of anger with the Prince; I must resume my ordinary gaiety, which will seem all the more attractive to these souls of mud, in the first place because I shall appear to be submitting with good grace to their Sovereign's will, secondly because, so far from laughing at them, I shall take good care to bring out all their pretty little qualities; for instance, I shall compliment Conte Zurla on the beauty of the white feather in his hat, which he has just had sent him from Lyons by courier, and which keeps him perfectly happy.

"Choose a lover from the Raversi's party. . . . If the Conte goes, that will be the party in office; there is where the power will lie. It will be a friend of the Raversi that will reign over the citadel, for Fabio Conti will take office as Minister. How in the world will the Prince, a man used to good society, a man of intelligence, accustomed to the charming collaboration of the Conte, be able to discuss business with that ox, that king of fools, whose whole life has been occupied with the fundamental problem: ought His Highness's troops to have seven buttons on their uniform, in front, or nine? It is all those brute beasts thoroughly jealous of myself, and that is where you are in danger, dear Fabrizio, it is those brute beasts who are going to decide my fate and yours! Well then, shall I not allow the Conte to hand in his resignation? Let him remain, even if he has to submit to humiliations. He always imagines that to resign is the greatest sacrifice a Prime Minister can make; and whenever his mirror tells him he is growing old, he offers me that sacrifice: a complete rupture, then; yes, and reconciliation only in the event of its being the sole method of prevailing upon him not to go. Naturally, I shall give him his dismissal in the friendliest possible way; but, after his courtierlike omission of the words *unjust proceedings* in the Prince's note, I feel that, if I am not to hate him, I need to spend some months without seeing him. On that decisive evening, I had no need of his cleverness; he had only to write down what I dictated to him, he had only to write those words *which I had obtained* by my own strength of character: he was led away by force of habit as a base courtier. He told me next day that he could not make the Prince sign an absurdity, that we should have had *letters of grace;* why, good God, with people like that, with those monsters of vanity and rancour who bear the name Farnese, one takes what one can get."

At the thought of this, all the Duchessa's anger was rekindled. "The Prince has betrayed me," she said to herself, "and in how dastardly a way! There is no excuse for the man: he has brains, discernment, he is capable of reasoning; there is nothing base in him but his passions. The Conte and I have noticed it a score of times; his mind becomes vulgar only when he imagines that some one has tried to insult him. Well, Fabrizio's crime has nothing to do with politics, it is a trifling homicide, just like a hundred others that are reported every day in his happy States, and the Conte has sworn to me that he has taken pains to procure the most accurate information, and that Fabrizio is innocent. That Giletti was certainly not lacking in courage: finding himself within a few yards of the frontier, he suddenly felt the temptation to rid himself of an attractive rival."

The Duchessa paused for a long time to consider whether it were possible to believe in Fabrizio's guilt, not that she felt that it would have been a very grave sin in a gentleman of her nephew's rank to rid himself of the impertinence of a mummer; but, in her despair, she was beginning to feel vaguely that she would be obliged to fight to prove Fabrizio's innocence. "No," she told herself finally, "here is a decisive proof: he is like poor Pietranera, he always has all his pockets stuffed with weapons, and that day he was carrying only a wretched singled-barrelled gun, and even that he had borrowed from one of the workmen.

"I hate the Prince because he has betrayed me, and betrayed me in the most dastardly fashion; after his written pardon, he had the poor boy seized at Bologna, and all that. But I shall settle that account." About five o'clock in the morning, the Duchessa, crushed by this prolonged fit of despair, rang for her women, who screamed. Seeing her on her bed, fully dressed, with her diamonds, pale as the sheet on which she lay and with closed eyes, it seemed to them as though they beheld her laid out in state after death. They would have supposed that she had completely lost consciousness had they not remembered that she had just rung for them. A few rare tears trickled from time to time down her insentient cheeks; her women gathered from a sign which she made that she wished to be put to bed.

Twice that evening after the party at the Minister Zurla's, the Conte had called on the Duchessa; being refused admittance, he wrote to her that he wished to ask her advice as to his conduct. Ought he to retain his post after the insult that they had dared to offer him? The Conte went on to say: "The young man is innocent; but, were he guilty, ought they to arrest him without first informing me, his acknowledged protector?" The Duchessa did not see this letter until the following day.

The Conte had no virtue; one may indeed add that what the Liberals understand by *virtue* (seeking the greatest happiness of the greatest number) seemed to him silly; he believed himself bound to seek first and foremost the happiness of Conte Mosca della Rovere; but he was entirely honourable, and perfectly sincere when he spoke of his resignation.

Never in his life had he told the Duchessa a lie; she, as it happened, did not pay the slightest attention to this letter; her attitude, and a very painful attitude it was, had been adopted: *to pretend to forget Fabrizio;* after that effort, nothing else mattered to her.

Next day, about noon, the Conte, who had called ten times at the *palazzo* Sanseverina, was at length admitted; he was appalled when he saw the Duchessa. . . . "She looks forty!" he said to himself; "and yesterday she was so brilliant, so young! . . . Everyone tells me that, during her long conversation with Clelia Conti, she looked every bit as young and far more attractive."

The Duchessa's voice, her tone were as strange as her personal appearance. This tone, divested of all passion, of all human interest, of all anger, turned the Conte pale; it reminded him of the manner of a friend of his who, a few months earlier, when on the point of death, and after receiving the Last Sacrament, had sent for him to talk to him.

After some minutes the Duchessa was able to speak to him. She looked at him, and her eyes remained dead.

"Let us part, my dear Conte," she said to him in a faint but quite articulate voice which she tried to make sound friendly; "let us part, we must! Heaven is my witness that, for five years, my behaviour towards you has been irreproachable. You have given me a brilliant existence, in place of the boredom which would have been my sad portion at the castle of Grianta; without you I should have reached old age several years sooner. . . . For my part, my sole occupation has been to try to make you find happiness. It is because I love you that I propose to you this parting *à l'amiable,* as they say in France."

The Conte did not understand; she was obliged to repeat her statement several times. He grew deadly pale, and, flinging himself on his knees by her bedside, said to her all the things that profound astonishment, followed by the keenest despair, can inspire in a man who is passionately in love. At every moment he offered to hand in his resignation and to follow his mistress to some retreat a thousand leagues from Parma.

"You dare to speak to me of departure, and Fabrizio is here!" she at length exclaimed, half rising. But seeing that the sound of Fabrizio's name made a painful impression, she added after a moment's quiet, gently pressing the Conte's hand: "No, dear friend, I am not going to tell you that

I have loved you with that passion and those transports which one no longer feels, it seems to me, after thirty, and I am already a long way past that age. They will have told you that I was in love with Fabrizio, for I know that the rumour has gone round in this *wicked* court." (Her eyes sparkled for the first time in this conversation, as she uttered the word *wicked*.) "I swear to you before God, and upon Fabrizio's life, that never has there passed between him and me the tiniest thing which could not have borne the eyes of a third person. Nor shall I say to you that I love him exactly as a sister might; I love him instinctively, so to speak. I love in him his courage, so simple and so perfect that, one may say, he is not aware of it himself; I remember that this sort of admiration began on his return from Waterloo. He was still a boy then, for all his seventeen years; his great anxiety was to know whether he had really been present at the battle, and, if so, whether he could say that he had fought, when he had not marched to the attack of any enemy battery or column. It was during the serious discussions which we used to have together on this important subject that I began to see in him a perfect charm. His great soul revealed itself to me; what sophisticated falsehoods would a well-bred young man, in his place, have flaunted! Well then, if he is not happy I cannot be happy. There, that is a statement which well describes the state of my heart; if it is not the truth it is at any rate all of it that I see." The Conte, encouraged by this tone of frankness and intimacy, tried to kiss her hand; she drew it back with a sort of horror. "The time is past," she said to him; "I am a woman of thirty-seven, I find myself on the threshold of old age, I already feel all its discouragements, and perhaps I have even drawn near to the tomb. That is a terrible moment, by all one hears, and yet it seems to me that I desire it. I feel the worst symptom of old age; my heart is extinguished by this frightful misfortune, I can no longer love. I see in you now, dear Conte, only the shade of someone who was dear to me. I shall say more, it is gratitude, simply and solely, that makes me speak to you thus."

"What is to become of me," the Conte repeated, "of me who feel that I am attached to you more passionately than in the first days of our friendship, when I saw you at the Scala?"

"Let me confess to you one thing, dear friend, this talk of love bores me, and seems to me indecent. Come," she said, trying to smile, but in vain, "courage! Be the man of spirit, the judicious man, the man of resource in all circumstances. Be with me what you really are in the eyes of strangers, the most able man and the greatest politician that Italy has produced for ages."

The Conte rose, and paced the room in silence for some moments.

"Impossible, dear friend," he said to her at length; "I am rent asunder by the most violent passion, and you ask me to consult my reason. There is no longer any reason for me!"

"Let us not speak of passion, I beg of you," she said in a dry tone; and this was the first time, after two hours of talk, that her voice assumed any expression whatever. The Conte, in despair himself, sought to console her.

"He has betrayed me," she cried without in any way considering the reasons for hope which the Conte was setting before her; "*he* has betrayed me in the most dastardly fashion!" Her deadly pallor ceased for a moment; but, even in this moment of violent excitement, the Conte noticed that she had not the strength to raise her arms.

"Great God! Can it be possible," he thought, "that she is only ill? In that case, though, it would be the beginning of some very serious illness." Then, filled with uneasiness, he proposed to call in the famous Razori, the leading physician in the place and in the whole of Italy.

"So you wish to give a stranger the pleasure of learning the whole extent of my despair? . . . Is that the counsel of a traitor or of a friend?" And she looked at him with strange eyes.

"It is all over," he said to himself with despair, "she has no longer any love for me! And worse still, she no longer includes me even among the common men of honour.

"I may tell you," the Conte went on, speaking with emphasis, "that I have been anxious above all things to obtain details of the arrest which has thrown us into despair, and the curious thing is that still I know nothing positive; I have had the constables at the nearest station questioned, they saw the prisoner arrive by the Castelnuovo road and received orders to follow his *sediola*. I at once sent off Bruno, whose zeal is as well known to you as his devotion; he has orders to go on from station to station until he finds out where and how Fabrizio was arrested."

On hearing him utter Fabrizio's name, the Duchessa was seized by a slight convulsion.

"Forgive me, my friend," she said to the Conte as soon as she was able to speak; "these details interest me greatly, give me them all, let me have a clear understanding of the smallest circumstances."

"Well, Signora," the Conte went on, assuming a somewhat lighter air in the hope of distracting her a little, "I have a good mind to send a confidential messenger to Bruno and to order him to push on as far as Bologna; it was from there, perhaps, that our young friend was carried off. What is the date of his last letter?"

"Tuesday, five days ago."

"Had it been opened in the post?"

"No trace of any opening. I ought to tell you that it was written on horrible paper; the address is in a woman's hand, and that address bears the name of an old laundress who is related to my maid. The laundress believes that it is something to do with a love affair, and Cecchina refunds her for the carriage of the letters without adding anything further." The Conte, who had adopted quite the tone of a man of business, tried to discover, by questioning the Duchessa, which could have been the day of the abduction from Bologna. He only then perceived, he who had ordinarily so much tact, that this was the right tone to adopt. These details interested the unhappy woman and seemed to distract her a little. If the Conte had not been in love, this simple idea would have occurred to him as soon as he entered the room. The Duchessa sent him away in order that he might without delay despatch fresh orders to the faithful Bruno. As they were momentarily considering the question whether there had been a sentence passed before the moment at which the Prince signed the note addressed to the Duchessa, the latter with a certain determination seized the opportunity to say to the Conte: "I shall not reproach you in the least for having omitted the words *unjust proceedings* in the letter which you wrote and he signed, it was the courtier's instinct that gripped you by the throat; unconsciously you preferred your master's interest to your friend's. You have placed your actions under my orders, dear Conte, and that for a long time past, but it is not in your power to change your nature; you have great talents for the part of Minister, but you have also the instinct of their trade. The suppression of the word *unjust* was my ruin; but far be it from me to reproach you for it in any way, it was the fault of your instinct and not of your will.

"Bear in mind," she went on, changing her tone, and with the most imperious air, "that I am by no means unduly afflicted by the abduction of Fabrizio, that I have never had the slightest intention of removing myself from this place, that I am full of respect for the Prince. That is what you have to say, and this is what I, for my part, wish to say to you: 'As I intend to have the entire control of my own behaviour for the future, I wish to part from you *à l'amiable*, that is to say as a good and old friend. Consider that I am sixty, the young woman is dead in me, I can no longer form an exaggerated idea of anything in the world, I can no longer love.' But I should be even more wretched than I am were I to compromise your future. It may enter into my plans to give myself the appearance of having a young lover, and I should not like to see you distressed. I can swear to you by Fabrizio's happiness"—she stopped for half a minute after these words —"that never have I been guilty of any infidelity to you, and that in five whole years. It is a long time," she said; she tried to smile; her pallid cheeks were convulsed, but her lips were unable to part. "I swear to you even that I have never either planned or wished such a thing. Now you understand that, leave me."

The Conte in despair left the *palazzo* Sanseverina: he could see in the Duchessa the deliberately formed intention to part from him, and never had he been so desperately in love. This is one of the points to which I am obliged frequently to revert, because they are improbable outside Italy. Returning home, he despatched as many as six different people along the road to Castelnuovo and Bologna, and gave them letters. "But that is not all," the unhappy Conte told himself: "the Prince may take it into his head to have this wretched boy executed, and that in revenge for the tone which the Duchessa adopted with him on the day of that fatal note. I felt that the Duchessa was exceeding a limit beyond which one ought never to go, and it was to compensate for this that I was so incredibly foolish as to suppress the words *unjust proceedings,* the only ones that bound the Sovereign. . . . But bah! Are those people bound by anything in the world? That is no doubt the greatest mistake of my life, I have risked everything that can bring me life's reward: it now remains to compensate for my folly by dint of activity and cunning; but after all, if I can obtain nothing, even by sacrificing a little of my dignity, I leave the man stranded; with his dreams of high politics, with his ideas of making himself Constitutional King of Lombardy, we shall see how he will fill my place. . . . Fabio Conti is nothing but a fool, Rassi's talent reduces itself to having a man legally hanged who is displeasing to Authority."

As soon as he had definitely made up his mind to resign from the Ministry if the rigour shewn Fabrizio went beyond that of simple detention, the Conte said to himself: "If a caprice of that man's vanity, rashly braved, should cost me my happiness, at least I shall have my honour left. . . . By that token, since I am throwing my portfolio to the winds, I may allow myself a hundred actions which, only this morning, would have seemed to be outside the bounds of possibility. For instance, I am going to attempt everything that is humanly feasible to secure Fabrizio's escape. . . . Great God!" exclaimed the Conte, breaking off in his soliloquy and opening his eyes wide as though at the sight of an unexpected happiness, "the Duchessa never said anything to me about an escape; can she have been wanting in sincerity for once in her life, and is the motive of her quarrel only a desire that I should betray the Prince? Upon my word, no sooner said than done!"

The Conte's eye had recovered all its satirical sublety. "That engaging Fiscal Rassi is paid by his master for all the sentences that disgrace us throughout Europe, but he is not the sort of man to refuse to be paid by me to betray the master's secrets. The animal has a mistress and a confessor, but the mistress is of too vile a sort for me to be able to tackle her, next day she would relate our interview to all the applewomen in the parish." The Conte, revived by this gleam of hope, was by this time on his way to the Cathedral; astonished at the alertness of his gait, he smiled in spite of his grief: "This is what it is," he said, "to be no longer a Minister!" This Cathedral, like many churches in Italy, serves as a passage from one street to another; the Conte saw as he entered one of the Archbishop's Grand Vicars crossing the nave.

"Since I have met you here," he said to him, "will you be so very good as to spare my gout the deadly fatigue of climbing to His Grace the Archbishop's. He would be doing me the greatest favour in the world if he would be so kind as to come down to the sacristy." The Archbishop was delighted by this message, he had a thousand things to say to the Minister on the subject of Fabrizio. But the Minister guessed that these things were no more than fine phrases, and refused to listen to any of them.

"What sort of man is Dugnani, the Vicar of San Paolo?"

"A small mind and a great ambition," replied the Archbishop; "few scruples and extreme poverty, for we too have our vices!"

"Egad, Monsignore," exclaimed the Minister, "you portray like Tacitus"; and he took leave of him, laughing. No sooner had he returned to his Ministry than he sent for Priore Dugnani.

"You direct the conscience of my excellent friend the Fiscal General Rassi; are you sure he has nothing to tell me?" And, without any further speech or ceremony, he dismissed Dugnani.

CHAPTER SEVENTEEN

THE CONTE regarded himself as out of office. "Let us see now," he said to himself, "how many horses we shall be able to have after my disgrace, for that is what they will call my resignation." He made a reckoning of his fortune: he had come to the Ministry with 80,000 francs to his name; greatly to his surprise, he found that, all told, his fortune at that moment did not amount to 500,000 francs: "that is an income of 20,000 lire at the most," he said to himself. "I must admit that I am a great simpleton! There is not a citizen in Parma who does not suppose me to have an income of 150,000 lire, and the Prince, in that respect, is more of a cit than any of them. When they see me in the ditch, they will say that I know how to hide my fortune. Egad!" he cried, "if I am still Minister in three months' time, we shall see that fortune doubled." He found in this idea an occasion for writing to the Duchessa, which he seized with avidity, but to bespeak her pardon for a letter, seeing the terms on which they were, he filled this with figures and calculations. "We shall have only 20,000 lire of income," he told her, "to live upon, all three of us, at Naples, Fabrizio, you and myself. Fabrizio and I shall have one saddle-horse between us." The Minister had barely sent off his letter when the Fiscal General Rassi was announced. He received him with a stiffness which bordered on impertinence.

"What, Sir," he said to him, "you seize and carry off from Bologna a conspirator who is under my protection; what is more, you propose to cut off his head, and you say nothing about it to me! Do you at least know the name of my successor? Is it General Conti, or yourself?"

Rassi was dumbfounded; he was too little accustomed to good society to know whether the Conte was speaking seriously: he blushed a deep red, mumbled a few scarcely intelligible words; the Conte watched him and enjoyed his embarrassment. Suddenly Rassi pulled himself together and exclaimed, with perfect ease and with the air of Figaro caught red-handed by Almaviva:

"Faith, Signor Conte, I shan't beat about the bush with Your Excellency: what will you give me to answer all your questions as I should those of my confessor?"

"The Cross of San Paolo" (which is the Parmesan Order) "or money, if you can find me an excuse for granting it to you."

"I prefer the Cross of San Paolo, because it ennobles me."

"What, my dear Fiscal, you still pay some regard to our poor nobility?"

"If I were of noble birth," replied Rassi with all the impudence of his trade, "the families of the people I have had hanged would hate me, but they would not feel contempt for me."

"Very well, I will save you from their contempt," said the Conte; "cure me of my ignorance. What do you intend to do with Fabrizio?"

"Faith, the Prince is greatly embarrassed; he is afraid that, seduced by the fine eyes of Armida—forgive my slightly bold language, they are the Sovereign's own words —he is afraid that, seduced by a certain pair of very fine eyes, which have touched him slightly himself, you may leave him stranded, and there is no one but you to handle the question of Lombardy. I will go so far as to say," Rassi went on, lowering his voice, "that there is a fine opportunity there for you, and one that is well worth the Cross of San Paolo which you are giving me. The Prince would grant you, as a reward from the nation, a fine estate worth 600,000 francs, which he would set apart from his own domains, or a gratuity of 300,000 scudi, if you would agree not to interfere in the affairs of Fabrizio del Dongo, or at any rate not to speak of them to him except in public."

"I expected something better than that," said the Conte; "not to interfere with Fabrizio means quarrelling with the Duchessa."

"There, that is just what the Prince says: the fact is that he is horribly enraged against the Signora Duchessa, this is between ourselves; and he is afraid that, to compensate yourself for the rupture with that charming lady, now that you are a widower, you may ask him for the hand of his cousin, the old Princess Isotta, who is only fifty."

"He has guessed aright," exclaimed the Conte; "our master is the shrewdest man in his States."

Never had the Conte entertained the grotesque idea of marrying this elderly Princess; nothing would less have suited a man whom the ceremonies of the court bored to death.

He began to tap with his snuff-box on the marble of a little table beside his chair. Rassi saw in this gesture of embarrassment the possibility of a fine windfall; his eye gleamed.

"As a favour, Signor Conte," he cried, "if Your Excellency decides to accept this estate of 600,000 francs or the gratuity in money, I beg that he will not choose any other intermediary than myself. I should make an effort," he added, lowering his voice, "to have the gratuity increased, or else to have a forest of some importance added to the land. If Your Excellency would deign to introduce a little gentleness and tact into his manner in speaking to the Prince of this youngster they've locked up, a Duchy might perhaps be created out of the lands which the nation's gratitude would offer him. I repeat to Your Excellency; the Prince, for the moment, abominates the Duchessa, but he is greatly embarrassed, so much so indeed that I have sometimes thought there must be some secret consideration which he dared not confess to me. Do you know, we may find a gold mine here, I selling you his most intimate secrets, and quite openly, for I am supposed to be your sworn enemy. After all, if he is furious with the Duchessa, he believes also, and so do we all, that you are the one man in the world who can carry through all the secret negotiations with regard to the Milanese. Will Your Excellency permit me to repeat to him textually the Sovereign's words?" said Rassi, growing heated; "there is often a character in the order of the words which no translation can render, and you may be able to see more in them than I see."

"I permit everything," said the Conte, as he went on, with an air of distraction, tapping the marble table with his gold snuff-box; "I permit everything, and I shall be grateful."

"Give me a patent of hereditary nobility independently of the Cross, and I shall be more than satisfied. When I speak of ennoblement to the Prince, he answers: 'A scoundrel like you, noble! I should have to shut up shop next day; nobody in Parma would wish to be ennobled again.' To come back to the business of the Milanese, the Prince said to me not three days ago: 'There is only that rascal to unravel the thread of our intrigues; if I send him away, or if he follows the Duchessa, I may as well abandon the hope of seeing myself one day the Liberal and beloved ruler of all Italy.' "

At this the Conte drew breath. "Fabrizio will not die," he said to himself.

Never in his life had Rassi been able to secure an intimate conversation with the Prime Minister. He was beside himself with joy: he saw himself on the eve of being able to discard the name Rassi, which had become synonymous throughout the country with everything that was base and vile. The lower orders gave the name Rassi to mad dogs; recently more than one soldier had fought a duel because one of his comrades had called him Rassi. Not a week passed, moreover, in which this ill-starred name did not figure in some atrocious sonnet. His son, a young and innocent schoolboy of sixteen, used to be driven out of the *caffè* on the strength of his name. It was the burning memory of all these little perquisites of his office that made him commit an imprudence. "I have an estate," he said to the Conte, drawing his chair closer to the Minister's; "it is called Riva. I should like to be Barone Riva."

"Why not?" said the Minister. Rassi was beside himself.

"Very well, Signor Conte, I shall take the liberty of being indiscreet. I shall venture to guess the object of your desires; you aspire to the hand of the Princess Isotta, and it is a noble ambition. Once you are of the family, you are sheltered from disgrace, you have our man *tied down*. I shall not conceal from you that he has a horror of this marriage with the Princess Isotta. But if your affairs were entrusted to some skilful and *well-paid* person, you would be in a position not to despair of success."

"I, my dear Barone, should despair of it; I disavow in advance everything that you can say in my name; but on the day on which that illustrious alliance comes at length to crown my wishes and to give me so exalted a position in the State, I will offer you, myself, 300,000 francs of my own money, or else recommend the Prince to accord you a mark of his favour which you yourself will prefer to that sum of money."

The reader finds this conversation long: and yet we are sparing him more than half of it; it continued for two hours more. Rassi left the Conte's presence mad with joy; the Conte was left with a great hope of saving Fabrizio, and more than ever determined to hand in his resignation. He found that his credit stood in need of renewal by the succession to power of persons such as Rassi and General Conti; he took an exquisite delight in a possible method which he had just discovered of avenging himself on the Prince: "He may send the Duchessa away," he cried, "but, by gad, he will have to abandon the hope of becoming Constitutional King of Lombardy." (This was an absurd fantasy: the Prince had abundance of brains, but, by dint of dreaming of it, he had fallen madly in love with the idea.)

The Conte could not contain himself for joy as he hurried to the Duchessa's to give her a report of his conversation with the Fiscal. He found the door closed to him; the porter scarcely dared admit to him the fact of this order, received from his mistress's own lips. The Conte went sadly back to the ministerial *palazzo;* the rebuff he had just encountered completely eclipsed the joy that his conversation with the Prince's confidant had given him. Having no longer the heart to devote himself to anything, the Conte was wandering gloomily through his picture gallery when, a quarter of an hour later, he received a note which ran as follows:

"Since it is true, dear and good friend, that we are nothing more now than friends, you must come to see me only three times in the week. In a fortnight we shall reduce these visits, always so dear to my heart, to two monthly. If you wish to please me, give publicity to this apparent rupture; if you wished to pay me back almost all the love that I once felt for you, you would choose a new mistress for yourself. As for myself, I have great plans of dissipation: I intend to go a great deal into society, perhaps I shall even find a man of parts to make me forget my misfortunes. Of course, in your capacity as a friend, the first place in my heart will always be kept for you; but I do not wish, for the future, that my actions should be said to have been dictated by your wisdom; above all, I wish it to be well known that I have lost all my influence over your decisions. In a word, dear Conte, be assured that you will always be my dearest friend, but never anything else. Do not, I beg you, entertain any idea of a resumption, it is all over. Count, always, upon my friendship."

This last stroke was too much for the Conte's courage: he
wrote a fine letter to the Prince resigning all his offices, and
addressed it to the Duchessa with a request that she would
forward it to the Palace. A moment later, he received his
resignation, torn across, and on one of the blank scraps of
the paper the Duchessa had condescended to write: *"No, a
thousand times no!"*

It would be difficult to describe the despair of the poor
Minister. "She is right, I quite agree," he kept saying to
himself at every moment; "my omission of the words *unjust
proceedings* is a dreadful misfortune; it will involve perhaps
the death of Fabrizio, and that will lead to my own." It was
with death in his heart that the Conte, who did not wish to
appear at the Sovereign's Palace before being summoned
there, wrote out with his own hand the *motu proprio* which
created Rassi Cavaliere of the Order of San Paolo and conferred on him hereditary nobility; the Conte appended to it
a report of half a page which set forth to the Prince the reasons of state which made this measure advisable. He found a
sort of melancholy joy in making a fair copy of each of
these documents, which he addressed to the Duchessa.

He lost himself in suppositions; he tried to guess what,
for the future, would be the plan of conduct of the woman
he loved. "She has no idea herself," he said to himself; "one
thing alone remains certain, which is that she would not for
anything in the world fail to adhere to any resolution once
she had announced it to me." What added still further to his
unhappiness was that he could not succeed in finding that
the Duchessa was to be blamed. "She has shewn me a favour
in loving me; she ceases to love me after a mistake, unin-
tentional, it is true, but one that may involve a horrible consequence; I have no right to complain." Next morning, the
Conte learned that the Duchessa had begun to go into society again; she had appeared the evening before in all the
houses in which parties were being given. What would have
happened if they had met in the same drawing-room? How
was he to speak to her? In what tone was he to address her?
And how could he not speak to her?

The day that followed was a day of gloom; the rumour had
gone abroad everywhere that Fabrizio was going to be put to
death, the town was stirred. It was added that the Prince,
having regard for his high birth, had deigned to decide that
he should have his head cut off.

"It is I that am killing him," the Conte said to himself;

"I can no longer aspire to see the Duchessa ever again." In spite of this fairly obvious conclusion, he could not restrain himself from going three times to her door; as a matter of fact, in order not to be noticed, he went to her house on foot. In his despair, he had even the courage to write to her. He had sent for Rassi twice; the Fiscal had not shewn his face. "The scoundrel is playing me false," the Conte said to himself.

The day after this, three great pieces of news excited the high society of Parma, and even the middle classes. The execution of Fabrizio was more certain than ever; and, a highly strange complement to this news, the Duchessa did not appear to be at all despairing. To all appearance, she bestowed only a quite moderate regret on her young lover; in any event, she made the most, with an unbounded art, of the pallor which was the legacy of a really serious indisposition, which had come to her at the time of Fabrizio's arrest. The middle classes saw clearly in these details the hard heart of a great lady of the court. In decency, however, and as a sacrifice to the shade of the young Fabrizio, she had broken with Conte Mosca. "What immorality!" exclaimed the Jansenists of Parma. But already the Duchessa, and this was incredible, seemed disposed to listen to the flatteries of the handsomest young men at court. It was observed, among other curious incidents, that she had been very gay in a conversation with Conte Baldi, the Raversi's reigning lover, and had teased him greatly over his frequent visits to the *castello* of Velleja. The lower middle class and the populace were indignant at the death of Fabrizio, which these good folk put down to the jealousy of Conte Mosca. The society of the court was also greatly taken up with the Conte, but only to laugh at him. The third of the great pieces of news to which we have referred was indeed nothing else than the Conte's resignation; everyone laughed at a ridiculous lover who, at the age of fifty-six, was sacrificing a magnificent position to his grief at being abandoned by a heartless woman, who moreover had long ago shewn her preference for a young man. The Archbishop alone had the intelligence or rather the heart to divine that honour forbade the Conte to remain Prime Minister in a country where they were going to cut off the head, and without consulting him, of a young man who was under his protection. The news of the Conte's resignation had the effect of curing General Fabio Conti of his gout, as we shall relate in due course, when we come to speak of the way in which poor Fabrizio was spending his time in the citadel, while the whole town was inquiring the hour of his execution.

On the following day the Conte saw Bruno, that faithful agent whom he had dispatched to Bologna: the Conte's heart melted at the moment when this man entered his cabinet; the sight of him recalled the happy state in which he had been when he sent him to Bologna, almost in concert with the Duchessa. Bruno came from Bologna, where he had discovered nothing; he had not been able to find Lodovico, whom the *podestà* of Castelnuovo had kept locked up in his village prison.

"I am going to send you to Bologna," said the Conte to Bruno; "the Duchessa wishes to give herself the melancholy pleasure of knowing the details of Fabrizio's disaster. Report yourself to the *brigadiere* of police in charge of the station at Castelnuovo. . . .

"No!" exclaimed the Conte, breaking off in his orders; "start at once for Lombardy, and distribute money lavishly among all our correspondents. My object is to obtain from all these people reports of the most encouraging nature." Bruno, after clearly grasping the object of his mission, set to work to write his letters of credit. As the Conte was giving him his final instructions, he received a letter which was entirely false, but extremely well written; one would have called it the letter of a friend writing to a friend to ask a favour of him. The friend who wrote it was none other than the Prince. Having heard mention of some idea of resignation, he besought his friend, Conte Mosca, to retain his office; he asked him this in the name of their friendship and of the *dangers that threatened the country,* and ordered him as his master. He added that, the King of —— having placed at his disposal two Cordons of his Order, he was keeping one for himself and was sending the other to his dear Conte Mosca.

"That animal is ruining me!" cried the Conte in a fury, before the astonished Bruno, "and he thinks to win me over by those same hypocritical phrases which we have planned together so many times to lime the twig for some fool." He declined the Order that was offered him, and in his reply spoke of the state of his health as allowing him but little hope of being able to carry on for much longer the arduous duties of the Ministry. The Conte was furious. A moment later was announced the Fiscal Rassi, whom he treated like a black.

"Well! Because I have made you noble, you are beginning to shew insolence! Why did you not come yesterday to thank me, as was your bounden duty, Master Drudge?"

Rassi was a long way below the reach of insult; it was in this tone that he was daily received by the Prince; but he was anxious to be a Barone, and justified himself with spirit. Nothing was easier.

"The Prince kept me glued to a table all day yesterday; I could not leave the Palace. His Highness made me copy out in my wretched attorney's script a number of diplomatic papers so stupid and so long-winded that I really believe his sole object was to keep me prisoner. When I was finally able to take my leave of him, about five o'clock, half dead with hunger, he gave me the order to go straight home and not to go out in the evening. As a matter of fact, I saw two of his private spies, well known to me, patrolling my street until nearly midnight. This morning, as soon as I could, I sent for a carriage which took me to the door of the Cathedral. I got down from the carriage very slowly, then at a quick pace walked through the church, and here I am. Your Excellency is at this moment the one man in the world whom I am most passionately anxious to please."

"And I, Master Joker, am not in the least taken in by all these more or less well-constructed stories. You refused to speak to me about Fabrizio the day before yesterday; I respected your scruples and your oaths of secrecy, although oaths, to a creature like you, are at the most means of evasion. To-day, I require the truth. What are these ridiculous rumours which make out that this young man is sentenced to death as the murderer of the comedian Giletti?"

"No one can give Your Excellency a better account of those rumours, for it was I myself who started them by the Sovereign's orders; and, I believe, it was perhaps to prevent me from informing you of this incident that he kept me prisoner all day yesterday. The Prince, who does not take me for a fool, could have no doubt that I should come to you with my Cross and ask you to fasten it in my buttonhole."

"To the point!" cried the Minister. "And no fine speeches."

"No doubt, the Prince would be glad to pass sentence of death on Signor del Dongo, but he has been sentenced, as you probably know, only to twenty years in irons, commuted by the Prince, on the very day after the sentence, to twelve years in a fortress, with fasting on bread and water every Friday and other religious observances."

"It is because I knew of this sentence to imprisonment only that I was alarmed by the rumours of immediate execution which are going about the town; I remember the death of Conte Palanza, which was such a clever trick on your part."

"It was then that I ought to have had the Cross!" cried Rassi, in no way disconcerted; "I ought to have forced him when I held him in my hand, and the man wished the prisoner killed. I was a fool then; and it is armed with that experience that I venture to advise you not to copy my example to-day." (This comparison seemed in the worst of taste to his hearer, who was obliged to restrain himself forcibly from kicking Rassi.)

"In the first place," the latter went on with the logic of a trained lawyer and the perfect assurance of a man whom no insult could offend, "in the first place there can be no question of the execution of the said del Dongo; the Prince would not dare, the times have altogether changed! Besides, I, who am noble and hope through you to become Barone, would not lend a hand in the matter. Now it is only from me, as Your Excellency knows, that the executioner of supreme penalties can receive orders, and, I swear to you, Cavaliere Rassi will never issue any such orders against Signor del Dongo."

"And you will be acting wisely," said the Conte with a severe air, taking his adversary's measure.

"Let us make a distinction," went on Rassi, smiling. "I myself figure only in the official death-roll, and if Signor del Dongo happens to die of a colic, do not go and put it down to me. The Prince is vexed, and I do not know why, with the Sanseverina." (Three days earlier Rassi would have said "the Duchessa," but, like everyone in the town, he knew of her breach with the Prime Minister.) The Conte was struck by the omission of her title on such lips, and the reader may judge of the pleasure that it afforded him; he darted at Rassi a glance charged with the keenest hatred. "My dear angel," he then said to himself, "I can shew you my love only by blind obedience to your orders.

"I must admit," he said to the Fiscal, "that I do not take any very passionate interest in the various caprices of the Signora Duchessa; only, since it was she who introduced to me this scapegrace of a Fabrizio, who would have done well to remain at Naples and not come here to complicate our affairs, I make a point of his not being put to death in my time, and I am quite ready to give you my word that you shall be Barone in the week following his release from prison."

"In that case, Signor Conte, I shall not be Barone for twelve whole years, for the Prince is furious, and his hatred of the Duchessa is so keen that he is trying to conceal it."

"His Highness is too good; what need has he to conceal his hatred, since his Prime Minister is no longer protecting the Duchessa? Only I do not wish that anyone should be able to accuse me of meanness, nor above all of jealousy: it was I who made the Duchessa come to this country, and if Fabrizio dies in prison you will not be Barone, but you will perhaps be stabbed with a dagger. But let us not talk about this trifle: the fact is that I have made an estimate of my fortune, at the most I may be able to put together an income of twenty thousand lire, on which I propose to offer my resignation, most humbly, to the Sovereign. I have some hope of finding employment with the King of Naples; that big town will offer me certain distractions which I need at this moment and which I cannot find in a hole like Parma; I should stay here only in the event of your obtaining for me the hand of the Princess Isotta," and so forth. The conversation on this subject was endless. As Rassi was rising to leave, the Conte said to him with an air of complete indifference:

"You know that people have said that Fabrizio was playing me false, in the sense that he was one of the Duchessa's lovers; I decline to accept that rumour, and, to give it the lie, I wish you to have this purse conveyed to Fabrizio."

"But, Signor Conte," said Rassi in alarm, looking at the purse, "there is an enormous sum here, and the regulations. . . ."

"To you, my dear Sir, it may be enormous," replied the Conte with an air of the most supreme contempt: "a cit like you, sending money to his friend in prison, thinks he is ruining himself if he gives him ten sequins; I, on the other hand, *wish* Fabrizio to receive these six thousand francs, and on no account is the Castle to know anything of the matter."

While the terrified Rassi was trying to answer, the Conte shut the door on him with impatience. "Those fellows," he said to himself, "cannot see power unless it is cloaked in insolence." So saying, this great Minister abandoned himself to an action so ridiculous that we have some misgivings about recording it. He ran to take from his desk a portrait in miniature of the Duchessa, and covered it with passionate kisses. "Forgive me, my dear angel," he cried, "if I did not

fling out of the window with my own hands that drudge who
dares to speak of you in a tone of familiarity; but, if I am
acting with this excess of patience, it is to obey you! And he
will lose nothing by waiting."

After a long conversation with the portrait, the Conte,
who felt his heart dead in his breast, had the idea of an
absurd action, and dashed into it with the eagerness of a
child. He sent for a coat on which his decorations were sewn
and went to pay a call on the elderly Princess Isotta. Never in
his life had he gone to her apartments, except on New Year's
Day. He found her surrounded by a number of dogs, and
tricked out in all her finery, including diamonds even, as
though she were going to court. The Conte having shewn
some fear lest he might be upsetting the arrangements of
Her Highness, who was probably going out, the lady replied
that a Princess of Parma owed it to herself to be always in
such array. For the first time since his disaster the Conte
felt an impulse of gaiety. "I have done well to appear here,"
he told himself, "and this very day I must make my declaration." The Princess had been delighted to receive a visit
from a man so renowned for his wit, and a Prime Minister;
the poor old maid was hardly accustomed to such visitors.
The Conte began by an adroit preamble, relative to the immense distance that must always separate from a plain gentleman the members of a reigning family.

"One must draw a distinction," said the Princess: "the
daughter of a King of France, for instance, has no hope of
ever succeeding to the Throne; but things are not like that
in the House of Parma. And that is why we Farnese must
always keep up a certain dignity in externals; and I, a poor
Princess such as you see me now, I cannot say that it is absolutely impossible that one day you may be my Prime
Minister."

This idea, by its fantastic unexpectedness, gave the poor
Conte a second momentary thrill of perfect gaiety.

On leaving the apartments of the Princess Isotta, who
had blushed deeply on receiving the avowal of the Prime
Minister's passion, he met one of the grooms from the
Palace: the Prince had sent for him in hot haste.

"I am unwell," replied the Minister, delighted at being
able to play a trick on his Prince. "Oh! Oh! You drive me
to extremes," he exclaimed in a fury, "and then you expect
me to serve you; but learn this, my Prince, that to have
received power from Providence is no longer enough in

these times: it requires great brains and a strong character to succeed in being a despot."

After dismissing the groom from the Palace, highly scandalised by the perfect health of this invalid, the Conte amused himself by going to see the two men at court who had the greatest influence over General Fabio Conti. The one thing that made the Minister shudder and robbed him of all his courage was that the governor of the citadel was accused of having once before made away with a captain, his personal enemy, by means of the *acquetta di Perugia*.

The Conte knew that during the last week the Duchessa had been squandering vast sums with a view to establishing communications with the citadel; but, in his opinion, there was small hope of success; all eyes were still too wide open. We shall not relate to the reader all the attempts at corruption made by this unhappy woman: she was in despair, and agents of every sort, all perfectly devoted, were supporting her. But there is perhaps only one kind of business which is done to perfection in small despotic courts, namely the custody of political prisoners. The Duchessa's gold had no other effect than to secure the dismissal from the citadel of nine or ten men of all ranks.

CHAPTER EIGHTEEN

THUS, WITH AN entire devotion to the prisoner, the Duchessa and the Prime Minister had been able to do but very little for him. The Prince was in a rage, the court as well as the public were *piqued* by Fabrizio, delighted to see him come to grief: he had been too fortunate. In spite of the gold which she spent in handfuls, the Duchessa had not succeeded in advancing an inch in her siege of the citadel; not a day passed but the Marchesa Raversi or Cavaliere Riscara had some fresh report to communicate to General Fabio Conti. They were supporting his weakness.

As we have already said, on the day of his imprisonment, Fabrizio was taken first of all to the *governor's palazzo*. This was a neat little building erected in the eighteenth century from the plans of Vanvitelli, who placed it one hundred and eighty feet above the ground, on the platform of the huge round tower. From the windows of this little *palazzo*, isolated on the back of the enormous tower like a camel's hump, Fabrizio could make out the country and the Alps to a great distance; he followed with his eye beneath the citadel the course of the Parma, a sort of torrent which, turning to the right four leagues from the town, empties its waters into the Po. Beyond the left bank of this river, which formed so to speak a series of huge white patches in the midst of the green fields, his enraptured eye caught distinctly each of the summits of the immense wall with which the Alps enclose Italy to the north. These summits, always covered in snow, even in the month of August which it then was, give one as it were a reminder of coolness in the midst of these scorching plains; the eye can follow them in the minutest detail, and yet they are more than thirty leagues from the citadel of Parma. This expansive view from the governor's charming *palazzo* is broken at one corner towards the south by the *Torre Farnese*, in which a room was being hastily prepared for Fabrizio. This second tower, as the reader may perhaps remember, was built on the platform of the great tower in honour of a Crown Prince who, unlike Hippolytus the son of Theseus, had by no means repelled the advances of a young stepmother. The Princess died in a few hours; the Prince's son regained his liberty only seventeen years later, when he ascended the throne on the death of his father. This Torre Farnese to which, after waiting for three quarters of an hour, Fabrizio was made to climb, of an extremely plain exterior, rises some fifty feet above the platform of the great tower, and is adorned with a number of lightning conductors. The Prince who, in his displeasure with his wife, built this prison visible from all parts of the country, had the singular design of trying to persuade his subjects that it had been there for many years: that is why he gave it the name of *Torre Farnese*. It was forbidden to speak of this construction, and from all parts of the town of Parma and the surrounding plains people could perfectly well see the masons laying each of the stones which compose this pentagonal edifice. In order to prove that it was old, there was placed above the door two feet wide and four feet high which forms its entrance a magnificent bas-relief representing Alessandro Farnese, the famous general, forcing Henri IV to withdraw from Paris. This Torre Farnese, standing in so conspicuous a position, consists of a hall on the ground floor, at least forty yards long, broad in proportion and filled with extremely squat pillars, for this disproportionately large room is not more than fifteen feet high. It is used as the guard-room, and in the middle of it the staircase rises in a spiral round one of the pillars; it is a small staircase of iron, very light, barely two feet in width and wrought in filigree. By this staircase, which shook beneath the weight of the gaolers who were escorting him, Fabrizio came to a set of vast rooms more than twenty feet high, forming a magnificent first floor. They had originally been furnished with the greatest luxury for the young Prince who spent in them the seventeen best years of his life. At one end of this apartment, the new prisoner was shewn a chapel of the greatest magnificence; the walls and ceiling were entirely covered in black marble; pillars, black also and of the noblest proportions, were placed in line along the black walls without touching them, and these walls were decorated with a number of skulls in white marble, of colossal proportions, elegantly carved and supported underneath by crossbones. "There is an invention of the hatred that cannot kill," thought Fabrizio, "and what a devilish idea to let me see it."

An iron staircase of light filigree, similarly coiled about a pillar, gave access to the second floor of this prison, and it was in the rooms of this second floor, which were some fifteen feet in height, that for the last year General Fabio Conti had given proof of his genius. First of all, under his direction, solid bars had been fixed in the windows of these rooms, originally occupied by the Prince's servants, and standing more than thirty feet above the stone slabs which paved the platform of the great round tower. It was by a dark corridor, running along the middle of this building, that one approached these rooms, each of which had two windows; and in this very narrow corridor Fabrizio noticed three iron gates in succession, formed of enormous bars and rising to the roof. It was the plans, sections and elevations of all these pretty inventions that, for two years past, had entitled the General to an audience of his master every week. A conspirator placed in one of these rooms could not complain to public opinion that he was being treated in an inhuman fashion, and yet was unable to communicate with anyone in the world, or to make a movement without being heard. The General had had placed in each room huge joists of oak in the form of trestles three feet high, and this was his paramount invention, which gave him a claim to the Ministry of Police. On these trestles he had set up a cell of planks, extremely resonant, ten feet high, and touching the wall only at the side where the windows were. On the other three sides ran a little corridor four feet wide, between the original wall of the prison, which consisted of huge blocks of dressed stone, and the wooden partitions of the cell. These partitions, formed of four double planks of walnut, oak and pine, were solidly held together by iron bolts and by innumerable nails.

It was into one of these rooms, constructed a year earlier, and the masterpiece of General Fabio Conti's inventive talent, which had received the sounding title of *Passive Obedience,* that Fabrizio was taken. He ran to the windows. The view that one had from these barred windows was sublime: one little piece of the horizon alone was hidden, to the north-west, by the terraced roof of the governor's *palazzo,* which had only two floors; the ground floor was occupied by the offices of the staff; and from the first Fabrizio's eyes were attracted to one of the windows of the upper floor, in which were to be seen, in pretty cages, a great number of birds of all sorts. Fabrizio amused himself in listening to their song and in watching them greet the last rays of the setting sun, while the gaolers busied themselves about him. This aviary window was not more than five-and-twenty feet from one of his, and stood five or six feet lower down, so that his eyes fell on the birds.

There was a moon that evening, and at the moment of Fabrizio's entering his prison it was rising majestically on the horizon to the right, over the chain of the Alps, towards Treviso. It was only half past eight, and, at the other extremity of the horizon, to the west, a brilliant orange-red sunset showed to perfection the outlines of Monviso and the other Alpine peaks which run inland from Nice towards Mont Cenis and Turin. Without a thought of his misfortunes, Fabrizio was moved and enraptured by this sublime spectacle. "So it is in this exquisite world that Clelia Conti dwells; with her pensive and serious nature, she must enjoy this view more than anyone; here it is like being alone in the mountains a hundred leagues from Parma." It was not until he had spent more than two hours at the window, admiring this horizon which spoke to his soul, and often also letting his eyes rest on the governor's charming *palazzo,* that Fabrizio suddenly exclaimed: "But is this really a prison? Is this what I have so greatly dreaded?" Instead of seeing at every turn discomforts and reasons for bitterness, our hero let himself be charmed by the attractions of his prison.

Suddenly his attention was forcibly recalled to reality by a terrifying din: his wooden cell, which was not unlike a cage and moreover was extremely resonant, was violently shaken; the barking of a dog and little shrill cries completed the strangest medley of sounds. "What now! Am I going to escape so soon?" thought Fabrizio. A moment later he was laughing as perhaps no one has ever laughed in a prison. By the General's orders, at the same time as the gaolers there had been sent up an English dog, extremely savage, which was set to guard officers of importance, and was to spend the night in the space so ingeniously contrived all round Fabrizio's cage. The dog and the gaoler were to sleep in the interval of three feet left between the stone pavement of the original floor and the wooden planks on which the prisoner could not move a step without being heard.

Now, when Fabrizio arrived, the room of the *Passive Obe-*

dience happened to be occupied by a hundred huge rats which took flight in every direction. The dog, a sort of spaniel crossed with an English fox-terrier, was no beauty, but to make up for this shewed a great alertness. He had been tied to the stone pavement beneath the planks of the wooden room; but when he heard the rats pass close by him, he made an effort so extraordinary that he succeeded in pulling his head out of his collar. Then came this splendid battle the din of which aroused Fabrizio, plunged in the least melancholy of dreams. The rats that had managed to escape the first assault of the dog's teeth took refuge in the wooden room, the dog came after them up the six steps which led from the stone floor to Fabrizio's cell. Then began a really terrifying din: the cell was shaken to its foundations. Fabrizio laughed like a madman until the tears ran down his cheeks: the gaoler Grillo, no less amused, had shut the door; the dog, in going after the rats, was not impeded by any furniture, for the room was completely bare; there was nothing to check the bounds of the hunting dog but an iron stove in one corner. When the dog had triumphed over all his enemies, Fabrizio called him, patted him, succeeded in winning his affection. "Should this fellow ever see me jumping over a wall," he said to himself, "he will not bark." But this far-seeing policy was a boast on his part: in the state of mind in which he was, he found his happiness in playing with this dog. By a paradox to which he gave no thought, a secret joy was reigning in the depths of his heart.

After he had made himself quite breathless by running about with the dog:

"What is your name?" Fabrizio asked the gaoler.

"Grillo, to serve Your Excellency in all that is allowed by the regulations."

"Very well, my dear Grillo, a certain Giletti tried to murder me on the broad highway, I defended myself, and killed him; I should kill him again if it had to be done, but I wish to lead a gay life for all that so long as I am your guest. Ask for authority from your chiefs, and go and procure linen for me from the *palazzo* Sanseverina; also, buy me lots of *nebiolo d'Asti*.

This is quite a good sparkling wine which is made in Piedmont, in Alfieri's country, and is highly esteemed, especially by the class of wine-tasters to which gaolers belong. Nine or ten of these gentlemen were engaged in transporting to Fabrizio's wooden room certain pieces of old furniture, highly gilded, which they took from the Prince's apartment on the first floor; all of them bore religiously in mind this recommendation of the wine of Asti. In spite of all they might do, Fabrizio's establishment for this first night was lamentable; but he appeared shocked only by the absence of a bottle of good *nebiolo*. "He seems a good lad," said the gaolers as they left him, "and there is only one thing to be hoped for, that our gentlemen will let him have plenty of money."

When he had recovered a little from all this din and confusion: "Is it possible that this is a prison?" Fabrizio asked himself, gazing at that vast horizon from Treviso to Monviso, the endless chain of the Alps, the peaks covered with snow, the stars, and everything, "and a first night in prison besides. I can conceive that Clelia Conti enjoys this airy solitude; here one is a thousand leagues above the pettinesses and wickednesses which occupy us down there. If those birds which are under my window there belong to her, I shall see her. . . . Will she blush when she catches sight of me?" It was while debating this important question that our hero, at a late hour of the night, fell asleep.

On the day following this night, the first spent in prison, in the course of which he never once lost his patience, Fabrizio was reduced to making conversation with Fox, the English dog; Grillo the gaoler did indeed greet him always with the friendliest expression, but a new order made him dumb, and he brought neither linen nor *nebiolo*.

"Shall I see Clelia?" Fabrizio asked himself as he awoke. "But are those birds hers?" The birds were beginning to utter little chirps and to sing, and at that height this was the only sound that was carried on the air. It was a sensation full of novelty and pleasure for Fabrizio, the vast silence which reigned at this height; he listened with rapture to the little chirpings, broken and so shrill, with which his neighbours the birds were greeting the day. "If they belong to her, she will appear for a moment in that room, there, beneath my window," and, while he examined the immense chains of the Alps, against the first foothills of which the citadel of Parma seemed to rise like an advanced redoubt, his eyes returned every moment to the sumptuous cages of lemon-wood and mahogany, which, adorned with gilt wires, filled the bright room which served as an aviary. What Fabrizio did not learn until later was that this room was the only one on the second floor of the *palazzo* which had any shade, between eleven o'clock and four: it was sheltered by the Torre Farnese.

"What will be my dismay," thought Fabrizio, "if, instead of those modest and pensive features for which I am waiting, and which will blush slightly perhaps if she catches sight of me, I see appear the coarse face of some thoroughly common maid, charged with the duty of looking after the birds! But if I do see Clelia, will she deign to notice me? Upon my soul, I must commit some indiscretion so as to be noticed; my position should have some privileges; besides, we are both alone here, and so far from the world! I am a prisoner, evidently what General Conti and the other wretches of his sort call one of their subordinates. . . . But she has so much intelligence, or, I should say, so much heart, so the Conte supposes, that possibly, by what he says, she despises her father's profession; which would account for her melancholy. A noble cause of sadness! But, after all, I am not exactly a stranger to her. With what grace, full of modesty, she greeted me yesterday evening! I remember quite well how, when we met near Como, I said to her: 'One day I shall come to see your beautiful pictures at Parma; will you remember this name: Fabrizio del Dongo?' Will she have forgotten it? She was so young then!

"But by the way," Fabrizio said to himself in astonishment, suddenly interrupting the current of his thoughts, "I am forgetting to be angry. Can I be one of those stout hearts of which antiquity has furnished the world with several examples? How is this, I who was so much afraid of prison, I am in prison, and I do not even remember to be sad! It is certainly a case where the fear was a hundred times worse than the evil. What! I have to convince myself before I can be distressed by this prison, which, as Blanès says, may as easily last ten years as ten months! Can it be the surprise of all these novel surroundings that is distracting me from the grief that I ought to feel? Perhaps this good humour which is independent of my will and not very reasonable will cease all of a sudden, perhaps in an instant I shall fall into the black misery which I ought to be feeling.

"In any case, it is indeed surprising to be in prison and to have to reason with oneself in order to be unhappy. Upon my soul, I come back to my theory, perhaps I have a great character."

Fabrizio's meditations were disturbed by the carpenter of the citadel, who came to take the measurements of a screen for his windows; it was the first time that this prison had been used, and they had forgotten to complete it in this essential detail.

"And so," thought Fabrizio, "I am going to be deprived of that sublime view." And he sought to derive sadness from this privation.

"But what's this?" he cried suddenly, addressing the carpenter. "Am I not to see those pretty birds any more?"

"Ah, the Signorina's birds, that she's so fond of," said the man, with a good-natured air, "hidden, eclipsed, blotted out like everything else."

Conversation was forbidden the carpenter just as strictly as it was the gaolers, but the man felt pity for the prisoner's youth: he informed him that these enormous shutters, resting on the sills of the two windows, and slanting upwards and away from the wall, were intended to leave the inmates with no view save of the sky. "It is done for their morals," he told him, "to increase a wholesome sadness and the desire to amend their ways in the hearts of the prisoners; the General," the carpenter added, "has also had the idea of taking the glass out of their windows and putting oiled paper there instead."

Fabrizio greatly enjoyed the epigrammatic turn of this conversation, extremely rare in Italy.

"I should very much like to have a bird to cheer me, I am madly fond of them; buy me one from Signorina Clelia Conti's maid."

"What, do you know her," cried the carpenter, "that you say her name so easily?"

"Who has not heard tell of so famous a beauty? But I have had the honour of meeting her several times at court."

"The poor young lady is very dull here," the carpenter went on; "she spends all her time there with her birds. This morning she sent out to buy some fine orange trees which they have placed by her orders at the door of the tower, under your window: if it weren't for the cornice, you would be able to see them." There were in this speech words that were very precious to Fabrizio; he found a tactful way of giving the carpenter money.

"I am breaking two rules at the same time," the man told him; "I am talking to Your Excellency and taking money. The day after to-morrow, when I come back with the shutters, I shall have a bird in my pocket, and if I am not alone, I shall pretend to let it escape; if I can, I shall bring you a prayer book: you must suffer by not being able to say your office."

"And so," Fabrizio said to himself as soon as he was alone, "those birds are hers, but in two days more I shall no longer see them." At this thought his eyes became tinged with regret. But finally, to his inexpressible joy, after so long a wait and so much anxious gazing, towards midday Clelia came to attend to her birds. Fabrizio remained motionless, and did not breathe; he was standing against the enormous bars of his window and pressed close to them. He observed that she did not raise her eyes to himself; but her movements had an air of embarrassment, like those of a person who knows that she is being overlooked. Had she wished to do so, the poor girl could not have forgotten the delicate smile she had seen hovering over the prisoner's lips the day before, when the constables brought him out of the guard-room.

Although to all appearance she was paying the most careful attention to what she was doing, at the moment when she approached the window of the aviary she blushed quite perceptibly. The first thought in Fabrizio's mind, as he stood glued to the iron bars of his window, was to indulge in the childish trick of tapping a little with his hand on those bars, and so making a slight noise; then the mere idea of such a want of delicacy horrified him. "It would serve me right if for the next week she sent her maid to look after the birds." This delicate thought would never have occurred to him at Naples or at Novara.

He followed her eagerly with his eyes: "Obviously," he said to himself, "she is going to leave the room without deigning to cast a glance at this poor window, and yet she is just opposite me." But, on turning back from the farther end of the room, which Fabrizio, thanks to his greater elevation, could see quite plainly, Clelia could not help looking furtively up at him, as she approached, and this was quite enough to make Fabrizio think himself authorised to salute her. "Are we not alone in the world here?" he asked himself, to give himself the courage to do so. At this salute the girl stood still and lowered her eyes; then Fabrizio saw her raise them very slowly; and, evidently making an effort to control herself, she greeted the prisoner with the most grave and *distant* gesture; but she could not impose silence on her eyes: without her knowing it, probably, they expressed for a moment the keenest pity. Fabrizio remarked that she blushed so deeply that the rosy tinge ran swiftly down to her shoulders, from which the heat had made her cast off, when she came to the aviary, a shawl of black lace. The unconscious stare with which Fabrizio replied to her glance doubled the girl's discomposure. "How happy that poor woman would be," she said to herself, thinking of the Duchessa, "if for a moment only she could see him as I see him now."

Fabrizio had had some slight hope of saluting her again as she left the room; but to avoid this further courtesy Clelia beat a skilful retreat by stages, from cage to cage, as if, at the end of her task, she had to attend to the birds nearest the door. At length she went out; Fabrizio stood motionless gazing at the door through which she had disappeared; he was another man.

From that moment the sole object of his thoughts was to discover how he might manage to continue to see her, even when they had set up that horrible screen outside the window that overlooked the governor's *palazzo*.

Overnight, before going to bed, he had set himself the long and tedious task of hiding the greater part of the gold that he had in several of the rat-holes which adorned his wooden cell. "This evening, I must hide my watch. Have I not heard it said that with patience and a watch-spring with a jagged edge one can cut through wood and even iron? So I shall be able to saw through this screen." The work of concealing his watch, which occupied him for hours, did not seem to him at all long; he was thinking of the different ways of attaining his object and of what he himself could do in the way of carpentering. "If I get to work the right way," he said to himself, "I shall be able to cut a section clean out of the oak plank which will form the screen, at the end which will be resting on the window-sill; I can take this piece out and put it back according to circumstances; I shall give everything I possess to Grillo, so that he may be kind enough not to notice this little device." All Fabrizio's happiness was now involved in the possibility of carrying out this task, and he could think of nothing else. "If I can only manage to see her, I am a happy man. . . . No," he reminded himself, "she must also see that I see her." All night long his head was filled with devices of carpentering, and perhaps never gave a single thought to the court of Parma, the Prince's anger, etc., etc. We must admit that he did not think either of the grief in which the Duchessa must be plunged. He waited impatiently for the morrow; but the carpenter did not appear again: evidently he was regarded in the prison as a Liberal. They took care to send another, a sour-faced fellow who made no reply except a growl that boded ill to all the pleasant words with which Fabrizio sought to cajole him. Some of the Duchessa's many attempts to open a correspondence with Fabrizio had been discovered by the Marchesa Raversi's many agents, and, by her, General Fabio Conti was daily warned, frightened, put on his mettle. Every eight hours six soldiers of the guard relieved the previous six in the great hall with the hundred pillars on the ground floor: in addition to these, the governor posted a gaoler on guard at each of the three successive iron gates of the corridor, and poor Grillo, the only one who saw the prisoner, was condemned to leave the Torre Farnese only once a week, at which he shewed great annoyance. He made his ill humour felt by Fabrizio, who had the sense to reply only in these words: "Plenty of good *nebiolo d'Asti*, my friend." And he gave him money.

"Well now, even this, which consoles us in all our troubles," exclaimed the indignant Grillo, in a voice barely loud enough to be heard by the prisoner, "we are forbidden to take, and I ought to refuse it, but I accept; however, it's money thrown away; I can tell you nothing about anything. Go on, you must be a rare bad lot, the whole citadel is upside down because of you; the Signora Duchessa's fine goings on have got three of us dismissed already."

"Will the screen be ready before midday?" This was the great question which made Fabrizio's heart throb throughout that long morning; he counted each quarter as it sounded from the citadel clock. Finally, when the last quarter before noon struck, the screen had not yet arrived; Clelia reappeared and looked after her birds. Cruel necessity had made Fabrizio's daring take such strides, and the risk of not seeing her again seemed to him so to transcend all others that he ventured, looking at Clelia, to make with his finger the gesture of sawing through the screen; it is true that as soon as she had perceived this gesture, so seditious in prison, she half bowed and withdrew.

"How now!" thought Fabrizio in amazement, "can she be so unreasonable as to see an absurd familiarity in a gesture dictated by the most imperious necessity? I meant to request her always to deign, when she is attending to her birds, to look now and again at the prison window, even when she finds it masked by an enormous wooden shutter; I meant to indicate to her that I shall do everything that is humanly possible to contrive to see her. Great God! Does this mean that she will not come tomorrow owing to that indiscreet gesture?" This fear, which troubled Fabrizio's sleep, was entirely justified; on the following day Clelia had not appeared at three o'clock, when the workman finished installing outside Fabrizio's windows the two enormous screens; they had been hauled up piecemeal, from the terrace of the great tower, by means of ropes and pulleys attached to the iron bars outside the windows. It is true that, hidden behind a shutter in her own room, Clelia had followed with anguish every movement of the workmen; she had seen quite plainly Fabrizio's mortal anxiety, but had nevertheless had the courage to keep the promise she had made to herself.

Clelia was a little devotee of Liberalism; in her girlhood she had taken seriously all the Liberal utterances which she had heard in the company of her father, who thought only of establishing his own position; from this she had come to feel a contempt, almost a horror for the flexible character of the courtier; whence her antipathy to marriage. Since Fabrizio's arrival, she had been racked by remorse: "And so," she said to herself, "my unworthy heart is taking the side of the people who seek to betray my father! He dares to make me the sign of sawing through a door! . . . But," she at once went on with anguish in her heart, "the whole town is talking of his approaching death! To-morrow may be the fatal day! With the monsters who govern us, what in the world is not possible? What meekness, what heroic serenity in those eyes, which perhaps are about to close for ever! God! What must be the Duchessa's anguish! They say that she is in a state of utter despair. If I were she, I would go and stab the Prince, like the heroic Charlotte Corday."

Throughout this third day of his imprisonment, Fabrizio was wild with anger, but solely at not having seen Clelia appear. "Anger for anger, I ought to have told her that I loved her," he cried; for he had arrived at this discovery. "No, it is not at all from greatness of heart that I am not thinking about prison, and am making Blanès's prophecy prove false: such honour is not mine. In spite of myself I think of that look of sweet pity which Clelia let fall on me when the constables led me out of the guard-room; that look has wiped out all my past life. Who would have said that I should find such sweet eyes in such a place, and at the moment when my own sight was offended by the faces of Barbone and the General-governor. Heaven appeared to me in the midst of

those vile creatures. And how can one help loving beauty and
seeking to see it again? No, it is certainly not greatness of
heart that makes me indifferent to all the little vexations
which prison heaps upon me." Fabrizio's imagination, passing
rapidly over every possibility in turn, arrived at that of his
being set at liberty. "No doubt the Duchessa's friendship
will do wonders for me. Well, I shall thank her for my liberty
only with my lips; this is not at all the sort of place to
which one returns! Once out of prison, separated as we are
socially, I should practically never see Clelia again! And,
after all, what harm is prison doing me? If Clelia deigned
not to crush me with her anger, what more should I have to
ask of heaven?"

On the evening of this day on which he had not seen his
pretty neighbour, he had a great idea: with the iron cross
of the rosary which is given to every prisoner on his admission to prison, he began, and with success, to bore a hole in
the shutter. "It is perhaps an imprudence," he told himself
before he began. "Did not the carpenters say in front of me
that the painters would be coming to-morrow in their place?
What will they say if they find the shutter with a hole in it?
But if I do not commit this imprudence, to-morrow I shall not
be able to see her. What! By my own inactivity am I to remain for a day without seeing her, and that after she has
turned from me in an ill humour?" Fabrizio's imprudence
was rewarded; after fifteen hours of work he saw Clelia, and,
to complete his happiness, as she had no idea that he was
looking at her, she stood for a long time without moving, her
gaze fixed on the huge screen; he had plenty of time to read
in her eyes the signs of the most tender pity. Towards the
end of the visit, she was even quite evidently neglecting her
duty to her birds, to stay for whole minutes gazing at the
window. Her heart was profoundly troubled; she was thinking of the Duchessa, whose extreme misfortune had inspired
in her so much pity, and at the same time she was beginning
to hate her. She understood nothing of the profound melancholy which had taken hold of her character, she felt out of
temper with herself. Two or three times, in the course of this
encounter, Fabrizio was impatient to try to shake the screen;
he felt that he was not happy so long as he could not indicate
to Clelia that he saw her. "However," he told himself, "if
she knew that I could see her so easily, timid and reserved as
she is, she would probably slip away out of my sight."

He was far more happy next day (out of what miseries does

love create its happiness!): while she was looking sadly at the huge screen, he succeeded in slipping a tiny piece of wire through the hole which the iron cross had bored, and made signs to her which she evidently understood, at least in the sense that they implied: "I am here and I see you."

Fabrizio was unfortunate on the days that followed. He was anxious to cut out of the colossal screen a piece of board the size of his hand, which could be replaced when he chose, and which would enable him to see and to be seen, that is to say to speak, by signs at least, of what was passing in his heart; but he found that the noise of the very imperfect little saw which he had made by notching the spring of his watch with the cross aroused Grillo, who came and spent long hours in his cell. It is true that he thought he noticed that Clelia's severity seemed to diminish as the material difficulties in the way of any communication between them increased; Fabrizio was fully aware that she no longer pretended to lower her eyes or to look at the birds when he was trying to shew her a sign of his presence by means of his wretched little piece of wire; he had the pleasure of seeing that she never failed to appear in the aviary at the precise moment when the quarter before noon struck, and he almost presumed to imagine himself to be the cause of this remarkable punctuality. Why? Such an idea does not seem reasonable; but love detects shades invisible to the indifferent eye, and draws endless conclusions from them. For instance, now that Clelia could no longer see the prisoner, almost immediately on entering the aviary she would raise her eyes to his window. These were the funereal days on which no one in Parma had any doubt that Fabrizio would shortly be put to death: he alone knew nothing; but this terrible thought never left Clelia's mind for a moment, and how could she reproach herself for the excessive interest which she felt in Fabrizio? He was about to perish—and for the cause of freedom! For it was too absurd to put a del Dongo to death for running his sword into a mummer. It was true that this attractive young man was attached to another woman! Clelia was profoundly unhappy, and without admitting to herself at all precisely the kind of interest that she took in his fate: "Certainly," she said to herself, "if they lead him out to die, I shall fly to a convent, and never in my life will I reappear in that society of the court; it horrifies me. Kid-gloved assassins!"

On the eighth day of Fabrizio's imprisonment, she had

good cause to blush: she was watching fixedly, absorbed in
her sorrowful thoughts, the screen that hid the prisoner's
window: suddenly a small piece of the screen, larger than a
man's hand, was removed by him; he looked at her with an
air of gaiety, and she could see his eyes which were greeting
her. She had not the strength to endure this unlooked-for
trial, she turned swiftly towards her birds and began to attend to them; but she trembled so much that she spilled the
water which she was pouring out for them, and Fabrizio
could perfectly well see her emotion; she could not endure
this situation, and took the prudent course of running from
the room.

This was the best moment in Fabrizio's life, beyond all
comparison. With what transports would he have refused his
freedom, had it been offered to him at that instant!

The following day was the day of the Duchessa's great
despair. Everyone in the town was certain that it was all
over with Fabrizio. Clelia had not the melancholy courage to
show him a harshness that was not in her heart, she spent an
hour and a half in the aviary, watched all his signals, and
often answered him, at least by an expression of the keenest
and sincerest interest; at certain moments she turned from
him so as not to let him see her tears. Her feminine coquetry
felt very strongly the inadequacy of the language employed:
if they could have spoken, in how many different ways could
she not have sought to discover what precisely was the nature
of the sentiments which Fabrizio felt for the Duchessa! Clelia
was now almost unable to delude herself any longer; her
feeling for Signora Sanseverina was one of hatred.

One night Fabrizio began to think somewhat seriously of
his aunt: he was amazed, he found a difficulty in recognising
her image; the memory that he kept of her had totally
changed; for him, at this moment, she was a woman of fifty.

"Great God!" he exclaimed with enthusiasm, "how well inspired I was not to tell her that I loved her!" He had reached
the point of being barely able to understand how he had
found her so good looking. In this connexion little
Marietta gave him the impression of a less perceptible
change: this was because he had never imagined that his
heart entered at all into his love for Marietta, while often he
had believed that his whole heart belonged to the Duchessa.
The Duchessa d'A—— and Marietta now had the effect on
him of two young doves whose whole charm would be in
weakness and innocence, whereas the sublime image of

Clelia Conti, taking entire possession of his heart, went so far as to inspire him with terror. He felt only too well that the eternal happiness of his life was to force him to reckon with the governor's daughter, and that it lay in her power to make of him the unhappiest of men. Every day he went in mortal fear of seeing brought to a sudden end, by a caprice of her will against which there was no appeal, this sort of singular and delicious life which he found in her presence; in any event she had already filled with joy the first two months of his imprisonment. It was the time when, twice a week, General Fabio Conti was saying to the Prince: "I can give Your Highness my word of honour that the prisoner del Dongo does not speak to a living soul, and is spending his life crushed by the most profound despair, or asleep."

Clelia came two or three times daily to visit her birds, sometimes for a few moments only; if Fabrizio had not loved her so well, he would have seen clearly that he was loved; but he had serious doubts on this head. Clelia had had a piano put in her aviary. As she struck the notes, that the sounds of the instrument might account for her presence there, and occupy the minds of the sentries who were patrolling beneath her windows, she replied with her eyes to Fabrizio's questions. On one subject alone she never made any answer, and indeed, on serious occasions, took flight, and sometimes disappeared for a whole day; this was when Fabrizio's signals indicated sentiments the import of which it was too difficult not to understand: on this point she was inexorable.

Thus, albeit straitly confined in a small enough cage, Fabrizio led a fully occupied life; it was entirely devoted to seeking the solution of this important problem: "Does she love me?" The result of thousands of observations, incessantly repeated, but also incessantly subjected to doubt, was as follows: "All her deliberate gestures say no, but what is involuntary in the movement of her eyes seems to admit that she is forming an affection for me."

Clelia hoped that she might never be brought to an avowal, and it was to avert this danger that she had repulsed, with an excessive show of anger, a prayer which Fabrizio had several times addressed to her. The wretchedness of the resources employed by the poor prisoner ought, it might seem, to have inspired greater pity in Clelia. He sought to correspond with her by means of letters which he traced on his hand with a piece of charcoal of which he had made the precious discovery in his stove; he would have formed the words letter by letter, in succession. This invention would have doubled the means of conversation, inasmuch as it would have allowed him to say actual words. His window was distant from Clelia's about twenty-five feet; it would have been too great a risk to speak aloud over the heads of the sentries patrolling outside the governor's *palazzo*. Fabrizio was in doubt whether he was loved; if he had had any experience of love, he would have had no doubt left: but never had a woman occupied his heart; he had, moreover, no suspicion of a secret which would have plunged him in despair had he known it: there was a serious question of the marriage of Clelia Conti to the Marchese Crescenzi, the richest man at court.

CHAPTER NINETEEN

GENERAL FABIO CONTI'S ambition, exalted to madness by the obstacles which were occurring in the career of the Prime Minister Mosca, and seemed to forebode his fall, had led him to make violent scenes before his daughter; he told her incessantly, and angrily, that she was ruining her own prospects if she did not finally make up her mind to choose a husband; at twenty and past it was time to make a match; this cruel state of isolation, in which her unreasonable obstinacy was plunging the General, must be brought to an end, and so forth.

It was originally to escape from these continual bursts of ill humour that Clelia had taken refuge in the aviary; it could be reached only by an extremely awkward wooden stair, which his gout made a serious obstacle to the governor.

For some weeks now Clelia's heart had been so agitated, she herself knew so little what she ought to decide, that, without giving any definite promise to her father, she had almost let herself be engaged. In one of his fits of rage, the General had shouted that he could easily send her to cool her heels in the most depressing convent in Parma, and that there he would let her stew until she deigned to make a choice.

"You know that our family, old as it is, cannot muster a rent-roll of 6,000 lire, while the Marchese Crescenzi's fortune amounts to more than 100,000 scudi a year. Everyone at court agrees that he has the sweetest temper; he has never given anyone cause for complaint; he is a fine looking man, young, popular with the Prince; and I say that you ought to be shut up in a madhouse if you reject his advances. If this were the first refusal, I might perhaps put up with it, but there have been five or six suitors now, all among the first men at court, whom you have rejected, like the little fool that you are. And what would become of you, I ask you, if I were to be put on half-pay? What a triumph for my enemies, if they saw me living in some second-floor apartment, I who have so often been talked of for the Ministry! No, begad, my good nature has let me play Cassandra quite long enough. You will kindly supply me with some valid objection to this poor Marchese Crescenzi, who is so kind as to be in love with you, to be willing to marry you without a dowry, and to make over to you a jointure of 30,000 lire a year, which will at least pay my rent; you will talk to me reasonably, or, by heaven, you will marry him in two months from now!"

One passage alone in the whole of this speech had struck Clelia; this was the threat to send her to a convent, and thereby remove her from the citadel, at the moment, moreover, when Fabrizio's life seemed to be hanging only by a thread, for not a month passed in which the rumour of his approaching death did not run afresh through the town and through the court. Whatever arguments she might use, she could not make up her mind to run this risk. To be separated from Fabrizio, and at the moment when she was trembling for his life! This was in her eyes the greatest of evils; it was at any rate the most immediate.

This is not to say that, even in not being parted from Fabrizio, her heart found any prospect of happiness; she believed him to be loved by the Duchessa, and her soul was torn by a deadly jealousy. Incessantly she thought of the advantages enjoyed by this woman who was so generally admired. The extreme reserve which she imposed on herself with regard to Fabrizio, the language of signs to which she had restricted him, from fear of falling into some indiscretion, all seemed to combine to take from her the means of arriving at any enlightenment as to his relations with the Duchessa. Thus, every day, she felt more cruelly than before the frightful misfortune of having a rival in the heart of Fabrizio, and every day she dared less to expose herself to the danger of giving him an opportunity to tell her the whole truth as to what was passing in that heart. But how charming it would be, nevertheless, to hear him make an avowal of his true feelings! What a joy for Clelia to be able to clear away those frightful suspicions which were poisoning her life!

Fabrizio was fickle; at Naples he had had the reputation of changing his mistress rather easily. Despite all the reserve imposed on the character of a young lady, since she had become a Canoness and had gone to court, Clelia, without ever asking questions, but by listening attentively, had succeeded in learning the reputation that had been made for themselves by the young men who in succession had sought her hand; very well, Fabrizio, when compared with all these young men, was the one who was charged with being most fickle in affairs of the heart. He was in prison, he was dull, he was paying court to the one woman to whom he could speak; what more simple? What, indeed, *more common?* And it was this that grieved Clelia. Even if, by a complete revelation, she should learn that Fabrizio no longer loved the Duchessa, what confidence could she have in his words? Even if she believed in the sincerity of what he said, what confidence could she have in the permanence of his feelings? And lastly, to drive the final stroke of despair into her heart, was not Fabrizio already far advanced in his career as a churchman? Was he not on the eve of binding himself by lifelong vows? Did not the highest dignities await him in that walk in life? "If the least glimmer of sense remained in my mind," the unhappy Clelia said to herself, "ought I not to take flight? Ought I not to beg my father to shut me up in some convent far away? And, as a last straw, it is precisely the fear of being sent away from the citadel and shut up in a convent that is governing all my conduct! It is that fear which is forcing me to hide the truth, which is obliging me to act the hideous and degrading lie of pretending to accept the public attentions of the Marchese Crescenzi."

Clelia was by nature profoundly reasonable; in the whole of her life she had never had to reproach herself with a single unconsidered step, and her conduct on this occasion was the height of unreason: one may judge of her sufferings! They were all the more cruel in that she let herself rest under no illusion. She was attaching herself to a man who was desperately loved by the most beautiful woman at court, a woman who had so many claims to be reckoned superior to Clelia herself! And this man himself, had he been at liberty, was incapable of a serious attachment, whereas she, as she felt only too well, would never have but this one attachment in her life.

It was, therefore, with a heart agitated by the most frightful remorse that Clelia came every day to the aviary: carried to this spot as though in spite of herself, her uneasiness changed its object and became less cruel, the remorse vanished for a few moments; she watched, with indescribable beatings of her heart, for the moments at which Fabrizio could open the sort of hatch that he had made in the enormous screen which masked his window. Often the presence of the gaoler Grillo in his cell prevented him from conversing by signs with his friend.

One evening, about eleven, Fabrizio heard sounds of the strangest nature in the citadel: at night, by leaning on the window-sill and poking his head out through the hatch, he could distinguish any noise at all loud that was made on the great staircase, called "of the three hundred steps," which led from the first courtyard, inside the round tower, to the stone platform on which had been built the governor's *palazzo* and the Farnese prison in which he himself was.

About halfway up, at the hundred and eightieth step, this staircase passed from the south side of a vast court to the north side; at this point there was an iron bridge, very light and very narrow, on the middle of which a turnkey was posted. This man was relieved every six hours, and was obliged to rise and stand to one side to enable anyone to pass over the bridge which he guarded, and by which alone one could reach the governor's *palazzo* and the Torre Farnese. Two turns of a spring, the key of which the governor carried on his person, were enough to hurl this iron bridge down into the court, more than a hundred feet below; this simple precaution once taken, as there was no other staircase in the whole of the citadel, and as every evening at midnight a serjeant brought to the governor's house, and placed in a closet which was reached through his bedroom, the ropes of all the wells, he was left completely inaccessible in his *palazzo*, and it would have been equally impossible for anyone in the world to reach the Torre Farnese. All this Fabrizio had thoroughly observed for himself on the day of his arrival at the citadel, while Grillo who, like all gaolers, loved to boast of his prison, had explained it to him many times since; thus he had but little hope of escape. At the same time he reminded himself of a maxim of Priore Blanès: "The lover thinks more often of reaching his mistress than the husband of guarding his wife; the prisoner thinks more often of escaping than the gaoler of shutting his door; and so, whatever the obstacles may be, the lover and the prisoner ought to succeed."

That evening Fabrizio could hear quite distinctly a considerable number of men cross the iron bridge, known as the Slave's Bridge, because once a Dalmatian slave had succeeded in escaping, by throwing the guardian of the bridge down into the court below.

"They are coming here to carry off somebody, perhaps they are going to take me out to hang me; but there may be some disorder, I must make the most of it." He had armed himself, he was already taking the gold from some of his hiding-places, when suddenly he stopped.

"Man is a quaint animal," he exclaimed, "I must admit! What would an invisible onlooker say if he saw my preparations? Do I by any chance wish to escape? What would happen to me the day after my return to Parma? Should I not be doing everything in the world to return to Clelia? If there is some disorder, let us profit by it to slip into the governor's *palazzo;* perhaps I may be able to speak to her, perhaps, encouraged by the disorder, I may venture to kiss her hand. General Conti, highly mistrustful by nature, and no less vain, has his *palazzo* guarded by five sentries, one at each corner of the building and a fifth outside the door, but fortunately the night is very dark." On tiptoe Fabrizio stole down to find out what the gaoler Grillo and his dog were doing: the gaoler was fast asleep in an oxhide suspended by four ropes and enclosed in a coarse net; the dog Fox opened his eyes, rose, and came quietly towards Fabrizio to lick his hand.

Our prisoner returned softly up the six steps which led to his wooden cell; the noise was becoming so loud at the foot of the Torre Farnese, and immediately opposite the door, that he thought that Grillo might easily awake. Fabrizio, armed with all his weapons, ready for action, was imagining that he was destined that night for great adventures, when suddenly he heard the most beautiful symphony in the world strike up: it was a serenade which was being given to the governor or his daughter. He was seized with a fit of wild laughter: "And I who was already dreaming of striking dagger-blows! As though a serenade were not infinitely more normal than an abduction requiring the presence of two dozen people in a prison, or than a mutiny!" The music was excellent, and seemed to Fabrizio delicious, his spirit having had no distraction for so many weeks; it made him shed very pleasant tears; in his delight he addressed the most irresistible speeches to the fair Clelia. But the following day, at noon, he found her in so sombre a melancholy, she was so pale, she directed at him a gaze in which he read at times such anger, that he did not feel himself to be sufficiently justified in putting any question to her as to the serenade; he was afraid of being impolite.

Clelia had every reason to be sad, it was a serenade given her by the Marchese Crescenzi; a step so public was in a sense the official announcement of their marriage. Until the very day of the serenade, and until nine o'clock that evening, Clelia had set up the bravest resistance, but she had had the weakness to yield to the threat of her being sent immediately to a convent, which had been held over her by her father.

"What! I should never see him again!" she had said to herself, weeping. It was in vain that her reason had added: "I should never see again that creature who will harm me in every possible way, I should never see again that lover of the Duchessa, I should never see again that man who had ten acknowledged mistresses at Naples, and was unfaithful to them all; I should never see again that ambitious young man who, if he survives the sentence that he is undergoing, is to take holy orders! It would be a crime for me to look at him again when he is out of his citadel, and his natural inconstancy will spare me the temptation; for, what am I to him? An excuse for spending less tediously a few hours of each of his days in prison." In the midst of all this abuse, Clelia happened to remember the smile with which he had looked at the constables who surrounded him when he came out of the turnkey's office to go up to the Torre Farnese. The tears welled into her eyes: "Dear friend, what would I not do for you? You will ruin me, I know; such is my fate; I am ruining myself in a terrible fashion by listening to-night to this frightful serenade; but to-morrow, at midday, I shall see your eyes again."

It was precisely on the morrow of that day on which Clelia had made such great sacrifices for the young prisoner, whom she loved with so strong a passion; it was on the morrow of that day on which, seeing all his faults, she had sacrificed her life to him, that Fabrizio was in despair at her coldness. If, even employing only the imperfect language of signs, he had done the slightest violence to Clelia's heart, probably she would not have been able to keep back her tears, and Fabrizio would have won an avowal of all that she felt for him; but he lacked the courage, he was in too deadly a fear of offending Clelia, she could punish him with too severe a penalty. In other words, Fabrizio had no experience of the emotion that is given one by a woman whom one loves; it was a sensation which he had never felt, even in the feeblest degree. It took him a week, from the day of the serenade, to place himself once more on the old footing of simple friendship with Clelia. The poor girl armed herself with severity, being half dead with fear of betraying herself, and it seemed to Fabrizio that every day he was losing ground with her.

One day (and Fabrizio had then been nearly three months in prison without having had any communication whatever with the outer world, and yet without feeling unhappy), Grillo had stayed very late in the morning in his cell: Fabrizio did not know how to get rid of him; in the end, half past twelve had already struck before he was able to open the two little traps, a foot high, which he had carved in the fatal screen.

Clelia was standing at the aviary window, her eyes fixed on Fabrizio's; her drawn features expressed the most violent despair. As soon as she saw Fabrizio, she made him a sign that all was lost: she dashed to her piano, and, pretending to sing a *recitativo* from the popular opera of the season, spoke to him in sentences broken by her despair and the fear of being overheard by the sentries who were patrolling beneath the window:

"Great God! You are still alive? How grateful I am to heaven! Barbone, the gaoler whose impudence you punished on the day of your coming here, disappeared, was not to be found in the citadel; the night before last he returned, and since yesterday I have had reason to believe that he is seeking to poison you. He comes prowling through the private kitchen of the *palazzo*, where your meals are prepared. I know nothing for certain, but my maid thinks that the horrible creature can only be coming to the *palazzo* kitchens with the object of taking your life. I was dying of anxiety when I did not see you appear, I thought you were dead. Abstain from all nourishment until further notice, I shall do everything possible to see that a little chocolate comes to you. In any case, this evening at nine, if the bounty of heaven wills that you have any thread, or that you can tie strips of your linen together in a riband, let it down from your window over the orange trees, I shall fasten a cord to it which you can pull up, and by means of the cord I shall keep you supplied with bread and chocolate."

Fabrizio had carefully treasured the piece of charcoal

which he had found in the stove in his cell: he hastened to make the most of Clelia's emotion, and wrote on his hand a series of letters which taken in order formed these words: "I love you, and life is dear to me only because I see you; at all costs, send me paper and a pencil."

As Fabrizio had hoped, the extreme terror which he read in Clelia's features prevented the girl from breaking off the conversation after this daring announcement, "I love you"; she was content with exhibiting great vexation. Fabrizio was inspired to add: "There is such a wind blowing to-day that I can only catch very faintly the advice you are so kind as to give me in your singing; the sound of the piano is drowning your voice. What is this poison, for instance, that you tell me of?"

At these words the girl's terror reappeared in its entirety; she began in haste to trace large letters in ink on the pages of a book which she tore out, and Fabrizio was transported with joy to see at length established, after three months of effort, this channel of correspondence for which he had so vainly begged. He had no thought of abandoning the little ruse which had proved so successful, his aim was to write real letters, and he pretended at every moment not to understand the words of which Clelia was holding up each letter in turn before his eyes.

She was obliged to leave the aviary to go to her father; she feared more than anything that he might come to look for her; his suspicious nature would not have been at all satisfied with the close proximity of the window of this aviary to the screen which masked that of the prisoner. Clelia herself had had the idea a few moments earlier, when Fabrizio's failure to appear was plunging her in so deadly an anxiety, that it might be possible to throw a small stone wrapped in a piece of paper over the top of this screen; if by a lucky chance the gaoler in charge of Fabrizio happened not to be in his cell at that moment, it was a certain method of corresponding with him.

Our hero hastened to make a riband of sorts out of his linen; and that evening, shortly after nine, he heard quite distinctly a series of little taps on the tubs of the orange trees which stood beneath his window; he let down his riband, which brought back with it a fine cord of great length with the help of which he drew up first of all a supply of chocolate, and then, to his unspeakable satisfaction, a roll of paper and a pencil. It was in vain that he let down the cord again, he received nothing more; apparently the sentries had come near the orange trees. But he was wild with joy. He hastened to write Clelia an endless letter: no sooner was it finished than he attached it to the cord and let it down. For more than three hours he waited in vain for it to be taken, and more than once drew it up again to make alterations. "If Clelia does not see my letter to-night," he said to himself, "while she is still upset by her idea of poison, to-morrow morning perhaps she will utterly reject the idea of receiving a letter."

The fact was that Clelia had been unable to avoid going down to the town with her father; Fabrizio almost guessed as much when he heard, about half past twelve, the General's carriage return; he recognised the trot of the horses. What was his joy when, a few minutes after he had heard the General cross the terrace and the sentries present arms to him, he felt a pull at the cord which he had not ceased to keep looped round his arm! A heavy weight was attached to this cord; two little tugs gave him the signal to draw it up. He had considerable difficulty in getting the heavy object that he was lifting past a cornice which jutted out some way beneath his window.

This object which he had so much difficulty in pulling up was a flask filled with water and wrapped in a shawl. It was with ecstasy that this poor young man, who had been living for so long in so complete a solitude, covered this shawl with his kisses. But we must abandon the attempt to describe his emotion when at last, after so many days of fruitless expectation, he discovered a little scrap of paper which was attached to the shawl by a pin.

"Drink nothing but this water, live upon chocolate; to-morrow I shall do everything in the world to get some bread to you, I shall mark it on each side with little crosses in ink. It is a terrible thing to say, but you must know it, perhaps Barbone has been ordered to poison you. How is it that you did not feel that the subject of which you treat in your pencilled letter was bound to displease me? Besides, I should not write to you, but for the danger that threatens us. I have just seen the Duchessa, she is well and so is the Conte, but she has grown very thin; do not write to me again on that subject; do you wish to make me angry?"

It required a great effort of virtue on Clelia's part to write the penultimate line of this letter. Everyone alleged, in the society at court, that Signora Sanseverina was becoming extremely friendly with Conte Baldi, that handsome man, the

former friend of the Marchesa Raversi. What was certain was
that he had quarrelled in the most open fashion with the
said Marchesa, who for six years had been a second mother to
him and had established him in society.

Clelia had been obliged to begin this hasty little note over
again, for, in the first draft, some allusion escaped her to the
fresh amours with which popular malice credited the
Duchessa.

"How base of me!" she had exclaimed, "to say things to
Fabrizio against the woman he loves!"

The following morning, long before it was light, Grillo
came into Fabrizio's cell, left there a package of some weight,
and vanished without saying a word. This package contained a loaf of bread of some size, adorned on every side
with little crosses traced in ink: Fabrizio covered them with
kisses; he was in love. Besides the bread there was a roll
wrapped in a large number of folds of paper; these enclosed
six hundred francs in sequins; last of all Fabrizio found a
handsome breviary, quite new: a hand which he was beginning to know had traced these words on the margin:

"*Poison!* Beware of water, wine, everything; live upon
chocolate, try to make the dog eat your untouched dinner;
you must not appear distrustful, the enemy would try some
other plan. Do nothing foolish, in heaven's name! No
frivolity!"

Fabrizio made haste to erase these dear words which
might compromise Clelia, and to tear a large number of
pages from the breviary, with the help of which he made
several alphabets; each letter was properly drawn with
crushed charcoal soaked in wine. These alphabets had dried
when at a quarter to twelve Clelia appeared, a few feet inside the aviary window. "The great thing now," Fabrizio
said to himself, "is that she shall consent to make use of
these." But, fortunately for him, it so happened that she had
a number of things to say to the young prisoner with regard to the attempt to poison him: a dog belonging to one of
the maidservants had died after eating a dish that was intended for him. Clelia, so far from raising any objection to
the use of the alphabets, had prepared a magnificent one for
herself, in ink. The conversation carried out by these means,
awkward enough in the first few moments, lasted not less
than an hour and a half, that is to say all the time that
Clelia was able to spend in the aviary. Two or three times,
when Fabrizio allowed himself forbidden liberties, she made

no answer, and turned away for a moment to give the necessary attention to her birds.

Fabrizio had obtained the concession that, in the evening, when she sent him his water, she would convey to him one of the alphabets which she had written in ink, and which were far more visible. He did not fail to write her a very long letter in which he took care not to include anything affectionate, in a manner at least that might give offence. This plan proved successful; his letter was accepted.

Next day, in their conversation by the alphabets, Clelia made him no reproach; she told him that the danger of poison was growing less; Barbone had been attacked and almost killed by the men who were keeping company with the kitchen-maids of the governor's *palazzo;* probably he would not venture to appear in the kitchens again. Clelia confessed to him that, for his sake, she had dared to steal an antidote from her father; she was sending it to him; the essential thing was to refuse at once all food in which he detected an unusual taste.

Clelia had put many questions to Don Cesare without succeeding in discovering who had sent the six hundred francs which Fabrizio had received; in any case, it was an excellent sign; the severity was decreasing.

This episode of the poison advanced our hero's position enormously; he was still unable ever to obtain the least admission that resembled love, but he had the happiness of living on the most intimate terms with Clelia. Every morning, and often in the evening, there was a long conversation with the alphabets; every evening, at nine o'clock, Clelia accepted a long letter, to which she sometimes replied in a few words; she sent him the newspaper and several books; finally, Grillo had been won over to the extent of bringing Fabrizio bread and wine, which were given him every day by Clelia's maid. The gaoler Grillo had concluded from this that the governor was not acting in concert with the people who had ordered Barbone to poison the young Monsignore, and was greatly relieved, as were all his fellows, for it had become a proverb in the prison that "you had only to look Monsignor del Dongo in the face for him to give you money."

Fabrizio had grown very pale; the complete want of exercise was affecting his health; apart from this, he had never in his life been so happy. The tone of the conversation between Clelia and himself was intimate, and at times quite gay. The only moments in Clelia's life that were not besieged by grim forebodings and remorse were those which she spent in talk with him. One day she was so rash as to say to him:

"I admire your delicacy; as I am the governor's daughter, you never speak to me of your desire to regain your freedom!"

"That is because I take good care not to feel so absurd a desire," was Fabrizio's answer; "once back in Parma, how should I see you again? And life would become insupportable if I could not tell you all that is in my mind—no, not quite all that is in my mind, you take good care of that: but still, in spite of your hard-heartedness, to live without seeing you every day would be to me a far worse punishment than this prison! Never in my life have I been so happy! . . . Is it not pleasant to find that happiness was awaiting me in prison?"

"There is a great deal more to be said about that," replied Clelia with an air which became of a sudden unduly serious and almost sinister.

"What!" cried Fabrizio, greatly alarmed, "is there a risk of my losing the tiny place I have managed to win in your heart, which constitutes my sole joy in this world?"

"Yes," she told him; "I have good reason to believe that you are lacking in frankness towards me, although you may be regarded generally as a great gentleman; but I do not wish to speak of this to-day."

This singular opening caused great embarrassment in their conversation, and often tears started to the eyes of both.

The Fiscal General Rassi was still anxious to change his name; he was tired to death of the name he had made for himself, and wished to become Barone Riva. Conte Mosca, for his part, was toiling, with all the skill of which he was capable, to strengthen in this venal judge his passion for the Barony, just as he was seeking to intensify in the Prince his mad hope of making himself Constitutional Monarch of Lombardy. They were the only means that he could invent of postponing the death of Fabrizio.

The Prince said to Rassi:

"A fortnight of despair and a fortnight of hope, it is by patiently carrying out this system that we shall succeed in subduing that proud woman's nature; it is by these alternatives of mildness and harshness that one manages to break the wildest horses. Apply the caustic firmly."

And indeed, every fortnight, one saw a fresh rumour come to birth in Parma announcing the death of Fabrizio in the near future. This talk plunged the unhappy Duchessa

in the utmost despair. Faithful to her resolution not to involve the Conte in her downfall, she saw him but twice
monthly; but she was punished for her cruelty towards that
poor man by the continual alternations of dark despair in
which she was passing her life. In vain did Conte Mosca,
overcoming the cruel jealousy inspired in him by the assi-
duities of Conte Baldi, that handsome man, write to the
Duchessa when he could not see her, and acquaint her with
all the intelligence that he owed to the zeal of the future
Barone Riva; the Duchessa would have needed (for strength
to resist the atrocious rumours that were incessantly going
about with regard to Fabrizio), to spend her life with a man
of intelligence and heart such as Mosca; the nullity of Baldi,
leaving her to her own thoughts, gave her an appalling existence, and the Conte could not succeed in communicating to
her his reasons for hope.

By means of various pretexts of considerable ingenuity
the Minister had succeeded in making the Prince agree to
his depositing in a friendly castle, in the very heart of Lombardy, the records of all the highly complicated intrigues by
means of which Ranuccio-Ernesto IV nourished the utterly
mad hope of making himself Constitutional Monarch of that
smiling land.

More than a score of these extremely compromising documents were in the Prince's hand, or bore his signature, and
in the event of Fabrizio's life being seriously threatened the
Conte had decided to announce to His Highness that he was
going to hand these documents over to a great power which
with a word could crush him.

Conte Mosca believed that he could rely upon the future
Barone Riva, he was afraid only of poison; Barbone's attempt had greatly alarmed him, and to such a point that he
had determined to risk taking a step which, to all appearance, was an act of madness. One morning he went to the
gate of the citadel and sent for General Fabio Conti, who
came down as far as the bastion above the gate; there, strolling with him in a friendly fashion, he had no hesitation in
saying to him, after a short preamble, acidulated but polite:

"If Fabrizio dies in any suspicious manner, his death may
be put down to me; I shall get a reputation for jealousy,
which would be an absurd and abominable stigma and one
that I am determined not to accept. So, to clear myself in the
matter, if he dies of illness, *I shall kill you with my own
hand;* you may count on that." General Fabio Conti made a

magnificent reply and spoke of his bravery, but the look in the Conte's eyes remained present in his thoughts.

A few days later, as though he were working in concert with the Conte, the Fiscal Rassi took a liberty which was indeed singular in a man of his sort. The public contempt attached to his name, which was proverbial among the rabble, had made him ill since he had acquired the hope of being able to change it. He addressed to General Fabio Conti an official copy of the sentence which condemned Fabrizio to twelve years in the citadel. According to the law, this was what should have been done on the very day after Fabrizio's admission to prison; but what was unheard-of at Parma, in that land of secret measures, was that Justice should allow itself to take such a step without an express order from the Sovereign. How indeed could the Prince entertain the hope of doubling every fortnight the Duchessa's alarm, and of subduing that proud spirit, to quote his own words, once an official copy of the sentence had gone out from the Chancellory of Justice? On the day before that on which General Fabio Conti received the official document from the Fiscal Rassi, he learned that the clerk Barbone had been beaten black and blue on returning rather late to the citadel; he concluded from this that there was no longer any question, in a certain quarter, of getting rid of Fabrizio; and, in a moment of prudence which saved Rassi from the immediate consequences of his folly, he said nothing to the Prince, at the next audience which he obtained of him, of the official copy of Fabrizio's sentence which had been transmitted to him. The Conte had discovered, happily for the peace of mind of the unfortunate Duchessa, that Barbone's clumsy attempt had been only an act of personal revenge, and had caused the clerk to be given the warning of which we have spoken.

Fabrizio was very agreeably surprised when, after one hundred and thirty-five days of confinement in a distinctly narrow cell, the good chaplain Don Cesare came to him one Thursday to take him for an airing on the dungeon of the Torre Farnese: he had not been there ten minutes before, unaccustomed to the fresh air, he began to feel faint.

Don Cesare made this accident an excuse to allow him half an hour's exercise every day. This was a mistake: these frequent airings soon restored to our hero a strength which he abused.

There were several serenades; the punctilious governor allowed them only because they created an engagement between the Marchese Crescenzi and his daughter Clelia, whose character alarmed him; he felt vaguely that there was no point of contact between her and himself, and was always afraid of some rash action on her part. She might fly to the convent, and he would be left helpless. At the same time, the General was afraid that all this music, the sound of which could penetrate into the deepest dungeons, reserved for the blackest Liberals, might contain signals. The musicians themselves, too, made him suspicious; and so no sooner was the serenade at an end than they were locked into the big rooms below the governor's *palazzo,* which by day served as an office for the staff, and the door was not opened to let them out until the following morning, when it was broad daylight. It was the governor himself who, stationed on the Slave's Bridge, had them searched in his presence and gave them their liberty, not without several times repeating that he would have hanged at once any of them who had the audacity to undertake the smallest commission for any prisoner. And they knew that, in his fear of giving offence, he was a man of his word, so that the Marchese Crescenzi was obliged to pay his musicians at a triple rate, they being greatly upset at thus having to spend a night in prison.

All that the Duchessa could obtain, and that with great difficulty, from the pusillanimity of one of these men was that he should take with him a letter to be handed to the governor. The letter was addressed to Fabrizio: the writer deplored the fatality which had brought it about that, after he had been more than five months in prison, his friends outside had not been able to establish any communication with him.

On entering the citadel, the bribed musician flung himself at the feet of General Fabio Conti, and confessed to him that a priest, unknown to him, had so insisted upon his taking a letter addressed to Signor del Dongo that he had not dared to refuse; but, faithful to his duty, he was hastening to place it in His Excellency's hands.

His Excellency was highly flattered: he knew the resources at the Duchessa's disposal, and was in great fear of being hoaxed. In his joy, the General went to submit this letter to the Prince, who was delighted.

"So, the firmness of my administration has brought me my

revenge! That proud woman has been suffering for more than six months! But one of these days we are going to have a scaffold erected, and her wild imagination will not fail to believe that it is intended for young del Dongo."

CHAPTER TWENTY

ONE NIGHT, about one o'clock in the morning, Fabrizio, leaning upon his window-sill, had slipped his head through the door cut in his screen and was contemplating the stars and the immense horizon which one enjoyed from the summit of the Torre Farnese. His eyes, roaming over the country in the direction of the lower Po and Ferrara, noticed quite by chance an extremely small but quite brilliant light which seemed to be shining from the top of a tower. "That light cannot be visible from the plain," Fabrizio said to himself, "the bulk of the tower prevents it from being seen from below; it will be some signal for a distant point." Suddenly he noticed that this light kept on appearing and disappearing at very short intervals. "It is some girl speaking to her lover in the next village." He counted nine flashes in succession. "That is an *I*," he said, "*I* being the ninth letter of the alphabet." There followed, after a pause, fourteen flashes: "That is *N*"; then, after another pause, a single flash: "It is an *A;* the word is *Ina.*"

What were his joy and surprise when the next series of flashes, still separated by short pauses, made up the following words:

INA PENSA A TE

Evidently, "Gina is thinking of you!"

He replied at once by flashing his own lamp through the smaller of the holes that he had made:

FABRIZIO T'AMA ("Fabrizio loves you!")

The conversation continued until daybreak. This night was

330

the one hundred and seventy-third of his imprisonment, and he was informed that for four months they had been making these signals every night. But anyone might see and read them; they began from this night to establish a system of abbreviations: three flashes in very quick succession meant the Duchessa; four, the Prince; two, Conte Mosca; two quick flashes followed by two slow ones meant *escape*. They agreed to use in future the old alphabet *alla Monaca*, which, so as not to be understood by unauthorised persons, changes the ordinary sequence of the letters, and gives them arbitrary values: *A,* for instance, is represented by 10, *B* by *Z;* that is to say three successive interruptions of the flash mean *B,* ten successive interruptions *A,* and so on; an interval of darkness separates the words. An appointment was made for the following night at one o'clock, and that night the Duchessa came to the tower, which was a quarter of a league from the town. Her eyes filled with tears as she saw the signals made by the Fabrizio whom she had so often imagined dead. She told him herself, by flashes of the lamp: *"I love you—courage —health—hope. Exercise your strength in your cell, you will need the strength of your arms.* —I have not seen him," she said to herself, "since that concert with Fausta, when he appeared at the door of my drawing-room dressed as a *chasseur.* Who would have said then what a fate was in store for him?"

The Duchessa had signals made which informed Fabrizio that presently he would be released THANKS TO THE PRINCE'S BOUNTY (these signals might be intercepted); then she returned to messages of affection; she could not tear herself from him. Only the representations made by Lodovico, who, because he had been of use to Fabrizio, had become her factotum, could prevail upon her, when day was already breaking, to discontinue signals which might attract the attention of some ill-disposed person. This announcement, several times repeated, of an approaching release, cast Fabrizio into a profound sorrow. Clelia, noticing this next day, was so imprudent as to inquire the cause of it.

"I can see myself on the point of giving the Duchessa serious grounds for displeasure."

"And what can she require of you that you would refuse her?" exclaimed Clelia, carried away by the most lively curiosity.

"She wishes me to leave this place," was his answer, "and that is what I will never consent to do."

Clelia could not reply: she looked at him and burst into

tears. If he had been able to speak to her face to face, then perhaps he would have received her avowal of feelings, his uncertainty as to which often plunged him in a profound discouragement; he felt keenly that life without Clelia's love could be for him only a succession of bitter griefs or intolerable tedium. He felt that it was no longer worth his while to live to rediscover those same pleasures that had seemed to him interesting before he knew what love was, and, albeit suicide has not yet become fashionable in Italy, he had thought of it as a last resource, if fate were to part him from Clelia.

Next day he received a long letter from her:

"You must, my friend, be told the truth: over and over again, since you have been here, it has been believed in Parma that your last day had come. It is true that you were sentenced only to twelve years in a fortress; but it is, unfortunately, impossible to doubt that an all-powerful hatred is bent on your destruction, and a score of times I have trembled for fear that poison was going to put an end to your days: you must therefore seize every *possible* means of escaping from here. You see that for your sake I am neglecting the most sacred duties; judge of the imminence of the danger by the things which I venture to say to you, and which are so out of place on my lips. If it is absolutely necessary, if there is no other way of safety, fly. Every moment that you spend in this fortress may put your life in the greatest peril; bear in mind that there is a party at court whom the prospect of crime has never deterred from carrying out their designs. And do you not see all the plans of that party constantly circumvented by the superior skill of Conte Mosca? Very well, they have found a sure way of banishing him from Parma, it is the Duchessa's desperation; and are they not only too sure of bringing about the desperation by the death of a certain young prisoner? This point alone, which is unanswerable, ought to make you form a judgment of your situation. You say that you feel friendship for me: think, first of all, that insurmountable obstacles must prevent that feeling from ever becoming at all definite between us. We may have met in our youth, we may each have held out a helping hand to the other in a time of trouble; fate may have set me in this grim place that I might lighten your suffering; but I should never cease to reproach myself if illusions, which nothing justifies or will ever justify, led you not to seize every possible opportunity of removing your life from so terrible a peril. I have lost all peace of mind through the cruel folly I have committed in exchanging with you certain signs of open friendship. If our childish pastimes, with alphabets, led you to form illusions which are so little warranted and which may be so fatal to yourself, it would be vain for me to seek to justify myself by reminding you of Barbone's attempt. I should be casting you myself into a far more terrible, far more certain peril, when I thought only to protect you from a momentary danger; and my imprudences are for ever unpardonable if they have given rise to feelings which may lead you to resist the Duchessa's advice. See what you oblige me to repeat to you: save yourself, I command you. . . ."

This letter was very long; certain passages, such as the *I command you* which we have just quoted, gave moments of exquisite hope to Fabrizio's love; it seemed to him that the sentiments underlying the words were distinctly tender, if the expressions used were remarkably prudent. In other instances he paid the penalty for his complete ignorance of this kind of warfare; he saw only simple friendship, or even a very ordinary humanity in this letter from Clelia.

Otherwise, nothing that she told him made him change his intentions for an instant: supposing that the perils which she depicted were indeed real, was it extravagant to purchase, with a few momentary dangers, the happiness of seeing her every day? What sort of life would he lead when he had fled once again to Bologna or to Florence? For, if he escaped from the citadel, he certainly could not hope for permission to live in Parma. And even so, when the Prince should change his mind sufficiently to set him at liberty (which was so highly improbable since he, Fabrizio, had become, for a powerful faction, one of the means of overthrowing Conte Mosca), what sort of life would he lead in Parma, separated from Clelia by all the hatred that divided the two parties? Once or twice in a month, perhaps, chance would place them in the same drawing-room; but even then, what sort of conversation could he hold with her? How could he recapture that perfect intimacy which, every day now, he enjoyed for several hours? What would be the conversation of the drawing-room, compared with that which they made by alphabets? "And, if I must purchase this life of enjoyment and this unique chance of happiness with a few little dangers, where is the harm in that? And would it not be a further happiness to find thus a feeble opportunity of giving her a proof of my love?"

Fabrizio saw nothing in Clelia's letter but an excuse for asking her for a meeting; it was the sole and constant object of all his desires. He had spoken to her of it once only, and then for an instant, at the moment of his entry into prison; and that was now more than two hundred days ago.

An easy way of meeting Clelia offered itself: the excellent Priore Don Cesare allowed Fabrizio half an hour's exercise on the terrace of the Torre Farnese every Thursday, during the day; but on the other days of the week this airing, which might be observed by all the inhabitants of Parma and the neighbouring villages, and might seriously compromise the governor, took place only at nightfall. To climb to the terrace of the Torre Farnese there was no other stair but that of the little belfry belonging to the chapel so lugubriously decorated in black and white marble, which the reader may perhaps remember. Grillo escorted Fabrizio to this chapel, and opened the little stair to the belfry for him: his duty would have been to accompany him; but, as the evenings were growing cold, the gaoler allowed him to go up by himself, locking him into this belfry which communicated with the terrace, and went back to keep warm in his cell. Very well; one evening, could not Clelia contrive to appear, escorted by her maid, in the black marble chapel?

The whole of the long letter in which Fabrizio replied to Clelia's was calculated to obtain this meeting. Otherwise, he confided to her, with perfect sincerity, and as though he were writing of someone else, all the reasons which made him decide not to leave the citadel.

"I would expose myself every day to the prospect of a thousand deaths to have the happiness of speaking to you with the help of our alphabets, which now never defeat us for a moment, and you wish me to be such a fool as to exile myself in Parma, or perhaps at Bologna, or even at Florence! You wish me to walk out of here so as to be farther from you! Understand that any such effort is impossible for me; it would be useless to give you my word, I could never keep it."

The result of this request for a meeting was an absence on the part of Clelia which lasted for no fewer then five days; for five days she came to the aviary only at times when she knew that Fabrizio could not make use of the little opening cut in the screen. Fabrizio was in despair; he concluded from this absence that, despite certain glances which had made him conceive wild hopes, he had never inspired in Clelia any sentiments other than those of a simple friendship. "In that case," he asked himself, "what good is life to me? Let the Prince take it from me, he will be welcome; another reason for not leaving the fortress." And it was with a profound feeling of disgust that, every night, he replied to the signals of the little lamp. The Duchessa thought him quite mad when she read, on the record of the messages which Lodovico brought to her every morning, these strange words: *"I do not wish to escape; I wish to die here!"*

During these five days, so cruel for Fabrizio, Clelia was more unhappy than he; she had had the idea, so poignant for a generous nature: "My duty is to take refuge in a convent, far from the citadel; when Fabrizio knows that I am no longer here, and I shall make Grillo and all the gaolers tell him, then he will decide upon an attempt at escape." But to go to a convent was to abandon for ever all hope of seeing Fabrizio again; and how abandon that hope, when he was furnishing so clear a proof that the sentiments which might at one time have attached him to the Duchessa no longer existed? What more touching proof of love could a young man give? After seven long months in prison, which had seriously affected his health, he refused to regain his liberty. A fickle creature, such as the talk of the courtiers had portrayed Fabrizio in Clelia's eyes as being, would have sacrificed a score of mistresses rather than remain another day in the citadel, and what would such a man not have done to escape from a prison in which, at any moment, poison might put an end to his life?

Clelia lacked courage; she made the signal mistake of not seeking refuge in a convent, a course which would at the same time have furnished her with a quite natural means of breaking with the Marchese Crescenzi. Once this mistake was made, how was she to resist this young man—so lovable, so natural, so tender—who was exposing his life to frightful perils to gain the simple pleasure of looking at her from one window to another? After five days of terrible struggles, interspersed with moments of self-contempt, Clelia

made up her mind to reply to the letter in which Fabrizio
begged for the pleasure of speaking to her in the black
marble chapel. To tell the truth, she refused, and in distinctly
firm language; but from that moment all peace of mind was
lost for her; at every instant her imagination portrayed to
her Fabrizio succumbing to the attack of the poisoner; she
came six or eight times in a day to her aviary, she felt the
passionate need of assuring herself with her own eyes that
Fabrizio was alive.

"If he is still in the fortress," she told herself, "if he is
exposed to all the horrors which the Raversi faction are perhaps plotting against him with the object of getting rid of
Conte Mosca, it is solely because I have had the cowardice
not to fly to the convent! What excuse could he have for
remaining here once he was certain that I had gone for
ever?"

This girl, at once so timid and so proud, brought herself
to the point of running the risk of a refusal on the part of
the gaoler Grillo; what was more, she exposed herself to all
the comments which the man might allow himself to make
on the singularity of her conduct. She stooped to the degree
of humiliation involved in sending for him, and telling
him in a tremulous voice which betrayed her whole secret
that within a few days Fabrizio was going to obtain his freedom, that the Duchessa Sanseverina, in the hope of this, was
taking the most active measures, that often it was necessary
to have without a moment's delay the prisoner's answer to
certain proposals which might be made, and that she wished
him, Grillo, to allow Fabrizio to make an opening in the
screen which masked his window, so that she might communicate to him by signs the instructions which she received several times daily from Signora Sanseverina.

Grillo smiled and gave her an assurance of his respect
and obedience. Clelia felt a boundless gratitude to him because he said nothing; it was evident that he knew quite
well all that had been going on for the last few months.

Scarcely had the gaoler left her presence when Clelia made
the signal by which she had arranged to call Fabrizio upon
important occasions; she confessed to him all that she had
just been doing. "You wish to perish by poison," she added:
"I hope to have the courage, one of these days, to leave
my father and escape to some remote convent. I shall be
indebted to you for that; then I hope that you will no longer
oppose the plans that may be proposed to you for getting you

away from here. So long as you are in prison, I have frightful and unreasonable moments; never in my life have I contributed to anyone's hurt, and I feel that I am to be the cause of your death. Such an idea in the case of a complete stranger would fill me with despair; judge of what I feel when I picture to myself that a friend, whose unreasonableness gives me serious cause for complaint, but whom, after all, I have been seeing every day for so long, is at this very moment a victim to the pangs of death. At times I feel the need to know from your own lips that you are alive.

"It was to escape from this frightful grief that I have just lowered myself so far as to ask a favour of a subordinate who might have refused it me, and may yet betray me. For that matter, I should perhaps be happy were he to come and denounce me to my father; at once I should leave for the convent, I should no longer be the most unwilling accomplice of your cruel folly. But, believe me, this cannot go on for long, you will obey the Duchessa's orders. Are you satisfied, cruel friend? It is I who am begging you to betray my father. Call Grillo, and give him a present."

Fabrizio was so deeply in love, the simplest expression of Clelia's wishes plunged him in such fear that even this strange communication gave him no certainty that he was loved. He summoned Grillo, whom he paid generously for his services in the past, and, as for the future, told him that for every day on which he allowed him to make use of the opening cut in the screen, he should receive a sequin. Grillo was delighted with these terms.

"I am going to speak to you with my hand on my heart, Monsignore; will you submit to eating your dinner cold every day? It is a very simple way of avoiding poison. But I ask you to use the utmost discretion; a gaoler has to see everything and know nothing," and so on. "Instead of one dog, I shall have several, and you yourself will make them taste all the dishes that you propose to eat; as for wine, I will give you my own, and you will touch only the bottles from which I have drunk. But if Your Excellency wishes to ruin me for ever, he has merely got to repeat these details even to Signorina Clelia; women will always be women; if to-morrow she quarrels with you, the day after, to have her revenge, she will tell the whole story to her father, whose greatest joy would be to find an excuse for having a gaoler hanged. After Barbone, he is perhaps the wickedest creature in the fortress, and that is where the real danger of your position lies; he knows how to handle poison, you may be sure of that, and he would never forgive me this idea of having three or four little dogs."

There was another serenade. This time Grillo answered all Fabrizio's questions: he had indeed promised himself always to be prudent, and not to betray Signorina Clelia, who according to him, while on the point of marrying the Marchese Crescenzi, the richest man in the States of Parma, was nevertheless making love, so far as the prison walls allowed, to the charming Monsignore del Dongo. He had answered the latter's final questions as to the serenade, when he was fool enough to add: "They think that he will marry her soon." One may judge of the effect of this simple statement on Fabrizio.

That night he replied to the signals of the lamp only to say that he was ill. The following morning, at ten o'clock, Clelia having appeared in the aviary, he asked her in a tone of ceremonious politeness which was quite novel between them, why she had not told him frankly that she was in love with the Marchese Crescenzi, and that she was on the point of marrying him.

"Because there is not a word of truth in the story," replied Clelia with impatience. It is true, however, that the rest of her answer was less precise: Fabrizio pointed this out to her, and took advantage of it to repeat his request for a meeting. Clelia, seeing a doubt cast on her sincerity, granted his request almost at once, reminding him at the same time that she was dishonouring herself for ever in Grillo's eyes. That evening, when it was quite dark, she appeared, accompanied by her maid, in the black marble chapel; she stopped in the middle, by the sanctuary lamp; the maid and Grillo retired thirty paces towards the door. Clelia, who was trembling all over, had prepared a fine speech: her object was to make no compromising admission, but the logic of passion is insistent; the profound interest which it feels in knowing the truth does not allow it to keep up vain pretences, while at the same time the extreme devotion that it feels to the object of its love takes from it the fear of giving offence. Fabrizio was dazzled at first by Clelia's beauty; for nearly eight months he had seen no one at such close range except gaolers. But the name of the Marchese Crescenzi revived all his fury, it increased when he saw quite clearly that Clelia was answering him only with tactful circumspection; Clelia herself realised that she was increasing his suspicions instead of dissipating them. This sensation was too cruel for her to bear.

"Will you be really glad," she said to him with a sort of anger and with tears in her eyes, "to have made me exceed all the bounds of what I owe to myself? Until the third of August last year I had never felt anything but aversion towards the men who sought to attract me. I had a boundless and probably exaggerated contempt for the character of the courtier, everyone who flourished at that court revolted me. I found, on the other hand, singular qualities in a prisoner who, on the third of August, was brought to this citadel. I felt, without noticing them at first, all the torments of jealousy. The attractions of a charming woman, and one whom I knew well, were like daggers thrust into my heart, because I believed, and I am still inclined to believe that this prisoner was attached to her. Presently the persecutions of the Marchese Crescenzi, who had sought my hand, were redoubled; he is extremely rich, and we have no fortune. I was rejecting them with the greatest boldness when my father uttered the fatal word convent; I realised that, if I left the citadel, I would no longer be able to watch over the life of the prisoner in whose fate I was interested. The triumph of my precautions had been that until that moment he had not the slightest suspicion of the appalling dangers that were threatening his life. I had promised myself never to betray either my father or my secret; but that woman of an admirable activity, a superior intelligence, a terrible will, who is protecting this prisoner, offered him, or so I suppose, means of escape: he rejected them, and sought to persuade me that he was refusing to leave the citadel in order not to be separated from me. Then I made a great mistake, I fought with myself for five days; I ought at once to have fled to the convent and to have left the fortress: that course offered me a very simple method of breaking with the Marchese Crescenzi. I had not the courage to leave the fortress, and I am a ruined girl: I have attached myself to a fickle man: I know what his conduct was at Naples; and what reason should I have to believe that his character has altered? Shut up in a harsh prison, he has paid his court to the one woman he could see; she has been a distraction from the dulness of his life. As he could speak to her only with a certain amount of difficulty, this amusement has assumed the false appearance of a passion. This prisoner, having made a name for himself in the world by his courage, imagines himself to be proving that his love is something more than a passing fancy by exposing himself to considerable dangers in order to continue to see the person whom he thinks that he loves. But as soon as he is in a big town, surrounded once more by the seductions of society, he will once more become what he has always been, a man of the world given to dissipation, to gallantry; and his poor prison companion will end her days in a convent, fogotten by this light-hearted creature, and with the undying regret that she has made him an avowal."

This historic speech, of which we give only the principal points, was, as one may imagine, interrupted a score of times by Fabrizio. He was desperately in love; also he was perfectly convinced that he had never loved before seeing Clelia, and that the destiny of his life was to live for her alone.

The reader will no doubt imagine the fine speeches that he was making when the maid warned her mistress that half past eleven had struck, and that the General might return at any moment; the parting was cruel.

"I am seeing you perhaps for the last time," said Celia to the prisoner: "a proceeding which is evidently in the interest of the Raversi cabal may furnish you with a cruel fashion of proving that you are not inconstant." Clelia parted from Fabrizio choked by her sobs and dying with shame at not being able to hide them entirely from her maid, nor, what was worse, from the gaoler Grillo. A second conversation was possible only when the General should announce his intention of spending an evening in society: and as, since Fabrizio's imprisonment, and the interest which it inspired in the curious courtiers, he had found it prudent to afflict himself with an almost continuous attack of gout, his excursions to the town, subjected to the requirements of an astute policy, were decided upon often only at the moment of his getting into the carriage.

After this evening in the marble chapel, Fabrizio's life was a succession of transports of joy. Serious obstacles, it was true, seemed still to stand in the way of his happiness; but now at last he had that supreme and scarcely hoped-for joy of being loved by the divine creature who occupied all his thoughts.

On the third evening after this conversation, the signals from the lamp finished quite early, almost at midnight; at the moment of their coming to an end Fabrizio almost had his skull broken by a huge ball of lead which, thrown over the top of the screen of his window, came crashing through its paper panes and fell into his room.

This huge ball was not nearly so heavy as appeared from its size. Fabrizio easily succeeded in opening it, and found inside a letter from the Duchessa. By the intervention of the Archbishop, to whom she paid sedulous attention, she had won over to her side a soldier in the garrison of the citadel. This man, a skilled slinger, had eluded the sentries posted at the corners and outside the door of the governor's *palazzo*, or had come to terms with them.

"You must escape with cords: I shudder as I give you this strange advice, I have been hesitating, for two whole months and more, to tell you this; but the official outlook grows darker every day, and one must be prepared for the worst. This being so, start signalling again at once with your lamp, to shew us that you have received this letter; send *P—B—G ala Monaca,* that is four, three and two: I shall not breathe until I have seen this signal. I am on the tower, we shall answer *N—O,* that is seven and five. On receiving the answer send no other signal, and attend to nothing but the meaning of my letter."

Fabrizio made haste to obey and sent the arranged signals, which were followed by the promised reply; then he went on reading the letter:

"We may be prepared for the worst; so I have been told by the three men in whom I have the greatest confidence, after I had made them swear on the Gospel that they would tell me the truth, however cruel it might be to me. The first of these men threatened the surgeon who betrayed you at Ferrara that he would fall upon him with an open knife in his hand; the second told you, on your return from Belgirate, that it would have been more strictly prudent to take your pistol and shoot the footman who came singing through the wood leading a fine horse, but a trifle thin; you do not know the third: he is a highway robber of my acquaintance, a man of action if ever there was one, and as full of courage as yourself; that is chiefly why I asked him to tell me what you ought to do. All three of them assured me, without knowing, any of them, that I was consulting the other two, that it was better to risk breaking your neck than to spend eleven years and four months in the continual fear of a highly probable poison.

"You must for the next month practise in your cell climbing up and down on a knotted cord. Then, on the night of some *festa* when the garrison of the citadel will have received an extra ration of wine, you will make the great attempt; you shall have three cords of silk and canvas, of the thickness of a swan's quill, the first of eighty feet to come down the thirty-five feet from the window to the orange trees; the second of three hundred feet, and that is where the difficulty will be on account of the weight, to come down the hundred and eighty feet which is the height of the wall of the great tower; a third of thirty feet will help you to climb down the rampart. I spend my life studying the great wall from the east, that is from the direction of Ferrara: a gap due to an earthquake has been filled by means of a buttress which forms an *inclined plane*. My highway robber assures me that he would undertake to climb down on that side without any great difficulty and at the risk only of a few scratches, by letting himself slide along the inclined plane formed by this buttress. The vertical drop is no more than twenty-eight feet, right at the bottom: that side is the least carefully guarded.

"However, all things considered, my robber, who has escaped three times from prison, and whom you would love if you knew him, though he abominates people of your class; my highway robber, I say, as agile and nimble as yourself, thinks that he would rather come down on the west side, exactly opposite the little *palazzo* formerly occupied by Fausta, which you know well. What would make him choose that side is that the wall, although very slightly inclined, is covered almost all the way down with shrubs; there are twigs on it, as thick as your little finger, which may easily scratch you if you do not take care, but are also excellent things to hold on to. Only this morning I examined this west side with an excellent telescope: the place to choose is precisely beneath a new stone which was fixed in the parapet two or three years ago. Directly beneath this stone you will find first of all a bare space of some twenty feet; you must go very slowly down this (you can imagine how my heart shudders in giving you these terrible instructions, but courage consists in knowing how to choose the lesser evil, frightful as it may be); after the bare space, you will find eighty or ninety feet of quite big shrubs, out of which one can see birds flying, then a space of thirty feet where there is nothing but grass, wall-flowers and creepers. Then, as you come near the ground, twenty feet of shrubs, and last of all twenty-five or thirty feet recently plastered.

"What would make me choose this side is that there, directly underneath the new stone in the parapet on top, there is a wooden hut built by a soldier in his garden, which the engineer captain employed at the fortress is trying to force him to pull down; it is seventeen feet high, and is roofed with thatch, and the roof touches the great wall of the citadel. It is this roof that tempts me; in the dreadful event of an accident, it would break your fall. Once you have reached this point, you are within the circle of the ramparts, which are none too carefully guarded; if they arrest you there, fire your pistol and put up a fight for a few minutes. Your friend of Ferrara and another stout-hearted man, he whom I call the high-way robber, will have ladders, and will not hesitate to scale this quite low rampart, and fly to your rescue.

"The rampart is only twenty-three feet high, and is built on an easy slope. I shall be at the foot of this last wall with a good number of armed men.

"I hope to be able to send you five or six letters by the same channel as this. I shall continue to repeat the same things in different words, so that we may fully understand one another. You can guess with what feelings I tell you that the man who said: '*Shoot the foot-man,*' who, after all, is the best of men, and is dying of compunction, thinks that you will get away with a broken arm. The highway robber, who has a wider ex-perience of this sort of expedition, thinks that, if you will climb down very carefully, and, above all, without hurrying, your liberty need cost you only a few scratches. The great difficulty is to supply the cords; and this is what has been occupying my whole mind during the last fortnight, in which this great idea has taken up all my time.

"I make no answer to that mad signal, the only stupid thing you have ever said in your life: 'I do not wish to escape!' The man who said: '*Shoot the footman,*' exclaimed that boredom had driven you mad. I shall not attempt to hide from you that we fear a very imminent danger, which will perhaps hasten the day of your flight. To warn you of this danger, the lamp will signal several times in succession:

The castle has taken fire.

You will reply:

Are my books burned?"

This letter contained five or six pages more of details; it was written in a microscopic hand on the thinnest paper.

"All that is very fine and very well thought out," Fabrizio said to himself; "I owe an eternal debt of gratitude to the Conte and the Duchessa; they will think perhaps that I am afraid, but I shall not try to escape. Did anyone ever escape from a place where he was at the height of happiness, to go and cast himself into a horrible exile where everything would be lacking, including air to breathe? What should I do after a month at Florence? I should put on a disguise to come and prowl round the gate of this fortress, and try to intercept a glance!"

Next day Fabrizio had an alarm; he was at his window, about eleven o'clock, admiring the magnificent view and awaiting the happy moment when he should see Clelia, when Grillo came breathless into his cell:

"Quick, quick, Monsignore! Fling yourself on your bed, pretend to be ill; there are three judges coming up! They are going to question you: think well before you speak; they have come to *entangle* you."

So saying, Grillo made haste to shut the little trap in the screen, thrust Fabrizio on to his bed and piled two or three cloaks on top of him.

"Tell them that you are very ill, and don't say much; above all make them repeat their questions, so as to have time to think."

The three judges entered. "Three escaped gaolbirds," thought Fabrizio on seeing their vile faces, "not three judges." They wore long black gowns. They bowed gravely and took possession, without saying a word, of the three chairs that were in the room.

"Signor Fabrizio del Dongo," said the eldest of the three, "we are pained by the sad duty which we have come to you to perform. We are here to announce to you the decease of His Excellency the Signor Marchese del Dongo, your father, Second Grand Majordomo Major of the Lombardo-Venetian Kingdom, Knight Grand Cross of the Orders of ——" a string of titles followed. Fabrizio burst into tears. The judge went on:

"The Signora Marchesa del Dongo, your mother, informs you of this event by a letter missive; but as she has added to the fact certain improper reflexions, by a decree issued yesterday, the Court of Justice has decided that her letter shall be communicated to you only by extract, and it is this extract which the Recorder Bona is now going to read to you."

This reading finished, the judge came across to Fabrizio, who was still lying down, and made him follow on his mother's letter the passages of which copies had been read to him. Fabrizio saw in the letter the words *unjust imprisonment, cruel punishment for a crime which is no crime at all,* and understood what had inspired the judges' visit. However, in his contempt for magistrates without honour, he did not actually say to them any more than:

"I am ill, gentlemen, I am dying of weakness, and you will excuse me if I do not rise."

When the judges had gone, Fabrizio wept again copiously, then said to himself: "Am I a hypocrite? I used to think that I did not love him at all."

On that day and the days that followed Clelia was very sad; she called him several times, but had barely the courage to say a few words. On the morning of the fifth day after their first meeting, she told him that she would come that evening to the marble chapel.

"I can only say a few words to you," she told him as she entered. She trembled so much that she had to lean on her maid. After sending the woman to wait at the chapel door: "You are going to give me your word of honour," she went on in a voice that was barely audible, "you are going to give me your word of honour that you will obey the Duchessa, and will attempt to escape on the day when she orders you and in the way that she will indicate to you, or else to-morrow morning I fly to a convent, and I swear to you here and now that never in my life will I utter a word to you again."

Fabrizio remained silent.

"Promise," said Clelia, the tears starting to her eyes and apparently quite beside herself, "or else we converse here for the last time. The life you have made me lead is intolerable: you are here on my account, and each day is perhaps the last of your existence." At this stage Clelia became so weak that she was obliged to seek the support of an enormous armchair that had originally stood in the middle of the chapel, for the use of the prisoner-prince; she was almost fainting.

"What must I promise?" asked Fabrizio with a beaten air.

"You know."

"I swear then to cast myself deliberately into a terrible disaster, and to condemn myself to live far from all that I love in the world."

"Make a definite promise."

"I swear to obey the Duchessa and to make my escape on the day she wishes and as she wishes. And what is to become of me once I am parted from you?"

"Swear to escape, whatever may happen to you."

"What! Have you made up your mind to marry the Marchese Crescenzi as soon as I am no longer here?"

"Oh, heavens! What sort of heart do you think I have? . . . But swear, or I shall not have another moment's peace."

"Very well, I swear to escape from here on the day on which Signora Sanseverina shall order me to do so, and whatever may happen to me between now and then."

This oath obtained, Clelia became so faint that she was obliged to retire after thanking Fabrizio.

"Everything was in readiness for my flight to-morrow morning," she told him, "had you persisted in refusing. I should have beheld you at this moment for the last time in my life, I had vowed that to the Madonna. Now, as soon as I can leave my room, I shall go and examine the terrible wall beneath the new stone in the parapet."

On the following day he found her so pale that he was keenly distressed. She said to him from the aviary window:

"Let us be under no illusion, my dear friend; as there is sin in our friendship, I have no doubt that misfortune will come to us. You will be discovered while seeking to make your escape, and ruined for ever, if it is no worse; however, we must satisfy the demands of human prudence, it orders us to leave nothing untried. You will need, to climb down the outside of the great tower, a strong cord more than two hundred feet long. In spite of all the efforts I have made since I learned of the Duchessa's plan, I have only been able to procure cords that together amount to barely fifty feet. By a standing order of the governor, all cords that may be seen in the fortress are burned, and every evening they remove the well-ropes, which for that matter are so frail that they often break when drawing up the light weight attached to them. But pray God to forgive me, I am betraying my father, and working, unnatural girl that I am, to cause him undying grief. Pray to God for me, and, if your life is saved, make a vow to consecrate every moment of it to His Glory.

"This is an idea that has come to me: in a week from now I shall leave the citadel to be present at the wedding of one of the Marchese Crescenzi's sisters. I shall come back that night, as I must, but I shall try in every possible way not to come in until very late, and perhaps Barbone will not dare to examine me too closely. All the greatest ladies of the court will be at this wedding of the Marchese's sister, and no doubt Signora Sanseverina among them. In heaven's name, make one of these ladies give me a parcel of cords tightly packed, not too large, and reduced to the smallest possible bulk. Were I to expose myself to a thousand deaths I shall employ every means, even the most dangerous, to introduce this parcel of cords into the citadel, in defiance, alas, of all my duties. If my father comes to hear of it, I shall never see you again; but whatever may be the fate that is in store for me, I shall be happy within the bounds of a sisterly friendship if I can help to save you."

That same evening, by their nocturnal correspondence with the lamps, Fabrizio gave the Duchessa warning of the unique opportunity that would shortly arise of conveying into the citadel a sufficient length of cord. But he begged her to keep this secret even from the Conte, which seemed to her odd. "He is mad," thought the Duchessa, "prison has altered him, he is taking things in a tragic spirit." Next day a ball of lead, thrown by the slinger, brought the prisoner news of the greatest possible peril; the person who undertook to convey the cords, he was told, would be literally saving his life. Fabrizio hastened to give this news to Clelia. This leaden ball brought him also a very careful drawing of the western wall by which he was to climb down from the top of the great tower into the space enclosed within the bastions; from this point it was then quite easy to escape, the ramparts being, as we know, only twenty-three feet in height. On the back of the plan was written in an exquisite hand a magnificent sonnet: a generous soul exhorted Fabrizio to take flight, and not to allow his soul to be debased and his body destroyed by the eleven years of captivity which he had still to undergo.

At this point a detail which is essential and will explain in part the courage that the Duchessa had found to recommend to Fabrizio so dangerous a flight, obliges us to interrupt for a moment the history of this bold enterprise.

Like all parties which are not in power, the Raversi party was not closely united. Cavaliere Riscara detested the Fiscal Rassi, whom he accused of having made him lose an important suit in which, as a matter of fact, he, Riscara, had been in the wrong. From Riscara the Prince received an anonymous message informing him that a copy of Fabrizio's sentence had been officially addressed to the governor of the citadel. The Marchesa Raversi, that skilled party leader, was extremely annoyed by this false move, and at once sent word of it to her friend the Fiscal General; she found it quite natural that he should have wished to secure something from the Minister Mosca while Mosca remained in power. Rassi presented himself boldly at the Palace, thinking that he would get out of the scrape with a few kicks; the Prince could not dispense with a talented jurist, and Rassi had procured the banishment as Liberals of a judge and a barrister, the only two men in the country who could have taken his place.

The Prince, beside himself with rage, hurled insults at him and advanced upon him to strike him.

"Why, it is only a clerk's mistake," replied Rassi with the utmost coolness; "the procedure is laid down by the law, it should have been done the day after Signor del Dongo was confined in the citadel. The clerk in his zeal thought it had been forgotten, and must have made me sign the covering letter as a formality."

"And you expect to take me in with a clumsy lie like that?" cried the Prince in a fury; "why not confess that you have sold yourself to that rascal Mosca, and that this is why he gave you the Cross. But, by heaven, you shall not escape with a thrashing: I shall have you brought to justice, I shall disgrace you publicly."

"I defy you to bring me to justice," replied Rassi with assurance; he knew that this was a sure way of calming the Prince: "the law is on my side, and you have not a second Rassi to find you a way round it. You will not disgrace me, because there are moments when your nature is severe; you then feel a thirst for blood, but at the same time you seek to retain the esteem of reasonable Italians; that esteem is a *sine qua non* for your ambition. And so you will recall me for the first act of severity of which your nature makes you feel the need, and as usual I shall procure you a quite regular sentence passed by timid judges who are fairly honest men, which will satisfy your passions. Find another man in your States as useful as myself!"

So saying, Rassi fled; he had got out of his scrape with a sharp reprimand and half-a-dozen kicks. On leaving the Palace he started for his estate of Riva; he had some fear of a dagger-thrust in the first impulse of anger, but had no doubt that within a fortnight a courier would summon him back to the capital. He employed the time which he spent in the country in organising a safe method of correspondence with Conte Mosca; he was madly in love with the title of Barone, and felt that the Prince made too much of that sublime thing, nobility, ever to confer it upon him; whereas the Conte, extremely proud of his own birth, respected nothing but nobility proved by titles anterior by the year 1400.

The Fiscal General had not been out in his forecast: he had been barely eight days on his estate when a friend of the Prince, who came there by chance, advised him to return to Parma without delay; the Prince received him with a laugh, then assumed a highly serious air, and made him swear on the Gospel that he would keep secret what was going to be confided to him. Rassi swore with great solemnity, and the Prince, his eye inflamed by hatred, cried that he would no longer be master in his own house so long as Fabrizio del Dongo was alive.

"I cannot," he went on, "either drive the Duchessa away or endure her presence; her eyes defy me and destroy my life."

Having allowed the Prince to explain himself at great length, Rassi, affecting extreme embarrassment, finally exclaimed:

"Your Highness shall be obeyed, of course, but the matter is one of a horrible difficulty: there is no possibility of condemning a del Dongo to death for the murder of a Giletti; it is already a masterly stroke to have made twelve years' imprisonment out of it. Besides, I suspect the Duchessa of having discovered three of the *contadini* who were employed on the excavations at Sanguigna, and were outside the trench at the moment when that brigand Giletti attacked del Dongo."

"And where are these witnesses?" said the Prince, irritated.

"Hiding in Piedmont, I suppose. It would require a conspiracy against Your Highness's life. . . ."

"There is a danger in that," said the Prince, "it makes people think of the reality."

"Well," said Rassi with a feint of innocence, "that is all my official arsenal."

"There remains poison. . . ."

"But who is to give it? Not that imbecile Conte?"

"From what one hears, it would not be his first attempt. . . ."

"He would have to be roused to anger first," Rassi went on; "and besides, when he made away with the captain he was not thirty, and he was in love, and infinitely less of a coward than he is in these days. No doubt, everything must give way to reasons of State; but, taken unawares like this and at first sight, I can see no one to carry out the Sovereign's orders but a certain Barbone, registry clerk in the prison, whom Signor del Dongo knocked down with a cuff in the face on the day of his admission there."

Once the Prince had been put at his ease, the conversation was endless; he brought it to a close by granting his Fiscal General a month in which to act; Rassi wished for two. Next day he received a secret present of a thousand sequins. For three days he reflected; on the fourth he returned to his original conclusion, which seemed to him self-evident: "Conte Mosca alone will have the heart to keep his word to me, because, in making me a Barone, he does not give me anything that he respects; secondly, by warning him, I save myself probably from a crime for which I am more or less paid in advance; thirdly, I have my revenge for the first humiliating blows which Cavaliere Rassi has received." The following night he communicated to Conte Mosca the whole of his conversation with the Prince.

The Conte was secretly paying his court to the Duchessa; it is quite true that he still did not see her in her own house more than once or twice in a month, but almost every week, and whenever he managed to create an occasion for speaking of Fabrizio, the Duchessa, accompanied by Cecchina, would come, late in the evening, to spend a few moments in the Conte's gardens. She managed even to deceive her coachman, who was devoted to her, and believed her to be visiting a neighbouring house.

One may imagine whether the Conte, after receiving the Fiscal's terrible confidence, at once made the signal arranged between them to the Duchessa. Although it was the middle of the night, she begged him by Cecchina to come to her for a moment. The Conte, enraptured, lover-like, by this prospect of intimate converse, yet hesitated before telling the Duchessa everything. He was afraid of seeing her driven mad by grief.

After first seeking veiled words in which to mitigate the fatal announcement, he ended by telling her all; it was not in his power to keep a secret which she asked of him. In the last nine months her extreme misery had had a great influence on this ardent soul, this had fortified her courage, and she did not give way to sobs or lamentations. On the following evening she sent Fabrizio the signal of great danger:

"The castle has taken fire."

He made the appropriate reply:

"Are my books burned?"

The same night she was fortunate enough to have a letter conveyed to him in a leaden ball. It was a week after this that the marriage of the Marchese Crescenzi's sister was celebrated, when the Duchessa was guilty of an enormously rash action of which we shall give an account in its proper place.

CHAPTER TWENTY-ONE

ALMOST A YEAR before the time of these calamities the Duchessa had made a singular acquaintance: one day when she had the *luna,* as they say in those parts, she had gone suddenly, towards evening, to her villa of Sacca, situated on the farther side of Colorno, on the hill commanding the Po. She was amusing herself in improving this property; she loved the vast forest which crowned the hill and reached to the house; she spent her time laying out paths in picturesque directions.

"You will have yourself carried off by brigands, fair Duchessa," the Prince said to her one day; "it is impossible that a forest in which it is known that you take the air should remain deserted." The Prince threw a glance at the Conte, whose jealousy he hoped to quicken.

"I have no fear, Serene Highness," replied the Duchessa with an innocent air, "when I go walking in my woods; I reassure myself with this thought: I have done no harm to anyone, who is there that could hate me?" This speech was considered daring, it recalled the insults offered by the Liberals of the country, who were most insolent people.

On the day of the walk in question, the Prince's words came back to the mind of the Duchessa as she observed a very ill-dressed man who was following her at a distance through the woods. At a sudden turn which she took in the course of her walk, this person came so near her that she felt alarmed. Her first impulse was to call her game-keeper whom she had left half a mile away, in the flower-garden close to the house. The stranger had time to overtake her and fling himself at her feet. He was young, extremely good looking, but horribly badly dressed; his clothes had rents in

352

them a foot long, but his eyes burned with the fire of an ardent soul.

"I am under sentence of death, I am the physician, Ferrante Palla, I am dying of hunger, I and my five children."

The Duchessa had noticed that he was terribly thin; but his eyes were so fine, and filled with so tender an exaltation that they took from him any suggestion of crime. "Pallagi," she thought, "might well have given eyes like those to the Saint John in the Desert he has just placed in the Cathedral." The idea of Saint John was suggested to her by the incredible thinness of the vagabond. The Duchessa gave him three sequins which she had in her purse, with an apology for offering him so little, because she had just paid her gardener's account. Ferrante thanked her effusively. "Alas!" he said to her, "once I lived in towns, I used to see beautiful women; now that in fulfilment of my duties as a citizen I have had myself sentenced to death, I live in the woods, and I was following you, not to demand alms of you nor to rob you, but like a savage fascinated by an angelic beauty. It is so long since I last saw a pair of lovely white hands."

"Rise, then," the Duchessa told him; for he had remained on his knees.

"Allow me to remain like this," said Ferrante; "this posture proves to me that I am not for the present engaged in robbery, and that soothes me; for you must know that I steal to live, now that I am prevented from practising my profession. But at this moment I am only a simple mortal who is adoring sublime beauty." The Duchessa gathered that he was slightly mad, but she was not at all afraid; she saw in the eyes of the man that he had a good and ardent soul, and besides she had no objection to extraordinary physiognomies.

"I am a physician, then, and I was making love to the wife of the apothecary Sarasine of Parma: he took us by surprise and drove us from the house, with three children whom he supposed, and rightly, to be mine and not his. I have had two since then. The mother and five children are living in the direst poverty in a sort of hut which I built with my own hands a league from here, in the wood. For I have to keep away from the police, and the poor woman refuses to be parted from me. I was sentenced to death, and quite justly; I was conspiring. I abominate the Prince, who is a tyrant. I did not fly the country, for want of money. My misfortunes have greatly increased, and I ought to have killed myself a thousand times over; I no longer love the unhappy woman who has borne me these five children and has ruined herself for me; I love another. But if I kill myself, the five children will literally starve to death." The man spoke with an accent of sincerity.

"But how do you live?" inquired the Duchessa, moved to compassion.

"The children's mother spins; the eldest girl is kept in a farm by some Liberals, where she tends the sheep; I am a highwayman on the road between Piacenza and Genoa."

"How do you harmonise highway robbery with your Liberal principles?"

"I keep a note of the people I rob, and if ever I have anything I shall restore to them the sums I have taken. I consider that a Tribune of the People like myself is performing work which, in view of its danger, is well worth a hundred francs monthly; and so I am careful not to take more than twelve hundred francs in a year.

"No, I am wrong, I steal a small sum in addition, for in that way I am able to meet the cost of printing my works."

"What works?"

"*Is —— ever to have a Chamber and a Budget?*"

"What," said the Duchessa in amazement, "it is you, Sir, who are one of the greatest poets of the age, the famous Ferrante Palla?"

"Famous perhaps, but most unfortunate; that is certain."

"And a man of your talent, Sir, is obliged to steal in order to live?"

"That is perhaps the calling for which I have some talent. Hitherto all our authors who have made themselves famous have been men paid by the government or the religion that they sought to undermine. I, in the first place, risk my life; in the second place, think, Signora, of the reflexions that disturb my mind when I go out to rob! Am I in the right, I ask myself. Does the office of Tribune render services that are really worth a hundred francs a month? I have two shirts, the coat in which you see me, a few worthless weapons, and I am sure to end by the rope; I venture to think that I am disinterested. I should be happy but for this fatal love which allows me to find only misery now in the company of the mother of my children. Poverty weighs upon me because it is ugly: I like fine clothes, white hands. . . ."

He looked at the Duchessa's in such a fashion that fear seized hold of her.

"Good-bye, Sir," she said to him: "can I be of any service to you in Parma?"

"Think sometimes of this question: his task is to awaken men's hearts and to prevent them from falling asleep in that false and wholly material happiness which is given by monarchies. Is the service that he renders to his fellow-citzens worth a hundred francs a month? . . . My misfortune is that I am in love," he said in the gentlest of tones, "and for nearly two years my heart has been occupied by you alone, but until now I have seen you without alarming you." And he took to his heels with a prodigious swiftness which astonished the Duchessa and reassured her. "The police would have hard work to catch him," she thought; "he must be mad, after all."

"He is mad," her servants informed her; "we have all known for a long time that the poor man was in love with the Signora; when the Signora is here we see him wandering in the highest parts of the woods, and as soon as the Signora has gone he never fails to come and sit in the very places where she has rested; he is careful to pick up any flowers that may have dropped from her nosegay and keeps them for a long time fastened in his battered hat."

"And you have never spoken to me of these eccentricities," said the Duchessa, almost in a tone of reproach.

"We were afraid that the Signora might tell the Minister Mosca. Poor Ferrante is such a good fellow! He has never done harm to anyone, and because he loves our Napoleon they have sentenced him to death."

She said no word to the Minister of this meeting, and, as in four years it was the first secret that she had kept from him, a dozen times she was obliged to stop short in the middle of a sentence. She returned to Sacca with a store of gold. Ferrante shewed no sign of life. She came again a fortnight later: Ferrante, after following her for some time, bounding through the wood at a distance of a hundred yards, fell upon her with the swiftness of a hawk, and flung himself at her feet as on the former occasion.

"Where were you a fortnight ago?"

"In the mountains, beyond Novi, robbing the muleteers who were returning from Milan where they had been selling oil."

"Take this purse."

Ferrante opened the purse, took from it a sequin which he kissed and thrust into his bosom, then handed it back to her.

"You give me back this purse, and you are a robber!"

"Certainly; my rule is that I must never possess more than a hundred francs; now, at this moment, the mother of my children has eight francs, and I have twenty-five; I am five francs to the bad, and if they were to hang me now I should feel remorse. I have taken this sequin because it comes from you and I love you."

The intonation of this very simple speech was perfect. "He does really love," the Duchessa said to herself.

That day he appeared quite distracted. He said that there were in Parma people who owed him six hundred francs, and that with that sum he could repair his hut in which now his poor children were catching cold.

"But I will make you a loan of those six hundred francs," said the Duchessa, genuinely moved.

"But then I, a public man—will not the opposite party have a chance to slander me, and say that I am selling myself?"

The Duchessa, in compassion, offered him a hiding-place in Parma if he would swear that for the time being he would not exercise his magistrature in that city, and above all would not carry out any of those sentences of death which, he said, he had *in petto*.

"And if they hang me, as a result of my rashness," said Ferrante gravely, "all those scoundrels, who are so obnoxious to the People, will live for long years to come, and by whose fault? What will my father say to me when he greets me up above?"

The Duchessa spoke to him at length of his young children, to whom the damp might give fatal illnesses; he ended by accepting the offer of the hiding place in Parma.

The Duca Sanseverina, during the solitary half-day which he had spent in Parma after his marriage, had shewn the Duchessa a highly singular hiding place which exists in the southern corner of the *palazzo* of that name. The wall in front, which dates from the middle ages, is eight feet thick; it has been hollowed out inside, so as to provide a secret chamber twenty feet in height but only two in width. It is close to where the visitor admires the reservoir mentioned in all the accounts of travels, a famous work of the twelfth century, constructed at the time of the siege of Parma by the Emperor Sigismund, and afterwards enclosed within the walls of the *palazzo* Sanseverina.

One enters the hiding place by turning an enormous stone on an iron axis which runs through the middle of the block.

The Duchessa was so profoundly touched by Ferrante's madness and by the hard lot of his children, for whom he obstinately refused every present of any value, that she allowed him to make use of this hiding place for a considerable time. She saw him again a month later, still in the woods of Sacca, and as on this occasion he was a little more calm, he recited to her one of his sonnets which seemed to her equal if not superior to any of the finest work written in Italy in the last two centuries. Ferrante obtained several interviews; but his love grew exalted, became importunate, and the Duchessa perceived that this passion was obeying the laws of all love-affairs in which one conceives the possibility of a ray of hope. She sent him back to the woods, forbade him to speak to her again: he obeyed immediately and with a perfect docility. Things had reached this point when Fabrizio was arrested. Three days later, at nightfall, a Capuchin presented himself at the door of the *palazzo* Sanseverina; he had, he said, an important secret to communicate to the lady of the house. She was so wretched that she had him admitted: it was Ferrante. "There is happening here a fresh iniquity of which the Tribune of the people ought to take cognisance," this man mad with love said to her. "On the other hand, acting as a private citizen," he added, "I can give the Signora Duchessa Sanseverina nothing but my life, and I lay it before her."

So sincere a devotion on the part of a robber and madman touched the Duchessa keenly. She talked for some time to this man who was considered the greatest poet in the North of Italy, and wept freely. "Here is a man who understands my heart," she said to herself. The following day he reappeared, again at the *Ave Maria,* disguised as a servant and wearing livery.

"I have not left Parma: I have heard tell of an atrocity which my lips shall not repeat; but here I am. Think, Signora, of what you are refusing! The being you see before you is not a doll of the court, he is a man!" He was on his knees as he uttered these words with an air which made them tell. "Yesterday I said to myself," he went on: "She has wept in my presence; therefore she is a little less unhappy."

"But, Sir, think of the dangers that surround you, you will be arrested in this town!"

"The Tribune will say to you: Signora, what is life when duty calls? The unhappy man, who has the grief of no longer feeling any passion for virtue now that he is burning with love, will add: Signora Duchessa, Fabrizio, a man of feeling, is perhaps about to perish, do not repulse another man of feeling who offers himself to you! Here is a body of iron and a heart which fears nothing in the world but your displeasure."

"If you speak to me again of your feelings, I close my door to you for ever."

It occurred to the Duchessa, that evening, to announce to Ferrante that she would make a small allowance to his children, but she was afraid that he would go straight from the house and kill himself.

No sooner had he left her than, filled with gloomy presentiments, she said to herself: "I too, I may die, and would to God I might, and that soon! If I found a man worthy of the name to whom to commend my poor Fabrizio."

An idea struck the Duchessa: she took a sheet of paper and drafted an acknowledgment, into which she introduced the few legal terms that she knew, that she had received from Signor Ferrante Palla the sum of 25,000 francs, on the express condition of paying every year a life-rent of 1,500 francs to Signora Sarasine and her five children. The Duchessa added: "In addition, I bequeath a life-rent of 300 francs to each of these five children, on condition that Ferrante Palla gives his professional services as a physician to my nephew Fabrizio del Dongo, and behaves to him as a brother. This I request him to do." She signed the document, ante-dated it by a year and folded the sheet.

Two days later, Ferrante reappeared. It was at the moment when the town was agitated by the rumour of the immediate execution of Fabrizio. Would this grim ceremony take place in the citadel, or under the trees of the public mall? Many of the populace took a walk that evening past the gate of the citadel, trying to see whether the scaffold were being erected; this spectacle had moved Ferrante. He found the Duchessa in floods of tears and unable to speak; she greeted him with her hand and pointed to a seat. Ferrante, disguised that day as a Capuchin, was superb; instead of seating himself he knelt, and prayed devoutly in an undertone. At a moment when the Duchessa seemed slightly more calm, without stirring from his posture, he broke off his prayer for an instant to say these words: "Once again he offers his life."

"Think of what you are saying," cried the Duchessa, with that haggard eye which, following tears, indicates that anger is overcoming emotion.

"He offers his life to place an obstacle in the way of Fabrizio's fate, or to avenge it."

"There are circumstances," replied the Duchessa, "in which I could accept the sacrifice of your life."

She gazed at him with a severe attention. A ray of joy gleamed in his eye; he rose swiftly and stretched out his arms towards heaven. The Duchessa went to find a paper hidden in the secret drawer of a walnut cabinet.

"Read this," she said to Ferrante. It was the deed in favour of his children, of which we have spoken.

Tears and sobs prevented Ferrante from reading it to the end; he fell on his knees.

"Give me back the paper," said the Duchessa, and, in his presence, burned it in the flame of a candle.

"My name," she explained, "must not appear if you are taken and executed, for your life will be at stake."

"My joy is to die in harming the tyrant: a far greater joy is to die for you. Once this is stated and clearly understood, be so kind as to make no further mention of this detail of money. I might see in it a suspicion that would be injurious to me."

"If you are compromised, I may be also," replied the Duchessa, "and Fabrizio as well as myself: it is for that reason, and not because I have any doubt of your bravery, that I require that the man who is lacerating my heart shall be poisoned and not stabbed. For the same reason which is so important to me, I order you to do everything in the world to save your own life."

"I shall execute the task faithfully, punctiliously and prudently. I foresee, Signora Duchessa, that my revenge will be combined with your own: were it not so, I should still obey you faithfully, punctiliously and prudently. I may not succeed, but I shall employ all my human strength."

"It is a question of poisoning Fabrizio's murderer."

"So I had guessed, and, during the twenty-seven months in which I have been leading this vagabond and abominable life, I have often thought of a similar action on my own account."

"If I am discovered and condemned as an accomplice," went on the Duchessa in a tone of pride, "I do not wish the charge to be imputed to me of having corrupted you. I order you to make no further attempt to see me until the time comes for our revenge: he must on no account be put to death before I have given you the signal. His death at the present moment, for instance, would be lamentable to me instead of being useful. Probably his death will occur only in several months' time, but it shall occur. I insist on his dying by poison, and I should prefer to leave him alive rather than see him shot. For considerations which I do not wish to explain to you, I insist upon your life's being saved."

Ferrante was delighted with the tone of authority which the Duchessa adopted with him: his eyes gleamed with a profound joy. As we have said, he was horribly thin; but one could see that he had been very handsome in his youth, and he imagined himself to be still what he had once been. "Am I mad?" he asked himself; "or will the Duchessa indeed one day, when I have given her this proof of my devotion, make me the happiest of men? And, when it comes to that, why not? Am I not worth as much as that doll of a Conte Mosca, who when the time came, could do nothing for her, not even enable Monsignor Fabrizio to escape?"

"I may wish his death to-morrow," the Duchessa continued, still with the same air of authority. "You know that immense reservoir of water which is at the corner of the *palazzo*, not far from the hiding-place which you have sometimes occupied; there is a secret way of letting all that water run out into the street: very well, that will be the signal for my revenge. You will see, if you are in Parma, or you will hear it said, if you are living in the woods, that the great reservoir of the *palazzo* Sanseverina has burst. Act at once but by poison, and above all risk your own life as little as possible. No one must ever know that I have had a hand in this affair."

"Words are useless," replied Ferrante, with an enthusiasm which he could ill conceal: "I have already fixed on the means which I shall employ. The life of that man has become more odious to me than it was before, since I shall not dare to see you again so long as he is alive. I shall await the signal of the reservoir flooding the street." He bowed abruptly and left the room. The Duchessa watched him go.

When he was in the next room, she recalled him.

"Ferrante!" she cried; "sublime man!"

He returned, as though impatient at being detained: his face at that moment was superb.

"And your children?"

"Signora, they will be richer than I; you will perhaps allow them some small pension."

"Wait," said the Duchessa as she handed him a sort of

large case of olive wood, "here are all the diamonds that I have left: they are worth 50,000 francs."

"Ah! Signora, you humiliate me!" said Ferrante with a gesture of horror; and his face completely altered.

"I shall not see you again before the deed: take them, I wish it," added the Duchessa with an air of pride which struck Ferrante dumb; he put the case in his pocket and left her.

The door had closed behind him. The Duchessa called him back once again; he returned with an uneasy air: the Duchessa was standing in the middle of the room; she threw herself into his arms. A moment later, Ferrante had almost fainted with happiness; the Duchessa released herself from his embrace, and with her eyes shewed him the door.

"There goes the one man who has understood me," she said to herself; "that is how Fabrizio would have acted, if he could have realised."

There were two salient points in the Duchessa's character: she always wished what she had once wished; she never gave any further consideration to what had once been decided. She used to quote in this connexion a saying of her first husband, the charming General Pietranera. "What insolence to myself!" he used to say; "Why should I suppose that I have more sense to-day than when I made up my mind?"

From that moment a sort of gaiety reappeared in the Duchessa's character. Before the fatal resolution, at each step that her mind took, at each new point that she saw, she had the feeling of her own inferiority to the Prince, of her weakness and gullibility; the Prince, according to her, had basely betrayed her, and Conte Mosca, as was natural to his courtier's spirit, albeit innocently, had supported the Prince. Once her revenge was settled, she felt her strength, every step that her mind took gave her happiness. I am inclined to think that the immoral happiness which the Italians find in revenge is due to the strength of their imagination; the people of other countries do not properly speaking forgive; they forget.

The Duchessa did not see Palla again until the last days of Fabrizio's imprisonment. As the reader may perhaps have guessed, it was he who gave her the idea of his escape: there was in the woods, two leagues from Sacca, a mediæval tower, half in ruins, and more than a hundred feet high; before speaking a second time to the Duchessa of an escape, Ferrante begged her to send Lodovico with a party of trustworthy men, to fasten a set of ladders against this tower. In the Duchessa's presence he climbed up by means of the ladders and down with an ordinary knotted cord; he repeated the experiment three times, then explained his idea again. A week later Lodovico too was prepared to climb down this old tower with a knotted cord; it was then that the Duchessa communicated the idea to Fabrizio.

In the final days before this attempt, which might lead to the death of the prisoner, and in more ways than one, the Duchessa could not secure a moment's rest unless she had Ferrante by her side; the courage of this man electrified her own; but it can be understood that she had to hide from the Conte this singular companionship. She was afraid, not that he would be revolted, but she would have been afflicted by his objections, which would have increased her uneasiness. "What! Take as an intimate adviser a madman known to be mad, and under sentence of death! And," added the Duchessa, speaking to herself, "a man who, in consequence, might do such strange things!" Ferrante happened to be in the Duchessa's drawing-room at the moment when the Conte came to give her a report of the Prince's conversation with Rassi; and, when the Conte had left her, she had great difficulty in preventing Ferrante from going straight away to the execution of a frightful plan.

"I am strong now," cried this madman; "I have no longer any doubt as to the lawfulness of the act!"

"But, in the moment of indignation which must inevitably follow, Fabrizio would be put to death!"

"Yes, but in that way we should spare him the danger of the climb: it is possible, indeed easy," he added; "but the young man lacks experience."

The marriage was celebrated of the Marchese Crescenzi's sister, and it was at the party given on this occasion that the Duchessa met Clelia, and was able to speak to her without causing any suspicion among the fashionable onlookers. The Duchessa herself handed to Clelia the parcel of cords in the garden, where the two ladies had gone for a moment's fresh air. These cords, prepared with the greatest care, of hemp and silk in equal parts, were knotted, very slender and fairly flexible; Lodovico had tested their strength, and, in every portion, they could bear without breaking a load of sixteen hundredweight. They had been packed in such a way as to form several packets each of the size and shape of a quarto volume; Clelia took charge of them, and promised the Duchessa that everything that was humanly possible would be done to deliver these packets in the Torre Farnese.

"But I am afraid of the timidity of your nature; and besides," the Duchessa added politely, "what interest can you feel in a stranger?"

"Signor del Dongo is in distress, *and I promise you that he shall be saved by me!*"

But the Duchessa, placing only a very moderate reliance on the presence of mind of a young person of twenty, had taken other precautions, of which she took care not to inform the governor's daughter. As might be expected, this governor was present at the party given for the marriage of the Marchese Crescenzi's sister. The Duchessa said to herself that, if she could make him be given a strong narcotic, it might be supposed, at first, that he had had an attack of apoplexy, and then, instead of his being placed in his carriage to be taken back to the citadel, it might, with a little arrangement, be possible to have the suggestion adopted of using a litter, which would happen to be in the house where the party was being given. There, too, would be gathered a body of intelligent men, dressed as workmen employed for the party, who, in the general confusion, would obligingly offer their services to transport the sick man to his *palazzo*, which stood at such a height. These men, under the direction of Lodovico, carried a sufficient quantity of cords, cleverly concealed beneath their clothing. One sees that the Duchessa's mind had become really unbalanced since she had begun to think seriously of Fabrizio's escape. The peril of this beloved creature was too much for her heart, and besides was lasting too long. By her excess of precaution, she nearly succeeded in preventing his escape, as we shall presently see. Everything went off as she had planned, with this one difference, that the narcotic produced too powerful an effect; everyone believed, including the medical profession, that the General had had an apoplectic stroke.

Fortunately, Clelia, who was in despair, had not the least suspicion of so criminal an attempt on the part of the Duchessa. The confusion was such at the moment when the litter, in which the General, half dead, was lying, entered the citadel, that Lodovico and his men passed in without challenge; they were subjected to a formal scrutiny only at the Slave's Bridge. When they had carried the General to his bedroom, they were taken to the kitchens, where the servants entertained them royally; but after this meal, which did not end until it was very nearly morning, it was explained to them that the rule of the prison required that, for the rest of the night, they should be locked up in the lower rooms of the *palazzo;* in the morning at daybreak they would be released by the governor's deputy.

These men had found an opportunity of handing to Lodovico the cords with which they had been loaded, but Lodovico had great difficulty in attracting Clelia's attention for a moment. At length, as she was passing from one room to another, he made her observe that he was laying down packets of cords in a dark corner of one of the drawing-rooms of the first floor. Clelia was profoundly struck by this strange circumstance; at once she conceived atrocious suspicions.

"Who are you?" she asked Lodovico.

And, on receiving his highly ambiguous reply, she added:

"I ought to have you arrested; you or your masters have poisoned my father! Confess this instant what is the nature of the poison you have used, so that the doctor of the citadel can apply the proper remedies; confess this instant, or else, you and your accomplices shall never go out of this citadel!"

"The Signorina does wrong to be alarmed," replied Lodovico, with a grace and politeness that were perfect; "there is no question of poison; someone has been rash enough to administer to the General a dose of laudanum, and it appears that the servant who was responsible for this crime poured a few drops too many into the glass; this we shall eternally regret; but the Signorina may be assured that, thank heaven, there is no sort of danger; the Signore must be treated for having taken, by mistake, too strong a dose of laudanum; but, I have the honour to repeat to the Signorina, the lackey responsible for the crime made no use of real poisons, as Barbone did, when he tried to poison Monsignor Fabrizio. There was no thought of revenge for the peril that Monsignor Fabrizio ran; nothing was given to this clumsy lackey but a bottle in which there was laudanum, that I swear to the Signorina! But it must be clearly understood that, if I were questioned officially, I should deny everything.

"Besides, if the Signorina speaks to anyone in the world of laudanum and poison, even to the excellent Don Cesare, Fabrizio is killed by the Signorina's own hand. She makes impossible for ever all the plans of escape; and the Signorina

knows better than I that it is not with laudanum that they
wish to poison Monsignore; she knows, too, that a certain
person has granted only a month's delay for that crime,
and that already more than a week has gone by since the
fatal order was received. So, if she has me arrested, or if
she merely says a word to Don Cesare or to anyone else,
she retards all our activities far more than a month, and I am
right in saying that she kills Monsignor Fabrizio with her
own hand."

Clelia was terrified by the strange tranquillity of Lodovico.

"And so," she said to herself, "here I am conversing for-
mally with my father's poisoner, who employs polite turns of
speech to address me! And it is love that has led me to all
these crimes! . . ."

Her remorse scarcely allowed her the strength to speak;
she said to Lodovico.

"I am going to lock you into this room. I shall run and
tell the doctor that it is only laudanum; but, great God, how
shall I tell him that I discovered this? I shall come back
afterwards to release you. But," said Clelia, running back
from the door, "did Fabrizio know anything of the laudanum?"

"Heavens, no, Signorina, he would never have consented
to that. And, besides, what good would it have done to make
an unnecessary confidence? We are acting with the strictest
prudence. It is a question of saving the life of Monsignore,
who will be poisoned in three weeks from now; the order
has been given by a person who is not accustomed to find any
obstacle to his wishes; and, to tell the Signorina everything,
they say that it was the terrible Fiscal General Rassi who
received these instructions."

Clelia fled in terror; she could so count on the perfect
probity of Don Cesare that, taking certain precautions, she
had the courage to tell him that the General had been given
laudanum, and nothing else. Without answering, without
putting any question, Don Cesare ran to the doctor.

Clelia returned to the room in which she had shut up
Lodovico, with the intention of plying him with questions
about the laudanum. She did not find him: he had managed
to escape. She saw on the table a purse full of sequins and a
box containing different kinds of poison. The sight of these
poisons made her shudder. "How can I be sure," she thought,
"that they have given nothing but laudanum to my father,

and that the Duchessa has not sought to avenge herself for Barbone's attempt?

"Great God!" she cried, "here am I in league with my father's poisoners. And I allow them to escape! And perhaps that man, when put to the question, would have confessed something else than laudanum!"

Clelia at once fell on her knees, burst into tears, and prayed to the Madonna with fervour.

Meanwhile the doctor of the citadel, greatly surprised by the information he had received from Don Cesare, according to which he had to deal only with laudanum, applied the appropriate remedies, which presently made the more alarming symptoms disappear. The General came to himself a little as day began to dawn. His first action that shewed any sign of consciousness was to hurl insults at the Colonel who was second in command of the citadel, and had taken upon himself to give certain orders, the simplest in the world, while the General was unconscious.

The governor next flew into a towering rage with a kitchen-maid who, when bringing him his soup, had been so rash as to utter the word apoplexy.

"Am I of an age," he cried, "to have apoplexies? It is only my deadly enemies who can find pleasure in spreading such reports. And besides, have I been bled, that slander itself dare speak of apoplexy?"

Fabrizio, wholly occupied with the preparations for his escape, could not understand the strange sounds that filled the citadel at the moment when the governor was brought in half dead. At first he had some idea that his sentence had been altered, and that they were coming to put him to death. Then, seeing that no one came to his cell, he thought that Clelia had been betrayed, that on her return to the fortress they had taken from her the cords which probably she was bringing back, and so, that his plans of escape were for the future impossible. Next day, at dawn, he saw come into his room a man unknown to him, who, without saying a word, laid down a basket of fruit: beneath the fruit was hidden the following letter:

"Penetrated by the keenest remorse for what has been done, not, thank heaven, by my consent, but as the outcome of an idea which I had, I have made a vow to the Blessed Virgin that if, by the effect of Her holy intercession my father is saved, I will never

refuse to obey any of his orders; I will marry the
Marchese as soon as he requires me to do so, and I
will never see you again. However, I consider it my
duty to finish what has been begun. Next Sunday, when
you return from mass, to which you will be taken at
my request (remember to prepare your soul, you may
kill yourself in the difficult enterprise); when you return
from mass, I say, put off as long as possible going
back to your room; you will find there what is necessary for the enterprise that you have in mind. If you
perish, my heart will be broken! Will you be able to accuse me of having contributed to your death? Has not
the Duchessa herself repeated to me upon several occasions that the Raversi faction is winning? They seek to
bind the Prince by an act of cruelty that must separate
him for ever from Conte Mosca. The Duchessa, with
floods of tears, has sworn to me that there remains only
this resource: you will perish unless you make an attempt. I cannot look at you again, I have made my vow;
but if on Sunday, towards evening, you see me dressed
entirely in black, at the usual window, it will be the
signal that everything will be ready that night so far as
my feeble means allow. After eleven, perhaps at midnight
or at one o'clock, a little lamp will appear in my
window, that will be the decisive moment; commend
yourself to your Holy Patron, dress yourself in haste
in the priestly habit with which you are provided, and
be off.

"Farewell, Fabrizio, I shall be at my prayers, and shed-
ding the most bitter tears, as you may well believe,
while you are running such great risks. If you perish, I
shall not outlive you a day; Great God! What am I
saying? But if you succeed, I shall never see you again.
On Sunday, after mass, you will find in your prison the
money, the poison, the cords, sent by that terrible
woman who loves you with passion, and who has three
times over assured me that this course must be adopted.
May God preserve you, and the Blessed Madonna!"

Fabio Conti was a gaoler who was always uneasy, always
unhappy, always seeing in his dreams one of his prisoners
escaping: he was loathed by everyone in the citadel; but
misfortune inspiring the same resolutions in all men, the
poor prisoners, even those who were chained in dungeons

three feet high, three feet wide and eight feet long, in which
they could neither stand nor sit, all the prisoners, even these,
I say, had the idea of ordering a *Te Deum* to be sung at their
own expense, when they knew that their governor was out
of danger. Two or three of these wretches composed sonnets
in honour of Fabio Conti. Oh, the effect of misery upon
men! May he who would blame them be led by his destiny
to spend a year in a cell three feet high, with eight ounces of
bread a day and *fasting* on Fridays!

Clelia, who left her father's room only to pray in the
chapel, said that the governor had decided that the rejoicings
should be confined to Sunday. On the morning of this Sunday, Fabrizio was present at mass and at the *Te Deum;* in
the evening there were fireworks, and in the lower rooms of
the *palazzo* the soldiers received a quantity of wine four times
that which the governor had allowed; an unknown hand had
even sent several barrels of brandy which the soldiers
broached. The generous spirit of the soldiers who were becoming intoxicated would not allow the five of their number
who were on duty as sentries outside the *palazzo* to suffer
accordingly; as soon as they arrived at their sentry-boxes, a
trusted servant gave them wine, and it was not known from
what hand those who came on duty at midnight and for the
rest of the night received also a glass each of brandy, while
the bottle was in each case forgotten and left by the sentry-
box (as was proved in the subsequent investigations).

The disorder lasted longer than Clelia had expected, and
it was not until nearly one o'clock that Fabrizio, who, more
than a week earlier, had sawn through two bars of his window, the window that did not look out on the aviary, began
to take down the screen; he was working almost over the
heads of the sentries who were guarding the governor's
palazzo, they heard nothing. He had made some fresh knots
only in the immense cord necessary for descending from that
terrible height of one hundred and eighty feet. He arranged
this cord as a bandolier about his body: it greatly embarrassed him, its bulk was enormous; the knots prevented it
from being wound close, and it projected more than eighteen
inches from his body. "This is the chief obstacle," said Fabrizio.

This cord once arranged as well as possible, Fabrizio took
the other with which he counted on climbing down the
thirty-five feet which separated his window from the terrace
on which the governor's *palazzo* stood. But inasmuch as,

however drunken the sentries might be, he could not descend exactly over their heads, he climbed out, as we have said, by the second window of his room, that which looked over the roof of a sort of vast guard-room. By a sick man's whim, as soon as General Fabio Conti was able to speak, he had ordered up two hundred soldiers into this old guard-room, disused for over a century. He said that after poisoning him, they would seek to murder him in his bed, and these two hundred soldiers were to guard him. One may judge of the effect which this unforeseen measure had on the heart of Clelia: that pious girl was fully conscious to what an extent she was betraying her father, and a father who had just been almost poisoned in the interests of the prisoner whom she loved. She almost saw in the unexpected arrival of these two hundred men an act of Providence which forbade her to go any farther and to give Fabrizio his freedom.

But everyone in Parma was talking of the immediate death of the prisoner. This grim subject had been discussed again at the party given on the occasion of the marriage of Donna Giulia Crescenzi. Since for such a mere trifle as a clumsy sword-thrust given to an actor, a man of Fabrizio's birth was not set at liberty at the end of nine months' imprisonment, and when he had the protection of the Prime Minister, it must be because politics entered into the case. And in that event, it was useless to think any more about him, people said; if it was not convenient to authority to put him to death in a public place, he would soon die of sickness. A locksmith who had been summoned to General Fabio Conti's *palazzo* spoke of Fabrizio as of a prisoner long since dispatched, whose death was being kept secret from motives of policy. This man's words decided Clelia.

CHAPTER TWENTY-TWO

D URING THE DAY Fabrizio was attacked by certain serious and disagreeable reflexions; but as he heard the hours strike that brought him nearer to the moment of action, he began to feel alert and ready. The Duchessa had written that he would feel the shock of the fresh air, and that once he was out of his prison he might find it impossible to walk; in that case it was better to run the risk of being caught than to let himself fall from a height of a hundred and eighty feet. "If I have that misfortune," said Fabrizio, "I shall lie down beneath the parapet, I shall sleep for an hour, then I shall start again. Since I have sworn to Clelia that I will make the attempt, I prefer to fall from the top of a rampart, however high, rather than always to have to think about the taste of the bread I eat. What horrible pains one must feel before the end, when one dies of poison! Fabio Conti will stand on no ceremony, he will make them give me the arsenic with which he kills the rats in his citadel."

Towards midnight, one of those thick white fogs in which the Po sometimes swathes its banks, spread first of all over the town, and then reached the esplanade and the bastions from the midst of which rises the great tower of the citadel. Fabrizio estimated that from the parapet of the platform it would be impossible to make out the young acacias that surrounded the gardens laid out by the soldiers at the foot of the hundred and eighty foot wall. "That, now, is excellent," he thought.

Shortly after half past twelve had struck, the signal of the little lamp appeared at the aviary window. Fabrizio was ready for action; he crossed himself, then fastened to his bed the fine cord intended to enable him to descend the thirty-five feet that separated him from the platform on which

the *palazzo* stood. He arrived without meeting any obstacle
on the roof of the guard-room occupied overnight by the re-
inforcement of two hundred soldiers of whom we have
spoken. Unfortunately, the soldiers, at a quarter to one in
the morning, as it now was, had not yet gone to sleep; while
he was creeping on tiptoe over the roof of large curved tiles,
Fabrizio could hear them saying that the devil was on the
roof, and that they must try to kill him with a shot from
a musket. Certain voices insisted that this desire savoured of
great impiety; others said that if a shot were fired without
killing anything, the governor would put them all in prison
for having alarmed the garrison without cause. The upshot
of this discussion was that Fabrizio walked across the roof as
quickly as possible and made a great deal more noise. The
fact remains that at the moment when, hanging by his cord,
he passed opposite the windows, mercifully at a distance of
four or five feet owing to the projection of the roof, they
were bristling with bayonets. Some accounts suggest that Fabrizio, mad as ever, had the idea of acting the part of the
devil, and that he flung these soldiers a handful of sequins.
One thing certain is that he had scattered sequins upon the
floor of his room, and that he scattered more on the platform on his way from the Torre Farnese to the parapet, so
as to give himself the chance of distracting the attention of
the soldiers who might come in pursuit of him.

Landing upon the platform where he was surrounded by
soldiers, who ordinarily called out every quarter of an hour
a whole sentence: "All's well around my post!" he directed
his steps towards the western parapet and sought for the new
stone.

The thing that appears incredible and might make one
doubt the truth of the story if the result had not had a whole
town for witnesses, is that the sentries posted along the
parapet did not see and arrest Fabrizio; as a matter of fact
the fog was beginning to rise, and Fabrizio said afterwards
that when he was on the platform the fog seemed to him to
have come already halfway up the Torre Farnese. But this
fog was by no means thick, and he could quite well see the
sentries, some of whom were moving. He added that, impelled as though by a supernatural force, he went to take up
his position boldly between two sentries who were quite
near one another. He calmly unwound the big cord which he
had round his body, and which twice became entangled; it
took him a long time to unravel it and spread it out on the

parapet. He heard the soldiers talking on all sides of him, and was quite determined to stab the first who advanced upon him. "I was not in the least anxious," he added, "I felt as though I were performing a ceremony."

He fastened his cord, when it was finally unravelled, through an opening cut in the parapet for the escape of rain-water, climbed on to the said parapet and prayed to God with fervour; then, like a hero of the days of chivalry, he thought for a moment of Clelia. "How different I am," he said to himself, "from the fickle, libertine Fabrizio of nine months ago!" At length he began to descend that astounding height. He acted mechanically, he said, and as he would have done in broad daylight, climbing down a wall before friends, to win a wager. About halfway down, he suddenly felt his arms lose their strength; he thought afterwards that he had even let go the cord for an instant, but he soon caught hold of it again; possibly, he said, he had held on to the bushes into which he slipped, receiving some scratches from them. He felt from time to time an agonising pain between his shoulders; it actually took away his breath. There was an extremely unpleasant swaying motion; he was constantly flung from the cord to the bushes. He was brushed by several birds which he aroused, and which dashed in at him in their flight. At first, he thought that he was being clutched by men who had come down from the citadel by the same way as himself in pursuit, and he prepared to defend his life. Finally he arrived at the base of the great tower without any inconvenience save that of having blood on his hands. He relates that, from the middle of the tower, the slope which it forms was of great use to him; he hugged the wall all the way down, and the plants growing between the stones gave him great support. On reaching the foot, among the soldiers' gardens, he fell upon an acacia which, looked at from above, had seemed to him to be four or five feet high, but was really fifteen or twenty. A drunken man who was lying asleep beneath it took him for a robber. In his fall from this tree, Fabrizio nearly dislocated his right arm. He started to run towards the rampart; but, as he said, his legs felt like cotton, he had no longer any strength. In spite of the danger, he sat down and drank a little brandy which he had left. He dozed off for a few minutes to the extent of not knowing where he was; on awaking, he could not understand how, lying in bed in his cell, he saw trees. Then the terrible truth came back to his mind. At once he stepped out to the rampart, and climbed it by a big stair. The sentry who was posted close beside this stair was snoring in his box. He found a cannon lying in the grass; he fastened his third cord to it; it proved to be a little too short, and he fell into a muddy ditch in which there was perhaps a foot of water. As he was picking himself up and trying to take his bearings, he felt himself seized by two men; he was afraid for a moment; but presently heard a voice close to his ear whisper very softly: "Ah! Monsignore, Monsignore!" He gathered vaguely that these men belonged to the Duchessa; at once he fell in a dead faint. A minute later, he felt that he was being carried by men who were marching in silence and very fast; then they stopped, which caused him great uneasiness. But he had not the strength either to speak or to open his eyes; he felt that he was being clasped in someone's arm; suddenly he recognised the scent of the Duchessa's clothing. This scent revived him; he opened his eyes; he was able to utter the words: "Ah! Dear friend!" Then once again he fainted away.

The faithful Bruno, with a squad of police all devoted to the Conte, was in reserve at a distance of two hundred yards; the Conte himself was hidden in a small house close to the place where the Duchessa was waiting. He would not have hesitated, had it been necessary, to take his sword in his hand, with a party of half-pay officers, his intimate friends; he regarded himself as obliged to save the life of Fabrizio, who seemed to him to be exposed to great risk, and would long ago have had his pardon signed by the Prince, if he, Mosca, had not been so foolish as to seek to avoid making the Sovereign write a foolish thing.

Since midnight the Duchessa, surrounded by men armed to the teeth, had been pacing in deep silence outside the ramparts of the citadel; she could not stay in one place, she thought that she would have to fight to rescue Fabrizio from the men who would pursue him. This ardent imagination had taken a hundred precautions, too long to be given here in detail, and of an incredible imprudence. It was calculated that more than eighty agents were afoot that night, in readiness to fight for something extraordinary. Fortunately Ferrante and Lodovico were at the head of all these men, and the Minister of Police was not hostile; but the Conte himself remarked that the Duchessa was not betrayed by anyone, and that he himself, as Minister, knew nothing.

The Duchessa lost her head altogether on seeing Fabrizio again; she clasped him convulsively in her arms, then was in despair on seeing herself covered in blood: it was the blood from Fabrizio's hands; she thought that he was dangerously wounded. With the assistance of one of her men, she was taking off his coat to bandage him when Lodovico, who fortunately happened to be on the spot, firmly put her and Fabrizio in one of the little carriages which were hidden in a garden near the gate of the town, and they set off at full gallop to cross the Po near Sacca. Ferrante, with a score of well-armed men, formed the rearguard, and had sworn on his head to stop the pursuit. The Conte, alone and on foot, did not leave the neighbourhood of the citadel until two hours later, when he saw that no one was stirring. "Look at me, committing high treason," he said to himself, mad with joy.

Lodovico had the excellent idea of placing in one of the carriages a young surgeon attached to the Duchessa's household, who was of much the same build as Fabrizio.

"Make your escape," he told him, "in the direction of Bologna; be as awkward as possible, try to have yourself arrested; then contradict yourself in your answers, and finally admit that you are Fabrizio del Dongo; above all, gain time. Use your skill in being awkward, you will get off with a month's imprisonment, and the Signora will give you fifty sequins."

"Does one think of money when one is serving the Signora?"

He set off, and was arrested a few hours later, an event which gave great joy to General Fabio Conti and also to Rassi, who, with Fabrizio's peril, saw his Barony taking flight.

The escape was not known at the citadel until about six o'clock in the morning, and it was not until ten that they dared inform the Prince. The Duchessa had been so well served that, in spite of Fabrizio's deep sleep, which she mistook for a dead faint, with the result that she stopped the carriage three times, she crossed the Po in a boat as four was striking. There were relays on the other side, they covered two leagues more at great speed, then were stopped for more than an hour for the examination of their passports. The Duchessa had every variety of these for herself and Fabrizio; but she was mad that day, and took it into her head to give ten napoleons to the clerk of the Austrian police, and to clasp his hand and burst into tears. This clerk, greatly alarmed, began the examination afresh. They took post; the

Duchessa paid in so extravagant a fashion that everywhere she aroused suspicions, in that land where every stranger is suspect. Lodovico came to the rescue again: he said that the Signora Duchessa was beside herself with grief at the protracted fever of young Conte Mosca, son of the Prime Minister of Parma, whom she was taking with her to consult the doctors of Pavia.

It was not until they were ten leagues beyond the Po that the prisoner really awoke; he had a dislocated shoulder and a number of slight cuts. The Duchessa again behaved in so extraordinary a fashion that the landlord of a village inn where they dined thought he was entertaining a Princess of the Imperial House, and was going to pay her the honours which he supposed to be due to her when Lodovico told him that the Princess would without fail have him put in prison if he thought of ordering the bells to be rung.

At length, about six o'clock in the evening, they reached Piedmontese territory. There for the first time Fabrizio was in complete safety; he was taken to a little village off the high road, the cuts on his hands were dressed, and he slept for several hours more.

It was in this village that the Duchessa allowed herself to take a step that was not only horrible from the moral point of view, but also fatal to the tranquillity of the rest of her life. Some weeks before Fabrizio's escape, on a day when the whole of Parma had gone to the gate of the citadel, hoping to see in the courtyard the scaffold that was being erected for his benefit, the Duchessa had shown to Lodovico, who had become the factotum of her household, the secret by which one raised from a little iron frame, very cunningly concealed, one of the stones forming the floor of the famous reservoir of the *palazzo* Sanseverina, a work of the thirteenth century, of which we have spoken already. While Fabrizio was lying asleep in the *trattoria* of this little village, the Duchessa sent for Lodovico. He thought that she had gone mad, so strange was the look that she gave him.

"You probably expect," she said to him, "that I am going to give you several thousand francs; well, I am not; I know you, you are a poet, you would soon squander it all. I am giving you the small *podere* of La Ricciarda, a league from Casalmaggiore." Lodovico flung himself at her feet, mad with joy, and protesting in heartfelt accents that it was not with any thought of earning money that he had helped to save Monsignor Fabrizio; that he had always loved him with a special affection since he had had the honour to drive him once, in his capacity as the Signora's third coachman. When this man, who was genuinely warm-hearted, thought that he had taken up enough of the time of so great a lady, he took his leave; but she, with flashing eyes, said to him:

"Wait!"

She paced without uttering a word the floor of this inn room, looking from time to time at Lodovico with incredible eyes. Finally the man, seeing that this strange exercise showed no sign of coming to an end, took it upon himself to address his mistress.

"The Signora has made me so extravagant a gift, one so far beyond anything that a poor man like me could imagine, and moreover so much greater than the humble services which I have had the honour to render, that I feel, on my conscience, that I cannot accept the *podere* of La Ricciarda. I have the honour to return this land to the Signora, and to beg her to grant me a pension of four hundred francs."

"How many times in your life," she said to him with the most sombre pride, "how many times have you heard it said that I had abandoned a project once I had made it?"

After uttering this sentence, the Duchessa continued to walk up and down the room for some minutes; then suddenly stopping, cried:

"It is by accident, and because he managed to attract that little girl, that Fabrizio's life has been saved! If he had not been attractive, he would now be dead. Can you deny that?" she asked, advancing on Lodovico with eyes in which the darkest fury blazed. Lodovico recoiled a few steps and thought her mad, which gave him great uneasiness as to the possession of his *podere* of La Ricciarda.

"Very well!" the Duchessa went on, in the most winning and light-hearted tone, completely changed, "I wish my good people of Sacca to have a mad holiday which they will long remember. You are going to return to Sacca; have you any objection? Do you think that you will be running any risk?"

"None to speak of, Signora: none of the people of Sacca will ever say that I was in Monsignor Fabrizio's service. Besides, if I may venture to say so to the Signora, I am burning to see *my* property at La Ricciarda: it seems so odd for me to be a landowner!"

"Your gaiety pleases me. The farmer at La Ricciarda owes me, I think, three or four years' rent; I make him a present of half of what he owes me, and the other half of all these arrears I give to you, but on this condition: you will go to Sacca, you will say there that the day after tomorrow is the *festa* of one of my patron saints, and, on the evening after your arrival, you will have my house illuminated in the most splendid fashion. Spare neither money nor trouble; remember that the occasion is the greatest happiness of my life. I have prepared for this illumination long beforehand; more than three months ago, I collected in the cellars of the house everything that can be used for this noble *festa;* I have put the gardener in charge of all the fireworks necessary for a magnificent display: you will let them off from the terrace overlooking the Po. I have eighty-nine large barrels of wine in my cellars, you will set up eighty-nine fountains of wine in my park. If next day there remains a single bottle which has not been drunk, I shall say that you do not love Fabrizio. When the fountains of wine, the illumination and the fireworks are well started, you will slip away cautiously, for it is possible, and it is my hope, that at Parma all these fine doings may appear an insolence."

"It is not possible, it is only a certainty; as it is certain too that the Fiscal Rassi, who signed Monsignore's sentence, will burst with rage. And indeed," added Lodovico timidly, "if the Signora wished to give more pleasure to her poor servant than by bestowing on him half the arrears of La Ricciarda, she would allow me to play a little joke on that Rassi. . . ."

"You are a stout fellow!" cried the Duchessa in a transport; "but I forbid you absolutely to do anything to Rassi: I have a plan of having him publicly hanged, later on. As for you, try not to have yourself arrested at Sacca; everything would be spoiled if I lost you."

"I, Signora! After I have said that I am celebrating the *festa* of one of the Signora's patrons, if the police sent thirty constables to upset things, you may be sure that before they had reached the Croce Rossa in the middle of the village, not one of them would be on his horse. They're no fools, the people of Sacca; finished smugglers all of them, and they worship the Signora."

"Finally," went on the Duchessa with a singularly detached air, "if I give wine to my good people of Sacca, I wish to flood the inhabitants of Parma; the same evening on which my house is illuminated, take the best horse in my stable, dash to my *palazzo* in Parma, and open the reservoir."

"Ah! What an excellent idea of the Signora!" cried Lodovico, laughing like a madman; "wine for the good people of Sacca, water for the cits of Parma, who were so sure, the wretches, that Monsignor Fabrizio was going to be poisoned like poor L——."

Lodovico's joy knew no end; the Duchessa complacently watched his wild laughter; he kept on repeating "Wine for the people of Sacca and water for the people of Parma! The Signora no doubt knows better than I that when they rashly emptied the reservoir, twenty years ago, there was as much as a foot of water in many of the streets of Parma."

"And water for the people of Parma," retorted the Duchessa with a laugh. "The avenue past the citadel would have been filled with people if they had cut off Fabrizio's head. . . . They all call him *the great culprit.* . . . But, above all, do everything carefully, so that not a living soul knows that the flood was started by you or ordered by me. Fabrizio, the Conte himself must be left in ignorance of this mad prank. . . . But I was forgetting the poor of Sacca: go and write a letter to my agent, which I shall sign; you will tell him that, for the *festa* of my holy patron, he must distribute a hundred sequins among the poor of Sacca, and tell him to obey you in everything to do with the illumination, the fireworks and the wine; and especially that there must not be a full bottle in my cellars next day."

"The Signora's agent will have no difficulty except in one thing: in the five years that the Signora has had the villa, she has not left ten poor persons in Sacca."

"And water for the people of Parma!" the Duchessa went on chanting. "How will you carry out this joke?"

"My plans are all made: I leave Sacca about nine o'clock, at half past ten my horse is at the inn of the Tre Ganasce, on the road to Casalmaggiore and to *my podere* of La Ricciarda; at eleven, I am in my room in the *palazzo,* and at a quarter past eleven water for the people of Parma, and more than they wish, to drink to the health of the great culprit. Ten minutes later, I leave the town by the Bologna road. I make, as I pass it, a profound bow to the citadel, which Monsignore's courage and the Signora's spirit have succeeded in disgracing; I take a path across country, which I know well, and I make my entry into La Ricciarda."

Lodovico raised his eyes to the Duchessa and was startled. She was staring fixedly at the blank wall six paces away from her, and, it must be admitted, her expression was terrible.

"Ah! My poor *podere!*" thought Lodovico. "The fact of the matter is, she is mad!" The Duchessa looked at him and read his thoughts.

"Ah! Signor Lodovico the great poet, you wish a deed of gift in writing: run and find me a sheet of paper." Lodovico did not wait to be told twice, and the Duchessa wrote out in her own hand a long form of receipt, ante-dated by a year, in which she declared that she had received from Lodovico San Micheli the sum of 80,000 francs, and had given him in pledge the lands of La Ricciarda. If after the lapse of twelve months the Duchessa had not restored the said 80,000 francs to Lodovico, the lands of La Ricciarda were to remain his property.

"It is a fine action," the Duchessa said to herself, "to give to a faithful servant nearly a third of what I have left for myself."

"Now then," she said to Lodovico, "after the joke of the reservoir, I give you just two days to enjoy yourself at Casalmaggiore. For the conveyance to hold good, say that it is a transaction which dates back more than a year. Come back and join me at Belgirate, and as quickly as possible; Fabrizio is perhaps going to England, where you will follow him."

Early the next day the Duchessa and Fabrizio were at Belgirate.

They took up their abode in that enchanting village; but a killing grief awaited the Duchessa on Lake Maggiore. Fabrizio was entirely changed; from the first moments in which he had awoken from his sleep, still somewhat lethargic, after his escape, the Duchessa had noticed that something out of the common was occurring in him. The deep-lying sentiment, which he took great pains to conceal, was distinctly odd, it was nothing less than this: he was in despair at being out of his prison. He was careful not to admit this cause of his sorrow, which would have led to questions which he did not wish to answer.

"What!" said the Duchessa, in amazement, "that horrible sensation when hunger forced you to feed, so as not to fall down, on one of those loathsome dishes supplied by the prison kitchen, that sensation: 'Is there some strange taste in this, am I poisoning myself at this moment?'—did not that sensation fill you with horror?"

"I thought of death," replied Fabrizio, "as I suppose soldiers think of it: it was a possible thing which I thought to avoid by taking care."

And so, what uneasiness, what grief for the Duchessa! This adored, singular, vivid, original creature was now before her eyes a prey to an endless train of fancies; he actually preferred solitude to the pleasure of talking of all manner of things, and with an open heart, to the best friend that he had in the world. Still he was always good, assiduous, grateful towards the Duchessa; he would, as before, have given his life a hundred times over for her; but his heart was elsewhere. They often went four or five leagues over that sublime lake without uttering a word. The conversation, the exchange of cold thoughts that from then onwards was possible between them might perhaps have seemed pleasant to others; but they remembered still, the Duchessa especially, what their conversation had been before that fatal fight with Giletti which had set them apart. Fabrizio owed the Duchessa an account of the nine months that he had spent in a horrible prison, and it appeared that he had nothing to say of this detention but brief and unfinished sentences.

"It was bound to happen sooner or later," the Duchessa told herself with a gloomy sadness. "Grief has aged me, or else he is really in love, and I have now only the second place in his heart." Demeaned, cast down by the greatest of all possible griefs, the Duchessa said to herself at times: "If, by the will of heaven, Ferrante should become mad altogether, or his courage should fail, I feel that I should be less unhappy." From that moment this half-remorse poisoned the esteem that the Duchessa had for her own character. "So," she said to herself bitterly, "I am repenting of a resolution I have already made. Then I am no longer a del Dongo!"

"It is the will of heaven," she would say: "Fabrizio is in love, and what right have I to wish that he should not be in love? Has one single word of genuine love ever passed between us?"

This idea, reasonable as it was, kept her from sleeping, and in short, a thing which shewed how old age and a weakening of the heart had come over her, she was a hundred times more unhappy than at Parma. As for the person who could be responsible for Fabrizio's strange abstraction, it was hardly possible to entertain any reasonable doubt: Clelia Conti, that pious girl, had betrayed her father since she had consented to make the garrison drunk, and never once did Fabrizio speak of Clelia! "But," added the Duchessa, beating her breast in desperation, "if the garrison had not been made drunk, all my stratagems, all my exertions became use-less; so it is she that saved him!"

It was with extreme difficulty that the Duchessa obtained from Fabrizio any details of the events of that night, which, she said to herself, "would at one time have been the sub-ject of an endlessly renewed discussion between us! In those happy times he would have talked for a whole day, with a force and gaiety endlessly renewed, of the smallest trifle which I thought of bringing forward."

As it was necessary to think of everything, the Duchessa had installed Fabrizio at the port of Locarno, a Swiss town at the head of Lake Maggiore. Every day she went to fetch him in a boat for long excursions over the lake. Well, on one occasion when she took it into her head to go up to his room, she found the walls lined with a number of views of the town of Parma, for which he had sent to Milan or to Parma it-self, a place which he ought to be holding in abomination. His little sitting-room, converted into a studio, was littered with all the apparatus of a painter in water-colours, and she found him finishing a third sketch of the Torre Farnese and the governor's *palazzo*.

"The only thing for you to do now," she said to him with an air of vexation, "is to make a portrait from memory of that charming governor whose only wish was to poison you. But, while I think of it," she went on, "you ought to write him a letter of apology for having taken the liberty of escaping and making his citadel look foolish."

The poor woman little knew how true her words were: no sooner had he arrived in a place of safety than Fabrizio's first thought had been to write General Fabio Conti a per-fectly polite and in a sense highly ridiculous letter; he asked his pardon for having escaped, offering as an excuse that a certain subordinate in the prison had been ordered to give him poison. Little did he care what he wrote, Fabrizio hoped that Clelia's eyes would see this letter, and his cheeks were wet with tears as he wrote it. He ended it with a very pleasant sentence: he ventured to say that, finding himself at liberty, he frequently had occasion to regret his little room in the Torre Farnese. This was the principal thought in his letter, he hoped that Clelia would understand it. In his writing vein, and always in the hope of being read by some-one, Fabrizio addressed his thanks to Don Cesare, that good chaplain who had lent him books on theology. A few days later Fabrizio arranged that the small bookseller of Locarno should make the journey to Milan, where this bookseller, a friend of the celebrated bibliomaniac Reina, bought the most sumptuous editions that he could find of the works that Don Cesare had lent Fabrizio. The good chaplain received these books and a handsome letter which informed him that, in moments of impatience, pardonable perhaps to a poor prisoner, the writer had covered the margins of his books with silly notes. He begged him, accordingly, to replace them in his library with the volumes which the most lively gratitude took the liberty of presenting to him.

Fabrizio was very modest in giving the simple name of notes to the endless scribblings with which he had covered the margins of a folio volume of the works of Saint Jerome. In the hope that he might be able to send back this book to the good chaplain, and exchange it for another, he had written day by day on the margins a very exact diary of all that occurred to him in prison; the great events were nothing else than ecstasies of *divine love* (this word *divine* took the place of another which he dared not write). At one moment this divine love led the prisoner to a profound despair, at other times a voice heard in the air restored some hope and caused transports of joy. All this, fortunately, was written with prison ink, made of wine, chocolate and soot, and Don Cesare had done no more than cast an eye over it as he put back on his shelves the volume of Saint Jerome. If he had studied the margins, he would have seen that one day the prisoner, believing himself to have been poisoned, was congratulating himself on dying at a distance of less than forty yards from what he had loved best in the world. But another eye than the good chaplain's had read this page since his escape. That fine idea: *To die near what one loves!* expressed in a hundred different fashions, was followed by a sonnet in which one saw that this soul, parted, after atrocious torments, from the frail body in which it had dwelt for three-and-twenty years, urged by that instinct for happiness natural to everything that has once existed, would not mount to heaven to mingle with the choirs of angels as soon as it should be free, and should the dread Judgment grant it pardon for its sins; but that, more fortunate after death than it had been in life, it would go a little way from the prison, where for so long it had groaned, to unite itself with all that it had loved in this world. And "So," said the last line of the sonnet, "I should find my earthly paradise."

Although they spoke of Fabrizio in the citadel of Parma

only as of an infamous traitor who had outraged the most sacred ties of duty, still the good priest Don Cesare was delighted by the sight of the fine books which an unknown hand had conveyed to him; for Fabrizio had decided to write to him only a few days after sending them, for fear lest his name might make the whole parcel be rejected with indignation. Don Cesare said no word of this kind attention to his brother, who flew into a rage at the mere name of Fabrizio; but since the latter's flight, he had returned to all his old intimacy with his charming niece; and as he had once taught her a few words of Latin, he let her see the fine books that he had received. Such had been the traveller's hope. Suddenly Clelia blushed deeply, she had recognised Fabrizio's handwriting. Long and very narrow strips of yellow paper were placed by way of markers in various parts of the volume. And as it is true to say that in the midst of the sordid pecuniary interests, and of the colourless coldness of the vulgar thoughts which fill our lives, the actions inspired by a true passion rarely fail to produce their effect; as though a propitious deity were taking the trouble to lead them by the hand, Clelia, guided by this instinct, and by the thought of one thing only in the world, asked her uncle to compare the old copy of Saint Jerome with the one that he had just received. How can I describe her rapture in the midst of the gloomy sadness in which Fabrizio's absence had plunged her, when she found on the margins of the old Saint Jerome the sonnet of which we have spoken, and the records, day by day, of the love that he had felt for her.

From the first day she knew the sonnet by heart; she would sing it, leaning on her window-sill, before the window, henceforward empty, where she had so often seen a little opening appear in the screen. This screen had been taken down to be placed in the office of the criminal court, and to serve as evidence in a ridiculous prosecution which Rassi was drawing up against Fabrizio, accused of the crime of having escaped, or, as the Fiscal said, laughing himself as he said it, *of having removed himself from the clemency of a magnanimous Prince!*

Each stage in Clelia's actions was for her a matter for keen remorse, and now that she was unhappy, her remorse was all the keener. She sought to mitigate somewhat the reproaches that she addressed to herself by reminding herself of the vow *never to see Fabrizio again,* which she had made to the Madonna at the time when the General was nearly poisoned, and since then had renewed daily.

Her father had been made ill by Fabrizio's escape, and, moreover, had been on the point of losing his post, when the Prince, in his anger, dismissed all the gaolers of the Torre Farnese, and sent them as prisoners to the town gaol. The General had been saved partly by the intercession of Conte Mosca, who preferred to see him shut up at the top of his citadel, rather than as an active and intriguing rival in court circles.

It was during the fortnight of uncertainty as to the disgrace of General Fabio Conti, who was really ill, that Clelia had the courage to carry out this sacrifice which she had announced to Fabrizio. She had had the sense to be ill on the day of the general rejoicings, which was also that of the prisoner's flight, as the reader may perhaps remember; she was ill also on the following day, and, in a word, managed things so well that, with the exception of Grillo, whose special duty it was to look after Fabrizio, no one had any suspicion of her complicity, and Grillo held his tongue.

But as soon as Clelia had no longer any anxiety in that direction, she was even more cruelly tormented by her just remorse. "What argument in the world," she asked herself, "can mitigate the crime of a daughter who betrays her father?"

One evening, after a day spent almost entirely in the chapel, and in tears, she begged her uncle, Don Cesare, to accompany her to the General, whose outbursts of rage alarmed her all the more since into every topic he introduced imprecations against Fabrizio, that abominable traitor.

Having come into her father's presence, she had the courage to say to him that if she had always refused to give her hand to the Marchese Crescenzi, it was because she did not feel any inclination towards him, and was certain of finding no happiness in such a union. At these words the General flew into a rage; and Clelia had some difficulty in making herself heard. She added that if her father, tempted by the Marchese's great fortune, felt himself bound to give her a definite order to marry him, she was prepared to obey. The General was quite astonished by this conclusion, which he had been far from expecting; he ended, however, by rejoicing at it. "So," he said to his brother, "I shall not be reduced to a lodging on a second floor, if that scoundrel Fabrizio makes me lose my post through his vile conduct."

Conte Mosca did not fail to shew himself profoundly scandalised by the flight of that *scapegrace* Fabrizio, and repeated when the occasion served the expression invented by Rassi to describe the base conduct of the young man—a very vulgar young man, to boot—who had removed himself from the clemency of the Prince. This witty expression, consecrated by good society, did not take hold at all of the people. Left to their own good sense, while fully believing in Fabrizio's guilt they admired the determination that he must have had to let himself down from so high a wall. Not a creature at court admired this courage. As for the police, greatly humiliated by this rebuff, they had officially discovered that a band of twenty soldiers, corrupted by the money distributed by the Duchessa, that woman of such atrocious ingratitude whose name was no longer uttered save with a sigh, had given Fabrizio four ladders tied together, each forty-five feet long; Fabrizio, having let down a cord which they had tied to these ladders, had had only the quite commonplace distinction of pulling the ladders up to where he was. Certain Liberals, well known for their imprudence, and among them Doctor C——, an agent paid directly by the Prince, added, but compromised themselves by adding that these atrocious police had had the barbarity to shoot eight of the unfortunate soldiers who had facilitated the flight of that wretch Fabrizio. Thereupon he was blamed even by the true Liberals, as having caused by his imprudence by the death of eight poor soldiers. It is thus that petty despotisms reduce to nothing the value of public opinion.

CHAPTER TWENTY-THREE

AMID THIS general uproar, Archbishop Landriani alone shewed himself loyal to the cause of his young friend; he made bold to repeat, even at the Princess's court, the legal maxim according to which, in every case, one ought to keep an ear free from all prejudice to hear the plea of an absent party.

The day after Fabrizio's escape a number of people had received a sonnet of no great merit which celebrated this flight as one of the fine actions of the age, and compared Fabrizio to an angel arriving on the earth with outspread wings. On the evening of the following day, the whole of Parma was repeating a sublime sonnet. It was Fabrizio's monologue as he let himself slide down the cord, and passed judgment on the different incidents of his life. This sonnet gave him a place in literature by two magnificent lines; all the experts recognised the style of Ferrante Palla.

But here I must seek the epic style: where can I find colours in which to paint the torrents of indignation that suddenly flooded every orthodox heart, when they learned of the frightful insolence of this illumination of the house at Sacca? There was but one outcry against the Duchessa; even the true Liberals decided that such an action compromised in a barbarous fashion the poor suspects detained in the various prisons, and needlessly exasperated the heart of the Sovereign. Conte Mosca declared that there was but one thing left for the Duchessa's former friends—to forget her. The concert of execration was therefore unanimous: a stranger passing through the town would have been struck by the energy of public opinion. But in the country, where they know how to appreciate the pleasure of revenge, the illumination and the admirable feast given in the park to more than six thousand *contadini* had an immense success. Everyone in Parma repeated that the Duchessa had distributed a thousand sequins among her *contadini;* thus they explained the somewhat harsh reception given to a party of thirty constables whom the police had been so foolish as to send to that small village, thirty-six hours after the sublime evening and the general intoxication that had followed it. The constables, greeted with showers of stones, had turned and fled, and two of their number, who fell from their horses, were flung into the Po.

As for the bursting of the great reservoir of the *palazzo* Sanseverina, it had passed almost unnoticed: it was during the night that several streets had been more or less flooded, next morning one would have said that it had *rained*. Lodovico had taken care to break the panes of a window in the *palazzo*, so as to account for the entry of robbers.

They had even found a little ladder. Only Conte Mosca recognised his friend's inventive genius.

Fabrizio was fully determined to return to Parma as soon as he could; he sent Lodovico with a long letter to the Archbishop, and this faithful servant came back to post at the first village in Piedmont, San Nazzaro, to the west of Pavia, a Latin epistle which the worthy prelate addressed to his young client. We may add here a detail which, like many others no doubt, will seem otiose in countries where there is no longer any need of precaution. The name of Fabrizio del Dongo was never written; all the letters that were intended for him were addressed to Lodovico San Micheli, at Locarno in Switzerland, or at Belgirate in Piedmont. The envelope was made of a coarse paper, the seal carelessly applied, the address barely legible and sometimes adorned with recommendations worthy of a cook; all the letters were dated from Naples six days before their actual date.

From the Piedmontese village of San Nazzaro, near Pavia, Lodovico returned in hot haste to Parma; he was charged with a mission to which Fabrizio attached the greatest importance; this was nothing less than to convey to Clelia Conti a handkerchief on which was printed a sonnet of Petrarch. It is true that a word was altered in this sonnet: Clelia found it on the table two days after she had received the thanks of the Marchese Crescenzi, who professed himself the happiest of men; and there is no need to say what impression this token of a still constant remembrance produced on her heart.

Lodovico was to try to procure all possible details as to

what was happening at the citadel. He it was who told Fabrizio the sad news that the Marchese Crescenzi's marriage seemed now to be definitely settled; scarcely a day passed without his giving a *festa* for Clelia, inside the citadel. A decisive proof of the marriage was that the Marchese, immensely rich and in consequence very avaricious, as is the custom among the opulent people of Northern Italy, was making immense preparations, and yet he was marrying a girl without a *portion*. It was true that General Fabio Conti, his vanity greatly shocked by this observation, the first to spring to the minds of all his compatriots, had just bought a property worth more than 300,000 francs; and for this property he, who had nothing, had paid in ready money, evidently with the Marchese's gold. Moreover, the General had said that he was giving this property to his daughter on her marriage. But the charges for the documents and other matters, which amounted to more than 12,000 francs, seemed a most ridiculous waste of money to the Marchese, a man of eminently logical mind. For his part he was having woven at Lyons a set of magnificent tapestries of admirably blended colours, calculated to charm the eye, by the famous Pallagi, the Bolognese painter. These tapestries, each of which embodied some deed of arms by the Crescenzi family, which, as the whole world knows, is descended from the famous Crescentius, Roman Consul in the year 985, were to furnish the seventeen saloons which composed the ground floor of the Marchese's *palazzo*. The tapestries, clocks and lustres sent to Parma cost more than 350,000 francs; the price of the new mirrors, in addition to those which the house already possessed, came to 200,000 francs. With the exception of two rooms, famous works of the Parmigianino, the greatest of local painters after the divine Correggio, all those of the first and second floors were now occupied by the leading painters of Florence, Rome and Milan, who were decorating them with paintings in fresco. Fokelberg, the great Swedish sculptor, Tenerani of Rome and Marchesi of Milan had been at work for the last year on ten bas-reliefs representing as many brave deeds of Crescentius, that truly great man. The majority of the ceilings, painted in fresco, also offered some allusion to his life. The ceiling most generally admired was that on which Hayez of Milan had represented Crescentius being received in the Elysian Fields by Francesco Sforza, Lorenzo the Magnificent, King Robert, the Tribune Cola di Rienzi, Machiavelli, Dante and the other great men of the middle ages. Admiration for these chosen spirits is supposed to be an epigram at the expense of the men in power.

All these sumptuous details occupied the exclusive attention of the nobility and burgesses of Parma, and pierced our hero's heart when he read of them, related with an artless admiration, in a long letter of more than twenty pages which Lodovico had dictated to a *doganiere* of Casalmaggiore.

"And I, who am so poor!" said Fabrizio, "an income of four thousand lire in all and for all! It is truly an impertinence in me to dare to be in love with Clelia Conti for whom all these miracles are being performed."

A single paragraph in Lodovico's long letter, but written, this, in his own villainous hand, announced to his master that he had met, at night and apparently in hiding, the unfortunate Grillo, his former gaoler, who had been put in prison and then released. The man had asked him for a sequin in charity, and Lodovico had given him four in the Duchessa's name. The old gaolers recently set at liberty, twelve in number, were preparing an entertainment with their knives (*un trattamento di cortellate*) for the new gaolers their successors, should they ever succeed in meeting them outside the citadel. Grillo had said that almost every day there was a serenade at the fortress, that Signorina Clelia was extremely pale, often ill, and *other things of the sort*. This absurd expression caused Lodovico to receive, by courier after courier, the order to return to Locarno. He returned, and the details which he supplied by word of mouth were even more depressing for Fabrizio.

One may judge what consideration he was shewing for the poor Duchessa; he would have suffered a thousand deaths rather than utter in her hearing the name of Clelia Conti. The Duchessa abhorred Parma; whereas, for Fabrizio, everything which recalled that city was at once sublime and touching.

Less than ever had the Duchessa forgotten her revenge; she had been so happy before the incident of Giletti's death —and now, what a fate was hers! She was living in expectation of a dire event of which she was careful not to say a word to Fabrizio, she who before, at the time of her arrangement with Ferrante, thought she would so delight Fabrizio by telling him that one day he would be avenged.

One can now form some idea of the pleasantness of Fabrizio's conversations with the Duchessa: a gloomy silence reigned almost invariably between them. To enhance the pleasantness of their relations, the Duchessa had yielded to the temptation to play a trick on this too dear nephew. The Conte wrote to her almost every day; evidently he was sending couriers as in the days of their infatuation, for his letters always bore the postmark of some little town in Switzerland. The poor man was torturing his mind so as not to speak too openly of his affection, and to construct amusing letters; barely did a distracted eye glance over them. What avails, alas, the fidelity of a respected lover when one's heart is pierced by the coldness of the other whom one sets above him?

In the space of two months the Duchessa answered him only once, and that was to engage him to explore how the land lay round the Princess, and to see whether, despite the impertinence of the fireworks, a letter from her, the Duchessa, would be received with pleasure. The letter which he was to present, if he thought fit, requested the post of *Cavaliere d'onore* to the Princess, which had recently fallen vacant, for the Marchese Crescenzi, and desired that it should be conferred upon him in consideration of his marriage. The Duchessa's letter was a masterpiece; it was a message of the most tender respect, expressed in the best possible terms; the writer had not admitted to this courtly style a single word the consequences, even the remotest consequences of which could be other than agreeable to the Princess. The reply also breathed a tender friendship, which was being tortured by the absence of its recipient.

"My son and I," the Princess told her, "have not spent one evening that could be called tolerable since your sudden departure. Does my dear Duchessa no longer remember that it was she who caused me to be consulted in the nomination of the officers of my household? Does she then think herself obliged to give me reasons for the Marchese's appointment, as if the expression of her desire was not for me the chief of reasons? The Marchese shall have the post, if I can do anything; and there will always be one in my heart, and that the first, for my dear Duchessa. My son employs absolutely the same expressions, a little strong perhaps on the lips of a great boy of one-and-twenty, and asks you for specimens of the minerals of the Val d'Orta, near Belgirate. You may address your letters, which will, I hope, be frequent, to the Conte, who still adores you and who is especially dear to me on account of these sentiments. The Archbishop also has

remained faithful to you. We all hope to see you again one
day: remember that it is your duty. The Marchesa Ghisleri,
my Grand Mistress, is preparing to leave this world for a better: the poor woman has done me much harm; she displeases
me still further by departing so inopportunely; her illness
makes me think of the name which I should once have set
with so much pleasure in the place of hers, if, that is, I could
have obtained that sacrifice of her independence from that
matchless woman who, in fleeing from us, has taken with her
all the joy of my little court," and so forth.

It was therefore with the consciousness of having sought
to hasten, so far as it lay in her power, the marriage which
was filling Fabrizio with despair, that the Duchessa saw him
every day. And so they spent sometimes four or five hours
in drifting together over the lake, without exchanging a
single word. The good feeling was entire and perfect on Fabrizio's part; but he was thinking of other things, and his
innocent and simple nature furnished him with nothing to
say. The Duchessa saw this, and it was her punishment.

We have forgotten to mention in the proper place that the
Duchessa had taken a house at Belgirate, a charming village
and one that contains everything which its name promises
(to wit a beautiful bend in the lake). From the window-sill
of her drawing-room, the Duchessa could set foot in her
boat. She had taken a quite simple one for which four rowers
would have sufficed; she engaged twelve, and arranged things
so as to have a man from each of the villages situated
in the neighbourhood of Belgirate. The third or fourth time
that she found herself in the middle of the lake with all of
these well-chosen men, she stopped the movement of their
oars.

"I regard you all as friends," she said to them, "and I
wish to confide a secret in you. My nephew Fabrizio has escaped from prison; and possibly by treachery they will seek
to recapture him, although he is on your lake, in a place of
freedom. Keep your ears open, and inform me of all that
you may hear. I authorise you to enter my room by day or
night."

The rowers replied with enthusiasm; she knew how to make
herself loved. But she did not think that there was any question of recapturing Fabrizio: it was for herself that all these
precautions were taken, and, before the fatal order to open

the reservoir of the *palazzo* Sanseverina, she would not have dreamed of them.

Her prudence had led her also to take an apartment at the port of Locarno for Fabrizio; every day he came to see her, or she herself crossed into Switzerland. One may judge of the pleasantness of their perpetual companionship by the following detail. The Marchesa and her daughter came twice to see them, and the presence of these strangers gave them pleasure; for, in spite of the ties of blood, we may call "stranger" a person who knows nothing of our dearest interests and whom we see but once in a year.

The Duchessa happened to be one evening at Locarno, in Fabrizio's rooms, with the Marchesa and her two daughters. The Archpriest of the place and the curate had come to pay their respects to these ladies: the Archpriest, who had an interest in a business house, and kept closely in touch with the news, was inspired to announce:

"The Prince of Parma is dead!"

The Duchessa turned extremely pale; she had barely the strength to say:

"Do they give any details?"

"No," replied the Archpriest; "the report is confined to the announcement of his death, which is certain."

The Duchessa looked at Fabrizio. "I have done this for him," she said to herself; "I would have done things a thousand times worse, and there he is standing before me indifferent, and dreaming of another!" It was beyond the Duchessa's strength to endure this frightful thought; she fell in a dead faint. Everyone hastened to her assistance; but, on coming to herself, she observed that Fabrizio was less active than the Archpriest and curate; he was dreaming as usual.

"He is thinking of returning to Parma," the Duchessa told herself, "and perhaps of breaking off Clelia's marriage to the Marchese; but I shall manage to prevent him." Then, remembering the presence of the two priests, she made haste to add:

"He was a good Prince, and has been greatly maligned! It is an immense loss for us!"

The priests took their leave, and the Duchessa, to be alone, announced that she was going to bed.

"No doubt," she said to herself, "prudence ordains that I should wait a month or two before returning to Parma; but I feel that I shall never have the patience; I am suffering too keenly here. Fabrizio's continual dreaming, his silence, are an intolerable spectacle for my heart. Who would ever have said that I should find it tedious to float on this charming lake, alone with him, and at the moment when I have done, to avenge him, more than I can tell him! After such a spectacle, death is nothing. It is now that I am paying for the transports of happiness and childish joy which I found in my *palazzo* at Parma when I welcomed Fabrizio there on his return from Naples. If I had said a word, all was at an end, and it may be that, tied to me, he would not have given a thought to that little Clelia; but that word filled me with a horrible repugnance. Now she has prevailed over me. What more simple? She is twenty; and I, altered by my anxieties, sick, I am twice her age! . . . I must die, I must make an end of things! A woman of forty is no longer anything save to the men who have loved her in her youth! Now I shall find nothing more but the pleasures of vanity; and are they worth the trouble of living? All the more reason for going to Parma, and amusing myself. If things took a certain turn, I should lose my life. Well, where is the harm? I shall make a magnificent death, and, before the end, but then only, I shall say to Fabrizio: 'Wretch! It is for you!' Yes, I can find no occupation for what little life remains to me save at Parma. I shall play the great lady there. What a blessing if I could be sensible now of all those distinctions which used to make the Raversi so unhappy! Then, in order to see my happiness, I had to look into the eyes of envy. . . . My vanity has one satisfaction; with the exception of the Conte perhaps, no one can have guessed what the event was that put an end to the life of my heart. . . . I shall love Fabrizio, I shall be devoted to his interests; but he must not be allowed to break off Clelia's marriage, and end by taking her himself. . . . No, that shall not be!"

The Duchessa had reached this point in her melancholy monologue, when she heard a great noise in the house.

"Good!" she said to herself, "they are coming to arrest me; Ferrante has let himself be caught, he must have spoken. Well, all the better! I am going to have an occupation, I am going to fight them for my head. But in the first place, I must not let myself be taken."

The Duchessa, half clad, fled to the bottom of her garden: she was already thinking of climbing a low wall and escaping across country; but she saw someone enter her room. She recognised Bruno, the Conte's confidential man; he was alone with her maid. She went up to the window. The man was telling her maid of the injuries he had received. The Duchessa entered the house. Bruno almost flung himself at her feet, imploring her not to tell the Conte of the preposterous hour at which he had arrived.

"Immediately after the Prince's death," he went on, "the Signor Conte gave the order to all the posts not to supply horses to subjects of the States of Parma. So that I had to go as far as the Po with the horses of the house, but on leaving the boat my carriage was overturned, broken, smashed, and I had such bad bruises that I could not get on a horse, as was my duty."

"Very well," said the Duchessa, "it is three o'clock in the morning: I shall say that you arrived at noon; but you must not go and give me away."

"I am very grateful for the Signora's kindness."

Politics in a work of literature are like a pistol-shot in the middle of a concert, something loud and vulgar and yet a thing to which it is not possible to refuse one's attention.

We are about to speak of very ugly matters, as to which, for more than one reason, we should like to keep silence; but we are forced to do so in order to come to happenings which are in our province, since they have for their theatre the hearts of our characters.

"But, great God, how did that great Prince die?" said the Duchessa to Bruno.

"He was out shooting the birds of passage, in the marshes, along by the Po, two leagues from Sacca. He fell into a hole hidden by a tuft of grass; he was all in a sweat, and caught cold; they carried him to a lonely house where he died in a few hours. Some say that Signor Catena and Signor Borone are dead as well, and that the whole accident arose from the copper pans in the *contadino's* house they went to, which were full of verdigris. They took their luncheon there. In fact, the swelled heads, the Jacobins, who say what they would like to be true, speak of poison. I know that my friend Toto, who is a groom at court, would have died but for the kind attention of a rustic who appeared to have a great knowledge of medicine, and gave him some very singular remedies. But they've ceased to talk of the Prince's death already; after all, he was a cruel man. When I left, the people were gathering to kill the Fiscal General Rassi: they were also proposing to set fire to the gates of the citadel, to enable the prisoners to escape. But it was said that Fabio Conti would fire his guns. Others were positive that the gunners at the citadel had poured water on their powder, and refused to massacre their fellow-citizens. But I can tell you something far more interesting: while the surgeon of Sandolaro was mending my poor arm, a man arrived from Parma who said that the mob had caught Barbone, the famous clerk from the citadel, in the street, and had beaten him, and were then going to hang him from the tree on the avenue nearest to the citadel. The mob were marching to break that fine statue of the Prince in the gardens of the court; but the Signor Conte took a battalion of the Guard, paraded them in front of the statue, and sent word to the people that no one who entered the gardens would go out of them alive, and the people took fright. But, what is a very curious thing, which the man who had come from Parma, who is an old constable, repeated several times, is that the Signor Conte kicked General P——, the commander of the Prince's Guard, and had him led out of the garden by two fusiliers, after tearing off his epaulettes."

"I can see the Conte doing that," cried the Duchessa with a transport of joy which she would not have believed possible a minute earlier: "he will never allow anyone to insult our Princess; and as for General P——, in his devotion to his rightful masters, he would never consent to serve the usurper, while the Conte, with less delicacy, fought through all the Spanish campaigns, and has often been reproached for it at court."

The Duchessa had opened the Conte's letter, but kept stopping as she read it to put a hundred questions to Bruno.

The letter was very pleasant; the Conte employed the most lugubrious terms, and yet the keenest joy broke out in every word; he avoided any detail of the Prince's death, and ended with the words:

"You will doubtless return, my dear angel, but I advise you to wait a day or two for the courier whom the Princess will send you, as I hope, to-day or to-morrow; your return must be as triumphant as your departure was bold. As for the great criminal who is with you, I count upon being able to have him tried by twelve judges selected from all parties in this State. But, to have the monster punished as he deserves, I must first be able to make spills of the other sentence, if it exists."

The Conte had opened his letter to add:

"Now for a very different matter: I have just issued

ammunition to the two battalions of the Guard; I am going to fight, and shall do my best to deserve the title of Cruel with which the Liberals have so long honoured me. That old mummy General P—— has dared to speak in the barracks of making a parley with the populace, who are more or less in revolt. I write to you from the street; I am going to the Palace, which they shall not enter save over my dead body. Good-bye! If I die, it will be worshipping you *all the same,* as I have lived. Do not forget to draw three hundred thousand francs which are deposited in my name with D—— of Lyons.

"Here is that poor devil Rassi, pale as death, and without his wig; you have no idea what he looks like. The people are absolutely determined to hang him; it would be doing him a great injustice, he deserves to be quartered. He took refuge in my *palazzo* and has run after me into the street; I hardly know what to do with him. . . . I do not wish to take him to the Prince's Palace, that would make the revolt break out there. F—— shall see whether I love him; my first word to Rassi was: I must have the sentence passed on Signor del Dongo, and all the copies that you may have of it; and say to all those unjust judges, who are the cause of this revolt, that I will have them all hanged, and you as well, my dear friend, if they breathe a word of that sentence, which never existed. In Fabrizio's name, I am sending a company of grenadiers to the Archbishop. Good-bye, dear angel! My *palazzo* is going to be burned, and I shall lose the charming portraits I have of you. I must run to the Palace to degrade that wretched General P——, who is at his tricks; he is basely flattering the people, as he used to flatter the late Prince. All these Generals are in the devil of a fright; I am going, I think, to have myself made Commander in Chief."

The Duchessa was unkind enough not to send to waken Fabrizio; she felt for the Conte a burst of admiration which was closely akin to love. "When all is said and done," she decided, "I shall have to marry him." She wrote to him at once and sent off one of her men. That night the Duchessa had no time to be unhappy.

Next day, about noon, she saw a boat manned by ten rowers which was swiftly cleaving the waters of the lake; Fabrizio and she soon recognised a man wearing the livery of the Prince of Parma: it was, in fact, one of his couriers who, before landing, cried to the Duchessa: "The revolt is suppressed!" This courier gave her several letters from the Conte, an admirable letter from the Princess, and an order from Prince Ranuccio-Ernesto V, on parchment, creating her Duchessa di San Giovanni and Grand Mistress to the Princess Dowager. The young Prince, an expert in mineralogy, whom she regarded as an imbecile, had had the intelligence to write her a little note; but there was love at the end of it. The note began thus:

"The Conte says, Signora Duchessa, that he is pleased with me; the fact is that I stood under fire by his side, and that my horse was hit: seeing the stir that is made about so small a matter, I am keen to take part in a real battle, but not against my subjects. I owe everything to the Conte; all my Generals, who have never been to war, ran like hares; I believe two or three have fled as far as Bologna. Since a great and deplorable event set me in power, I have signed no order which has given me so much pleasure as this which appoints you Grand Mistress to my mother. My mother and I both remembered a day when you admired the fine view one has from the *palazzetto* of San Giovanni, which once belonged to Petrarch, or so they say at least; my mother wished to give you that little property: and I, not knowing what to give you, and not venturing to offer you all that is rightly yours, have made you Duchessa in my country; I do not know whether you are learned enough in these matters to be aware that Sanseverina is a Roman title. I have just given the Grand Cordon of my Order to our worthy Archbishop, who has shown a firmness very rare in men of seventy. You will not be angry with me for having recalled all the ladies from exile. I am told that I must now sign only after writing the words *your affectionate;* it annoys me that I should be made to scatter broadcast what is completely true only when I write to you.

"*Your affectionate*

"RANUCCIO-ERNESTO

Who would not have said, from such language, that the Duchessa was about to enjoy the highest favour? And yet she found something very strange in other letters from the

Conte, which she received an hour or two later. He offered no special reason, but advised her to postpone for some days her return to Parma, and to write to the Princess that she was seriously unwell. The Duchessa and Fabrizio set off, nevertheless, for Parma immediately after dinner. The Duchessa's object, which however she did not admit to herself, was to hasten the Marchese Crescenzi's marriage; Fabrizio, for his part, spent the journey in wild transports of joy, which seemed to his aunt absurd. He was in hopes of seeing Clelia again soon; he fully counted upon carrying her off, against her will, if there should be no other way of preventing her marriage.

The Duchessa and her nephew made a very gay journey. At a post before Parma, Fabrizio stopped for a minute to change into the ecclesiastical habit; ordinarily he dressed as a layman in mourning. When he returned to the Duchessa's room:

"I find something suspicious and inexplicable," she said to him, "in the Conte's letters. If you would take my advice you would spend a few hours here; I shall send you a courier after I have spoken to that great Minister."

It was with great reluctance that Fabrizio consented to accept this sensible warning. Transports of joy worthy of a boy of fifteen were the note of the reception which the Conte gave to the Duchessa, whom he called his wife. It was long before he would speak of politics, and when at last they came down to cold reason:

"You did very well to prevent Fabrizio from arriving officially; we are in the full swing of reaction here. Just guess the colleague that the Prince has given me as Minister of Justice! Rassi, my dear, Rassi, whom I treated like the ruffian that he is, on the day of our great adventure. By the way, I must warn you that we have suppressed everything that has happened here. If you read our *Gazette* you will see that a clerk at the citadel, named Barbone, has died as the result of falling from a carriage. As for the sixty odd rascals whom I dispatched with powder and shot, when they were attacking the Prince's statue in the gardens, they are in the best of health, only they are travelling abroad. Conte Zurla, the Minister of the Interior, has gone in person to the house of each of these unfortunate heroes, and has handed fifteen sequins to his family or his friends, with the order to say that the deceased is abroad, and a very definite threat of imprisonment should they let it be understood that he is dead. A man from my own Ministry, the Foreign Office, has been sent on a mission to the journalists of Milan and Turin, so that they shall not speak of the *unfortunate event* —that is the recognised expression; he is to go on to Paris and London, to insert a correction in all the newspapers, semi-officially, of anything that they may say about our troubles. Another agent has posted off to Bologna and Florence. I have shrugged my shoulders.

"But the delightful thing, at my age, is that I felt a moment of enthusiasm when I was speaking to the soldiers of the Guard, and when I tore the epaulettes off that contemptible General P——. At that moment, I would have given my life, without hesitating, for the Prince: I admit now that it would have been a very stupid way of ending it. To-day the Prince, excellent young fellow as he is, would give a hundred scudi to see me die in my bed; he has not yet dared to ask for my resignation, but we speak to each other as seldom as possible, and I send him a number of little reports in writing, as I used to do with the late Prince, after Fabrizio's imprisonment. By the way, I have not yet made spills out of the sentence they passed on Fabrizio, for the simple reason that that scoundrel Rassi has not let me have it. So you are very wise to prevent Fabrizio from arriving here officially. The sentence still holds good; at the same time I do not think that Rassi would dare to have our nephew arrested now, but it is possible that he will in another fortnight. If Fabrizio absolutely insists on returning to town, let him come and stay with me."

"But the reason for all this?" cried the Duchessa in astonishment.

"They have persuaded the Prince that I am giving myself the airs of a dictator and a saviour of the country, and that I wish to lead him about like a boy; what is more, in speaking of him, I seem to have uttered the fatal words: *that boy*. It may be so, I was excited that day; for instance, I looked on him as a great man, because he was not unduly frightened by the first shots he had ever heard fired in his life. He is not lacking in spirit, indeed he has a better tone than his father; in fact, I cannot repeat it too often, in his heart of hearts he is honest and good; but that sincere and youthful heart shudders when they tell him of any dastardly trick, and he thinks he must have a very dark soul himself to notice such things: think of the upbringing he has had!"

"Your Excellency ought to have remembered that one day

he would be master, and to have placed an intelligent man with him."

"For one thing, we have the example of the Abbé de Condillac, who, when appointed by the Marchese di Felino, my predecessor, could make nothing more of his pupil than a King of fools. He succeeded in due course, and, in 1796, he had not the sense to treat with General Bonaparte, who would have tripled the area of his States. In the second place, I never expected to remain Minister for ten years in succession. Now that I have lost all interest in the business, as I have for the last month, I intend to amass a million before leaving this bedlam I have rescued to its own devices. But for me, Parma would have been a Republic for two months, with the poet Ferrante Palla as Dictator."

This made the Duchessa blush; the Conte knew nothing of what had happened.

"We are going to fall back into the ordinary Monarchy of the eighteenth century; the confessor and the mistress. At heart the Prince cares for nothing but mineralogy, and perhaps yourself, Signora. Since he began to reign, his valet, whose brother I have just made a captain, this brother having nine months' service, his valet, I say, has gone and stuffed into his head that he ought to be the happiest of men because his profile is going to appear on the scudi. This bright idea has been followed by boredom.

"What he now needs is an Aide-de-Camp, as a remedy for boredom. Well, even if he were to offer me that famous million which is necessary for us to live comfortably in Naples or Paris, I would not be his remedy for boredom, and spend four or five hours every day with His Highness. Besides, as I have more brains than he, at the end of a month he would regard me as a monster.

"The late Prince was evil-minded and jealous, but he had been on service and had commanded army corps, which had given him a bearing; he had the stuff in him of which Princes are made, and I could be his Minister, for better or worse. With this honest fellow of a son, who is candid and really good, I am forced to be an intriguer. You see me now the rival of the humblest little woman in the Castle, and a very inferior rival, for I shall scorn all the hundred essential details. For instance, three days ago, one of those women who put out the clean towels every morning in the rooms, took it into her head to make the Prince lose the key of one of his English desks. Whereupon His Highness refused to deal

with any of the business the papers of which happened to
be in this desk; as a matter of fact, for twenty francs, they
could have taken off the wooden bottom, or used skeleton
keys; but Ranuccio-Ernesto V told me that that would be
teaching the court locksmith bad habits.

"Up to the present, it has been absolutely impossible for
him to adhere to any decision for three days running. If he
had been born Marchese so-and-so, with an ample fortune,
this young Prince would have been one of the most estimable
men at court, a sort of Louis XVI; but how, with his pious
simplicity, is he to resist all the cunningly laid snares that
surround him? And so the drawing-room of your enemy the
Marchesa Raversi is more powerful than ever; they have
discovered there that I, who gave the order to fire on the
people, and was determined to kill three thousand men if
necessary, rather than let them outrage the statue of the
Prince who had been my master, am a red-hot Liberal, that I
wished him to sign a Constitution, and a hundred such
absurdities. With all this talk of a Republic, the fools would
prevent us from enjoying the best of Monarchies. In short,
Signora, you are the only member of the present Liberal
Party of which my enemies make me the head, at whose expense the Prince has not expressed himself in offensive
terms; the Archbishop, always perfectly honest, for having
spoken in reasonable language of what I did on *the unhappy
day,* is in deep disgrace.

"On the morrow of the day which was not then called
unhappy, when it was still true that the revolt had existed,
the Prince told the Archbishop that, so that you should not
have to take an inferior title on marrying me, he would make
me a Duca. To-day I fancy that it is Rassi, ennobled by me
when he sold me the late Prince's secrets, who is going to
be made Conte. In the face of such a promotion as that, I
shall cut a sorry figure."

"And the poor Prince will bespatter himself with mud."

"No doubt; but after all he is *master,* a position which,
in less than a fortnight, makes the *ridiculous* element disappear. So, dear Duchessa, as at the game of tric-trac, *let us
get out.*"

"But we shall not be exactly rich."

"After all, neither you nor I have any need of luxury. If
you give me, at Naples, a seat in a box at San Carlo and a
horse, I am more than satisfied; it will never be the amount
of luxury with which we live that will give you and me our

position, it is the pleasure which the intelligent people of the
place may perhaps find in coming to take a dish of tea with
you."

"But," the Duchessa went on, "what would have happened, on the *unhappy day,* if you had held aloof, as I hope
you will in future?"

"The troops would have fraternised with the people, there
would have been three days of bloodshed and incendiarism
(for it would take a hundred years in this country for the
Republic to be anything more than an absurdity), then a
fortnight of pillage, until two or three regiments supplied
from abroad came to put a stop to it. Ferrante Palla was in
the thick of the crowd, full of courage and raging as usual;
he had probably a dozen friends who were acting in collu-
sion with him, which Rassi will make into a superb conspiracy. One thing certain is that, wearing an incredibly dilapidated coat, he was scattering gold with both hands."

The Duchessa, bewildered by all this information, went in
haste to thank the Princess.

As she entered the room the Lady of the Bedchamber
handed her a little gold key, which is worn in the belt, and
is the badge of supreme authority in the part of the Palace
which belongs to the Princess. Clara-Paolina hastened to
dismiss all the company; and, once she was alone with her
friend, persisted for some moments in giving only fragmen-
tary explanations. The Duchessa found it hard to understand
what she meant, and answered only with considerable reserve. At length the Princess burst into tears, and, flinging
herself into the Duchessa's arms, cried: "The days of my
misery are going to begin again; my son will treat me worse
than his father did!"

"That is what I shall prevent," the Duchessa replied with
emphasis. "But first of all," she went on, "I must ask Your
Serene Highness to deign to accept this offering of all my
gratitude and my profound respect."

"What do you mean?" cried the Princess, full of uneasiness, and fearing a resignation.

"I ask that whenever Your Serene Highness shall permit
me to turn to the right the head of that nodding mandarin
on her chimneypiece, she will permit me also to call things
by their true names."

"Is that all, my dear Duchessa?" cried Clara-Paolina, rising from her seat and hastening herself to put the mandarin's head in the right position: "speak then, with the utmost

freedom, Signora Maggiordoma," she said in a charming tone.

"Ma'am," the Duchessa went on, "Your Highness has grasped the situation perfectly; you and I are both running the greatest risk; the sentence passed on Fabrizio has not been quashed; consequently, on the day when they wish to rid themselves of me and to insult you, they will put him back in prison. Our position is as bad as ever. As for me personally, I am marrying the Conte, and we are going to set up house in Naples or Paris. The final stroke of ingratitude of which the Conte is at this moment the victim has entirely disgusted him with public life, and but for the interest Your Serene Highness takes in him, I should advise him to remain in this mess only on condition of the Prince's giving him an enormous sum. I shall ask leave of Your Highness to explain that the Conte, who had 130,000 francs when he came into office, has to-day an income of barely 20,000 lire. In vain did I long urge him to think of his pocket. In my absence, he has picked a quarrel with the Prince's Farmers-General, who were rascals; he has replaced them with other rascals, who have given him 800,000 francs."

"What!" cried the Princess in astonishment; "Heavens, I am extremely annoyed to hear that!"

"Ma'am," replied the Duchessa with the greatest coolness, "must I turn the mandarin's head back to the left?"

"Good heavens, no," exclaimed the Princess; "but I am annoyed that a man of the Conte's character should have thought of enriching himself in such a way."

"But for this peculation he would be despised by all the honest folk."

"Great heavens! Is it possible?"

"Ma'am," went on the Duchessa, "except for my friend, the Marchese Crescenzi, who has an income of three or four hundred thousand lire, everyone here steals; and how should they not steal in a country where the recognition of the greatest services lasts for not quite a month? It means that there is nothing real, nothing that survives disgrace, save money. I am going to take the liberty, Ma'am, of saying some terrible truths."

"You have my permission," said the Princess with a deep sigh, "and yet they are painfully unpleasant to me."

"Very well, Ma'am, the Prince your son, a perfectly honest man, is capable of making you far more unhappy than his father ever did; the late Prince was a man of character more or less like everyone else. Our present Sovereign is not sure of wishing the same thing for three days on end, and so, in order that one may make sure of him, one must live continually with him and not allow him to speak to anyone. As this truth is not very difficult to guess, the new Ultra Party, ruled by those two excellent heads, Rassi and the Marchesa Raversi, are going to try to provide the Prince with a mistress. This mistress will have permission to make her own fortune and to distribute various minor posts; but she will have to answer to the Party for the constancy of the master's will.

"I, to be properly established at Your Highness's court, require that Rassi be exiled and degraded; I desire, in addition, that Fabrizio be tried by the most honest judges that can be found: if these gentlemen admit, as I hope, that he is innocent, it will be natural to grant the petition of His Grace the Archbishop that Fabrizio shall be his Coadjutor with eventual succession. If I fail, the Conte and I retire; in that case, I leave this parting advice with Your Serene Highness: she must never pardon Rassi, nor must she ever leave her son's States. While she is with him, that worthy son will never do her any serious harm."

"I have followed your arguments with the close attention they require," the Princess replied, smiling; "ought I, then, to take upon myself the responsibility of providing my son with a mistress?"

"Not at all, Ma'am, but see first of all that your drawing-room is the only one which he finds amusing."

The conversation on this topic was endless, the scales fell from the eyes of the innocent and intelligent Princess.

One of the Duchessa's couriers went to tell Fabrizio that he might enter the town, but must hide himself. He was barely noticed: he spent his time disguised as a *contadino* in the wooden booth of a chestnut-seller, erected opposite the gate of the citadel, beneath the trees of the avenue.

CHAPTER TWENTY-FOUR

THE DUCHESSA arranged a series of charming evenings at the Palace, which had never seen such gaiety: never had she been more delightful than during this winter, and yet she was living in the midst of the greatest dangers; but at the same time, during this critical period, it so happened that she did not think twice with any appreciable regret of the strange alteration in Fabrizio. The young Prince used to appear very early at his mother's parties, where she always said to him:

"Away with you and govern; I wager there are at least a score of reports on your desk awaiting a definite answer, and I do not wish to have the rest of Europe accuse me of making you a mere figurehead in order to reign in your place."

These counsels had the disadvantage of being offered always at the most inopportune moments, that is to say when His Highness, having overcome his timidity, was taking part in some acted charade which amused him greatly. Twice a week there were parties in the country to which on the pretext of winning for the new Sovereign the affection of his people, the Princess admitted the prettiest women of the middle classes. The Duchessa, who was the life and soul of this joyous court, hoped that these handsome women, all of whom looked with a mortal envy on the great prosperity of the burgess Rassi, would inform the Prince of some of the countless rascalities of that Minister. For, among other childish ideas, the Prince claimed to have a *moral* Ministry.

Rassi had too much sense not to feel how dangerous these brilliant evenings at the Princess's court, with his enemy in command of them, were to himself. He had not chosen to return to Conte Mosca the perfectly legal sentence passed on

405

Fabrizio; it was inevitable therefore that either the Duchessa or he must vanish from the court.

On the day of that popular movement, the existence of which it was now in good taste to deny, someone had distributed money among the populace. Rassi started from that point: worse dressed even than was his habit, he climbed to the most wretched attics in the town, and spent whole hours in serious conversation with their needy inhabitants. He was well rewarded for all his trouble: after a fortnight of this kind of life he had acquired the certainty that Ferrante Palla had been the secret head of the insurrection, and furthermore, that this creature, a pauper all his life as a great poet would be, had sent nine or ten diamonds to be sold at Genoa.

Among others were mentioned five valuable stones which were really worth more than 40,000 francs, and which, *ten days before the death of the Prince,* had been sacrificed for 35,000 francs, because, the vendor said, *he was in need of money.*

What words can describe the rapture of the Minister of Justice on making this discovery? He had learned that every day he was being made a laughing stock at the court of the Princess Dowager, and on several occasions the Prince, when discussing business with him, laughed in his face with all the frankness of his youth. It must be admitted that Rassi had some singularly plebeian habits: for instance, as soon as a discussion began to interest him, he would cross his legs and take his foot in his hand; if the interest increased, he would spread his red cotton handkerchief over his knee, and so forth. The Prince had laughed heartily at the wit of one of the prettiest women of the middle class, who, being aware incidentally that she had a very shapely leg, had begun to imitate this elegant gesture of the Minister of Justice.

Rassi requested an extraordinary audience and said to the Prince:

"Would Your Highness be willing to give a hundred thousand francs to know definitely in what manner his august father met his death? With that sum, the authorities would be in a position to arrest the guilty parties, if such exist."

The Prince's reply left no room for doubt.

A little while later, Cecchina informed the Duchessa that she had been offered a large sum to allow her mistress's diamonds to be examined by a jeweller; she had indignantly refused. The Duchessa scolded her for having refused; and, a week later, Cecchina had the diamonds to shew. On the day appointed for this exhibition of the diamonds, the Conte posted a couple of trustworthy men at every jeweller's in Parma, and towards midnight he came to tell the Duchessa that the inquisitive jeweller was none other than Rassi's brother. The Duchessa, who was very gay that evening (they were playing at the Palace a *commedia dell'arte*, that is to say one in which each character invents the dialogue as he goes on, only the plot of the play being posted up in the green-room), the Duchessa, who was playing a part, had as her lover in the piece Conte Baldi, the former friend of the Marchesa Raversi, who was present. The Prince, the shyest man in his States, but an extremely good looking youth and one endowed with the tenderest of hearts, was studying Conte Baldi's part, which he intended to take at the second performance.

"I have very little time," the Duchessa told the Conte; "I am appearing in the first scene of the second act: let us go into the guard-room."

There, surrounded by a score of the body-guard, all wide awake and closely attentive to the conversation between the Prime Minister and the Grand Mistress, the Duchessa said with a laugh to her friend:

"You always scold me when I tell you unnecessary secrets. It was I who summoned Ernesto V to the throne; it was a question of avenging Fabrizio, whom I loved then far more than I do to-day, although always quite innocently. I know very well that you have little belief in my innocence, but that does not matter, since you love me in spite of my crimes. Very well, here is a real crime: I gave all my diamonds to a sort of lunatic, a most interesting man, named Ferrante Palla, I even kissed him so that he should destroy the man who wished to have Fabrizio poisoned. Where is the harm in that?"

"Ah! So that is where Ferrante had found money for his rising!" said the Conte, slightly taken aback; "and you tell me all this in the guard-room!"

"It is because I am in a hurry, and now Rassi is on the track of the crime. It is quite true that I never mentioned an insurrection, for I abhor Jacobins. Think it over, and let me have your advice after the play."

"I will tell you at once that you must make the Prince fall in love with you. But perfectly honourably, please."

The Duchessa was called to return to the stage. She fled.

Some days later the Duchessa received by post a long and ridiculous letter, signed with the name of a former maid of her own; the woman asked to be employed at the court, but the Duchessa had seen from the first glance that the letter was neither in her handwriting nor in her style. On opening the sheet to read the second page, she saw fall at her feet a little miraculous image of the Madonna, folded in a printed leaf from an old book. After glancing at the image, the Duchessa read a few lines of the printed page. Her eyes shone, she found on it these words:

"The Tribune has taken one hundred francs monthly, not more; with the rest it was decided to rekindle the sacred fire in souls which had become frozen by selfishness. The fox is upon my track, that is why I have not sought to see for the last time the adored being. I said to myself, she does not love the Republic, she who is superior to me in mind as well as by her graces and her beauty. Besides, how is one to create a Republic without Republicans? Can I be mistaken? In six months I shall visit, microscope in hand, and on foot, the small towns of America, I shall see whether I ought still to love the sole rival that you have in my heart. If you receive this letter, Signora Baronessa, and no profane eye has read it before yours, tell them to break one of the young ash trees planted twenty paces from the spot where I dared to speak to you for the first time. I shall then have buried, under the great box tree in the garden to which you called attention once in my happy days, a box in which will be found some of those things which lead to the slandering of people of my way of thinking. You may be sure that I should have taken care not to write if the fox were not on my track, and there were not a risk of his reaching that heavenly being; examine the box tree in a fortnight's time."

"Since he has a printing press at his command," the Duchessa said to herself, "we shall soon have a volume of sonnets; heaven knows what name he will give me!"

The Duchessa's coquetry led her to make a venture; for a week she was indisposed, and the court had no more pleasant evenings. The Princess, greatly shocked by all that her fear of her son was obliging her to do in the first moments of her widowhood, went to spend this week in a convent attached to the church in which the late Prince was buried.

This interruption of the evening parties threw upon the Prince an enormous burden of leisure and brought a noteworthy check to the credit of the Minister of Justice. Ernesto V realised all the boredom that threatened him if the Duchessa left his court, or merely ceased to diffuse joy in it. The evenings began again, and the Prince shewed himself more and more interested in the *commedia dell'arte*. He had the intention of taking a part, but dared not confess this ambition. One day, blushing deeply, he said to the Duchessa: "Why should not I act, also?"

"We are all at Your Highness's orders here; if he deigns to give me the order, I will arrange the plot of a comedy, all the chief scenes in Your Highness's part will be with me, and as, on the first evenings, everyone falters a little, if Your Highness will please to watch me closely, I will tell him the answers that he ought to make." Everything was arranged, and with infinite skill. The very shy Prince was ashamed of being shy, the pains that the Duchessa took not to let this innate shyness suffer made a deep impression on the young Sovereign.

On the day of his first appearance, the performance began half an hour earlier than usual, and there were in the drawing-room, when the party moved into the theatre, only nine or ten elderly women. This audience had but little effect on the Prince, and besides, having been brought up at Munich on sound monarchical principles, they always applauded. Using her authority as Grand Mistress, the Duchessa turned the key in the door by which the common herd of courtiers were admitted to the performance. The Prince, who had a *literary* mind and a fine figure, came very well out of his opening scenes; he repeated with intelligence the lines which he read in the Duchessa's eyes, or with which she prompted him in an undertone. At a moment when the few spectators were applauding with all their might, the Duchessa gave a signal, the door of honour was thrown open, and the theatre filled in a moment with all the pretty women of the court, who, finding that the Prince cut a charming figure and seemed thoroughly happy, began to applaud; the Prince flushed with joy. He was playing the part of a lover to the Duchessa. So far from having to suggest his speeches to him, she was soon obliged to request him to curtail those speeches; he spoke of love with an enthusiasm which often embarrassed the actress; his replies lasted five minutes. The Duchessa was no longer the dazzling beauty of the year before: Fabrizio's imprisonment, and, far more than that, her stay by Lake Maggiore with a Fabrizio grown morose and silent, had added ten years to the fair Gina's age. Her features had become marked, they shewed more intelligence and less youth.

They had now only very rarely the playfulness of early youth; but on the stage, with the aid of rouge and all the expedients which art supplies to actresses, she was still the prettiest woman at court. The passionate addresses uttered by the Prince put the courtiers on the alert; they were all saying to themselves this evening: "There is the Balbi of this new reign." The Conte felt himself inwardly revolted. The play ended, the Duchessa said to the Prince before all the court:

"Your Highness acts too well; people will say that you are in love with a woman of eight-and-thirty, which will put a stop to my arrangement with the Conte. And so I will not act any more with Your Highness, unless the Prince swears to me to address me as he would a woman of a certain age, the Signora Marchesa Raversi, for example."

The same play was three times repeated; the Prince was madly happy; but one evening he appeared very thoughtful.

"Either I am greatly mistaken," said the Grand Mistress to the Princess, "or Rassi is seeking to play some trick upon us; I should advise Your Highness to choose a play for to-morrow; the Prince will act badly, and in his despair will tell you something."

The Prince did indeed act very badly; one could barely hear him, and he no longer knew how to end his sentences. At the end of the first act he almost had tears in his eyes; the Duchessa stayed beside him, but was cold and un-moved. The Prince, finding himself alone with her for a moment, in the actors' green-room, went to shut the door.

"I shall never," he said to her, "be able to play in the second and third acts; I absolutely decline to be applauded out of kindness; the applause they gave me this evening cut me to the heart. Give me your advice, what ought I to do?"

"I shall appear on the stage, make a profound reverence to Her Highness, another to the audience, like a real stage manager, and say that, the actor who was playing the part of Lelio having suddenly been taken ill, the performance will conclude with some pieces of music. Conte Rusca and little Ghisolfi will be delighted to be able to shew off their harsh voices to so brilliant an assembly."

The Prince took the Duchessa's hand, which he kissed with rapture.

"Why are you not a man?" he said to her; "you would give me good advice. Rassi has just laid on my desk one hundred and eighty-two depositions against the alleged assassins of my father. Apart from the depositions, there is a formal accusation of more than two hundred pages; I shall have to read all that, and, besides, I have given my word not to say anything to the Conte. All this is leading straight to executions, already he wants me to fetch back from France, from near Antibes, Ferrante Palla, that great poet whom I admire so much. He is there under the name of Poncet."

"The day on which you have a Liberal hanged, Rassi will be bound to the Ministry by chains of iron, and that is what he wishes more than anything: but Your Highness will no longer be able to speak of leaving the Palace two hours in advance. I shall say nothing either to the Princess or to the Conte of the cry of grief which has just escaped you; but, since I am bound on oath to keep nothing secret from the Princess, I should be glad if Your Highness would say to his mother the same things that he has let fall with me."

This idea provided a diversion to the misery of the hissed actor which was crushing the Sovereign.

"Very well, go and tell my mother; I shall be in her big cabinet."

The Prince left the stage, found his way to the drawing-room from which one entered the theatre, harshly dismissed the Great Chamberlain and the Aide-de-Camp on duty who were following him; the Princess, meanwhile, hurriedly left the play; entering the big cabinet, the Grand Mistress made a profound reverence to mother and son, and left them alone. One may imagine the agitation of the court, these are the things that make it so amusing. At the end of an hour the Prince himself appeared at the door of the cabinet and summoned the Duchessa; the Princess was in tears; her son's expression had entirely altered.

"These are weak creatures who are out of temper," the Grand Mistress said to herself, "and are seeking some good excuse to be angry with somebody." At first the mother and son began both to speak at once to tell the details to the Duchessa, who in her answers took great care not to put forward any idea. For two mortal hours, the three actors in this tedious scene did not step out of the parts which we have indicated. The Prince went in person to fetch the two enormous portfolios which Rassi had deposited on his desk; on leaving his mother's cabinet, he found the whole court awaiting him. "Go away, leave me alone!" he cried in a most impolite tone which was quite without precedent in him. The Prince did not wish to be seen carrying the two portfolios himself, a Prince ought not to carry anything. The courtiers vanished in the twinkling of an eye. On his return the Prince encountered no one but the footmen who were blowing out the candles; he dismissed them with fury, also poor Fontana, the Aide-de-Camp on duty, who had been so tactless as to remain, in his zeal.

"Everyone is doing his utmost to try my patience this evening," he said crossly to the Duchessa, as he entered the cabinet; he credited her with great intelligence, and was furious at her evident refusal to offer him any advice. She, for her part, was determined to say nothing so long as she was not asked for her advice *quite expressly*. Another long half hour elapsed before the Prince, who had a sense of his own dignity, could make up his mind to say to her: "But, Signora, you say nothing."

"I am here to serve the Princess, and to forget very quickly what is said before me."

"Very well, Signora," said the Prince, blushing deeply, "I order you to give me your opinion."

"One punishes crimes to prevent their recurrence. Was the late Prince poisoned? That is a very doubtful question. Was he poisoned by the Jacobins? That is what Rassi would dearly like to prove, for then he becomes for Your Highness a permanently necessary instrument. In that case Your Highness, whose reign is just beginning, can promise himself many evenings like this. Your subjects say on the whole, what is quite true, that Your Highness has a strain of goodness in his nature; so long as he has not had any Liberal hanged, he will enjoy that reputation, and most certainly no one will ever dream of planning to poison him."

"Your conclusion is evident," cried the Princess angrily; "you do not wish us to punish my husband's assassins!"

"Apparently, Ma'am, because I am bound to them by ties of tender affection."

The Duchessa could see in the Prince's eyes that he believed her to be perfectly in accord with his mother as to dictating a plan of action to him. There followed between the two women a fairly rapid succession of bitter repartees, at the end of which the Duchessa protested that she would not utter a single word more, and adhered to her resolution; but the Prince, after a long discussion with his mother, ordered her once more to express her opinion.

"That is what I swear to Your Highnesses that I will not do!"

"But this is really childish!" exclaimed the Prince.

"I beg you to speak, Signora Duchessa," said the Princess with an air of dignity.

"That is what I implore you to excuse me from doing, Ma'am; but Your Highness," the Duchessa went on, addressing the Prince, "reads French perfectly: to calm our agitated minds, would he read *us* a fable by La Fontaine?"

The Princess thought this *"us"* extremely insolent, but assumed an air at once of surprise and of amusement when the Grand Mistress, who had gone with the utmost coolness to open the bookcase, returned with a volume of La Fontaine's *Fables;* she turned the pages for some moments, then said to the Prince, handing him the book:

"I beg your Highness to read *the whole* of the fable."

THE GARDENER AND THE LORD OF THE MANOR

A devotee of gardening there was,
Between the peasant and the yeoman class,
Who on the outskirts of a certain village
Owned a neat garden with a bit of tillage.
He made a quickset hedge to fence it in,
And there grew lettuce, pink and jessamine,
Such as win prizes at the local show,
Or make a birthday bouquet for Margot.
 One day he called upon the neighbouring Squire
To ask his help with a marauding hare.
"The brute," says he, "comes guzzling everywhere,
And simply laughs at all my traps and wire.
No stick or stone will hit him—I declare
He's a magician." "Rubbish! I don't care
If he's the Deuce himself," replied the other,
"I warrant he shan't give you much more bother.
Miraut, in spite of all his cunning,

For this translation of La Fontaine's fable I am indebted to my friend Mr. Edward Marsh, who allows me to reprint the lines from his *Forty-two Fables of La Fontaine* (William Heinemann, Ltd., 1924). C. K. S. M.

Won't take much time to get him running."
"But when?" "To-morrow, sure as here I stand."
 Next morning he rides up with all his band.
"Now then, we'll lunch! Those chickens don't look bad."

*   *   *   *   *   *   *

 The luncheon over, all was preparation,
Bustle and buzz and animation,
Horns blowing, hounds barking, such a hullabaloo,
The good man feared the worst. His fear came true!
The kitchen-garden was a total wreck
Under the trampling, not a speck
Of pot or frame survived. Good-bye
To onion, leek, and chicory,
Good-bye to marrows and their bravery,
Good-bye to all that makes soup savoury!

*   *   *   *   *   *   *

 The wretched owner saw no sense
In this grand style of doing things;
But no one marked his mutterings.
The hounds and riders in a single trice
Had wrought more havoc in his paradise
Than all the hares in the vicinity
Could have achieved throughout infinity.

So far the story—now the moral:
Each petty Prince should settle his own quarrel.
If once he gets a King for an ally,
He's certain to regret it by and by.

This reading was followed by a long silence. The Prince
paced up and down the cabinet, after going himself to put
the volume back in its place.

"Well, Signora," said the Princess, "will you deign to
speak?"

"No, indeed, Ma'am, until such time as His Highness shall
appoint me his Minister; by speaking here, I should run the
risk of losing my place as Grand Mistress."

A fresh silence, lasting a full quarter of an hour; finally
the Princess remembered the part that had been played in the
past by Marie de' Medici, the mother of Louis XIII: for
the last few days the Grand Mistress had made the *lettrice*
read aloud the excellent *History of Louis XIII*, by M. Bazin.
The Princess, although greatly annoyed, thought that the
Duchessa might easily leave the country, and then Rassi,

who filled her with mortal terror, might quite well imitate Richelieu and have her banished by her son. At this moment the Princess would have given everything in the world to humiliate her Grand Mistress; but she could not. She rose, and came, with a smile that was slightly exaggerated, to take the Duchessa's hand and say to her:

"Come, Signora, give me a proof of your friendship by speaking."

"Very well! Two words, and no more: burn, in the grate there, all the papers collected by that viper Rassi, and never reveal to him that they have been burned."

She added in a whisper, and in a familiar tone, in the Princess's ear:

"Rassi may become Richelieu!"

"But, damn it, those papers are costing me more than 80,000 francs!" the Prince exclaimed angrily.

"Prince," replied the Duchessa with emphasis, "that is what it costs to employ scoundrels of low birth. Would to God you could lose a million and never put your trust in the base rascals who kept your father from sleeping during the last six years of his reign."

The words *low birth* had greatly delighted the Princess, who felt that the Conte and his friend had too exclusive a regard for brains, always slightly akin to Jacobinism.

During the short interval of profound silence, filled by the Princess's reflections, the castle clock struck three. The Princess rose, made a profound reverence to her son, and said to him: "My health does not allow me to prolong the discussion further. Never have a Minister of *low birth;* you will not disabuse me of the idea that your Rassi has stolen half the money he has made you spend on spies." The Princess took two candles from the brackets and put them in the fireplace in such a way that they should not blow out; then, going up to her son, she added: "La Fontaine's fable prevails, in my mind, over the lawful desire to avenge a husband. Will Your Highness permit me to burn *these writings?*" The Prince remained motionless.

"His face is really stupid," the Duchessa said to herself; "the Conte is right: the late Prince would not have kept us out of our beds until three o'clock in the morning, before making up his mind."

The Princess, still standing, went on:

"That little attorney would be very proud, if he knew that his papers stuffed with lies, and arranged so as to secure his own advancement, had occupied the two greatest personages in the States for a whole night."

The Prince dashed at one of the portfolios like a madman, and emptied its contents into the fireplace. The mass of papers nearly extinguished the two candles; the room filled with smoke. The Princess saw in her son's eyes that he was tempted to seize a jug of water and save these papers, which were costing him eighty thousand francs.

"Open the window!" she cried angrily to the Duchessa. The Duchessa made haste to obey; at once all the papers took light together; there was a great roar in the chimney, and it soon became evident that it was on fire.

The Prince had a petty nature in all matters of money; he thought he saw his Palace in flames, and all the treasures that it contained destroyed; he ran to the window and called the guard in a voice completely altered. The soldiers in a tumult rushed into the courtyard at the sound of the Prince's voice, he returned to the fireplace which was sucking in the air from the open window with a really alarming sound; he grew impatient, swore, took two or three turns up and down the room like a man out of his mind, and finally ran out.

The Princess and the Grand Mistress remained standing, face to face, and preserving a profound silence.

"Is the storm going to begin again?" the Duchessa asked herself; "upon my word, my cause is won." And she was preparing to be highly impertinent in her replies, when a sudden thought came to her; she saw the second portfolio intact. "No, my cause is only half won!" She said to the Princess, in a distinctly cold tone:

"Does Ma'am order me to burn the rest of these papers?"

"And where will you burn them?" asked the Princess angrily.

"In the drawing-room fire; if I throw them in one after another, there is no danger."

The Duchessa put under her arm the portfolio bursting with papers, took a candle and went into the next room. She looked first to see that the portfolio was that which contained the depositions, put in her shawl five or six bundles of papers, burned the rest with great care, then disappeared without taking leave of the Princess.

"There is a fine piece of impertinence," she said to herself, with a laugh, "but her affectations of inconsolable widowhood came very near to making me lose my head on a scaffold."

On hearing the sound of the Duchessa's carriage, the

Princess was beside herself with rage at her Grand Mistress.

In spite of the lateness of the hour, the Duchessa sent for the Conte; he was at the fire at the Castle, but soon appeared with the news that it was all over. "That little Prince has really shewn great courage, and I have complimented him on it effusively."

"Examine these depositions quickly, and let us burn them as soon as possible."

The Conte read them, and turned pale.

"Upon my soul, they have come very near the truth; their procedure has been very cleverly managed, they are positively on the track of Ferrante Palla; and, if he speaks, we have a difficult part to play."

"But he will not speak," cried the Duchessa; "he is a man of honour: burn them, burn them."

"Not yet. Allow me to take down the names of a dozen or fifteen dangerous witnesses, whom I shall take the liberty of removing, if Rassi ever thinks of beginning again."

"I may remind Your Excellency that the Prince has given his word to say nothing to his Minister of Justice of our midnight escapade."

"From cowardice and fear of a scene he will keep it."

"Now, my friend, this is a night that has greatly hastened our marriage; I should not have wished to bring you as my portion a criminal trial, still less for a sin which I was led to commit by my interest in another man."

The Conte was in love; he took her hand with an exclamation; tears stood in his eyes.

"Before you go, give me some advice as to the way I ought to behave with the Princess; I am utterly worn out, I have been play-acting for an hour on the stage and for five in her cabinet."

"You have avenged yourself quite sufficiently for the Princess's sour speeches, which were due only to weakness, by the impertinence with which you left her. Address her to-morrow in the tone you used this morning; Rassi is not yet in prison or in exile, and we have not yet torn up Fabrizio's sentence.

"You were asking the Princess to come to a decision, which is a thing that always annoys Princes and even Prime Ministers; also you are her Grand Mistress, that is to say her little servant. By a reversion which is inevitable in weak people, in three days Rassi will be more in favour than ever;

he will try to have someone hanged: so long as he has not compromised the Prince, he is sure of nothing.

"There has been a man injured in to-night's fire; he is a tailor, who, upon my word, shewed an extraordinary intrepidity. To-morrow I am going to ask the Prince to take my arm and come with me to pay the tailor a visit; I shall be armed to the teeth and shall keep a sharp look-out; but anyhow, this young Prince is not hated at all as yet. I wish to make him accustomed to walking in the streets, it is a trick I am playing on Rassi, who is certainly going to succeed me, and will not be able to allow such imprudences. On our way back from the tailor's, I shall take the Prince past his father's statue; he will notice the marks of the stones which have broken the Roman toga in which the idiot of a sculptor dressed it up; and, in short, he will have to be a great fool if he does not on his own initiative make the comment: 'This is what one gains by having Jacobins hanged.' To which I shall reply: 'You must hang either ten thousand or none at all: the Saint-Bartholomew destroyed the Protestants in France.'

"To-morrow, dear friend, before this excursion, send your name in to the Prince, and say to him: 'Yesterday evening, I performed the duties of a Minister to you, and, by your orders, have incurred the Princess's displeasure. You will have to pay me.' He will expect a demand for money, and will knit his brows; you will leave him plunged in this unhappy thought for as long as you can; then you will say: 'I beg Your Highness to order that Fabrizio be tried *in contradittorio*' (which means, in his presence) 'by the twelve most respected judges in your States.' *And*, without losing any time, you will present for his signature a little order written out by your own fair hand, which I am going to dictate to you; I shall of course include the clause that the former sentence is quashed. To this there is only one objection; but, if you press the matter warmly, it will not occur to the Prince's mind. He may say to you: 'Fabrizio must first make himself a prisoner in the citadel.' To which you will reply: 'He will make himself a prisoner in the town prison' (you know that I am the master there; every evening your nephew will come to see us). If the Prince answers: 'No, his escape has tarnished the honour of my citadel, and I desire, for form's sake, that he return to the cell in which he was'; you in turn will reply: 'No, for there he would be at the disposal of my enemy Rassi'; and, in one of those feminine sentences which you utter so effectively, you will give him to understand that, to make Rassi yield, you have only to tell him of to-night's *auto-da-fè;* if he insists, you will announce that you are going to spend a fortnight at your place at Sacca.

"You will send for Fabrizio, and consult him as to this step which may land him in prison. If, to anticipate everything while he is under lock and key, Rassi should grow too impatient and have me poisoned, Fabrizio may run a certain risk. But that is hardly probable; you know that I have imported a French cook, who is the merriest of men, and makes puns; well, punning is incompatible with poison. I have already told our friend Fabrizio that I have managed to find all the witnesses of his fine and courageous action; it was evidently that fellow Giletti who tried to murder him. I have not spoken to you of these witnesses, because I wished to give you a surprise, but the plan has failed; the Prince refused to sign. I have told our friend Fabrizio that certainly I should procure him a high ecclesiastical dignity; but I shall have great difficulty if his enemies can raise the objection in the Roman Curia of a charge of murder.

"Do you realise, Signora, that, if he is not tried and judged in the most solemn fashion, all his life long the name of Giletti will be a reproach to him? It would be a great act of cowardice not to have oneself tried, when one is sure of one's innocence. Besides, even if he were guilty, I should make them acquit him. When I spoke to him, the fiery youngster would not allow me to finish, he picked up the official almanac, and we went through it together choosing the twelve most upright and learned judges; when we had made the list, we cancelled six names for which we substituted those of six counsel, my personal enemies, and, as we could find only two enemies, we filled up the gaps with four rascals who are devoted to Rassi."

This proposal filled the Duchessa with a mortal anxiety, and not without cause; at length she yielded to reason, and, at the Minister's dictation, wrote out the order appointing the judges.

The Conte did not leave her until six o'clock in the morning; she endeavoured to sleep, but in vain. At nine o'clock, she took breakfast with Fabrizio, whom she found burning with a desire to be tried; at ten, she waited on the Princess, who was not visible; at eleven, she saw the Prince, who was holding his levee, and signed the order without the slightest objection. The Duchessa sent the order to the Conte, and retired to bed.

It would be pleasant perhaps to relate Rassi's fury when the Conte obliged him to countersign, in the Prince's presence, the order signed that morning by the Prince himself; but we must go on with our story.

The Conte discussed the merits of each judge, and offered to change the names. But the reader is perhaps a little tired of all these details of procedure, no less than of all these court intrigues. From the whole business one can derive this moral, that the man who mingles with a court compromises his happiness, if he is happy, and, in any event, makes his future depend on the intrigues of a chambermaid.

On the other hand in America, in the Republic, one has to spend the whole weary day paying serious court to the shopkeepers in the street, and must become as stupid as they are; and there, one has no Opera.

The Duchessa, when she rose in the evening, had a moment of keen anxiety: Fabrizio was not to be found; finally, towards midnight, during the performance at court, she received a letter from him. Instead of making himself a prisoner *in the town prison*, where the Conte was in control, he had gone back to occupy his old cell in the citadel, only too happy to be living within a few feet of Clelia.

This was an event of vast consequence: in this place he was exposed to the risk of poison more than ever. This act of folly filled the Duchessa with despair; she forgave the cause of it, a mad love for Clelia, because unquestionably in a few days' time that young lady was going to marry the rich Marchese Crescenzi. This folly restored to Fabrizio all the influence he had originally enjoyed over the Duchessa's heart.

"It is that cursed paper which I went and made the Prince sign that will be his death! What fools men are with their ideas of honour! As if one needed to think of honour under absolute governments, in countries where a Rassi is Minister of Justice! He ought to have accepted the pardon outright, which the Prince would have signed just as readily as the order convening this extraordinary tribunal. What does it matter, after all, that a man of Fabrizio's birth should be more or less accused of having himself, sword in hand, killed an actor like Giletti?"

No sooner had she received Fabrizio's note than the Duchessa ran to the Conte, whom she found deadly pale.

"Great God! Dear friend, I am most unlucky in handling

that boy, and you will be vexed with me again. I can prove to you that I made the gaoler of the town prison come here yesterday evening; every day your nephew would have come to take tea with you. What is so terrible is that it is impossible for you and me to say to the Prince that there is fear of poison, and of poison administered by Rassi; the suspicion would seem to him the height of immorality. However, if you insist, I am ready to go up to the Palace; but I am certain of the answer. I am going to say more; I offer you a stratagem which I would not employ for myself. Since I have been in power in this country, I have not caused the death of a single man, and you know that I am so sensitive in that respect that sometimes, at the close of day, I still think of those two spies whom I had shot, rather too light-heartedly, in Spain. Very well, do you wish me to get rid of Rassi? The danger in which he is placing Fabrizio is un-bounded; he has there a sure way of sending me packing."

This proposal pleased the Duchessa extremely, but she did not adopt it.

"I do not wish," she said to the Conte, "that in our retire-ment, beneath the beautiful sky of Naples, you should have dark thoughts in the evenings."

"But, dear friend, it seems to me that we have only the choice between one dark thought and another. What will you do, what will I do myself, if Fabrizio is carried off by an ill-ness?"

The discussion returned to dwell upon this idea, and the Duchessa ended it with this speech:

"Rassi owes his life to the fact that I love you more than Fabrizio; no, I do not wish to poison all the evenings of the old age which we are going to spend together."

The Duchessa hastened to the fortress; General Fabio Conti was delighted at having to stop her with the strict letter of the military regulations: no one might enter a state prison without an order signed by the Prince.

"But the Marchese Crescenzi and his musicians come every day to the citadel?"

"Because I obtained an order for them from the Prince."

The poor Duchessa did not know the full tale of her troubles. General Fabio Conti had regarded himself as per-sonally dishonoured by Fabrizio's escape: when he saw him arrive at the citadel, he ought not to have admitted him, for he had no order to that effect. "But," he said to himself, "it is Heaven that is sending him to me to restore my honour, and

to save me from the ridicule which would assail my military
career. This opportunity must not be missed: doubtless they
are going to acquit him, and I have only a few days for my
revenge."

CHAPTER TWENTY-FIVE

THE ARRIVAL OF our hero threw Clelia into despair: the poor girl, pious and sincere with herself, could not avoid the reflexion that there would never be any happiness for her apart from Fabrizio; but she had made a vow to the Madonna, at the time when her father was nearly poisoned, that she would offer him the sacrifice of marrying the Marchese Crescenzi. She had made the vow that she would never see Fabrizio, and already she was a prey to the most fearful remorse over the admission she had been led to make in the letter she had written Fabrizio on the eve of his escape. How is one to depict what occurred in that sorrowful heart when, occupied in a melancholy way with watching her birds flit to and fro, and raising her eyes from habit, and with affection, towards the window from which formerly Fabrizio used to look at her, she saw him there once again, greeting her with tender respect.

She imagined it to be a vision which Heaven had allowed for her punishment; then the atrocious reality became apparent to her reason. "They have caught him again," she said to herself, "and he is lost!" She remembered the things that had been said in the fortress after the escape; the humblest of the gaolers regarded themselves as mortally insulted. Clelia looked at Fabrizio, and in spite of herself that look portrayed in full the passion that had thrown her into despair.

"Do you suppose," she seemed to be saying to Fabrizio, "that I shall find happiness in that sumptuous palace which they are making ready for me? My father repeats to me till I am weary that you are as poor as ourselves; but, great God, with what joy would I share that poverty! But, alas, we must never see one another again!"

423

Clelia had not the strength to make use of the alphabets: as she looked at Fabrizio she felt faint and sank upon a chair that stood beside the window. Her head rested upon the ledge of this window, and as she had been anxious to see him until the last moment, her face was turned towards Fabrizio, who had a perfect view of it. When, after a few moments, she opened her eyes again, her first glance was at Fabrizio: she saw tears in his eyes, but those tears were the effect of extreme happiness; he saw that absence had by no means made him forgotten. The two poor young things remained for some time as though spell-bound by the sight of each other. Fabrizio ventured to sing, as if he were accompanying himself on the guitar, a few improvised lines which said: *"It is to see you again* that I have returned to prison; *they are going to try me."*

These words seemed to awaken all Clelia's dormant virtue: she rose swiftly, and hid her eyes; and, by the most vivid gestures, sought to express to him that she must never see him again; she had promised this to the Madonna, and had looked at him just now in a moment of forgetfulness. Fabrizio venturing once more to express his love, Clelia fled from the room indignant, and swearing to herself that never would she see him again, for such were the precise words of her vow to the Madonna: *"My eyes shall never see him again."* She had written them on a little slip of paper which her uncle Don Cesare had allowed her to burn upon the altar at the moment of the oblation, while he was saying mass.

But, oaths or no oaths, Fabrizio's presence in the Torre Farnese had restored to Clelia all her old habits and activities. Normally she passed all her days in solitude, in her room. No sooner had she recovered from the unforeseen disturbance in which the sight of Fabrizio had plunged her, than she began to wander through the *palazzo,* and, so to speak, to renew her acquaintance with all her humble friends. A very loquacious old woman, employed in the kitchen, said to her with an air of mystery: "This time, Signor Fabrizio will not leave the citadel."

"He will not make the mistake of going over the walls again," said Clelia, "but he will leave by the door if he is acquitted."

"I say, and I can assure Your Excellency that he will go out of the citadel feet first."

Clelia turned extremely pale, a change which was remarked

by the old woman and stopped the flow of her eloquence. She said to herself that she had been guilty of an imprudence in speaking thus before the governor's daughter, whose duty it would be to tell everybody that Fabrizio had died a natural death. As she went up to her room, Clelia met the prison doctor, an honest sort of man but timid, who told her with a terrified air that Fabrizio was seriously ill. Clelia could hardly keep on her feet; she sought everywhere for her uncle, the good Don Cesare, and at length found him in the chapel, where he was praying fervently: from his face he appeared upset. The dinner bell rang. At table, not a word was exchanged between the brothers; only, towards the end of the meal, the General addressed a few very harsh words to his brother. The latter looked at the servants, who left the room.

"General," said Don Cesare to the governor, "I have the honour to inform you that I am leaving the citadel: I give you my resignation."

"*Bravo! Bravissimo!* So that I shall be suspect! . . . And your reason, if you please?"

"My conscience."

"Go on, you're only a frock! You know nothing about honour."

"Fabrizio is dead," thought Clelia; "they have poisoned him at dinner, or it is arranged for to-morrow." She ran to the aviary, resolved to sing, accompanying herself on the piano. "I shall go to confession," she said to herself, "and I shall be forgiven for having broken my vow to save a man's life." What was her consternation when, on reaching the aviary, she saw that the screens had been replaced by planks fastened to the iron bars. In desperation she tried to give the prisoner a warning in a few words shouted rather than sung. There was no response of any sort: a deathly silence already reigned in the Torre Farnese. "It is all over," she said to herself. Beside herself, she went downstairs, then returned to equip herself with the little money she had and some small diamond earrings; she took also, on her way out, the bread that remained from dinner, which had been placed in a sideboard. "If he still lives, my duty is to save him." She advanced with a haughty air to the little door of the tower; this door stood open, and eight soldiers had just been posted in the pillared room on the ground floor. She faced these soldiers boldly; Clelia counted on speaking to the serjeant who would be in charge of them: this man was absent. Clelia rushed on to the little iron staircase which wound in a spiral round one of the pillars; the soldiers looked at her with great stupefaction but, evidently on account of her lace shawl and her hat, dared not say anything to her. On the first landing there was no one; but, when she reached the second, at the entrance to the corridor which, as the reader may remember, was closed by three barred gates and led to Fabrizio's cell, she found a turnkey who was a stranger to her, and said to her with a terrified air:

"He has not dined yet."

"I know that," said Clelia haughtily. The man dared not stop her. Twenty paces farther, Clelia found sitting upon the first of the six wooden steps which led to Fabrizio's cell, another turnkey, elderly and very cross, who said to her firmly:

"Signorina, have you an order from the governor?"

"Do you mean to say that you do not know me?"

Clelia, at that moment, was animated by a supernatural force, she was beside herself. "I am going to save my husband," she said to herself.

While the old turnkey was exclaiming: "But my duty does not allow me. . . ." Clelia hastened up the six steps; she hurled herself against the door: an enormous key was in the lock; she required all her strength to make it turn. At that moment, the old turnkey, who was half intoxicated, seized the hem of her gown, she went quickly into the room, shut the door behind her, tearing her gown, and, as the turnkey was pushing the door to follow her, closed it with a bolt which lay to her hand. She looked into the cell and saw Fabrizio seated at a small table upon which his dinner was laid. She dashed at the table, overturned it, and, seizing Fabrizio by the arm, said to him:

"Hai mangiato?"

This use of the singular form delighted Fabrizio. In her confusion, Clelia forgot for the first time her feminine reserve, and let her love appear.

Fabrizio had been going to begin the fatal meal; he took her in his arms and covered her with kisses. "This dinner was poisoned," was his thought: "if I tell her that I have not touched it, religion regains its hold, and Clelia flies. If, on the other hand, she regards me as a dying man, I shall obtain from her a promise not to leave me. She wishes to find some way of breaking off her abominable marriage and here chance offers us one: the gaolers will collect, they

will break down the door, and then there will be such a
scandal that perhaps the Marchese Crescenzi will fight shy,
and the marriage be broken off."

During the moment of silence occupied by these reflexions
Fabrizio felt that already Clelia was seeking to free herself
from his embrace.

"I feel no pain as yet," he said to her, "but presently
it will prostrate me at your feet; help me to die."

"O my only friend!" was her answer, "I will die with
thee." She clasped him in her arms with a convulsive movement.

She was so beautiful, half unclad and in this state of
intense passion, that Fabrizio could not resist an almost
unconscious impulse. No resistance was offered him.

In the enthusiasm of passion and generous instincts which
follows an extreme happiness, he said to her fatuously:

"I must not allow an unworthy falsehood to soil the first
moments of our happiness: but for your courage, I should
now be only a corpse, or writhing in atrocious pain, but
I was going to begin my dinner when you came in, and I
have not touched these dishes at all."

Fabrizio dwelt upon these appalling images to conjure
away the indignation which he could already read in Clelia's
eyes. She looked at him for some moments, while two violent
and conflicting sentiments fought within her, then flung herself into his arms. They heard a great noise in the corridor,
the three iron doors were violently opened and shut, voices
shouted.

"Ah! If I had arms!" cried Fabrizio; "they made me give
them up before they would let me in. No doubt they are
coming to kill me. Farewell, my Clelia, I bless my death
since it has been the cause of my happiness." Clelia embraced him and gave him a little dagger with an ivory
handle, the blade of which was scarcely longer than that of a
pen-knife.

"Do not let yourself be killed," she said to him, "and
defend yourself to the last moment; if my uncle the Priore
hears the noise, he is a man of courage and virtue, he will
save you." So saying she rushed to the door.

"If you are not killed," she said with exaltation, holding
the bolt of the door in her hand and turning her head towards him, "let yourself die of hunger rather than touch
anything. Carry this bread always on you." The noise came
nearer, Fabrizio seized her round the body, stepped into her

place by the door, and, opening it with fury, dashed down the six steps of the wooden staircase. He had in his hand the little dagger with the ivory handle, and was on the point of piercing with it the waistcoat of General Fontana, Aide-de-Camp to the Prince, who recoiled with great alacrity, crying in a panic: "But I am coming to save you, Signor del Dongo."

Fabrizio went up the six steps, called into the cell: "Fontana has come to save me"; then, returning to the General, on the wooden steps, discussed matters coldly with him. He begged him at great length to pardon him a movement of anger. "They wished to poison me; the dinner that is there on my table is poisoned; I had the sense not to touch it, but I may admit to you that this procedure has given me a shock. When I heard you on the stair, I thought that they were coming to finish me off with their dirks. Signor Generale, I request you to order that no one shall enter my cell: they would remove the poison, and our good Prince must know all."

The General, very pale and completely taken aback, passed on the orders suggested by Fabrizio to the picked body of gaolers who were following him: these men, greatly dismayed at finding the poison discovered, hastened downstairs; they went first, ostensibly so as not to delay the Prince's Aide-de-Camp on the narrow staircase, actually in order to escape themselves and vanish. To the great surprise of General Fontana, Fabrizio kept him for fully a quarter of an hour on the little iron staircase which ran round the pillar of the ground floor; he wished to give Clelia time to hide on the floor above.

It was the Duchessa who, after various wild attempts, had managed to get General Fontana sent to the citadel; it was only by chance that she succeeded. On leaving Conte Mosca, as alarmed as she was herself, she had hastened to the Palace. The Princess, who had a marked repugnance for energy, which seemed to her vulgar, thought her mad and did not appear at all disposed to attempt any unusual measures on her behalf. The Duchessa, out of her senses, was weeping hot tears, she could do nothing but repeat, every moment:

"But, Ma'am, in a quarter of an hour Fabrizio will be dead, poisoned."

Seeing the Princess remain perfectly composed, the Duchessa became mad with grief. She completely overlooked the moral reflexion which would not have escaped a woman brought up in one of those Northern religions which allow self-examination: "I was the first to use poison, and I am perishing by poison." In Italy reflexions of that sort, in moments of passion, appear in the poorest of taste, as a pun would seem in Paris in similar circumstances.

The Duchessa, in desperation, risked going into the drawing-room where she found the Marchese Crescenzi, who was in waiting that day. On her return to Parma he had thanked her effusively for the place of *Cavaliere d'onore*, to which, but for her, he would never have had any claim. Protestations of unbounded devotion had not been lacking on his part. The Duchessa appealed to him in these words:

"Rassi is going to have Fabrizio, who is in the citadel, poisoned. Take in your pocket some chocolate and a bottle of water which I shall give you. Go up to the citadel, and save my life by saying to General Fabio Conti that you will break off your marriage with his daughter if he does not allow you to give the water and the chocolate to Fabrizio with your own hands."

The Marchese turned pale, and his features, so far from shewing any animation at these words, presented a picture of the dullest embarrassment; he could not believe in the possibility of so shocking a crime in a town as moral as Parma, and one over which so great a Prince reigned, and so forth; these platitudes, moreover, he uttered slowly. In a word, the Duchessa found an honest man, but the weakest imaginable, and one who could not make up his mind to act. After a score of similar phrases interrupted by cries of impatience from Signora Sanseverina, he hit upon an excellent idea: the oath which he had given as *Cavaliere d'onore* forbade him to take part in any action against the Government.

Who can conceive the anxiety and despair of the Duchessa, who felt that time was flying?

"But, at least, see the governor; tell him that I shall pursue Fabrizio's murderers to hell itself!"

Despair increased the Duchessa's natural eloquence, but all this fire only made the Marchese more alarmed and doubled his irresolution; at the end of an hour he was less disposed to act than at the first moment.

This unhappy woman, who had reached the utmost limits of despair and knew well that the governor would refuse nothing to so rich a son-in-law, went so far as to fling herself at his feet; at this the Marchese's pusillanimity seemed to increase still further; he himself, at the sight of this strange spectacle, was afraid of being compromised unawares; but a singular thing happened: the Marchese, a good man at heart, was touched by the tears and by the posture, at his feet, of so beautiful and, above all, so influential a woman.

"I myself, noble and rich as I am," he said to himself, "will perhaps one day be at the feet of some Republican!" The Marchese burst into tears, and finally it was agreed that the Duchessa, in her capacity as Grand Mistress, should present him to the Princess, who would give him permission to convey to Fabrizio a little hamper, of the contents of which he would declare himself to know nothing.

The previous evening, before the Duchessa knew of Fabrizio's act of folly in going to the citadel, they had played at court a *commedia dell'arte,* and the Prince, who always reserved for himself the lover's part to be played with the Duchessa, had been so passionate in speaking to her of his affection that he would have been absurd, if, in Italy, an impassioned man or a Prince could ever be thought so.

The Prince, extremely shy, but always intensely serious in matters of love, met, in one of the corridors of the Castle, the Duchessa who was carrying off the Marchese Crescenzi, in great distress, to the Princess. He was so surprised and dazzled by the beauty, full of emotion, which her despair gave the Grand Mistress, that for the first time in his life he shewed character. With a more than imperious gesture he dismissed the Marchese, and began to make a declaration of love, according to all the rules, to the Duchessa. The Prince had doubtless prepared this speech long beforehand, for there were things in it that were quite reasonable.

"Since the conventions of my rank forbid me to give myself the supreme happiness of marrying you, I will swear to you upon the Blessed Sacrament never to marry without your permission in writing. I am well aware," he added, "that I am making you forfeit the hand of a Prime Minister, a clever and extremely amiable man; but after all he is fifty-six, and I am not yet two-and-twenty. I should consider myself to be insulting you, and to deserve your refusal if I spoke to you of the advantages that there are apart from love; but everyone who takes an interest in money at my court speaks with admiration of the proof of his love which the Conte gives you, in leaving you the custodian of all that he possesses. I shall be only too happy to copy him in that respect. You will make a better use of my fortune than I, and you shall have the entire disposal of the annual sum which my Ministers hand over to the Intendant General of my Crown; so that it will be you, Signora Duchessa, who will decide upon the sums which I may spend each month." The Duchessa found all these details very long; Fabrizio's dangers pierced her heart.

"Then you do not know, Prince," she cried, "that at this moment they are poisoning Fabrizio in your citadel! Save him! I accept everything."

The arrangement of this speech was perfect in its clumsiness. At the mere mention of poison all the ease, all the good faith which this poor, moral Prince was putting into the conversation vanished in the twinkling of an eye; the Duchessa did not notice her tactlessness until it was too late to remedy it, and her despair was intensified, a thing she had believed to be impossible. "If I had not spoken of poison," she said to herself, "he would grant me Fabrizio's freedom. . . . O my dear Fabrizio," she added, "so it is fated that it is I who must pierce your heart by my foolishness!"

It took the Duchessa all her time and all her coquetry to get the Prince back to his talk of passionate love; but even then he remained deeply offended. It was his mind alone that spoke; his heart had been frozen by the idea first of all of poison, and then by the other idea, as displeasing as the first was terrible: "They administer poison in my States, and without telling me! So Rassi wishes to dishonour me in the eyes of Europe! And God knows what I shall read next month in the Paris newspapers!"

Suddenly the heart of this shy young man was silent, his mind arrived at an idea.

"Dear Duchessa! You know whether I am attached to you. Your terrible ideas about poison are unfounded, I prefer to think; still, they give me food for thought, they make me almost forget for an instant the passion that I feel for you, which is the only passion that I have ever felt in all my life. I know that I am not attractive; I am only a boy, hopelessly in love; still, put me to the test."

The Prince grew quite animated in using this language.

"Save Fabrizio, and I accept everything! No doubt I am carried away by the foolish fears of a mother's heart; but send this moment to fetch Fabrizio from the citadel, that I may see him. If he is still alive, send him from the Palace to the town prison, where he can remain for months on end, if Your Highness requires, until his trial."

The Duchessa saw with despair that the Prince, instead of granting with a word so simple a request, had turned sombre; he was very red, he looked at the Duchessa, then lowered his eyes, and his cheeks grew pale. The idea of poison put forward at the wrong moment, had suggested to him an idea worthy of his father or of Philip II; but he dared not express it in words.

"Listen, Signora," he said at length, as though forcing himself to speak, and in a tone that was by no means gracious, "you look down on me as a child and, what is more, a creature without graces: very well, I am going to say something which is horrible, but which has just been suggested to me by the deep and true passion that I feel for you. If I believed for one moment in this poison, I should have taken action already, as in duty bound; but I see in your request only a passionate fancy, and one of which, I beg leave to state, I do not see all the consequences. You desire that I should act without consulting my Ministers, I who have been reigning for barely three months! You ask of me a great exception to my ordinary mode of action, which I regard as highly reasonable. It is you, Signora, who are here and now the Absolute Sovereign, you give me reason to hope in a matter which is everything to me; but, in an hour's time, when this imaginary poison, when this nightmare has vanished, my presence will become an annoyance to you, I shall forfeit your favour, Signora. Very well, I require an oath: swear to me, Signora, that if Fabrizio is restored to you safe and sound I shall obtain from you, in three months from now, all that my love can desire; you will assure the happiness of my entire life by placing at my disposal an hour of your own, and you will be wholly mine."

At that moment, the Castle clock struck two. "Ah! It is too late, perhaps," thought the Duchessa.

"I swear it," she cried, with a wild look in her eyes.

At once the Prince became another man; he ran to the far end of the gallery, where the Aide-de-Camp's room was.

"General Fontana, dash off to the citadel this instant, go up as quickly as possible to the room in which they have put Signor del Dongo, and bring him to me; I must speak to him within twenty minutes, fifteen if possible."

"Ah, General," cried the Duchessa, who had followed the Prince, "one minute may decide my life. A report which is doubtless false makes me fear poison for Fabrizio: shout to him, as soon as you are within earshot, not to eat. If he has touched his dinner, make him swallow an emetic; tell him that it is I who wish it, employ force if necessary; tell him that I am following close behind you, and I shall be obliged to you all my life."

"Signora Duchessa, my horse is saddled, I am generally considered a pretty good horseman, and I shall ride hell for leather; I shall be at the citadel eight minutes before you."

"And I, Signora Duchessa," cried the Prince, "I ask of you four of those eight minutes."

The Aide-de-Camp had vanished, he was a man who had no other merit than that of his horsemanship. No sooner had he shut the door than the young Prince, who seemed to have acquired some character, seized the Duchessa's hand.

"Condescend, Signora," he said to her with passion, "to come with me to the chapel." The Duchessa, at a loss for the first time in her life, followed him without uttering a word. The Prince and she passed rapidly down the whole length of the great gallery of the Palace, the chapel being at the other end. On entering the chapel, the Prince fell on his knees, almost as much before the Duchessa as before the altar.

"Repeat the oath," he said with passion: "if you had been fair, if the wretched fact of my being a Prince had not been against me, you would have granted me out of pity for my love what you now owe me because you have sworn it."

"If I see Fabrizio again not poisoned, if he is alive in a week from now, if His Highness will appoint him Coadjutor with eventual succession to Archbishop Landriani, my honour, my womanly dignity, everything shall be trampled under foot, and I will give myself to His Highness."

"But, *dear friend,*" said the Prince with a blend of timid anxiety and affection which was quite pleasing, "I am afraid of some ambush which I do not understand, and which might destroy my happiness; that would kill me. If the Archbishop opposes me with one of those ecclesiastical reasons which keep things dragging on for year after year, what will become of me? You see that I am behaving towards you with entire good faith; are you going to be a little Jesuit with me?"

"No: in good faith, if Fabrizio is saved, if, so far as lies in your power, you make him Coadjutor and a future Archbishop, I dishonour myself and I am yours.

"Your Highness undertakes to write *approved* on the margin of a request which His Grace the Archbishop will present to you in a week from now."

"I will sign you a blank sheet; reign over me and over my States," cried the Prince, colouring with happiness and really beside himself. He demanded a second oath. He was so deeply moved that he forgot the shyness that came so naturally to him, and, in this Palace chapel in which they were alone, murmured in an undertone to the Duchessa things which, uttered three days earlier, would have altered the opinion that she held of him. But in her the despair which Fabrizio's danger had caused her had given place to horror at the promise which had been wrung from her.

The Duchessa was completely upset by what she had just done. If she did not yet feel all the fearful bitterness of the word she had given, it was because her attention was occupied in wondering whether General Fontana would be able to reach the citadel in time.

To free herself from the madly amorous speeches of this boy, and to change the topic of conversation, she praised a famous picture by the Parmigianino, which hung over the high altar of the chapel.

"Be so good as to permit me to send it to you," said the Prince.

"I accept," replied the Duchessa; "but allow me to go and meet Fabrizio."

With a distracted air she told her coachman to put his horses into a gallop. On the bridge over the moat of the citadel she met General Fontana and Fabrizio, who were coming out on foot.

"Have you eaten?"

"No, by a miracle."

The Duchessa flung her arms round Fabrizio's neck and fell in a faint which lasted for an hour, and gave fears first for her life and afterwards for her reason.

The governor Fabio Conti had turned white with rage at the sight of General Fontana: he had been so slow in obeying the Prince's orders that the Aide-de-Camp, who supposed that the Duchessa was going to occupy the position of reigning mistress, had ended by losing his temper. The governor reckoned upon making Fabrizio's illness last for two or three days, and "now," he said to himself, "the General, a man

from the court, will find that insolent fellow writhing in the
agony which is my revenge for his escape."

Fabio Conti, lost in thought, stopped in the guard-room
on the ground floor of the Torre Farnese, from which he
hastily dismissed the soldiers: he did not wish to have any
witnesses of the scene which was about to be played. Five
minutes later he was petrified with astonishment on hearing
Fabrizio's voice, on seeing him, alive and alert, giving
General Fontana an account of his imprisonment. He
vanished.

Fabrizio shewed himself a perfect "gentleman" in his interview with the Prince. For one thing, he did not wish to
assume the air of a boy who takes fright at nothing. The
Prince asked him kindly how he felt: "Like a man, Serene
Highness, who is dying of hunger, having fortunately neither
broken my fast nor dined." After having had the honour to
thank the Prince, he requested permission to visit the Archbishop before surrendering himself at the town prison. The
Prince had turned prodigiously pale, when his boyish head
had been penetrated by the idea that this poison was not
altogether a chimæra of the Duchessa's imagination. Absorbed in this cruel thought, he did not at first reply to the
request to see the Archbishop which Fabrizio addressed to
him; then he felt himself obliged to atone for his distraction
by a profusion of graciousness.

"Go out alone, Signore, walk through the streets of my
capital unguarded. About ten or eleven o'clock you will return to prison, where I hope that you will not long remain."

On the morrow of this great day, the most remarkable of
his life, the Prince fancied himself a little Napoleon; he had
read that that great man had been kindly treated by several
of the beauties of his court. Once established as a Napoleon
in love, he remembered that he had been one also under fire.
His heart was still quite enraptured by the firmness of his
conduct with the Duchessa. The consciousness of having done
something difficult made him another man altogether for a
fortnight; he became susceptible to generous considerations;
he had some character.

He began this day by burning the patent of Conte made
out in favour of Rassi, which had been lying on his desk for
a month. He degraded General Fabio Conti, and called upon
Colonel Lange, his successor, for the truth as to the poison.
Lange, a gallant Polish officer, intimidated the gaolers, and
reported that there had been a design to poison Signor del

Dongo's breakfast; but too many people would have had to be taken into confidence. Arrangements to deal with his dinner were more successful; and, but for the arrival of General Fontana, Signor del Dongo was a dead man. The Prince was dismayed; but, as he was really in love, it was a consolation for him to be able to say to himself: "It appears that I really did save Signor del Dongo's life, and the Duchessa will never dare fail to keep the word she has given me." Another idea struck him: "My business is a great deal more difficult than I thought; everyone is agreed that the Duchessa is a woman of infinite cleverness, here my policy and my heart go together. It would be divine for me if she would consent to be my Prime Minister."

That evening, the Prince was so infuriated by the horrors that he had discovered that he would not take part in the play.

"I should be more than happy," he said to the Duchessa, "if you would reign over my States as you reign over my heart. To begin with, I am going to tell you how I have spent my day." He then told her everything, very exactly: the burning of Conte Rassi's patent, the appointment of Lange, his report on the poisoning, and so forth. "I find that I have very little experience for ruling. The Conte humiliates me by his jokes. He makes jokes even at the Council; and, in society, he says things the truth of which you are going to disprove; he says that I am a boy whom he leads wherever he chooses. Though one is a Prince, Signora, one is none the less a man, and these things annoy one. In order to give an air of improbability to the stories which Signor Mosca may repeat, they have made me summon to the Ministry that dangerous scoundrel Rassi, and now there is that General Conti who believes him to be still so powerful that he dare not admit that it was he or the Raversi who ordered him to destroy your nephew; I have a good mind simply to send General Fabio Conti before the court; the judges will see whether he is guilty of attempted poisoning."

"But, Prince, have you judges?"

"What!" said the Prince in astonishment.

"You have certain learned counsel who walk the streets with a solemn air; apart from that they always give the judgment that will please the dominant party at your court."

While the young Prince, now scandalised, uttered expressions which shewed his candour far more than his sagacity, the Duchessa was saying to herself:

"Does it really suit me to let Conti be disgraced? No, certainly not; for then his daughter's marriage with that honest simpleton the Marchese Crescenzi becomes impossible."

On this topic there was an endless discussion between the Duchessa and the Prince. The Prince was dazed with admiration. In consideration of the marriage of Clelia Conti to the Marchese Crescenzi, but on that express condition, which he laid down in an angry scene with the ex-governor, the Prince pardoned his attempt to poison; but, on the Duchessa's advice, banished him until the date of his daughter's marriage. The Duchessa imagined that it was no longer love that she felt for Fabrizio, but she was still passionately anxious for the marriage of Clelia Conti to the Marchese; there lay in that the vague hope that gradually she might see Fabrizio's preoccupation disappear.

The Prince, rapturously happy, wished that same evening publicly to disgrace the Minister Rassi. The Duchessa said to him with a laugh:

"Do you know a saying of Napoleon? A man placed in an exalted position, with the eyes of the whole world on him, ought never to allow himself to make violent movements. But this evening it is too late, let us leave business till to-morrow."

She wished to give herself time to consult the Conte, to whom she repeated very accurately the whole of the evening's conversation, suppressing however the frequent allusions to a promise which was poisoning her life. The Duchessa hoped to make herself so indispensable that she would be able to obtain an indefinite adjournment by saying to the Prince: "If you have the barbarity to insist upon subjecting me to that humiliation, which I will never forgive you, I leave your States the day after."

Consulted by the Duchessa as to the fate of Rassi, the Conte shewed himself most philosophic. General Fabio Conti and he went for a tour of Piedmont.

A singular difficulty arose in the trial of Fabrizio: the judges wished to acquit him by acclamation, and at the first sitting of the court. The Conte was obliged to use threats to enforce that the trial should last for at least a week, and the judges take the trouble to hear all the witnesses. "These fellows are always the same," he said to himself.

The day after his acquittal, Fabrizio del Dongo at last took possession of the place of Grand Vicar to the worthy Archbishop Landriani. On the same day the Prince signed the dispatches necessary to obtain Fabrizio's nomination as Coadjutor with eventual succession, and less than two months afterwards he was installed in that office.

Everyone complimented the Duchessa on her nephew's air of gravity; the fact was that he was in despair. The day after his deliverance, followed by the dismissal and banishment of General Fabio Conti and the Duchessa's arrival in high favour, Clelia had taken refuge with Contessa Contarini, her aunt, a woman of great wealth and great age, occupied exclusively in looking after her health. Clelia could, had she wished, have seen Fabrizio; but anyone acquainted with her previous commitments who had seen her behaviour now might have thought that with her lover's danger her love for him also had ceased. Not only did Fabrizio pass as often as he decently could before the *palazzo* Contarini, he had also succeeded, after endless trouble, in taking a little apartment opposite the windows of its first floor. On one occasion Clelia, having gone to the window without thinking, to see a procession pass, drew back at once, as though terror-stricken; she had caught sight of Fabrizio, dressed in black, but as a workman in very humble circumstances, looking at her from one of the windows of this rookery, which had panes of oiled paper, like his cell in the Torre Farnese. Fabrizio would fain have been able to persuade himself that Clelia was shunning him in consequence of her father's disgrace, which current report put down to the Duchessa; but he knew only too well another cause for this aloofness, and nothing could distract him from his melancholy.

He had been left unmoved by his acquittal, his installation in a fine office, the first that he had had to fill in his life, by his fine position in society, and finally by the assiduous court that was paid to him by all the ecclesiastics and all the devout laity in the diocese. The charming apartment that he occupied in the *palazzo* Sanseverina was no longer adequate. Greatly to her delight, the Duchessa was obliged to give up to him all the second floor of her *palazzo* and two fine rooms on the first, which were always filled with people awaiting their turn to pay their respects to the young Coadjutor. The clause securing his eventual succession had created a surprising effect in the country; people now ascribed to Fabrizio as virtues all those firm qualities in his character which before had so greatly scandalised the poor, foolish courtiers.

It was a great lesson in philosophy to Fabrizio to find himself perfectly insensible of all these honours, and far more unhappy in this magnificent apartment, with ten flunkeys wearing his livery, than he had been in his wooden cell in the Torre Farnese, surrounded by hideous gaolers, and always in fear for his life. His mother and sister, the Duchessa V——, who came to Parma to see him in his glory, were struck by his profound melancholy. The Marchesa del Dongo, now the least romantic of women, was so greatly alarmed by it that she imagined that they must, in the Torre Farnese, have given him some slow poison. Despite her extreme discretion, she felt it her duty to speak of so extraordinary a melancholy, and Fabrizio replied only by tears.

A swarm of advantages, due to his brilliant position, produced no other effect on him than to make him ill-tempered. His brother, that vain soul gangrened by the vilest selfishness, wrote him what was almost an official letter of congratulation, and in this letter was enclosed a draft for fifty thousand francs, in order that he might, said the new Marchese, purchase horses and a carriage worthy of his name. Fabrizio sent this money to his younger sister, who was poorly married.

Conte Mosca had ordered a fine translation to be made, in Italian, of the genealogy of the family Valserra del Dongo, originally published in Latin by Fabrizio, Archbishop of Parma. He had it splendidly printed, with the Latin text on alternate pages; the engravings had been reproduced by superb lithographs made in Paris. The Duchessa had asked that a fine portrait of Fabrizio should be placed opposite that of the old Archbishop. This translation was published as being the work of Fabrizio during his first imprisonment. But all the spirit was crushed out of our hero; even the vanity so natural to mankind; he did not deign to read a single page of this work which was attributed to himself. His social position made it incumbent upon him to present a magnificently bound copy to the Prince, who felt that he owed him some compensation for the cruel death to which he had come so near, and accorded him the grand entry into his bedchamber, a favour which confers the rank of *Excellency*.

CHAPTER TWENTY-SIX

THE ONLY MOMENTS in which Fabrizio had any chance of escaping from his profound melancholy were those which he spent hidden behind a pane, the glass of which he had had replaced by a sheet of oiled paper, in the window of his apartment opposite the *palazzo* Contarini, in which, as we know, Clelia had taken refuge; on the few occasions on which he had seen her since his leaving the citadel, he had been profoundly distressed by a striking change, and one that seemed to him of the most evil augury. Since her fall, Clelia's face had assumed a character of nobility and seriousness that was truly remarkable; one would have called her a woman of thirty. In this extraordinary change, Fabrizio caught the reflexion of some firm resolution. "At every moment of the day," he said to himself, "she is swearing to herself to be faithful to the vow she made to the Madonna, and never to see me again."

Fabrizio guessed a part only of Clelia's miseries; she knew that her father, having fallen into deep disgrace, could not return to Parma and reappear at court (without which life for him was impossible) until the day of her marriage to the Marchese Crescenzi; she wrote to her father that she desired this marriage. The General had then retired to Turin, where he was ill with grief. Truly, the counter-effect of that desperate remedy had been to add ten years to her age.

She had soon discovered that Fabrizio had a window opposite the *palazzo* Contarini; but only once had she had the misfortune to behold him; as soon as she saw the poise of a head or a man's figure that in any way resembled his, she at once shut her eyes. Her profound piety and her confidence in the help of the Madonna were from then onwards her sole resources. She had the grief of feeling no respect for her father; the character of her future husband seemed to her perfectly lifeless and on a par with the emotional manners of high society; finally she adored a man whom she must never see again, and who at the same time had certain rights over her. She would need, after her marriage, to go and live two hundred leagues from Parma.

Fabrizio was aware of Clelia's intense modesty, he knew how greatly any extraordinary enterprise, that might form a subject for gossip, were it discovered, was bound to displease her. And yet, driven to extremes by the excess of his melancholy and by Clelia's constantly turning away her eyes from him, he made bold to try to purchase two of the servants of Signora Contarini, her aunt. One day, at nightfall, Fabrizio, dressed as a prosperous countryman, presented himself at the door of the *palazzo*, where one of the servants whom he had bribed was waiting for him; he announced himself as coming from Turin and bearing letters for Clelia from her father. The servant went to deliver the message, and took him up to an immense ante-room on the first floor of the *palazzo*. It was here that Fabrizio passed what was perhaps the most anxious quarter of an hour in his life. If Clelia rejected him, there was no more hope of peace for his mind. "To put an end to the incessant worries which my new dignity heaps upon me, I shall remove from the Church an unworthy priest, and, under an assumed name, seek refuge in some Charterhouse." At length the servant came to inform him that Signorina Clelia Conti was willing to receive him. Our hero's courage failed him completely; he almost collapsed with fear as he climbed the stair to the second floor.

Clelia was sitting at a little table on which stood a single candle. No sooner had she recognised Fabrizio under his disguise than she rose and fled, hiding at the far end of the room.

"This is how you care for my salvation!" she cried to him, hiding her face in her hands. "You know very well, when my father was at the point of death after taking poison, I made a vow to the Madonna that I would never see you. I have never failed to keep that vow save on that day, the most wretched day of my life, when I felt myself bound by conscience to snatch you from death. It is already far more than you deserve if, by a strained and no doubt criminal interpretation of my vow, I consent to listen to you."

This last sentence so astonished Fabrizio that it took him some moments to grasp its joyful meaning. He had expected the most fiery anger, and to see Clelia fly from the room; at length his presence of mind returned, and he extinguished the one candle. Although he believed that he had understood Clelia's orders, he was trembling all over as he advanced towards the end of the room, where she had taken refuge behind a sofa; he did not know whether it would offend her if he kissed her hand; she was all tremulous with love and threw herself into his arms.

"Dear Fabrizio," she said to him, "how long you have been in coming! I can only speak to you for a moment, for I am sure it is a great sin; and when I promised never to see you, I am sure I meant also to promise not to hear you speak. But how could you pursue with such barbarity the idea of vengeance that my poor father had? For, after all, it was he who was first nearly poisoned to assist your escape. Ought you not to do something for me, who have exposed my reputation to such risks in order to save you? And besides you are now bound absolutely in Holy Orders; you could not marry me any longer, even though I should find a way of getting rid of that odious Marchese. And then how did you dare, on the afternoon of the procession, have the effrontery to look at me in broad daylight, and so violate, in the most flagrant fashion, the holy promise that I had made to the Madonna?"

Fabrizio clasped her in his arms, carried out of himself by his surprise and joy.

A conversation which began with such a quantity of things to be said could not finish for a long time. Fabrizio told her the exact truth as to her father's banishment; the Duchessa had had no part in it whatsoever, for the simple reason that she had never for a single instant believed that the idea of poison had originated with General Conti; she had always thought that it was a little game on the part of the Raversi faction, who wished to drive Conte Mosca from Parma. This historical truth developed at great length made Clelia very happy; she was wretched at having to hate anyone who belonged to Fabrizio. Now she no longer regarded the Duchessa with a jealous eye.

The happiness established by this evening lasted only a few days.

The worthy Don Cesare arrived from Turin; and, taking courage in the perfect honesty of his heart, ventured to send in his name to the Duchessa. After asking her to give him her word that she would not abuse the confidence he was about to repose in her, he admitted that his brother, led astray by a false point of honour, and thinking himself challenged and lowered in public opinion by Fabrizio's escape, had felt bound to avenge himself.

Don Cesare had not been speaking for two minutes before his cause was won: his perfect goodness had touched the Duchessa, who was by no means accustomed to such a spectacle. He appealed to her as a novelty.

"Hasten the marriage between the General's daughter and the Marchese Crescenzi, and I give you my word that I will do all that lies in my power to ensure that the General is received as though he were returning from a tour abroad. I shall invite him to dinner; does that satisfy you? No doubt there will be some coolness at the beginning, and the General must on no account be in a hurry to ask for his place as governor of the citadel. But you know that I have a friendly feeling for the Marchese, and I shall retain no rancour towards his father-in-law."

Fortified by these words, Don Cesare came to tell his niece that she held in her hands the life of her father, who was ill with despair. For many months past he had not appeared at any court.

Clelia decided to go to visit her father, who was hiding under an assumed name in a village near Turin; for he had supposed that the court of Parma would demand his extradition from that of Turin, to put him on his trial. She found him ill and almost insane. That same evening she wrote Fabrizio a letter threatening an eternal rupture. On receiving this letter, Fabrizio, who was developing a character closely resembling that of his mistress, went into retreat in the convent of Velleja, situated in the mountains, ten leagues from Parma. Clelia wrote him a letter of ten pages: she had sworn to him, before, that she would never marry the Marchese without his consent; now she asked this of him, and Fabrizio granted it from his retreat at Valleja, in a letter full of the purest friendship.

On receiving this letter, the friendliness of which, it must be admitted, irritated her, Clelia herself fixed the day of her wedding, the festivities surrounding which enhanced still further the brilliance with which the court of Parma, that winter, shone.

Ranuccio-Ernesto V was a miser at heart; but he was desperately in love, and he hoped to establish the Duchessa permanently at his court; he begged his mother to accept a very considerable sum of money, and to give entertainments. The Grand Mistress contrived to make an admirable use of this increase of wealth; the entertainments at Parma, that winter, recalled the great days of the court of Milan and of that charming Prince Eugène, Viceroy of Italy, whose virtues have left so lasting a memory.

His duties as Coadjutor had summoned Fabrizio back to Parma; but he announced that, for spiritual reasons, he would continue his retreat in the small apartment which his protector, Monsignor Landriani, had forced him to take in the Archbishop's Palace; and he went to shut himself up there, accompanied by a single servant. Thus he was present at none of the brilliant festivities of the court, an abstention which won for him at Parma, and throughout his future diocese, an immense reputation for sanctity. An unforeseen consequence of this retreat, inspired in Fabrizio solely by his profound and hopeless sorrow, was that the good Archbishop Landriani, who had always loved him, began to be slightly jealous of him. The Archbishop felt it his duty (and rightly) to attend all the festivities at court, as is the custom in Italy. On these occasions he wore a ceremonial costume, which was, more or less, the same as that in which he was to be seen in the choir of his Cathedral. The hundreds of servants gathered in the colonnaded ante-chamber of the Palace never failed to rise and ask for a blessing from Monsignore, who was kind enough to stop and give it them. It was in one of these moments of solemn silence that Monsignor Landriani heard a voice say: "Our Archbishop goes out to balls, and Monsignor del Dongo never leaves his room!"

From that moment the immense favour that Fabrizio had enjoyed in the Archbishop's Palace was at an end; but he could now fly with his own wings. All this conduct, which had been inspired only by the despair in which Clelia's marriage plunged him, was regarded as due to a simple and sublime piety, and the faithful read, as a work of edification, the translation of the genealogy of his family, which reeked of the most insane vanity. The booksellers prepared a lithographed edition of his portrait, which was bought up in a few days, and mainly by the humbler classes; the engraver, in his ignorance, had reproduced round Fabrizio's portrait a number of the ornaments which ought only to be found on the portraits of Bishops, and to which a Coadjutor could have no claim. The Archbishop saw one of these portraits, and his rage knew no bounds; he sent for Fabrizio and addressed him in the harshest words, and in terms which his

passion rendered at times extremely coarse. Fabrizio required
no effort, as may well be imagined, to conduct himself as
Fénelon would have done in similar circumstances; he
listened to the Archbishop with all the humility and respect
possible; and, when the prelate had ceased speaking, told
him the whole story of the translation of the genealogy
made by Conte Mosca's orders, at the time of his first imprisonment. It had been published with a worldly object,
which had always seemed to him hardly befitting a man of
his cloth. As for the portrait, he had been entirely uncon-
cerned with the second edition, as with the first; and the
bookseller having sent to him, at the Archbishop's Palace,
during his retreat, twenty-four copies of this second edition,
he had sent his servant to buy a twenty-fifth; and, having
learned in this way that the portrait was being sold for thirty
soldi, he had sent a hundred francs in payment of the
twenty-four copies.

All these arguments, albeit set forth in the most reasonable terms by a man who had many other sorrows in his
heart, lashed the Archbishop's anger to madness; he went
so far as to accuse Fabrizio of hypocrisy.

"That is what these common people are like," Fabrizio
said to himself, "even when they have brains!"

He had at the time a more serious anxiety; this was his
aunt's letters, in which she absolutely insisted on his coming
back to occupy his apartment in the *palazzo* Sanseverina,
or at least coming to see her sometimes. There Fabrizio was
certain of hearing talk of the splendid festivities given by
the Marchese Crescenzi on the occasion of his marriage; and
this was what he was not sure of his ability to endure without creating a scene.

When the marriage ceremony was celebrated, for eight
whole days in succession Fabrizio vowed himself to the most
complete silence, after ordering his servant and the members of the Archbishop's household with whom he had any
dealings never to utter a word to him.

Monsignor Landriani having learned of this new affectation sent for Fabrizio far more often than usual, and tried
to engage him in long conversations; he even obliged him
to attend conferences with certain Canons from the country,
who complained that the Archbishop had infringed their
privileges. Fabrizio took all these things with the perfect
indifference of a man who has other thoughts on his mind.
"It would be better for me," he thought, "to become a

Carthusian; I should suffer less among the rocks of Velleja."

He went to see his aunt, and could not restrain his tears as he embraced her. She found him so greatly altered, his eyes, still more enlarged by his extreme thinness, had so much the air of starting from his head, and he himself presented so pinched and unhappy an appearance, that at this first encounter the Duchessa herself could not restrain her tears either; but a moment later, when she had reminded herself that all this change in the appearance of this handsome young man had been caused by Clelia's marriage, her feelings were almost equal in vehemence to those of the Archbishop, although more skilfully controlled. She was so barbarous as to discourse at length of certain picturesque details which had been a feature of the charming entertainments given by the Marchese Crescenzi. Fabrizio made no reply; but his eyes closed slightly with a convulsive movement, and he became even paler than he already was, which at first sight would have seemed impossible. In these moments of keen grief, his pallor assumed a greenish hue.

Conte Mosca joined them, and what he then saw, a thing which seemed to him incredible, finally and completely cured him of the jealousy which Fabrizio had never ceased to inspire in him. This able man employed the most delicate and ingenious turns of speech in an attempt to restore to Fabrizio some interest in the things of this world. The Conte had always felt for him a great esteem and a certain degree of friendship; this friendship, being no longer counterbalanced by jealousy, became at that moment almost devotion. "There's no denying it, he has paid dearly for his fine fortune," he said to himself, going over the tale of Fabrizio's misadventures. On the pretext of letting him see the picture by the Parmigianino which the Prince had sent to the Duchessa, the Conte drew Fabrizio aside.

"Now, my friend, let us speak as man to man: can I help you in any way? You need not be afraid of any questions on my part; still, can money be of use to you, can power help you? Speak, I am at your orders; if you prefer to write, write to me."

Fabrizio embraced him tenderly and spoke of the picture.

"Your conduct is a masterpiece of the finest policy," the Conte said to him, returning to the light tone of their previous conversation; "you are laying up for yourself a very agreeable future, the Prince respects you, the people venerate you, your little-worn black coat gives Monsignor Landriani some bad nights. I have some experience of life, and I can swear to you that I should not know what advice to give you to improve upon what I see. Your first step in the world at the age of twenty-five has carried you to perfection. People talk of you a great deal at court; and do you know to what you owe that distinction, unique at your age? To the little-worn black coat. The Duchessa and I have at our disposal, as you know, Petrarch's old house on that fine slope in the middle of the forest, near the Po; if ever you are weary of the little mischief-makings of envy, it has occurred to me that you might be the successor of Petrarch, whose fame will enhance your own." The Conte was racking his brains to make a smile appear on that anchorite face, but failed. What made the change more striking was that, before this latest phase, if Fabrizio's features had a defect, it was that of presenting sometimes, at the wrong moment, an expression of gaiety and pleasure.

The Conte did not let him go without telling him that, notwithstanding his retreat, it would be perhaps an affectation if he did not appear at court the following Saturday, which was the Princess's birthday. These words were a dagger-thrust to Fabrizio. "Great God!" he thought, "what have I let myself in for here?" He could not think without shuddering of the meeting that might occur at court. This idea absorbed every other; he thought that the only thing left to him was to arrive at the Palace at the precise moment at which the doors of the rooms would be opened.

And so it happened that the name of Monsignor del Dongo was one of the first to be announced on the evening of the gala reception, and the Princess greeted him with the greatest possible distinction. Fabrizio's eyes were fastened on the clock, and, at the instant at which it marked the twentieth minute of his presence in the room, he was rising to take his leave, when the Prince joined his mother. After paying his respects to him for some moments, Fabrizio was again, by a skilful stratagem, making his way to the door, when there befell at his expense one of those little trifling points of court etiquette which the Grand Mistress knew so well how to handle: the Chamberlain in waiting ran after him to tell him that he had been put down to make up the Prince's table at whist. At Parma this was a signal honour, and far above the rank which the Coadjutor held in society. To play whist with the Prince was a marked honour even for the Archbishop. At the Chamberlain's words Fabrizio felt his heart pierced, and although a lifelong enemy of anything like a scene in public, he was on the point of going to tell him that he had been seized with a sudden fit of giddiness; but he reflected that he would be exposed to questions and polite expressions of sympathy, more intolerable even than the game. That day he had a horror of speaking.

Fortunately the General of the Friars Minor happened to be one of the prominent personages who had come to pay their respects to the Princess. This friar, a most learned man, a worthy rival of the Fontanas and the Duvoisins, had taken his place in a far corner of the room: Fabrizio took up a position facing him, so that he could not see the door, and began to talk theology. But he could not prevent his ear from hearing a servant announce the Signor Marchese and Signora Marchesa Crescenzi. Fabrizio, to his surprise, felt a violent impulse of anger.

"If I were Borso Valserra," he said to himself (this being one of the generals of the first Sforza), "I should go and stab that lout of a Marchese, and with that very same dagger with the ivory handle which Clelia gave me on that happy day, and I should teach him to have the insolence to present himself with his Marchesa in a room in which I am."

His expression altered so greatly that the General of the Friars Minor said to him:

"Does Your Excellency feel unwell?"

"I have a raging headache . . . these lights are hurting me . . . and I am staying here only because I have been put down for the Prince's whist-table."

On hearing this the General of the Friars Minor, who was of plebeian origin, was so disconcerted that, not knowing what to do, he began to bow to Fabrizio, who, for his part, far more seriously disturbed than the General, started to talk with a strange volubility: he noticed that there was a great silence in the room behind him, but would not turn round to look. Suddenly a baton tapped a desk; a *ritornello* was played, and the famous Signora P—— sang that air of Cimarosa, at one time so popular: *Quelle pupille tenere!*

Fabrizio stood firm throughout the opening bars, but presently his anger melted away, and he felt a compelling need to shed tears. "Great God!" he said to himself, "what a ridiculous scene! and with my cloth, too!" He felt it wiser to talk about himself.

"These violent headaches, when I do anything to thwart them, as I am doing this evening," he said to the General of the Minorites, "end in floods of tears which provide food for scandal in a man of our calling; and so I request Your Illustrious Reverence to allow me to look at him while I cry, and not to pay any attention."

"Our Father Provincial at Catanzaro suffers from the same disability," said the General of the Minorites. And he began in an undertone a long narrative.

The absurdity of this story, which included the details of the Father Provincial's evening meals, made Fabrizio smile, a thing which had not happened to him for a long time; but presently he ceased to listen to the General of the Minorites. Signora P—— was singing, with divine talent, an air of Pergolese (the Duchessa had a fondness for old music). She was interrupted by a slight sound, a few feet away from Fabrizio; for the first time in the evening, he turned his head, to look. The chair that had been the cause of this faint creak in the woodwork of the floor was occupied by the Marchesa Crescenzi whose eyes, filled with tears, met the direct gaze of Fabrizio's which were in much the same state. The Marchesa bent her head; Fabrizio continued to gaze at her for some moments: he made a thorough study of that head loaded with diamonds; but his gaze expressed anger and disdain. Then, saying to himself: *"and my eyes shall never look upon you,"* he turned back to his Father General, and said to him:

"There, now, my weakness is taking me worse than ever."

And indeed, Fabrizio wept hot tears for more than half an hour. Fortunately, a Symphony of Mozart, horribly mutilated, as is the way in Italy, came to his rescue and helped him to dry his tears.

He stood firm and did not turn his eyes towards the Marchesa Crescenzi; but Signora P—— sang again, and Fabrizio's soul, soothed by his tears, arrived at a state of perfect repose. Then life appeared to him in a new light. "Am I pretending," he asked himself, "to be able to forget her in the first few moments? Would such a thing be possible?" The idea came to him: "Can I be more unhappy than I have been for the last two months? Then, if nothing can add to my anguish, why resist the pleasure of seeing her? She has forgotten her vows; she is fickle: are not all women so? But who could deny her a heavenly beauty? She has a look in her eyes that sends me into ecstasies, whereas I have to make an effort to force myself to look at the women who are considered the greatest beauties! Very well, why not let myself be enraptured? It will be at least a moment of respite."

Fabrizio had some knowledge of men, but no experience of the passions, otherwise he would have told himself that this momentary pleasure, to which he was about to yield, would render futile all the efforts that he had been making for the last two months to forget Clelia.

That poor woman would not have come to this party save under compulsion from her husband; even then she wished to slip away after half an hour, on the excuse of her health, but the Marchese assured her that to send for her carriage to go away, when many carriages were still arriving, would be a thing absolutely without precedent, which might even be interpreted as an indirect criticism of the party given by the Princess.

"In my capacity as *Cavaliere d'onore*," the Marchese added, "I have to remain in the drawing-room at the Princess's orders, until everyone has gone. There may be and no doubt will be orders to be given to the servants, they are so careless! And would you have a mere Gentleman Usher usurp that honour?"

Clelia resigned herself; she had not seen Fabrizio; she still hoped that he might not have come to this party. But at the moment when the concert was about to begin, the Princess having given the ladies leave to be seated, Clelia, who was not at all alert in that sort of thing, let all the best places near the Princess be snatched from her, and was obliged to go and look for a chair at the end of the room, in the very corner to which Fabrizio had withdrawn. When she reached her chair, the costume, unusual in such a place, of the General of the Friars Minor caught her eye, and at first she did not observe the other man, slim and dressed in a plain black coat, who was talking to him; nevertheless a certain secret impulse brought her gaze to rest on this man. "Everyone here is wearing uniform, or a richly embroidered coat: who can that young man be in such a plain black coat?" She was looking at him, profoundly attentive, when a lady, taking her seat beside her, caused her chair to move. Fabrizio turned his head: she did not recognise him, he had so altered. At first she said to herself: "That is like him, it must be his elder brother; but I thought there were only a few years between them, and that is a man of forty." Suddenly she recognised him by a movement of his lips.

"Poor man, how he has suffered!" she said to herself. And she bent her head, bowed down by grief, and not in fidelity to her vow. Her heart was convulsed with pity; "after nine months in prison, he did not look anything like that." She did not look at him again; but, without actually turning her eyes in his direction, she could see all his movements.

After the concert, she saw him go up to the Prince's card-table, placed a few feet from the throne; she breathed a sigh of relief when Fabrizio was thus removed to a certain distance from her.

But the Marchese Crescenzi had been greatly annoyed to see his wife relegated to a place so far from the throne; all evening he had been occupied in persuading a lady seated three chairs away from the Princess, whose husband was under a financial obligation to him, that she would do well to change places with the Marchesa. The poor woman resisting, as was natural, he went in search of the debtor husband, who let his better half hear the sad voice of reason, and finally the Marchese had the pleasure of effecting the exchange; he went to find his wife. "You are always too modest," he said to her. "Why walk like that with downcast eyes? Anyone would take you for one of those cits' wives astonished at finding themselves here, whom everyone else is astonished, too, to see here. That fool of a Grand Mistress does nothing else but collect them! And they talk of retarding the advance of Jacobinism! Remember that your husband occupies the first position, among the gentlemen, at the Princess's court; and that even should the Republicans succeed in suppressing the court, and even the nobility, your husband would still be the richest man in this State. That is an idea which you do not keep sufficiently in your head."

The chair on which the Marchese had the pleasure of installing his wife was but six paces from the Prince's card-table: she saw Fabrizio only in profile, but she found him grown so thin, he had, above all, the air of being so far above everything that might happen in this world, he who before would never let any incident pass without making his comment, that she finally arrived at the terrible conclusion: Fabrizio had altogether changed; he had forgotten her; if he had grown so thin, that was the effect of the severe fasts to which his piety subjected him. Clelia was confirmed in this sad thought by the conversation of all her neighbours: the name of the Coadjutor was on every tongue; they sought a reason for the signal favour which they saw conferred upon him: for him, so young, to be admitted to the Prince's table! They marvelled at the polite indifference and the air of pride with which he threw down his cards, even when he had His Highness for a partner.

"But this is incredible!" cried certain old courtiers; "his aunt's favour has quite turned his head. . . . But, mercifully, it won't last; our Sovereign does not like people to put on these little airs of superiority." The Duchessa approached the Prince; the courtiers, who kept at a most respectful distance from the card-table, so that they could hear only a few stray words of the Prince's conversation, noticed that Fabrizio blushed deeply. "His aunt has been teaching him a lesson," they said to themselves, "about those grand airs of indifference." Fabrizio had just caught the sound of Clelia's voice, she was replying to the Princess, who, in making her tour of the ball-room, had addressed a few words to the wife of her *Cavaliere d'onore*. The moment arrived when Fabrizio had to change his place at the whist-table; he then found himself directly opposite Clelia, and gave himself up repeatedly to the pleasure of contemplating her. The poor Marchesa, feeling his gaze rest upon her, lost countenance altogether. More than once she forgot what she owed to her vow: in her desire to read what was going on in Fabrizio's heart, she fixed her eyes on him.

The Prince's game ended, the ladies rose to go into the supper-room. There was some slight confusion. Fabrizio found himself close to Clelia; his mind was still quite made up, but he happened to recognise a faint perfume which she used on her clothes; this sensation overthrew all the resolutions that he had made. He approached her and repeated, in an undertone and as though he were speaking to himself, two lines from that sonnet of Petrarch which he had sent her from Lake Maggiore, printed on a silk handkerchief:

"Nessum visse giammai più di me lieto;
    Nessun vive più tristo e giorni e notti."

"No, he has not forgotten me," Clelia told herself with a transport of joy. "That fine soul is not inconstant!"

"Esser po in prima ogni impossibil cosa
    Ch'altri che morte od ella sani il colpo

Ch'Amor co' suoi begli occhi al cor m'impresse,"

Clelia ventured to repeat to herself these lines of Petrarch.

The Princess withdrew immediately after supper; the Prince had gone with her to her room and did not appear again in the reception rooms. As soon as this became known, everyone wished to leave at once; there was complete confusion in the ante-rooms; Clelia found herself close to Fabrizio; the profound misery depicted on his features moved her to pity. "Let us forget the past," she said to him, "and keep this reminder of *friendship*." As she said these words, she held out her fan so that he might take it.

Everything changed in Fabrizio's eyes; in an instant he was another man; the following day he announced that his retreat was at an end, and returned to occupy his magnificent apartment in the *palazzo* Sanseverina. The Archbishop said, and believed, that the favour which the Prince had shewn him in admitting him to his game had completely turned the head of this new saint: the Duchessa saw that he had come to terms with Clelia. This thought, coming to intensify the misery that was caused her by the memory of a fatal promise, finally decided her to absent herself for a while. People marvelled at her folly. What! Leave the court at the moment when the favour that she enjoyed appeared to have no bounds! The Conte, perfectly happy since he had seen that there was no love between Fabrizio and the Duchessa, said to his friend: "This new Prince is virtue incarnate, but I have called him *that boy:* will he ever forgive me? I can see only one way of putting myself back in his good books, that is absence. I am going to shew myself a perfect model of courtesy and respect, after which I shall be ill, and shall ask leave to retire. You will allow me that, now that Fabrizio's fortune is assured. But will you make me the immense sacrifice," he added, laughing, "of exchanging the sublime title of Duchessa for another greatly inferior? For my own amusement, I am leaving everything here in an inextricable confusion; I had four or five workers in my various Ministries, I placed them all on the pension list two months ago, because they read the French newspapers; and I have filled their places with blockheads of the first order.

"After our departure, the Prince will find himself in such difficulties that, in spite of the horror that he feels for Rassi's character, I have no doubt that he will be obliged to recall him, and I myself am only awaiting an order from the tyrant who disposes of my fate to write a letter of tender friendship to my friend Rassi, and tell him that I have every reason to hope that presently justice will be done to his merits."

CHAPTER TWENTY-SEVEN

THIS SERIOUS conversation was held on the day following Fabrizio's return to the *palazzo* Sanseverina; the Duchessa was still overcome by the joy that radiated from Fabrizio's every action. "So," she said to herself, "that little saint has deceived me! She has not been able to hold out against her lover for three months even."

The certainty of a happy ending had given that pusillanimous creature, the young Prince, the courage to love; he knew something of the preparations for flight that were being made at the *palazzo* Sanseverina; and his French valet, who had little belief in the virtue of great ladies, gave him courage with respect to the Duchessa. Ernesto V allowed himself to take a step for which he was severely reproved by the Princess and all the sensible people at court; to the populace it appeared to set the seal on the astonishing favour which the Duchessa enjoyed. The Prince went to see her in her *palazzo*.

"You are leaving," he said to her in a serious tone which the Duchessa thought odious; "you are leaving, you are going to play me false and violate your oath! And yet, if I had delayed ten minutes in granting you Fabrizio's pardon, he would have been dead. And you leave me in this wretched state! When but for your oath I should never have had the courage to love you as I do! Have you no sense of honour, then?"

"Think for a little, Prince. In the whole of your life has there been a period equal in happiness to the four months that have just gone by? Your glory as Sovereign, and, I venture to think, your happiness as a man, have never risen to such a pitch. This is the compact that I propose; if you deign to consent to it, I shall not be your

455

mistress for a fleeting instant, and by virtue of an oath extorted by fear, but I shall consecrate every moment of my life to procuring your happiness, I shall be always what I have been for the last four months, and perhaps love will come to crown friendship. I would not swear to the contrary."

"Very well," said the Prince, delighted, "take on another part, be something more still, reign at once over my heart and over my States, be my Prime Minister; I offer you such a marriage as is permitted by the regrettable conventions of my rank; we have an example close at hand: the King of Naples has recently married the Duchessa di Partana. I offer you all that I have to offer, a marriage of the same sort. I am going to add a distressing political consideration to shew you that I am no longer a mere boy, and that I have thought of everything. I lay no stress on the condition which I impose on myself of being the last Sovereign of my race, the sorrow of seeing in my lifetime the Great Powers dispose of my succession; I bless these very genuine drawbacks, since they offer me additional means of proving to you my esteem and my passion."

The Duchessa did not hesitate for an instant; the Prince bored her, and the Conte seemed to her perfectly suitable; there was only one man in the world who could be preferred to him. Besides, she ruled the Conte, and the Prince, dominated by the exigencies of his rank, would more or less rule her. Then, too, he might become unfaithful to her, and take mistresses; the difference of age would seem, in a very few years, to give him the right to do so.

From the first moment, the prospect of boredom had settled the whole question; however, the Duchessa, who wished to be as charming as possible, asked leave to reflect.

It would take too long to recount here the almost loving turns of speech and the infinitely graceful terms in which she managed to clothe her refusal. The Prince flew into a rage; he saw all his happiness escaping. What was to become of him when the Duchessa had left his court? Besides, what a humiliation to be refused! "And what will my French valet say when I tell him of my defeat?"

The Duchessa knew how to calm the Prince, and to bring the discussion back gradually to her actual terms.

"If Your Highness deigns to consent not to press for the fulfilment of a fatal promise, and one that is horrible in my eyes, as making me incur my own contempt, I shall spend my life at his court, and that court will always be what it has been this winter; every moment of my time will be devoted to contributing to his happiness as a man, and to his glory as a Sovereign. If he insists on binding me by my oath, he will be destroying the rest of my life, and will at once see me leave his States, never to return. The day on which I shall have lost my honour will be also the last day on which I shall set eyes on you."

But the Prince was obstinate, like all pusillanimous creatures; moreover his pride as a man and a Sovereign was irritated by the refusal of his hand; he thought of all the difficulties which he would have had to overcome to make this marriage be accepted, difficulties which, nevertheless, he was determined to conquer.

For the next three hours, the same arguments were repeated on either side, often interspersed with very sharp words. The Prince exclaimed:

"Do you then wish me to believe, Signora, that you are lacking in honour? If I had hesitated so long on the day when General Fabio Conti was giving Fabrizio poison, you would at present be occupied in erecting a tomb to him in one of the churches of Parma."

"Not at Parma, certainly, in this land of poisoners."

"Very well then, go, Signora Duchessa," retorted the Prince angrily, "and you will take with you my contempt."

As he was leaving, the Duchessa said to him in a whisper:

"Very well, be here at ten o'clock this evening, in the strictest incognito, and you shall have your fool's bargain. You will then have seen me for the last time, and I would have devoted my life to making you as happy as an Absolute Prince can be in this age of Jacobins. And think what your court will be when I am no longer here to extricate it by force from its innate dulness and mischief."

"For your part, you refuse the crown of Parma, and more than the crown, for you would not have been the ordinary Princess, married for political reasons and without being loved; my heart is all yours, and you would have seen yourself for ever the absolute mistress of my actions as of my government."

"Yes, but the Princess your mother would have the right to look down upon me as a vile intriguer."

"What then; I should banish the Princess with a pension."

There were still three quarters of an hour of cutting retorts. The Prince, who had a delicate nature, could not make up his mind either to enjoy his rights, or to let the Duchessa go. He had been told that after the first moment has been obtained, no matter how, women come back.

Driven from the house by the indignant Duchessa, he had the temerity to return, trembling all over and extremely unhappy, at three minutes to ten. At half past ten the Duchessa stepped into her carriage and started for Bologna. She wrote to the Conte as soon as she was outside the Prince's States:

"The sacrifice has been made. Do not ask me to be merry for a month. I shall not see Fabrizio again; I await you at Bologna, and when you please I will be the Contessa Mosca. I ask you one thing only, do not ever force me to appear again in the land I am leaving, and remember always that instead of an income of 150,000 lire, you are going to have thirty or forty thousand at the very most. All the fools have been watching you with gaping mouths, and for the future you will be respected only so long as you demean yourself to understand all their petty ideas. *Tu l'as voulu, George Dandin!*"

A week later their marriage was celebrated at Perugia, in a church in which the Conte's ancestors were buried. The Prince was in despair. The Duchessa had received from him three or four couriers, and had not failed to return his letters to him, in fresh envelopes, with their seals unbroken. Ernesto V had bestowed a magnificent pension on the Conte, and had given the Grand Cordon of his order to Fabrizio.

"That is what pleased me most in his farewells. We parted," said the Conte to the new Contessa Mosca della Rovere, "the best friends in the world; he gave me a Spanish Grand Cordon, and diamonds which are worth quite as much as the Grand Cordon. He told me that he would make me a Duca, but he wished to keep that in reserve, as a way of bringing you back to his States. And so I am charged to inform you, a fine mission for a husband, that if you deign to return to Parma, be it only for a month, I shall be made Duca, with whatever title you may select, and you shall have a fine estate."

This the Duchessa refused with an expression of horror.

After the scene that had occurred at the ball at court, which seemed fairly decisive, Clelia seemed to retain no memory of the love which she had for a moment reciprocated; the most violent remorse had seized hold of that virtuous and Christian soul. All this Fabrizio understood quite well, and in spite of all the hopes that he sought to entertain, a sombre misery took possession similarly of his soul. This time, however, his misery did not send him into retreat, as on the occasion of Clelia's marriage.

The Conte had requested *his nephew* to keep him exactly informed of all that went on at court, and Fabrizio, who was beginning to realise all that he owed to him, had promised himself that he would carry out this mission faithfully.

Like everyone in the town and at court, Fabrizio had no doubt that the Conte intended to return to the Ministry, and with more power than he had ever had before. The Conte's forecasts were not long in taking effect: in less than six weeks after his departure, Rassi was Prime Minister, Fabio Conti Minister of War, and the prisons, which the Conte had nearly emptied, began to fill again. The Prince, in summoning these men to power, thought that he was avenging himself on the Duchessa; he was madly in love and above all hated Conte Mosca as a rival.

Fabrizio had plenty to do; Monsignor Landriani, now seventy-two years old, had declined into a state of great languor, and as he now hardly ever left his Palace, it fell to his Coadjutor to take his place in almost all his functions.

The Marchesa Crescenzi, crushed by remorse, and frightened by her spiritual director, had found an excellent way of withdrawing herself from Fabrizio's gaze. Taking as an excuse the last months of a first confinement, she had given herself as a prison her own *palazzo;* but this *palazzo* had an immense garden. Fabrizio managed to find a way into it, and placed on the path which Clelia most affected flowers tied up in nosegays, and arranged in such a way as to form a language, like the flowers which she had sent up to him every evening in the last days of his imprisonment in the Torre Farnese.

The Marchesa was greatly annoyed by this overture; the motions of her soul were swayed at one time by remorse, at another by passion. For several months she did not allow herself to go down once to the garden of her *palazzo;* she had scruples even about looking at it from the windows.

Fabrizio began to think that she was parted from him for ever, and despair began to seize hold of his soul also. The world in which he was obliged to live disgusted him unspeakably, and had he not been convinced in his heart that the Conte could not find peace of mind apart from his Ministry, he would have gone into retreat in his small apartment in the Archbishop's Palace. It would have been pleasant for him to live entirely in his thoughts and never more to hear the human voice save in the exercise of his functions.

"But," he said to himself, "in the interest of the Conte and Contessa Mosca, there is no one to take my place."

The Prince continued to treat him with a distinction which placed him in the highest rank at that court, and this favour he owed in great measure to himself. The extreme reserve which, in Fabrizio, sprang from an indifference bordering on disgust for all the affections or petty passions that fill the lives of men, had pricked the young Prince's vanity; he often remarked that Fabrizio had as much character as his aunt. The Prince's candid nature had in part perceived a truth: namely that no one approached him with the same feelings in his heart as Fabrizio. What could not escape the notice even of the common herd of courtiers was that the consideration won by Fabrizio was not that given to a mere Coadjutor, but actually exceeded the respect which the Sovereign shewed to the Archbishop. Fabrizio wrote to the Conte that if ever the Prince had enough intelligence to perceive the mess into which the Ministers, Rassi, Fabio Conti, Zurla and others of like capacity had thrown his affairs, he, Fabrizio, would be the natural channel through which he would take action without unduly compromising his self-esteem.

"But for the memory of those fatal words, *that boy*," he told Contessa Mosca, "applied by a man of talent to an august personage, the august personage would already have cried: 'Return at once and rid me of these rascals!' At this very moment, if the wife of the man of talent deigned to make an advance, of however little significance, the Conte would be recalled with joy: but he will return through a far nobler door, if he is willing to wait until the fruit is ripe. Meanwhile everyone is bored to death at the Princess's drawing-rooms, they have nothing to amuse them but the absurdity of Rassi, who, now that he is a Conte, has become a maniac for nobility. Strict orders have just been issued that anyone who cannot produce eight quarterings of nobility *must no longer dare* to present himself at the Princess's evenings (these are the exact words of the proclamation). All the men who already possess the right to enter the great gallery in the mornings, and to remain in the Sovereign's presence when he passes on his way to mass, are to continue to enjoy that privilege; but newcomers will have to shew proof of their eight quarterings. Which has given rise to the saying that it is clear that Rassi gives no quarter."

It may be imagined that such letters were not entrusted to the post. Contessa Mosca replied from Naples: "We have a concert every Thursday, and a *conversazione* on Sundays; there is no room to move in our rooms. The Conte is enchanted with his excavations, he devotes a thousand francs a month to them, and has just brought some labourers down from the mountains of the Abruzzi, who cost him only three and twenty soldi a day. You must really come and see us. This is the twentieth time and more, you ungrateful man, that I have given you this invitation."

Fabrizio had no thought of obeying the summons: the letter which he wrote every day to the Conte or Contessa seemed in itself an almost insupportable burden. The reader will forgive him when he learns that a whole year passed in this way, without his being able to address a single word to the Marchesa. All his attempts to establish some correspondence with her had been repulsed with horror. The habitual silence which, in his boredom with life, Fabrizio preserved everywhere, except in the exercise of his functions and at court, added to the spotless purity of his morals, made him the object of a veneration so extraordinary that he finally decided to pay heed to his aunt's advice.

"The Prince has such a veneration for you," she wrote to him, "that you must be on the look-out for disgrace; he will lavish on you signs of indifference, and the atrocious contempt of the courtiers will follow on the heels of his. These petty despots, however honest they may be, change like the fashions, and for the same reason: boredom. You will find no strength to resist the Sovereign's caprices except in preaching. You improvise so well in verse! Try to speak for half an hour on religion; you will utter heresies at first; but hire a learned and discreet theologian to help you with your sermons, and warn you of your mistakes, you can put them right the day after."

The kind of misery which a crossed love brings to the soul has this effect, that everything which requires attention and action becomes an atrocious burden. But Fabrizio told himself that his influence with the people, if he acquired any, might one day be of use to his aunt, and also to the Conte, his veneration for whom increased daily, as his public life taught him to realise the dishonesty of mankind. He decided to preach, and his success, prepared for him by his thinness and his worn coat, was without precedent. People found in his utterances a fragrance of profound sadness, which, combined with his charming appearance and the stories of the high favour that he enjoyed at court, captivated every woman's heart. They invented the legend that he had been one of the most gallant captains in Napoleon's army. Soon this absurd rumour had passed beyond the stage of doubt. Seats were reserved in the churches in which he was to preach; the poor used to take their places there as a speculation from five o'clock in the morning.

His success was such that Fabrizio finally conceived the idea, which altered his whole nature, that, were it only from simple curiosity, the Marchesa Crescenzi might very well come one day to listen to one of his sermons. Suddenly the enraptured public became aware that his talent had increased twofold. He allowed himself, when he was moved, to use imagery the boldness of which would have made the most practised orators shudder; at times, forgetting himself completely, he gave way to moments of passionate inspiration, and his whole audience melted in tears. But it was in vain that his *aggrottato* eye sought among all the faces turned towards the pulpit that one face the presence of which would have been so great an event for him.

"But if ever I do have that happiness," he said to himself, "either I shall be taken ill, or I shall stop short altogether." To obviate the latter misfortune, he had composed a sort of prayer, tender and impassioned, which he always placed in the pulpit, on a footstool; his plan was to begin reading this piece, should the Marchesa's presence ever place him at a loss for a word.

He learned one day, through those of the Marchesa's servants who were in his pay, that orders had been given to prepare for the following evening the box of the *casa* Crescenzi at the principal theatre. It was a year since the Marchesa had appeared at any public spectacle, and it was a tenor who was creating a furore and filling the house every evening that was making her depart from her habit. Fabrizio's first impulse was an intense joy. "At last I can look at her for a whole evening! They say she is very pale." And he sought to imagine what that charming face could be like, with its colours half obliterated by the war that had been waged in her soul.

His friend Lodovico, in consternation at what he called

his master's madness, found, with great difficulty, a box on the fourth tier, almost opposite the Marchesa's. An idea suggested itself to Fabrizio; "I hope to put it into her head to come to a sermon, and I shall choose a church that is quite small, so as to be able to see her properly." As a rule, Fabrizio preached at three o'clock. On the morning of the day on which the Marchesa was to go to the theatre, he gave out that, as he would be detained all day at the Palace by professional duties, he would preach as a special exception at half past eight in the evening, in the little church of Santa Maria della Visitazione, situated precisely opposite one of the wings of the *palazzo* Crescenzi. Lodovico, on his behalf, presented an enormous quantity of candles to the nuns of the Visitation, with the request that they would illuminate their church during the day. He had a whole company of Grenadier Guards, a sentry was posted, with fixed bayonet, outside each chapel, to prevent pilfering.

The sermon was announced for half past eight only, and by two o'clock the church was completely filled; one may imagine the din that there was in the quiet street over which towered the noble structure of the *palazzo* Crescenzi. Fabrizio had published the announcement that, in honour of Our Lady of Pity, he would preach on the pity which a generous soul ought to feel for one in misfortune, even when he is guilty.

Disguised with all possible care, Fabrizio reached his box in the theatre at the moment when the doors were opened, and when there were still no lights. The performance began about eight o'clock, and a few minutes later he had that joy which no mind can conceive that has not also felt it, he saw the door of the Crescenzi box open; a little later the Marchesa appeared; he had not had so clear a view of her since the day on which she had given him her fan. Fabrizio thought that he would suffocate with joy; he was conscious of emotions so extraordinary that he said to himself: "Perhaps I am going to die! What a charming way of ending this sad life! Perhaps I am going to collapse in this box; the faithful gathered at the Visitation will wait for me in vain, and to-morrow they will learn that their future Archbishop forgot himself in a box at the Opera, and, what is more, disguised as a servant and wearing livery! Farewell my whole reputation! And what does my reputation mean to me?"

However, about a quarter to nine, Fabrizio collected himself with an effort; he left his box on the fourth tier and had the greatest difficulty in reaching, on foot, the place where he was to doff his livery and put on a more suitable costume. It was not until nearly nine o'clock that he arrived at the Visitation, in such a state of pallor and weakness that the rumour went round the church that the Signor Coadiutore would not be able to preach that evening. One may imagine the attention that was lavished on him by the Sisters at the grille of their inner parlour, to which he had retired. These ladies talked incessantly; Fabrizio asked to be left alone for a few moments, then hastened to the pulpit. One of his assistants had informed him, about three o'clock, that the Church of the Visitation was packed to the doors, but with people of the lowest class, attracted apparently by the spectacle of the illumination. On entering the pulpit, Fabrizio was agreeably surprised to find all the chairs occupied by young men of fashion, and by people of the highest distinction.

A few words of excuse began his sermon, and were received with suppressed cries of admiration. Next came the impassioned description of the unfortunate wretch whom one must pity, to honour worthily the Madonna della Pietà, who, herself, had so greatly suffered when on earth. The orator was greatly moved; there were moments when he could barely pronounce his words so as to be heard in every part of this small church. In the eyes of all the women, and of a good many of the men, he had himself the air of the wretch whom one ought to pity, so extreme was his pallor. A few minutes after the words of apology with which he had begun his discourse, it was noticed that he was not in his normal state; it was felt that his melancholy, this evening, was more profound and more tender than usual. Once he was seen to have tears in his eyes; in a moment there rose through the congregation a general sob, so loud that the sermon was completely interrupted.

This first interruption was followed by a dozen others; his listeners uttered cries of admiration, there were outbursts of tears; one heard at every moment such exclamations as: "Ah! Santa Madonna!" "Ah! Gran Dio!" The emotion was so general and so irrepressible in this select public, that no one was ashamed of uttering these cries, and the people who were carried away by them did not seem to their neighbours to be in the least absurd.

During the rest which it is customary to take in the middle

of the sermon, Fabrizio was informed that there was absolutely no one left in the theatre; one lady only was still to be seen in her box, the Marchesa Crescenzi. During this brief interval, a great clamour was suddenly heard proceeding from the church; it was the faithful who were voting a statue to the Signor Coadiutore. His success in the second part of the discourse was so wild and worldly, the bursts of Christian contrition gave place so completely to cries of admiration that were altogether profane, that he felt it his duty to address, on leaving the pulpit, a sort of reprimand to his hearers. Whereupon they all left at once with a movement that was singularly formal; and, on reaching the street, all began to applaud with frenzy, and to shout: *"Evviva del Dongo!"*

Fabrizio hastily consulted his watch, and ran to a little barred window which lighted the narrow passage from the organ gallery to the interior of the convent. Out of politeness to the unprecedented and incredible crowd which filled the street, the porter of the *palazzo* Crescenzi had placed a dozen torches in those iron sconces which one sees projecting from the outer walls of *palazzi* built in the middle ages. After some minutes, and long before the shouting had ceased, the event for which Fabrizio was waiting with such anxiety occurred, the Marchesa's carriage, returning from the theatre, appeared in the street; the coachman was obliged to stop, and it was only at a crawling pace, and by dint of shouts, that the carriage was able to reach the door.

The Marchesa had been touched by the sublime music, as is the way with sorrowing hearts, but far more by the complete solitude in which she sat, when she learned the reason for it. In the middle of the second act, and while the tenor was on the stage, even the people in the pit had suddenly abandoned their seats to go and tempt fortune by trying to force their way into the Church of the Visitation. The Marchesa, finding herself stopped by the crowd outside her door, burst into tears. "I had not made a bad choice," she said to herself.

But precisely on account of this momentary weakening, she firmly resisted the pressure put upon her by the Marchese and the friends of the family, who could not conceive her not going to see so astonishing a preacher.

"Really," they said, "he beats even the best tenor in Italy!"

"If I see him, I am lost!" the Marchesa said to herself.

It was in vain that Fabrizio, whose talent seemed more

brilliant every day, preached several times more in the same little church, opposite the *palazzo* Crescenzi, never did he catch sight of Clelia, who indeed took offence finally at this affection of coming to disturb her quiet street, after he had already driven her from her own garden.

In letting his eye run over the faces of the women who listened to him, Fabrizio had noticed some time back a little face of dark complexion, very pretty, and with eyes that darted fire. As a rule these magnificent eyes were drowned in tears at the ninth or tenth sentence in the sermon. When Fabrizio was obliged to say things at some length, which were tedious to himself, he would very readily let his eyes rest on that head, the youthfulness of which pleased him. He learned that this young person was called Annetta Marini, the only daughter and heiress of the richest cloth merchant in Parma, who had died a few months before.

Presently the name of this Annetta Marini, the cloth merchant's daughter, was on every tongue; she had fallen desperately in love with Fabrizio. When the famous sermons began, her marriage had been arranged with Giacomo Rassi, eldest son of the Minister of Justice, who was by no means unattractive to her; but she had barely listened twice to Monsignor Fabrizio before she declared that she no longer wished to marry; and, since she was asked the reason for so singular a change of mind, she replied that it was not fitting for an honourable girl to marry one man when she had fallen madly in love with another. Her family sought to discover, at first without success, who this other might be.

But the burning tears which Annetta shed at the sermon put them on the way to the truth; her mother and uncles having asked her if she loved Monsignor Fabrizio, she replied boldly that, since the truth had been discovered, she would not demean herself with a lie; she added that, having no hope of marrying the man whom she adored, she wished at least no longer to have her eyes offended by the ridiculous figure of Contino Rassi. This speech in ridicule of the son of a man who was pursued by the envy of the entire middle class became in a couple of days the talk of the whole town. Annetta Marini's reply was thought charming, and everyone repeated it. People spoke of it at the *palazzo* Crescenzi as everywhere else.

Clelia took good care not to open her mouth on such a topic in her own drawing-room; but she plied her maid with questions, and, the following Sunday, after hearing mass in the chapel of her *palazzo*, bade her maid come with her in her carriage and went in search of a second mass at Signora Marini's parish church. She found assembled there all the gallants of the town, drawn by the same attraction; these gentlemen were standing by the door. Presently, from the great stir which they made, the Marchesa gathered that this Signorina Marini was entering the church; she found herself excellently placed to see her, and, for all her piety, paid little attention to the mass. Clelia found in this middle class beauty a little air of decision which, to her mind, would have suited, if anyone, a woman who had been married for a good many years. Otherwise, she was admirably built on her small scale, and her eyes, as they say in Lombardy, seemed to make conversation with the things at which she looked. The Marchesa escaped before the end of mass.

The following day the friends of the Crescenzi household, who came regularly to spend the evening there, related a fresh absurdity on the part of Annetta Marini. Since her mother, afraid of her doing something foolish, left only a little money at her disposal, Annetta had gone and offered a magnificent diamond ring, a gift from her father, to the famous Hayez, then at Parma decorating the drawing-rooms of the *palazzo* Crescenzi, and had asked him to paint the portrait of Signor del Dongo; but she wished that in this portrait he should simply be dressed in black, and not in the priestly habit. Well, the previous evening, Annetta's mother had been greatly surprised, and even more shocked to find in her daughter's room a magnificent portrait of Fabrizio del Dongo, set in the finest frame that had been gilded in Parma in the last twenty years.

CHAPTER TWENTY-EIGHT

CARRIED AWAY by the train of events, we have not had time to sketch the comic race of courtiers who swarm at the court of Parma and who made fatuous comments on the incidents which we have related. What in that country makes a small noble, adorned with an income of three or four thousand lire, worthy to figure in black stockings at the Prince's levees, is, first and foremost, that he shall never have read Voltaire and Rousseau: this condition it is not very difficult to fulfil. He must then know how to speak with emotion of the Sovereign's cold, or of the latest case of mineralogical specimens that has come to him from Saxony. If, after this, you were not absent from mass for a single day in the year, if you could include in the number of your intimate friends two or three prominent monks, the Prince deigned to address a few words to you once every year, a fortnight before or a fortnight after the first of January, which brought you great relief in your parish, and the tax collector dared not press you unduly if you were in arrears with the annual sum of one hundred francs with which your small estate was burdened.

Signor Gonzo was a poor devil of this sort, very noble, who, apart from possessing some little fortune of his own, had obtained, through the Marchese Crescenzi's influence, a magnificent post which brought him in eleven hundred and fifty francs annually. This man might have dined at home; but he had one passion: he was never at his ease and happy except when he found himself in the drawing-room of some great personage who said to him from time to time: "Hold your tongue, Gonzo, you're a perfect fool." This judgment was prompted by ill temper, for Gonzo had almost always more intelligence than the great personage. He would discuss anything, and quite gracefully, besides, he was ready to change his opinion on a grimace from the master of the house. To tell the truth, although of a profound subtlety in securing his own interests, he had not an idea in his head, and, when the Prince had not a cold, was sometimes embarrassed as he came into a drawing-room.

What had, in Parma, won Gonzo a reputation was a magnificent cocked hat, adorned with a slightly dilapidated black plume, which he wore even with evening dress; but you ought to have seen the way in which he carried this plume, whether upon his head or in his hand; there were talent and importance combined. He inquired with genuine anxiety after the health of the Marchesa's little dog, and, if the *palazzo* Crescenzi had caught fire, he would have risked his life to save one of those fine armchairs in gold brocade, which for so many years had caught in his black silk breeches, whenever it so happened that he ventured to sit down for a moment.

Seven or eight persons of this species appeared every evening at seven o'clock in the Marchesa Crescenzi's drawing-room. No sooner had they sat down than a lackey, magnificently attired in a daffodil-yellow livery, covered all over with silver braid, as was the red waistcoat which completed his magnificence, came to take the poor devils' hats and canes. He was immediately followed by a footman carrying an infinitesimal cup of coffee, supported on a stem of silver filigree; and every half hour a butler, wearing a sword and a magnificent coat, in the French style, brought round ices.

Half an hour after the threadbare little courtiers, one saw arrive five or six officers, talking in loud voices and with a very military air, and usually discussing the number of buttons which ought to be on the soldiers' uniform in order that the Commander in Chief might gain victories. It would not have been prudent to quote a French newspaper in this drawing-room; for, even when the news itself was of the most agreeable kind, as for instance that fifty Liberals had been shot in Spain, the speaker none the less remained convicted of having read a French newspaper. The crowning effort of all these people's skill was to obtain every ten years an increase of 150 francs in their pensions. It is thus that the Prince shares with his nobility the pleasure of reigning over all the peasants and burgesses of the land.

The principal personage, beyond all question, of the Crescenzi drawing-room, was the Cavaliere Foscarini, an entirely honest man; in consequence of which he had been in prison off and on, under every government. He had been a member of that famous Chamber of Deputies which, at Milan, rejected the Registration Law presented to them by Napoleon, an action of very rare occurrence in history. Cavaliere Foscarini, after having been for twenty years a friend of the Marchese's mother, had remained the influential man in the household. He had always some amusing story to tell, but nothing escaped his shrewd perception; and the young Marchesa, who felt herself guilty at heart, trembled before him.

As Gonzo had a regular passion for the great gentleman, who said rude things to him and moved him to tears once or twice every year, his mania was to seek to do him trifling services; and, if he had not been paralysed by the habits of an extreme poverty, he might sometimes have succeeded, for he was not lacking in a certain ingredient of shrewdness, and a far greater effrontery.

Gonzo, as we have seen him, felt some contempt for the Marchesa Crescenzi, for never in her life had she addressed a word to him that was not quite civil; but after all she was the wife of the famous Marchese Crescenzi, *Cavaliere d'onore* to the Princess, who, once or twice in a month, used to say to Gonzo: "Hold your tongue, Gonzo, you're a perfect fool."

Gonzo observed that everything which was said about little Annetta Marini made the Marchesa emerge for a moment from the state of dreamy indifference in which as a rule she remained plunged until the clock struck eleven; then she made tea, and offered a cup to each of the men present, addressing him by name. After which, at the moment of her withdrawing to her room, she seemed to find a momentary gaiety, and this was the time chosen for repeating to her satirical sonnets.

They compose such sonnets admirably in Italy: it is the one kind of literature that has still a little vitality; as a matter of fact, it is not subjected to the censor, and the courtiers of the *casa* Crescenzi invariably prefaced their sonnets with these words: "Will the Signora Marchesa permit one to repeat to her a very bad sonnet?" And when the sonnet had been greeted with laughter and had been repeated several times, one of the officers would not fail to exclaim: "The Minister of Police ought to see about giving a bit of hanging to the authors of such atrocities." Middle class society, on the other hand, welcomes these sonnets with the most open admiration, and the lawyers' clerks sell copies of them.

From the sort of curiosity shown by the Marchesa, Gonzo imagined that too much had been said in front of her of the beauty of the little Marini, who moreover had a fortune of a million, and that the other woman was jealous of her. As, with his incessant smile and his complete effrontery towards all that was not noble, Gonzo found his way everywhere, on the very next day he arrived in the Marchesa's drawing-room, carrying his plumed hat in a triumphant fashion which was to be seen perhaps only once or twice in the year, when the Prince had said to him: *"Addio, Gonzo."*

After respectfully greeting the Marchesa, Gonzo did not withdraw as usual to take his seat on the chair which had just been pushed forward for him. He took his stand in the middle of the circle and exclaimed bluntly: "I have seen the portrait of Monsignor del Dongo." Clelia was so surprised that she was obliged to lean upon the arm of her chair; she tried to face the storm, but presently was obliged to leave the room.

"You must agree, my poor Gonzo, that your tactlessness is unique," came arrogantly from one of the officers, who was finishing his fourth ice. "Don't you know that the Coadjutor, who was one of the most gallant Colonels in Napoleon's army, played a trick that ought to have hanged him on the Marchesa's father, when he walked out of the citadel where General Fabio Conti was in command, as he might have walked out of the Steccata?" (The Steccata is the principal church in Parma.)

"Indeed I am ignorant of many things, my dear Captain, and I am a poor imbecile who makes blunders all day long."

This reply, quite to the Italian taste, caused a laugh at the expense of the brilliant officer. The Marchesa soon returned; she had armed herself with courage, and was not without hope of being able herself to admire this portrait, which was said to be excellent. She spoke with praise of the talent of Hayez, who had painted it. Unconsciously she addressed charming smiles at Gonzo, who looked malevolently at the officer. As all the other courtiers of the house indulged in the same pastime, the officer took flight, not without vowing a deadly hatred against Gonzo; the latter was triumphant, and later in the evening, when he took his leave, was invited to dine next day.

"I can tell you something more," cried Gonzo, the following evening, after dinner, when the servants had left the room: "the latest thing is that our Coadjutor has fallen in love with the little Marini!"

One may judge of the agitation that arose in Clelia's heart on hearing so extraordinary an announcement. The Marchese himself was moved.

"But, Gonzo my friend, you are off the track, as usual! And you ought to speak with a little more caution of a person who has had the honour to sit down eleven times at his Highness's whist-table."

"Well, Signor Marchese," replied Gonzo with the coarseness of people of his sort, "I can promise you that he would just as soon sit down to the little Marini. But it is enough that these details displease you; they no longer exist for me, who desire above all things not to shock my beloved Marchese."

Regularly, after dinner, the Marchese used to retire to take a *siesta*. He let the time pass that day; but Gonzo would sooner have cut out his tongue than have said another word about the little Marini; and, every moment, he began a speech, so planned that the Marchese might hope that he was about to return to the subject of the little lady's love affairs. Gonzo had in a superior degree that Italian quality of mind which consists in exquisitely delaying the launching of the word for which one's hearer longs. The poor Marchese, dying of curiosity, was obliged to make advances; he told Gonzo that, when he had the pleasure of dining with him, he ate twice as much as usual. Gonzo did not take the hint, he began to describe a magnificent collection of pictures which the Marchesa Balbi, the late Prince's mistress, was forming; three or four times he spoke of Hayez, in a slow and measured tone full of the most profound admiration. The Marchese said to himself: "Now he is coming to the portrait which the little Marini ordered!" But this was what Gonzo took good care not to do. Five o'clock struck, which put the Marchese in the worst of tempers, for he was in the habit of getting into his carriage at half past five, after his *siesta*, to drive to the Corso.

"This is what you do with your stupid talk!" he said rudely to Gonzo: "you are making me reach the Corso after the Princess, whose *Cavaliere d'onore* I am, when she may have orders to give me. Come along! Hurry up! Tell me in a few words, if you can, what is this so-called love affair of the Coadjutor?"

But Gonzo wished to keep this anecdote for the Marchesa, who had invited him to dine; he did *hurry up,* in a very few words, the story demanded of him, and the Marchese, half asleep, ran off to take his *siesta.* Gonzo adopted a wholly different manner with the poor Marchesa. She had remained so young and natural in spite of her high position, that she felt it her duty to make amends for the rudeness with which the Marchese had just spoken to Gonzo. Charmed by this success, her guest recovered all his eloquence, and made it a pleasure, no less than a duty, to enter into endless details with her.

Little Annetta Marini gave as much as a sequin for each place that was kept for her for the sermons; she always arrived with two of her aunts and her father's old cashier. These places, which were reserved for her overnight, were generally chosen almost opposite the pulpit, but slightly in the direction of the high altar, for she had noticed that the Coadjutor often turned towards the altar. Now, what the public also had noticed was that, *not infrequently,* those speaking eyes of the young preacher rested with evident pleasure on the young heiress, that striking beauty; and apparently with some attention, for, when he had his eyes fixed on her, his sermon became learned; the quotations began to abound in it, there was no more sign of that eloquence which springs from the heart; and the ladies, whose interest ceased almost at once, began to look at the Marini and to find fault with her.

Clelia made him repeat to her three times over all these singular details. At the third repetition she became lost in meditation; she was calculating that just fourteen months had passed since she last saw Fabrizio. "Would it be very wrong," she asked herself, "to spend an hour in a church, not to see Fabrizio but to hear a famous preacher? Besides, I shall take a seat a long way from the pulpit, and I shall look at Fabrizio only once as I go in and once more at the end of the sermon. . . . No," Clelia said to herself, "it is not Fabrizio I am going to see, I am going to hear the astounding preacher!" In the midst of all these reasonings, the Marchesa felt some remorse; her conduct had been so exemplary for fourteen months! "Well," she said to herself, in order to secure some peace of mind, "if the first woman to arrive this evening has been to hear Monsignor del Dongo, I shall go too; if she has not been, I shall stay away."

Having come to this decision, the Marchesa made Gonzo happy by saying to him:

"Try to find out on what day the Coadjutor will be preaching, and in what church. This evening, before you go, I shall perhaps have a commission to give you."

No sooner had Gonzo set off for the Corso than Clelia went to take the air in the garden of her *palazzo*. She did not consider the objection that for ten months she had not set foot in it. She was lively, animated; she had a colour. That evening, as each boring visitor entered the room, her heart throbbed with emotion. At length they announced Gonzo, who at the first glance saw that he was going to be the indispensable person for the next week; "The Marchesa is jealous of the little Marini, and, upon my word, it would be a fine drama to put on the stage," he said to himself, "with the Marchesa playing the leading lady, little Annetta the juvenile, and Monsignor del Dongo the lover! Upon my word, the seats would not be too dear at two francs." He was beside himself with joy, and throughout the evening cut everybody short, and told the most ridiculous stories (that, for example, of the famous actress and the Marquis de Pequigny, which he had heard the day before from a French visitor). The Marchesa, for her part, could not stay in one place; she moved about the drawing-room, she passed into a gallery adjoining it into which the Marchese had admitted no picture that had not cost more than twenty thousand francs. These pictures spoke in so clear a language that evening that they wore out the Marchesa's heart with the force of her emotion. At last she heard the double doors open, she ran to the drawing-room: it was the Marchesa Raversi! But, on making her the customary polite speeches, Clelia felt that her voice was failing her. The Marchesa made her repeat twice the question: "What do you think of the fashionable preacher?" which she had not heard at first.

"I did regard him as a little intriguer, a most worthy nephew of the illustrious Contessa Mosca, but the last time he preached; why, it was at the Church of the Visitation, opposite you, he was so sublime, that I could not hate him any longer, and I regard him as the most eloquent man I have ever heard."

"So you have been to hear his sermons?" said Clelia, trembling with happiness.

"Why," the Marchesa laughed, "haven't you been listening? I wouldn't miss one for anything in the world. They

say that his lungs are affected, and that soon he will have
to give up preaching."

No sooner had the Marchesa left than Clelia called Gonzo
to the gallery.

"I have almost decided," she told him, "to hear this
preacher who is so highly praised. When does he preach?"

"Next Monday, that is to say in three days from now; and
one would say that he had guessed Your Excellency's intention, for he is coming to preach in the Church of the
Visitation."

There was more to be settled; but Clelia could no longer
muster enough voice to speak: she took five or six turns of
the gallery without adding a word. Gonzo said to himself:
"There is vengeance at work. How can anyone have the
insolence to escape from a prison, especially when he is
guarded by a hero like General Fabio Conti?

"However, you must make haste," he added with delicate
irony; "his lungs are affected. I heard Doctor Rambo say
that he has not a year to live; God is punishing him for having broken his bond by treacherously escaping from the
citadel."

The Marchesa sat down on the divan in the gallery, and
made a sign to Gonzo to follow her example. After some
moments of silence she handed him a little purse in which
she had a few sequins ready. "Reserve four places for me."

"Will it be permitted for poor Gonzo to slip in, in Your
Excellency's train?"

"Certainly. Reserve five places. . . . I do not in the least
mind," she added, "whether I am near the pulpit; but I
should like to see Signorina Marini, who they say is so
pretty."

The Marchesa could not live through the three days that
separated her from the famous Monday, the day of the
sermon. Gonzo, inasmuch as it was a signal honour to be
seen in the company of so great a lady, had put on his
French coat with his sword; this was not all, taking advantage
of the proximity of the *palazzo*, he had had carried into the
church a magnificent gilt armchair for the Marchesa, which
was thought the last word in insolence by the middle classes.
One may imagine how the poor Marchesa felt when she saw
this armchair, which had been placed directly opposite the
pulpit. Clelia was in such confusion, with downcast eyes,
shrinking into a corner of the huge chair, that she had not
even the courage to look at the little Marini, whom Gonzo

pointed out to her with his hand with an effrontery which amazed her. Everyone not of noble birth was absolutely nothing in the eyes of this courtier.

Fabrizio appeared in the pulpit; he was so thin, so pale, so *consumed,* that Clelia's eyes immediately filled with tears. Fabrizio uttered a few words, then stopped, as though his voice had suddenly failed; he tried in vain to begin various sentences; he turned round and took up a sheet of paper:

"Brethren," he said, "an unhappy soul and one well worthy of all your pity requests you, through my lips, to pray for the ending of his torments, which will cease only with his life."

Fabrizio read the rest of his paper very slowly; but the expression of his voice was such that before he was half-way through the prayer, everyone was weeping, even Gonzo. "At any rate, I shall not be noticed," thought the Marchesa, bursting into tears.

While he was reading from the paper, Fabrizio found two or three ideas concerning the state of the unhappy man for whom he had come to beg the prayers of the faithful. Presently thoughts came to him in abundance. While he appeared to be addressing the public, he spoke only to the Marchesa. He ended his discourse a little sooner than was usual, because, in spite of his efforts to control them, his tears got the better of him to such a point that he was no longer able to pronounce his words in an intelligible manner. The good judges found this sermon strange but quite equal, in pathos at least, to the famous sermon preached with the lighted candles. As for Clelia, no sooner had she heard the first ten lines of the prayer read by Fabrizio than it seemed to her an atrocious crime to have been able to spend fourteen months without seeing him. On her return home she took to her bed, to be able to think of Fabrizio with perfect freedom; and next morning, at an early hour, Fabrizio received a note couched in the following terms:

"We rely upon your honour; find four *bravi,* of whose discretion you can be sure, and to-morrow, when midnight sounds from the Steccata, be by a little door which bears the number 19, in the Strada San Paolo. Remember that you may be attacked, do not come alone."

On recognising that heavenly script, Fabrizio fell on his

knees and burst into tears. "At last," he cried, "after fourteen months and eight days! Farewell to preaching."

It would take too long to describe all the varieties of folly to which the hearts of Fabrizio and Clelia were a prey that day. The little door indicated in the note was none other than that of the orangery of the *palazzo* Crescenzi, and ten times in the day Fabrizio found an excuse to visit it. He armed himself, and alone, shortly before midnight, with a rapid step, was passing by the door when, to his inexpressible joy, he heard a well-known voice say in a very low whisper:

"Come in here, friend of my heart."

Fabrizio entered cautiously and found himself actually in the orangery, but opposite a window heavily barred which stood three or four feet above the ground. The darkness was intense. Fabrizio had heard a slight sound in this window, and was exploring the bars with his hand, when he felt another hand, slipped through the bars, take hold of his and carry it to a pair of lips which gave it a kiss.

"It is I," said a dear voice, "who have come here to tell you that I love you, and to ask you if you are willing to obey me."

One may imagine the answer, the joy, the astonishment of Fabrizio; after the first transports, Clelia said to him:

"I have made a vow to the Madonna, as you know, never to see you; that is why I receive you in this profound darkness. I wish you to understand clearly that, should you ever force me to look at you in the daylight, all would be over between us. But first of all, I do not wish you to preach before Annetta Marini, and do not go and think that it was I who was so foolish as to have an armchair carried into the House of God."

"My dear angel, I shall never preach again before anyone; I have been preaching only in the hope that one day I might see you."

"Do not speak like that, remember that it is not permitted to me to see you."

Here we shall ask leave to pass over, without saying a single word about them, an interval of three years.

At the time when our story is resumed, Conte Mosca had long since returned to Parma, as Prime Minister, and was more powerful than ever.

After three years of divine happiness, Fabrizio's heart underwent a caprice of affection which led to a complete change

in his circumstances. The Marchesa had a charming little boy
two years old, Sandrino, who was his mother's joy; he was
always with her or on the knees of the Marchese Crescenzi;
Fabrizio, on the other hand, hardly ever saw him; he did
not wish him to become accustomed to loving another father.
He formed the plan of taking the child away before his
memories should have grown distinct.

In the long hours of each day when the Marchesa could
not see her lover, Sandrino's company consoled her; for we
have to confess a thing which will seem strange north of the
Alps; in spite of her errors she had remained true to her vow;
she had promised the Madonna, as the reader may perhaps
remember, never to *see* Fabrizio; these had been her exact
words; consequently she received him only at night, and
there was never any light in the room.

But every evening he was received by his mistress; and,
what is worthy of admiration, in the midst of a court devoured by curiosity and envy, Fabrizio's precautions had
been so ably calculated that this *amicizia,* as it is called in
Lombardy, had never even been suspected. Their love was
too intense for quarrels not to occur; Clelia was extremely
given to jealousy, but almost always their quarrels sprang
from another cause. Fabrizio had made use of some public
ceremony in order to be in the same place as the Marchesa
and to look at her; she then seized a pretext to escape quickly,
and for a long time afterwards banished her lover.

Amazement was felt at the court of Parma that no
intrigue should be known of a woman so remarkable both for
her beauty and for the loftiness of her mind; she gave rise
to passions which inspired many foolish actions, and often
Fabrizio too was jealous.

The good Archbishop Landriani had long been dead; the
piety, the exemplary morals, the eloquence of Fabrizio had
made him be forgotten; his own elder brother was dead and
all the wealth of his family had come to him. From this
time onwards he distributed annually among the vicars and
curates of his diocese the hundred odd thousand francs which
the Archbishopric of Parma brought him in.

It would be difficult to imagine a life more honoured, more
honourable or more useful than Fabrizio had made for himself, when everything was upset by this unfortunate caprice
of paternal affection.

"According to the vow which I respect and which nevertheless is the bane of my life, since you refuse to see me

during the day," he said once to Clelia, "I am obliged to live perpetually alone, with no other distraction than my work; and besides I have not enough work. In the course of this stern and sad way of passing the long hours of each day, an idea has occurred to me, which is now torturing me, and against which I have been striving in vain for six months: my son will not love me at all; he never hears my name mentioned. Brought up amid all the pleasing luxury of the *palazzo* Crescenzi, he barely knows me. On the rare occasions when I do see him, I think of his mother, whose heavenly beauty he recalls to me, and whom I may not see, and he must find me a serious person, which, with children, means sad."

"Well," said the Marchesa, "to what is all this speech leading? It frightens me."

"To my having my son; I wish him to live with me; I wish to see him every day; I wish him to grow accustomed to loving me; I wish to love him myself at my leisure. Since a fatality without counterpart in the world decrees that I must be deprived of that happiness which so many other tender hearts enjoy, and forbids me to pass my life with all that I adore, I wish at least to have beside me a creature who recalls you to my heart, who to some extent takes your place. Men and affairs are a burden to me in my enforced solitude; you know that ambition has always been a vain word to me, since the moment when I had the good fortune to be locked up by Barbone; and anything that is not felt in my heart seems to me fatuous in the melancholy which in your absence overwhelms me."

One can imagine the keen anguish with which her lover's grief filled the heart of poor Clelia; her sorrow was all the more intense, as she felt that Fabrizio had some justification. She went the length of wondering whether she ought not to try to obtain a release from her vow. Then she would receive Fabrizio during the day like any other person in society, and her reputation for sagacity was too well established for any scandal to arise. She told herself that by spending enough money she could procure a dispensation from her vow; but she felt also that this purely worldly arrangement would not set her conscience at rest, and that an angry heaven might perhaps punish her for this fresh crime.

On the other hand, if she consented to yield to so natural a desire on the part of Fabrizio, if she sought not to hurt that tender heart which she knew so well, and whose tranquillity her singular vow so strangely jeopardised, what chance was there of abducting the only son of one of the greatest nobles in Italy without the fraud's being discovered? The Marchese Crescenzi would spend enormous sums, would himself conduct the investigations, and sooner or later the facts of the abduction would become known. There was only one way of meeting this danger, the child must be sent abroad, to Edinburgh, for instance, or to Paris; but this was a course to which the mother's affection could never consent. The other plan proposed by Fabrizio, which was indeed the more reasonable of the two, had something sinister about it, and was almost more alarming still in the eyes of this despairing mother; she must, said Fabrizio, feign an illness for the child; he would grow steadily worse, until finally he died in the Marchese Crescenzi's absence.

A repugnance which, in Clelia, amounted to terror, caused a rupture that could not last.

Clelia insisted that they must not tempt God; that this beloved son was the fruit of a crime, and that if they provoked the divine anger further, God would not fail to call him back to Himself. Fabrizio spoke again of his strange destiny: "The station to which chance has called me," he said to Clelia, "and my love oblige me to dwell in an eternal solitude, I cannot, like the majority of my brethren, taste the pleasures of an intimate society, since you will receive me only in the darkness, which reduces to a few moments, so to speak, the part of my life which I may spend with you."

Tears flowed in abundance. Clelia fell ill; but she loved Fabrizio too well to maintain her opposition to the terrible sacrifice that he demanded of her. Apparently, Sandrino fell ill; the Marchese sent in haste for the most celebrated doctors, and Clelia at once encountered a terrible difficulty which she had not foreseen: she must prevent this adored child from taking any of the remedies ordered by the doctors; it was no small matter.

The child, kept in bed longer than was good for his health, became really ill. How was one to explain to the doctors the cause of his malady? Torn asunder by two conflicting interests both so dear to her, Clelia was within an ace of losing her reason. Must she consent to an apparent recovery, and so sacrifice all the results of that long and painful make-believe? Fabrizio, for his part, could neither forgive himself the violence he was doing to the heart of his mistress nor abandon his project. He had found a way of being admitted every night to the sick child's room, which had led to another complication. The Marchesa came to attend to her son, and sometimes Fabrizio was obliged to see her by candle-light, which seemed to the poor sick heart of Clelia a horrible sin and one that foreboded the death of Sandrino. In vain had the most famous casuists, consulted as to the necessity of adherence to a vow in a case where its performance would obviously do harm, replied that the vow could not be regarded as broken in a criminal fashion, so long as the person bound by a promise to God failed to keep that promise not for a vain pleasure of the senses but so as not to cause an obvious evil. The Marchesa was none the less in despair, and Fabrizio could see the time coming when his strange idea was going to bring about the death of Clelia and that of his son.

He had recourse to his intimate friend, Conte Mosca, who, for all the old Minister that he was, was moved by this tale of love of which to a great extent he had been ignorant.

"I can procure for you the Marchese's absence for five or six days at least: when do you require it?"

A little later, Fabrizio came to inform the Conte that everything was in readiness now for them to take advantage of the Marchese's absence.

Two days after this, as the Marchese was riding home from one of his estates in the neighbourhood of Mantua, a party of brigands, evidently hired to execute some personal vengeance, carried him off, without maltreating him in any way, and placed him in a boat which took three days to travel down the Po, making the same journey that Fabrizio had made long ago, after the famous affair with Giletti. On the fourth day, the brigands marooned the Marchese on a desert island in the Po, taking care first to rob him completely, and to leave him no money or other object that had the slightest value. It was two whole days before the Marchese managed to reach his *palazzo* in Parma; he found it draped in black and all his household in mourning.

This abduction, very skilfully carried out, had a deplorable consequence: Sandrino, secretly installed in a large and fine house where the Marchesa came to see him almost every day, died after a few months. Clelia imagined herself to have been visited with a just punishment, for having been unfaithful to her vow to the Madonna: she had seen Fabrizio so often by candle-light, and indeed twice in broad daylight and with such rapturous affection, during Sandrino's illness. She survived by a few months only this beloved son, but had the joy of dying in the arms of her lover.

Fabrizio was too much in love and too religious to have recourse to suicide; he hoped to meet Clelia again in a better world, but he had too much intelligence not to feel that he had first to atone for many faults.

A few days after Clelia's death, he signed several settlements by which he assured a pension of one thousand francs to each of his servants, and reserved a similar pension for himself; he gave landed property, of an annual value of 100,000 lire or thereabouts, to Contessa Mosca; a similar estate to the Marchesa del Dongo, his mother, and such residue as there might be of the paternal fortune to one of his sisters who was poorly married. On the following day, having forwarded to the proper authorities his resignation of his Archbishopric and of all the posts which the favour of Ernesto V and the Prime Minister's friendship had successively heaped upon him, he retired to the *Charterhouse of Parma,* situated in the woods adjoining the Po, two leagues from Sacca.

Contessa Mosca had strongly approved, at the time, her husband's return to office, but she herself would never on any account consent to cross the frontier of the States of Ernesto V. She held her court at Vignano, a quarter of a league from Casalmaggiore, on the left bank of the Po, and consequently in the Austrian States. In this magnificent palace of Vignano, which the Conte had built for her, she entertained every Thursday all the high society of Parma, and every day her own many friends. Fabrizio had never missed a day in going to Vignano. The Contessa, in a word, combined all the outward appearances of happiness, but she lived for a very short time only after Fabrizio, whom she adored, and who spent but one year in his Charterhouse.

The prisons of Parma were empty, the Conte immensely rich, Ernesto V adored by his subjects, who compared his rule to that of the Grand Dukes of Tuscany.

TO THE HAPPY FEW

APPENDIX

THIS TRANSLATION of *La Chartreuse de Parme* has been made from the reprint in two volumes of the first edition (Paris, Les éditions G. Crès et Cie. MCMXXII), with reference also to the stereotyped edition published by MM. Calmann Lévy and to the reprint issued by M. Flammarion in his series, *Les meilleurs auteurs classiques* (1921). I am also indebted to the extremely literal version by Signora Maria Ortiz (Biblioteca Sansoniana Straniera—*La Certosa di Parma* —G. C. Sansoni, Firenze, 1922), which has thrown a ray of light on several dark passages.

The *Chartreuse* was written in (and not a distance of three hundred leagues from) Paris, and in the short interval between November 4, 1838, and December 26 of that year. So much the author reveals in a note, which I do not translate: "The Char, made 4 novembre 1838—26 décembre id. The 3 septembre 1838, I had the idea of the Char. I begined it after a tour in Britanny, I suppose, or to the Havre. I begined the 4 nov. till the 26 décembre. The 26 dec. I send the 6 énormes cahiers to Kol for les faire voir to the bookseller." His object in pretending to have written the book in 1830 may have been to establish a prescriptive immunity from any charge of traducing the government of Louis-Philippe; if so, it is by a characteristic slip that he speaks of having written it *towards the end of* 1830.

Kol., otherwise Romain Colomb, Beyle's executor, relates in the *Notice Biographique* prefixed to *Armance* that in January, 1839, while the *Chartreuse* was going through the press, a *cahier* of sixty pages of the manuscript was mislaid. Unable to find it among the mass of papers that littered his room, Beyle rewrote the sixty pages, and the new version was already in type when he told Colomb of his loss. Colomb at once searched for and found the missing *cahier*, whereupon Beyle, "stupefied by the ease of my discovery, dreading, in a sense, the sight of this manuscript, would not even glance over it, much less compare it with the pages that had taken its place."

It was published in March, 1839. In the same year, Beyle began to correct, reduce and amplify the whole work, before he was moved by Balzac's criticism to condense the first fifty-four pages into four or five. Three copies thus annotated are in existence, one of which has been reproduced in facsimile in an extremely limited edition: (Paris, Edouard Champion, 3 vols. 1921—100 copies only.) In 1904 M. Casimir Stryienski reprinted in the first volume of *Les Soirées du Stendhal Club* (Mercure de France) the two fragments of which a translation follows. The first is intended for inclusion in Chapter V, in the brief account of Fabrizio's convalescence at Amiens. Colonel Le Baron, the wounded officer whom he met and left at the White Horse Inn at the end of Chapter IV, is now re-introduced as returning to his family at Amiens, and a story is told them which supersedes the account of General Pietranera's death in Chapter II. The second fragment is a small expansion of the already overlong Chapter VI.

Visitors to Parma will look in vain for most of the architectural monuments which met the gaze of Fabrizio. The Torre Farnese has never existed, though it may have been suggested, as to mass, by the huge fragment of the Palazzo Farnese at Piacenza, as well as by the Castel Sant'Angelo in Rome, and as to origin, by the story of Parisina and Ugo d'Este, told in English by Gibbon and Byron. In appearance, it would have been not unlike the tower, also damaged by an earthquake, which stands in the background of Mantegna's fresco of the *Martyrdom of Saint James*, in the Church of the Eremitani at Padua. The problem of how a road running out of Parma to the south could lead directly to Sacca and the Po is as insoluble as that of the guarded permission given to Fabrizio in 1815 to read the novels of Walter Scott.

The Steccata of course exists, and the Church of San Giovanni, but the latter is singularly bare of monumental tombs. There is even a Charterhouse, at San Lazzaro Parmense, though it has escaped the attention of Baedeker. There were Farnese, but the last of them died, of the pleasures of the table, in 1731; a portrait of him in his corpulence may be seen by the curious in the Reale Galleria in the Pilotta—

another large Farnese Palace also unfinished. There is indeed a Cathedral, but there is no Archbishop, and the Bishop's Palace is an untidy piece of patched-up antiquity.

It is probable that Beyle was led to place the scene of his story at Parma, which, in *Rome, Naples et Florence,* he had dismissed, not unjustly, as *ville d'ailleurs assez plate,* precisely because there was not, in 1838, any reigning *dynasty* in that State. The Duchy of Parma was held and admirably governed by Marie-Louise, the wife and widow of Napoleon, from 1815 until after Beyle's death in 1843, when she was still in the prime of life, being by some years his junior. Suddenly, in 1847, she died. The Bourbon dynasty, which had been transplanted to the brief Kingdom of Etruria, and in 1814 had been placated with the Republic of Lucca as a temporary Duchy (which Charles II had finally sold, a few months earlier, to its legal heir, the Grand Duke of Tuscany), returned, and rapidly converted Stendhal's fiction into historical fact. Charles II was almost at once obliged to abdicate. His son, Charles III, proceeded to emulate the career of Ranuccio-Ernesto IV until, in 1854, he met a similar fate. His widow, a daughter of the Duc de Berri, then acted as Regent for her son Robert I, until in 1859 the Risorgimento swept them for ever from their Duchy. Duke Robert died in 1907, the father of twenty children, one of whom, Prince Sixte de Bourbon-Parme, shewed in the late war some reflexion of the spirit of Fabrizio del Dongo, as the curious English reader may find in my translation of his *L'Autriche et la paix séparée* (*Austria's Peace Offer,* London, Constable and Co., Ltd., 1921). Another is the Empress Zita, while a third has re-established the Bourbon dynasty in Northern Europe by becoming the father of the Hereditary Grand Duke of Luxembourg.

Francesco Hayez, the Milanese painter immortalised by his decoration of the *palazzo* Crescenzi and by his portrait of Fabrizio del Dongo, died at a great age in 1882, having outlived the date appointed by Beyle for his own immortality.

C. K. S. M.

FRAGMENT I

BIRAGUE'S NARRATIVE

FABRIZIO, WELL received in this house which seemed to him very pleasant, sought never to speak of the battle, since memories of that sort depressed the Colonel; but as he thought without ceasing of the details of which he had been a witness, he would sometimes return to the topic; then the Colonel placed a finger on his lips with a smile, and spoke of something else. On the other hand, Fabrizio was careful never to say anything that might let it be guessed by what succession of chances he had been brought into the neighbourhood of Waterloo. The ladies especially were constantly placing him under the necessity of finding polite answers which should tell them nothing of what they desired to know. At every moment, by phrases which betrayed the keenest interest, they placed him under the necessity of telling them something; but he got well out of the trap and the ladies knew absolutely nothing, except that he was called Vasi, and even then they had good reason to believe that this name was assumed.

Colonel Le Baron, his wife and the ladies of their acquaintance were therefore devoured by curiosity, this young man's adventures must indeed be extraordinary.

"All that I can say positively," repeated the Colonel, "is that he is endowed with the truest courage, the most simple, the most innocent, so to speak. When I was so stupid as to set him on picket at the head of the bridge of La Sainte, and he fought there, one against ten, I would wager that he was drawing a sabre for the first time."

"And his passport which you went to verify at the municipality is really made out: Vasi, dealer in barometers, travelling with his wares?" ...

The ladies, that day, plied him with a thousand artful

questions about the barometers, he extricated himself with a laugh and very neatly; they consulted him as to the state of the barometer in the house, which they put in his hands, he remembered the tone that, in similar circumstances, Conte Pietranera would have adopted, and, justified by the fun that was being made of him, replied in a tone of the most lively gallantry. His appearance was so modest and his tone was in so strange a contrast to his ordinary manner that it was by no means ill received, the ladies went into fits of laughter. That same evening the Colonel said to them:

"Chance has just offered me a way of finding out our young man's position; you know that resurrected-looking creature who has come to him from Italy, the man is a lawyer and is called Birague, but besides that he is dying of fright; he speaks bad French, but I hope that his gibberish may not offend you, for he is so driven by fear that each of his sentences says something. This morning, this lawyer who, for some days, has always followed me with his eye at the *café*, has at last found an excuse for, as he says, presenting his respects to me; I at once thought that perhaps you would deign not to be put off by his speech, which for that matter greatly resembles your young favourite's; and so I have invited this strange creature to take tea with us this evening, and, if you give me leave, I shall now send Beloir to fetch him from the *café*."

Ten minutes later, Trooper Beloir announced at the door of the drawing-room: "M. Birague, *avocat*."

The conversation lasted for fully two hours, the ladies heaped every attention on the poor lawyer, who did everything in his power to please them, but it was in vain that they sought to extract from him anything that bore upon Fabrizio; they had lost patience with his discretion, which was not lacking in polite forms of speech, when the Colonel exclaimed:

"I must say, my dear *avocat*, that you are a very brave man, how could you dare enter France in the present state of things? They are kind enough to give me in the army a certain reputation for bravery, but I must confess to you that in your place, and (I tell you frankly) speaking a French so different from that spoken by the natives of the country, I should never have ventured to penetrate into so disturbed a country. Now I see that you have made a conquest of these ladies, you have an air of sincerity which pleases me and I should like to give you my protection. Madame's uncle

is Mayor of Amiens; I ought to tell you that, since you are
not recommended by an Ambassador, your fate lies in his
hands. M. le Maire Leborgne has a savage nature, he will
never believe that you have come to Amiens for your health,"
and so forth.

The ladies were quick in taking the hint given them by
the Colonel; they took the utmost pains to give the Milanese
lawyer a strong impression of the cruel nature of the worthy
M. Leborgne, Mayor of Amiens. Birague turned paler than
his shirt, than the white cravat and enormous hat in which
he had attired himself that evening to be presented to ladies;
but he found himself so well treated that finally about eleven
o'clock he ventured to ask the Colonel if he had any horses.
The Colonel asked him whether, at that time of night, he
wished to go for a ride, saying that he had only two horses,
which indeed were a pair of screws, but that he placed them
willingly at his service.

"I should not think of going out by the gate at this hour,
and running the risk of seeing myself questioned by the police, but I find so estimable a humanity in your heart and in
the hearts of these good ladies that I venture to make a request of you; allow me to spend the night in your horses'
hayloft: as it is an idea that has just occurred to me, the
terrible Mayor Leborgne would never hear of it and I should
spend one night at least in peace and quiet. I am lodging
with His Excellency, M. Vasi, but he has committed the
imprudence, as a matter of fact long before my arrival, of
refusing to see any more of the Duprez family, who are
greatly annoyed and who, I have no doubt, would be glad to
have their revenge. I have not attempted to hide my feelings
in the matter from M. Vasi, I have taken the liberty of saying that this step was rash on his part; but your experience,
Monsieur le Colonel, must have taught you what the rashness
of youth is. M. Vasi's answer was that he would have been
stifled by boredom if he had continued to spend his evenings with the Duprez family.

"In the present state of things, the Duprez, who, no
doubt, desire to be avenged, will not dare to attack a man
like M. Vasi, but they will take it out of a poor devil like
myself," and so on.

The Colonel ended by giving M. Birague a letter of recommendation addressed to the Mayor of Amiens, in which
he declared that he would answer with his life for M. Bi-

rague, a respectable lawyer of Milan, whom he had known when he was stationed in that city.

"Carry this letter on you while you are on your way to the Grand Monarque, and burn all the written or printed documents which you may have in your room; spend a quiet night, but you see that I am answering for you, come to-morrow and tell me your whole history so that, if the Mayor questions me closely, I can make a show of having known you for a long time; say nothing to M. Vasi of what I am doing for you."

One may imagine whether this evening was amusing for the ladies, but they were afraid of having alarmed M. Birague unduly.

"Really, the man's appearance was incredible," said Mme. Le Baron.

"But," put in one of her friends, "it becomes more and more likely that our young *protégé* Vasi is a man of consequence in his own country."

The Colonel had to employ stratagems for a week; M. Birague spoke as freely as could be desired of his own affairs, but was impenetrable on everything that related to Fabrizio. Mme. Le Baron and her friends invited him to luncheon one day when the Colonel was absent and played so cruelly upon M. Birague's alarm that he ended by saying to them with tears:

"Oh, well, I see that you are good ladies, I see that you would not wish to ruin me, you have immense influence with the Mayor of Amiens, give me your word that you will obtain for me a passport for England signed by the Mayor and I shall at least be able to fly to London in case of danger; my father ordered me to travel by London so as to be able to return to Milan without fear of Barone Binder, the Chief of Police there; he is a man of the same sort as your Mayor, it is not easy to get out of his prisons, once one has got into them."

"Very well," exclaimed Mme. Le Baron, "if you are frank with us, I give you my word that to-morrow you shall have your passport for London; we wish no harm to M. Vasi, far from it, this lady," she pointed to the youngest of her friends, "has a tender regard for him."

Birague was slightly astonished by the shout of laughter which greeted this admission; he had some difficulty in replying with any clarity to the hundred questions by which he was at once overwhelmed.

The ladies knew already that Vasi was an assumed name, that Fabrizio del Dongo was the second son of the Marchese del Dongo, Second Grand Majordomo Major of the Lombardo-Venetian Kingdom, one of the greatest noblemen in that country, to whom his, Birague's father, was steward. On the news of Napoleon's landing from the Gulf of Granti, in June, regardless of the alarm of his aunt and mother, Fabrizio had fled from his father's magnificent castle, situated at Grianta, on the Lake of Como, six leagues from the Swiss frontier.

Birague was at this stage in his narrative when the Colonel returned; he was told all that Birague had already said; as his regiment had been stationed for some time at Lodi, a few leagues from Milan, he knew all the principal personages of the court of Prince Eugène.

"What," he cried, "that Contessa Gina Pietranera, of whom you are speaking to these ladies as the aunt of Fabrizio, is she that famous Contessa Pietranera, the most beautiful woman in Milan in the days of the Viceroy, whose word was law at his court?"

"The very same, Colonel."

"And what age might she be now?"

"Twenty-seven or twenty-eight; she is more beautiful than ever, but she is completely ruined, her husband was murdered in what they called a duel, and the Contessa was furious at not being able to avenge his death: the General was out shooting in the mountains of Bergamo with some officers of the Ultra Party; he, as you know, although belonging to a family of the old nobility, had always served with the troops of the Cisalpine Republic; there was a luncheon in the course of this shooting party, one of the Ultra officers took the liberty of belittling the courage of the Cisalpine troops; the General struck him a blow, the luncheon was interrupted; as they had no weapons but guns, they fought with those, the poor General fell stone dead, with two bullets in his body; but the details of this duel made such a stir in Milan that all the officers who had been present were obliged to go and travel in Switzerland. The local surgeon who examined the General's body certified that the bullet which caused his death had entered from the back. This statement by the surgeon came to the Signor Barone Binder, Director General of the Police, Contessa Pietranera knew of it at once, for she can do anything she likes at Milan; all the important people of the place are her friends and are at her service. Twenty-four hours later, there arrived a second statement by the country surgeon from the Bergamo district; it contradicted the first and stated that the bullet which caused the death had entered by the stomach and that the second bullet which had passed through the thigh had also entered from in front; but they said that this surgeon had received a large sum of money. On the very night after the arrival of this second statement, the officers who had been present at the duel left for Switzerland; the funeral was held next day; they were afraid of being mobbed by the crowd, and the strangest thing of all was that the surgeon also left for Switzerland, where he still is. He has never dared to shew his face again in his own neighbourhood; the Bergamasks have sworn to exterminate him; and they don't take things lightly in that part of the world. It was after that that there was the famous quarrel between Signora Pietranera and her friend Limercati."

"What, is that the famous Limercati who, in 1811, had such fine English horses, seven of them?"

"No doubt, Lodovico Limercati; he had forty horses in his stables, he has an income of over two hundred thousand lire; my cousin Ercole is his factor; but there's a bad relation for you, he has never thought of employing me as lawyer to the rich Limercati estate."

"It is terrible, frightful," cried Mme. Le Baron, "but you spoke of a letter which, I must tell you, excites my curiosity greatly."

FRAGMENT II

CONTE ZORAFI, THE PRINCE'S "PRESS"

CONTE ZURLA, the Minister of the Interior, brought to Signora Sanseverina's Conte Zorafi, who was the Press of Parma.

At the gatherings at which he appeared, that silence, which is often painful at official gatherings, could not find a place, and, in a country which has a terrible police and a State Prison the tower of which, one hundred and eighty feet high, may be seen at the end of every street, all gatherings of more than two persons may be considered official.

One thing that may be said in praise of Zorafi is that he was no more of a spy than any other gentleman at court; in fact, at heart he was ridiculous, but not at all wicked. No other gentleman at court could, without risk to his friends, have seen the Sovereign daily. Zorafi fancied himself a Minister, and was afraid of Conte Mosca. At the same time he was obliged, ten times in a month perhaps, to speak evil of him. When the Conte had scored a marked success in any affair, he was certain to be blamed, the day after, by the Prince's Press.

Conte Zorafi was a man of spirit who could not bear to have fifty napoleons in his desk. As soon as he saw that sum, or indeed a much less considerable sum in his possession, he would think of spending it. For instance, on the day on which we shall do him the honour of presenting him to the reader, he will have just bought for forty-five napoleons a magnificent English lustre. The purchase made, not knowing where to place it and already caring less about it, he has asked Prinote, the famous jeweller, to keep it in his shop.

This Conte had spent his youth in composing sonnets in an emphatic style over which the people of Lombardy had gone so mad as to compare them to the sonnets of Monti. Now, in some connexion or other, someone had ventured to say in public that this style, which was so emphatic, was emphatic with the simple character of Napoleon; it had required only this comment to make Zorafi's sonnets fall into disrepute.

And, a surprising thing, Zorafi, whose character was precisely that of a conceited child, had not shewn the slightest annoyance. Besides what was more serious than the decline of his sonnets, he had an income of barely nine or ten thousand lire and spent twenty-five.

In spite of these 25,000 lire he frequently had debts, and these debts were paid every year by an unseen hand.

What then was Zorafi? He was the Prince's *Press*.

He was a Conte, as everyone is in Italy, but besides that he had enjoyed the greatest literary renown for ten years. Zorafi was not at all wicked, or at least had only the ill temper of a child. He had the purest Sienese accent. The sentences flowed from his lips with a perfect facility, he spoke of everything with charm, in a word nothing would have been lacking if from time to time he could have found some idea to place in his sentences.

A little time since, the Prince had given Zorafi a carriage, but this was on condition of his paying at least twenty-five visits daily.

"It does not suit me at present to have a newspaper printed," the Prince had said to him in making him a present of the carriage, with horses attached, and a coachman and groom to boot. "A newspaper conducted by a man of your sort would have a crowd of subscribers; very well, have a crowd of friends and tell them, with the spirit for which you are distinguished, the articles that you would print, if you had the privilege of the newspaper. One day, you shall have this newspaper, and it will bring you in an income of 50,000 lire. For I shall give you plenty of liberty, you will speak of the measures adopted by my Government."

Once they had observed this mania in Zorafi, people listened to him in society, as in another place they read the *Journal Officiel*.

CHRONOLOGY OF EVENTS

IN *THE CHARTERHOUSE OF PARMA*

May 15, 1796	French army under Bonaparte enters Milan
1798	Birth of Fabrizio del Dongo.
1814	Fabrizio hears of Napoleon's return from Elba.
1815	Fabrizio goes to Paris.
June 18, 1815	Fabrizio at Waterloo.
1816-20	Fabrizio at seminary in Naples.
1826	Fabrizio imprisoned in the tower, to serve 12 years.
1827	Fabrizio escapes. His son is born.
1829	Death of Clelia and her son. Fabrizio retires to Charterhouse.
1830	Death of Fabrizio and the Duchess Sanseverina.

AFTERWORD

Two manifestations of the human spirit, above all others, preoccupied Stendhal as man and as artist: passion and politics. One might think that these were but two forms of the same driving emotion, for we commonly speak of political passion. But for Stendhal the two were opposites. He knew passionate politicians, of course, and portrayed the type under the name of Conte Mosca in the present book. And he understood the politics of love, which he also depicted with a minute and intent curiosity. But passion and politics remained for him opposites, for passion is abandon and politics is calculation. The one is introspective and irresistible; it is a disease, as Stendhal says and as its root meaning of "suffering" implies, and one gives in to the ailment with one's whole being; whereas the other, politics, is all externals and façade and adroit make-believe, which require detachment and the healthiest attention to visible detail. In love one must be ecstatically content to be deceived by what Stendhal called the "crystallization" of beauty around the beloved object. In politics one must never be deceived into forgetting suspicion or relaxing contrivance. There is no charm in politics; there is only success.

These convictions explain why Stendhal chose Italy as the scene of so many tales and of his second great novel. Down to his own time Italy had been the theater of the most heroic love episodes and of the most ruthless political deeds. Stendhal knew the country well, having lived in it for long periods and being, toward the end of his life, French consul at Civita-Vecchia, near Rome. It was during the dull moments of this incumbency that he came across another manuscript chronicle of Renaissance days, such as he loved to collect and decipher. It had to do with the stormy youth of Alexander Farnese, later Pope Paul the Third, and it proved to be a dramatic tangle of love and ambitious intrigue. Stendhal apparently toyed for a time with the idea of retelling the high-colored events in fictional form, as he had done with other chronicles on several occasions. But suddenly, during a longish vacation in Paris, while he enjoyed the revigorating amenities of

the French capital and was musing over his lost passions and
political disappointments, the idea struck him of transposing
the general outline of the old chronicle into a modern novel,
borrowing episodes from the Memoirs of Benvenuto Cellini
(another man of passion and politics), and drawing even
more largely on his own stock of adventure and observation.
La Chartreuse de Parme was dictated with incredible speed
in the fifty-two days between November 4 and Christmas
1838, and was published in two volumes in April 1839.

Stendhal was then fifty-six years old. He was known in
France as a writer on a variety of subjects—music, painting,
travel, critical theory—and also as a producer of singular
tales which were printed and read but not especially relished.
Nine years earlier he had given the world a masterpiece
called *The Red and the Black,* but the world, while seeing
merit in it, thought that on the whole its author was one of
those brilliant failures who enliven salon conversation and
now and then throw off fine passages in the midst of their
otherwise ill-favored productions. Stendhal, the leading critics
were sure, lacked direction in his efforts; in any case, his
concerns were not central to any of the main tendencies of
the day. He was, in short, eccentric, or as we now like to
say, offbeat—in his life, in his work, and in his view of
human affairs.

Why, in the first place, did this Frenchman from Grenoble
write under a vaguely German pseudonym, but call himself
a born Milanese? Why did he espouse liberal principles, but
admire all the antiliberal virtues embodied in the figure of
Napoleon? What could bring a man of good family and re-
fined manners, descended from solid bourgeois in the south-
eastern province of Dauphiné, to boast that on his mother's
side he had an Italian ancestor who had fled to France centuries back "because of a few little murders"? His Parisian
friends knew, moreover, that the propounder of this brag-
gadocio—not the mythical Stendhal, but the broad-faced,
thin-lipped, stocky figure named Henri Beyle—was also a
man of the tenderest sensibilities, frequently moved to tears
by love and friendship, by scenery and music; a man whose
behavior in society was guided by the greatest delicacy—
that is, when he was not deliberately rude out of boredom.
And women, or at least some women, noticed that Beyle was
often timid in their presence, although they had heard re-
liable reports of his bravery in the grueling retreat of Napoleon from Moscow. Knowing all this too, are we to find

in Beyle-Stendhal the first example of that sentimentality overlaid by assumed toughness which has inspired so much of our fiction from Hemingway to the angry theater? Is this likeness the reason Stendhal has come into his own only recently, more than a century after his death, as he himself predicted?

I do not think the explanation sufficient. Stendhal's is a much more complicated case than that of any of our disillusioned, abolitionist writers, even though his disillusion shows some common elements with ours. Born and reared in a stuffy, well-to-do environment, Stendhal hated his unattractive father and adored his beautiful mother, whom he lost when he was seven years old. He grew up a self-contained, rebellious boy during the years of the French Revolution, but soon found in Bonaparte the symbol and the means of liberation from dullness, mediocrity, and petty ambitions. Through cousins high in power at the capital, Stendhal was early attached to the army commissariat, and he roamed Europe. He learned English and Italian, became a journalist, took part in the literary battle on the side of the Romanticists, and after giving up poetry and playwriting (he wanted to become the modern Molière), devoted himself unceasingly to observation and self-analysis. Novel writing was but one of his devices of research. A disciple of the eighteenth-century psychologists, Stendhal was persuaded that absolute fidelity to minute facts—*le petit fait vrai*—would yield a complete understanding of man's soul.

He therefore studied himself and his friends, took notes on current and historical crimes and scandals, kept voluminous diaries, sought experience in art, love, and war, and scanned men and women for whatever was spontaneous, strong, untrammeled by convention and base fears.

This double tendency in Stendhal—the love of impulse and the rage for observing—is what produced the seemingly contradictory character and also his puzzling books, in which passion (the ungovernable) and politics (ruling the self to rule others) interact and give off strange resonances. What brought Stendhal disillusionment was not, therefore, as with us, the chaos of life in an era of wars. Violence was to him (as one sees in *The Charterhouse*) a madness thanks to which men break the chains of convention or tyranny. Stendhal condemned his hero, Napoleon, for his warring mania, but he condemned the ensuing peace even more for its petrified sterility.

Nor was Stendhal distrustful of love as we are. He wrote a long work, *On Love*, to demonstrate that this disease, this other madness, was the greatest thing in life. Mere sexual dalliance might amuse for a brief instant; vanity-love had its place in an idle society; and a sentimental attachment could be a sweetly grateful experience; but passion-love was the highest form of self-realization. Not only were its pleasures good in themselves, as all partakers have always averred, but pleasures and pains alike gave the soul its barest view and fullest knowledge of itself. In both his great novels, accordingly, Stendhal studies the varieties of love, not in the abstract, but under the precise conditions of time and place as he knew them, including politics.

In *The Charterhouse of Parma*, the hero finds passion-love only at the end, with Clelia, after he has tasted the fruits of vanity with Fausta, physical pleasure with the thoughtless, attractive Marietta, and a mixture of sentiment and undeveloped passion with his beautiful aunt, the Duchess Sanseverina. Amid this education of the feelings, Fabrizio is taught the varied lessons that political danger instills; he learns to be a man, which is to say a double soul—all passion and all calculation.

Stendhal had a notion that a different novel ought to be written in every degree of latitude, so powerful is the effect of environment on men and morals. But it is not the mores of a violent people under absolute repression that strike us most forcibly in *The Charterhouse*. The first and strongest impression made on the reader is that of the enormous gap between the experience of love and commerce with society. A passion has an independent life of its own. Society breaks into that life, mars its form and quality, and ends by denaturing or destroying it. The superior man, the soul of fire, is he who can withstand these contending powers, can master society without uprooting love. This is the clue to Stendhal's meanderings through the maze of "little true facts."

The world was aware before Stendhal that great love stories are tragic because of this duel waged by passion and the world for possession of the highest spirits. But no one before had made the truth plain by the assault of multitudinous facts on our sensibilities. Compare the intentional sketchiness of the political element in, say, *Romeo and Juliet*, with the richness of incident and nuance in *The Charterhouse of Parma*, a richness so evenly divided between the inner life

of love and the outer life of politics that at times the reader
almost resents the author's impartiality. The sagacious Prime
Minister and the cunning of his enemy Rassi, the diverse
natures of the two Princes, the diplomatic instinct which the
Duchessa spoils by her impulsive pride, the dubious role of
the Church, the liberals, money, and the state—all are seen
through the same watchmaker's eye that records the fluctua-
tions of love in Fabrizio and his Clelia, as well as in the private selves of the scheming Prime Minister and his Duchessa.

Stendhal knew the dangers of this detachment, better
suited to the psychologist than to the artist. In three of his
novels he offered an apology in nearly identical words: "Politics in a work of literature is like a pistol shot in a concert
—something uncouth, yet something to which one can't help
paying attention." But the fault, if it was one, did not keep
Stendhal from writing what are, first and last, novels of adventure, The Charterhouse more persistently so than any
other. His reading of old chronicles was to Stendhal what
the reading of street ballads was to Wordsworth—it supplied the spur to imagination a modern writer might find in
gangster stories and other cheap shockers. The residue in
The Charterhouse is the solid substance of melodrama: intrigue, murder, disguise, imprisonment, escape, help and en-
mity from the powerful, anxious fear and love rivalry in the
hearts of contrasted women.

What makes the book differ from a thriller, and what
moved Balzac in his enthusiastic review to call The Charterhouse "the masterpiece of the literature of ideas in our
time," is the ease with which Stendhal was able to fuse
with the excitement of events the freshness and force of
his peculiar outlook. He had done this once before, in The
Red and the Black, based on two contemporary scandals of
love and murder. In that novel Stendhal discharged the anger
and irony of his thwarted ambition in a world of ferocious
nonentities. In The Charterhouse, he has grown appeased
and is amused by the same spectacle. Looking back on his
full life, he endows all that is lovable in the book with the
graces of his own tender recollections. His best-loved mistresses live again in the Duchessa Sanseverina. His charming
friendship with young Mlle. de Montijo, later the Empress
Eugénie, informs the figure of Clelia. His Napoleonic youth
incites him to bring Fabrizio to Waterloo in that astonishing
battle scene where no armies fight. His entranced reading

of Rousseau and discovery of Italy and the Swiss Alps inspire the glowing or misty landscapes of the novel. His own superstitions mingle with old hearsay to produce the touching eccentricities of the Abbé Blanès. Finally, his stock of wisdom and liberal hopes reappear transformed into the enchanting cynicism and passionate good nature of Conte Mosca. Balzac believed that the Conte was a portrait of Metternich, but Stendhal denied this. A shrewder hit of Balzac's was the comparison of the whole novel to Machiavelli's *Prince*. For Stendhal, like the historian of Florentine intrigue, who was also a writer of comedies and an alienated patriot, was projecting himself, without rancor, into the role of the statesman he would have wished to be. So much so that Balzac, characteristically downright, asks why "this observer of the first rank, this profound diplomat" is only a consul in a small town; why not ambassador to the Pope?

It is easy enough to answer that question, and in Stendhal's own words. How make an ambassador of one who preaches as a moral principle "the infinite respect which a man worthy of the name must show for all the motions of his soul"? And how could politicians rely on a man who pursued the kind of passion that "seeks but to satisfy itself and not to give our neighbor a magnificent idea of our person"?

It is even a question how far the advanced thinker of today can trust "the animal," as Stendhal used to call himself. Surely the leading thought of the twentieth century disavows the artist who pours his own life candidly into his books, as Stendhal did; who says that art (and music especially) is meant to arouse emotion and self-centered reminiscence, as Stendhal thought; who believes that love is all in all and ridicule of no account, as Stendhal felt; who admires heroes and seeks power, as Stendhal was ever ready to do; who is indifferent to craftsmanship, form, structure, and the rest of the esthetic baggage, as Stendhal was; who—the list of his refusals to cooperate with our prejudices is long and would infallibly exclude him from any charmed circle of our time.

Only his genius for seizing and showing the mixed psychology of the self-conscious mind saves him from our neglect—I almost said: from our contempt. Even in France his name is more notable than popular; he still addresses the Happy Few, and his fame seems at times a mere by-product of the huge scholarly research made necessary by his eccentric habits of writing, his mixing of fact and fiction, his plagiarism, and his love of elaborate secrecy. This last point suggests that our present perception of his genius may well be heightened by the curious similarity between the Italian principalities Stendhal depicted (his Parma was actually Modena) and our delightful postwar civilization, both alike embellished with spying, censorship, treacheries, executions, political witch hunts, and puppet regimes.

Some modern critics, to be sure, have tried to acclimate Stendhal still further to our atmosphere by finding in his works an extensive symbolism of the approved kind. For example, when Fabrizio wanders around the family castle, its walls are surmised to have the meaning of a barrier standing between him and the society into which he was born, excluded as he is by his father's and brother's hatred and his presumable illegitimacy. Stendhal would have been delighted to learn that walls mean barriers and keep out those who stand outside. He might even have deduced that when Fabrizio is inside, the significance is: the hero shut in by a repressive society. Unfortunately, these subtleties are not necessary, for Stendhal tells us what he means, and since he wrote always with real objects and persons in his mind's eye, his castles had walls and people stood on one side or the other.

It must be admitted in the critics' defense that in Stendhalian narrative there is always something beyond the reach of sense that has to be explained; the prose has at times an obscurity which is all the more baffling that the language is simple. Stendhal was himself aware of this difficulty and made jottings in his copy of *The Charterhouse* for a revised edition he never prepared. "In composing," he says, "I thought only of the point. I think such a style is a strain on the reader's attention because it does not provide enough details that are easy to grasp." Here is, perhaps, an example of what Stendhal means. The passage refers to Fabrizio: "He was still far from spending time in the patient observation of the true particulars of things, so as to guess their cause. Reality still seemed to him dull and murky. I can understand that one may not like to contemplate it, but then one should not reason about it. Above all, one should not make objections out of the fragments of one's ignorance." It is both the intrusion of the novelist and the jerky succession of ideas that occasion the difficulty and—when one knows Stendhal—the pleasure. The jerkiness he honestly believed he wanted to correct; actually, he preferred to let it stand, loathing as he did the rounded periods of some of his renowned contemporaries: "it is their noble language that will make them unreadable forty years hence."

He was right. His own style has kept its freshness. It seemed stiff and even monotonous to the professional lyricists, but it has a variety and range that permit Stendhal to modulate from the description of love to that of lakes and mountains and from political theory to specifications about buildings and asides on money. The pages are packed with everything except dialogue, which he disliked as being an impediment to telling and seeing. He also thought his chapters too long—"the subject being passionate and without embellishments, they must not exceed twenty pages"—but he did not redivide them, fortunately, for their density conveys a sense of populousness and entanglement which impels us to believe that the affairs of Parma and the troubles of Fabrizio matter, and are a paradigm of the wide world.

In truth, the whole effect is produced because Stendhal, having lived and loved and scribbled a full lifetime, was able at the right moment to decant the wine of his experience as it came, without premeditation. "I never knew while dictating one chapter what was going to happen in the next." When he had finished, his publisher made him abridge the conclusion, to save money; which is why the characters are hustled offstage rather curtly. But this does not spoil the work as it would in a lesser man's book. Stendhal belongs with those artists who are great by virtue of the stuff they make, not by virtue of the skillful fashioning of common materials. That is why it is very risky to apply to Stendhal our century's rather precious modes of judgment. Still worse it is to push him into our ways of thinking about life, making him exclusively a cool and sharp ironist subject to moments of weakness. He thinks about life as no one ever did; his irony *is* cool and sharp, and yet is not blunted or made tepid by passion and tenderness. It was a man all of one piece who created Gina Sanseverina and said he "copied her from Correggio—that is, to produce in my soul the same effect as Correggio," and who in the Foreword to his novel is dryly ironic about both his creation and his critics, saying: "The canon's niece, who knew and even loved the Duchessa Sanseverina, asks me to alter nothing in the account of her adventures, which are blamable."

Jacques Barzun

Columbia University

SELECTED BIBLIOGRAPHY

OTHER WORKS BY STENDHAL

Rome, Naples and Florence, 1817 Travel
On Love, 1822 Essay, autobiography, and fiction
The Life of Rossini, 1823 Discussion of opera, music, and the fine arts
Racine and Shakespeare, 1823-25 Critical principles of Romanticism
Armance, 1827 Novel
The Red and the Black, 1830 Novel
The Abbess of Castro and Other Tales, 1839 Five short stories
Journal 1801-1818, 1888
Lamiel, 1889 Novel (incomplete)
The Life of Henri Brulard, 1890 Unfinished autobiography
Memoirs of an Egotist 1822-1830, 1892 Unfinished autobiography
Lucien Leuwen, 1894 Novel, 2 vols., lacking conclusion

SELECTED BIOGRAPHY AND CRITICISM

Adams, Robert M. *Stendhal: Notes on a Novelist.* New York: The Noonday Press; London: Merlin Press, Ltd., 1959.

Brombart, Victor (ed.). *Stendhal: A Collection of Essays.* Englewood Cliffs, N. J.: Prentice-Hall, Inc. (Spectrum Books), 1962.

Dutourd, Jean. *The Man of Sensibility.* Tr. Robin Chancellor. New York: Simon & Schuster, Inc., 1961.

Fineshriber, W. H., Jr. *Stendhal, The Romantic Rationalist.* Princeton, N. J.: Princeton University Press, 1932.

Giraud, R. *The Unheroic Hero in the Novels of Stendhal, Balzac and Flaubert.* New Brunswick, N. J.: Rutgers University Press, 1957.

Josephson, Matthew. *Stendhal, or The Pursuit of Happiness.* New York: Doubleday & Company, Inc., 1946.

Krutch, Joseph Wood. "Stendhal," *Five Masters: A Study in the Mutations of the Novel.* Bloomington, Ind.: Indiana University Press (Midland Books); London: Mark Paterson & Company, Ltd., 1959.

Turnell, Martin. "Stendhal," *The Novel in France.* New York: Alfred A. Knopf, Inc. (Vintage Books), 1958.

SIGNET CLASSICS by French Authors

L'ASSOMMOIR *by Emile Zola*

A scathing indictment, in the idiom of the Parisian working classes, of the evils of drinking. Newly translated by Atwood Townsend. Afterword by Angus Wilson.   (#CT128—75¢)

CANDIDE, ZADIG AND SELECTED STORIES *by Voltaire*

Voltaire satirizes with ruthless wit the social, religious, and human vanities of his day in sixteen biting stories. A new translation with an Introduction by Donald Frame. (#CD35—50¢)

MANON LESCAUT *by Abbé Prevost*

The first modern "novel of passion" on which the operas of Massenet and Puccini are based. Newly translated with an Introduction by Donald Frame.   (#CP96—60¢)

THE PRINCESS OF CLEVES *by Mme. de Lafayette*

A profound and delicate psychological novel about a woman involved in a triangle. Newly translated with a Foreword by Walter J. Cobb.   (#CD89—50¢)

NIGHT FLIGHT *by Antoine de St. Exupéry*

A novel of beauty and power about the intrepid flyers of the early, heroic age of aviation. Translated by Stuart Gilbert. Foreword by André Gide.   (#CD46—50¢)

LES LIAISONS DANGEREUSES *by Choderlos de Laclos*

The diabolical story of the systematic corruption of the innocent by two partners in jealousy exposes the tragic folly of hyper-rationality in 18th century France. Translated by Richard Aldington with a Foreword by Harry Levin.   (#CT127—75¢)

ATALA AND RENE *by Francois René de Chateaubriand*

Two charming romantic tales, whose heroes are American Indians, by the French author who had been called "the true founder of Romanticism in France." Newly translated, with a Foreword by Walter J. Cobb.   (#CD103—50¢)

TO OUR READERS: If your dealer does not have the SIGNET and MENTOR books you want, you may order them by mail, enclosing the list price plus 5¢ a copy to cover mailing. If you would like our free catalog, please request it by postcard. The New American Library of World Literature, Inc., P. O. Box 2310, Grand Central Station, N. Y. 17, N. Y.